T0065048

You Were There
Before My Eyes

ALSO BY MARIA RIVA

Marlene Dietrich: The Life

You Were There Before My Eyes

A Novel

MARIA RIVA

PEGASUS BOOKS
NEW YORK LONDON

YOU WERE THERE BEFORE MY EYES

Pegasus Books Ltd.
148 W 37th Street, 13th Floor
New York, NY 10018

First Pegasus Books edition October 2017

Interior design by Maria Fernandez

Library of Congress Cataloging-in-Publication Data is available.

ISBN: 978-1-68177-507-4

10 9 8 7 6 5 4 3 2 1

Printed in the United States of America
Distributed by W. W. Norton & Company

For all immigrants and those left behind

You were there, before my eyes,
but I had deserted even my own self.
I could not find myself, much less find you.

—St. Augustine

You Were There
Before My Eyes

1

The morning her mother died, Giovanna gave up on God. The protective loving Shepherd had become a fraud. No more kneeling on cold stone, begging Him for impossible things. He never listened! Even the Madonna, so beautiful with her deep blue cloak and carmine mouth, was, after all, only a plaster lady, painted compassion, pretending Divinity.

Tall for her age, spindly thin yet exuding a skeletal strength, at the age of eight Giovanna now looked at life with disenchanted eyes, their brown velvet softness already coarsened by too much reality seen too soon.

The widows of the village, come to prepare her mother for burial, assigned her the task of "the washing of the feet." Carefully, Giovanna poured wine onto the white linen napkin, its lace border instantly stained red as it soaked up the dark liquid. Gently, she began washing between her mother's rigid toes, as the wine dripped catching it in a special basin encircled by a crown of porcelain thorns.

Like blood, the child thought. Giovanna bent to her serious task, *Cold . . . Mamma was always cold, even when she was half-well . . . icy when the Demons possessed her . . . once when the village priest tied Mamma to their strongest chair . . . how she screamed and kicked—but he was a big man, the knots he tied held her for three whole days . . .*

Giovanna remembered those days, especially the smell of them, as it had been her duty to wash down her mother's legs whenever she relieved herself. *Funny, washing Mamma . . . always washing Mamma.*

The attending widows respectfully drew back into the shadows, murmuring amongst themselves the platitudes required for such tragic occasions. "What a blessing! . . . A divine blessing! . . . At last, the Angel of Death has released this poor tormented creature from the Devil's possession!"

Giovanna watched the midwife place tall candles on either side of her mother's still face. Their light flickered across the inert form on the long wooden table. Hardly moving, Giovanna stood, tensed, waiting. Not that she expected to actually see anything materialize, but the nuns had taught her of the special wonder of all beings having a soul that must rise, leave what was newly dead, and although she knew this particular soul would not, could not, desert her mother—still, she felt compelled to wait out its required time to do so.

"Look! The child is standing vigil!" the widows whispered, impressed. Giovanna heard them as faint background to her concentration. Hugging herself, her eyes fixed on her mother's body, she tensed, ready to catch her soul, push it back, protect it from the flames of Hell she was so certain would be waiting to consume it.

"Giovanna! Go!" Her father, scrubbed newly clean, the smell of lye and brilliantine mingled with the scent of warmed beeswax. "Go, I said go!"

But Papa won't know what to do if it appears! A soul can't be easy to see! Her eyes pleaded. *Maybe Papa won't even try!* But she went, did as she was told, obeyed his order.

As an only child, she had a room all to herself, an envied treasure that set her apart from her schoolmates. Tonight, it seemed especially forlorn. Not lighting her bedside candle, she climbed onto the small trestle bed. Fully clothed, thin arms crossed upon her chest, she lay like her mother below and cried. Throughout her life, Giovanna would grieve in this way, without moving, without sound, in silent sorrow.

By seventeen she had a spinster's body; flat-chested, angular, soft flesh absent from too much work and not enough meals. In her somber wool, her shrouded frame all bone and sinew, she resembled a young crow. Even her eyes were birdlike, dark, intense, focused beyond her immediate visual range as though searching far horizons. Too tall to be considered a true "romantic," Giovanna thought her carriage "regal" and liked it; her small breasts quite sufficient, different enough from those of her amply bosomed friends to give her the distinction of difference she courted. Being motherless had added to her distinctiveness. The nuns especially were forever praying over her, sometimes even marking her copybooks with a better grade than she knew she deserved. There had been moments over the years when she missed her mother, not from any special attachment or feeling of love—for the memory of madness was ever sharp. Of actual mothering? Vague, defused by time. An aloneness had been a part of Giovanna, long before her mother's death. A sorrowing childhood begets emotional voids that remain to haunt. But as most assumed a young daughter's lingering grief to be the obvious reason for Giovanna's unusual remoteness, she let them. At an early age she had found people liked to believe they alone knew things no one had actually ever given them the right to know. Sharing feelings, confiding one's inner emotions, the way other girls did, blushing and giggling, whispering in hushed tones with many furtive glances, irritated her. Giovanna's longings were her own, as unattainable as were miracles. It was the summer of 1913, and her life was about to begin.

Perched within its alpine range, the village of Cirié smoldered in the intense summer heat. Behind faded shutters, women loosened their stays, lay in homespun shifts, hoping for rest. In the piazza, men in shirtsleeves and broad suspenders, the brims of their black hats pulled low, drank cellar-cooled wine in the mottled shade of the taverna's vine-covered canopy. Up in the orchards, peasants left their tall ladders to seek refuge beneath the laden trees. Women shifted shawl slings from their backs to suckle their babes cradled within, while their men ate, slept—waiting for the cooling of late afternoon.

In their convent's subterranean chapel, white-robed nuns knelt in unified prayer, fingered ebony beads. In the Benedictine monastery above, the male counterparts of their illustrious order did not stop to rest, for this was July—their busiest season! No time for languid *Reposas*, not even prayer. The fame of their delectable Cherry Cordial depended on their devotion to vats, casks, secret formulas, and vigilant pressings! As the diligent Sisters ran not only the village school but everything else they considered worthy of their administrative skills, the busy Fathers had, long ago, relinquished their expected dominance to them, in their consummate need to nurture, bring to fruition the glorious ruby-red elixir they adored, which depended on them so. The village of Cirié, enormously proud of its chemist monks, forgave them whatever shortcomings arose in their most holy duties.

As had been their custom since their First Communion, Giovanna and her friends, Camilla, Teresa, and Antonia, brought their high-backed chairs to the village square to sit and work lace in the dense shade of its mighty chestnut; a tree so ancient no one was left who could vouch for its beginning.

It was only when Father Tomasso Innocente proclaimed that the Holy Virgin Mother herself must have surely commanded the mountain winds to blow—to carry the seed of their glorious tree to nestle amidst the granite, there to take root for the sole purpose of bringing comforting shade to her beloved flock of the village of Cirié—that everyone had finally acepted this Holy Dictum.

Regardless, the four girls were grateful for the mighty chestnut's welcoming shade. Small work pillows positioned securely on their laps, they began fashioning lace. Each rapid movement, studied and precise, their practiced fingers flipping bobbins, pinning, twisting, knotting the fine cotton threads over and under, back and forth, they formed the intricate patterns of delicate lace indigenous to their region of Piedmont, which would later be sold in the elegant city of Turin, down the mountain path only six hours away on foot, even less if one rode a mule or had the luxury of a horse-drawn cart.

Camilla, pink, plump, and pretty, liked little glass beads to weigh her bobbins. Whenever the gypsy peddlers came to the village, she searched through their leather pouches for hours, hoping to find some in her favorite colors of leaf green and palest rose. Once tied to her bobbins in little bunches, the tinkling sound they made when she flipped them was pretty, and their colors in motion delighted her.

Antonia, a cool Madonna with passionate eyes, preferred bits of bleached bone, delicately carved into animal shapes by her father's surgeon hands.

Teresa, a docile girl, already the designated nun of her large family, used weights her mother found when she was seventeen during an exciting summer journey down to the sea; fragile shells, curled and spiraled, with tiny holes just right for thread.

Giovanna made do with small buttons. They did the job, even jingled softly like the others.

Their weighted bobbins bouncing, playing their individual tunes, the girls worked in accustomed companionship. Sitting so straight on their high-backed chairs, glossy dark heads bent in determined concentration, their classic profiles as though chiseled from finest marble, they looked like an artist's rendering of what they were—four Italian virgins fashioning lace at the beginning of their womanhood and their century.

A drawn-out snore drifted across from the taverna. Somewhere a baby cried, a dog rooted through his coarse hair searching for fleas, teeth clicking in excited anticipation, a cart-horse, head down, dozing, flicked flies with a matted tail, a woman in a red flowered wrapper, one buttock balanced on her windowsill, sat fanning herself, looking nowhere in particular.

Ever curious, Camilla was the first to interrupt their bobbins' rhythm.

"Where are the sisters?"

Their friends Gina and her younger sister, Celestina, were always referred to as a unit. They were so perfectly matched, they reversed each other. Where one was confident, the other was uncertain; one bubbled, never far from laughter, the other brooded, suspicious of good fortune. Sometimes they switched characteristics, as though to better understand each other, but mostly they were content within their perfect counterbalance. As Gina grew into what the village believed would become a possible beauty, Antonia, who had known her since they were babes in arms, decided she had never really liked her even then. She now answered Camilla, "Probably she has gone with their mamma on one of their errands of charity. Whenever these three appear, it's like the Holy procession . . . the saintly old goose, followed by Gina, the strutting peacock, and, bringing up the rear, Celestina, the giggling chicken."

The picture was so perfect, they all laughed, even Teresa, who quickly recovered, ashamed of herself, reprimanded Antonia for being unkind. Antonia's eye's blazed; Camilla, who hated confrontations, jumped into the breach. "Did you hear? He's back! Did you see him? . . . Well, did you? What do you think? . . . I think he's too short to be really handsome . . . but he is strong! Really *strong*! Even under his city coat, I could see his muscles—rows and rows of them! Mamma even noticed them! Then she saw me looking and got angry and told me not to stare and made me go back into the house but she stayed outside, sweeping the stoop that I had just been sweeping for hours!" Camilla giggled, looked expectantly at her three friends.

Teresa, fussing with a tangle, trying to correct a mistake she had made in the pattern of her lace collar, was too busy to offer a comment. Giovanna remained silent. Antonia, very pleased to be given a really good reason to stop working, looked up with interest.

"Who? Who has muscles? Camilla, what *are* you talking about?"

"The sisters' brother, Giovanni. He had that big fight with his papa about . . . Oh! I don't know WHAT it was . . . My papa told my mamma it had to be something again about machines . . . something about 'always those damned machines . . . Fight, fight, fight! All the Ricassolis are nothing but stuck-up trouble,' Papa said. Anyway, he's back and . . . guess what? He found work! In l'America! Just like he said he would." Camilla stopped to fan herself—even in the shade, it was just too hot today for all this accelerated talking. Antonia, having decided the weight of her hair was bothering her, removed the long pins from the knot at the nape of her neck, splayed its beauty with her fingers, and began plaiting it into two thick braids instead. "Why isn't he handsome then? If he has muscles, has work in America, and is rich . . . short isn't so bad!"

"Once I saw a real fistfight at the fair. My brothers let me watch . . . it was awful! One man got a broken nose . . . the blood poured out and . . ."

"Teresa, what has that got to do with what we are talking about?" Antonia asked in that tone of aristocratic annoyance she used whenever she felt something was about to elude her.

"Well, if you ever gave someone time to finish what they are trying to say, you would know without having to ask in that superior way!"

Antonia stopped her braiding and glared.

Teresa continued, uncowed, "As I was GOING TO SAY, when I saw this fight at the fair, I noticed that one of those sweaty men—the one who broke the nose, not the one who got it broken—he had short legs AND THEY WERE BOWED! So, I can tell you—I know! Short legs are not handsome . . . not handsome at all!" Having said her piece, handed on her superior knowledge, Teresa felt all had been said that could, or at least should, be mentioned by innocent maidens on the subject of male anatomy. She picked up her bobbins and resumed her pattern at the point where she had left off.

"I have never heard such nonsense!" Antonia's tone was worthy of a real *principessa*. "Really! If you saw some of the illustrations I have seen in my father's books, you would probably have hysterics for weeks. Swoon dead away! . . . Of course, I am absolutely forbidden to look inside those books . . . but I sneak into my papa's study whenever I know it's safe . . . and see things you couldn't imagine if you tried for a thousand years!"

"Antonia," Camilla asked, just a little breathless, "do you know what makes babies? I once asked Mamma and she sent me to my room, without supper! When I asked my brothers, they laughed at me, said I was stupid and told me all I had to do was 'watch the animals and find out everything.' Well, I did . . . and . . . it is—ugly! Really, really UGLY! That can't have anything to do with making sweet little babies! Can it? . . . I don't dare ask Sister Bertine . . . she'd be so shocked I would be kneeling for weeks!"

Everyone giggled, self-consciously half-afraid of being overheard in what would surely be interpreted as mocking the Church!

Giovanna asked quietly, "So? Did you find out why he came back?"

"Who?"

"Giovanni . . . the Ricassoli boy! Weren't you all just talking about him?"

"Oh, him! Giovanna, that was hours ago! Weren't you listening?" Camilla could sound like her ever-exasperated mother without even trying an imitation.

"Oh, Camilla . . . Really! Don't be silly! I'm hot, my eyes hurt from working in this darkness. I still have to lay the fire, bake bread, cook Papa's meal, iron his Sunday suit, and blacken his shoes for church before I can come back here, draw water, carry it back for his bath. All I asked was a simple answer to a simple question!"

"Well, really! We all draw water from the well . . . What a big fuss! You'd think you were the only one!" Camilla sniffed, offended.

"That does it!" Giovanna secured her bobbins, preparing to leave.

"I don't think Camilla really knows why he's back, Giovanna." Teresa liked everyone to be nice to each other.

"Anyway, she was too busy swooning over his bulging muscles to ask!" Antonia chuckled, fluffing out the ends of her sumptuous braids.

"You're mean! You're all mean! I AM GOING HOME!" and, picking up her chair, cushion, and pride, Camilla stormed off.

Undisturbed, Antonia remarked, "I think that the old grandmother Ricassoli is sinking. I heard Papa say something about being called in and that it is now 'only a matter of time.'"

"That must be it!" Teresa caught fire. "Only yesterday my mamma said, 'Mark my words! There'll be a funeral soon . . . I felt a cold shadow hovering over my left shoulder . . . then my polenta burned without a reason. I was there, the whole time, every second—I was stirring, yet my polenta scorched! A sure sign—the Angel of Death is near!'" Teresa always committed to memory whatever her mother said. For some reason, at an early age she had convinced herself that it was very important to do so. No one had figured out why, least of all Teresa's mother, who, at first flattered by her daughter's habit of absorbing her every word, now that she had turned seventeen and was still doing it, had become slightly apprehensive.

"Well, then that must be the reason Giovanni came back." Giovanna had her answer, and the girls picked up their chairs and went home.

After Mass on Sundays, when the village square became a bustling meeting place, the girls usually met by the tall clump of oleanders that shadowed the low stone wall bordering the terraced path that wound its way down from the monastery above. Dressed in their Sunday best, starched white shirtwaists and long black skirts, they perched like swallows, surveying the sloping meadow of alpine flowers at their dangling feet. Work pillows ready on their laps, they sat, enjoying the beauty spread before them. The toll of church bells drifted up from the valley below, the faint echo of tin bells drifted down from above as sure-footed goats searched steep crags for their favorite bitter herbs.

As usual Camilla was late. Confession always took up a great deal of her time. Giovanna, who resented the ritualistic dogma of Confession, avoided the confessional whenever possible. Besides having nothing of real importance to beg forgiveness for, it made her uncomfortable in taking up the busy priest's time. She knew her friends looked forward to those sequestered moments amidst the scent of sandalwood and incense, especially if, when they finally emerged, their given penance took up most of their remaining day, by its very length giving proof to all of their blossoming maturity. Just once, Giovanna wished she could have something really shocking to confess—see what stirred her most, the Prayers of Contrition or the sin that had fostered them.

A fat bee bumped into her black-stockinged ankle, and gently she pushed it off with the tip of her shoe. Teresa sighed and began preparing her bobbins. Antonia undid the taffeta ribbon of her Sunday braid, smoothing it between her fingers before rolling it up. Then she began combing her long hair with the wide tortoiseshell comb she had bought with her lace money from the gypsy tinker.

"Antonia, can you sit on it yet?" Giovanna asked, admiring the glorious sepia-colored silk curtain being groomed, a little envious that her own hair refused to grow any further than her waist, even frizzed when it rained.

"When I lift my chin and have no clothes on, I can. Papa says it's hereditary. All the women in his family have long, beautiful hair . . . but Mamma says no, it's the olive oil that she rubbed onto my head the second after she bore me."

"Did you see the Rossini twins?" Teresa asked in a tone heralding dramatic news.

Without interrupting her comb's hypnotic strokes, Antonia turned in anticipation. "No, why?"

"They're shaved!"

"NO!" her friends gasped.

"Yes! They're BALD! Not a single hair left on their heads! Like babies' behinds . . . both of them! Well, with scarletina, you have to shave off all the hair. *You* should know that, Antonia!"

"Of course I know that! But what I didn't know is that they had it. Papa said it was varicella. But, Mamma said it had to be 'the fever' because Mario and Stephano were quarantined for so long so, when they finally came out, their hair was GONE!"

Camilla came puffing up the path, straw bonnet trailing from one listless hand, tears glistening in her pretty gray eyes.

"I lost my pillow . . . Well, I didn't really . . . I know exactly where I left it. I had it next to me on the bench in the confessional and I couldn't go back to get it because the Rossini twins went in . . . both of them at once! What they can have to confess after being locked up for weeks is beyond me . . . and they were in there forever! Signora Fellice was waiting to be next, tapping her cane, furious she had to wait! . . . So, I just have to try and find it when I confess tonight." Out of breath, very depressed, Camilla settled herself on the wall next to Antonia and dangled her feet.

"What do you expect to do for the rest of the day so that you will still have something left to confess this evening?" Teresa asked with genuine interest.

Antonia, slipping her precious comb carefully into the wide belt at her waist, laughed. "Camilla will make up something. She always does. Of course, nothing ever really happens to her . . . but . . ."

"Sister Bertine says just thinking sinful thoughts is a sin," Teresa observed without looking up.

"Pooh!" Antonia snorted and took up her bobbins of bone.

Camilla kicked a fuzzy dandelion with the tip of her high-buttoned Sunday shoe, watched its soft explosion drift away. In a tone filled with anguished doom, she whispered, "My papa took the widow Angelli . . ."

Bobbins stopped in midair! Three incredulous gasps of "What?" filled it.

"Don't make me say it again! I can't! I just can't say it again . . . ever . . . ever!"

"Where?" asked Antonia.

"I don't believe it!" Teresa had turned as white as her thread.

"And how would you even know such a thing?" Giovanna, the ever practical one, said not unkindly.

"Well . . . I DO know . . . It's true! Mamma saw them! In the barn, when she went to collect the eggs!"

"They were there in your own barn? . . . In broad daylight?" Antonia shook her head in disbelief.

"And you said nothing of this yesterday?" Teresa was very put out that Camilla had kept such a shocking tragedy from her closest friends.

"How could I? It only happened this morning!" Camilla wailed.

"On a Sunday!?" Teresa crossed herself.

"But the widow Angelli has a beard! . . . And lives with goats!" Antonia exclaimed, very disgusted.

"Well, Mamma has gone to see Father Innocente . . . Sister Bertine is accompanying her up there. My second married sister, Lucia, is in early labor from the shock! All my brothers have disappeared somewhere . . . the rest of my sisters are weeping and lighting candles in the chapel . . . and Papa is getting drunk! I only came up here because I couldn't stay hidden all day in the confessional . . . and I thought that my dearest friends would understand and help!"

Tears that had begun to fall at the beginning of the first sentence of this sad litany now flowed freely at the close of it. Hugs and Sunday handkerchiefs were offered, with many "There . . . theres" and "Easy . . . easys" until Camilla was able to regain her composure.

"'Beasts!' My mother has always said, 'All men are beasts—deep down beasts!' I never believed her, but now, after this, I do—I do!" sighed a thoroughly disillusioned Teresa, who crossed herself anew.

Antonia felt it was up to her to take charge. "Camilla—now don't take this the wrong way and PLEASE, do not swoon, for I must tell you something. Something very important. It seems that men, all kinds of men, sometimes have what is described as 'Urges'. . . and when these 'Urges' come upon them, they do all sorts of very strange things. You must also know that for men, these 'Spells' are considered to be . . . no more than . . . well . . . than eating a really fine risotto . . . just . . . a normal appetite!"

Camilla had ceased to breathe. Teresa felt faint. Giovanna thought Antonia terribly brave. A shadow fell across their shoulders and a deep male voice said, "Hi, girls!"

Camilla shrieked, sprang off the wall, ran down the path towards the village, as though the Devil himself was in hot pursuit! Teresa trembled—Giovanna patted her hand. Antonia, her black eyes sparkling, smiled up into the handsome face of the adventuresome Giovanni Ricassoli, who exclaimed, "My God! What's wrong with Camilla? . . . That was Camilla, wasn't it?"

"Yes! She had to get home. Don't pay any attention to her. She just had a bad shock today. She didn't mean to be rude." Antonia patted the place newly vacated by her side. "Welcome home, Giovanni!"

"Welcome," Giovanna joined in the greeting of one of their childhood friends. He had been the only one of the older boys who had never been mean, teased the girls as they walked, eyes downcast, two by two to their convent school, never pelted them with icy snowballs. If only in memory of that, he deserved a proper welcome. He looked a little like she remembered him—stocky and strong, like a fine plow horse, all rippling muscles and gloss, with that strange beauty of controlled power all its own. Now this seemed overlaid with a man's self-assurance, and she wasn't sure if she would like him as much.

"I think I should go and see to Camilla. Besides, I have to help my mamma with the babies." Teresa rolled up her bobbins, smiled a hasty good-bye, and took the shortcut through the buttercups on her way down the hill.

Left on either side of the young man, Antonia and Giovanna worked their lace. Lying back against the grassy knoll behind, he pillowed his head in his hands, looked up at the clean, clear sky.

"When you smell grease all day . . . you forget . . ."

"Grease?" Antonia turned to look down at him lying beside her, suddenly made shy by the faint feeling of excitement this caused.

"I work with machines. They have to be lubricated to . . ." The young man stopped himself, as though explaining a private passion to others might defile it somehow.

Antonia thought his abrupt silence boorish. Tossing her heavy hair back over her shoulders, she slipped off the wall. The young man jumped to attention, eager to be the one allowed to accompany this village beauty back down to her front door. Antonia took stock. Camilla had been right—he was certainly not tall . . . that made it a bit awkward if one wanted to gaze up beguilingly, so she did the next best thing and looked deep into his level eyes, gave him her very best look of softest, helpless need. When he hesitantly touched her elbow, she allowed him to assist her along the twisted path towards the village. At the first bend, they remembered, turned, and waved a belated friendly good-bye in Giovanna's direction, who, watching them, waved back before slapping a bumblebee that had dared to settle on her pillow.

The next day, only Giovanna came to the piazza to work in the shade of its ancient tree. Camilla, being part of a family scandal that had the village buzzing, was too ashamed to step outside her door. Teresa, who had offered to light candles and prayers to the saint in charge of lecherous fathers, was on her tenth round of Hail Marys, and Antonia, having decided not to wait until the full moon, was busy washing her mighty mane two weeks earlier than her monthly schedule called for.

"Hi! Where's everybody? . . . My God! It's hot!" Giovanni sank down on the worn cobblestones, near Giovanna's chair. "What a tree! It feels wonderful . . . like being in an icebox!"

"What did you say? What's a . . . that funny first word? The other one I think I can figure out because it sounds a little like French." The Benedictines retained their close bonds with France, taught those given into their academic care the beauty of its language. Giovanna, being a natural linguist, could not only read and write French but speak it with only a trace of her Italian cadence. Although *box* was close enough to its equivalent word in French for her to figure its meaning, the hissing sound of *ice* was a complete mystery.

Giovanni laughed, such an honest sound that it made those who heard it long for the feelings that produced it. Not at all embarrassed by her question, Giovanna laughed with him, suddenly feeling happy for no special reason. Carefully he explained what an "icebox" was, what it looked like, what it was for, what it did and how it did it. He seemed to know everything about them.

"Sometimes I'm there when the iceman comes to deliver the block for the one my landlady keeps on her back porch." Giovanna listened, enthralled. Amazed not only that such a marvel had been invented, but that it could be owned by one of the working class.

"Oh, Giovanna—l'America is full of so many wonderful things!"

Giovanna sprang to her village's defense. "Well, here too we can keep all sorts of things cool during the heat of summer . . . We hang fish in the mountain streams, keep roots and cheese in deep cellar. Still, it must be very special to own such a splendid boite."

"No, no. The correct word is *box*—sharp and quick! L'America is full of quick words, like the country, like the people . . . fast, everything to the point. No one has time to waste . . . Everything must be quick . . . like my name. You want to hear what my name is in American?"

"Oh, yes!"

"John! Just . . . John. See—short and quick! Everyone where I work calls me John." His voice held a tone of pride.

"I don't think that sounds as nice as Giovanni!"

"Well, I like it! In America, you would be a Jane!"

"Oh, dear—that sounds just as bad." The young man smiled. "Antonia says that in America, all the ladies wear large hats decorated with stuffed birds. Is that true?"

"I've seen some," he answered with obvious disinterest.

"And long velvet coats trimmed with fine fur?"

He frowned. This girlish interest in fashionable ladies did not suit her character somehow, and it annoyed him. Afraid he considered her questions frivolous, Giovanna hastened to explain.

"Oh, I'm not interested in wearing such fine things . . . I want to make them! I am skilled with the needle. I wanted to go to the Institute in Torino, to learn to be a seamstress so I could get work in a fine dress shop . . . but Papa said he didn't have money to waste on a girl. If he had a son, then it would have been worthwhile for him to learn a trade, but for a girl? That was just 'senseless extravagance'!"

"In America, many young ladies are employed. I don't know any who sew, but I know one who works in the office for our Mr. Willis. She even knows how to operate a machine that prints letters onto paper. She is a stenographer."

Giovanna hung on his every word.

"What is the name of her machine?"

"A typing machine."

"Does she have to wear a special uniform to work it?"

"Well, if you consider a crisp, high-necked shirtwaist and a long black skirt that just shows her ankles a special uniform, then I suppose she does. But men don't notice such things."

"If I were a man, I would go . . . make my way to Genova, stow away on a great ship bound for China . . . see the whole world—and maybe never ever come back!"

"Well, you're not a man! But don't worry, someday someone will marry you! Until then, your father needs a woman to look after him."

Oh, why did he have to say that! She had so enjoyed the novelty of speaking without reserve, as though she were his equal. Now he had reminded her that she was not and spoiled it. When she answered him, the bitterness of her disappointment lingered. "Yes, someday, some man will take pity on me and save me from the cardinal sin of spinsterhood. Until then, Papa needs me to polish his boots, scrub his floors, wash his clothes, cook his food . . . a woman must know her proper place and be grateful for being given it."

"You know, Giovanna . . . you are a very strange girl."

"Yes, I know," she answered, her voice bereft of all emotion.

He ran his fingers through his hair, uncurled his body with an athlete's grace, stood brushing off his trouser leg. "Tomorrow—is it the chestnut or the oleanders?"

That made her smile. "The oleanders."

"Think Camilla will be there?"

Giovanna lowered her head, flipped her bobbins, answered, "Maybe not Camilla . . . but Antonia will surely be."

"See you then . . . Jane!"

The effect of his laugh lingered long after he had gone.

Waiting, Giovanna began pinning the first row of a newly begun collar. For no particular reason, she had decided to come especially early to the meeting place by the oleanders. Already the morning heat lay heavy, dampening sound, the jingle of her bobbins muffled, as though the effort of their twisting dance exhausted them.

"Hello!" He stood against the sun. She sat in his shadow, the sudden cooling a pleasure. "Been waiting for me?" Bracing his arms, he hoisted his body to sit beside her on the ancient stone wall. She shifted away from him. He had always been cocky! Always so sure of himself, with his dreams and his big plans—making all the girls notice him!

Without looking up, she answered, "No!" The sharpness in her voice startled her when she heard it.

"Hey!" He bent his head towards her, trying to see her face. "You angry with me? Why? I was only teasing . . ."

Giovanna felt silly. She usually never reacted in this way, got upset so easily and for such little things—it was not like her at all! She wondered why she had. Embarrassed by her own confusion, she smiled quickly to cover it up.

"That's better! After yesterday, I thought we were friends."

Giovanna stopped working, lifted her head, ready to apologize for her strange reaction to his greeting, and found that he wasn't paying the slightest attention to her.

Like a vision drawn by Botticelli, Antonia, in thistle-mauve and eyelet petticoats, appeared along the path. Approaching, her mouth stained crimson from the juice of ripe currants she had been gathering, she said in a breathless purr, "Oh, there you are, Giovanni. What a surprise! I only came to keep Giovanna company because she is always so alone." And allowing him to clasp her small waist, lift her up, settled herself next to him on the low wall. "Want some? They are so sweet this year . . ." Stretching a graceful arm across him, she offered her open palm filled with the shiny fruit to Giovanna, who selected one tiny red currant, just to be polite. "Giovanni? . . ." Antonia turned the full intensity of her beautiful amber eyes to lock with his. "You take some . . . they're so wonderfully sweet this year," and, tipping her hand, let her bounty spill into his lap, inquired, "Are the others coming, Giovanna?"

Who murmured, "I don't know . . . I came early," very engrossed with a particular section of her lace that seemed suddenly to refuse to lie flat.

"Today, it's much too hot to walk all the way up here . . . I don't know why I even attempted it." Sighing, Antonia removed the pins from her hair, letting it cascade down her back, raising her arms high to lift its shining weight, allow the air to touch and cool the nape of her milky white neck; that upward stretch accentuating to perfection the outline of her full breasts beneath the taut cloth of her bodice. From the moment of her appearance, the young man's eyes had never left her, riveted, mesmerized by the delicious picture she made.

The shadow of a kestrel startled a colony of green finches to seek safety within a dark pine. The soft drone of bumblebees mingled with church bells, calling across from another valley, a lark sang. The three sat, listening to their secret thoughts.

He is still looking at me. He can't take his eyes off me . . . I knew he would be here waiting for me . . . I was right! Antonia tingled, shivers of delight running all the way down to the very tips of her toes.

What a piece! She's magnificent! What a whore she would make. If she keeps this up, I will . . . careful, my boy . . . Remember, this is an Italian virgin AND the physician's only daughter . . . but . . . she may, just may . . . be worth the risk! If Giovanna hadn't been there, Giovanni would surely have thrown all caution to the wind, grabbed the so seductive Antonia into his aching arms.

Temptress! If she stretches her arms any higher, she'll split that badly stitched bodice and those big melon breasts of hers will pop out . . . in full view! . . . And look at him! . . . Sits

there completely stunned! . . . Even his eyes are glazed! Really—if Father Innocente comes
strolling by here now and sees this . . . he'll have an apoplectic fit!

Deciding to avoid being a witness to such a very deplorable and probable confrontation, Giovanna rolled up her bobbins, slipped off the wall, and strode down
the winding path towards the village. Antonia and her latest conquest didn't even
notice she had left.

The next day, Giovanna was so filled with remorse for having had such shocking
thoughts about one of her dearest and oldest friends that she marched up the hill
towards the oleanders, determined to make amends. How exactly she was going to
manage that when Antonia didn't even know the thoughts she was wanting to make
amends for, Giovanna didn't know . . . but surely something appropriate would come
to her, once the right moment presented itself. Out of breath, full of good intentions,
she arrived to find the wall deserted, except for the figure of Giovanni stretched out on
the grassy knoll above it. Well, might just as well get him over with too; her thoughts
about him had been just as mean, she really owed him a little atonement as well.

Not knowing how to begin, what to say, she stood looking down at him, hoping
he was asleep. Raising his hand to shield his eyes, he looked up at her, his face expres-
sionless. Giovanna hesitated, tongue-tied, suddenly shy. He reached up, caught her
wrist, and pulled her down beside him.

"What's the matter, little one? A raven got your tongue?" His strong hand kept
its hold on her thin wrist.

"Don't make fun of me!" she snapped.

"NOW what have I done wrong again? I'm not making fun of you!"

"Yes, you are . . . I'm not 'little'! I'm tall . . . lanky and spindly. In school Sister
Marie-Agnesia always called me the Fishing Pole. Don't you remember?"

"No, I never heard that one . . . but I wasn't thinking of the way you look . . . I
don't know why I said 'little'. . . It just came out!"

"Then I am sorry. I shouldn't have made a fuss." Giovanna moved away from him
and settled herself on the wall. "I know I must seem terribly touchy about absolutely
everything, but I'm really not. Everyone always says how quiet I am, how controlled,
practically unfeeling . . . Sister Bertine shakes her head over me constantly . . . She
is very concerned about what she calls my 'complete lack of fervor'! Of course, she's
alluding to religious fervor. Still, she has a point. I do try, I do . . . all the time . . .
but . . ." Giovanna stopped, aghast! She was prattling! Saying anything that came into
her head—and to a man—practically a stranger! Thoroughly shocked with herself,
she fussed with her cushion, unrolled her bobbins, and, lips tightly compressed, took
refuge in her lace.

Eyes half closed, he watched her in profile. High forehead framed by its chestnut brown hair, center parted, pulled back, secured with many pins, stationed on a neck so long—rising from a spine so straight—it had a military carriage. Maybe it was this that interested him, her bearing—it kept reminding him of a soldier he had once met, who'd told of battlefields, all the while appearing unaffected by his anguished tale. She had his same air of sad detachment that had moved him, had impressed itself onto his memory. He came to sit beside her.

"Friends?"

"Yes, thank you." Nice of him. A man never needed to ask permission of a woman for anything. "Please, before the others come, would you tell me some more about America?"

"What do you want to know?"

"What do you do there?"

"I build motorcars!"

"Oh . . . horseless carriages. Those are only for the very, very rich."

"In my factory, we build thirty every day!"

"Are there that many millionaires in America?"

"Daimler, the German, he builds his motorcars for the rich—but *we, we* know how to build them so that even the common man can afford to own one." Giovanna, lace forgotten, hung on his every word. "Already in the big cities we have some surfaced roads that the invention of the bicycle brought, and soon there will be more."

"It did? I have seen one. When Papa had his bad chest, I had to travel down to Torino to deliver our lace and I saw a street all smooth like that. But I didn't know those came about because of the bicycle. It must be exciting to ride on one of those."

"The cycle has its uses, but it takes human energy. It is slow . . . solitary transportation. But a motorcar—that is true liberty! It makes any man who can own one the master of his time and destination. Only the rich had such luxury of choice, until my boss made his dream come true. 'I shall build an auto for the masses,' he vowed and we did! It's not sleek—no racing lines, no ornamentation. You can't even say the design is beautiful, and since last year, only black can be its color . . . but you should see that little car go! Nothing stops her. Climbs the steepest grade like a mountain goat, then comes down just as sure-footed. She is so light, rides so high on her special chassis, impassable country roads, mud, ice, snow—nothing stops her. She can even cross rivers without getting bogged down. She's more dependable than the best horse ever born! That's why the first men to buy her were country doctors. They knew that nothing could stop her once she made up her mind!"

"Why do you say 'she'?"

"We all do. She's 'our girl'! Something about it just seems alive, as though it has a heart. It is strange how she makes you proud and not just us who build her but the everyday people who own her. She's America's Sweetheart!"

"What's that?"

"An American expression . . . it means a girl your heart likes."

"Do you have one?"

"Someday I will—and I'll take her everywhere. But first we must find a faster way to produce her! We are working on it to meet the huge demand."

Giovanna thought to correct him, then thought better of it and asked, instead, "But the horses—what will happen to them?"

"Oh, they have already disappeared from the big cities and their stinking manure with them! They still work the land and are the aristocrats' playthings, as they always have been." Her eyes had not left his face. What an extraordinary new world he believed in. Still, she just had to ask and so ventured a hesitant, "You're not making all this up, are you?"

"No. It has happened and I . . . I am part of it."

He said it like a vow and she believed him. He sat looking across the valley as though alone. Hardly breathing, not wanting to disturb the moment, she watched him.

After a while he remembered she was there. "The men that I work with say, 'Never get John Ricassoli started on his love affair with Tin Lizzie'!"

"Who's that?"

"She's now so famous, people give her names."

"You mean your wondrous motorcar is made of TIN?"

"Of course not! They only say that because she is so light—we use a special steel. The Americans like to joke!"

"It all sounds very exciting, what you do," Giovanna, newly awed, said, adding, "your landlady, the one who owns the . . . no, no, don't help me . . . I'll get it . . . 'izz boite.'"

"Pretty good! What about my landlady with the marvelous wooden boite?"

"You live there, in her house?"

"Yes, I rent a room and take my evening meal downstairs with the other lodgers. She's a good woman. She likes me . . . 'So tell me . . . what is my Italian baby boy up to?' she always says. I'm her youngest lodger—so she calls me her baby. Her husband brought her with him when he came over from Germany. He and I work together . . . that's how I found a place to live."

Giovanna felt relieved. For a young man alone, it was so much more fitting to live under the roof of a married lady whose husband was also in residence.

Streaks of orange glowed across the fading sky, touching mountains turned silhouette, a tiny bat flitted by on its first twilight foray; an awakening owl announced the beginning of its darkening day. Giovanna rolled up her bobbins. "It's late! I must go! Papa gets angry if his meal isn't ready waiting for him. And I haven't done my lace . . . and now I won't be able to finish it in time and Papa expects the money! I'll have to work on it after he's gone to sleep . . . I must hurry . . ."

Giovanni slid off the ledge and reached up to help her down.

"Will you come tomorrow?" he asked, not knowing why he did.

"Yes," she answered, not knowing why she wanted to so badly.

She had rushed and the sauce had not had enough time to thicken properly, so her father had been angry. Of course, he had had every right to be, for it was her fault for being late.

She banked the embers in the iron stove, moved the candle over to the low sideboard, began wiping down the long wooden table . . . seeing her mother's form as it lay upon it. This happened every evening. Over the years she had come to terms with it—accepting it as one of the hurting things that belonged to her.

She rolled up the threadbare rug, knelt, dipped the brush into the leather pail, began scrubbing the stone floor when suddenly she remembered her father's cup. In the summer, he drank his coffee outside their door, and tonight she had forgotten to collect it! He must be wondering what was wrong with her. Wiping her hands on her apron, she hurried outside to fetch it.

His chair tipped against the rough stone of his house, black hat cushioning the back of his head, her father's scarecrow frame sat balanced, smoking his pipe. Knowing how he hated being disturbed during what he called his "interlude of digestion," she looked for the cup, but being a moonless night, she couldn't find it in the gloom and had to ask, "Papa—the cup?"

"On the ground, by my foot! Eyes are for looking!"

"Sorry, Papa." She bent to retrieve the small cup and turned to take it inside.

"Wait!" He spoke without removing his pipe. Over the years, it had become a part of the configuration of his stone-cut face. "Why was my meal not ready on time? What were you doing?"

"I said I was sorry when I explained about the sauce . . ."

"You seem to be 'sorry' about a lot of things tonight! Well? Out with it, girl. Answer me!"

"I walked up to the oleanders to do my work . . . the Ricassoli boy . . . the one who ran off to America and now has returned . . . he was there waiting . . ."

Her father's jeer stopped her. "For you?"

"No, of course not me . . . for Antonia."

"So, he's after our saintly doctor's pretty daughter, is he? She'll make him dance to the Devil's tune! Runs off to be a fancy man in America but when he needs a wife, he comes scurrying back!"

"Oh, no, Papa! It is said the old nonna, the grandmother's illness brought him back."

"No, the only reason that young rascal came back here was to find himself a good Italian wife to service him—in more ways than one." Chuckling behind his pipe, he rocked his chair with the heel of his boot.

A sharp crack startled him. "What the Devil . . ."

"I'm sorry, Papa—I dropped it." Giovanna gathered up the pieces of the broken cup and went inside.

They met by chance the next day; he stretched on the grassy knoll, Giovanna on her way down from the convent above. Hoping he was asleep, she didn't stop. "You weren't here today and now it's too late to talk," he said, making her turn, ignoring Giovanni now an impossibility.

"Oh . . . it's you. I didn't see you! No, I couldn't today. Once a week I sew for the Sisters. Mend sheets and re-hem habits for those who have rheumatism and can't. Well?" she said, her tone impatient.

"Well, what?"

"Was there something you wanted to talk to *me* about—or one of the others?"

"Who said I wanted to talk?"

"You did . . . just now you said . . ."

"Oh, forget it." He got up, turned looking across the darkening valley. He was close enough to touch and yet seemed not there at all.

She should have left, instead remained, unable to come to a decision to leave. Suspended silence stretched between them into discomfort. Purple-rose stained the evening sky. The call to Vespers sounded.

"It's late," he said.

"Yes," she murmured, turning to leave.

"Don't go."

"Why?"

"Has anyone ever told you that you love questions?"

"No, but I suppose I do. It's a way of learning and knowing where one stands."

"Giovanna, sometimes you speak like a man."

"I am a motherless child, reared by a father who never liked her."

"It isn't proper for a girl to speak in that way!" Surprise and censure colored his tone.

"I know. I have real trouble being what I know I am supposed to be. Most of the time, I feel I am very different from other girls."

"Camilla is a real girl," he mused, as though he were alone.

"Giovanni, they say you returned to find a wife to take back with you. Is that true?"

"None of your business!"

"Is it true?"

"Yes!"

"Take me!"

Shocked, he backed away from her. Now that she had started, unable to stop, Giovanna advanced towards him. "TAKE ME! *Please*, take me! I can cook, clean, and sew. I'll take good care of you! I'll never interfere in your life, never be a burden to you. I swear I'll never ask for anything more! Just take me, TAKE ME WITH YOU TO AMERICA!"

"You're crazy! As crazy as your mother!"

With a snarl she jumped him, steel fingers gripped his throat. "I'm NOT! Damn you! I am NOT like my mother!"

His fury matching hers, he tore her hands from his throat, slapped her across the face and strode down the hill. Giovanna, stunned—more by her shocking loss of control than his blow—watched him disappear.

The next day, the chestnut sheltered only three. The sisters, excited about their brother's sudden decision to declare his honorable intentions to Camilla's father, couldn't even think of working lace, and, now that Camilla's future was being decided, her proud mamma had forbidden her virgin daughter to venture from within the protection of her father's house until Giovanni's actual proposal and her papa's certain consent.

Teresa, always brought to fever pitch by anything remotely suggestive of romance or ritual, now that the immediate future might hold the melding of both, was breathless with anticipation.

"Antonia, do you think he will marry her here? Well, he'll have to . . . they can't travel together without being man and wife. Just think—a marriage feast here! And our Camilla the lucky bride! Isn't it exciting? I asked my mamma if I can please, please wear my hair up for such an important event and you know what she said? She said, 'Yes!' and that she would even allow me to borrow her ivory comb. Do you think Mamma might let me dance? I am going to wear my flowered skirt—you know the one, but maybe with a new sash and dance with Mario Rossini. He looks nice now—his hair has grown back and Mamma says it is alright if I enjoy myself just a little before I renounce all worldly pleasures and give myself to Christ."

"You can rattle on longer than anyone I know," Antonia snapped. "If there ever *is* a wedding feast and your mamma *does* let you dance, which I doubt, don't do it with a Rossini twin—or you'll find yourself twirling in the bushes. Anyway . . ." Antonia continued in her principessa tone, "this morning my father spoke to Father Innocente to ask his opinion of all these goings-on and our saintly Abbot didn't know anything about it! And we all know that *he* of all people would be the very first to be informed if a nuptial was being planned."

A faint breeze rustled the broad chestnut leaves, joining the jingle of their busy bobbins.

"Oh! One of my shells has split!" Teresa, lips trembling, picked at her bundle, ready to weep.

"Well—just ask the Virgin to send you down another," retorted Antonia, which made Teresa's lips tremble even more.

Giovanna worked in silence.

"No . . . I don't think it's split *all* the way through." Teresa rolled the tiny spiral shell around in her palm, examining it, making sure the disaster she had first expected had been spared her. "Antonia, you must not take the name of our Holy Mother in vain—no matter how upset you are. It is a sin, Sister Bertine says so."

"You and your eternal prattle about your precious Sister Bertine! Why don't you just go into your convent right now, take the veil, lock yourself away and be done with it!"

Giovanna looked up. "Antonia, I think this time you have gone too far! You owe Teresa an apology."

"How dare you speak to me in that superior tone—I have never been so insulted!" Looking every inch the enraged aristocrat, Antonia marched off, dragging her chair behind her.

Teresa sighed, "Poor Antonia! She is so very disappointed Giovanni didn't choose her . . . but who knows . . . even Mamma said, 'I'll believe it when I see it. Nothing is ever what it seems—even if the foxes cry, Spring can be late in coming!' I don't know what she means by that but she always says it. My mamma's sort of partial to fox sayings . . . One of her favorites is 'Hens and boys beware of a vixen seen in the light of a new moon!' . . . I don't know what that one means either but she says that one *all* the time . . . and then there's . . ."

"Teresa," even Giovanna could take just so much of Teresa's mamma. "Do you really believe Camilla's father will give his consent?"

"Why not? Millionaires don't come along every day."

"Giovanni isn't a millionaire!"

"Well! Don't *you* think, with five daughters still left to marry off, wouldn't Camilla's papa be overjoyed to welcome any acceptable suitor who comes to his door?"

Giovanna sighed, tucked her work pillow under her arm, picked up her chair, and, shoulders drooping, stepped from beneath the comforting shade into the white glare of midday. Teresa watched her friend go, the compassion in her gaze belying her untried youth.

Having asked for Camilla's hand in marriage and been accepted by a grateful father, Giovanni left for Turin to make the necessary travel arrangements for himself and his bride. Now that everything was finally settled, all hesitation behind him, he could concentrate on getting back to work as quickly as possible. All accomplished, he returned, took a thorough bath in his mother's kitchen, slicked his hair, brushed his derby, shined his boots, and, clutching a bunch of daisies, pulled the plaited cord that rang the brass bell of the mayor's house. Camilla's mamma, in churchgoing finery, flung open the door and embraced her future son-in-law with unbridled delight.

"Welcome! Welcome, my dear Giovanni. Camilla awaits. Ready in the parlor." An anxious mother's slight exaggeration, for Camilla, propped amongst tasseled pillows on a very uncomfortable love seat, in a dress of palest yellow, her panic pallor having taken on a hue of curdled cream, was far from ready for anything. Camilla's mamma bustled about the room, indicating a broad footstool positioned at her daughter's feet. As with all of her daughters, Mamma believed in orchestrating proposals for their most romantic effectiveness. Giovanni lowered himself into the position of ardent suitor. Although her girlish bosom fluttered, no words of welcome left Camilla's pale lips. Mamma, in a bit of a quandary whether she needed to remain as chaperone, hesitated, then decided as they were already betrothed, she could leave them together long enough to tend to her soup for the evening meal. At the door, she turned, gave Giovanni a meaningful look, and left the two lovebirds to get on with it.

Gazing up at his bride-to-be, Giovanni began laying his plans for their future before her. Just as his profession demanded utmost attention to detail, precision in its execution, he approached life with the same attitude. Knowing all would be new to her, he proceeded to give her an explicit account of the arduous journey that lay before them, the endless days and nights in third-class carriages on trains, assuring her that sleeping sitting up was not as uncomfortable as she might think, it was simply a matter of getting used to. Once, having arrived in the port of the city of Le Havre, she would have to be extremely careful not to draw attention to herself or him, for, once spotted as possible immigrants, things could be dangerous. Thieves and, worse, ruthless swindlers took one's money, promised lodgings that then did not exist or were unfit for humans. But he would protect her, knew of a tavern where an affordable room could be found, where she might even be able to indulge in a bath in its kitchen, as such luxury would not be possible again for many weeks until after they had reached America. He wanted her to know that having survived the cattle conditions of steerage on his first crossing, he had sworn then that never would he be a part of such misery again, nor would anyone in his care need to endure it. He was proud that now he was in a position to keep that promise, he had been able to afford second-class accommodations for both of them. Although extremely small, the ship's cabins were not only safe but afforded precious privacy. He would share his with three other men, she with three other ladies. He hastened to add that communal facilities for private acts would only be a short distance in another part of the ship and certainly better than the open pails used by those in steerage. And when they encountered the usual heavy seas, being seasick with three ladies for company would be a comfort to her. Once safely arrived, the next journey by various trains would probably seem endless, for America was large, its distances farther than anyone from across the sea could ever imagine but she had his solemn promise that they would get to their final destination, eventually.

"We will make our first home in the room I rent. It is not big but sufficient. I work a nine-hour day, so you will have plenty of time to do your housework and learn to speak American. Frau Geiger, my landlady, is a kind woman—she will help you. I bet in no time you two will be boiling your wash together and making your soap in the huge kettle she keeps on the back porch of the house."

Throughout this travelogue of delights, Camilla's already enormous eyes had widened even further. Now, with the softest meow, she fainted dead away.

"Signora! Signora!" Giovanni dashed into the pungent kitchen. "Your daughter . . ."

"Santa Maria! What have you done to my child?" Mamma threw her spoon into the bubbling minestrone, hurried to her daughter spread-eagled on the horsehair love seat.

"Signora—believe me! All I said was we were going to America—I swear!"

"Did you remember to tell her first she would be going as your lawfully wedded wife?" Mamma asked, chafing her daughter's limp wrist.

"Of course she knew that, Signora!" Giovanni retorted, very put out at even the slightest hint of impropriety on his part.

"Then why should she faint?" pressured Mamma. Receiving only a dumbfounded look as answer, she hastened to reassure him. "Of course Camilla can be at times a little overdramatic. Nothing serious of course. Nothing for you, dear Giovanni, to have to be concerned about. You will see, once she has gotten used to the idea she will be as pleased as we all are with your offer."

This sensible speech somewhat placated Camilla's future husband as it was intended to. With a sharp pat on her newly resurrected daughter's cheek plus a warning look that spoke volumes, Mamma returned to her kitchen, leaving the young lovers to continue their courtship where they had left off.

"Camilla, are you alright?" Giovanni sat next to the trembling girl, anxious to repair whatever damage he might have done. He had no clue as to what it could have been that had put her into such a tizzy, still was more than willing to take the blame if it made her feel any better. To give her time to collect herself, he stroked her little white hand. Admiring its soft delicacy, he spoke again of their future.

"STOP! OH, PLEASE, please stop!" wailed Camilla, tears splashing down her cheeks, little hiccups getting in the way of words that tumbled out of her pretty mouth like cherry pits. "I CAN'T! I just can't! I don't want to die in the sea! I don't want to be seasick! I don't want to go to a big strange place full of savages I can't talk to! I don't want to be married to you! I don't want to leave my mamma! I don't want to make SOAP! GO AWAY!"

Giovanni fled.

2

Did you hear? She turned him down!" At the village fountain the shocking news of Camilla's refusal flowed like the water. Some shook their heads in disbelief; others nodded their approval of a true virgin's fears. In the chapel, Teresa, her longed-for wedding feast fading, knelt in ardent prayer, asking guidance for her friend's obvious confusion. A gleam in her eye, Antonia chuckled, washed her luscious mane, began preparing her father for the inevitable visit she was convinced Giovanni would now be making to her door, while Giovanna, with no hope whatsoever, went about her daily chores, pretending the excitement over this village romance had no effect on her.

Giovanni was furious. He had come home to get himself a woman to look after him, and by God he'd find one before the boat sailed! It no longer mattered who she was, as long as she was suitable. Precious hard-earned money had been laid out for a wife's passage, and by all the saints in Heaven, he was going to have one by sailing time!

Camilla no longer came to the piazza to seek the shade; neither did Antonia. One was in disgrace, locked in her room for shaming her father's given word, the other primped and paced, waiting for that expected suitor. Of course, Giovanni's sisters were far too upset over their brother's big trouble to even think of lace.

Alone, Teresa and Giovanna worked in silence. Their bobbins bounced but missed their usual friendly accompaniment. Anchoring pins to form the sunburst points of her collar, Teresa broke into their concentration, "Giovanna, isn't there something we can do to help poor Camilla? I mean besides praying—which you don't ever do anyway. I feel so sorry for her. Why wouldn't she be frightened—and I don't even mean having to marry, be WITH a man as a wife, that's scary enough but to have to leave all you have ever known—brave storms and unknown hardships and THEN, even if you manage to get there alive, savages scalp you?"

"You are as bad as Camilla. Shipwrecks and savages. Really! I don't know where everyone gets these silly ideas. First, how can he work in a big factory that makes wonderful motorcars that hundreds of people are able to buy if there are savages running around scalping everybody?" Fascinated, Teresa looked at her friend in amazement. "Yes, it's true. He told me about it. Oh, Teresa, *I* would go! I don't believe what people say, not even that all the streets are paved with gold, but I know why it is called the Land of Opportunity. Because everything is possible there, for everyone, no matter where you come from. I wouldn't care if I had to cross the most dangerous oceans in the world just to be a part of it! That's what I wan . . . wanted to tell him . . ." Giovanna stopped; she had almost blurted out what she was still too ashamed to admit—even to herself.

"Giovanna, do you hate it here?"

"Hate? Oh no, not really. Anyway, you always say that hate erodes the soul, so I wouldn't dare." Teresa smiled, knowing her friend was stalling, trying to find an answer to a question never asked her before. "Maybe I'm just different."

"How?"

"I don't know. Maybe it's a longing—a feeling of wanting more, something more than this—" Giovanna's arm swept the air as though encompassing her small world. "Well, haven't *you* ever longed to get away . . . see new worlds . . . learn . . . become somebody . . . ?"

Teresa looked up from her pillow. "To serve God is the greatest adventure of all."

"Oh, Teresa! Will you really? Are you sure? To spend your whole life on your knees in meaningless prayer, how . . ."

"Giovanna, don't blaspheme!! For the sake of your soul—not mine—you mustn't!"

"Oh, for heaven's sake. It's nonsense, all of it—just a lot of nonsense." Giovanna's tone held a finality. Teresa, eyes lowered to her pillow, murmured, "I shall pray for you."

A tense interval of conscientious work, then, in a voice that still held a hint of her irritation with Divinity, Giovanna asked, "Teresa—tell me—haven't you ever felt lost?"

"No. Never!"

"I do all the time. It's like I don't really belong . . . anywhere. Sometimes when the feeling gets really bad, I think, What if there really isn't anywhere for me? And then I wonder what will become of me if that is so. But I must try—I have to—AND I'm not like my mother, truly I'm not!" Giovanna swallowed a threatening sob. Teresa reached out, covered her friend's hands clenched in her lap, stilling their agitation with her touch. Lace forgotten, they sat, watching the perimeter of their shade. One lost, seeking peace at any price; the other content having found, without search, all that was necessary. In the cool of early evening, they walked home together. As they parted, Giovanna, in a rush of courage, confessed, "Teresa, I asked Giovanni to take me. Oh, I know it was a shocking thing to do and, of course, he was furious. But I had to . . . I just had to try. And now, what do you think? Can I ask him again?"

"Oh, dear!" fluttered an uncertain Teresa. Cast down to bare human need, completely out of her element, she said the first thing that presented itself. "Well, if you have already done it once, why not again? Who knows? Mamma always says, 'Men are very peculiar.'"

Giovanna kissed her cheek and ran.

The sisters, putting their heads together and agreeing on all important points, went in search of their brother. They found Giovanni in the blackest of moods, sharpening an axe in their father's toolshed. Courageous Celestina was the first to speak. "Giovanni, we, your sisters, have come to speak with you on a most delicate matter which we consider of utmost importance."

"So please don't get angry at us." Confrontation made Gina nervous. Being politely beautiful she considered much more advantageous.

"And please, stop this noise and"—Celestina held up a hand—"don't speak, because if I am stopped now, I'll forget what we thought through and agreed to say!"

Giovanni glowered at the two girls . . . If they said one thing in defense of that stupid Camilla, he'd murder them.

"Well? What's *so* important?"

Looking at her sister, making sure one last time that what had been decided between them still stood, Celestina took a deep breath and plunged, "Gina and I think you should consider Giovanna Zanchetta!"

"You're both as crazy as she is!"

"No, no. She isn't crazy! All our lives we have been friends. Her mother was crazy, everyone knows that, but that doesn't mean Giovanna is." Celestina, warmed to her task, rushed on to present their conclusions. "Now listen, please! You came all the way back home to get yourself a sensible wife . . . and what do you do . . . you go and ask that Camilla. She's pretty and all that silly stuff that you men seem to like so much . . . but really, Giovanni, she hasn't a sensible bone in her whole spine and she has not too much up in her head either! Instead of having someone who could take proper care of you, you would have to spend all your time and money taking care of her. We, your loving sisters, think it was your very good fortune that Camilla turned you down!"

"And you better be careful that ambitious mamma of hers doesn't force Camilla to change her mind and THEN you will really be in the soup!" Gina chimed in as Celestina was catching her breath, gearing up for the next assault.

"Gina's right about the mamma. Now—we certainly don't want you to find some Detroit lady to marry. Papa and Mamma would die. Their grandsons not Italian? What a thought! Now, as the good nuns love to say, 'Let us look at the whole picture!' You need a wife. Everybody agrees about that—healthy, strong, frugal . . . someone you can depend on. You said yourself how very, very hard the journey is to reach l'America . . . so what you need is a wife who can take the hardships you have told us about, who won't have the vapors every two minutes, who can bear you healthy sons, save you money, and, also, has brains to learn to speak American so you won't have to be ashamed of a wife as though you married an ignorant peasant from the South! Giovanna Zanchetta is not pretty, but she is dependable and all those other things I just said—and, as Teresa's mamma always says, 'Better an ass that carries than a horse that throws!' And you know what is the best of all? Giovanna will never be able to run home to her mamma . . . because SHE HASN'T GOT ONE!"

Giovanni threw back his head and roared with laughter. Encouraged by his reaction, the sisters hugged each other, delighted.

"Come here, you two scamps!" and each received a brother's kiss on their flushed cheeks.

Too much time was passing. Soon the ship would sail and with it an angry, disappointed bachelor. Giovanni, pressured by an imminent departure, made his decision, resigned himself to second best—more likely fourth or even fifth best, had anyone dared to question him—and so one evening presented himself at the Zanchettas' front door.

Taken aback, Giovanna admitted him, presented him to her glowering father, and faded into the shadows, heart pounding. Giovanni wasted no time.

"Sir, I know the hour is late, but I have come to ask for your daughter's hand in marriage. Please, before you answer, I wish you to know that I do not expect, nor do I have the need to accept, the required dowry. Should you give your consent I must warn you that any wife of mine will have to be ready to leave with me for America within the next two weeks."

Giovanna's father did not stir. His hawklike eyes focused on the young man before him, as though he were discovered prey.

"Couldn't get the one you really wanted, so you're desperate . . . *boy*?"

"No . . . *sir*." Giovanni's dislike of this man was hard to hide.

"Well, you can't have this one! This one's mine! She stays here where she belongs, to look after me."

"And what about Giovanna? She is to have nothing to say . . . ?"

"Don't you bring your evil foreign ways into my house! My daughter belongs to me! She will do what I say! GET OUT!"

Giovanni was more than ready. This bastard for a father-in-law? Nothing was worth that.

The soft "no" stopped his retreat. Despite his need to escape, Giovanni paused, intrigued. Stepping from the shadows into the circle of light, Giovanna faced her father's chair.

"No, Papa! I am leaving. I shall go with Giovanni as his wife or not. I have no false pride in such things. If he will take me to America, I will go with thankfulness."

Her voice calm, her manner assured, she turned, lifted her woolen shawl from its nail by the door, motioned the stunned young man to follow her, and stepped outside. The night was cold, darkened by a moonless sky. Arms folded, she stood looking up. He watched her, a little afraid of this young girl with the passionate convictions of a woman twice her age. Apprehensive silence lay between them.

I wish he'd say something! Anything! Get it over with. He won't want to take me now after all this—so let him say it and get it over with. I'm tired of wanting too much! She tensed for his words, certain they would hurt.

Convinced he was making a catastrophic mistake, he turned her towards him. "Well, Giovanna Zanchetta, are you coming with me to America?"

"Yes," she whispered, afraid to believe him.

"Thank God *that's* settled! First we get your papers, then we marry . . ."

"You don't have to, I meant what—"

"I know exactly what you meant in there. Where you get such craz—" Just in time, he caught himself. "STRANGE ideas is beyond me. Of course we have to be married. Mr. Henry Ford expects his workers to be respectable!"

She wore her mother's summer hat, a bunch of wild irises her only finery. Her suitcase of straw, secured by its leather strap, contained the few mementos of a life already relegated to the past.

Nearly the whole village came to see them off. Sister Bertine and Sister Marie-Agnesia smiled benignly, slightly nervous as they always were when face-to-face with acts of coupling in the outer world. Father Innocente beamed. He loved the very thought that by nightfall of this very day these two young people would be one. Camilla, forgiven by everyone but her mamma, brought a pretty basket of fruit for the long train journey. The sisters wept, joy mingled with fear. When, if ever, would they see their favorite brother again? And what if, through their good intentions, they and they alone had condemned this bridal pair to death in the ominous depths of the Atlantic Ocean? Antonia wished Giovanna well, offered her a gift of a vial containing her father's special concoction for the treatment of severe seasickness, cautioning her that as it contained laudanum, it could kill. Teresa pressed a small St. Benedict medallion into Giovanna's reluctant hand, whispered as she held her close one last time, "May the Lord keep you, make His eyes shine upon you, guide you till the end of your days."

The loud hiss of steam! Giovanna curtsied to her father-in-law, Giovanni embraced his mother, the sisters hugged their brother. The stationmaster, father to the Rossini twins, checked his large pocket watch, blew his special trumpet. Giovanna, following her husband, boarded the train.

"Bonna Fortuna! Bonna Fortuna!" Everyone waved.

Clutching her precious hat, Giovanna leaned out of the window to catch a last look of her childhood friends. She hung there, searching for their faces, long after coal smoke had enveloped them in ghostly shrouds.

Her great adventure had begun. The fledgling dream she had given her pride for was about to become her reality. Now, suddenly this frightened her. Marriage vows parroted, not felt, a barrier of mutual embarrassment, they sat facing each other like strangers waiting to alight at separate stations.

"Close the window, Giovanna."

She did, giving its broad leather strap an extra tug to make certain it would hold. Her knees shook; sitting, she pressed her palms against them hoping he wouldn't notice. Ashamed at her loss of courage, hiding her eyes, she focused on the tops of descending pines as they slowly passed by the window. She wished she could unbutton the high collar of her shirtwaist, but that would be an unladylike thing to do. She hoped the sweat beginning to form on her face would not be considered equally unladylike. It startled her, this sudden concern for propriety. It was not like her at all. Could a few sanctimonious incantations have such a radical effect? And so quickly? Better not to dwell on it. The deed was done. No turning back—besides, nothing to turn back to.

"Your face is covered in soot. Here . . ." Giovanni offered his handkerchief.

Shaking her head, Giovanna took from her jacket pocket one of the ones she had made for herself. Using the dim reflection of herself in the window to wipe her face, she acknowledged, as she often did, that she was truly plain. A reality accepted long ago—then learned to live with. Turning to him, her eyes questioned if her face was now clean.

"Yes, Giovanna. You must be more careful. You cannot lean out when a train is in motion. You could have gotten cinders in your eyes, and that can be serious. When they examine you, if the doctors find anything wrong with your eyes, you won't be allowed to enter America. I'll go on, of course, but you? You will be sent back, alone!"

Giovanni fingered the pockets of his vest, searching for a match to light one of the thin cheroots he seemed to have an endless supply of.

She was going to be examined? By strange men in a strange land—maybe then abandoned? Whatever had possessed her to want to leave Cirié, marry, journey across half the world with a man who, though he didn't love her, could at least like her enough to not leave her like a sack of weeviled potatoes just because her eyes might be judged unsuitable? And what else would those strange doctors do to her, want to examine? She decided to ask.

"Giovanni, I am very healthy, so what—"

He interrupted her. "I know. I checked with the nuns."

"You . . . did?" Giovanna barely contained her outrage.

"Of course. Camilla too! 'Good family health is most important,' Mr. Ford says."

"Oh, your Mr. Ford is interested in health? Not only with the making of motorcars?"

"Mr. Henry Ford takes care of his workers in everything!" bristled Giovanni.

Giovanna remained silent. Giovanni dozed; it had been an exasperating week.

Hesitant, as though afraid to slip, the small train rattled on towards the city below.

Later, whenever Giovanna tried to describe their arrival in Turin's opulent station, she could never quite manage to convey the enormity of that vast canvas of people in motion engulfed by smoke and turmoil. The indescribable noise, the shouts, clanging bells, trains in motion, hissing steam streaming upwards towards the vaulted glass ceiling, amplifying itself as it ricocheted back down to shatter eardrums and composure. And how it stood, mighty, its own majesty, as though no human effort could have created it. Its visual impact of power so overwhelming that Giovanna, standing rooted below, looking up at it, caught her breath in fearful awe.

Intent on finding a pump to refill their water bottles, Giovanni lost sight of his wife. She, mesmerized by the first true locomotive she had ever seen, didn't even miss him. His anger when he finally found her didn't penetrate either. He shouted above the din, "I had to look for you! Don't you *ever* make me do that again! Understand? Where I go, you follow!"

Trance broken, Giovanna switched her rapt gaze to him, asking, "This? This will pull *our* train?"

"Yes, it's a locomotive. Now take the water and food." Handing her the laden string bags, he turned and barked, "Come on!" over his shoulder, and hurried along the platform. Bottles and bags bumping against her legs, Giovanna stumbled after him.

Inside the crowded third-class carriage, people slid over, making room for them to sit together. Giovanni got organized. On the roped rack above, he stacked their two suitcases, on top of which he placed their overcoats, neatly folded inside out. As hats needed to be worn for propriety as well as station, they represented no problem of storage. The string bags holding their bottles of water he placed on the floor behind his legs; the one with their provisions, behind Giovanna's. Removing his jacket carefully, reversing its sleeves, he instructed his wife to observe, follow his example, explaining that in this way, folded twice, a comfortable padding could be arrived at, making the sitting on wooden slats for long periods of time at least bearable. Following his instruction, Giovanna saw some of their fellow travelers, on hearing this advice, doing the same. On entering, she had noticed the way the men looked at her husband. They, in their workman's clothes and cloth caps, sizing up the stranger in a store-bought suit, sporting a boss's derby.

Giovanni pulled the tasseled curtain across the open window. It swayed with the undulation of the train, but no breeze made it flutter. Women unknotted their headscarves, wiped their faces before folding the cloths into damp triangles. Their men fanned themselves—those who could read—with their folded newspapers, others using their caps. One, sweat-stained, addressed Giovanni in Piedmontese, the dialect of the region. If he had done so in any of the hundreds of dialects passing for Italian within the country, neither Giovanni nor Giovanna would have understood him. Italians actually became Italians only outside their country's borders. Within, their language was shaped by the region they came from, their identity by the former kingdoms—the duchies they lived in. So, a Neapolitan introduced himself as such to a Venetian, a Milanese to a Florentine, a Roman to a Genovese. Shakespeare's Juliet was a Veronesa. If Romeo had called her an Italian, he would probably never have been allowed up that balcony vine.

Their women in attentive silence, the men in multi-dialects—aided by expressive gestures and vehement emotions—set about getting acquainted. By the time they reached their various destinations, they would know each other's angers, if not each other.

As the only one who had actually seen the land of milk and honey, its streets of pure gold, Giovanni was questioned, listened to without interruption except for ahs of disbelief and incredulous "Gesu Marias."

Knowing what they wanted to hear, he spoke of only good things. Now was not the time to tell them of cities where the Irish immigrants ruled. Of their belief that their Catholicism was the only one sanctioned by the Holy Trinity, whereas Italians were the "Christ Killers," their religion solely one of superstition, proving their inherent ignorance and worthlessness. That Italian immigrants, those mostly from the South, were considered not fit for employment in higher-ranking jobs and were reduced to seeking out their livelihood as pushcart vendors, ragmen, and organ grinders, their women sweatshop captives, their children street acrobats, bootblacks, and beggars, their social position only slightly above those considered even lower than they—the "conniving Jews," closely followed by the "uncivilized darkies."

No, Giovanni did not tell of these sad truths within that wonderful country—that symbol of hope sought by so many of Europe's hopeless. He had learned not to disturb dreams. Immigrants needed them to survive the realities awaiting them.

Watching her husband, his authority acknowledged, sanctioned by men older than he, Giovanna felt a pride in belonging to him. She who had such aversion to ownership of all kinds found herself as the bride one looked up to, showing off her new wedding band to women who believed her more fortunate than they. Respect, even by association, was a heady experience.

Flipping open the ornate lid of his pocket watch, a Milanese checked the time, carefully winding his precious possession, scrutinizing its face before announcing to the carriage at large, the precise hour, minute, and seconds of the approaching night.

Pain awakened her before she knew why she hurt and then she realized it was just another dead of night on wooden slats. Kneading the ache in her neck, she turned. Next to her the space was empty, Giovanni's jacket pad gone. He had left her! He had decided marrying her was after all a terrible mistake—gotten off the train, was now far away on his way to America unencumbered by an unwanted wife. So convinced was she of this calamity that she didn't even check the overhead rack for his bag until the worn corner of it caught her eye. Giovanni might abandon her, but his fine American clothes? Never! Reassured, she sat admonishing herself severely. Really, she was no better than silly Camilla, getting so excited, imagining all sorts of dramas in the slightest of things.

Just because he said "abandoned" once doesn't mean he really would. Such childish behavior! Really, Giovanna! Wholly involved in the scolding of herself, his sudden voice startled her.

"Here, I found a fruit vendor." He handed her a small cornucopia of grayish paper.

"On the train?"

Even to Giovanna, her question sounded lame—but the rush of joyous relief on seeing him was so bewildering, a sudden shyness engulfed her.

"No, of course not—outside, on the platform."

"Oh, has the train stopped? Are we in a station?"

Giovanni looked at his wife.

Thoroughly confused with herself, Giovanna peered intensely through the grimy window, wondering where they were and whatever was the matter with her. Feeling her husband's speculative gaze, she tried to eliminate the awkward moment by asking, "I can't see the name of the station—is this Paris?"

Giovanni was torn between the urge to laugh or shake her until her senses returned. But knowing that exhaustion could make one light-headed, he sat down beside her, stretched out his legs, pulled his derby down over his eyes, and murmured, "Eat your cherries, then rest. We have a long way still." And fell sound asleep.

The train picked up speed, piercing the night with its mournful wail—the loneliest sound Giovanna had ever heard. The cry so mighty—from one so strong that compassion would not be given it, or comfort. It was so with people—the strong, the apparently capable, were left to pull their loads alone, cry unseen, iron casing in place, hiding vulnerability. The soft received spontaneous support, for they advertised so well their need of it. Giovanna wondered if the black iron giant she had so admired ever wailed into the night because of sorrow or only to announce its approach. A cherry spilled from the small cornucopia on her lap, reminding her how thirsty she was. Never, not even those picked from Father Tomasso's orchard, ever tasted so truly wonderful. Always, Giovanna remembered the taste of their syrupy juice that night, never forgot it.

Glowing ocher, umbers reflecting sunrise and sunsets as though they were made of them, scattered houses terra-cotta shingles askew, everywhere haphazard untidiness made picturesque virtue in a landscape suited to it; followed by high mountain passes holding forever captive seasonless snows; then, suddenly as though a page in a child's picture book had been turned, lush fields, grazing cows, turrets, curled iron balconies, everything embellished, new, pin neat, nothing left to chance or irresponsible nature.

Giovanna, her nose pressed to the window she yearned to be allowed to open, was overwhelmed by all she saw.

"Oh, look! A castle!" Even as tired as she had to have been by now, her enthusiasm was still intact. Giovanni liked that in his bride.

Smiling, he corrected her. "No, we have left Italy. Now we are in France. That was a château. A small one. The French like to show off their riches."

"But then the robbers will know where to go!" observed a thoroughly confused Giovanna, whose prosperous countrymen hid their wealth behind inner courtyard walls and unassuming outer doors.

"I suppose so, but outward beauty is very important to the French. They seem to live for it. You should see the automobiles they buy. Speed and sparkle—the more of both, the better they like them."

"Oh! There—a yellow field! Do you see it? Brighter than sunshine. What was that?"

"Mustard. Another French passion," said Giovanni and went to sleep.

Giovanna's eyes and spirit moved with the glorious countryside passing before her. By the time another night blackened her view, she was convinced that French cows gave only cream, those engorged udders they dragged about with them couldn't contain anything as plain as everyday milk, all French farmers must be princes—dukes at the very least—and Giovanni, who could be fascinating when holding forth on subjects that interested him, could be a rather boring travel companion. Even if he had seen it all before, that was no reason to simply ignore everything. After a while, when her excited questions received only curt replies or snores, she stopped asking them.

Endless days, endless nights. Despite her clothes cushion, the wooden slats seemed to have grown themselves into Giovanna's backside. Pain radiated up and through her spine, reaching every bone in her exhausted body, but she refused to succumb to it. Any minute she might wake up—find herself back in Cirié—this whole marvelous adventure just another one of her many dreams; so, while this one lasted, she was determined to stay wide awake to revel in it.

"Hurry!" Giovanni lifted their bags down from the overhead rack. "Don't gawk! We have to change stations." The screech of iron on iron, the recoil of a stopping train, one last blast of escaping steam and Giovanna Francesca Zanchetta, village girl, was in Paris! And it wasn't a dream after all!

Weaving, dodging like a prizefighter in the ring, Giovanni made his way through the milling crowds, his wife in hot pursuit.

Once outside, Giovanna just had time to register the startling whiteness of daylight intensifying the blue of workers' smocks before her waist was clutched and, suitcases dangling from both arms, she was hauled off the sidewalk, plopped onto the small platform of a moving trolley car. Out of breath, making sure her hat hadn't been lost in the wild maneuver, she clung to the wooden railing as Giovanni squeezed in beside her.

"We made it! Look! Look, over there! A Hispano-Suiza! See? The steering wheel still on the right? But those lines . . . Magnificent!"

Had he been exclaiming over a beautiful woman, he couldn't have sounded more adoring. Clutching the railing to keep from falling against him, Giovanna thought that to become so enthused by a motorcar when the tip of what must be the so wondrous Tower of Eiffel could be seen on the horizon was a huge exaggeration, yet she had to admit those immaculate driving coats, white as the elegant tires and especially the ladies' chiffon tied hats, had been spectacular. Stopping and starting, clanging its bells, the trolley scooted along until Giovanni shouted, "Move! We're here! Give me the bags—get off!"

Here too, Giovanna was given no time to marvel at vaulted domes of cut glass, tall columns adorned with acanthus leaves edged in gilt, or the steaming black giants arrayed like horses in their stalls, but was hustled into a catacomb room of darkened oak reached through a massive door sporting a small white porcelain plaque that read SALLE D'ATTENTE 3EME CLASSE. Indicating a free space on one of the long benches lining the room, Giovanni told his wife to sit and wait for him, adding as an afterthought that he would return.

Giovanna sat, waiting, wondering where in this rather ominous enclosure a place to relieve oneself might be hidden and, should Giovanni be gone longer than expected, how she would manage to ask directions to it and what did he think one did *but* wait in a waiting room, when suddenly, utterly astounded, she realized that not only had she been able to read the sign on the door but, from the moment of their arrival, during all the dashing and confusion, she had understood the babble of voices surrounding her, all the while completely unaware that she could. French, of course! Everyone had been speaking French—a language she knew well! She liked the comforting feeling, the new sense of security, that this discovery gave her. *I am not a tongue-tied foreigner in a strange land—I can understand them. And they will understand me*, Giovanna marveled, quite impressed with herself. Now all she had to do was learn American. As soon as the proper moment presented itself, she would ask Giovanni to teach her.

Rearranging the heavy folds of her long skirt, Giovanna waited, idly observing her fellow travelers. Some seemed as weary as she. She noticed that being the only woman wearing a lady's hat, she was scrutinized by those whose head coverings were tied beneath their chins. Across from her, a young mother, her wooden clogs protruding from a voluminous, patterned skirt, kept eyeing the tips of Giovanna's leather shoes, which were visible beneath the fashionable blue serge of her traveling costume. Seeming not to notice, as if quite by chance, adjusting the angle of her body, Giovanna exposed to full view her prized high-button shoes for inspection, enjoying, quite without shame, the hint of raw envy they inspired.

Giovanni returned to find his wife most anxious to leave.

"You have to pay the attendant to get in. Here," he said, handing her a coin, adding, "and take our soap. You can wash in there." From the string bag, Giovanna took their precious cake wrapped in its protective sheet of oilskin and, not at all uncertain, turned to leave.

"Go through the door at the far end, then turn left. Be careful—don't go into the wrong side. Yours will have a sign marked with the letters D-A-M-E-S."

"Oh, really? I wouldn't have known that!" snapped Giovanna. Realizing how very tired she must be to have resorted to sarcasm, she hurried away before her husband could reprimand her for it.

Giovanna never forgot the discovery of that inner sanctum marked DAMES—that awesome palace of tile, its endless gleam of pristine white, the lidless seats that lined a whole wall, each with its own cubicle, giving utmost privacy when its door was secured by a large hook, the tidy bundle of cut-up newsprint that hung by a string so conveniently at arm's length, the long chain with its porcelain teardrop weight that, when she pulled it out of curiosity, produced such a gush of water, it made her jump up in fear, peer down, watch a mighty swirl as it disappeared into the depth of nowhere. Fascinated at how water seemed to materialize from everything, the small, three-spoked porcelain wheels that, when twisted, produced theirs that then poured into a basin beneath, where she washed her face and hands and, full of excitement, exited the DAMES.

Careful not to get lost, remembering each turn in reverse, she returned and was greeted by "What took you so long? I was beginning to wonder if you got yourself lost!"

That opened up the floodgates of her discovery. By the time she got around to the pull chain that produced such gushing magic of its own, her husband was laughing. A little at her but mostly just laughter without a hint of ridicule, so she didn't mind at all. When he began to explain in the minutest detail the intricacies of something called "plumbing," later becoming rhapsodic when describing the engineering marvels of the Paris sewers, Giovanna listened, completely enthralled. The hours flew. He taught—she learned.

Giovanni was beginning to enjoy her. Once or twice, he had felt it only proper to inquire if she was alright, was their arduous journey beginning to take its toll, and each time she had turned to him, eyes aglow in a tired face, assuring him that no aching bones, no yearning for a bath, a hot meal—absolutely nothing could spoil the wonders she was seeing of a world so unknown to her before. It came to him that maybe he had not made such a bad choice after all, but, ever cautious, knowing what still lay ahead, he reserved his final opinion of her until they had crossed the sea and arrived safely in Detroit. That Giovanna was adaptable, he was beginning to learn. Just *how* adaptable, he would still wait and see. It did puzzle him that she seemed so completely oblivious of her new state of wifehood, her attitude so devoid of any bridal coyness or feminine sham. Not one flirtatious look, no inviting gesture had been directed his way. What he was so used to from women, he now found completely lacking in the one he had taken to wife. He assured himself this was actually a relief . . . still, it piqued his vanity that she had not even given him the opportunity to rebuff her. Of course, this could still change once they found themselves in proper lodgings, in a private room with a bed. Still, it irritated him that this lanky girl, with her plain face, seemed so unaware of him as a male. Or was she pretending? Could there be a passionate woman hidden beneath the excellent traveling companion not given to feminine frailties? Somehow, he doubted it. No, a sensible housekeeper he had come for, and a sensible housekeeper he had acquired. A real woman to moan under him he could find anywhere. Giovanni checked his pocket watch against the big wooden clock on the waiting room wall and, putting on his coat and hat, motioned Giovanna to pick up their bags and follow him out the door. Another swaying carriage—this one so long one couldn't see the faces of one's fellow passengers sitting at the far end of it, with real linen curtains, their edges stitched, and padded armrests covered in pebbly leather. Everything was so elegant; there was even a private place to relieve oneself, and the slats of the benches were placed so close together, they actually touched. Thoroughly impressed, Giovanna settled into her corner, a little sad she was leaving. Oh, the DAMES had certainly been a marvel, the tip of Monsieur Eiffel's Tower too, to say nothing of the trolley car ride—yet there had to be more of such marvels in Paris, and she wished she had been given the chance to see those too.

The train hurried towards the night's horizon as though anxious to reach the sea. Giovanna yearned to see what it would look like, yet wondered if by its very vastness it might make her fear to journey upon its ominous surface, and that would never do. When taking her marriage vows, she had silently made one of her own: never to show fear, thereby embarrass, hinder, become a burden to the man who, by making her his wife, was taking her to the land of opportunity and freedom. Though a vow did not carry any religious obligation for Giovanna, her gratitude to Giovanni did, and for him she intended to keep it, no matter what the future might demand of her.

Too dark now to watch the moving images, she turned from the window, observing her husband as he read the English-language newspaper he had bought for himself from the station kiosk. Of course, she had assumed that he could read. Having such important employment would require it. Still, it was reassuring to actually witness him doing so. Quite unexpectedly she caught herself wondering if this man sitting across from her might be considered by others to be handsome. Antonia had certainly thought so. But then, without meaning to be unkind, Antonia found men in general interesting, so her opinion didn't really count. Actually, his face was rather nice, maybe his mouth the best part of it, especially when he smiled. He didn't do that often, but when he did, it felt worth waiting for. There was that contradiction about him that had always intrigued her, even when they were growing up. A difference from all the other boys—subtle, yet obvious. Like his strangely beautiful hands that showed none of the strength she knew they possessed, that belonged more to a sensitive artist or a fine gentleman than to a common man of the people. She had always liked that about him—his lack of coarseness, this unschooled elegance that seemed to be such an unself-conscious part of him. The distant lights of an approaching city attracted her eyes away from him, yet her thoughts held in place. In Torino, when he had helped her down off the train; in Paris, when he'd lifted her off the sidewalk, her body had remembered his touch as though it had had need of it. The confusion this had caused her had been so newly uncomfortable that she had immediately decided to forget it, and now, suddenly, she found that she had not. Whatever was the matter with her? Just tiredness! *So stop it!* she admonished herself and turned her full attention to the night passing by the window.

Giovanni folded his paper, placed it with his hat on the rack above, took his coat, and, leaning forward, draped it across Giovanna's chest. Assuming her slight recoil to be involuntary, he settled himself for the long night. Eyes closed, Giovanna pretended sleep, hopeful that whatever was wrong with her would be cured and gone by morning.

By the time they finally arrived at their port of embarkation, her body had acquired a tiredness quite beyond its capacity of youth. It swayed regardless of where it stood, as if it now possessed a new rhythm for her to exist by. She was so afraid she might fall that she closed her eyes, hoping to regain her balance, but only for a second, for losing Giovanni in the surging crowd of travelers was even more frightening. Taking a deep breath, she stumbled after him, eyes riveted on his dodging derby headed towards the docks.

The echo cry of gulls, the acrid smell of creosote and iodine. The sea! For the first time, Giovanna smelled its distinctive odor, felt its salt sting as wind whipped her face.

"The Atlantic Ocean!" she gasped, completely overcome.

"No, the English Channel," said her husband and hurried on.

Oh, dear! She always knew she should have paid more attention in Sister Bertine's geography class. Still, if she knew everything, Giovanni wouldn't need to correct her as often, so, as he seemed to welcome every opportunity to do so, it could be argued that she was actually doing him a favor. Very satisfied with this solution to her new status of slightly backward wife, she hurried after him. If only he would stop, just for a minute, that's all she needed to catch her breath. But he didn't, and suddenly she felt like crying. If she allowed that to happen, tears would blind her, she would really lose sight of him, and he would never forgive her and, lost, all alone, wandering dank, dark alleys, some sinister white slaver would find her, knock her over the head, sell her to a Chinaman in a haze-filled opium den! Slightly dazed by her vision of Oriental lust, Giovanna shook her head to clear it, pinned her hat back from where it had wobbled to, squared her shoulders, mustered up her last remaining strength, and, determined not to sway even if it killed her, keeping his bobbing derby fixed in her sights, followed it through the milling crowds along the quay, catching up just as Giovanni was opening a weathered door to an establishment that looked to have withstood years of lashing storms.

"Oh, there you are. Good." Giovanni acknowledged his wife's presence and, stepping inside, motioned her to follow. The narrow hall smelled of entrenched mildew. In a circle of orange light, burly men in thick wool, light-eyed as though the glare of many seas had bleached their irises, played frayed cards from thickened hands. The smell of their cheap wine and black tobacco mingled with the one of the hall.

"Madame, I require a room. I am John Ricassoli, and this is my wife," her husband said in the most atrocious imitation of French Giovanna had ever heard. But the wizened woman behind the desk, her nostrils sprouting nearly as much hair as her bearded customers in the bar, seemed to understand. Nodding, she plucked a large key from its nail and, pointing, indicated that their room was directly over her head. Giovanna followed her husband up the threadbare stairs into a room equally run-down but, thankfully, clean.

"We are lucky. That crone may look like a witch, but she is one of the very few who don't rob immigrants—especially Italians, not even Jews." Hanging his coat and vest over the back of the only chair, he removed his collar and cuffs, rolled up his sleeves, unwrapped their soap and towel, poured water from the cracked pitcher into its chipped bowl, and washed. No need to shave—he would do that in the morning.

Giovanna hung her jacket on the newel post of the double bed, wondering if she too could wash, perhaps even change into a clean shirtwaist. Giovanni emptied his wash water into the slop pail, informed her that he had left enough in the pitcher for her, not to forget that when she was through, to wipe the soap dry before rewrapping it or it would become gelatinous. Then he slipped down his suspenders, stripped off his shirt, pulled a fresh one from his bag, unbuttoned his trousers, smoothed down its tail, re-dressed, and, without the slightest hint of self-consciousness, said that a hot meal could be had downstairs—she needed to hurry before it was all gone and shouldn't forget to lock their door—then handed her the key before leaving. Giovanna picked up his shirt from where he had flung it, not certain if there was time to launder it or if she needed to wait until they were aboard the ship. Deciding not to take the time to change, she washed, dried the soap as instructed, repinned her hair, and, anxious to escape the lingering picture of Giovanni's naked torso, hastened from the room, locking the door securely before rushing downstairs.

Leek and potatoes, thick and hot. Never had anything tasted so truly wonderful. Her exhausted body welcomed that soup as though it was life-giving and, in a way, it was. After two whole bowls, she felt deliciously drowsy. Smiling, Giovanni reached across the low table, lifted her drooping chin. "Giovanna—you're falling asleep. Go, go up to bed."

The seagulls' cries woke her. To be able to stretch out, sleep in a bed after such a very long time, had been a little like dying pleasantly. Stretching, she sighed at the thought of having to leave such comfort.

"Giovanna . . ."

Startled, she sat up, surprised someone was in the room, then realized it was Giovanni, fully dressed.

"I am going out to buy provisions. We need vinegar for disinfectant and medicinal purposes and extra tobacco for bribes, always important to have if it becomes necessary. I will also try to find some lemons—although they are very expensive, especially on the docks, but at least one that you can suck on when you become seasick. Get dressed, have your breakfast—I've paid for it in advance. Don't forget to refill the water. Have everything done, be ready to leave when I return. We sail on the afternoon tide." And he left.

His manner seemed even more brisk than usual. Giovanna wondered if he might be angry. Trying to think back, she couldn't find a reason. All she had done was sleep through the night and . . . here her thoughts stopped dead in their tracks. Oh! Perhaps he had expected . . . ? This part of her impulsive plea to be taken to America had never actually entered her mind. Being married had meant freedom, leaving, embarking on a great adventure, whatever physical act required endurance necessary for that, automatic. Yet the physical act required by marriage had never been a part of that. Now, she had spent a night in bed with a man who had the right to take what belonged to him, and it shocked her that she had not thought of this before. Last night mutual exhaustion had saved her. From what exactly, she wasn't completely certain but felt saved from it nevertheless. Still, in all fairness, she had to acknowledge that Giovanni had the just right to be annoyed. He *had* made her his wife and she had a debt to pay, should be ready, willing to do whatever he might demand of her. A bargain was a bargain. Bags packed and strapped, her hat in place, water bottles filled, she was ready when her husband returned.

Putting a fat lemon into her hand as though it were a jewel, he said, "Here. Keep it safe. Don't let others see it or they will steal it. Now, we *go!*"

They boarded the ship by twos. *Like Noah's ark*, thought Giovanna, surprised she would conjure up an image from the Bible at such a momentous moment. But Teresa would have been pleased she was capable of doing so. Unconsciously fingering the small St. Benedictine medal where she had sewn it into the lining of her jacket pocket, Giovanna entered the cavernous bowels of the great ship that would carry her to the Promised Land.

3

A shoebox enclosure, two narrow bunks stacked on either side, the top ones mere inches beneath a stained ceiling glowing murky brown in the pale light of a single bulb. The smell of rancid wax overlaid that of accumulated metal polish. Two young women, one pallid, one flushed, sat opposite each other, their knees touching in the confined space, and looked up as Giovanna stood hesitating in the doorway of the cabin. Tallness seems to generate an immediate response of apprehension in all species—as now did Giovanna's. Possibly this imposing creature would threaten their possession of the coveted lower berths they had claimed for themselves. Eyes speculative, they looked her over. Friend or foe?

Entering, Giovanna removed her hat, placed it and her suitcase on one of the top bunks.

"Hello," said the one, whose curly hair matched the rosy color of her cheeks. "My name is Megan Flannigan from County Cork and me husband is waiting for me in a place they call Virginia. Have you maybe heard of it? . . . Oh—I do hope you can understand English!" Her pretty mouth in a petulant pout, pointing to the girl across from her, she lamented, "This one doesn't!"

Loudly enunciating every syllable as though to one hard of hearing, Giovanna introduced herself in Italian—and got nowhere. So she tried it in French. The transformation in the pallid one was cataclysmic. Eyes alight, sparkling with sudden life,

she babbled in relieved abandon that she was French and her name was Eugenie—
after the beautiful princess of course—although her dearest Maman had wished to
name her eldest daughter, which she was . . . Oh, Mon Dieu! What had she been "en
train de" to relate? . . . oh, yes, of course, her name. Most dearest Maman had wished
her to be Josephine but Monsieur Le Papa had been adamant—no offspring of his
would ever carry a name associated with that usurper Napoleon Bonaparte, so here
she was, Eugenie, on her way to join the loyal husband who had sent for her where
they would live in a fine house in an elegant city called Philadelphia of course, she
must have heard of it, as it was such a well-known place, where her Etienne, now a
most successful salesman of ladies' shoes, had promised he would give her a maid
of her very own. Catching her breath, her violet eyes misting at the very thought of
such awaiting luxury, looking up at Giovanna, Eugenie asked, "This Philadelphia . . .
do *you* know where one finds it?"

When Giovanna informed her that she would ask her husband, who was on the
ship personally accompanying her to their destination, she saw envy in the French
girl's eyes.

Wondering who would be the fourth to share their tiny cabin, the three girls busied
themselves stowing their few belongings into the meager space available to them.

Ship's bells began their call announcing departure.

"Oh, it is time. France . . . I must wave *au revoir* to my beautiful France. I may
never, ever see her again—oh, what a tragedy that would be! My heart breaks even
now at the very thought . . . you come too, yes?" and out dashed Eugenie, lyric drama
in high-button shoes and straw boater. Giovanna, not knowing where the men's
quarters were located, followed as did Megan, still pouting at not having understood
a single word of all that talk between her fellow travelers, yet as eager to witness their
ship leaving the harbor.

The great ship shivered, as though, tied in its stall, it wanted to tear loose its fetters
and run free! Four funnels belching, it began to move. Passengers crowded the open
decks to catch the last glimpse of land; that split moment when vague regret mingles
with the excitement of anticipated adventure united their faces before individuality
took over. The waving of those who had someone left behind to wave to, the tears,
the shouts of words left unsaid before, now needing to be said even if impossible to
be heard above the din, the joyous laughter of those shedding the old world for the
new. Slowly, the ship moved its human cargo into the Channel and out onto the
Atlantic Ocean.

Megan's excellent sense of direction brought the girls safely back down to their
small cabin, where they surprised a very buxom woman unpacking her belongings

into a cubicle allotted to one of the lower bunks. Megan's eyes blazed, "OH NO! That one's mine! I was here first!" The fourth fellow traveler of their cabin, her potato face taking on the color of her accuser's hair as she wielded a very large salami, threatening mayhem, braced for a fight like the bull terrier she resembled, growling a language none of them had ever heard before. Giovanna tried to take charge in oil-upon-the-waters Italian, Eugenie twittered in philosophical French, Megan cursed in merciless Gaelic, while the as yet nameless terrier spluttered Polish. "Me Bela, ten-year wife of Lotar Zankowsky, iron miner, Missouri!"

The cabin door opened and Giovanni stood surveying the Tower of female Babel before him. Suddenly, with a man in their midst, docile female silence was instantly restored.

"Giovanna! I leave you to get properly settled and what happens? I find you squabbling like some peasant. This is NOT the behavior I expect from my wife!" and not waiting for any explanation, Giovanna's husband strode out, slamming the heavy door behind him. As a man's angry disapproval belongs to that unassailable realm of universal language, making translation unnecessary, the women duly chastised, eyes downcast, careful not to bump into each other, arranged their individual spaces without another word. Bela Zankowsky tossed her sausage up onto the remaining bunk and laboriously climbed the precarious ladder with Slavic resignation.

The first days out, when the trumpet sounded for meals, no one in Giovanna's cabin paid the slightest attention—all were seasick. Fortunately, not all at once, so those not yet could minister to those not caring if they lived or died. Bela was the first to become seaworthy and, true to her name if not exactly her looks, took on the labors of ministering angel. Held foreheads over chamber pots, fetched water from some discovered source, applied cool compresses, patted limp hands reassuringly, and, when nothing else seemed to do as well, sang soft lullabies, mothering her young as though they were really hers. Giovanna shared her precious lemon with nonhesitant generosity and everyone agreed that *it* and Bela were the sole reasons they eventually survived the demon sea. Eugenie did continue to linger on the brink, whenever the steam from boiling cabbage, so necessary to all German ships, drifted by her sensitive nose, but as she claimed she was actually sensitive all over, soon no one took any notice of her daily vapors.

The first evening after a dinner that had miraculously stayed down, Giovanna approached her husband as he sat smoking in the men's section.

"Giovanni, I need to ask a favor."

"I see you have recovered," he flicked off the ash. "Your cabin is back to normal?"

"Oh, yes—but it was truly awful. I nearly used Antonia's potion, then thought better not. But now we are all well again, and so I really must learn to speak and understand American. Megan, the Irish girl, glares when Eugenie and I talk together in French. Bela doesn't seem to care as much. I think she is quite used to no one ever knowing Polish—but poor Megan, she really needs to talk and, as I need to learn, would you please teach me right away?"

Pleased, Giovanni agreed. Every morning, bright and early before the dining hall became the hub, the meeting place, with her copybook spread open before her on the long table, pencil in hand and penknife ready to resharpen it, Giovanna received intensive instruction in the use of conversational English. Giovanni was a strict teacher, she a fast pupil, and so one evening when preparing for bed, Giovanna turned to Megan and said, with proud assurance, "Good night, Megan. I wish you good to sleep," placing the accent on the last syllable of the girl's name, whose delighted chuckle spoke volumes.

"Oh, my! What a fancy name I have! Go on! I like it—say it again!"

While Bela knitted yet another pair of thick socks for a husband with unusually large feet and Eugenie, feeling very sorry for herself, trimmed her boater with paper roses, Megan now chatted away like a chipmunk in spring. Although most of what she said was often far beyond Giovanna's English language skills, she listened, recognizing the Irish girl's need to confide her good fortune to someone.

"Patrick, that's his name. Oh, if you could but see him! Hair black as a raven's wing seen by moonlight, with eyes blue—blue as the sky—with his grin that can break a girl's heart if not meant for her. Would you believe it? Found employment right off as head groom on a grand estate that breeds Thoroughbreds. I am not certain where it is exactly . . . a place called Virginia where me Patrick says even the grass is rich. The fine lady of the manor house, needing a serving girl to polish her silver, said I too could come work for her and someday, when we have saved enough, we will return home, buy the land on the Bluff, build us a grand house of our own, be looked up to. Look . . ." Jumping off the bunk, Megan pulled her trunk out from beneath, opened its battered lid, displayed its interior wooden tray filled with linen. "See . . . it's me very own bridal sheets. I stitched them meself and . . . here . . ." Carefully, lovingly, she pulled from its paper wrapping a long apron, so starched it crackled, its square yolk edged in Irish Point openwork, a thing of true beauty. "This too I made with a proper dust cap to match. I mean to wear it on me very first day as a serving maid in a grand American home!"

Even Eugenie, permitted to admire the fine needlework, agreed that the apron was beyond criticism, would be deemed acceptable in the finest châteaus.

Naturally, now it was the French girl who was miffed, showing her disdain at being ignored by flouncing from the cabin whenever Giovanna practiced her newly acquired

American, but Bela stayed, clicked her knitting needles, after a while joining in the sessions of practicing conversation. Using each other's language skills, correcting each other, by the end of the many days at sea, they would be a triumphant duo of basic language for the country of their destination. Each could name themselves, their marital status, their homeland, their final destination, ask for food, water, washroom, and the price of things.

For those in the Upper Cabin classes, shipboard life settled into its structured routine. Men bonded over endless card games, exchanged impressive opinions engulfed in thick clouds of tobacco smoke, marched briskly circling decks on daily constitutionals, adhering to the strict boundaries of their class. Their women tended bored children, strolled while gossiping, crocheted, wrote into Morocco bound diaries that could be locked with very small keys.

Since the tragic sinking of the "Unsinkable Titanic" the year before, daily life-boat drills were strictly observed. Everyone made certain they knew where their life jackets were at all times, some carrying them about, slung on one shoulder as though they were a part of clothing. Giovanna solved her problem of where to place her life jacket for fastest retrieval by wearing it to bed. She reasoned that as disasters at sea most often occurred in the dead of night, this was her most intelligent option. In daylight, she felt quite capable of taking whatever came in her stride. At first, Megan laughed when she saw Giovanna strapped into her bulky harness, then decided why not, and followed her lead. Eugenie refused, saying even if it meant she must drown, she would not wear it. Its rough canvas and wood slats would chafe her so delicate skin and whatever would Etienne say if his wife arrived covered in blotches! *Quelle horreur!* Bela's bunk was already so crowded by her ample bulk to say nothing of the sausage she had sworn an oath to never let out of her sight, and bring to the waiting arms of a husband, that she hung hers on the door handle, hoping none of the girls would knock it off when rushing out to save themselves while she was still struggling to get down her ladder.

Below the water line in steerage, Giovanna's ship designated it as Third Class, 1,074 immigrants also bonded. Like abused animals, they clustered, seeking comfort, safety within their languages and nationalities in order to survive.

In a secluded spot she had discovered for herself on deck, Giovanna watched as from below overcrowded, airless holds this human flotsam emerged each day as though released from some undeserved captivity, blinking in the sudden brightness of daylight, faces lifted gratefully to the open sky. From her vantage point above, Giovanna marveled at the resilience of these hordes of desperate people willing to endure whatever they must to achieve a dream. She did not equate her condition with theirs. She knew the difference between her security and their precarious, possibly doomed, search for it. A roof, food, and protection were guaranteed her therefore her quest for a new life could not be compared with theirs and so felt the privilege of her status as Giovanni's wife. Once he too had been one of them, endured, struggled to make a place for himself—a stranger in a foreign land—had succeeded, not only found work but his pride within it! Now, she, as wife to this courageous man, was reaping the rewards and, for the first time since her irrational request, Giovanna considered the man not only what he represented, her means of escape, from what she still could not identify only knew her need of it. For a long time she watched the people below her, thankful she was not one of them, wondering what lives awaited them—what waited for her.

Entering the Gulf Stream, the sea became strangely calm, its mirrorlike surface reflecting a chalk gray sky. Putting away her learning things, Giovanna went in search of her husband. He who had crossed this vast ocean twice before would be able to tell her, know if it was preparing a tumultuous storm or just lying still without any malevolent intentions. When she couldn't find him anywhere, she went up on deck to her private spot to take a good look at the sea and try to figure it out for herself. Leaning on the railing, a faint breeze making her skirt ripple against her ankles, she studied the endless horizon. The sudden thought that Columbus must have seen what she was seeing made her smile. Now that she knew being seasick was not a fatal condition, she liked the sea. Its unpredictability, even its frightening power, an intriguing challenge. *If I were a man, I'd be an explorer, live my whole life on a ship, circle the world!* The low sound of a man's voice disturbed Giovanna's musings. It came again, clearer, more emphatic this time and she recognized it was Giovanni speaking to someone directly below from where she stood. What was he doing down there? In Third Class? Second Class passengers weren't allowed there—so who was he talking to? Crouching down straining to hear, Giovanna listened.

"All of you who understand Italian, listen to me carefully. I have knowledge that is important for you to hear. I will come here every morning at this time to speak to you of the things that you must know before you are taken to be processed on Ellis Island." A low murmur greeted the name. "Yes, I know, some of you have heard it called The Island of Tears and that is one of the reasons I have come. I know it—I have been there, I was able to pass through to America and found work, good work and so will you. But there are some tricks that can help get you through and I know them. Those of you who speak other languages can translate my words to the other groups—or ask around. Try the Russian Jews, they are usually good linguists. Tomorrow we meet. I must go. Take heart, from now on, the sea will remain calm, so they may allow you to sleep up on deck."

The next day at the appointed time, Giovanna was crouched by her listening post, ear pressed to the bottom railing as Giovanni began speaking to his attentive flock that now comprised representative Poles, Romanians, Bohemians, Germans, Hungarians, and Hollanders amongst the Italian men.

"Once we have arrived, you will be unloaded onto smaller boats and ferried to Ellis Island. Once there, you will be told to leave all of your belongings to be reclaimed when you are through. I cannot tell you that this will be so—for such things are often stolen, disappear—even the Promised Land has its thieves, so take what is most precious to you, put it with your papers and your money on your person for safety. Next, you will be herded into the Great Hall. It is called so because it truly is—greater than you have ever seen before, with many aisles marked off by iron pipes to contain the thousands of people being moved towards the stairs that lead up to the inner balcony that circles the hall. Remember ours will not be the only ship to arrive, the harbor will be full of ships from many ports, all filled with people like you. Tell your women they must hold onto the children, never let go of their hands or they will lose them in the crush of people. Yes, it is frightening, even for men. But you must not allow fear to take control of you or be seen, for then bad mistakes can happen. The guards will move you towards the steps where men who look like the police . . ." Alarmed voices interrupted him. "No, no—they are not real policemen. They are doctors in special uniforms and they are there to watch you. Watch how you climb the stairs. If you stumble, have a difficulty and they think there may be something wrong with you, with their piece of chalk, they will mark you with a C—which means Cripple, so the other doctors upstairs will know 'here is one who has to be examined more thoroughly.' If you seem out of breath, they move you up at a fast pace for that reason, you could get an H on your back for Heart. So, remember, watch out how you climb, place your foot firmly one after the other . . . tell those of your women whose skirts are very long, to shorten them before we arrive. It is safer and remember, when you climb the stairs, to calm yourself, so your breathing comes easy. Anyone here with children who are deaf mutes? Come closer." There was a shuffling of feet as some pressed forward. "Now, while you still have the time, teach them that when they see you talking to them, they must nod their heads as though they can understand. They must also be taught to keep their eyes open and their heads up to look alert. This is true for everyone, all of you—no downcast eyes, even from your women. If you don't look straight at them, the doctors and the officers think maybe you are trying to hide something and then they will single you out. Don't ever give anyone a reason to be suspicious of you. Don't shuffle—don't look down, don't mumble, don't hesitate. Never appear confused even when you are. Look as though you understand, even when you don't. Those who can't read or write, find those who can and stay close to them for help. Try to make everyone understand this—how very important all this is. The worst chalk mark that you can receive, the one that can mean great tragedy for your whole family, is an X, for it means Mental Deficient and the special doctors for that will put you through tests that even those who have nothing wrong with them often fail—then America will be lost to you, you will not be allowed to enter. They will send you back where you came from—separated forever from those of your family who are healthy and allowed to stay. I must go. Tomorrow I will talk about the purchase of railway tickets and money matters in general." The men crowded around him, questioning, eager to hear more, finally let him go when they realized, young as he was, here was a man who could not be cajoled into changing his mind. Murmuring their gratitude, the men dispersed.

For a long while Giovanna remained where she was, thinking through all she had heard, trying to understand the enormity of what lay behind Giovanni's words, the need that had prompted them. His amazing generosity beguiled her. She found she liked him, was enormously proud of him. Love was so foreign to Giovanna, she wasn't aware she was taking the first step towards it.

During the evening meal, first making sure no one near them understood Italian, keeping her voice low, Giovanna confessed, surprised that her husband was not angry at her eavesdropping as she had expected, she dared to ask, "But aren't you frightening them?"

"They are already frightened. It is always better to know than to imagine."

"Giovanni, would you allow me to accompany you down there? It is not easy to catch all the words from above and I too want to hear what you have to say."

He hesitated, then replied, "Maybe seeing you there might encourage the women to come and listen. Their fears are so much worse for they have children to protect. Yes, it is a good idea. You may come."

The next morning, Giovanna met her husband at the appointed rendezvous, making sure their passage was unobserved, followed him down secluded stairs, along half-hidden walkways, finally ducking under the chained barrier separating classes. The men were waiting, many more than Giovanna had expected.

"*Buon giorno.* Last night, not so many were seasick—right?" A few wan smiles acknowledged Giovanni's greeting. "Even in the dead of winter, it is better when they allow you to sleep on deck. Here, this is my wife, Giovanna. Like you, she is crossing the ocean for the first time to accompany me to my home in America." Slightly uncomfortable, the men acknowledged the female stranger in their midst, as two young women, one obviously pregnant carrying a small boy on her hip, the other holding two little girls by the hand, sidled up to the back of the group. Seeing them, Giovanni raised his voice, hoping to attract the other women who watched, afraid to come nearer in case this being man's business they were excluded.

"Before I begin, let me make one important observation. Not all the women here are fortunate enough to be accompanied by their men. Some, as many hundreds before them, are traveling alone, some with children, to be reunited with husbands, fathers, or brothers who have saved enough to send them their passage to join them in America. So they must be allowed to listen—make room for them. First, the sum of money that is now required of all immigrants who enter America through the port of New York City. This is not a law—only the man who rules New York demands it—so you must have this ready. You all have this? Safe? At Ellis Island there is a special room where you can change your money into the dollars of the United States. There they will not cheat you . . ." As though something disturbed him, Giovanni stopped, hesitated, then continued. "Some of you have heard of the examination of the eyes and what they do to you. I cannot make that easier for you. I wish I could but I can't. You will have to endure it. They will use a buttonhook to fold back your eyelids, while the doctor looks for infection, understand?" The stillness that froze the crowd was answer enough.

"Once you get through, and most of you will, believe me, you will be taken by ferries to American land and left. Those of you who are already contracted, you now will find the agents of those enterprises waiting to make sure that their gangs get to where they are expected to work. But those of you, single or in family groups who must travel on, may be approached, greeted by a very friendly man speaking your language—he may even say he comes from your village—who will offer to help you.

"Do not believe him! Do not go with him! No matter how much you want to. Some of our own countrymen have turned into hungry wolves who pray on the newly arrived—using your fears, your confusion, your innocence to steal the little money you have. Remember that your twenty-five dollars, though it is a large amount of money, is all you have to live on for you and your family until you reach your final destination and there find work.

"If you have far to go, you must remember you will no longer be in a small country but one that is so vast . . . I can't even describe it to you. Where else can you travel on a fast train a whole four days and four nights and when you finally arrive, you are only next door to the state you started from? If you must wait between trains, or miss a connection, always stay in a station waiting room and wait there for the next. And practice! Practice saying where you must go, the name of the town and, very important, also the name of the state it is in. America is so large it has many towns with the same name—only if you know what state your destination is in, can you be sure to get to the right one. Most of all, above all else, remember. All of you, even the children, burn this into your heart, into your soul. No matter what awaits you—no matter how hard your new life may be, all of it will, in the end, will have been worth it! If you work hard, never give up, you can make a good life because in America all things are possible. There is no place in all the world with such a generous heart—believe me—I know. *Buona fortuna!*"

Respectfully, the men removed their caps, crowded around this benefactor, anxious to shake his hand. Their women curtsied to Giovanna, shyly acknowledging their respect for the wife of such a moving orator.

Soon they would arrive and go their separate ways. As the only one of her cabin who had an actual address, Giovanna asked Giovanni to please write it out for her, so she could copy it, then give one to each of her shipboard companions, adding that she planned to keep the original on her person—in case she ever lost him, she would know where to go and to be sure not to omit the correct state his Detroit could be found in.

Passing Coney Island, the ship made its way through the narrows towards the upper reaches of New York Harbor. On every level, passengers crowded the open decks, pushed, shoved, jockeyed for whatever space was available to catch a glimpse of the land that held such promise for so many and there, engulfed in late summer sun, standing tall, as though a Divinity risen from out of the sea, She greeted them. The one they had all heard of, dreamt someday of meeting and a mighty cheer rolled out to greet her, a cry of recognition for all She represented. Babies were held high, children hoisted onto shoulders to see the symbol of their glorious future. Giovanna never forgot that moment. The sound of it, all those jubilant voices hailing a thing of iron and that, for some inexplicable reason, hers was amongst them.

Giovanni and she watched as their ship unloaded its human cargo onto the ferries alongside. Battered baggage, boxes, bundles, sacks, bales, whole lives, whole cultures tied with rope, thong and cloth, being herded aboard with practiced efficiency. Had Giovanna ever seen the Chicago stockyards, she might have used them as reference point; as it was, the scene below her became its own reference. She took out her handkerchief and waved it in farewell.

In the dining hall, converted for the official processing on board of the cabin classes, Giovanna waited with the others to be examined. Sitting on one of the chairs now lined against the walls, she wondered how the buttonhook would be hooked on her eyelids and how much it would hurt. Moving up the line each time a chair was vacated, she finally arrived at her turn.

"Stand up," said a deep voice from somewhere far above her and, when she obeyed, found that for the first time in her whole life, she needed to look up at someone's face to see them. A very tall man, the tight leggings of his field uniform making him appear even taller, lifted her lids with feather-light fingers, peered through thick spectacles into her eyes for a suspended moment, then gestured dismissal, moving her on. The doctor who thumped her chest, then listened through his rubber stethoscope stood on tiptoes to do so, but he too found nothing and moved her on.

Breathless with relief, Giovanna hurried off to find Giovanni, who was being questioned at another table by an official speaking rapid English interrupting himself with loud bangs of his rubber stamp. Though impatient, Giovanna waited until she heard "Next," the important word that Giovanni had taught her to listen for, then quickly whispered, "Giovanni! The eyes—I passed! But the doctor was gentle and no buttonhook. I thought you said . . ."

Giovanni, preoccupied, checking the official stamps and signatures on their papers of entrance, commented, "If you had been one of the poor from below, you would have gotten the buttonhook and the pain. For those who can pay, there are always privileges, so, you got gentle hands and no hook! Now, go collect your things and say your good-byes. We will be docking. I will come to fetch you when it is time to leave the ship."

The small cabin was a beehive of last-minute emergencies. Megan, sprawled under her bunk was searching for a lost shoe, berating St. Anthony for not doing his appointed duty. Eugenie was tearing her bed apart in a frantic search for a precious hatpin while Bela on her top bunk, out of harm's way, fully dressed, the salami cradled in one arm, her satchel in the other was beating out the rhythm with her booted feet as she practiced her name and destination in English. After things calmed down a bit, Giovanna handed Megan the paper with her address.

"To this you write, to me, please, if you wish about your Patrick and his nice horses," Giovanna said very carefully to get all the words right and in their proper order. The Irish girl, much too excited to really pay attention, tucked the small piece of paper into her satchel and gave Giovanna a fast hug of farewell.

"Eugenie, this is for you. My address in America. You can write me in French, of course. I know you will be terribly busy moving into that fine new house but maybe, afterwards you will find some time to give me news of your exciting life and that maid of your very own."

The French girl, her eyes a little misty by excited apprehension, nodded. Stuffing the paper into the pocket of her summer mousseline de soie that matched the color of her violet eyes, formally kissed Giovanna on both cheeks as though she was being given a medal—and was gone. Bela took hers, folded it in four, placed it carefully inside a small coin purse. Cupping Giovanna's face in her large hands, said in her new English, "You good girl. Husband good. Like mine Lotar. We come Detroit—ha? Maybe?" And, hefting her suitcase and dilapidated hat from the bunk, left their cabin.

Watertight doors were opened, gangplanks attached, hundreds of anxious people looking up searching, as those on board looking down, did the same. Megan was the first to spot the face she was looking for, shrieked, dashed down the gangplank, catapulted herself into the open arms of a handsome young man in a pinstripe suit sporting a pearl gray fedora set at a rakish angle.

"Little darlin'," he murmured, kissing her soundly. The two men flanking him stepped back in deference, smiled, appreciating the scene. Releasing the breathless girl, the man drew on his gray suede gloves, tucked Megan under one arm, his silver-tipped ebony cane under the other and, motioning for the men to take charge of his wife's trunk, led her towards the exit. Giovanni, having observed the romantic reunion below, commented, "That's no stable hand."

A tree trunk of a man, the stoop of hard labor giving him the deceptive look of advanced age, plowed his way through the crowds, looking up, searching for the face he needed to see. Bela saw him first, waving the salami for positive identification, she yelled, "Lotar! Lotar!" Giovanna often wondered if it was that ridiculous sausage or his wife's face that brought that big hulk of a man to a sudden standstill but, the way he caught Bela's outstretched hands as she reached him, the joy that transformed him into a much younger man, that was hers alone.

Eugenie, in her rose-adorned boater and matching parasol, looking as pretty as a rotogravure on the sheet music of a love song, sat on her leather trunk waiting to be found. Giovanni hurried them out of the arrivals' shed onto the teeming street.

The heat of a New York summer hit Giovanna with such force, she recoiled from it as though it were something alive wanting to devour her.

"Take your jacket off and roll up your sleeves," instructed Giovanni doing the same. Seeing her astonishment, he laughed, "You are in America now! Freedom—my girl—freedom! Remember?"

So there stood Giovanna on a big city street in broad daylight, undressing and not one of the hurrying multitude paid the slightest attention. The sudden thought of how far could she could go before anyone did notice made her want to giggle but she didn't, for that would really have been going too far even for the first day of a new life. For a fleeting second, she did think of the gossips of Cirié, then forgot them forever.

"Giovanna! Farewell!" Megan called as she was being handled into a gleaming, bright yellow motorcar that looked as though it belonged on a racetrack in constant motion, not parked sedately at a city curb by a fire hydrant. Handing Giovanna his coat to carry with her, Giovanni informed his wife that the gleaming beauty was actually a 1912 Four-Door Runabout converted with wire wheels, a monocle windshield, an oval gas tank and the removal of running-board panels into a special Ford Speedster and that Megan's paragon of a hardworking, so dependable husband was, without a doubt, a most successful bookie and that he would explain what that meant when next he had time to do so, but now they had to hurry, catch the trolley about to leave without them, adding, "Don't stop to look up—you can see tall buildings later!"

Running, they caught it. As the trolley began to move, a welcome breeze entered through its open sides, bringing a little relief. *We're packed together like barreled olives*, thought Giovanna and suddenly realized that from the very moment of setting foot on land, there had been nothing but people; masses and masses of them everywhere she looked.

Incessantly clanging its bell, the trolley rattled along broad streets, scattering speeding motorcars and courageous pedestrians alike. Everywhere, bustle, constant motion, hither and yon, as though without it meant some expected disaster, with it a form of salvation. Fascinated by so much frenzy exposed, Giovanna remembered what Giovanni had said when he first told her of America beneath the chestnut tree. Now she understood what he had meant, admired so about this new world. No time to dawdle! Here life was a race, its goal expected prosperity. The ones who ran the fastest would have their reward of success—those who lagged behind justified their failure. This very day, the first in her new homeland, she too would give it her contribution, start off correctly. Looking up at Giovanni swaying by a leather strap beside her, Giovanna shouted above the din, "Giovanni—from today, please call me Jane and I will call you John." Clutching at her hat as the trolley swayed precariously, she gasped, "This is very exciting!"

Her husband's answering laughter had a boyish ring. Ever since their arrival, she had noticed a youthfulness about him, as though he were happy. Although she had never experienced it herself, she knew that very often happiness accompanied a sense of homecoming and this could be the reason for her husband's sudden lightness of spirit.

"Jane! Look! There! Our Model T! See it? And there . . ." Craning to see, nearly falling off the skittish trolley, Jane saw her first Ford and thought, What a funny-looking thing. Hopping about on its big thin wheels so high off the ground it looked like a black baby stork, shuddering as though in the throes of unstoppable hiccups.

This was his so famous motorcar? Certainly there were a lot of them bouncing along, chasing others of exact likeness as though they were all friends playing tag.

"All of those? All are 'Lizzies'?" Jane shouted.

"Yes! 'Watch the Fords go by,'" shouted John in English, enjoying himself enormously.

"What?"

"That's our slogan. Never mind, I'll explain later . . . get ready, we're nearly there." Pushing his way rapidly through the crowd, he called over his shoulder, "We're here—follow me!" and jumped off, pulling Jane down after him.

"We have to cross the street—watch where you step! They still use horses here!"

He needn't have worried, for the intense heat had already dried the mounds of manure into a fine powder that swirled in the hot breeze creating its own haze, before settling wherever it wished. Jane, still clutching their jackets, her suitcases, trying to catch her breath, lifted her eyes to follow him and remained rooted where she stood. Nothing could have prepared her for what lay before her.

The kaleidoscope of colors and sounds, the sights, the sheer pageantry of it all. Everywhere pushcarts, peddlers announcing their wares, shouts of *"Frutta Fresca,"* scissor grinder, wheel and treadle strapped to his back, ringing his bell, the toot of a ragman's horn, livery horses snorting stomping flies off scabbed legs, the cackle of soup chickens, their flag red cockscombs waving from out of flimsy crates, Puccini cranked from a hurdy-gurdy, its leering monkey chattering angrily plucking at the high collar of its garish costume, a marching lady in navy, adorned with red, hitting a small tambourine with the heel of a black gloved hand, girls in dark pinafores over white dresses their long braids bouncing, singsonging patter playing hopscotch, scruffy boys in knee britches and narrow suspenders clinking variegated marbles within chalked circles, others kicking a can with booted gusto, old men in buttoned under vests and brimmed hats on kitchen chairs brought outside for watching, errant children searching for the ice wagon, and women of all ages in voluminous aprons and tight head cloths gossiping. Suddenly at the sound of a policeman's whistle, they stopped, peered down, and watched as a burly man in a woolen uniform shaking his truncheon, his official dome-shaped hat wobbling, chased a clutch of jeering boys, waving stolen licorice laces like lariats egging him on.

John, seeing his wife still standing across the street, mesmerized, called to her. "Giovanna—wake up! Come over here!" in his impatience resorting to her Italian name. Still in a daze, circumventing a pushcart heaped high with dented pans and scrap iron, Jane made her way across the teeming cobblestone street. Motioning his wife to follow him, John strode along the busy sidewalk, stopping as he reached a house whose glass transom above its front door displayed a large number nine. Gingerly stepping between the bodies lounging on the stoop, he mounted the steps and, pulling a polished brass ball, rang the bell, and waited for the door to open.

"Johnny! My Johnny! Back so soon! Come here! . . ." chortled an immense woman as broad as the double doorway she stood in. Reaching out, she pressed him to her as though she were a hungry grizzly, he a brimming honeycomb. They kissed. Finally finished, pushing away from him, her beringed fingers retaining their hold, she examined the woman standing beside him and inquired, "And this? This is the wife?" Receiving an affirmative nod, she observed in a tone of practiced appraisal, "Aha! . . . Well . . . a little thin . . . but strong and good hips for breeding—she'll do for you!" and she ushered them into her house.

That night, Jane was given a spare bed in the attic room occupied by two pretty women who appeared very cross because they had the sniffles and were therefore not allowed downstairs. They eyed her with suspicion when first introduced, then quickly became friendly when Jane undressed and they saw her sensible underthings. Although the bed seemed to sway as though it too had a sea beneath it, Jane slept. Even the night noises of this strange new place didn't penetrate enough to wake her completely.

Jane didn't quite understand that place. The muffled footsteps, the comings and goings, up then down stairs that creaked no matter how cautiously they were crept upon. Nor why Mamma Cantonocci allowed so many of her young nieces not only to live with her, but sit around the big kitchen in the mornings in flimsy kimonos doing absolutely nothing to help. When she questioned John where he had been given a bed and what about all those many nieces, he answered very curtly, "Mamma 'Nocci' is a generous relative—she always finds a spare bed for an old friend like me!" By his tone, Jane knew the subject was firmly closed and so turning her curiosity to more pressing things, went in search of her companions of the attic to ask if they thought the wonder of a bath was at all possible in such a busy establishment.

Lily, a cream pale blonde, blew her nose. Iris, a slow-eyed brunette, considered the problem, then both relinquished their daily right to bathe to the yearning immigrant before them.

Like adoptive hens to a newly hatched chick, they fussed, getting into the spirit of things. An elegant copper bath was dragged into the kitchen, water heated, then filled to its beveled edge; Lily, sprinting to the attic to fetch her essence of violets, insisting that a bath without a drop of it couldn't be considered a bath at all, while Iris climbed onto the kitchen stool, stood on tiptoes to reach the topmost shelf of the china cupboard to steal a cake of the special oatmeal soap kept hidden there. To shield their chick from the possibility of a draft, they positioned a lacquered screen, its panels depicting coy Japanese ladies peeping out between branches of cherry blossoms in full bloom and urged Jane to hurry, get into the water before it turned tepid. Bringing chairs, placing them in front of the tub, they sat as though they were about to attend a special performance at the Hippodrome. Flimsy kimonos askew, revealing camisoles trimmed with tiny rosebuds and bows nestled amidst rushing of Venetian lace, legs crossed, a hint of milky thigh above white hose of silken lisle, one foot dangling a seductive boudoir slipper imported from France, they waited for the show to begin. The enjoyment they derived from their good deed was so infectious that it freed Jane of all shyness. Amidst the steamy scent of wood violets, she scrubbed while her new friends applauded, enchanted by the virgin in their midst.

Later, all heavenly clean, Jane was shown the front parlor and understood why her two new friends had been so upset at being denied it because of silly sniffles. It was truly an astounding, awe-inspiring sight! Emerald green, the golden glow from its electrified crystal chandelier giving it the look of soft velvet, it resembled a secret glen in some enchanted forest. Jane wondered if she would ever possess a front parlor as resplendent as this and, if so, how would she ever manage to dust it!

John was given another kiss, this one lasting even longer as it was one of farewell. Jane was bear hugged, given a loving slap on her behind, admonished to be good to fine "Johnny" the apple of Mamma Nocci's eye—and everyone knew that her eye was never wrong—to make lots of healthy babies, adding that when they were old enough, to bring them to New York City for her to look them over. Most of the nieces followed them out, their colorful kimonos decorating the stoop as they waved good-bye. Shouts of "Good Luck!" "All the Saints protect you!" mingled with the clanging of the trolley carrying John and his bride to the railway station and the train that would carry them to their next stop, a place called Buffalo. Now she sat on a padded bench that even had armrests, on a train so long, like some giant snake it undulated, its tail forever lost from view. Sights whizzed by at an alarming rate at times resulting in unidentifiable blurs. Jane wanted to ask when she could expect to see her first whooping Indians chasing alongside, but didn't. She was rapidly learning the many things that seemed to annoy her husband and disturbing him with childish questions while he was reading his newspaper was one of them. So she concentrated on the blurs, hoping one of them would metamorphose into an Indian chief, feather headdress flying, astride a spotted horse. After a while, this made her dizzy and she turned from the window to observe their fellow travelers instead. It seemed that here in America even unaccompanied ladies journeyed. Their travel attire, obviously store-bought of finest workmanship, the piping of corded braid on lapels and cuffs, most elegant, their skirts never sweeping the dusty ground, yet hanging below the heel of their high laced shoes as convention demanded.

Gloved hands held books that they read, oblivious, even disinterested, in the exciting sights and sounds surrounding them. Their easy self-assurance so intrigued Jane, her eyes kept returning to study them. Even those obviously married, at their husband's side, children claiming their attention, had an air about them that was foreign to Jane's experience. She couldn't quite explain it to herself, yet something unusual was there, even in the way they sat, erect, shoulders back yet completely relaxed. None of the self-conscious tension so inherent in the women of her old homeland and, when they spoke, their voices had an ease as though they never had to wait to be given first permission to do so—as if certain they would be listened to.

John, noticing his wife's concentrated interest in the American women, felt it necessary to comment, "It is considered rude to stare," before unfolding his paper to the next page.

Jane turned back to the blurs. In time these became endless vistas interrupted by too many people encircled by too many buildings. It seemed that everything in her new country was overly large—maybe even had to be, abundance in volume as well as size. It could make one reared within the restricted confines of the old world feel of no consequence. Yet she found this very exaggeration exciting. Like the train, her spirit welcomed the approach of every bend, anxious to see what would lie beyond.

Across from her, John sat, silent, all boyishness gone. She wondered why. She had liked him being "young." Maybe she should try to make conversation like she had seen the American ladies do with their husbands, elegantly conversing about, what seemed from their expression, to be topics lacking drama, bland in nature. Now that she was to be one of them, she should really try out some of the behaviors belonging to them. Straightening her spine, yet relaxed as though nonchalance wasn't new to her, she spoke. "John, I enjoyed the city of New York very much. Iris and Lily were delightful, ever so helpful." Folding her hands, Giovanna settled back in her seat as she had seen the other ladies do, expecting a cozy conversation. Her husband behaved as though he hadn't even heard her speak. She tried again. "I was wondering, why are all the nieces named after flowers? I met a plump Rose and a shy Violet, who didn't say much. And a Daisy was busy and, when I asked why the one named Honey wasn't a flower, Lily said she was, a Honeysuckle which is a flower in America."

Her husband got up and went in search of a lavatory in the next carriage. He returned to find his wife doubled over, holding her hat, trying to see up beyond the frame of the window.

"What in God's name are you doing?"

"Trying to see the tops of pine trees," came the muffled reply from down below.

"Well, you won't. American pines are too tall—so sit up and behave yourself!"

She did. Until they had to change trains in Buffalo and, while waiting, just had to ask what that persistent sound like distant thunder was. When he explained it came from a giant waterfall quite some miles away, she didn't even blink an eye. Again just another inexplicable wonder of a country that just didn't seem to have any boundaries for such things. But it irritated her, being constantly reduced to an awestruck infant, its mouth hanging open in perpetual bedazzled confusion. Besides not liking this picture of herself at all, she was equally certain that the man who had married her without wanting to, was liking it even less. What was she to do? How could she cope, absorb all the overwhelming newness and still not be overcome by it? It was not like her to flounder, her character forbade it and so, she resolved that henceforth, she would accept unconditionally whatever was in store for her in this astounding country with quiet assurance devoid of awed histrionics whenever possible. She did not consciously decide this to please her husband. Her knowledge of him was still too much in progress—it was quite simply how Jane coped with life in general, its intricacies in particular, first facing truths, evaluating their importance, then searching, expecting eventually to find an answer that would accommodate an acceptable solution.

Their next train out of Buffalo, despite its equally impressive length, chugged, its wheels clickety-clacked, billows of snow-white smoke dipped down by the windows looking like masses of whipped cream tumbled off a giant ice cream cone.

She noticed that some of the ladies, now sharing their carriage, had removed their broad-brimmed hats, securing their long hatpins, before placing them in the overhead nets. So, as it seemed permissible, she followed their lead even to the removal of her gloves. In America, freedom seemed to reach even into the category of wearables. She liked that. Smoothing the fingers of her gloves before rolling them into a neat ball, like a pair of men's hose, she placed them beneath her hat—then noticed John watching her. How long had he been doing that? And why? Not certain how to react, what to say, made suddenly shy—which in itself was an unnerving sensation—she looked out the window, pretending that something outside had caught her interest, not he. His gaze remained on her. It became so disturbing she turned, met it head-on, silently challenging its reason. Still he didn't speak. Running a hand over her hair, she waited. He had better say something because she was certainly not going to make another abortive attempt at polite conversation. Finally, his tone serious, he asked, "This may seem a strange question but tell me, have you got anything against making soap?"

Jane had to laugh. "Of course not. Why? As a matter of fact, I make very good soap. I don't use as much lye with the potash as one is supposed to. I always wanted to add a little oil of rose but it is too expensive—so I couldn't."

"When we get home, I'll buy you some."

"Oh, thank you! I will make you a nice batch for your baths. Will I have a strong pot large enough?"

"My landlady has one."

"Oh. That lady of yours seems to have everything, how convenient."

Jane had the feeling that the making of soap was not the reason her husband had been watching her but, as he seemed inclined to talk, she didn't want to lose this rare opportunity. But what could they talk about? What could bring this man to life? What would pique his interest, capture his attention? Hoping time wasn't running out, Jane evaluated possible subjects, then decided, she plunged, "John, you have never described where you do your so interesting work? Is it in a shed? Of course, I realize it must be a big one. Is it?"

Her husband grinned, "Yes, I think you could call it big. Actually, it is often referred to as 'mammoth' in the newspapers as it is the largest single manufacturing institution in the world."

She had him! Smiling, she said, "Please, tell me all about it," and, settling back in her seat, allowed his enthusiasm to wash over her.

"Three years ago, in 1910, we made the move from Piquette to the new plant in Highland Park. Its size is nearly impossible to describe. If I tell you it is as large as two American football fields, you wouldn't know what I am talking about. The area used to be a racetrack, maybe that will give you some idea. But you have to actually see it to believe it and, even then, it's hard. One day I'll take you and show it to you. But no words can prepare you for what you will feel when you actually stand before it! It's called Henry Ford's Crystal Palace! A self-contained world that has never existed before."

Eyes amazed saucers, all fine resolutions to remain cool and collected no matter what, completely gone, Jane sat spellbound.

"We have our own railroad yard, so we can load directly . . . our power house was inspected and approved by Thomas Edison himself. The great man even praised our exceptional dynamos!"

His audience of one just sat there. No reaction forthcoming that such a glorious occurrence warranted, John stopped his proud oratory to comment, "Even the great Henry Ford bows down to the genius who harnessed light—you must know who he is!" Jane shook her head. "The incandescent lamp, my girl! My God! What have you been doing with your life? Flipping your bobbins all day?"

It was the sharp tone of that "my girl" that woke her. Its biting censure broke through her trance, making coherent speech once more available to answer him. "We lived our life as we expected to."

"Amazing! Lace and religion! Timeless isolation encased in granite!"

"Is that why you left?"

"Isn't that why you needed to?"

He had a way of surprising her. When suddenly, as now, his strangely hidden sensitivity appeared, made itself known by the truth it had surmised. Perhaps this was what she liked about him the most, this instinctive knowing, then the practically casual way he had of voicing what he had felt, perceived in another. Even in its rawest state, it had a childlike honesty that Jane found utterly disarming. It just might be difficult to retain one's anger at such a man.

"This place you call Highland Park—is it there we will live?"

"Yes."

"But Detroit? My address paper says . . ."

"It's on the outskirts of Detroit. Now, it is late, get some sleep. We still have a long way to go before we get to Ohio."

"Ohio?" Jane stumbled over the pronunciation.

"Ohio, that's Iroquois Indian language for 'Fine River.' It comes before Michigan, which means 'Great Water' in Chippewa. Now we're only just leaving the State of New York for the State of Pennsylvania."

"All this long time has only been one United state?" Jane gasped, convinced he must be playing a joke on her.

"Just go to sleep. The size of America is also too impossible to explain." Thinking that perhaps he had sounded undeservedly severe, he took his jacket and, folding it into a pillow, tucked it by Jane's head. She thought that was especially nice of him and, settling her head into it, obediently closed her eyes.

Pennsylvania seemed endless, Ohio too, and had a lake that John told her was so large one couldn't see across it, but to wait until he showed her a Lake Huron that was even larger but small compared to the one called Michigan . . . that was so huge it lay by Chicago, which was in another state entirely, called Illinois—which meant 'Great Warrior' in Algonquin. Finally, she just gave up trying to understand the entire phenomenon of American geographical marvels but, resolved that once arrived in Highland Park, once a racetrack now an outskirt of Detroit, in the State of Michigan, that in Indian language meant 'Great Water,' she would find herself a map and figure out where she was, once and for all!

4

Puddles of early morning rain mirrored a colorless sky. Barren trees sentineled the narrow street of porched houses, clapboard and gabled, separated by thread-thin alleys; each one alike, devoid of individuality, as though placed by an exacting child playing with uniform building blocks.

A sharp wind pulled at Jane's shawl. She clutched it closer, glad she had thought to pull it from her case on arrival before they had hurried out of the streetcar into the rain. Weeks of endless travel had taken their toll—images blurred, experiences muted, excitement and wonder dulled by exhaustion. Fellow travelers and destination had become interchangeable, memories defused, the endurance required, leaving nothing in reserve. Jane felt the late summer cold as though it were the one of winter. Her arms ached, the straw of her case had taken on added weight from the rain, as had her precious shoes, the ground still swayed as though it would never stop; there was a painful knot in the pit of her stomach. Now that she had come to the end of her journey, she found she was frightened of the one about to begin for her.

She reprimanded herself, as she often did when confused.

Well now, Giovanna, here you are in the Highland Park of America—and what do you do? Cold and tired and scared like a mouse. Here it is where you will be a wife, so wipe your nose and follow your man where he leads you. Squaring her shoulders, she followed him up the porch steps of a gray house, to its painted door that opened before he could knock.

"Ach! *Da bist du*, finally! My baby John has come home! And vid de little Italian bride!" exclaimed a woman of Valkyrian proportions, face beaming, dimpled and plump, topped by a towering knot of straw-colored hair, its tangled confusion escaping pins of various shapes and sizes trying desperately to contain it. "Come, come into de house, get warm quick!"

Jane had the fleeting impression that this face belonged on a body of diminutive proportions, not this towering Amazon, before she was grabbed, pressed against a bouncing bosom that smelled of lavender sachet and cleanliness—then, with equal force, pushed away as eyes, blue as forget-me-nots, surveyed her with what seemed to the startled girl military scrutiny. "But? She is not 'little'? No 'dark pools.' No 'angel curls'? No 'curves'?! So vat is dis? Wrong vife?" Jane still held in a vicelike grip trembled.

John had the grace to be embarrassed, murmured, "This is my wife. Her name is Jane."

"Vell, it is not vat you told us! All dat so big stories about a little dainty sweetheart back home. We vere expecting maybe some sugar plum fairy! But dis one? Dis one is much better for a vife. She vill give you strong sons mit no hanky-panky flirty! Now, children off mit de vet tings—quick!" Pulling off Jane's soggy hat and coat, she handed the mess to John, instructing him to be a good baby boy and do the same. Putting a comforting arm around Jane's shoulders, her eyes giving her another fast going-over, she led her down the hall towards a big kitchen. "Now, my little scared rabbit, you come mit Hannah. First, get dry and cozy, den some good hot chicken soup! After dat—to bed! Now here, Vifey, sit! Baby John, you take off de child's vet shoes. I poke coals around for to heat up de soup." Jane, looking down at her husband kneeling before her, obediently unbuttoning her shoes, felt like giggling but controlled herself just in time. Slapping butter on thick slices of still steaming bread, ladling out her justly famous chicken soup, Hannah Geiger filled John in on some neighborhood news.

"Frau Feldmann, remember? De one in de house dat needs a good coat of paint not dat cheap stuff already mit de peeling—down the block? Her husband, Rudolph, he is home two days, lost a finger by de drill press. Frau Powdonsky, across de street a little down? She lost a lodger to dat stuck-up Mrs. Adams four streets over, who talks de fine la-de-da English, but swallow her cooking you can't, he . . ." All of a sudden Hannah stopped. "Ach! Mein Gott! John, your Vifey? She maybe not understand English? And me rattling on!"

Jane, warming her hands around the porcelain bowl, spoke before her husband could answer. "Signora Geiger, I speak not too well, but I understand better. I am very happy to be here in the United States of America and I thank you."

"She speaks! Vhat a wonder! Already mit de English and so pretty singsongy!" Wiping her hands on her apron, Hannah was delighted.

"I have been giving Jane lessons. She is a very good student for languages. She also speaks French—the nuns taught her."

The pride in her husband's voice made Jane's heart beat faster. *My intelligence pleases him!* she thought.

"Nuns?" Hannah shrugged, her tone dismissive. "Now, little one—up! A vash, a varm bed, a good night kiss, no more! Husband, you hear dat?" Hannah's eyes pierced John, as though she had slapped him. "Den, in de morning you vake up, be a brand-new girl—de vorld all shiny good!" By Hannah decreed, so be it!

In the Geiger boardinghouse, things were done her way. Her husband Fritz never questioning her good sense, nor her ability to run their life as thoroughly as she did everyone else's. So Jane's first day in her new home went according to her landlady's dictum, all except the "good night kiss" that turned into an offhand, though friendly, verbal "Good night, Jane," even though it was only late afternoon.

She woke feeling guilty. Her husband's side of the bed was empty. He must have already gone to work—and here she was, languishing under a mountainous feather bed as though she had no wifely duties to perform. Jumping up, chiding herself for such outrageous negligence,she realized that as they had arrived on a Saturday, this day must be a Sunday! Still, even Sundays required attending to one's husband's needs and, throwing off her nightclothes—that she had no recollection of how she had gotten into—she washed, plaited, knotted her hair, turned from the small framed mirror to find that her suitcase was nowhere to be seen.

Standing naked, feeling very self-conscious, she looked about the room seeing for the first time what was to be her home. Small, bare, except for essential pieces of brooding furniture, it had the look of transient occupation. The iron bedstead painted white, giving it an institutional look, dominated; two chairs mismatched, one cushioned, a slate-topped washstand, its doors decorated with borders of Bavarian hearts and spindly geese. On an ink-stained library table by a small window, a jelly glass with lavender sweet peas attested to a landlady's welcome. In a massive wardrobe that seemed to dwarf the room further, Jane found her few belongings hung next to those of her husband's, his so neatly aligned, no one would have suspected they were the belongings of a bachelor. His best suit, the one he had worn to be married in, seemed to be missing. Being Sunday, he must be wearing it. Perhaps he had gone to early Mass or expected later to be going to church, his wife by his side. Half dressed, Jane sat on the edge of the bed, to think how best to handle her refusal to do so, then remembered her husband's scorn when criticizing her for not knowing who the Man of Light was. The practically degrading way he had pronounced *religion* did not, to her way of thinking, indicate an overly devout churchgoer. The more she mulled this over, the more convinced she became that Providence must surely have been on her side. Not only had she married a man completely unknown, who as yet had not surprised her unduly, but now it seemed, by mere chance, had found one who, by all indications, might not be a zealous Catholic, ruled by dogma, stoically oblivious to all reality. With such a man, this marriage of hers might be much easier to bear than first envisioned. Dressed, her spirits high, feeling ready for anything, she left the room.

Hearing voices, she followed their sound down the narrow stairs to a windowless room where men at a long linen-covered table sat within the perimeter of light from a shaded chandelier, having breakfast. Jane hesitated in the arched entrance as one of the men, his guttural accent identifying him as one of Balkan origin, said, "The flywheel magneto line before you left, John, no good! But now it works. Tomorrow—come—I show you."

Hannah, moving down the table filling blue and white patterned cups from a large graniteware coffeepot, exclaimed, "Ach! Here! Our new Vifey, she is here! Come—come in, little one." Waving her over. "Here, sit here by de blushing husband!"

Jane, feeling the speculative scrutiny of the now silent men, sat. At the head of the table, a stocky man, in Sunday vest and shirt garters, his Santa Claus face clean-shaven, broke the uncomfortable silence. In a booming voice, its German-Yiddish cadence matching his wife's, he introduced himself as Fritz Geiger, husband of the "Boss"—adding, in a swallowed aside, "No manners—my Frau."

Hannah, who could hear if a pin dropped in a house up the block, called from the kitchen, "Again, you criticize, Mr. Big Shot? First, I feed de so-tin wife—den comes your fancy manners!" Pots and pans slammed in emphasis.

Avoiding Jane's eyes, the men drank their coffee. Smiling, John ladled sugar into his.

"Here, Child—eat!" Hannah plunked a tower of steaming flapjacks oozing butter and glistening syrup in front of Jane, shook out a large linen napkin, tied it under her chin, and, giving her back an encouraging shove towards the plate, took up her coffeepot. Suddenly ravenous, Jane did as she was told. Never had she tasted anything as good, but didn't dare to ask what it was she was enjoying so. This time choosing to do so in German, Fritz Geiger complained to his wife for instigating an uncomfortable tension around the Sunday breakfast table. Hannah, pouring coffee, ignored him. Taking a last swallow of the strong black brew, Jane unknotting her bib, feeling wonderful, smiled, acknowledging her fellow boarders.

"See what I mean? *Now* de child is ready for de big meeting of everybody." Hannah delighted, right as always, put down her pot, cleared her throat, and began. "Now, new Vifey, pay attention. Dat handsome baby boy next to you? Him you know. Maybe not yet so good, but soon maybe too much?" That brought chuckles. The boarders loved Hannah's performances, now sensing one in the making, leaned back in their chairs, ready to enjoy it. "On de udder side of you, sits our Polish ox. Big important, rim-wheel man. Puts more tires on veels faster dan any udder—vas recommended by foreman, got even mentioned in our special *Ford Times* paper . . . Mr. Peter Clutovich, I introduce if you please!" A gentle giant, head and neck seeming fused, reddish hair standing like a scrubbing brush atop an innocent face, rose, extended a callused paw and, careful not to crush it, shook Jane's hand, growling, "Welcome, Lady."

Hannah beamed. "Very nice. Now from him, down de line, sits our Casanova Fancy Man. Very clever mit de Lizzies. Every time he mounts one, he dreams maybe it is his sweetie Frederika who still is vaiting in a stall in his Austria because she is maybe a cow! . . . Mr. Rudy Zegelmann, still bachelor!"

Laughing, not at all put out, a strapping tow-headed young man with delicate features took Jane's extended hand and bending low, brushed the back of it with his lips. The audience applauded.

"Ach! De real Austrian! Enough horse-playing! Dis is serious good manners!" Hannah, keeping a straight face, continued, "Now ve come to Rumanian gypsy, also bachelor—Mr. Dark Silent—alvays mit de pomade in de so black hair and de beautiful moustache he fondles like it vas a lady love—best japanning man in de Ford business—watch out for him, Vifey . . . Mr. Stanislav Bartok—Stan for every day."

A reedlike man, long angular face, pale background to a gleaming ebony moustache, curled tips waxed, bowed, shook Jane's hand with a feathery touch.

"More coffee, Boys?" Those still not introduced thinking they had escaped, chorused, "Yes!"

"Aha! Veaseling out? I make fresh after. So, next. Here ve got a real beauty! Answer to a maiden's prayer—strong, good earner, good looker and best, not too bright. Girlies lead him by de long nose easy! Our special real Englishman, who likes to eat good, so here he is mit Hannah, not de stuck up Mrs. Adams four-streets-over . . . Mr. very, very proper, Jimmy Weatherby, foundry big shot." A tall man in a buttoned jacket and tie stood, reached across the table to shake Jane's hand with shy deference.

"Vifey, two Poles ve got, ain't ve lucky! Here is our number two—him the big cheese foreman on magneto line. Soon, Vifey, you vill know vat all dis means. In dis house ve have so much Ford big shots ve can build our own Model T. So now say hello to Mr. 'Know-It-All'. . . Carl Baldechek."

The gravel-voiced man Jane had heard on entering, got up, walked around the table, pumped Jane's hand, slapped John's back congratulating him on an excellent choice and beaming, returned to his place. "See—big shot! Now comes our new Hollander. Him married, even a Papa already so won't stay long but his Vifey not over yet—still saving up. So every day, poor man, dead tired and sad missing everybody. Very proper, never no hanky-panky like some I know, just sweet, lonely boy . . . Mr. Johann Niedellander, specialist mit de pistons." Pink and scrubbed, thin blond hair falling over one eye, his shy young smile welcomed Jane across the table from him. "See vat a sveetheart boy? Next . . . Mr. 'Buzzing Fly.' Sits quiet, only to eat—even in bed he tvitches, so I hear from who I can't tell. Him, special tester—big shot, everybody has to listen to our Bulgarian Mr. Zoltan, mit a last name you can't pronounce." A smallish man, wiry as though under tension, with piercing black eyes above a sensuous mouth, jumped up, moved quickly to Jane's side, shook her hand as though in a frantic hurry to go somewhere, then sat down again.

"Come on, Hannah, now Fritz—and make it good!" the men chimed, egging their landlady on.

"And last, dere he sits . . . Mr. Supreme, 'De Man of de House.' Bestest leather man trimmer, so good dat Mr. Ford himself says 'Hello' to him. So delicate, he stitches the diamond shapes like a fine needle-lady he isn't! A good man, in bed and out . . . Mr. Fritz Vilhelm Georg Geiger! Maybe now, Papa, you should give de new Vifey a kiss, yes?"

Her husband, face red as a beet, rose, took one step, stopped, turned back, picked up his napkin, dunked one corner into his coffee, wiped his mouth thoroughly, then walking over to Jane, bent down, gave her a ringing smack right on her lips and returned to his place at the head of the table amidst appreciative applause. Hannah left, returned from the kitchen, bearing a huge platter laden with yeasty doughnuts, red jelly oozing, the men groaned, "No more!"

"Just a little nosh! Von't hurt."

As the men talked, Hannah refilled their cups, watched with smug satisfaction as her baking bounty disappeared. Jane, munching her first jelly doughnut, trying to understand what everyone was saying, their different accents so distinctive, thought her husband's fellow workers were fascinating and the fact that none of them seemed to be in the slightest hurry to rush off to church, endeared them even more than when she first shook their capable hands and had decided, she liked them.

Being the only other woman present, Jane felt it only right to assume the female duties of helping in the kitchen. As she washed dishes, she was torn between admiring what she was washing them in and trying to overhear, hopefully understand, what the men were discussing in the dining room. All that filtered through was the booming voice of Fritz Geiger.

"Good to have you back, John. As Carl says, the moving line idea can work, but that we knew when we tried it with the ropes. We still have many problems, I tell you . . ."

Hannah drying and stacking, having noticed Jane's admiration of her washing receptacle, began informing her that this magnificence was called a sink, but not just any old, what-others-might-have sink, but a porcelain-enameled-iron-roll-rim one that had cost the fortune of eleven dollars and twenty-five cents—a whole week's pay!

"Vonderful, no? See, every time ven you twist handle, vater runs out. No pumping like old times! Long, long times we save, went mitout, so poor we lived. All de time only dreaming someday to buy a house, have like dis sink . . . valls covered mit quality vallpaper, real electricity light—oh, everyting! Maybe whole of Mr. Sears and Mr. Roebuck and dat Mr. Montgomery Ward Company mail order catalog books." Handing Jane a dishtowel, she whispered, "Here. Stop vashing, dry hands—ve sneak avay a minute—I show you someting also not to be believed. Come!" Her accent even more pronounced by excitement, Hannah grabbed Jane's hand and pulling her, hurried out of the kitchen, up the stairs, down a hall wallpapered in shepherdesses and their flocks, to a door bearing a white porcelain plaque.

"Now, Vifey, take a breath and I vill show you vat in America is called My Pride and Joy." A perfunctory knock, a breathless hesitation, then, getting no response, she flung open the door—stepping aside so that Jane could receive the full impact of what was exposed. Jane struck speechless, did not disappoint. "Vonderbar, yes? Look—look—" pulling Jane further into the gleaming bathroom. "Only de bestest battubs have like lion feet—and cold and even hot runs direct into! . . . And dis, de inside house water closet and it can, as it's called, flush! Can't do it now, de whole house hears. My Fritz fixed de plumbing—Vell?"

"It is, how you say it? Magnifico!"

"Downstairs, by de back porch, I have anudder inside house closet but de golden oak box dere is high, high up de wall and a chain hang down to pull—dat one not so noisy—dat I don't know vy. Puzzles me!" About to lead Jane out of her porcelain palace, Hannah had a sudden thought. She was prone to explosive inspiration. "Vifey, vile so new husband downstairs, out of de vay, busy mit de big talking of dis and dat of de Lizzies, you, quiet like a mouse, take a bat! Yes? All over one. I mean it! I go fetch nice big towel and my soap mit lavender. You den soak. No hurry. Take your time. Don't vorry. Next I give dem strudel, dey sit all day! Till it's time for Sunday Supper Special!"

Out she scooted. Back in what seemed seconds, with towel, soap, and a big fluffy sponge, patted the stunned girl's cheek, saying, "Come, come—never mind daytime and you all dressed—undo! Now is good time. Nobody need special batroom!" And closing the door behind her with a last look, "Lock—mit de hook dere is," hurried downstairs to perform more magic in her kitchen.

After Sunday supper that was again consumed as though no one had seen food for weeks, the men, as was their custom, moved to the small parlor, as Hannah put it, to digest. They settled themselves into a copious selection of overstuffed armchairs, elegantly upholstered in muted shades of maroon plush, each with its own small side table and padded footstool. Men who were on their feet for nine-hour stretches under highly intensified working conditions, welcomed such considerations so far beyond the usual boardinghouse benefits. Their gratitude, at times, was quite touching, their genuine affection for the one responsible for this added care, an automatic result. Home and homeland left far behind—striving to succeed—make a new life in a foreign land that promised so much yet gave only to those who could endure, lonely, often uncertain, fearing their ability might not suffice to carry them towards their longed-for goal, immigrants soaked up any kindness shown them like parched earth water. The Geiger boardinghouse run on the premise that everyone in it was Hannah's child, could justly boast that, as she often remarked, "Empty bed? Ve never got!"

In the sufficient light provided, the men read their newspapers, smoked—some, legs stretched out, dozed. Factory talk gave way to contentment overlaid by a weariness that Sunday was nearly over and Monday loomed.

In the kitchen, the dishes were done, preparations made for very early morning breakfast, the dining table laid, the yeast starter for Hannah's sweet rolls rested in its crock.

"Thank you, Vifey, you big help. No need, you know, but nice doing mit company dat smells so good from lavender. Now, little one, go up, get ready for to sleep. Tomorrow is anudder day. Don't vorry. I tell boys good night for you and send husband up after," giving Jane a fast peck on the cheek, Hannah shooed her out of the kitchen.

Slowly, Jane climbed the stairs to their room, a faint apprehension disturbed her. She wondered where it came from, what caused it, then shook it off, started to get ready for bed.

⚜

As methodically as her husband designed tools for Henry Ford, he made Jane his wife. Neither love nor discernable passion entered into the act, efficiency did. When it was over, she lay beneath him numbed by the experience, though not shocked by it. It had been too bereft of emotion to warrant any.

That she hadn't liked it, that she knew. That she could tolerate it being done again, she also knew. After all, it was an expected consequence of marriage that had been spared her until now and, if this was all that was required, it would not disturb her existence overmuch. As John moved off her, Jane turned away from him and slept.

She woke to the sounds of her husband hurrying to leave the room. Not knowing what wifely duties were expected of her at the beginning of a working day, she used that excuse for herself to pretend sleep. The noises of hasty breakfasts filtered up from below, the commotion as men left for work.

Jumping out of bed, she inspected it. It was a small stain—she hadn't bled much—it would be easy to wash out. Stripping the sheet off the bed, she bunched it, threw it down by the door, put on her flannel wrapper and, knowing the house was now empty of men, hurried on legs strangely unsteady, to the wondrous bathroom to wash. Later hoping she could pass as trim and proper, telltale sheet tucked under her arm, she descended the stairs in search of her landlady.

In the kitchen, pungent with the lingering perfume of fried bacon and warm cinnamon, she found Hannah putting away the breakfast dishes.

"Ach! Dere you are, Vifey!" A welcoming smile on her flushed face, her sharp eyes having seen the sheet the second Jane had entered. "First, coffee. Mit a fresh Schnecke made dis morning by me personal, here called a danish—why? Don't ask! A riddle. Come, child, sit—give me—" She reached out for the bundle. Jane backed away, clung to her sheet. "Ach, so!" What was she to do with this skittish fawn that looked more like a self-sufficient stork? Poor frightened child, pretending so hard to be a grown woman. She, who had once too been this innocent—now remembered that long-lost time and when she looked at Jane clutching her sheet, her eyes showed a tenderness the girl had never seen nor experienced, not even with Teresa. Now like a magnet, it drew her to this woman's side and into her arms. As though this was quite natural, an often-repeated gesture, not the least extraordinary, they stood holding each other—the barren woman and the motherless child. Both had come home—but didn't know it just then.

Suddenly shy, Jane asked, "Where, please?"

Hannah gestured for her to follow, led her to the back porch, pointed to an enormous zinc washtub already filled with steaming water.

"Monday—vash day. I show you how ve do it—hard part boiling de vater, den carrying out already done! Now, we take Fels-Naptha bar one hand, sharp knife in udder and scrape. Make curly chips fall into tub. Are you vatching?" Jane nodded. "Now, mit hand, svoosh like dis, make pretty bubbles—see? For whites, like dis—take dis can, here . . . but careful! Sal-soda. Scoop out some, svoosh around some more . . . now, put sheet in—oh, give me already! No shame, child." Throwing the sheet into the water, she pushed it down with a wooden paddle that resembled a broken-off oar. "Now, here ve have really American miracle, dis called 'washboard.' See—sturdy wood frame around glass—yes, true! It is glass, like little steps but not delicate—vatch—ve put in, steady inside tub and now . . . rub up and down—up and down, rub-a-dub-tub, come clean as a vistle, no one de viser—dat's American saying. Someday I learn you German, too, yes?" Expertly, Hannah wrung the now clean sheet, threw it with a mighty "plop" into the second tub for rinsing. "Come, bring de basket dere—good time—much to do. Den I show you anudder miracle I got. Dis one is called a wringer. When you crank handle, it squeezes de vater all out—so big hard hand squeezing no more! Real modern American my house, no?"

"Oh, yes, Signora. It is full of wonder," said Jane, truly impressed as she tipped the contents of the big wash basket into the tub. All morning they scrubbed, rinsed, wrung, lugging pails of water from the kitchen out to the back porch, taking turns with the miracles. Stretched, then hung sheets, pillowcases, tablecloths, napkins and shirts on long rows of clothesline that traversed the small back yard, helping themselves to the clothes-pegs that hung in a big cloth sack.

"Signora . . ."

Hannah held up a warning hand. "Little one, ve stop mit de stranger talk. Hannah, dat's my name—so please use it. Yes?" Jane smiled her pleasure, nearly dropping the clothes-peg held between her lips.

"So?" asked Hannah, bending down to the wash basket.

"Oh, I just wonder if Herr Geiger and you have seen the city of New York."

"Ven ve got passed from dat Ellis Island, vere ve vere, ve vent. Stayed mit Hyman, school friend of my Fritz, vere he lived a place called Hester Street. Nice name, not so nice street—too much like old country. Vy go all de vay across de sea to so big America to live all squeezed? Everybody on top of everybody like bees, but no honey. Everybody still poor, so vork hard daytime, even all de nights. Bring piece vork sewing home—so whole family stitches. Even de little children so hard dey vork . . . but nice, too—all togedder, safe vere everybody speaks de same. De talking I miss—sometime. But not good to hold on too much on tings too gone avay. Ven I become American citizen, I am one hundred percent United States!" Hannah shook out a sheet, its wetness cracking the air. "So, child, why you ask?"

"Oh, I wonder if you know Signora Cantonocci. We stay with her overnight."

"You did? Vat happened?"

"Happened? Nothing. I see her beautiful green parlor with—how you say 'statues'? And so many nieces, very pretty." Bending to pick up the empty basket, Jane did not see Hannah's expression. Even if she had, she probably would not have understood why her landlady suddenly looked so cross.

Before supper that evening, Hannah cornered her "baby" John in the hall. Her low voice ominous, an accusative finger poking his chest to the rhythm of her words, she hissed, "Okay, Fancy Boy. You explain to me, right here and now vy you take a so new innocent Vifey to dat House of Hanky-Panky in dat city full of it!"

John, under attack, about to hang up his hat on the hall tree, stopped in mid-reach. "Who told you that?"

"Your sweet Vifey—who knows not a ting—tinks only nieces and so pretty parlor! You should be ashamed!"

"I'm sorry, Hannah, but it was the only place where it wouldn't cost anything for the night!"

"Cost? It vould have cost you plenty! Count your lucky stars you got avay mit it! Dat hot stuff Daisy—she dere still?" That last barb Hannah threw at him over her shoulder as she hurried back to the kitchen and her simmering stew.

One morning that heralded what Hannah proclaimed would be a late summer scorcher, she placed a numbered card in her front window, covered the kitchen floor all the way out to the back porch with old newspaper, poured a tall glass of her sweet lemonade and sat peeling potatoes anticipating something. Jane, in the back yard hanging her wash, heard the loud clip-clop of a heavy horse, when Hannah called, "Vifey! Iceman here! Come, come see!"

Dropping her clothes-pegs, Jane ran. In front of the house stood a thick, muscled horse, hitched to a splendid wagon that reminded her of those gypsy tinkers who came to Cirié on festival days. Its rear wheels high, front ones low, painted bright red; the sides of its enclosed body elaborately decorated with ornate lettering that curved above and below a large oval-shaped scene depicting two happy polar bears in an artistic arctic setting. A big scale swung merrily from its back; but Hannah said Mr. Kennec, the Ice Man, always "guesstimated"—he was so good at it that he never needed to weigh her fifty-pound block. His baggy pants held up precariously by very old suspenders half attached, Mr. Kennec was as chunky as his horse. Everything about him gave the impression he was in the process of coming apart at the seams. On seeing

Hannah and Jane, he doffed his cap, hailed them with, "Mornin' Ladies!" as he swung his pincers, biting into a large block of ice that he hoisted onto his shoulder padded by a piece of soggy sheepskin. Up the back porch stairs, into the kitchen, melting ice dripping, mixing with the mud from his boots, Jane, following, understood why the need for the newspaper on the floors. From a loop on his belt, Mr. Kennec lifted an ice pick of lethal proportions—as Hannah exclaimed, "Vifey—now vatch! Dis is beautiful! Real talent dis man got! He do it here inside for me."

Fist clenching his mighty weapon, the iceman raised a bulging arm and struck! Crack! Ice chips spewed up into the air like silver fireworks! Once more a mighty blow and Hannah cried out in wondrous delight. "See! Presto! It fits! Into my icebox it fits like hand in glove!" Mr. Kennec sheathed his stiletto-like weapon, beamed, basking in her approval. "Come, now, drink lemonade—all ready for you like alvays. Oh, excuse . . . dis here new vife of my Italian boarder—Missus Jane, just come over from de old country!"

"Howdy, Ma'am, pleased I'm sure." Mr. Kennec tipped his cap, drank down his lemonade in one gulp, smacked his lips, collected his twenty cents and doffing his headgear once again, said in a tone of sad farewell, "Next summer then, Missus Geiger. Good winter to ya. You take care now. You too, Miss," and left.

Hannah gazed after him as though a good friend had departed on a long journey, then began picking up wet newspaper.

"Nice man. In vinter time big Lake Erie makes special ice. But is so big hard work to cut out. Den, de ice vaits in de big icehouses for me to get ven hot time summer comes around again. Clever, no?"

Jane nodded in agreement. That day, under the chestnut tree when she had heard of an icebox for the very first time, having the chance of actually ever seeing one had been quite inconceivable, yet here she was, in the same room with one, had witnessed ice splinters in splendid explosion and Jane was now convinced that she had finally seen it all!

As summer ended, time became sectioned by routine, the women's days as structured as those of the men punching time clocks. Beds stripped, aired, remade, carpets beaten, everything dusted, polished, brushed and shined, peeled, cut, sliced, pounded, kneaded and cooked. Interrupted by exciting adventures of long walks to the grocery man and butcher to select, discuss and argue prices. Jane observed new wonders as they applied to the preset structures of daily life. Those still to be discovered just had to wait out their time.

She learned how one could feed eight men and still have pennies left to hide away in a sugar bowl for "dat rainy day dat oh, God in Heaven shouldn't come," that the big broad paddle really did help stir the wash when hands and arms felt they would drop off. That a little salt, sprinkled into boiling starch kept it from sticking, that a tub half filled with ashes and water made such a strong supply of lye that, when added to water, it turned it soft as rain. How one padded the kitchen table, heated an iron, pressed upon it mountains of shirts and still had it cleared in time to prepare supper. How to brush a man's suit correctly so it would look as though newly store-bought, that a coarse broom was for cellar, yard and porch, while a soft broom was for inside only.

The scrubbing of floors—that she knew, but even there Hannah had a few tricks to teach her that she said would make it easier when Jane had a home of her own and would be "big mit child!" No matter how used Jane got to Hannah's way of speaking her mind, there were times when she still could shock her. Being "with child" was not part of the bargain she had made. No matter how many women commented favorably on her capability to produce, Jane had no intention of doing so. Mothering was foreign to her—to be one a disturbing intrusion, even an unpleasant one. She was sure by willpower alone she would avoid it.

In bed at night, her husband continued his right to her. She, not knowing that this required anything of her, lay submissive as always, waiting for the whole mysterious gyrations to be over, reducing the act to mere bodily exertion, love a misnomer.

That John was patient, with overtones of disinterest, did not help her introduction. That his true passion was the consummation of his work made sex within their marriage a routine of duty, practiced when the reminder of its obligation arose. If Jane had loved him, perhaps that emotion might have propelled her into a needing physical maturity. As it was, he emptied himself, she received, without reaction or complaint. It would take quite a long time before she would learn what it was she had been missing. For the present, she thought that marriage, once entered into for its paramount reason, held few advantages after its initial need had been realized.

What bothered her though, and that she should be bothered at all she found irritating, so out of character for herself, was the physical regularity. Her husband's so predictable punctuality of availing himself of her, that brought her at times to the brink of inner fury. She astonished herself for being affected by something so basically common, for if she analyzed the whole strange procedure, parts of it could be considered even pleasant. The touch of another's body held a certain comforting warmth, even its encompassing weight could not, in all fairness, be judged wholly dislikable. So why was she suddenly so resentful?

Whenever Jane confronted self-confusion and got no immediate satisfactory solution, she turned whatever was bothering her around, distilling it to pseudo nonimportance. Slowly, Jane became a housewife, if not a wife.

She baked bread that only had air holes where they ought to be, was introduced to the consummate skill of producing an American pie crust. Became so proficient in lemon meringue pies that Hannah stopped making them altogether, letting Jane be the one to receive the men's accolades whenever she paraded hers into the dining room, while Hannah perfected her already perfect apple instead. The men threw themselves into what they perceived as a pie rivalry between the two women. Tasting, looking serious, tasting some more, feigning indecision to taste again. "Yesterday Jane's lemon was just a little tart—Hannah's apple was just right . . . but, I'm not sure . . . so you better give me another slice, just to be sure . . ." As Sundays were exclusively reserved for strudel and doughnuts, during the week, like small boys, they played their tasting game consuming an astounding amount of pie in the process—never fully aware that the two women were enjoying themselves as much as they. Jane found there was something in the very act of baking an American pie that seemed joyous, wholly inexplicable, yet true. As the seasons changed, so did the fillings. Jane gave up on pumpkin when it just refused to become one of her accomplishments—but that was all right with everybody because in pumpkin pie, Hannah was untouchable. In a world of backbreaking work and dedicated concentration to hold on to it, child-like behavior often serves a vital function. To become an untroubled child, even for minute spaces of time, allows a burdened spirit rest.

In her kitchen apron, escaped tendrils of hair framing her face, Jane opened the door for her husband, greeting him in Italian. "Good evening, John. You have time to wash up for supper. Fritz and the others are home already. Oh, in our room, you will find a bushel basket I have lined with some cloth that Hannah let me have. From now on, please place your dirty wash into it, not as you have been doing, on the floor. Now that I am here, Hannah should no longer collect and wash your clothes. Also, by next payday, I shall have an accounting book, then you can give me the allowance for our household purchases. It is time for me to learn how such things are acquired and accounted for in the American way." Slightly taken aback, John informed his wife that he was used to leaving all such things to capable Hannah and was answered, "Well, now that you have a wife, it is no longer the responsibility of another. Go wash . . . supper will be ready in six minutes," and Jane marched off to the kitchen.

In a foul mood, John ate his meatloaf, not even looking up when his wife, having taken on the chore of serving the evening meal, asked him if he wanted more gravy on his mashed potatoes. Hannah, having been told to sit for a change, eat with the men, enjoyed the unexpected luxury as much as John's reaction to Jane taking charge. "Vifey" was no longer the poor little thing she had first welcomed into her house. Not disliking this new self-sufficiency in the young woman, still it interested her what was really responsible for its appearance. Love could bring such self-awareness, satisfactory sex even more so, yet Hannah's unfailing instinct told her neither of these reasons were correct. No, this tall girl-child, with all her sensible seriousness, her cool calm, was still unawakened, a virgin emotionally, if no longer in body. Hannah's thoughts corrected themselves, no—even the body part not a woman yet. She would have to have a little serious talk with her Baby John for sure. There was something there he was not doing right by that good girl she had come to love.

The next day, John brought home a present for his wife, wrapped in brown paper, tied with string.

"Here, for you." He handed it to her, adding, "Mr. Ford says every good American home should have one of these. Open it." Watching as she unknotted the string, winding it around her fingers before putting it into her apron pocket, smoothing the paper to use it again, she unwrapped her first book, entitled *McGuffey's Eclectic Primer*. "This one is for you to keep. The office will let me borrow more later when you have learned this one." She was about to thank him, when he continued, "Jane, I wish to speak to you. Although in English you are making excellent progress, your pronunciation is beginning to sound like Hannah's. You must watch that. Your ear for language is much too fine to allow yourself to speak so badly. Please try to remember that not all words beginning with a W are pronounced as though they start with a V and that *the* starts with the sound of *th*, not a *d*."

Jane thanked her husband for the lesson and the primer, in Italian, and left to help Hannah in the kitchen.

As scrubbing floors required one to be down on one's knees, Hannah decreed that German, the language of force and conscientious labor was in its correct setting to be learned. Hanging wash, on the other hand, could lend itself to learning that a W was not a V—that is, when one remembered to take the clothes-peg out of one's mouth first. Jane, a true linguist, eventually became quite proficient in German, although for the rest of her life, she retained a slight Yiddish cadence when speaking it and though Hannah did finally master her "whats," "wheres," and "whens," *th* remained her unconquerable enemy forever.

In between chores, Jane waded through her primer and thought how utterly boring; but plodded on diligently until she arrived at Lesson L-1 and, suddenly, everyone was replaced by "the Lord and all His so Holy Goodness" and took over the text like punctuated clobber onto the mind. That stopped her cold and she switched to deciphering the old newspapers that were kept bundled up in the attic. Whenever a little time could be stolen, feeling guilty yet determined, Jane would creep up there, sit on the floor beneath the low-slung roof and teach herself to read in English. She found many interesting things had happened the year before. A Mr. Wilson, with a strange first name, had been elected as a president; the greatest ocean liner ever built, an unsinkable "Floating Palace," on her maiden voyage had struck an iceberg and sank with the loss of 1,503 lives—a real millionaire among the dead, heralded as "The Tragedy of the Century." Another gentleman had actually reached the South Pole and a place called Boston had defeated New York in something called the World Series. 1912 intrigued her so, she couldn't wait to go back further to find out what 1911 had been like—but that would have to wait. She had still so much to learn. What she really could not decipher, she skipped—hoping it would clarify later when she knew more and could come back to it.

Whenever her husband inquired how she was coming along with her *McGuffey's Eclectic Reader*, adding that he would be disappointed in her if she failed to follow Mr. Ford's so excellent curriculum, she lied in Italian, assuring him of her dedication to its contents. Once she nearly made a slip, when, at the breakfast table, Johann, the Hollander, asked what street Mr. Ford's house was on and she blurted, "Sixty-six Edison Avenue in Detroit. Well, last year anyway," having just the day before devoured an old society section. When everyone stopped eating and stared at her, she tried to cover quickly by explaining she must have overheard it while listening to some ladies gossiping at the butcher's. Fortunately Hannah let the coffee boil over just then and that diverted the men's attention.

After supper Jane usually took her mending downstairs to work quietly in the parlor. While the men talked, she listened—pretending that she wasn't.

John lit his cigar, leaned back in his chair expelling a bluish haze that joined the air already thick with the smoky aromas of assorted tobaccos.

Stan Bartok, fanning a lit match across the bowl of his pipe, mumbled, "John, I don't agree with the whole idea. The damn place is in an uproar. It's chaos! What's wrong? Our work no good—no more?"

The men of the Geiger Boardinghouse, whose life's blood not only financially but emotionally was their involvement with Ford, were split as to the merits of the revolutionary idea that was being tested, implemented in specified sections of the plant. Rudy Zegelmann, his black eyes snapping, for once their seductive gaze erased, agreed, "Damn right! So what do I do? Just stand there? Wait for my little chassis to arrive, pinch it on the behind and wave bye-bye? No way to work!" Cursing in Austrian dialect, he took a small pouch and paper from his coat pocket and began rolling a cigarette.

"Oh, Rudy, come on! Now it takes twelve and a half hours to assemble a Model T. If the Boss wants it quicker, new ideas maybe work. Watch and see!" said Peter

Clutovich who since his congratulatory encounter within the pages of the *Ford Times*, was known to have a doglike loyalty to his masters that bordered occasionally on blind adulation.

Stan Bartok turned to John. "You always know statistics. Last season, how many Ts did we turn out?"

"Seventy-eight thousand four hundred and forty."

"And what's the goal now?"

"Two hundred sixty-seven thousand, last time I heard—but demand is more!"

Jane nearly gasped out loud, the men smoked in silence. John flicked the ash off his cigar.

"What's wrong with bringing the work to the men—instead of the men to the work? That's how the meat packers do it in Chicago!"

"Come on, John. Assembling an automobile that has more than five thousand parts is not like cutting up a dead cow!" Carl Baldechek grunted.

"Why not? We are talking about piecework—precision piecework—every action timed . . . individualized. My God, man, can't you see it? Thousands of men in stationary motion. Every movement controlled, timed by the rhythm of a line that is *moving*! Jesus, Carl, that's the future!"

It was times like these that her husband's passionate enthusiasm reawakened Jane's first memories of him and she found, once again, how attractive this made him.

"Listen," John continued, "you're the one who *knows* it works, Carl."

"But when they set up the line to move and gave twenty men the twenty-nine separate operations, what happened?"

"We turned out one hundred and thirty-two every hour," Carl answered begrudgingly.

"Of course! I saw the results on paper. One man needed twenty minutes before the assembly line moved. After it was put in motion, it took thirteen minutes ten seconds. My God, can't you see what that means?"

Stan stroked his moustache, shaking his head, "I still don't trust it."

"And who's going to set the speed?" Stan challenged.

"Ja!" Fritz joined the discussion. "With orders already more than what we can produce, Mr. Couzens for sure now will want that kind of speedup quick for all operations."

Sensing a slight censure in Fritz's tone, John hastened to comment. "Henry Ford knows what he is doing. Trust him."

"Sorenson is the one to trust. If it can be done, he is the one who will do it for sure!" Carl corrected him.

Fritz looked up at the ornate cuckoo clock, said it was late as Hannah entered and shooed her "boys" to bed. Jane remained to help tidy up the parlor, turn off the lights, check the windows and doors, then followed her husband up to bed. That night, when he fell asleep without touching her, she shocked herself by wondering why he hadn't.

The more Jane found herself thinking about her status as wife, the more this confused her. Why should she be concerned, even influenced by a man's moods, his attitudes? Why should it mater, all of a sudden how he reacted to her? She knew she was not like Camilla, who came unstuck if a man just looked at her, and an Antonia—she was most emphatically not; going around needing to entice a man as though always hungry, looking for nourishment—Jane thought debasing. Yet she remembered how John had been attracted by just that. So why hadn't he chosen Antonia, who by all indications, would probably relish the so punctual nightly exercise. And why was she taking the time thinking such ridiculous thoughts when she had work to do and should be doing it? Well, the next time John touched her, she would be the one to turn away—go to sleep. See how he would like that! As Hannah would say, "tit-for-tat." Do him good.

Most evenings now, the Ford men talked shop. In the testing sections, the new assembly system was giving everyone trouble; by demanding that workers remained stationary while a line moved, not only its rate of speed but its height became a crucial point of discussion. Men who knew their craft, had been in command of their every move to execute its skilled perfection, now were being asked to perform within a stationary position—rooted in place, as assembly, broken down to a wide range of separate components passed by, dictating the rhythm of their every action. Jane in her usual corner, darning needle busy, listened, as always fascinated by anything to do with her husband's idol and his so famous "flivver" that had given the common man his freedom to roam.

As foreman, always a mother-hen type when dedicated, Carl worried about his men. "John, lifting the line to waist level may solve the stooping problem but still . . . Okay—I know—they clocked us when we walked and it took too long . . . still, we knew what we were doing . . . all of us. We did our job right." His voice sounded even gruffer than usual.

Stan, his Rumanian heritage contributing to his usual somber distrust, now made his point. "What kind of worker you think will now pull down wages? Nine hours standing in one spot, doing one simple action over and over, a monkey can do—takes no brains—just endurance."

Johann stretched out his long legs.

John proclaimed, "I bet you that in six months' time, by spring, every line at the plant will be in constant motion. We all know that a moving line works, so why are you all excited?"

"Excited? Who's excited!" Fritz sucked on his pipe.

"Come on, John. Since you've been gone, and this thing started, you know how many men have quit?" Not waiting for an answer, Carl continued, "We lose maybe forty men every week and . . ."

"Why, for God's sake?!" John interrupted. "Who'd be dumb enough to leave Ford?"

"These are no boobs—these are skilled men and most of them go over to the Dodge Brothers." Carl's tone held censure.

"Handwork, John, is still craftsmanship to some," observed the Englishman.

"Well, Jimmy, I'll answer that with the words of Henry Ford, 'Man minus the machine is a slave—Man plus the machine is a free man.'"

"You really believe that?"

"Sure! All of us here, we are building a machine that is freeing a whole nation!"

"Yeah—while its builders maybe are losing theirs!" murmured Stan.

John turned on him. "If you think that, why haven't you gone over to the Dodge Brothers?"

Before the Rumanian could answer, Johann jumped in. "Stan, what is Mr. Sorenson doing in all this?"

"'Cast-Iron Charlie'? He's everywhere, watching—making notes—correcting. Heard he has some idea of bringing from my top floor some of the big parts down from above—sort of continuous shoot the chutes. Soon our Highland Park plant is going to get a new name. From Crystal Palace to Ford Motor Company Amusement Park."

"I hear maybe we too get pulleys up high, like trolleys to come from floor to floor. How can that be done?" Peter, the wheel man, sounded thoroughly confused.

Rudy's gaze took in the men assembled in the parlor. "So, you all are going to be happy being a monkey?"

Preferring to ignore its implication, no one rose to the bait. Fritz checked the clock, wound his pocket watch.

"John, you know that new man who came in to clear up the wage structures? Well, my friend, now, we got only three levels and the big news is, because you have now wife to feed, you go up to level C-One—and that means you're getting a raise! Me too, also Johann, but, our so happy-go-lucky bachelor boys here? They gotta get hitched before they can get the raises!" Fritz chuckled, "See how clever our John? Gets himself married just at the right time!"

Zoltan jumped up.

"I'm off—good night!" and hurried from the room. The others followed suit. Jane caught her husband's eye and, when he nodded, picked up her work basket and followed him upstairs to bed.

Other evenings, the parlor talk took a lighter course. Flivver jokes were retold as were the latest wonders achieved by their precious motorcar. As Jane became more and more familiar with the language and the Ford men who spoke it, she often felt she was listening to lovesick boys, extolling the virtues of a girl they all adored.

"Hey, Carl, did you hear the one about a patron of a large department store who asked for tires for his T, then was directed to the 'rubber band' department? Wait . . . I heard another . . . what time is it when one Ford follows another? Tin after tin!"

"Isn't that a lulu!" Peter slapped his thigh.

Carl joined the fun. "Heard the one of the parson who's giving a sermon on better church attendance?"

Everyone became attentive.

"Well, this parson, he is preaching that it's the demon automobile that is taking people away on Sunday outings to have good times—instead of to church—so he says, 'The Model T has taken more people to Hell than any other thing I can mention' when a lady in the congregation starts clapping her hands, moaning 'Glory to God! Praise the Lord!' 'What's the matter, sister?' asks the parson and the old lady answers, 'A Ford never went anyplace that it couldn't come back from, so I reckon all them folks in Hell will be comin' back someday. Praise the Lord!'"

Some evenings, becoming suddenly aware that there was a newcomer in their midst, who not only seemed interested in their lady-love but eager to know more, the men fell over themselves telling Jane all about her.

"First, she was built all by hand in a little secret room hidden away where only Mr. Ford and special men he trusted were allowed in. That was way back in the years 1907 to '08 and then, when finally, there she stood, all perfect, tested, finished—you know what they did, Missus Jane?" Fritz paused, letting the suspense take effect.

Jane, fully affected, breathed, "What?"

"Mr. Henry Ford said, 'Now, boys . . . take her apart!'—and, that they did! Piece by piece, bolt by bolt. Everything! They laid out all the pieces like a giant puzzle right there on the floor of the secret room, so to make the drawings, the plans, so everyone will know for always how to put together again their so perfect Model T! No one sing 'Happy Birthday,' but that's what it was that day for our Lizzie!"

"What are you rascals teaching my wife?" John asked good-naturedly as he entered the parlor.

"We were only trying to explain how to start Lizzie up!"

John settled in his chair, stretched out his legs. "Nothing to it! First you sweet-talk her—then you crank like crazy!"

Carl gave him a look.

"My boy, watch your tongue. Your lady wife will think we are a bunch of bully-boys!"

"Oh, my Jane is no shrinking violet. She has a sensible head on her shoulders and knows how to use it!" For some reason, this remark of her husband's both pleased and rankled and, for the life of her, Jane couldn't think why.

The next evening, on the way to his chair, Zoltan first bowed in Jane's direction, then hurried over to whisper, "Last night they forgot to tell you—she holds the world's hill-climbing record. Just point her nose downhill and reverse her up it—and with the crankcase oil? Once it warms up a little, she settles right down like the good girl she is," and he scurried off to sit in his chair.

"Zoltan! Whispering sweet nothings to my wife?"

"Oh, goodness! No!" Zoltan, flustered, shook his head like a quail on the run. "Only thought your Missus should be informed of what was left out last evening . . ."

John, trying not to laugh, continued in the tone of a suspicious husband, "And, what was that?"

"What? Oh dear!" One eyebrow developing a tick, Zoltan's eyes darted about the room looking for help. The men hid behind their papers, pretending disinterest. John's questioning gaze remained fixed on the squirming tester, who, nearly stuttering, beseeched his would-be accuser. "The warming of the crankcase oil! So she settles! The Lizzie." By now, both eyebrows were twitching. "To start her up is tricky climbing—well . . ."

John could hold it no longer, his laughter exploded. The men howled. Zoltan, the butt of a joke, was miffed.

"That was not fair, John. Putting me on! Thought you were serious. Not good for the nerves! Not good at all!" and opening his paper with noisy flourish, he disappeared behind it, refusing to be spoken to for the rest of the evening.

As time passed and the men kept singing her praises, the Lizzie became sort of human, even to Jane. Her indomitable courage, her honorable dependability, her devotion to her owner, her spunk, appealed to Jane, like someone real one would want to meet, call a friend. That little black motorcar had a way of capturing one's heart; this might be considered foolish to admit but "by gum," Jane was learning all sorts of American expressions, it sure felt right to love it! Secretly, she determined, no matter how long she might have to wait, that someday she would ride in a Model T, have Lizzie show her the freedom of the open road!

5

The first time Jane laid a fire in the coal stove, poured on the kerosene, then lit it—thick smoke spewed from its iron belly, engulfing everything. Hearing the mighty swoosh, Hannah rushed into her kitchen and, seeing the blackened apparition, doubled over with laughter, slapping her thighs.

"A minstrel—in my kitchen! I got a minstrel! Hey, you gonna play me a fine toon on your banjo now, ya? What a ninnie!"

Jane, covered in soot, just stood there, feeling very foolish yet grateful Hannah wasn't angry, thinking it would take days to wipe all traces clean! That evening, over supper, the boarders were treated to a full theatrical performance of what became known as the Big Black Minstrel Explosion. As it was embroidered with fascinating additions whenever retold—it was requested whenever they felt Hannah was in the mood to perform her rendition of "De Camptown Races," strut and all. It was from this that Jane received her very first nickname, the one that John used from then on. To hear her husband call her Ninnie was a joyous warmth she held on to—until the very end. But her first reaction to it surprised her because she liked it so much! Perhaps, as with some nicknames that seem to change one's character in order to suit them better, for her, Ninnie by its lilting sound indicated a lightness, a girlishness, a special femininity, even a prettiness that as a plain Jane she secretly aspired to, so that when she heard herself called by it, she had the feeling of being actually pretty.

October passed, but not before Jane was introduced to Halloween. She had dreaded the arrival of November and its macabre beginning of All Saints' Day as she remembered it from Cirié. The candles, the incense, the sanctimonious reawakened mourning for those long since turned to dust, mostly forgotten. So, when Hannah, all smiles, solicited donations from her boarders for something called penny candy—saying that this year she would be adding Neccos to her trove of Jub-Jubs—Jane, intrigued, asked her what those were and why.

"Oh, Vifey! I forget—dis your first. I tell you. Last nighttime of dis month, October, children, some naughty, some not so, come—in sheets—mit sock full mit flour. You puzzled, right?" Jane nodded. "I explain. First, dey sing-a-ling—'Trick or treat!' What that means? Dat mean if no treat, you get a bang mit de sock, flour mess all over your nice front door. So what you do? Give quick a candy treat, Jub-Jub, maybe even a peppermint stick—or sometime licorice twist—den dey happy . . . go away. Dat's American Halloween!"

Jane digested this for a minute, then questioned, "Why sheets?"

"For de ghost dressing up!"

"Ghosts—are fun?"

"Sure, only children playing—not serious—good to have fun mit de ghosts, not so scary den for little children such tings. Tomorrow night, Vifey, you watch door—you learn. If we lucky, dis year maybe we even get some witches!"

Stationed by the front door, supplies of sticky treats awaiting the arrival of Happy Ghosts, Jane, ready at her post, filched a Necco from the brown paper sack and, though surprised that a child's sweet should taste of lavender, had to admit once gotten over the initial shock, that it was delicious. Hannah, keeping one eye on her bubbling goulash, the other on her front door, enjoyed the parade of little ghosts as much as Jane's obvious delight with her first introduction to an American holiday.

Now that winter was coming, Hannah's sumptuous soup tureen, so diligently transported from an old life to dispense its warming comfort to a new, took its rightful place at suppertime. Carl floated chunks of crusty bread in his favorite lentil soup.

"Saw young Edsel did his summer job real well. Every machine has its brass plaque—everyone identified—nice and tidy. Good boy that!"

"Hey, did you notice he always carried a notebook, just like the Boss? Keeps jotting things into it, just like him, too." Rudy took a swig of beer.

"Mr. Ford is proud of his boy. Rightly so. He's a credit to him and his Missus," Carl observed.

"You watch, someday that boy will surprise his proud Papa. Has a head on his shoulders, thinks for himself." Stan admired the spindly youth who liked to work in the plant during his summer vacations.

"He don't look down on nobody. Could, being son of big Boss!" said Peter. The men nodded in agreement.

Jimmy wiped his mouth. "I find the whole idea rather astonishing."

"What?" Fritz asked.

"Henry Ford, letting the boy work, like one of his men, no favors shown."

"That's because Edsel will be boss someday. Good, learn what it takes now, to work for a living. Being rich born not teach you how hard that is."

"Quite right, Fritz." Jimmy acknowledged the older man's opinion.

Jane, helping Hannah clear, heard her murmur to herself. "Dat's American way, Mr. Jimmy Englishman, everybody equal."

"In one way, I agree with Jimmy," Johann looked at Fritz. "Now that Edsel has graduated, why not let him go get himself a fine college education—the money sure is there, so why not? Why have him join the company?"

"Why? Because the Boss is getting his boy ready to run his Ford Motor Company one day! Teach him more here what he needs to know than fancy college full of other rich sons!"

"Heard Edsel has himself a girl," John announced.

"Already? So young?" Fritz exclaimed.

"Good for him!" Stan approved.

"Okay with the Boss?" Rudy asked.

"Oh, nothing serious," John chuckled, "still only good clean fun."

"Well, soon the boy need to marry—important we have sons, make Mr. Ford happy grandpapa—know his company then safe for always." Fritz pushed back his chair, rose, led the procession of men to the parlor.

Jane, clearing the table, wondered as she often did, at the intense interest Henry Ford's workers had for anything that concerned him, like a father with many children—they felt they were a part of him. Everything he did, his very thoughts were a part of their lives. That this man's children numbered more than fourteen thousand workers, as well as the astounding sum of Model T owners, Ford dealers, and assembly shop personnel across America as well as foreign lands, made this so intimate interest in the boss of this vast empire that much more beguiling.

Jane was becoming a "Ford wife" and it pleased her. This amazing man, who had elevated the common man to the equal mobility of his superiors, was now about to change the concept of quantity production for all time, had captured her imagination.

She, whose need for limitless horizons had propelled her across the sea, bound her to an unloved stranger, felt a longing kinship with one whose dream had become reality. Each evening, she rushed to be settled in her corner, ready to listen—fascination growing as the Ford men talked.

"Today overhead wheel line move so fast, make you hurry up so don't miss something, 'til you feel like machine, too," announced Peter, his tone tinged with guilt for voicing what might be construed as a criticism.

Jimmy struck a match against the heel of his boot. "Joke going around, your boys on the line drop a wrench, bend down to pick it up—three Ts have passed you by."

"Like I said, if this goes on, monkeys will wear our badges, punch time cards and we? We'll have to move to Flint!" Stan was not joking.

John, ever the defender of his hero, answered him. "You forget Henry Ford is a mechanic. He has always respected his men. And what about Couzens and Sorenson? Even Avery. You really believe, Stan, such men would allow inferior workmanship to increase production?"

"Yes, I do."

"Well, I don't!"

"Have it your way, John," Stan murmured, not wanting to get into a fight.

John, opening his paper, changed direction if not the subject of their evening's discussion.

"Fritz, tomorrow put down your nimble thimble, come down from your eagle nest and I'll show you how we now turn out crankcases. You've got to see this. Right, Jimmy?"

Fritz put down his paper. "Another new thing?"

"You bet . . . and it's fantastic! On an overhead automatic conveyer system— they now go direct from the pressed steel department to the paint tank, onto the drying ovens—that before, took up miles of floor space . . . time and men at hard labor."

Zoltan sneezed, excused himself, adding, "Everything dangling above the heads— hope that's safe."

"I say, we should put the whole car assembly on a continuous line!"

"John, that's plain crazy!" Rudy blew a smoke ring. John shrugged.

"Heard today a man out West has invented a hand pump that can pump gasoline into a gas tank. They said he calls it a 'Filling Station' because it has wheels, can be rolled right to a curb." Johann looked around for a reaction and got one from Stan.

"A curb? How many towns do you know that even have streets?"

"Not a bad idea, though," Fritz observed.

"Now everybody's inventing something. There's a company offering T owners a Speed-O-Meter. Sells for twelve dollars. Who can afford that?"

"And what about the one offering gasoline gages," Rudy sounded excited. "Can you beat that? If you own one of those, you don't have to get your ruler out of the toolbox—make your girl get out to pull up the front seat to get to the tank and measure to see what you got left in there!"

Johann laughed. "There's even a man who swears he's invented an alarm that will ring when the Henry is about to go dry!"

Jane wondered just how many more names one little automobile could be known by.

"Yes, I hear there have been letters on that." Carl agreed.

"There are letters on everything! Evangeline saw one from a lady in Virginia, who complained that when one squeezed the bulb on Lizzie's horn it sounded like a duck with a bad case of *catarrh*!"

Everyone laughed, except Jane, who didn't know what *catarrh* meant.

Carl turned to John. "So, you saw the fair Evangeline!"

"Hey, Missus Jane—you better watch your fella! He's associating with dynamite!"

"Quit it, Rudy." John was not amused.

"Yes, boys—no teasing John's Missus. She still new—not knows our joking way." Fritz sounded stern.

Silenced, the men took up their evening's reading—Jane, her darning forgotten, was trying to digest what she had heard.

"Hannah?"

It was Friday, Noodle Day, and Jane was rolling dough into thick sausages, ready for cutting.

"Yes, child, you got trouble?" Hannah turned from the sink.

"Oh, no, not the noodles. I just wondered if you know an Evangeline?"

Hannah dried her hands on her apron. Her usual effusive verbal output reduced to a solitary "Sure," which hung in the air as though looking for a place to land safely.

Jane, concentrating on cutting the rolled dough into quarter-inch-wide sections, murmured, "Is she someone who works in the plant?"

"Yes." Again a one-word answer from Hannah, a most unusual occurrence.

Jane continued cutting. Whatever was worrying her could not be permitted to interfere with the prescribed width of Hannah's egg noodles.

"Does she work in the dynamite department?"

That did it! Hannah fell onto the kitchen chair and burst out laughing.

"Oh, Vifey Vifey! Dat is funniest ting I hear for long, long time! Oh, my!" Wiping her eyes, gasping for breath, Hannah tried to collect herself. "How come you hear of her? Never mind! She not work with dynamite. She IS de dynamite! Very sprightly, sort of soft little bundle of 'Squeeze-me-come-on, fella' type she is. But no floozy. Mit all dat, she is still a lady, dat I gotta say."

"She's that pretty?" Jane asked, wondering why her stomach suddenly felt so queasy.

"Ya—dat's why de Boss so smitten. Everybody has idea maybe Miss Evangeline soon his special friend!"

"The Boss?" Jane breathed.

"Who else? Everybody knows, sort of. Even his smart so good missus maybe. But dat's dere business—if okay by dem, okay by us who work for boss of good and decent Ford Company. Why you ask?"

Jane, very busy suddenly, fluffing out the perfectly cut noodles, answered her as though completely disinterested.

"Oh, nothing really. I heard the name and just wondered who she was."

Smiling, Hannah returned to her sink to scrape carrots for supper.

November winds whipped across the Great Lakes beginning to freeze over. Morning dew no longer lay silent waiting to evaporate, acquired an opaqueness that powdered when disturbed. Daylight, foreshortened, took on the color of a tarnished blade. The North American winter had taken up its residence along the Border States.

Not even amidst the glacial granite of her mountain village had Jane ever experienced such bone-twisting cold, known it could exist where civilized beings needed to go about their daily lives. She marveled at the accustomed acceptance of the people around her—their casual explanation "that's Michigan" when one's breath seemed it would freeze in midair. Even that there had ever been a time when the arrival of Mr. Kennec, the iceman, had been welcomed seemed now only two months later, quite inconceivable.

Even before Halloween, the Geiger boardinghouse had been readied to withstand the attack of winter. With Fritz as marshalling foreman, the boarders were organized into an efficient squad of handymen. Hannah and Fritz's ultimate pride, their Acme Hummer Heating and Ventilation Hot Air Furnace, courtesy of the ever dependable Messrs. Sears and Roebuck, stood freshly reamed, cleaned, and swept, waiting in the cellar domain ready to do its duty. Every pipe was wrapped in shrouds of newsprint and flannel scraps that Hannah collected in her rag-bag throughout the year, windows corked and puttied, every door had its very own threshold "snake"— a Hannah whimsy of thick sausages made of remnants, twisted, entwined, then sewn with carpet thread to keep out lethal drafts. Their name of "snake" derived from Hannah's proclamation that as dead cloth sausages lying about depressed her, she had decided to bring them to life by giving them button eyes. Jane became especially fond of the one that reclined along the base of their bedroom door. One of its buttons, being smaller than the other, gave it a cross-eyed myopic expression of perpetual surprise. She christened it Francis after an illustration she remembered from one of Sister Bertine's favorite class books dealing with the lives of saints, in which the monk of Assisi had been depicted as close-eyed as his birds. Hannah so loved this idea of affording her snakes personal identities, she christened the fattest one stretched beneath the back porch door Hercules—because, of all his brothers, who kept out drafts, he was the one who had the toughest job to do.

Heads swathed in woolen mufflers, mittened hands clumsy, Hannah and Jane were taking wash off the line. Hannah sighed, "Winter here, Vifey. No more hanging out. Wash freeze—snap right in two. Everyting now have to hang on pulley rods from ceiling in warm kitchen." Jane, too cold to speak, nodded. "Soon de holidays coming and den we go into big city of Detroit, you and me, yes?"

"Oh, yes, Hannah, please!" Jane's words muffled by the scarf Hannah had tied over her mouth, saying "Freezed lips no good for kisses."

"Now you speak so good American and you no greenhorn no more, maybe time you look it smart for de so fine city shopping."

"But, Hannah—I won't be able to make anything in time!"

"No—no—not make! Ready-made from a store bought by de mail-ordering American way." Grabbing the handle of the full basket, Hannah motioned Jane to take the other and between them, they carried the wash up the back porch and into the kitchen.

Unwinding her mufflers, Jane protested, "Anyway, I can make them better . . . and store-bought costs too much!"

"You want to look Italian Mountain Woman, fresh off de boat? Or American married lady mit husband steady working, even mit raise, in biggest motor company in whole world?" Not waiting for an answer, Hannah plunked one of her precious mail-order house catalogs onto the kitchen table, opening it to the Ladies' Garments section. Peeling off her mittens, unwrapping herself from yards of knitted wool, she sat, patting the seat of the kitchen chair next to hers.

"Come, child, sit . . . nice and cozy . . . we look for outfitting you as befits." An inner excitement stirring, Jane sat. "See, right away—here is nice skirt. Says 'serge' better dat dan dolman cloth—lasts longer. Oh, looky here—coat perfection for de skirt—just right. Sturdy overcoat too you need—Michigan cold for long, long time—so money well spent for into future!" Wetting a finger on her tongue, Hannah turned pages, pointed, delighted, "Here! Look! We got de hats! All first quality . . . dis one—dat will look special smart on you—not too fancy like floozy, but good classy ladylike. Good shoes already you got. Real leater soles very important. People notice. Like in old country, look—decide about you right off. But in America, here you can look what you want to be—not be stuck what you are. Important what your purse holds, not where you first come from. My Fritz say, maybe dat not so good dis for people sometime, but I say, work hard, behave yourself, do everyting right, so when time comes you can show off—why not? Be proud! Enjoy!"

That evening after supper, the men were minus their usual attentive listener—Jane, captive in the kitchen, was being measured, schooled in the fine art of writing out requests for her winter finery to be sent to her by the so-efficient United States Postal Service and the anticipatory visit of Hannah's secret admirer, Mr. Henry Johnson, Mailman.

The next evening Jane cornered her husband as he was about to leave their room to go down for supper, speaking Italian, as was their habit when alone, "John, it has been brought to my attention that before going into the grand city of Detroit, I need to be properly attired as befits your wife."

"Who put that silly idea into your head?"

"I do not think it is silly, as you put it. Besides, it was Hannah who said it," countered Jane.

"Well, if she thinks you need some new clothes, tell me how much you will need for the cloth and I'll give it to you." John turned to leave.

Jane's "Oh, no!" stopped him. Her Italian came in a rush, "I must have a ready-made from a store-bought complete outfit. This includes a hat in fashion, a full ensemble and a proper winter overcoat with real buttons, maybe even a velveteen collar, and for all this, I shall need the rather large sum of seventeen dollars and eighty-five cents, if you please."

"What? Seventeen dollars for a skirt, coat, and overcoat—who do you think you're married to? J. P. Morgan?"

"That was seventeen dollars *and* eighty-five cents and you forgot the hat. If I needed a pair of proper leather shoes and gloves, which I already have, it would cost much, much more!"

"What has *that* got to do with it?"

"Please, you're shouting. Hannah will get upset. It was she who thought I should be dressed to complement your station of high employment—not me. If you cannot afford to dress your wife . . ." She let it trail. Italian was such an effective language to infer criticism without actually having to spell it out.

"Dress my wife? Who said I can't dress my wife? Here . . ." and stepping back into their room, he strode to the wardrobe, opened it, pulled out his metal cash box from behind his good shoes and, unlocking it with a key attached to his watch fob, counted out seventeen dollars and eighty-five cents in change, placing it into Jane's outstretched hand.

"Thank you, John. If at all possible, I shall try to require less and then return what is left over." Stuffing the precious money into the deep pocket of her apron, Jane hurried downstairs before her husband could change his mind and ask for the treasure's return.

She could hide it from herself no longer. She was with child and this appalled her. It was not the physical process that she feared, but the enslavement it represented, would demand of her. This annex to marriage that women were schooled to accept without rebellion Jane had believed she would escape, if only by determination alone.

Now reality mocked her naïve complacency, forcing her to take stock. She realized her compulsive search for unfettered freedom at any price had but shifted her direction—not her destiny—had propelled her into a life of socially accepted bondage for which she might as well have remained where she was. After all, bondage was bondage, regardless of its geographical encampment. She did not want to be a mother, rejected the image of herself as one, yet knew now it was up to her to find the disciplined acceptance of becoming one. She absolved her husband from blame in all this, for she blamed only herself for the confinement she found herself in. Having learned at much too early an age to hide her anguish, Jane told no one, kept her inner conflict hidden, suppressed, as though it were of too little consequence to warrant serious concern. Throughout her life, Jane chose this path of injuring herself with what often appeared as an ever-ready willingness for self-harm. Now, as she faced her first pregnancy, its joylessness her secret, an imperceptible hardening began to encroach onto the fledgling softness that had just begun to blossom under the encompassing warmth of Hannah's mothering affection and a man's not unkind protection. As the child grew inside her, the inner escape route of her childhood resurrected itself. Once again, she used it to detach herself from overt life, reducing it to mere experience instead of passionate involvement. Spectator to her own existence, she stood apart. This self-protective reflex to negate what might offer her salvation would come to haunt her.

Hannah, who had witnessed Jane turning green at the sight of boiling cabbage, noticed her sudden aversion to early morning coffee, knew exactly what was going on but waited, though impatiently, for the official announcement that surely by late spring of the new year, a miracle would be occurring under her very roof. Due to her repeated bouts of nausea, the truth of Jane's condition could not be hidden for long, and, finally, one evening she was forced to confess. Hannah clucked, kissed, hugged, clapped her hands, danced about her kitchen with such joyous abandon, Jane felt guilty she couldn't join her happiness.

"A baby! I knew! I knew! We are having a little bundle of joy! Mazel tov God willing!" Hannah chanted, quite overcome. Wiping away tears with her apron, she asked, "John know he is going to be a proud Papa?" Jane shook her head. "Now good time as any," and pulling the reluctant girl behind her, stormed into the parlor.

Startled, the men looked up from their papers. Although they were now used to having Jane in their midst, it was very unusual for Hannah to make an appearance during their digesting hour. Dwarfing the doorway, Jane hiding behind her, Hannah in a voice most often used for Royal Proclamation from flag-draped balconies, announced, "John, your Vifey—she has de wonderful news! First to whisper private in your ear. Den for all to know and cheer!" and pushed a reluctant Jane towards her husband's chair.

John's reaction to his wife's embarrassed whisper amused everyone—even her. It took a moment for the news to sink in, then, when it did, he looked with wonder upon his wife, as though he couldn't understand how she ever could have achieved such an amazing feat all by herself.

Hannah could wait no longer for John to come to his senses.

"A BABY! John and his Vifey are expecting!" she blurted. "Now, we celebrate! I get Schnapps!" and rushed off.

John, still speechless, sat glued to his chair. Jane, standing before him, wondered what she should do or say next.

Rudy started to laugh. "The birds and the bees, John! Remember?" which Stan had to top with "Hey! Maybe we all got it wrong! Could it be it's Hannah's beau, Mr. Johnson the Mailman?!"

Carl shut him up with a look. Stan jumped up, motioned to Rudy to take Jane's arm, between them they conducted her to his comfortable armchair, insisting she sit as though birth was imminent. Clasping John in a fatherly hug, Fritz beamed, "You a Papa! Just a boy first time we meet—now you a Papa! My, my!"

Grinning from ear to ear, Peter punched John's shoulder, then dared to kiss Jane's cheek. As the only father among them, Johann started giving John sage advice, while Jimmy began reciting suitable boys' names, appropriate for a future true American born.

Zoltan, very affected, blew his nose, rose, crossed over to John, shook his hand, murmured his heartfelt felicitations, bowed in Jane's direction before heading back to his chair. If he had been wearing his derby, he would surely have tipped it to young motherhood.

Hannah reappeared, bearing a tray with her very best crystal and a bottle of precious Schnapps that was kept under lock and key until momentous occurrences called for its laudatory kick of 100 proof.

Everyone toasted John and his Missus. Fritz wiped his eyes, overcome when John asked him to be godfather. Beaming, Carl exclaimed he was going to be an uncle, the rest correcting him—saying that he would be only one of many!

Hannah raised her glass. "I got another toast. Everybody—to our NEW BOARDER!" Jane felt John's arm encircle her waist, drawing her against him. Forcing a smile, she wondered how a happy mother-to-be should react, hoping she was fooling them to their satisfaction, not to disappoint.

That night, John left his sexual prerogative aside, held his wife as though she had acquired a sudden fragility. For the first time in her marriage, Jane felt the magic of feeling cherished and, when John murmured, "Good night, Ninnie, you now need your rest," she slept lying against him, not turned away.

"Missus Jane, you feeling okay?" How often did she hear that? Not a day went by when one or another of the boarders didn't ask after her state of health, anxiously hanging on her reply.

"You tink you got only one husband? You got EIGHT worrying Papas—dat, I tink must be a record!" Hannah would laugh, enjoying every minute of her pregnancy by proxy. She who had prayed for a child of her own, been denied this joy, now gloried in the participation granted her of soon bringing a child into her world.

Henry Johnson, mail carrier by chosen profession, took his duty to the United States Postal Service very seriously. He believed without the slightest reservation in its credo that neither snow, nor rain, nor heat, nor gloom of night should stay him from the swift completion of his appointed rounds. So one bitter morning, not far from death by freezing, there he stood before the boardinghouse door. Chunky galoshes, like stovepipes tied beneath his knees—hands in multiple mittens resembling the paws of a grizzly, the tip of a purpled nose above a sumptuous moustache whose handlebars, once proudly waxed, erect, now sagged beneath the weight of tiny icicles, the only proof that amidst the layers of scarves, there must be a face.

His syncopated knock brought Hannah scurrying to her front door, flinging it open, knowing it was he.

"Ach, Mein Gott! Mr. Henry! Come—come quick, inside! Get melted!!"

"No, no!" protested the mailman from between blue lips. "I'll drip!"

"Drip—Schmip!" She pulled him inside.

"No, it's not proper!"

"No arguing! What's dis mit de 'proper'? You sick or someting? Hot coffee, a little nosh—you feel like a new man!" By this time she had him into the kitchen. "So, sit!"

Henry Johnson sat, eyes downcast, watching the melting ice begin to pool around his galoshes. Hannah knowing how it upset him to mess up a floor, handed him an old newspaper.

"Here, Silly! Put!"

The mailman shoved it under his feet, began peeling himself as though he were an onion—multiple mittens first. Jane, at the sink, breakfast dishes forgotten, watched fascinated as each new layer made its colorful appearance. Hannah, noticing Jane's amazement at the rainbow array, explained, "Mr. Henry—he bachelor, lives mit his sister—a widow lady. So many children she left mit to raise—she knits for dem everyting. Each one get a different color so know which belongs to which. When any wool left, she knit mittins for her brother mit de leftovers. Oh, please excuse—Mr. Henry, here by the sink is our very special Missus Jane. She expecting, so no get ideas! Vifey, here before you melting, sits Number One biggest heartbreaker, Mr. Henry Johnson, by the United States Government employed."

The mailman unwrapped his head, exposing a confusing face. Its gaunt hardness bordering on ugliness in which the softest eyes shone like enticing beacons in a darkening storm. Then, Mr. Henry smiled and Jane's mouth fell open—her heart turned somersaults, Mr. Henry's smile oozed seduction.

"You keep your special smiles for my doughnuts, you Rascal Man!" chuckled Hannah, poking him in the ribs. "Dis is a 'Good' girl—so mit her no hanky-panky allowed!"

Slender hands wrapped around his coffee cup, Mr. Henry turned his devastating smile on his benefactress and achieved an answering giggle—accompanied by a saucy wink. Stunned, Jane watched their interplay.

"Rascal Man, what you do mit dat poor girl you was playing around mit, out in Polishtown? She still mooning mit heartbreaking for you?"

And then, Mr. Henry spoke—and it was as though silk were sliding on melted chocolate and the butterflies that suddenly fluttered inside Jane's stomach had nothing to do with her delicate condition.

"Why, Missus Hannah—how you do go on!" Wiping powdered sugar from his lips with unconscious elegance, the mailman rose, uncurling his frame as though he were rising from bed. "Seen that little redhead charmer at Twenty-two Puritan? A real looker, that one. Know her?" He began replacing his many mittens, yellows first.

"You out of luck dere, Honey Boy. She's new engaged mit a big Irish rowdy. You make eyes, he knock you silly!"

"Oh, a brute is he? Well, well." Kelly green followed, then came ones of baby blue. "She'll soon tire of that. A pretty girl like that, all pink and soft deserves something better—someone who will appreciate what she's got to give," he reached for mittens of bright red.

"Aha! Like you maybe? You watch out, my boy!"

Mr. Henry covered his rainbow paws with final Postal Service gray. "Missus Hannah, you know if you weren't already taken, I could settle down, be saved from all temptations. Nothing like a strapping woman to tame a sinner like me!"

"Rascal Man! You got post for me? So? Give and out! Go deliver!"

Grinning, Mr. Henry plunked the packages on the table, rewrapped himself, hefted his mail sack, blew Jane a kiss, gave Hannah a mighty squeeze and ran out of the house—she laughing, swinging a frying pan in hot pursuit. Panting, she returned to the kitchen, where Jane still stood, rooted by the sink.

"Dat man! Such a joker! Full of de Devil! He break de hearts everywhere he goes—up and down de streets women he's got waiting. Mammas know—time for de letters coming? Run—lock up quick de daughters! But, Mr. Henry not really bad—just naughty! Come, Vifey, now we open de treasures. See how smart you are outfitted from dat Mr. Montgomery Ward of big Chicago!" Her fingers were busy undoing knots of twine, "But de eyes—you see de way Mr. Henry can look mit dem? A tingle it gives. He's someting, no?"

The ordered overcoat was magnificent. Heavy and durable, it would last for years. Its velveteen collar, perhaps even its eight buttons might need renewing in the distant future but that didn't worry Jane. Her seamstress eye delighted in the expert cut of its cloth—its tailored perfection.

Hannah, excited, overcome by her own genius of having managed not only to instigate the need but the successful completion of Jane's transformation into American Womanhood, insisted everything had to be tried on right there and then, make sure it fit, matched exactly the illustrations of the items they had chosen.

"Vifey, run upstairs—get the shoes you got, also de waist you make so pretty mit de little lace collar—no good try on new tings mitout everyting all togedder—see complete effect." Jane ran.

The velour hat, soft and shapeless with only its small brim to give it form was slightly intimidating, until Hannah pushed its crown down, arranging it at an angle that suited Jane's face perfectly, enhancing its patrician lines. Finally, dressed, prodded, pulled, arranged to Hannah's satisfaction, they raced upstairs to the looking glass that stood by her bedroom window, hung in its tall oval frame of lustrous cherrywood.

Jane looked at the reflection of herself as though encountering a stranger—doubtless a young lady of the upper class whom she would be very pleased to make the acquaintance of.

"Dat's you, Vifey! Dat smart American Lady—dat's you, child!" Hannah wiped away a tear.

Jane stared at herself. She, who had never taken notice of her looks except in derision, for the first time in her young life thought herself attractive and the shock robbed her of speech. Hannah shook her. "It's getting late. Now put finery away safe—den come down. I got to get my pot roast making—work to do!"

Changed, her apron tied, Jane didn't walk downstairs into the kitchen, she floated!

Hannah, busy cutting out biscuits, was already making mental plans that the very next day they would need to write out an order for proper hose—not the thick cotton kind, but ones Mr. Ward called "Silky Lisle Imported." Very expensive at forty cents for only one pair but utterly necessary for when a country girl needed to know further she could be a pretty lady.

Their evening newspapers in hand the men headed for their parlor chairs. Rudy, winking at Fritz, called out to Hannah, stopping her in the doorway.

"Hey—heard your beau was here today!"

"So? What's it to you, Mr. Nosey?"

With an exaggerated rustle, Fritz opened his paper. Zoltan sneezed, excused himself. Peter wished him health. John tried not to laugh. Stan jumped in with, "God, it was cold today! This winter is going to be a real corker!"

Jimmy, packing his pipe, nodded his agreement. Without a backward glance, Hannah left the parlor. Fritz peeked out from behind his paper, gave Rudy a conspiratorial grin.

"You two—you shouldn't tease her," John chided. "All the ladies like it when Henry Johnson comes to their door."

"Yeah, I hear some are so smitten, they write letters to themselves—so he has to come to deliver them!" Johann laughed.

"But our Hannah? No—she never would do such a thing?" Peter sounded troubled.

"Of course not," Carl reassured him. "Johann meant the young ones—Henry is a good catch."

"If he ever lets himself get 'catched'!"

"Johann is right!" Rudy lit his cigarette. "That smart rascal loves the chase too much to let himself get tied to any apron strings!"

Stan adjusted his footstool, stretched out his legs. "Well, if you ask me—I don't trust him."

"But . . . I do," murmured Fritz.

Silenced, the men concentrated on their reading. In her corner, Jane opened the lid of her mending box.

"Hey, John—I heard today the company wants to lower the price of the Touring another fifty, somewhere down to around four hundred and forty dollars," said Carl.

"What did I tell you! The more cars you can turn out, the more you can sell, the less you can sell them for—the more can afford to buy them, the more profit you make!" John loved those moments when he was proven right in his often euphoric-sounding predictions. "Any of you seen last season's inventory lists?" He continued, knowing the answer would be no.

"Why?" asked Carl.

"I happened to see them in the office today. Seeing it all written out like that—it strikes you. I wrote some of it down . . ." Taking the notebook he always carried, like Henry Ford, John flipped pages, until arriving at what he was looking for, read out loud to no one in particular. "One million lamps, eight hundred thousand wheels, eight hundred thousand tires, ninety thousand tons of steel, two million square feet of glass for windshields, twelve thousand hickory billets for wheel spokes . . . it took thirty-five thousand freight cars to ship our year's production . . ."

"Well, I'm sure your wife enjoyed that bit of information. Right, Missus Jane?" said Carl, giving her a wink.

Perhaps emboldened by the still vivid reflection of herself, Jane dared to ask, "Someday, may I see a Lizzie up close?"

John frowned. He often forgot she was in the room. Now, being made aware she was there, it startled him.

Stan looked over at Fritz. "Isn't it time for our Fishbein to show up?"

"That's right! Before the holidays—he comes always!" Peter agreed, excited.

Fritz looked up. "You have to ask Hannah. She has a sixth sense about him. Somehow, she always knows when he is about to arrive in town from somewhere!"

"So, Missus Jane—you just may get that wish of yours. For Mr. Fishbein is our traveling salesman of no equal who has given up the rails for good—bought himself his very own Model T 2-Seater Runabout."

"How he manages to crank it is beyond me," Johann exclaimed, smiling.

"How his feet ever reach the pedals is even more astounding!" Jimmy laughed. "Mr. Fishbein is so gallant, he may even allow you, Missus Jane to touch his most precious possession."

"Wait till you see him. You won't believe it." Rudy joined in the laughter.

Stan turned to the sports page. "We who build them just ride trolleys."

Fritz put down his paper. "Something is going on."

"You don't say!" Stan's sarcasm filled the air.

Rudy rolled another cigarette. "Today we were timing the chassis. Big shots all over the floor, clicking stop watches, shaking their heads, running around . . . like crazy squirrels." He was not amused.

"I told you it's the uniform speed rate. The secret is all in the timing," John murmured from behind his paper.

Carl disagreed, "It's our standardization of parts that's the key—without that, no newfangled idea of production would stand a chance!"

"Well, that was proven long ago, Carl!" Jimmy joined the discussion. "Every one of our assembly plants across the country couldn't exist without our revolutionary system of fully interchangeable parts."

"A T sure ain't a Daimler."

Startled by the first inferred criticism of Lizzie she had heard, Jane stared at Stan, her mending forgotten.

"What do you want, Stan? A handcrafted unique jewel, weighing a ton, that must sell for a fortune?"

"Stop the preaching, John. We all know the answer to that. But don't tell me *you* never miss the days when we built an automobile with our hands."

"Of course I do—but we haven't got time for that now! Those times are gone! It's a new world, Stan—and it's Henry Ford who made it!"

"Looking back never good," said Peter. "We lucky good work we got. Many don't have any!"

"Before, when I said that something is going on, I meant something is happening—nothing to do with the new moving line. Something else . . ."

"What? Fritz, not *again* something new?"

"No Carl, I don't think so—it's a feeling I got that's got me worried."

Zoltan slowly folded his paper. "Fritz, what kind of a feeling is this 'feeling'?"

"I just told you—I don't know. If I knew, I wouldn't be worried!"

Zoltan's eyes swept the parlor.

"In all the years I have known this man, never has he been wrong with 'feelings.' You who were there, remember? That day at the old Piquette plant? He shouted, 'ACCIDENT' so loud over the noise, they heard him but it's too late, couldn't stop the Latvian from falling through the hole in the roof? . . . but still, Fritz knew something—and what about the time when Stolz lost his eye from the hot metal chip—that morning Fritz also had a 'feeling'!"

"Hey, don't forget to tell us when you got it figured out! In the meantime, I'm taking me and my rabbit's foot to bed." Rudy waved good night.

Fritz looked up at the clock. Zoltan coughed, squirmed in his chair. Peter heaved his bulk from his and, saying good night, led the procession of men upstairs to bed.

Jane stayed to tidy up, filching a *Detroit Free Press* left behind, so she could once read news that was happening instead of long ago; besides, it was cold up in the attic—then hurried to the kitchen to help. Hannah, having set out her sweet roll dough for Sunday breakfast, was heating the pressing irons on the stove, getting them ready for the ironing of the week's wash. She chose to do this grueling task on Saturday nights because, as she explained, nighttime was good for the doing of "quiet" work and, Saturday being the day before the only day in the week one could sleep a little longer and had no lunch boxes to prepare, it made sense.

As one of the heavy irons began to glow, wrapping a flannel around its handle, she lifted it off the stove—banging it down onto its trivet with such force, the table shook.

"Dat nosey Rudy! . . . Someday I get dat smarty Austrian good!"

Jane, trying not to laugh, unrolled the bundle of dampened shirts. "Hannah let me do the ironing."

"No! Not good now for you to do long standing work. You a Mama long before your baby come out. Remember dat. You can help mit de beans. Sack of dem is on de porch. For cleaning and snapping you can sit. Peeling, like potatoes, also okay. So—maybe, while you expecting I make you my special vegetable girl, just like de fancy cooks in de fine houses got!"

Jane fetched the sack of string beans and, with bowl on lap, sack, pot by her chair, settled herself by the kitchen table. Hannah folded an expertly ironed shirt, adding it to the stack beginning to grow.

"Vifey—tomorrow night—right after dishes done, put away, you and me, we go up to sleep early. Reason for dis is dat dis Monday, washday gotta start even before de dawn comes. Dis week coming much work. Is time for de most special American day called Tanksgiving. Old custom from American beginning days, when Englishmen called Puritans . . . why I don't know . . . got friendly mit de Indians because dey bring dem gifts to eat so de Palefaces shouldn't starve in de bad wintertime. Dat's how American peoples got to know about pumpkin and buttered corn . . . Oh! It's vonderful . . . vait and see! Everybody eat till de buttons pop off! . . . Hearts, too dey want to burst out mit so much tanks in dem, Indians not scalped everybody—so now dis vonderful country is safe and hearty!"

Though slightly confused, Hannah's infectious joy swept Jane along the preparing of a feast that even by Hannah's generous culinary standard was to be astounding. The hunt for just the right turkey was an adventure in itself!

Like Moses arrived on the shores of the Red Sea, Hannah—in galoshes, long winter coat, muffler, and second-best hat, carrying her grandfather's walking staff—stood surveying the seemingly endless sea of gobbling fowl, as though about to command it to part, make way for her choosing. Mr. Rabinowitz, Turkey Farmer, knowing her only too well, kept his sales pitch to himself.

Like a general choosing a volunteer for a dangerous mission she strode amongst the hysterical fowl until a proud tom, not too old, not too young, in his meaty prime caught her expert eye and his fate was sealed!

She agreed to pay the extra three cents to have him killed but not the five cents to have him plucked and dressed, saying, "What I pay for I keep. Feet good for soup, turkey feather dusters good for de spiderwebs!"

The long table, resplendent, decorated with Hannah's best linen cloth, its wide border embroidered in a cross-stitch pattern and Mr. Tom, regal, lustrous, his crisp skin glistening mahogany like the chestnuts of his stuffing, yams bubbling beneath their crust of maple sugar, peas nestled against orange carrot wheels, Brussels sprouts, vinegared beets, piled high mashed potatoes dripping gravy, glassy cranberries steam popping their bright skins, pickled watermelon rind put up the summer before—around this bounty stood the men, resplendent in their vested suits, fresh shirts, high collars newly starched, sporting ties. Fritz took his wife's hand . . . pulled her to stand by his side and spoke. "Today we think of those who have nothing—no freedom, no home, no work, no food, no one who cares—and we say, 'Thank you.' For here, in this house, in this country, we have." Kissing Hannah's hand clasped in his, Fritz lifted his eyes. "Amen! Mazel tov! . . . Now! We eat!"

Years later, far from home, whenever November was about to end, Jane's memory of her first Thanksgiving would stir, making her long for America and Hannah.

6

J ohn," Jane caught him in the hall as he was getting ready to leave. "Just a
moment, please. I need to ask you something." He was hurrying, folding one
trouser leg ready for the bicycle clip.

"What?"

"Hannah keeps talking of gifts under a tree and I think she said—hose filled with
something, hanging—I'm not sure where. Is that how Christmas is done in America?"

"Yes."

"The Befana—she doesn't bring them, here?"

John straightened up, reached for his overcoat.

"You know, I had forgotten about her—it's been so long." He smiled at the memory
of that hook-nosed hag, riding her broomstick, that brought presents to Italian children long after Christmas day had passed.

"Well? Does she or doesn't she?" Jane wanted to get it straight.

"In America, witches are only used for Halloween." He pulled the flaps of his
winter cap down over his ears. "I never could understand why anything so ugly and
mean would bring presents! But then, most Italian customs so influenced by superstition and the Church don't make much sense." He wound his muffler around his
neck, tucking in its end. "Stick with Hannah's menorah and Jolly Saint Nick—that
combination is much more fun!"

And he was off, racing down the street, bicycle wheels spinning, slipping on the ice.

Hannah, welcoming any excuse to make of life a festive occasion, took Hanukah, Saint Nicholas, and the birth of Christ and rolled them all into one glorious ecumenical celebration. As December's darkening skies threatened snow and frost chalked barren trees, the Geiger boardinghouse glowed with joyous anticipation of the holiday season about to begin. Cookie cutters, mountains of them, were unearthed from their boxed lairs, little tin candle holders, their pincers ready for the branches of a pine, were checked, repaired; shepherds, kings, Madonna and Babe unwrapped, reglued, candles counted, all placed by the freshly polished brass Menorah—everything ready and waiting for their moment of individual glory.

Finally the time came for Hannah to make her biannual expedition into the city of Detroit for the essential spices she could not do without. This year taking Jane along, she announced her intentions one evening during supper. "Time for de spices special shopping at Mr. Hirt's in de city. I will go dis Wednesday—and taking Vifey mit me. So, boys, you on your own!"

Fritz, Carl, John, and Zoltan—who had been through Hannah's holiday frenzies more than once, knew what to do, what was expected of them. The others were instructed to just follow their leads, and take orders without squabbling. Breakfast would be served at 5:30, a half hour earlier than usual. Those who paid for a daily lunch pail would find theirs ready on the kitchen sideboard as they were used to, but the washing up, drying and tidying of the kitchen that morning would be the boarders' responsibility, as the ladies needed this time to change into their proper city attire. Later, after their nine-hour shift was done, the men were cautioned not to waste any time getting home, for light housework awaited their attention, as well as the laying of the dinner table, the reheating of Hannah's supper already prepared—everything to be ready in time for when the ladies of the house returned from their expedition.

Dressed in her store-bought American finery, Jane descended the stairs to find her husband staring up at her. For a moment, she faltered, wondered if he might now forbid her to journey to the city without him. Apprehensive, she pulled on her gloves, buttoning them at the wrist as she arrived to where he stood.

"Ninnie, you look grand!"

Jane held on to the banister, knees gone suddenly wobbly.

Hannah, her already imposing stature enhanced by a voluminous greatcoat, neck wrapped in a ferret's fur, wearing a merry widow hat on which nestled a bluebird that had seen better days, strode into the hall, carrying an extra pair of galoshes.

"Here, put!" she said, handing them to Jane.

"Oh, Hannah—must I?"

"Yes," answered John.

Jane sat on the bottom step, pulling on the ugly galoshes over her best shoes, thinking that now her whole exciting effect would be spoiled. Fritz came to bid them good-bye.

"You two enjoy yourselves. Hannachen, you have the money safe? Pickpockets in the city! Watch the money!"

"And watch out for the white slavers! They fancy tall women. More of 'em, so they fetch a bigger price!" Rudy and Stan doing dishes chorused from the kitchen.

"Don't take any wooden nickels!" Peter and Carl, getting a jump on bed making, called down from the landing.

Zoltan, wearing one of Hannah's aprons tied under his armpits, appeared in the hall. "Now, don't you worry about a thing. I have taken charge so that your orders will be carried out to a T!" and waving his dishcloth in farewell, disappeared back into the kitchen.

"Go already! You'll miss the tram! Here . . . take." Fritz handed Hannah her basket.

Jimmy poked his head out from the parlor he was supposed to dust. "Hannah, I would advise you to take your umbrella—it looks like rain or maybe sleet."

John handed it to her. "Be careful, the streets are icy."

"Go!" Fritz pushed them out of the door, closing it quickly against the cold.

Heads down, clutching their hats, bent against the wind, the two women made their way to the Highland Park Inter-Urban Railway trolley stop, only a mile away on Woodward Avenue.

Hannah touched her shoulder, "Next stop us!"

By the time they arrived at the Market Square, it had begun to drizzle its wash of infinite colors muted by the milky grayness of winter light as though covered by a gossamer veil. Without sound or motion, the square would have been like a vast canvas depicting a market day painted by an artist whose eyesight was failing. But sound and motion there was, bringing it into vibrant life. Horses neighed, pushcarts rumbled, beneath long open roofed structures farmers shouted their wares, eulogizing their perfection. Ladies in sealskin coats and stylish hats fingered produce with gloved hands, followed by domestics carrying their baskets; others in shawls and head scarves, carrying protesting children, men in assorted headgear denoting their occupations, others bare-headed in long rubber aprons and gum boots amidst the high-pitched cackle, quack and hiss of penned chickens, ducks and geese. The ebb and flow of continuous sound, the sheer volume of bodies in continuous motion as people in concentrated hurry inspected, searched, evaluated, priced, haggled, moved on, decided, bought, sold, wrapped accompanied by the repetitive clink of coins, their metallic echo enhanced by the cold.

Opening her old umbrella, Hannah hurried across the square towards a large brick building, calling over her shoulder, "Come, Vifey. First we go to Hirt . . . open market after, maybe."

With a longing backward glance at the pageantry she wanted to join, Jane followed, doubling her pace so as not to lose sight of Hannah's bluebird in the milling crowd.

It was so warm in Mr. Hirt's Aladdin's cave, the pungent aroma from hanging sausages and hams melded with that of an endless assortment of cheeses and roasted coffee beans. On long electrical cords, single lightbulbs suspended down the length of the store from the ceiling gave off their yellowish glow, contributing to the illusion that all was golden treasure within.

Jane stood on tiptoes, glad her shoes were protected, for already so early in the morning, the sawdust covering the floor had turned to soggy mush. Her eyes ran along rows upon rows of japanned tins in all sizes, wooden boxes of all shapes, stone crocks, earthenware jars, labeled drawers, along laden counters up to the rafters where pots, pans and strainers dangled, crowding each other for any remaining space, down to the rows of open barrels and gunnysacks.

All day they shopped. Their basket becoming heavier as the day wore on. Although Hannah had her select tradesmen in Highland Park, the butchers and fishmongers that were housed in separate buildings bordering the square were visited to look and see what was being offered to fancy Detroiters and at what exaggerated prices. It seemed to Jane that Hannah longed for more than she bought. Coming face-to-face with a mighty carp, so fresh one had the impression one could hear the roar of its sea, she looked it in the eye, murmuring under her breath. "Ach—you beautiful ting. How I would like to take you home mit me, treat you right—make you New Year feast!" then bade him farewell, knowing such a luxury was not to be. Jane, puzzled by such longing for a fish, asked, "Why, Hannah? You like carp that much?"

"In Germany, very important dat fish. For de welcoming of de New Year you gotta have whole fish, head to tail, steamed mit peppercorns, onions, lemons and big bunches of dill. Everybody have to eat it to have good luck. Also goes perfect mit champagne drinking. Next day, no one have de upset stomach—so start de New Year feeling Honkey Dorey. I don't like carp much, but to be lucky? I eat plenty!"

Now the open sheds were deserted. Amidst mounds of wilting vegetable trimmings and broken crates, the square lay silent. Against a darkening sky, snow was beginning to fall. Tired, yet satisfied, their basket filled with treasures, Hannah and Jane started home. On the way, Hannah pointed out important landmarks, while Jane marveled at the electrical illumination of the city. Everywhere lights were beginning to shine so bright, signs could be read without the slightest difficulty as though it were day. But it was the sight of her first traffic light that impressed Jane the most on that already exceptional day of wonders. The way it stood on its very own island, its conical roof atop a small guardhouse in which a uniformed gentleman waved his white-clad arms at automobiles and trolley cars whizzing in all directions directly below. How, by simply illuminating, changing its three colors, the traffic light took absolute control, commandeered instant response, from men and their machines alike. To think that such an invention should even be necessary was in itself astounding.

When the trolley passed the drugstore where the first ice-cream soda was invented, Hannah became rhapsodic, explaining how it came to be, the shape of the special glass it was always served in, so, as Hannah put it "de foam can have de room to bubble over de ice-cream ball Vifey, I tell you dis also a greatest Detroit invention—so delicious it is, angels would like a sip! Maybe in summertime after de baby come, we go—okay? Den you can have strawberry—my favorite! From de fresh berries, soda gets pink! My treat! . . . . Look, Vifey. See? Dat's Mr. S. S. Kresge's big Five and Ten Cent store. In dere everyting costs only dat little. Next time I take you dere . . . You like today, child?"

Jane nodded, eyes shining.

On their return, supper awaited them. The men beaming, proud of having accomplished all their household duties as instructed, pulled out Hannah's chair, made her sit, insisted she not lift a finger, have a drink of their beer while they bustled about serving her stew, her noodles, her bread, her pie as though they had prepared it all themselves from scratch. That evening, she regaled them with snippets of the day's adventure, lauded them for being such good, reliable boys, then reminded them that for the next two weeks, she would not permit the slamming of doors, the making of the slightest drafts—for now that she had her spices, the serious Christmas baking would begin.

The next day, Mr. Henry, sporting a new, ingeniously knitted head covering, with slits permitting only his eyes, nostrils and lower lip to brave the elements, delivered into Jane's hands the very first letter she had ever received. Allowing himself to be hauled into the kitchen as though defenseless against Hannah's superior strength, he called back over his shoulder that if Jane was not partial to collecting postmarks, he would be more than pleased to receive the foreign one on her envelope. Leaving the two to their flirtatious banter, Jane raced upstairs, glad that as John had gone with Fritz to a meeting of the German Harmonie Club in the city, she could read her letter in private, not have to share it until later.

In her feathery script, Teresa conferred on her God's blessing, as she was permitted to write letters, hoped that this one would not only reach America but find Giovanna well. She had entered the Benedictine Order, was now a postulate in its convent in Reims that she might become fluent in French in the pious hope that when she had taken her vows, she might be chosen to serve as a nursing Sister of her order in the Belgian Congo.

Teresa was full of news. Her sisters were married, babies born, others on the way on a regular basis. This depressed her Mamma enormously, as she had always planned to have more than just one nun among her brood of daughters. It did not help that even some of her brothers still hesitated between celibacy and husbandry, although Marcus—surely Giovanna remembered him . . . the youngest, who never could find work but could juggle four stones all at one time—was now a Franciscan monk. As poverty seemed to suit him, by taking their vow for it, this would give Brother Marcus the sanctified allowance to pursue it further.

Jane chuckled. That streak of off-hand humor that she always found so appealing in her friend was still there and this cheered her.

> . . . I am aware that I have referred to myself in the first person which is a sin—to be confessed, penance done. One reason why the writer of this letter still much too conscious of self, finds it is difficult to communicate on paper, except for news apart from her.
>
> By the time this reaches you, dear friend, your life will have changed in so many ways I cannot even begin to imagine. Has it been as fine, as liberating as you first dreamt it might be? I pray all is well with you. And what about America? It too must be a revelation—life so very different from the quiet shady hours beneath our tree, our wall by the blooms of the oleander. A Sister here, who teaches pharmacology with skill, has told me that oleander is a deadly poison when its bitter leaves are distilled, then ingested. I found that rather disheartening, thinking back to such pleasant innocence experienced in its shade.
>
> Write me. We are permitted to receive letters once they have been approved, deemed acceptable by the Mother Superior as nondisruptive to our state of mind and discipline. So write me, please!
>
> The candle splutters and my eyes are strained. It would be more sensible to pray—for then they could rest. Seeing into one's soul requires a different sight. So, this sinner shall be sensible—but not until she has wished you

well, with a heart filled with affection for the time of our youth that has
passed—yet never lost.

May the Lord watch over you and yours. You are always in my prayers.
Having chosen Marie-Luke, she signs it here for the first time . . .

A tidal wave of sudden longing surged through Jane that startled her by its ferocity. Until that moment, she had been convinced there was nothing of her past worthy of such remembrance. Carefully, she folded Teresa's letter, returned it to its envelope, then tucked it down inside her sewing box. Turning off the lamp, she noticed her hand was shaking—and wondered why. When John returned, she told him of the letter and its news but not how it had affected her.

When it was time to get the tree, Hannah reminded Fritz that the one he and Peter dragged home all the way from Polishtown the year before had not only been not worth the trip, but had cost too much for what it wasn't. For days, heated discussions filled the house, until it was decided that this year, Fritz would go across town to see what the Irish were offering in pine.

"De Catholics—only de Catholics have de good trees—so go to de Irish . . . who else do you know who is mit de praying and de bead telling all de time, have a Virgin who can have a baby? So, go already, take Stan to help—bring me back a nice tree, mit de pins all on! But don't spend more dan twenty-five cents at most!"

The tree when first seen did not elicit Hannah's full approval. Although she did approve of its needles that did not drop when she shook it, she complained that it was much too small, but when Rudy had nailed its wooden stand and placed it next to the parlor table by the window and its height suited that of the menorah next to it perfectly, Hannah beamed, declaring it, after all, just right, blandly ignoring the overly exaggerated sighs of dramatic relief of the men teasing her.

Now, in the evenings, Hannah popped corn, spread it out on the kitchen table for Jane, her darning needle ready to thread it into garlands. Then it was the ginger-boys' turn to be joined so that they too could adorn the small tree as though they were dancing amongst its fluffy corn. Hoarded tin foil from a Hershey chocolate bar was cut into the shape of a six-pronged star, backed with brown paper and paste to stiffen it, then attached with wire to the pinnacle of the tree. When Johann, on seeing it, slightly confused commented on its rather unconventional shape, Hannah was heard to retort, "A star is a star, Mr. Smarty. You know maybe de exact shape dey all are up in de sky?"

As the menorah gained its daily light, the Christmas tree beside it took on its festive finery. Rudy and Stan built an enclosure from dried twigs and glue, decorated it with bits of straw they had found and, with Zoltan standing back to get proper perspective giving directions, set up the Nativity figures beneath the tree, while the others, with Fritz as foreman, clipped the small candle holders onto its branches.

On Christmas Eve, when the little candles were lit, they all agreed that this was the very best tree they had ever had. Everyone had a gift to give. Jimmy sang an old English carol. His voice light, like a bird, warmly gentle in a man usually so cool. Carl played "O Tannenbaum" on his harmonica as though he was performing it in a concert hall, Peter did a fine rendition of "Jingle Bells" on a paper-wrapped comb, with Rudy accompanying him, playing spoons. Zoltan, who had worked in secret on a conjuring act, with John as his able assistant, did clever tricks with copper pennies, playing cards and bits of colored silk. Johann and Stan had rehearsed a tandem version of "A Visit from Saint Nicholas," but Stan had to go on alone when Johann, missing his children, choked up during the naming of all the reindeer. Hannah beamed, applauded, proud of her gifted boys, served steaming cider pungent with a special cinnamon stick and clove from Mr. Hirt's Emporium, accompanied by her gingerbread with its sugar glaze. Fritz, having waited for just the right moment, when it came, sang softly "Brahms's Lullaby" as he brought the cradle he had fashioned to the young expectant mother in their midst. Jane, kissing his cheek, thanking him, felt the first joy of carrying a child. The candlelit room became still. Men, lonely for home and family, let their thoughts drift back across the sea, yet were content and that was Hannah's Christmas gift to those in her care.

Rudy broke the trancelike quiet. "Midnight Mass! If we go now we can make it. Who's coming?"

John looked at his wife to see if she wanted to go. She shook her head. Carl, Stan, and Peter joined Rudy already in the hall hurrying, putting on his galoshes, calling, "Don't wait up for us. Merry Christmas!"

The front door banged and they were gone. Jane began collecting the cider cups, Fritz rose to blow out the light of the tree—the mood of celebration was at an end.

Christmas day everyone went skating on the big pond next to the Ford plant. Zoltan insisted on lending Jane his skates so the men could teach her how to glide upon the ice Hannah giving them strict orders to make certain she did not fall. Although it was the most exhilarating activity Jane had ever experienced, by the time she had skidded, stumbled and nearly fallen more times than she wanted to count, she returned to where Zoltan was sitting, all forlorn, handed back his skates with heartfelt thanks, assuring him that the time had come for him to enjoy himself while she did the watching. So beautifully did Hannah and Fritz waltz upon the ice, they looked as though they were dancing in a grand ballroom, that other skaters stood aside making room for them. Everyone had a marvelous time. Even the sun came out to join in the fun.

Production at the Ford plant having been closed down for its usual layoff period that began on the eve of Christmas, and now that festivities were over, the boarders became restless, chafing under the imposed idleness. Their seniority being in trusted positions, their jobs were not in jeopardy, as were so many others' during these forced, unprotected layoffs without pay, still having no work to go to bothered them. Irritable, house-bound, constantly underfoot, like bored children, they kept getting in Hannah's way—until finally she'd had enough and, like the mother she was, took her boys to task, telling them in no uncertain terms, to find something constructive to do with their time or else . . . neither her doughnuts not even her strudel would ever exit her kitchen again!

This shocking threat had immediate results. Zoltan scurried to his room to read *Crime and Punishment* from the small collection of books he had brought with him from Bulgaria. Jimmy bundled up in rough tweed, took long walks, wishing he had a gundog at his side. Johann wrote letters home, then gave in to the call of his Hollander blood and went skating, coaxing Rudy and Stan to accompany him by reminding them of the many young ladies always to be found on the great pond in need of a man's steadying arm to cling to. John, always in a foul mood when separated from his passion, stopped brooding, jumped on his bicycle, and rode to the plant to observe the installation of two more automated assembly lines. Fritz, Carl, and Peter tinkered, repaired whatever Hannah pointed to, generally made themselves useful.

The old year was at an end,1914 was ready, impatient to set its benchmark on the history of the world. Nothing would ever be quite the same again.

"Fritz!" Shaking snow off himself like a dog returned home, John called again. Hearing an answer from below, he descended the stairs leading down to the cellar. Concerned by the note of urgency in John's voice, Fritz looked up from what he was doing.

"Fritz, remember when you said something was going to happen? You had one of your feelings?"

"So?"

"Well, you were right! Something *is* going on! I don't know *what*, but whatever it is, it's important!"

As though disinterested, Fritz put down his sandpaper, fitted the rung into the back of the kitchen chair he was repairing, checked if it was ready for gluing in place.

"Well Fritz? Aren't you interested?"

"Sure," Fritz applied dabs of glue, "but you say you don't know. So?"

"Fritz, it's got to be important. An executive meeting held in secret and on New Year's Day? You think that was only so they could all wish each other Happy New Year?"

"Maybe." Fritz began to sandpaper another rung.

"There's a rumor . . ."

"Rumors . . . all the time rumors!"

"Just listen! It seems that someone . . ."

"Ach! Again a someone!" Fritz shook his head.

"Will you listen . . . !"

"Calm down, my boy. Why so excited?"

"You drive me crazy when you do this!"

"This what?" Fritz's voice held a tone of exaggerated innocence.

"You know exactly what I mean . . . you do this every time one of your *feelings* pays off!"

"Ach! How our baby boy knows me!"

"You . . . you son of a gun! You know! You already know there was a secret meeting! . . . How?"

"Hermann. His missus is friendly with one of the nighttime cleaning women, said in the Boss's office his blackboard was full of scribbles, no chalk left, pencil shavings all over—but the wastepaper baskets? All empty! Not a thing in them! . . . Interesting?"

"So, it's not just a rumor! . . . What else did he tell you?"

"No more." Fritz fit in the last rung.

"I wish we knew who was there with Ford . . ."

"Who knows? Had to be Couzens for sure. Willis and Hawkins maybe."

"I don't suppose the woman could read what was left on the blackboard?"

"No, I don't think so. Hermann said she is a simple peasant, just come over from Slovenia."

"Damn!"

Fritz lifted the repaired chair down from the worktable.

"Only thing she knows real good is the signs for American money."

"Yeah, first thing we all learned when we got here." John started up the stairs.

Fritz pulled the string extinguishing the overhead light, followed him.

"Well, she said that the blackboard was covered all over with dollar signs."

"What? So she *did* see something!! What do you think? With the new system in place—the assembly plant nearly fully automated . . . could be just projections for this year's production?"

Fritz shook his head.

"Don't think so. On New Year's Day *and* in secret? Not like the Boss. Whatever was said in that room was important. More important than usual things." Putting an arm around John's shoulders, Fritz walked him down the hall. "Come, supper nearly ready—we go wash up. With other thing, we wait and see. When Henry Ford is ready, he'll tell us what's on his mind, like always. I have a feeling . . ."

Zoltan, at the top of the stairs about to start down, heard, stopped dead in his tracks.

"Feelings?! You got one of your feelings again? What, Fritz? What?"

Fritz held up a hand. "Don't get excited! It's only the old one."

"Oh, *that* one." Zoltan, relieved he had nothing new to worry about, hurried past them down the stairs.

They didn't have long to wait. Just three days later, at noon on the fifth of January, following his own advice printed in his company's *Ford Times*—"Early to bed and early to rise, work like hell and advertise"—representatives of Detroit's press were summoned to Highland Park to be read what would become a historic announcement.

The Ford Motor Company, the greatest and most successful automobile manufacturing company in the world will, on January 12, inaugurate the greatest revolution in the matter of rewards to its workers ever known to the industrial world . . . at one stroke it will reduce the hours of labor from nine to eight and add to every man's pay a share of the profits of the house. The smallest amount to be received by a man 22 years old and upwards will be $5.00 per day . . .

There followed the stipulations, the eligibility required to share in the ten million dollars that the company vowed to distribute over and above the regular wages of its men.

By afternoon, Detroit's newspapers carried banner headlines, telegrams flashed across the nation, cablegrams proclaimed it to the world. By the sixth of January, Henry Ford was a national hero—by the seventh, an international celebrity.

For men whose wage scale stood at $2.34 or less for a grueling nine-hour day, the effect of the Ford Motor Company's sweeping announcement was cataclysmic. In one fell stroke because of one man's generosity, laborers saw themselves as future equals to the rich. Henry Ford had proven the truth of the American Dream—that all things were possible.

The Geiger boardinghouse celebrated. Never in the history of all their lives had anything quite as marvelous, as unexpected, happened. Every one of them was going to be a millionaire!

Fritz, his Santa Claus face flushed by excitement and a little too much Schnapps, danced a jig, singing.

Hooray! Hooray!
Five dollars a day,
So Henry Ford say . . .
And so it's even more
Now just eight . . .
Then home we can go . . .
Through the big Ford gate!

Grabbing Hannah, he danced her around the kitchen, through the dining room, across the parlor, down the hall and back into the kitchen, the boarders and Jane following in joyous procession. Hannah, hugging him, kept repeating, "I don't believe it! I don't believe it! Five whole dollars a day! A fortune!"

That evening, the men read their papers out loud, each one trying to top each other's news. Zoltan was so excited, he sneezed incessantly—but that didn't stop him. "Listen—here they say, *'God bless Henry Ford of the Ford Motor Company . . .'*"

"My paper calls him one of 'God's noblemen,'" Carl announced.

Rudy chuckled, "Notice how the company news has knocked the marriage of President Wilson's daughter off the front pages?"

"Hey—even the latest on Ty Cobb," Johann added.

Zoltan, knowing that he was about to be rich, had afforded himself the luxury of out-of-town newspapers, cleared his throat. "Here's a good one out of Cleveland: the company's announcement 'shot like a blinding rocket through the dark clouds of the present industrial depression.' How's that for lyrical prose!"

Fritz looked up.

"I got a lulu!! Listen to this one—'When you see his modest little car running by, take your hat off!' If this goes on, we better pump up production fast!"

"Anybody got comments from other manufacturers?" Stan asked.

"I have," Jimmy called out. "Pittsburgh Plate Glass is quoted as saying that if other employers follow Ford's lead, it will mean the ruin of all business in this country. That Ford himself will find he cannot afford to pay five dollars a day."

"Just jealous. Never the Boss promises what he can't deliver."

"True." For once, Stan had to agree with Peter. John, his paper still folded on his lap, hands behind his head, legs stretched out before him, his often overzealous adulation of Henry Ford now fully vindicated, was trying his best not to gloat. Catching his eye, Jane acknowledged his right to do so, received an answering smile as reward for her perceptiveness. All in all, it was an evening long remembered for the pride they felt in being part of the Ford Motor Company and its magnanimous founder.

Far into the night, they talked—exchanging each other's papers, reading the praises heaped upon their Boss until Hannah had to remind them it was time for bed. Sighing their reluctance to put an end to this special day, they knocked out their pipes, folded their newspapers, leaving them on their chairs to be reread in the morning and, saying goodnight, began to leave the parlor. Zoltan topped off the evening when, on his way out, he turned, walked back to Fritz and, in a voice filled with respect tinged with awe, exclaimed, "Fritz! This *feeling*—this one was a real humdinger!"

John was still laughing as he closed the door to their room.

"That Zoltan—I'm going to miss him." He began to undress.

"Why? Is he leaving?" Jane unpinned her hair.

"Not that I know of, but we will be." He hung up his pants, letting the suspenders dangle.

"We? Are we leaving?"

Hearing the tremor in her voice, John turned to look at her.

"Not right away. The profit sharing will take time to get set in place but then, it will be time. I never intended to remain here. A boardinghouse is not a place to raise a family." Getting into bed, he turned on his side, murmured, "*Buonanotte*, Ninnie," and fell asleep.

Jane, wide-eyed, imagined a time without Hannah and felt quite lost.

By the introduction of the moving assembly line into the industrial workplace, now capped by the sweeping wage structure of his company, its further announcement that a third shift would be necessary in order to turn out his only product to satisfy demand, Henry Ford's personal fame began to surpass even that of his acclaimed automobile. Within days, Detroit and its Ford Motor Company became the Mecca of hungry men—the Highland Park plant their goal. Statistically, no company, no matter how vast or willing, could accommodate these hordes of men looking for work in this Five-Dollar-Day Utopia. But hunger never fostered reason—and so they came. From New York, Ohio, Pennsylvania, Indiana, Illinois, within Michigan, Wisconsin, the border states, out of the deep South, many paying the fare with their last dollar, most riding the rails. An invasion of desperate men was underway.

"Fritz?! Carl?!" Slamming the front door behind him, John hurried into the kitchen. "Hannah! Where the hell is Fritz?"

"In de basement, fixing. What's wrong? Why you home? What's . . ."

Not stopping to answer, John ran back into the hall, bellowing. "Fritz! Come up! Where's Carl? Is Zoltan here?"

"Where's the fire?" Fritz appeared from below.

"My God, you've got to see it! You gotta see it to believe it! Hurry, put your coat on and come. We've got to get the others—Hannah—who's home?"

"Rudy, Stan." Hannah never wasted words when an emergency seemed to be in progress, turned to Jane. "You see Zoltan?"

"He was in his room."

"Ninnie—get him down here." Jane hesitated. "Move!"

"John, if I find any of the others you . . ."

"Anybody! Tell them to get down here—NOW!"

Jane ran. Within minutes the boarders were assembled in the hall, John throwing their overcoats at them.

"Don't ask questions! Put them on. It's freezing out there—and follow me to the plant. You got to see this!"

The door slammed behind them—they were gone. Hannah snapped into action.

"Okay, we go make coffee. Big pot—get ready for what's coming, maybe trouble."

Jane followed her into the kitchen.

"What trouble?"

"Who knows! But dat excited no man gets witout a big reason. So we prepare, den wait till we get to know what de big fuss is. Maybe we better bring de big pot mit my chicken soup also in case dis is serious."

Waiting, neither concentrating on what they were actually doing, Jane darned a sock that didn't need to be, Hannah tidied what was tidy. Time dragged. They began preparing for the evening meal, unsure if it would be eaten.

Faces flushed, eyes tearing from the cold, inner excitement making their words tumble over each other, still in their hats and coats, the boarders strode into the kitchen crowding the doorway.

"Hannahchen," his voice hoarse, Fritz pulled off his cap, twisting it in his hands. "What I have seen today, never never will I forget!"

"My God! You should see it! It . . ." Rudy searched for words.

Zoltan collapsed onto a kitchen chair, utterly speechless.

"As far as the eye could see, men—thousands of men!" Jimmy, hand shaking, swept the air.

"The whole length of Manchester, around and down Woodward, jam-packed with men waiting for the hiring to begin. An unbelievable sight!" Carl looked at John. "You know when they got there?"

"I saw them at dawn, but they started arriving long before that."

Johann shook his head in disbelief.

Pulling off his gloves, Stan asked, "Got any idea how many, John?"

"One of the reporters said fifteen thousand."

"*Gott im Himmel!*" Hannah gasped, looking at Fritz.

"Ja, looked like could be that many. Fifteen thousand! My God! What's going to happen? We can't use that many new men! But what a sight! Never, if I live to be a hundred, will I ever forget. There are more people outside our plant than in the whole village I come from!"

"Mine, too!" Peter agreed.

"And mine." Stan strode into the hall to hang up his coat and cap, the others talking amongst themselves followed him. Hannah heaved a sigh of relief.

"Well—dat's over! Tank de heavens no big trouble—only big excitement . . . so we get going mit de supper—boys will tell us more later. Vifey, you please start mit de potatoes mashing. I do de gravy." Banging pots and pans, she muttered, "*Gott im Himmel!* What a day! Every day someting new getting everybody topsy-turvy!"

Monday, January 12, in the darkness of a bitter winter dawn, an icy wind swirling snow, the thermometer registering two above zero, some four thousand Ford employees wearing their identity badges, returned to work. Arriving at the plant, six thousand job seekers, having waited throughout the freezing night for the hiring to begin, surged towards them hoping to gain admittance, get inside the plant behind them. Police in place ever since the first announcement of the Five-Dollar-Day, and Ford security guards who had been circulated undercover amongst the crowd, now sprang into action using any means at hand to beat back the tidal wave of desperate men. Hemmed in, surrounded, the Ford workers, determined to hold on to their jobs, clock in on time for their morning shift, began fighting their way towards the only entrance that had been opened for them. The angered mob pushed forward, blocking their advance and a full riot was underway. The fire brigade, called out, rushed to the Ford plant. As men began scaling the tall factory gates shut against them, the order was given to train the fire hoses on them, douse them with water, force them down. In that bitter cold, as the water hit, it froze. Like human icicles men hung, where they had been hit and on the streets below, the mob went wild! Stampeded, rushed the hoses, overturned, trampled the lunch and tobacco stands that serviced Ford employees, hurled bricks, smashed windows, attacked anything that stood in their way. By the time the Ford men were able to gain the safety of the plant, many were bloodied, their clothing ripped, their badges lost.

The news that a riot had occurred at the plant traveled like wildfire along the grapevine of the Ford wives. When Missus-Schneider-eight-blocks-over ran with the news, Hannah's first reaction was typical. She offered her a nice cup of coffee, accompanied by a baked-this-morning doughnut, listened calmly as the frightened woman gulped out what she had heard. Giving no indication of her own fear, Hannah reassured her that as her Bruno was one of Fritz's men, she should take heart—all her worries were groundless, for her Fritz always took care of his men, then gently shoved the distraught lady out.

"Dat woman—fluster, fluster, fluster! Good midwife. When pulling out de babies, she's fine—but all udder times? Too nervous making!" Seeing Jane's worried face, she motioned her to sit. "Come, Vifey, fearing inside not good for your baby. We have coffee, a little nosh of someting sweet, keep busy, wait for boys. Time enough to hear trouble den."

The men came home in silence. Without comment, John handed Jane his torn coat. Taking it, she wondered how she could possibly repair it in time for him to wear it to work the next day. Their voices strangely hushed, Rudy and Stan asked if she would have a look at theirs, see what could be done. Peter touched the bandage above his eye, as though he couldn't remember why it was there. Carl kept looking at the blood down the sleeve of his overcoat, wondered aloud if it would wash out. As though in passing, Zoltan mentioned his scarf was lost. Jimmy, that his derby had been trampled. Their voices low, as though not wanting to disturb someone asleep, they had about them a lethargic calm like that of shock.

Without acknowledging the two women, they climbed the stairs and disappeared into their rooms. Worried, Jane started to follow, Hannah stopped her. "No, child. Not now. Dis looks like man alone time. When someting very wrong in de soul, dey always creep away. Like de animals do, to lick de wounds. Women talk out big troubles—but men, dey brood. Tonight for sure is my chicken soup!"

By the time they had settled into their parlor chairs, the men were back. This evening Hannah for once ignoring her kitchen, stayed in the room by Fritz. Lighting his pipe, Carl complimented her on the soup.

"Hit the spot, Hannah. Just right, just what we all needed."

For a while there was silence. Then Stan took the bull by the horns.

"Okay! Anybody here know what idiot called out the fire brigade?"

"Who knows?" Rudy sounded relieved that what was troubling them had been brought out into the open.

"I heard that long before hiring began, there were Ford agents milling amongst the crowds during the night, secretly handing out employment slips to those they decided qualified. Anyone else hear that?" Johann asked.

"If that is true, no wonder those poor bastards were angry. They had every right to be!"

"But not go on a rampage like that, Stan!"

"Why not? You travel hundreds of miles, probably hidden in some stinking boxcar, no food, maybe not even water, finally get yourself to Highland Park and—what do you find? You find there are thousands just like you already there before you! So now you stand for endless hours in zero weather, no overcoat, not even a blanket, nearly freeze to death so you can hold your place in line—THEN, some son of a bitch hires a guy a mile *behind* you because he likes his looks?! Jeez!"

"More likely because he found one who spoke English!" Rudy added.

"Who said 'Desperate men resort to desperate action'?" Jimmy lit his pipe.

"Don't know, but it was sure true today!" Fritz sighed.

"I thought I was going to be trampled along with my poor derby!"

"Me, too."

"I was scared," said Peter, like a small boy.

The men nodded. Zoltan looked about the room.

"Today was a disgrace—should not have happened!"

"Who already had the police there?" Johann wanted to know.

"They've been there every day since the announcement," Rudy answered him. "And why was only one entrance open? We couldn't move our men inside fast enough!"

Carl looked at Fritz. "Where, in God's name, was Couzens? He could have talked some sense into them!"

"He must have been there."

"And where the hell was the Boss?"

"He's still in New York City for the auto show."

"No. He came back this morning." John ground out his cigarette.

Zoltan got up from his chair. "You watch—the papers will leave nothing out. They'll describe every lurid detail, state it was a disgrace! And Henry Ford himself will be held accountable for the way his company handled the whole shocking situation. I've had enough! I'm off to bed." And he left.

The others got ready to follow. Peter looked at John, and said, "Tomorrow—I got no badge."

"I have mine, Peter. I'll take you in."

The Riot, as it became known, once discussed, dissected, evaluated by the senior Ford men, was never referred to again. Like a deep splinter once removed, after a while the place it had entered became nondiscernable, yet remained ever tender to the touch. To retain their loyalty to the company and its founder, it was best left alone.

But neither riots nor rumors could dampen the nation's enthusiasm for their new hero. Every day brought new accolades for the man who now symbolized the reality of the American Dream. When Henry Ford was quoted as having told a New York reporter that he believed dying rich was a sin, the nation's newspapers had another field day. The man who was about to bring mass production into the industrial workplace so suited legend that at times even truth seemed it must be pure invention. Humble farm boy, childhood repairer of watches, youthful wage earner, trusted employee of the great Alva Edison, skilled mechanic, brilliant engineer, tireless dreamer, inspired inventor, champion of the common man, the self-made millionaire! Even Ford's appearance suited the mold of an American icon. His gaunt frame, those slightly haggard features, the eagle gaze hinting melancholy, conjured an uncanny resemblance to Lincoln.

John, devouring the newspapers that each day found something new, exciting and exhilarating about the man and his company, preened as though he alone had been aware of true greatness, long before others had discovered it. Mr. Ford this and Mr. Ford that became the basis of most of his conversation. Sometimes, when her husband spoke of his idol, Jane was reminded of Father Innocente giving his most fatuous Lenten sermon. No matter how great and glorious Henry Ford might be, God he was not! But Jane had the impression that John didn't quite realize the truth of that and, if ever confronted, wouldn't be able to accept it. It was in one of these moods of rebellion that she decided to put a halt, once and for all on the constant, irritating supply of McGuffey readers. She was trying to think of a way to broach this delicate subject when, while getting dressed one morning, John did it for her.

"How are you getting on with your new McGuffey reader?"

"I just finished 'Don't Kill the Birds.'"

"That's one of Mr. Ford's favorite lessons. He is very partial to birds," adding, as he pulled on his trousers, "he's a very keen bird-watcher, you know."

Jane, plaiting her hair, was relieved he didn't ask her opinion of the lesson she had found excruciatingly boring. Feeling it was now or never, she plunged, "John, please do not bring me any more McGuffeys." John, stuffing in his shirttail, stopped and stared. "Really, I can read English very well now, so they are no longer necessary." She hoped that would do.

"Very well, Ninnie, if you are so certain you are really that advanced, I'll bring you one of Mr. Ralph Waldo Emerson's. Mr. Ford admires him greatly as well."

She thanked her husband for his continued interest in her education in a tone so glacial, John stopped what he was doing, and watched as his wife left their room.

Deciding he had married a most confusing woman he rarely understood, he resumed tying his tie, not overly concerned.

"Ach, dere you are, Vifey!" Hannah handed Jane a bowl of eggs. "Here, please beat!" Jane attacked the yolks as though they could do her harm. "Enough, enough already! I ask you beat—not kill!" Hannah retrieved her bowl, spooned sugar onto the still quivering mass, gave it a very gentle stir. "My, my . . . storm clouds around here heavy dis morning . . . de trouble, I should know about?"

"Mr. Ford this and Mr. Ford that . . ."

"What? You angry with de Boss?" Sheer disbelief made Hannah's voice rise an octave higher.

"No! Not really. It's John. Oh, it's everybody! Every time somebody opens their mouth, it's 'how wonderful, how great, how perfect.' Everybody behaves like Henry Ford is God Almighty!"

"Well, not really—but close."

"You see! Even you! What gets into people?" Jane wasn't really expecting an answer but Hannah gave her one anyway. "Sure me! De poor eggs you just beat de stuffing out of, Mr. Henry Ford—he got dem. Dis nice warm kitchen we are in—he give us. De house, a safe roof over our head, he make it possible—and why? Because he have a special brain dat gives him great ideas—so he can build a company big as a whole country where many people like my Fritz and your John can work, be proud. And now, even going to get highest pay ever in de whole state of Michigan, even whole East and West! So, you tell me, why not 'hooray Mr. Henry Ford'?"

"I'm sorry, Hannah. You're right. I was just . . . how do you say it . . . fed up?"

Hannah wiped flour off her hands with her apron. "Dat's okay—expecting makes cranky. And mit your John, I tink you got maybe a point. Sometimes when he talks, he sounds like one of de twelve Apostles and Mr. Ford his Holy Man. But don't worry, your man know de difference between de one up in Heaven and de one on de Earth he work for." Hannah slid her cake into the oven, secured the latch of its iron door. "Boys will like dis cake . . . now we are rich, I put in currants. Now I start de meatloaf—you scrape de carrots." On her way to the back porch to get the meat from the icebox that now it was winter was referred to as "keeping box," she called back over her shoulder, "Vifey—you know, it is better have a husband in love mit his work den mit another woman instead of you." Reentering the kitchen, she gave Jane a look, see if her words had sunk in. Then, satisfied that they had, got busy chopping onions, pleased by the beginning signs of jealousy she had detected in this untried wife in her care.

7

Naked to the waist, dressed only in his trousers, John was shaving. Already dressed, Jane was making the bed. Outside their window, pale February sun seemed to be trying its best to give the impression of a sunny day.

"Ninnie," John stopped to sharpen his razor along the worn strap. Jane waited for him to continue. "If the weather holds, I thought being Sunday, we might walk over to the plant. I remember I promised to show it to you one day. Would you like to go?"

"Oh, yes! Please!"

"Hannah said a mile is not too far, would even do you good." John went back to shaving his upper lip.

Feeling the dragging weight of her pregnancy, secretly Jane would have welcomed a shorter distance but her eagerness to finally see where all the wonders were taking place outweighed her physical discomfort.

Hannah having bundled her up as though she was embarking on a Polar expedition, Jane arrived, red of nose but warm inside, at the corner of Woodward Avenue and Manchester Street and time stopped! Her breath caught in her throat—for a suspended moment she had the feeling she might fall—then recovered sufficiently to realize what her eyes were seeing.

Oh, John had been right! Nothing, nothing could prepare one for a sight such as this! This was not a factory—this was a world of its own! Giant, endless, overpowering, magnificent! Buildings that seemed to have no end stretching towards their own horizon, walkways, chutes, inner streets, loading docks, railway yards, boxcars, trains, and locomotives, power house—its mighty funnels soaring towards the sky, water towers, each emblazoned with the distinctive emblem of one man's signature! All this vast grandeur for just one chunky little motorcar named Lizzie!

John hadn't taken his eyes off his wife since their arrival. Her enthralled amazement delighted him—women so often lacked the imagination necessary to appreciate wonders such as this. Grinning, he poked her shoulder to waken her. Incredulous eyes shifted to his face. "You? And Fritz? And Carl and Zoltan and the others? You come *here*?"

Laughing, John pointed to the mile-high letters on top of the mammoth main building.

"Ninnie, what does that say?

"THE FORD MOTOR COMPANY," breathed Jane.

"So? Do I work here?"

"Oh, Giovanni! Now I understand why you can't wait to get here. Why you rush so in the mornings! If I could build something marvelous here, I would rush too!"

And John took her in his arms and kissed her and when they walked back home, he held her hand tucked inside the pocket of his overcoat.

As she quickly changed in order to help Hannah with Sunday supper, John, sitting on the bed watching, promised that someday, after the baby, he would take her, show her the inside of the great assembly plant. When she ran down to the kitchen, it felt like she had wings on her feet.

Hannah, stirring a huge pot with an equally huge wooden spoon, looked at Jane's shining face and with an underlying smugness utterly deserved, greeted her with "Wonderful walk, Vifey?" And when she got a lilting "Oh, yes! Just wonderful!" she was more than satisfied.

Was it that winter morning that her husband began to love her? Jane never knew, only that he was never as casual after that. From then on, his touch held a tenderness, quite new, that awakened feelings within her that confused, as much as they pleased. No longer did she turn from him, slept cradled in his embrace, as though this had been their habit from the start. Sex remained unto itself, separate from this affection. Still a duty to be received, though not as coolly accepted as before. As her pregnancy progressed, the nightly demands lessened, finally stopping altogether. Both changes needed adjusting to. Of the two, the swelling of her body was the one she least appreciated. So foreign to her was curvaceous femininity that seeing it take possession of her lanky frame seemed an intrusion of her inner privacy. To love the seed, she would have needed to love the giver of it. Having so little experience with this emotion, Jane lacked the aptitude for recognizing its existence.

Hannah, who would have gloried in the visible proof of carrying a child, if been permitted such joyous reality, watched and worried. Wondered what it would take to push this so self-sheltered girl across the emotional threshold into passionate womanhood. That this could mean Jane's eventual salvation—she was certain. How to accomplish such a feat puzzled, if not stymied even Hannah's formidable talent for becoming actively involved in people's lives. She wished she could talk to Fritz but knew he would only resort to his usual escape route of telling her not to meddle in what was not, should not, be her concern. For one so given to generous impulse, to retreat, stand back, was a difficult decision—but Hannah, loving Jane, made it, convinced that if she but bided her time, divine inspiration was bound to strike—show her what she could do.

The added benefits of being a Ford Man began to show themselves in bursts of unrelated pleasures. When Stan, wearing his company badge traveled to the city to look, see if he could afford a new suit, he was treated with fawning respect given instant credit by a most delighted establishment, returned home triumphant, wearing a vested suit of best-quality serge. Tradesmen were so courteous and obliging when spotting a Ford Company badge that men began wearing theirs outside the workplace. Where once this identity had proclaimed a man's skill, it now stood for his ability to pay. Banks, which had considered immigrant laborers within the automotive industry bad risks, now courted those employed by Ford—offering mortgages as though they were now all Vanderbilts.

Johann began looking for a house, wrote his wife to start packing, that as soon as he had found a home, he would send the passage money for her and their children to join him in America.

As his shift ended at four, Zoltan took to jumping on the railway trolley that whisked him to the city, where he roamed secondhand bookstores, often returning clutching a precious find, to have Hannah bawl him out for being late for supper.

Rudy purchased a few sheets of expensive letter paper and, after a serious consultation with Hannah as to what women liked to hear and how, proposed marriage to his Frederika left waiting amidst the pastures of the Austro-Hungarian Empire.

Carl bought himself a new overcoat but refused the credit offered him. Still owing money on something he was already wearing seemed to him like having stolen it.

Shaking his head over all the excitement, Fritz bought himself a better brand of tobacco that smelled so much nicer than his old one, Hannah approved.

One afternoon, returning from work, John brought his wife a rose, murmured, "Happy Valentine's Day," kissed her cheek before removing his coat. Jane stood in the dimly lit hallway, holding the gift as though fearful of damaging its beauty. A red rose! In the middle of winter! It must have cost a fortune! On the front porch, the boarders, having stomped ice off their boots, now crowded inside, shouting, "HANNAH!" Running, she appeared, sure something was wrong. They must have rehearsed it for, as one, the six men fell to one knee, extending their surprise, a scarlet heart filled with fancy chocolates.

"Sweets to the sweet! Hannah, be our Valentine!" they chorused, grinning from ear to ear, while the object of their affection curtsied, blushing the vivid color of Jane's rose.

In the parlor that evening, Hannah handed around her heart—sharing its chocolate contents as she did. Knowing Zoltan was partial to soft centers, Jimmy to toffee, Peter and Carl to nougat, Rudy and Johann to nut clusters, she kept those safe to one side, until she reached their chairs. Returning to Fritz, she handed him his favorite, the chocolate-covered cherry. The men munched and talked.

"How many men were needed for a third shift?" Jimmy asked.

"Around five thousand—maybe more," Carl answered.

"ALL unskilled?"

"Most of 'em. With the new system running—who needs skill! The man who places the nut doesn't turn it—the man who turns it doesn't tighten it."

"On the chassis assembly line a continuous line of men, each doing one single action—over and over for eight hours . . ."

Stan interrupted, "Long ago I told you—monkeys! Lines of monkeys as far as the eye can see."

"You know the new conditions, John?" Johann thinking he had written his wife sooner than he should have, sounded worried.

John hastened to reassure him. "Nothing for us to be worried about. One of the conditions to qualify for profit sharing is that a man must have been employed by the company for a period of no less than six months, he must be married . . ." Stan cursed. John continued, ". . . the only earner in his family. Bachelors do not qualify, unless they can prove they are the sole breadwinners of their family."

Stan leaned back in his chair. "My friend, it's called profit sharing, so that if the company has no profit, what's to share?!"

Hannah motioned to Fritz it was getting late. Jane put away her mending, picked up the soda pop bottle holding her lovely rose and, saying, "Good night," followed John upstairs.

Jane tended the rose until all her efforts were in vain, then pressed it between pieces of John's blotting paper and laid it to rest beside Teresa's letter.

By the time Hannah commemorated the birth of George Washington with her special sour cherry pies, Detroit, with its beckoning Five-Dollar-Day, had taken on the characteristics of a boomtown. Saloons and brothels, pool parlors, cardsharps, con men and shantytowns; in this era of mass emigration, the beginnings of over-crowding soon to be slums, appeared. The Ford Motor Company, following its founder's credo that better pay made a better man, now formed an organization whose overall purpose was to make certain that the company's willing generosity to share its profits would go only to those worthy of it. The Sociological Department, one of Henry Ford's pet projects, employed men given absolute autonomy to inspect, evaluate, report on the habits, living conditions, and morals of Ford employees. When the first rumors of this new department and its purpose filtered down the vine, Hannah was livid.

The mere idea that a total stranger would have the right to enter her house without needing her permission, then once inside investigate her cleanliness, both actual and moral, made her so furious, for once words failed her. Fritz and John kept insisting that the Sociological Department had been formed solely for the purpose of giving aid to those newly arrived, uneducated immigrants from such poverty-stricken regions as the Ukraine, Eastern Europe, and southern Italy, who could not be expected to fend for themselves, manage sensibly their new exorbitant wage. Therefore, the Geiger boardinghouse, with its occupants all being respected long-standing Ford employees, English speaking, some even in possession of "First Papers" towards American citi-zenship, would be safe, exempt from any and all inspections.

"Hannahchen, I am tired of telling you—the Boss only wants to help. There are men with wife and many children, all of them living in one room, no running water, no heat, outhouse in the back alley, rats running everywhere. Ford wage, first big money they have ever seen, so suddenly he feels like a big shot in America, gets drunk, whores, gambles. So, when Ford money gone—what happens? Family starves."

"Listen to him, Hannah," John tried to help Fritz. "This new venture only proves what a great humanitarian Henry Ford is. A true guardian of the men."

Hannah, ladling out potato soup from the big tureen, passed soup plates down the table without comment. Jane, dispensing beer from a big glass pitcher, knew Hannah was angry but didn't exactly understand why.

After supper, the men and Jane settled in their usual places. Hannah remained in her kitchen, its door closed.

John lit his cheroot. "I was told the Boss is going to start a school program for all the non-English-speaking workers that have flooded in."

"Now that's a good idea! I haven't heard anything I could understand in months!" Rudy was pleased.

"Somebody said we've got now more than twenty nationalities. Is that true?" Fritz looked at Carl.

"Double that. It's like a Tower of Babel on the line."

"Why start a school at all—monkeys don't need to talk." Stan opened his paper.

"At the moment, the count of non-English-speaking men is around three thousand," offered Johann.

"Three thousand pupils! Quite a school!" Jimmy took out his pipe.

"I heard it's going to be in some big hall—with words written on blackboards and teachers making them repeat after them," Zoltan continued.

"You're kidding!"

"Now, that's really right for your monkeys, Stan." Johann laughed.

"Those poor bastards are so frightened to lose their jobs, they'll do anything the Boss orders."

"Oh, come on, Stan. It's not orders exactly. He's offering these men advantages so they can better themselves." Jimmy corrected.

"Uh-huh! Just see if anyone refuses."

Zoltan put down his paper. "They want those of us educated who speak English to volunteer one evening a week to . . ."

"To do what? Spank the kiddies?" Stan laughed.

Zoltan ignoring him, continued, "It's going to be done like this. First, you print a word on your blackboard, then—pointing to it with your ruler, pronounce it, then have them repeat it after you, until they get it right."

"How many teachers per how many men?" Fritz wanted to know.

"Exactly I don't know, but something like forty for each section of, say, fifty men."

"That's nearly two thousand men! Under one roof? All yelling out words—all at the same time?" Even John had to laugh.

"Did I say monkeys? I take it all back. No, my friends, we've got ourselves two thousand parrots!"

Jimmy lit his pipe. "Joke if you must Stan, but I hear those are the orders. One evening a week is going to be school night and some of us should volunteer. Diplomacy, my friends. Diplomacy!"

"You going to?" asked Rudy.

"Most probably. John, what about you?"

"I think it's a good idea."

"Mr. Ford's or you volunteering?" Fritz asked.

"Both. All he wants is to give these men a chance to be good Americans. In order to do that, they must understand as well as speak the language."

"I'm going with you, just so I can hear two thousand parrots repeat after me 'Bless America and its almighty God, Henry Ford!'"

"That's not funny, Stan. You have no cause to say something like that." Fritz sounded shocked.

Carl rose. "It's late. Tomorrow again I have new men to train."

John motioned to Jane to pack up her sewing.

"Me too—and I tell you, if they understood just a little of what I was saying, it would be a lot easier."

"You said it!" Zoltan sighed.

Fritz knocked out his pipe. "Okay! When the time comes, we volunteer! John, you can take on the Italians. Stan, the Rumanians, Johann the Hollanders, Carl and Peter the Poles. Rudy and me, we will take the Germans. We'll get my friend Bruno for the Serbs and Hermann for the Slovaks! Well, good night, everybody!"

Jane, following her husband upstairs, couldn't help wondering what an endless room would sound like, filled with thousands of men all shouting words at one time!

The Michigan winter dragged on. Jane, now well advanced into her pregnancy, became housebound. Once they showed, ladies did not parade their condition in public. Although she thought such exaggerated public delicacy overdone, Jane knew she had to obey Hannah's instructions not to embarrass convention. Besides, she agreed that her now misshapen body was not a pleasant sight, even to herself. That John did not have her aversion to it puzzled her. Helping Hannah with the housework, finishing the new drapes for the parlor, kept Jane busy and out of sight, in her spare time becoming acquainted with Mr. Emerson's idealistic philosophy for living. A little difficult to grasp, but much more stimulating than Mr. McGuffey's stoic parables.

They hung the new drapes made up from a bolt of patterned velveteen they had found on special offer in one of the catalogs. Hannah stood back to admire Jane's handiwork and the color she had chosen.

"Goes perfect mit de chairs—and look how good dey hang! No bubbles, no place! Better den store made—wonderful! Vifey, you so good wit needle and big help wit de wash and de pressing, I've been contemplating, I split money with you for dat! Only right."

"Oh, no Hannah!" Jane protested.

"Yes! Fair is fair! Anyway, good for you have a little someting—no beg husband for to have. You work hard, you get paid! American way! Shush! When Hannah make up her mind—stop right dere!"

So Jane took to poring over Hannah's catalogs, marveling at the wonders that Mr. Sears and Mr. Roebuck had to offer, counted her precious coins, hoping that by Christmas she would have enough saved to send away for a new razor strap for John.

Deep in sylvan woods with Ralph Waldo Emerson, Jane heard Hannah's excited voice calling her. "Vifey! Come! Come down quick—in de parlor! He is here our salesman who travels!"

On entering the parlor, Jane thought the wizened little man perched on the love seat, bowed legs barely touching the floor, an apparition from a child's fairy tale whose name escaped her. But, when he jumped to his little feet, bowed gallantly before her, she knew! Mr. Ebberhardt Isador Fishbein, salesman in ladies' unmentionables, that included an astonishing diverse selection of corsets was, for Jane, always Rumpelstiltskin. No other name suited him so well. Having been Hannah's very first boarder, he was a cherished figure of the Geiger boardinghouse coming and going at will as he covered his territory laden down by his sample cases that seemed bigger than he. Whenever Rumpelstiltskin was in residence, everyone hung on the words of one who had seen big cities—been as far as Missouri and beyond.

Mr. Fishbein was not at all sensitive about his size. On the contrary, he considered his arrested appearance to be a most valuable asset. "Like a child I am, a small boy!" was his way of describing his diminutive stature and, because of it an innocence of all things lascivious was automatically assumed. Husband and lovers thought him harmless, ladies could inspect, evaluate the most intimate of undergarments without the slightest embarrassment at having a grown man present. Rumpelstiltskin's sales book was like a fascinating travelogue. Moistening a fingertip, he would flip pages until he found an entry worthy of his listener's attention, then launch himself into entertaining them. "Poughkeepsie—sold one Madame Fry's. #1.50 one dozen Barters Duplex corsets—sizes 18 to 30. $9.00. Have you ever been to Poughkeepsie? If you haven't—count yourself lucky" was one of his favorite opening lines.

The morning when Jane first met Hannah's traveling salesman and she asked him where he had been this time, Rumpelstiltskin put down his coffee cup, took a deep breath and replied, "San Francisco!" in the voice of a man in love. "Now there is a city! A true Phoenix, risen from the ashes. It inspires one to poetry! And the ladies, Oiy! You should see the ladies! Powdered and perfumed—they rustle when they walk. That's because their petticoats are of the finest imported taffeta. Only the best will do for my ladies up on Knob Hill. That's where the wealthy barons have built their mansions. Beautiful vistas. I never schlep my case of cottons up that hill—only the one containing silks and satins, maybe some French dimity, light as air, if it's summer and, of course, no matter what time of the year, as they are always in great demand—my beribboned peignoirs for wealthy ladies that are so rich, they lounge."

Jane, agog, asked, "What is that?"

With a tip of a tiny finger, Rumpelstiltskin flicked a cake crumb from his bottom lip. "Well, my dear. If you have never done it, it is rather difficult to describe." Turning to Hannah, "Isn't that so, Sweet Lady?" She, knowing how much he was enjoying himself, smiled. "You see, our dear Hannah agrees. Mrs. Jane, having just made your charming acquaintance, may I be so forward as to address you by your Christian name?" Jane, mesmerized, nodded. "Kind of you, much obliged. Now where were we? Oh yes! To lounge. The art of lounging, for it is an art, requires first and foremost a suitable piece of furniture to do it on. Preferably ornate, upholstered in either peach or baby blue damask—long enough to take the full length of a form supine. This reclined form must be languid. Preferably one alabaster arm tucked in back of the head, the other trailing, wrist limpid. The bias-cut skirt of my top-line peignoir cascading to the floor in casual perfection. A pale pink rose in one hand resting against a porcelain-like cheek would also do, but is not a pivotal necessity. What *is* essential is the mood of ennui, ennui, and more ennui!"

Hannah applauded, Rumpelstiltskin giggled, and Jane was thoroughly at sea.

"Ach! My Ebbely, how you talk! Forever I could listen! But—look vat you do to dis poor child. She doesn't know you—so can't figger if you joking or what."

A penitent Ebberhardt Fishbein jumped down from the love seat and, going over to Jane, bowed.

"Forgive my theatrical nature, oh so Statuesque Mother-to-be, but a new audience is such temptation—I simply can't help myself! By the way of making amends, dear lady, allow me to offer you a pair of my top-of-the-line ladies' garters, trimmed in genuine Chantilly lace of cream and baby rosebuds."

"Vifey, now you know how come dis man can sell anyting to anybody. Even de ice to de Eskimos, I swear!"

So rare was the sight of an automobile standing on the street, the boarders knew immediately that Ebberhardt Fishbein had arrived.

"Where is he? Where's our mighty shrimp?" Fritz and John called, at the same time.

"Hannah, stop kissing your precious Ebbely and let us have him!" the others shouted.

As the little man appeared, the boarders pounced on him as though he were a favorite ball they all wanted to play with. Pretending fright, he took refuge behind Hannah's height, so they twirled her about, as he ran down the hall the men in hot pursuit. Everyone was having a whale of a time.

Hannah, clutching her sides, gulped for air.

"My ribs, dey are splitting! Dey always like dis crazy when he comes back. Vifey, quick—while de boys play, we get de supper going." Still laughing she marched back into the kitchen, "And me—always want so much have children? I got 'em here already!"

That evening, suppertime never ended. There was so much to tell, so much to listen to, no one wanted to break it up by leaving the table. First, Mr. Fishbein was minutely questioned on the performance of his very own Model T. Had she broken down and, if so, why and under what hazardous conditions? Had she proven as reliable as the men knew she was? How many miles had she withstood before needing an oil change—on and on they questioned, interrogated, eager to hear from the only one of them who possessed, drove what they could only build, until Ebbely, they all called him by Hannah's affectionate diminutive of his given name, held up his tiny hands in mock dismay. "Stop already! You're giving me a headache! That pile of black tin parked outside? Well, let me tell all of you everything in just one word, Perfection! A marvel! A joy! I should find a woman like that!"

"You son of a gun—that good, huh?"

They could have kissed him.

"Nothing better. If she could cook, I'd marry her!" Looking up at Hannah, he inquired, "Sweet Lady, any more of this heavenly borsch?" For such a small person, Rumpelstiltskin could consume an amazing quantity of food. Hannah, delighted, rushed to serve him. "Delectable as always. Home cooking! And Hannah's! You lucky devils! You don't deserve her! Fritz does, but you don't!! Now, tell me *your* news. I already know all about Henry Ford's announcement. The whole country is buzzing! Every town I went through, the newspapers were full of it! Truly, an amazing gesture by an amazing man. By the time I come through here again, you'll be so rich you'll be too big for your britches! Oh, before I forget, John—allow me to offer you my sincere congratulations. Nice lady you got there. We got acquainted this afternoon and I like her . . . no frou-frou like the others." Zoltan coughed. "Still got that cough I see, Zolly. I told you the last time, a little horehound dissolved in warmed brandy never fails."

"If Mr. Rich Traveling Man would bring me some, I'll do it!" Zoltan retorted.

"Hey, Ebbely. I'm looking to buy a house and I've already written Henrietta to come, bring the children. By summer we should be settled in our own home."

"Johann—at last! After all these years! How delightful!"

"And I, I have asked Frederika to marry me," Rudy announced proudly.

"Sweet Lady, what are you? A landlady or a marriage broker? I don't know if I should leave you all for such long periods of time—can't trust you to behave!!"

"Ebbely, how far were you this time?" Jimmy asked.

"Oregon—wettest state in the Union! Excellent territory for long drawers!"

"What does the rest of the country think of President Wilson?" Fritz asked.

"Personally, I am still of the same mind. He's not to my taste. Such a haughty man cannot know the needs of the common man. As for my clientele, although they haven't the vote, their influence over their husbands is considerable. The ladies are charmed having a 'true' gentleman in the White House. 'How lovely! How refreshing! How cultured! And how he adores his sister.'" The table applauded the little man's talent for perfect mimicry of dithering womanhood.

Although Jane knew it was men's privilege to discuss subjects deemed too intricate for women's comprehension, she ventured to ask the table at large, "Excuse me, please—but in a free country like America, why does it not allow women to vote?"

"Because they know nothing about politics and belong in the kitchen," answered Fritz before his wife smacked the top of his head with the soup ladle. Sheepishly, wiping dollops of borsch from his moist pate, Fritz gave Jane a look as though blaming her for bringing up the subject that got him into trouble. Jane, eyes downcast giving her full attention to the soup before her, heard her husband fill the momentary embarrassed silence with a good-natured, "Don't mind my wife. She is always sticking her nose in where it doesn't belong."

This produced a few chuckles, the atmosphere eased. Jane swallowed her soup as though it contained nails.

"Mrs. Jane, now that we are so well acquainted, permit me the liberty of asking when you plan to deliver!"

"Early May, Mr. Fishbein."

"Then I shall plan to return around that time bearing a gift or two."

"That would be most kind, Mr. Fishbein."

"No, no, my dear. Hannah made me an 'Ebbely' and here, Ebbely I am."

Jane smiled her gratitude for much more than the use of a name. Hannah, clearing the soup plates, kissed the top of Rumpelstiltskin's head as she removed his plate.

"Jimmy, this time I overnighted in the grand city of Chicago. Needed to restock on one of my best-selling items, camisoles of such pure cashmere they float. Like an infant's sigh. So as a lark, I treated myself to a moving picture show. Very amusing. Laughed a lot. A funny little man . . . I believe a compatriot of yours . . . Charlie something or other. Oh, and fedoras, mostly pearl with wide bands of darker ribbed silk are now the rage in Chicago and other Eastern cities. The rest of the country is still partial to our bowlers except, of course, farmers and field hands who wear straw."

Hannah paraded in a huge platter of succulent chickens, roasted to perfection, nestled amongst whipped potatoes, glazed carrots, and peas—Rumpelstiltskin's favorite dish. Creamy gravy, flaky biscuits were passed around, everyone complimenting the cook by eating in silence, not wanting to stop in order to talk.

"What a feast!" the guest of honor sighed, mopping his brow, "the energy! The energy it takes to consume such a meal! I'm quite exhausted! Don't make me move, Hannah—don't make me move, I implore you!"

"There he goes again!" Johann laughed.

"Ebbely never tells his stories right after eating," said Peter, slightly disappointed.

"Where do you put it all?"

"Away, dear Zoltan, away! Before I forget, there is something I want to ask all of you. When are you going to get around to closing the T? I freeze my ass off—sorry, ladies—in this weather, give me something! A heater? Anything!"

All the strudel had been eaten, all the coffee drunk, being a weeknight, it was time for bed. Hannah hit the table to catch everyone's attention. "Boys, here de setup for tonight's sleeping arrangements. John goes in mit Zoltan, I sleep mit Jane, so Ebbely get our bed by himself because Fritz on de settee tonight will be sleeping!"

Nobody laughed, although they all knew why and wanted to.

"Dear Lady, in that great big bed of yours? I shall get lost!"

"You need good, peaceful sleeping, Traveling Man. No discussion—orders!"

Climbing the stairs, Zoltan asked his roommate for the night, "In the morning, John, shouldn't we give it a quick once-over?"

Peter joined in. "Yes—I want to have a good look at the tire frames."

John agreed. "Ebbely, how about if before we all leave in the morning, we check out your Lizzie? Okay with you?"

"Much obliged. Nothing like being gone over by Ford's crème de la crème. She'll love it!"

"Okay. But first get Hannah to give you some blankets. We've got to cover her or she'll be frozen by morning!"

Early the next day, long before their usual rising time, Rumpelstiltskin, still snoring peacefully cocooned in Hannah's featherbed, eight eager men were fondling his automobile like a bunch of love-struck swains. Oblivious, one was under the car, Zoltan was cranking, Peter checking the wheels pinched her tires, inside Fritz was stroking the upholstery for any loose threads, John and Carl had their heads buried in her engine. Stan, after making sure the body had no scratches, was inspecting the gear-box, tightening pedals, Jimmy had taken on the lights.

They were so happy, they forgot all about breakfast until Jane called them in. Afterwards, good-byes were swift. Reminding Ebbely he had promised to return in time for Hannah's Passover, the men rushed off to work.

Ready to reconquer the open road, Rumpelstiltskin pulled Hannah's face down to receive his devoted kiss, presented Jane with the promised frilly garters and was off.

Ignoring the cold, Hannah stood on the front porch, waving good-bye. "Be careful, Ebbely. Come back soon!" As his Lizzie wobbled away at the breakneck speed of ten miles an hour.

8

I cy rains swept down the streets, rattling windows as though knocking to be let in. Jane wondered if spring ever came to Michigan.

She had so much to learn, so much needed to be absorbed, and understood. The child within her stirred, waking her. The pungent aroma of brewing coffee tickled her nose. Hannah was already downstairs, busy in the kitchen—she had overslept! Jumping out of bed, she washed, dressed, hurried downstairs to help with breakfast.

Zoltan poured the syrup onto his stack of steaming flapjacks, then handed it on to Stan.

"Nearly Easter and Passover, Hannah. Got any feelings of our Ebbely?"

"No." She poured him coffee. "My bones don't say nutting about him. Must be still far away."

"Bones?" John helped himself to sausages. "What about your heart?"

"Yeah, Hannah, what's your heart saying?" Peter spooned sugar into his cup.

"Quit de teasing. Is possible dis year our Ebbely won't say de Seder for us, so Fritz will have to. Now, quit de talking. Finish and get to work."

Rudy, anxiously waiting for Frederika's answer, half in hope, half in trepidation that he might have been in too much of a hurry to propose, got up, pushed his chair into the table. "I'm going crazy. Hannah, you've got to ask that mailman again. Frederika must have answered—something! Her letter should have been here by now!"

"Rudy, don't worry. Every day I ask, 'Now, today you finally got a letter for my Rudy Zegelmann?' Believe me, Mr. Henry he knows for sure how much you are waiting. Now go already!"

Still, no letter for Rudy that day, but there was one for Jane.

> *Dear Giovanna, wife to Giovanni,*
>
> *I hope you remember me. I hope you do. I am the Bela from the boat cabin. A good friend of my Lotar knows how to write the English so he is writing down the words I am speaking for me. I speak good now. My Lotar says he is proud I do so good but the reading and the writing I cannot. Here in this mine camp is hard life. Everybody live in shacks, get so cold when new babies born in the night many they freeze and die at their poor Mama's breast. Many so sad things happen here. Frozen babies just some of it. My Lotar say soon we will leave. When enough dollars saved for train, we go far to where the sun shines to find gold. Lotar say that better than dying here in Missouri iron mine. Here we hear much talk of bad, bad trouble. Strike in copper mines. Many killed, even children, by stomping on when they run to get away when someone cried fire. Hope this place they call Calumet is not where your Giovanni works. The friend who is writing this down says I have to stop. Strike talk he don't want to have anything to do with it—even when writing down words only I am speaking. So, thank you for address you give me. Now I give you mine after my name that I do in my own hand.*
> *Your friend,*
> *Bela*

Jane shared her letter with John, then composed her answer. Aware that someone would have to read it out loud, she wrote it in print, giving Bela her news in simple terms, leaving wordy embroidery aside for clarity. In the hall the next morning, John offered to take her letter to work with him, saying he would give it to Evangeline to frank, put it with the outgoing correspondence. This casually familiar reference to the ever-intriguing Evangeline raised a few eyebrows amongst the boarders but none ventured a comment.

Mr. Henry had become so involved in Rudy's suspenseful romance that only a letter delivered by his very own hand could solve, that when it finally arrived, he rushed to the Geiger house, not even stopping to put on any of his mittens.

"It's come! I've got it! It's here!" Hannah snatched the envelope, pulling him inside. "No, no—can't stop! Must get back. Left everything behind! Let me know what she answered—yes—or no!" And waving, he sprinted down the street.

That evening, Hannah stood by the front door, waiting for Rudy to get home from work. As he stepped inside, she pounced. "IT'S HERE! Quick, open! . . . So? She say 'yes' to you?"

Giving him no chance to escape upstairs, read in private, she watched his face as he skimmed the lines, caught the beginning of a grin and, clapping her hands, cried, "She say—'yes'! Clever girl!"

As the others came through the door, Hannah pointed to Rudy holding Frederika's letter, mouthed an ecstatic *yes*!

"I've got to find a house—buy furniture . . ." stammered Rudy in a daze.

"Easy, my boy . . . don't go crazy!" Fritz cautioned, hanging up his coat.

"Congratulations!" The men shook Rudy's hand. Hannah gave Fritz a fast hug.

"First, we get a baby coming. Now we got a wedding wit de Catholic organ music and all de candles flickering—what a time!! Okay, boys—don't stand around, wash, and tidy for supper. Tonight we make a toast for coming wedding bells."

Settled into their parlor chairs, they sipped the fiery liquid that Johann had contributed to toast Rudy's good fortune.

"Well, *I* will not be bought," declared Stan to no one in particular.

"Now what's wrong?" asked Fritz, his tone impatient.

"I'll tell you what's wrong. Rules. More damn rules than you can shake a stick at—*that's* what's wrong!"

Zoltan put down his glass. "Yes, you better watch out, Fritz! I heard the Boss wants no more rooming houses nor boardinghouses run by Ford wives. Thinks that when their husbands are away at work, having other men in the house will be too much of a temptation for them to resist—and poof! There go the profit-sharing benefits!"

"Sin and profit sharing, they don't mix!" Jimmy chanted.

"Yeah, so tell Hannah not to creep into my bed no more!" chuckled Rudy.

Fritz glared at him. "No joking! This is a serious matter."

"It's just a rumor, Fritz. It'll never happen," placated Carl.

"Well, the Sociological Department is sure in full swing!" said Peter.

"Cleanliness is next to Godliness. Henry's own words."

Jane looked at Jimmy, not sure if he was joking or serious.

"Is that really what this new department is all about?" Johann asked John.

"I told you, all I know is that the Boss wants to make sure that any worker eligible for profit sharing deserves it."

"And that is going to depend on how clean his wife and kids are?"

"Come on, Johann. These people are raw immigrants. Mostly farm laborers, they have no knowledge how to live a decent city life, make use of their newfound prosperity."

"And you, John? Were you never a raw immigrant maybe?" Fritz's voice held censure.

"Sure, but I had a trade—I was schooled. And, I was single. I only had myself to look after." The room fell silent. John lit a cheroot. "It's not just that. You know as well as I do, you can tell a good, trustworthy worker by the way he lives, feeds and houses his family. A drunk or a gambler has nothing to show for his wages but debts and squalor. That's what the Ford inspectors are there for—to find out—try and set them on the right path. They won't come to check on us, you know."

Zoltan coughed, "I wonder. This time, John, you might just be wrong."

"Tell me honestly, John, you think it right that before you can receive what you have earned, your wife is inspected?" Carl challenged.

"Not my wife—not Fritz's, none of ours. The company knows us . . ."

"Yeah," Rudy interrupted. "Henry Ford's inspectors won't dare to touch us."

"Well, I hope you're right, John. I hope you're right, but allow me my opinion that with this, you may not be!" Zoltan said very quietly.

"Yes, I agree." Carl sounded troubled. "I don't like it! I don't like it at all. Something wrong there. And, who will these *inspectors* be? What kind of men will they choose for the job? Make them so important, so they can go into where man and his family live—with the Ford given right to inspect and judge him?"

"And what he writes down in his report to the Boss that can decide a man's pay," added Rudy.

"I bet you they'll be offered bribes and some will take them," said Johann.

"And I'll bet they'll take more than money if the wife is pretty!"

"Stan, that's enough. There is a lady present," Fritz reprimanded.

Stan, unrepentant, replied, "Well, then she better have her eyes opened to what is about to happen in the latest of Henry Ford's crusades to own his workers."

"Why is it, Stan, that you always insist on seeing the wrong side of such a giant of a man?" asked John.

"Why? Because ever since the success of the Highland Park scheme—his revolutionary assembly, his Five-Dollar-Day—to the people, Henry Ford has become a sort of God and I think he is beginning to believe it himself. This may not scare you, my friend, but it sure scares the hell out of me!"

"Well, I don't know about this God stuff," Carl packed his pipe. "But yes, the place has gotten too big. Everything! Jesus! Three shifts working full out and still they want to increase the speed of the lines! And they will—and if that doesn't kill the men, the constant pressure will!"

John stretched out in his chair.

"Tell me, Stan. Are you a union man?"

The question so often speculated on but never voiced had finally been asked. The room fell silent. Everyone wondered what Stan's answer would be but it was Rudy who spoke. "Why don't you ask me, John?"

Zoltan, knowing where this type of talk could lead, opened his paper to hide behind.

"We don't need any unions to protect us. We are Ford men. Our Boss takes care of us," proclaimed Peter as though no further discussions on this subject were permissible.

Zoltan giggled behind his paper. "Anyone see this latest cartoon about us? It's hilarious!"

"Is it the one where the man in a fur coat, silk top hat, spats and cane, wearing his Ford badge says to his liveried chauffeur, 'James, be so good my man and pick up my wages'?" said Jimmy, laughing.

"Yes," answered Zoltan, disappointed. He had anticipated telling the joke himself and certainly in a far more humorous way.

Frowning, Rudy looked over at Johann. "Maybe I shouldn't get married?"

"To be eligible for the new benefits, you have to be."

"Or get your parents to come," John advised.

"You mean that works, too?" Zoltan asked intrigued.

"Yes, as long as you can prove you are the sole breadwinner of your family—you are eligible."

"So, to make Henry Ford happy we all now have to lumber ourselves with mouths to feed!" Stan grumbled.

"I'm not going to get into another argument with you over that." John flicked the ashes off his cheroot.

"Well, Frederika has accepted me, so it's too late now anyway. Besides, my mother would never leave Austria."

"Listen, Rudy." Johann put away his paper. "I heard of a house that may be for sale. After work tomorrow, come with me. We'll have a look. If it turns out to be too small for what I need, it might be just right for you and your bride."

The evening that had started on such a happy note ended when it was finally recaptured.

One morning, its chill unhampered by sunshine still too weak, Jane found an errant crocus hiding by the backyard fence. Soon it would be her time. She wondered if it would be a boy. Begetting sons was so important to men, whereas daughters were relegated to being a comfort to their mothers. Jane, not quite certain how she could handle that, hoped she was carrying a boy. Finally as Hannah had promised, Spring appeared, with it, Passover, and Jane's introduction to the solemn beauty of its ritual, its spiritual meaning—then Easter, its celebration so familiar, her nonacceptance of it hidden beneath the mood of celebration that Hannah infused into everything.

The Ford Motor Company, having become the pot of gold at the end of an immigrant's rainbow, and Highland Park, once a country village far outside Detroit, was now a teeming suburb of more than ten thousand new inhabitants. To accommodate the flood of new workers and their dependents pouring into the area, single-family houses were going up like weeds, existing ones were being split down the middle, making them into two-family homes that shared the roof and porch but had their own front door. Johann, having found one that suited him whose adjacent side was also for sale, persuaded Rudy to join him and together they bought the house, financing their purchase through the newly established Ford Company Housing plan.

By the beginning of May, still experimenting, installing ever new revolutionary concepts that would, one day, carry the term *mass production*, Ford's Highland Park plant was turning out twelve hundred automobiles a day—an unheard-of volume in 1914. All Model Ts, the Runabout, the Touring and the Town, all black, their parts interchangeable. The motor assembly had been broken down into eighty-four different operations for five hundred men stationed at several continuously moving lines. Chassis assembly now consisted of forty-five different operations, chain drives wove their endless way overhead like metered roller coasters, the designing and redesigning of innovative machinery and tools was constant. Construction of new buildings and annexes had begun to acquire ever more floor space to augment production. Henry Ford was considering establishing a comprehensive hospital for his workers as his English school program got underway. Some grumbled, some resented the loss of their free time but, in the end, everyone who had volunteered reported to their assigned groups of yelling parrots.

When everything was ready, their new homes awaiting only the imminent arrival of their ladies, Johann and Rudy decided it was time to move. They left one evening when everyone was there to say good-bye, wish them well. Hannah handed each a small packet. "Here, dis is for de new home. A little salt, a piece of bread—means 'good luck so never hunger can come your house ever.'"

Johann kissed her cheek.

"I won't be far away. It's just four houses down from Missus Schneider . . ."

"Ja, eight blocks away."

"We'll visit. Wait till you meet the children and you'll like Henrietta. You can take her under your wing, just like you did John's Jane." Giving her a hug, he whispered, "Thank you, Hannah," and was gone.

Rudy doffed his cap, kissed Hannah's hand as though she were a queen. "We'll be back, I won't say good-bye," and followed Johann.

Fritz closed and locked the front door. The boarders murmured good night, and went upstairs to their rooms. Taking a handkerchief out of her apron pocket, Hannah blew her nose, then marched into the sanctuary of her kitchen to set out breakfast for the next day. Jane, following, saw her reach for the usual count of coffee cups, hesitate for a moment, then return two back inside the china cupboard.

With her flaxen hair and china blue eyes, Johann's Henrietta deserved Hannah's enthusiastic description when she first saw her. "A porcelain doll! Johann, you lucky fella! A doll you marry and wit two baby dolls exactly like! Why you never tell us all so pretty!"

Two wide-eyed little girls, one five, the other six, clung to their mother's skirts. Their father had become a distant stranger and this lady beaming down at them was so huge! Whipped cream floating on hot cocoa, bread and jam, apple pie and currant cakes, soon they were munching, their fears forgotten while their mother was being introduced to her husband's friends, finally putting faces to the names Henrietta knew so well, had read of so often in Johann's letters.

"Hi, everybody! And here is mine!" Rudy stood in the doorway of the dining room, proudly holding the slender, gloved hand of his Frederika. Skin of pearl, hair black as a raven's wing, agate eyes fringed by midnight, their gaze fixed like that of a fishing heron, poised enchantment.

"Anudder beauty! Rudy, come. Come, child, sit, eat, have a little something. You so tiny, all bones!" Hannah couldn't get over that such a bird of a girl had braved the arduous sea journey all by herself and survived. She clucked and fussed over her as though Frederika were indeed a fledgling fallen from its nest before its time. Removing her kid gloves, the delicate creature smiled and, in a voice both musical and cool, instructed Rudy to present those present to her.

When the children's eyes began to close and the youngest wanted to crawl onto her mother's lap to sleep, Johann took Henrietta and his family home.

Excusing herself, Frederika accompanied Rudy into the hall, permitted him a chaste kiss on one cheek, then pushed him out the door. Retracing her steps, she stopped in the entrance of the dining room, interrupted the lively conversation with an imperious "Frau Geiger, as I am to remain here until such time as I am properly wed, please be so good as to show me to my room," said in such perfect convent-bred German that Hannah jumped as though a servent's bell had rung, then caught herself, recapturing her self-assurance, ushered the young Austrian upstairs.

The tea things had been cleared, the table re-laid for Sunday supper. Jane peeled potatoes, while Hannah chopped onions with her favorite knife, a cleaver the size of an executioner's axe. Eyes streaming, intermittently wiping her nose, Hannah took stock.

"Johann and Rudy, my two happy-go-lucky boys. Now dey have to be good behaved husbands. Okay mit Johann, he already a papa and knows. But Rudy? Once de sugar is off de gingerbread? Tink maybe, trouble. What you tink?"

"Why would Rudy want such a wife?"

"Oh, dat is easy. He likes de wildness dat's dere."

"Wildness?" Startled, Jane almost cut her finger.

Hannah carried the chopping board over to the stove, scraped the mound of onions into her big iron pot.

"Inside, my Ninnie—inside dat dark beauty, dere is someting. Someting like waiting to pounce." She looked over her shoulder. "Next, I chop de cabbages for de coleslaw—you got dem dere?" Jane nodded. "Johann's Henrietta, she's nice and, right away you can see, a good mama." Hannah attacked the cabbage. "A turtle dove on one side and a fox in de udder. Dat will be a house to watch!"

"A 'fox'? Why, Hannah? My first impression of Frederika was birdlike."

"Me too—but dat was first moment. Now, I'm not so sure. It's a feeling . . . someting dere for certain is not Kosher!"

"What's Kosher?"

"Oh, dat, means lots of tings—like pure, clean, correct sometimes, sometimes even Holy. Vifey, now you speak de Italian, de English, even de German so good, next I teach you Yiddish! How about dat? When you know dat—you can talk to half de world!"

⚜

In high starched collar, a brand-new expensive fifteen-dollar suit, courtesy of Gold's Emporium, Rudy made a most fashionable bridegroom. His Frederika, in pale green summer lace, shocked a few for not being attired in virginal white, but when they saw she was carrying a small ivory-bound Bible from which dangled a silver rosary, she was forgiven for her shade of green.

Fritz checked the clock. "It's been a long day, tomorrow work, so, everybody now to bed. Hannah, tonight you leave the dishes—in the morning we all get up a little early and help."

"Vifey, you feeling okay?" Hannah asked as they slowly climbed the stairs together.

"Yes, I think so . . . I'm just tired, although I slept all afternoon."

"Uh-huh. Feel down below new heaviness maybe?"

"Is that a sign that it's time?"

"We will see. But, I tink maybe soon now, your baby get fed up living in de dark—want to come out, see de light of day."

Thunder in the early summer air, her back strained against a persistent dull ache, she made her awkward way downstairs wishing it wasn't Monday washday. From the big washtub, steam already fogged the kitchen window, Hannah turned to greet her, saw Jane's face, looked quickly at the clock on the wall, told her to sit, handed her instead of the usual milky coffee, a cup of hot lemon water instead.

"Have an ache in de back by de hips, child?" Jane nodded. "Aha! By tonight I tink we have a baby!"

Clapping her hands with glee, Hannah bustled about her kitchen, canceling all preparations for washday in anticipation of birthing day, while Jane sipped water, wished it were the usual coffee and it was, after all, the dreaded washday and nothing out of the ordinary was about to happen.

Her kitchen ready, battened down, coal stove banked down until it would be needed, Hannah took charge. Taking Jane by the hand, she propelled her into the hall, took her shawl and everyday hat from the cloak stand and marched them out the front door onto the street.

"But Hannah! I can't!" gasped Jane, adding plaintively, "I don't have my hat on!"

"Now it is de time to walk! Up de block, down de block and so forth. No time for hat—come! We walk! Good for you and baby coming!"

Jane always remembered that endless up then down, then up again as the morning dragged on, Hannah trying to distract her, talking incessantly, telling her stories as though reading out loud from a book of fairy tales. By the time Hansel and Gretel had given way to the poor Match Girl shivering on a wintry corner, Jane's labor had begun and, when a frog was about to be kissed by a real princess, Hannah satisfied, said they had now walked enough, it was time to go back inside—Jane upstairs to her room, while she prepared for what would be needed.

"How long?" Jane asked, feeling awful.

"Long time still. Dis your first, so don't go fast. First time babies got big job to do, making de way so de next know where to go, get out. You go take de clothes off, put on clean nightdress, get nice and comfortable in de bed, I come up keep you company. Go, child, go!"

Hannah filled her big pots, put them on the back of the stove so the water would take its time to boil, tore the flannel she had saved into swaddling lengths, positioned the drying screen by the stove on which to hang them to warm, then with her arms full of towels and sheets, giving the clock an anxious look, Hannah went upstairs to keep Jane company.

Looking white and more than a little scared, Jane greeted Hannah's reappearance with undisguised relief. "Hannah, be grateful you never had to go through this!"

"Hush! Dat's de fear making you talk silly! Now we say nice prayer for de baby. Pass time!"

"No."

"No? You not friendly wit God?"

"No."

"Why, child? You Italian. You have de Saints for everyting. Popes even! And so many fancy churches—even better den de Irish, because dey don't paint so beautiful like Italians—so dey just drink, sing and confess. So what's wrong mit you?" A labor pain got in the way of an appropriate answer. "Dat was a nice one. You know, mit de Catholics and de udders, I never understand no nutting. Why everyone so different, hate de udders when dey all supposed to be believing in de same ting! In de old country we have dose troubles too. Dere we had also Lutherans—not bad people, just snooty!"

"Snooty? What's that?"

"Nose in de air, like rich people."

"All rich people are snooty?"

"Most. Even here, where a poor man can get important rich, become even president of de whole country—dey forget where dey come from first and look down on poor people. All over, people are people—no matter what. Dat's why God so sorry He make them, tries to fix it all de time. Like de big flood he made and so forth. But he's not willy-nilly. He knows de good ones from de bad ones, like wit de Passover times . . . like even smart animals always know who."

"Hannah?"

"Yes, child?"

"How did you meet Fritz?"

"In school. When I was little my mama she braided my hair so I look proper for school going. Fritz, he dunked de tail into de inkwell and I punched his nose."

Jane laughed, "How old were you?"

"Oh, I tink six. I didn't like him until I was ten—no dat's wrong—eleven, when some boys trow stones at me and Fritz beat dem up for it!"

Jane waited for a pain to pass before asking, "Why were boys throwing stones at you?"

"Because dey don't like Jewish people."

"Why?"

"Many hatings in de world 'why' can't answer. Children learn what their papa and mama teach them. You remember dat—when you're a mama, it is important get it right de first time. Come to tink of it, I never tell you of Fritz and me in de old country—I tell you a little while we wait for labor to begin, okay?"

Jane gasped, "These pains aren't it!?"

"No, dese just announcing it's coming—take more time before real ones start. Don't worry. Very interesting dis having a baby—every woman say dat when it is at last all over, all de big pain right away is poof! All forgotten because of de great big joy!"

Jane, not convinced, thought that women probably used such self-delusions in order to face the repeated birthing that was their lot which, if she survived this one, she had definitely decided she would never do again.

"Vell, let's see, me and Fritz. Ve come from a small village, not so high up like yours in mountains, we more rolling up and down mit fat cows all over pretty countryside mit churches—oy vey! Have we got churches! When de bells start ringing—a noise to get a headache from . . ." Jane laughed. "What? I make a funny?" Jane, panting, nodded. "Inside dose churches, you should see!! Everywhere gold and baby angels flying . . . and precious jewels. You tink everyone must be very rich up dere in dat special Heaven. Fritz's papa, he is vood carver. Very fine. Downstairs, my dining room set? He made dat, for our vedding present. Dat's why my Fritz so special wit his hands, de artistic is in him from his papa . . . untighten, Vifey . . . breathe, don't be afraid, everyting going fine—normal. Now, where was I? . . . Oh, de papas. Mine, he is dead now. Vas shoemaker, very respected because he could read and write, so peoples came to him for letter writing and reading—not just for soles."

Holding Jane's hand, Hannah talked, led her through the waiting hours until she knew the time had come for her to run, fetch Missus-Schneider-eight-blocks-over.

Having been trotted the full eight blocks by a relentless Hannah, the midwife, bosom heaving, removed her summer hat adorned with trembling daisies, put down her basket, extracted silver scissors, threw them into the pot of boiling water, fished them out by the ribbon attached to them, washed her hands, put on a voluminous white apron and, picking up her basket, telling Hannah to follow with boiled water, went upstairs to deliver Jane's baby with practiced efficiency. She smacked, it wailed, cord tied and cleaned, she handed the newborn fury over to Hannah, then concentrated on what she considered her most vital duty, to make every effort to save the mother from developing childbed fever and possible death because of an afterbirth not fully expelled.

"Good! Wunderbar. All clean."

The midwife acknowledged Jane as a bona fide living mother, gave her a satisfied smile of approval for the excellent assist she had managed during delivery, washed her down, dried her off, turned to Hannah, who, entranced by the bundle in her hands wasn't paying the slightest attention, startling her into action with "Well, what are you waiting for? Put the child in the cradle. Now, we change the sheets—then the mother can sleep before the husband comes home and wants his supper."

And so, Jane's son was born in the bed he had been conceived in.

When the men came home, Hannah, putting on a serious face, greeted them with "Tonight—no usual supper. Tonight only sandwiches you have." And allowed them to register disappointment before breaking into a big smile and announcing, "Dat's because today we got a new boarder! Vifey had her baby—A BOY!" And that's how John got the news he was a father. "So go up already! New Papa!"

"Is it alright? Can I?" John asked, uncertain how one should behave at such a time.

"Up—up wit you! Go!" John sprinted upstairs. "Rest of you boys—wash up, but make no noise when come down for de eating!"

Later in the parlor, when John brought him down, the men were introduced to the new boarder. Carl got misty-eyed when the baby curled its tiny fingers around one of his, Zoltan asked if he might stroke the silken head and when he did, his hand had a tremor. Peter shook his head vehemently when offered the bundle to hold, saying he wasn't clean enough, but it was obvious he was only frightened of dropping it. Having returned in time, Rumpelstiltskin had no such fear and cradled the baby cooing softly.

"Ah, the miracle of birth . . . the miracle of birth . . . divine!"

Jimmy said the boy was the spitting image of John. Stan disagreed, how could that be when he had Jane's eyes! Everyone fussed and marveled, clapped John on the back, told him how proud he should be and to offer their heartfelt congratulations to the new mother. Hannah, her house having been honored by a first-generation American, was bursting with joy. Hugging Fritz, she declared, "We got our first real Yankee Doodle Dandy!"

The next day, Jane was ready to resume her wifely duties, relieved that, for a while at least, the ones expected in bed would not be included. What she would do after this reprieve, she wasn't sure of yet but determined to find some way of escaping another pregnancy. Having once been told, by whom she couldn't remember but thought it could have been Antonia, that suckling a child protected a woman from conceiving another, Jane threw herself into the feeding of her son with fierce dedication. This enraptured the baby as much as it startled Hannah.

With a son to carry on his name, John, for the first time, felt truly married. Anxiety followed close behind. The responsibility of a defenseless life, its precarious existence of his making, was reality not faced with ease—any regret now an impossibility. To be aware of a woman as a wife was one thing; to accept her status as mother of one's son required an adjustment wholly apart, totally new. Somehow, the willing, interested girl that had begun to attract him, now was *mother*—its connotation of saintliness inescapable. When Jane nursed, visions of Madonnas kept superimposing themselves onto her face, making him uncomfortable, a sudden outsider. Neither John nor Jane being conformist parent material, this was a confusing time for both but, as neither knew why and marriage in their time was a state of being not an open forum for verbal communication, both made do—accepted what they had, without the slightest realization that either had the power to change their individual destiny.

John named his son Michael. Jane, relieved that the subject of an immediate church christening did not come up, hoped it might even be forgotten in time, but knew it probably wouldn't. It had always puzzled her why everyone was in such a hurry, felt such religious zeal to *bring a child to God*, as the good Sisters insisted, when babies were constantly referred to as *having come from God* in the first place. Was Original Sin besmirching the miracle of birth? Somewhere there seemed a confusion of Christian dogma, one she had found often, as though pure belief was never good enough until sanctified by man-made interference of ritualized pomp.

Jane found she was not a natural mother. This did not surprise her, for the one from whom she might have learned by example had been denied her and nuns, as virgin brides, women incased in Divine Chastity, not earthly bonds, lacked such experience except in faded retrospect. Though never abusive in the physical sense, it was Jane's very lack of exhibited emotion that eliminated the recognition of spontaneous affection from her child's life. It was her way. If overt loving preordained the loss of it, then it was better not to venture into it at all. This catechism of self-protection against eventual emotional pain that had replaced her God at such a young age—matured, until she became what she was unaware of, a cool creature contained, not given to introspection of her lack of human passion.

Due to the devoted mothering of Hannah and Rumpelstiltskin by day, in the evenings passed around to delighted boarders, Michael was a happy baby, given to cooing appreciably to all who held him tenderly enchanted by his brown velvet gaze of trust and contemplation. Except for feeding him, Jane found her mother's duties unnecessary for her child's well-being. As this did not bother her in the least, Hannah could indulge her longing for motherhood by proxy, without any danger of overstepping emotional boundaries belonging to another. So, Michael thrived. Adored by one, accepted by another, his father proud—his friends besotted and, when Henrietta's little girls came to play and tickled his toes, he was in seventh heaven. A child loved and loving, his charm infectious tonic to all he encountered, Michael was, as such children often are, sacrifice to future tragedy. But, for now, it was his time still whole, unblemished and life welcomed him with open arms.

9

Rumors that Henry Ford believed boardinghouses were potential harborers of rampant sin persisted. His belief was that women being weak, easily tempted creatures with their husbands away at work, any lodger so inclined could have his lascivious way with his landlady without encountering any resistance. Every day there were new speculations as to when Ford's Sociological Department would be given the order to close all boardinghouses as well as rooming houses run by the wives of his employees. This, plus the conditions demanded for eligibility to share in the company's profits, now forced the still unmarried men of the Geiger house to act.

Carl, who had only taken a fancy to one of the Irish typists at the plant, now began courting her in earnest, telling Hannah, who worried he was rushing into matrimony for the wrong reasons, that he was only doing so out of the simple needs of a normal man, not simply to conform to the Boss's rules. When the only obstacle that stood in the way of his lady love's acceptance of his marriage proposal was her refusal to abandon her parents, Carl bought the house they were living in, married his Rosie, and moved over to Irishtown. Peter found himself a comely widow lady willing to shed her memories, married and moved over to Polishtown. For a while, Jane sewed so much wedding finery, she was too busy to contemplate the changes that were taking place. Zoltan, who categorically refused to marry, sent for his mother.

While waiting for her to make the journey from Bulgaria, he began searching for a place to install her in to keep house for him. Jimmy, when offered a promotion if he returned to England to take up an advisory position at the Ford assembly plant in Manchester, accepted, gloating that he had found a way of escaping the shackles of marriage by simply returning from whence he had come. They threw him a farewell party—Hannah outdoing herself, constructing a resplendent trifle made with mountains of cream and real sherry! There were lots of jokes about the mania for drinking tea, pomp and circumstance, old world class distinctions but, despite the jovial mood, its gaiety was a bit forced, as though everyone had made up their mind to make Jimmy's farewell evening something it just couldn't be—a happy occasion. Even Stan finally capitulated, and found himself a woman. A fiery Sicilian, magnificent in rage as she was in displayed passion that Hannah swore had to be a practicing witch. Having looked forward to chatting with her in Italian, Jane found her southern dialect impossible to decipher but, as Serafina spoke some English, they could communicate.

Despite an inner fury, Hannah knew her days as mothering landlady were coming to an end, realized that the benefits to be gained by the approval of the company inspectors would eventually outweigh those of personal liberty. Now, in the evenings when the boarders took their places in the parlor, empty chairs stood as silent reminders of absent friends. For the first time, the Geiger boardinghouse had empty beds to fill and Fritz mentioned there were Hungarians looking for room and board.

"Hungarians? I don't want! Stay one week, den disappear with all de silver spoons!"

"Be careful, Hannachen!" said her husband in German, "that is not American fair thinking."

"Oh? What is fair American, please tell me? Not taking into any boardinghouses black skins?"

Fritz decided to go back to the safety of his newspaper. Even the high wage of Five-Dollars-a-Day could not compensate for the loss of income from steady boarders. Hannah, not willing to take in unskilled laborers whose languages no one could understand, began to worry.

It was then that Mr. Ebberhardt Fishbein, traveling salesman of perfection, decided he needed roots. A place of permanence to welcome him when returning from his many arduous travels on the rutted roads of the Middle West. And so, one morning, he approached Hannah as she was putting away the breakfast dishes.

"Dear Frau Geiger," the little man always reverted to formal address when conducting business.

Hannah, knowing this, replied in kind. "Yes, Mr. Fishbein. What can I do for you?"

"I have been giving this matter much thought. Actually, it has taken deep contemplation and I have come to the conclusion that I wish to rent permanent accommodations, here, in your so excellent establishment. Please, note the use of the word *permanent*. For this, I would require *two* rooms, preferably connecting, with full board when in residence, of course none when absent. This arrangement would also need to include the laundering and pressing of such various intimate articles as shirts, collars and cuffs, the degree of starch to be decided at a later date. If this would meet with you and your dear husband's approval, I would be more than pleased to negotiate a fair and binding yearly sum."

Hannah's love of theatrics always blossomed when her Ebbely performed. Looking down at him as he stood before her looking up, he acting the suppliant aristocrat now fallen on hard times, needing shelter in a boardinghouse, she curtsied, replied she would be overjoyed to welcome such a distinguished gentleman as himself to take up permanent residence in her humble abode, reached down, lifted him off the floor, kissed his little forehead and plunked him back down. Mr. Fishbein beamed.

Their game over, Hannah got serious.

"Ebbely, sit. No, no, we discuss de money later—first, we got to talk. You want coffee? A little something?" Frowning, the little man declined, wondering what was bothering her. "Now, listen good. If dis ting wit de boardinghouse dat Mr. Henry Ford dey say has de bug up his nose about, happens and I gotta close, what den? What happens to you? Only fair we discuss dis before you bring all your stuff. I know you! *Gott im Himmel*—will you have stuff! Little carpets, lamps mit fringes, porcelain dancing ladies. Wit de bric-and-de-bracs, loaded you will be!"

"Ah! How you do know me!"

"See! So what happens mit all dat if Mr. Ford make me close?"

"Dear lady, am I not a relative? Some sister's husband, perhaps? Cousin? Brother-in-law? . . . All quite possible categories, perfectly legitimately acceptable to the Master of Highland Park. Do not worry—*mum* shall be the word and cleverness the game. We manipulate whenever possible, resign only when impossible! By dawn tomorrow, I shall move in, lock-stock and ladies' underwear."

Hannah could have kissed him again but he scurried out of the kitchen before she got a hold on him.

Having been given the idea that relatives would be acceptable as paying boarders, Hannah decided to grant her sister's wish for her eldest to immigrate to America, there to make his fortune under the protective eye of his affluent aunt. Never having been overly fond of him even as a child, Hannah had been putting her insistent sister off by the rightful claim of having no room. But now, with her house emptying at an alarming rate, she relented—hoping the intervening years had changed her nephew sufficiently so she wouldn't have to regret having changed her mind.

Now most Sunday suppers became small reunions, as those who had left returned, brought wives and sweethearts, sat around the big table, once again enjoyed Hannah's cooking, feeling at home—as though nothing had changed. Hannah gloried in these evenings, fussing all week preparing for them, hoping as many who could would show up—their ravenous appetites intact. Johann's family fitted into these congenial times, as did Carl's Rosie and Peter's Dora; even Serafina, whenever Stan brought her, only Rudy's Frederika remained the aloof stranger visiting another's home. But then, being such a rare bird, most places, most people seemed too foreign for her to feel comfortable with. This did not seem to bother Rudy, not even Frederika—only their friends.

The baby sleeping contentedly in his cradle under the kitchen table, Jane helped serve, carrying in the sauceboats of onion gravy for Hannah's Sunday Special.

"Pot roast! My God! How I've missed Hannah's magic!" Johann cheered, then, catching himself quickly added, "Henrietta, you are such an excellent cook yourself, you must get Hannah to give you her recipe!"

His wife, busy tying bibs around their children's necks, smiled, "Even with it, mine would never come out so perfect!" And she meant it.

"Ach! Only trick is de right black iron pot, den de slow, slow, long time smallest simmering, den you got it! A little bay leaf and de sweet paprika maybe also, den noting to it, Dolly." As *Vifey* had been given Jane, so Henrietta was now a dominative *doll*, Hannah's concession to her possible embarrassment leaving off the *China* that belonged to it. "Mashed potatoes, glazed carrots, and de coleslaw on de way also got gherkins." Hannah bustled back into the kitchen, as Jane arrived with the beer.

"John," Zoltan looked up from his plate, "this latest innovation at the plant—what do you think of it?"

"Which one?" John asked, not trying to make a joke.

"He's talking about the Boss's Moving Pictures Department," Rudy answered. "Can you believe it! Now we are going to make moving picture shows?"

"For an automobile?" Stan passed the potatoes to Johann.

"Our Lizzie is going to be in the flicks," Rudy laughed.

"Ja," Fritz helped himself to gherkins. "That little Mary Pickford better watch her curls!"

"Starting up a whole moving pictures operation, right inside a manufacturing plant—no one has ever done that before! Whatever is that man going to think of next?" Zoltan was impressed.

"Well, I tell you, if they put on celluloid the assembly lines—it's going to revolutionize how we sell in the future!" John helped himself to carrots. "If the Boss plans to use this new device to advertise, those seven thousand Ford dealers across the country . . ."

"We've got that many now?" Fritz interrupted.

"Yes. Evangeline just got the latest count." Jane noticed that at the mention of this ever-reoccurring name, the women grouped at the end of the table became interested. John continued, "When those dealerships can see our production in actual motion, their eyes will pop out!"

"Damn right they will!!" Rudy agreed.

"You swearing in front of your lady wife and the others?" Fritz reprimanded.

"Sorry, ladies."

Rosie giggled, Henrietta smiled forgiveness. Serafina, always bored by Ford Talk, hadn't understood a word, ate in stony silence, helped herself to more pot roast, while Frederika wiped an imaginary smudge off the rim of her glass, causing Hannah to look in her direction, which she ignored, repeating the action. Jane, engrossed in the men's conversation, blurted, "Pictures that move? How is that done?" and opened the floodgates to their enthusiasm.

Tumbling over themselves, each one trying to explain this relatively new phenomenon before another might do it better, strange words flew around the table like spitballs. From out of the jumble of *peepshow, penny arcade, nickelodeon, loop, reel, celluloid, projection*, only one—*Edison*—Jane recognized. It seemed to her that he had a way of cropping up in anything exciting as often as Henry Ford.

Rudy held up his hand. "Hold everything! I've got an idea! Next Sunday, I'm taking Jane and Hannah to see a real moving picture show—my treat!"

"Aha! Now de big time rich chassis man!" Hannah shook a finger at him. "No! No reason spending now you got it just to go see floozies in de dark!" But the look of saddest disappointment on Jane's face broke through Hannah's frugal nature, not to mention the one of censure on Frederika's because of her husband's extravagant gesture; so Hannah relented, promised that the subject of such an unusual outing could be discussed further at another time and left to refill the coleslaw bowl.

"Anybody know how the building is going out in Dearborn?" asked Fritz.

"I hear the Boss has already built himself a power house. A real marvel." Peter poured himself more beer.

"That's going to be some mansion when they finally get it finished."

"Limestone, I hear," observed Fritz as Hannah returned.

"Missus Schneider . . ."

"Eight-Blocks-Over!!" chorused the men in unison.

"Ach! You boys making de fun of me!" complained Hannah, loving every minute of their familiar banter. "But dat lady, whose name I will not repeat, so dere! She said she heard say Missus Clara Ford will get a boat of her own to go sailing down dat River Rouge, like for de finest lady, she is!"

"I can see it now—Missus Henry Ford, drifting down the river . . . our very own Cleopatra!" Stan jeered, buttering a thick slice of bread.

"And why not, Mr. All-de-time-Smarty? De queen of Detroit, she is—so? She can go drifting down any river her so important husband gives her! She don't need no Marc Antony—she's got a Henry Ford!" and, as though punctuating her proclamation, Hannah sat, and served herself some of her own pot roast.

"How much land do you think he has actually acquired?" asked Zoltan, trying not to laugh.

"Some say it must be at least a thousand acres, others insist it's more." John finished his beer.

"Well, with all that untouched countryside at his disposal, Henry Ford will finally get to see enough of his precious birds!" Stan put down his napkin.

"That and their childhood memories is probably why he decided to buy most of Dearborn," Johann added.

"How long do you think before the Boss and his Missus can move in?"

"I don't know, Peter." John leaned back in his chair. "The rumor is at least another year, or it could be not until the beginning of 1916."

The women began clearing. Henrietta gave her girls permission to leave the table, go play pick-up-sticks in the parlor until it was time for dessert. Jane, hearing the baby's cry, went to feed him.

Over pie and coffee, the men discussed the new compulsory three-shift rotation system that none of them liked, as well as the latest right of foremen and department superintendents spotting exceptional talent, to relocate such workers to positions where they could serve the company best, which they all approved of. Their own specialized skills having brought them to their elevated positions with Ford, the men welcomed giving those who showed they were capable of more than repetitive, unskilled labor a chance to prove their worth. At the opposite end of the table, the women who could understand each other talked amongst themselves, exchanging tidbits on fashions and household furnishings. Soon it was time to leave, Serafina, knowing Stan would start translating what had been said around the supper table, hoped he wouldn't take all night explaining what she wasn't really interested in. To be escorted to her father's front door, there to be thoroughly kissed—would suffice. Rosie, eager to get to bed, have Carl make love to her, rushed him out of the house, worried they might miss their trolley. Holding the children's hands between them, Johann and Rudy walked home together, their wives following behind, each carrying one of Hannah's apple pies.

Fritz began extinguishing lights, securing the house for the night. Zoltan thanked Hannah for yet another delicious meal, reminded her to keep looking out for a letter from his mother announcing the date of her arrival and, waving good night, disappeared upstairs. John cautioned his wife not to take too long changing his son, settling him down, kissed Hannah good night and went to bed. Ebbely followed suit.

Hannah hung the damp dishtowels on the rack to dry, prepared for the next day's breakfast, while Jane laid the table; wondering if Stan would return, should she lay a place for him, then took care of the baby, carried him in his cradle upstairs to their room. It had been a long day and she was tired. Before falling asleep, she wondered what it would be like, to see pictures moving right before one's eyes and if Rudy really would take her to see them someday.

"I have bought a house. I am certain it will please you to have a home of your own to take care of. Besides, it is time," was how John announced the purchase of their first home. Jane recovered sufficiently to ask, "Where?"

"One street down, three blocks over on Louise." Hannah would still be near, was Jane's first thought. "Within a month, we will move. Now, with merchants eager to extend credit to Ford employees, furniture can be bought on time. The house has its own indoor bathroom, complete with water closet. On Sunday, we can walk over and I will show it to you." John left for work.

Jane stood in the center of their room, wondering why this moment was not filled with the elation it warranted. What woman wouldn't want a house of her own, a husband who could afford to buy one, present it to her on a silver platter without her having to lift a finger? She should be jumping with joy, instead of feeling somehow resentful.

Really Giovanna, she took herself to task. *How very ungrateful of you! At least, he did volunteer to show it to you. Maybe he will even let you see the furniture before he buys it on this time—whatever that means!* and she hurried downstairs to tell Hannah the news.

Hannah's eyes filled with tears then insisted so vehemently that they were only ones of joy that Jane knew they weren't.

"The best thing of all, it's only one street down and three streets over. I think John said Louise."

Hannah brushed away the tears and beamed, "Louise? *Gott im Himmel*! Dat's only away a hop and a skip! Not *serious* leaving. So, now Vifey, we both Big Shot house owners!! Good for you, Ninnie and your baby be where you belong. John do right by you. Oh! And all dose extras I keep!! De attic is full of dem. You take, make de house cozy fine and save de money." Hannah pulled Jane's arm, "Come, bread on second rising, baby sleeping, ve got time go inspect, see what is hidden. Oy, such excitement! And not yet noon!" Pulling Jane behind her, Hannah hurried to the stairs leading to her attic.

A small house in a row resembling it, its clapboard exterior greenish-gray, front porch gabled, a piece of lawn in a small back yard giving it a grandeur of land owned. Walking through the empty rooms, their peeling wallpaper witness to neglect, Jane felt an aura of desertion as though the house challenged her to prove that she would not. The way station to responsible marriage that Hannah's home had become was about to end, its shelter of an untried wife removed. Jane, sensing this, was apprehensive. To leave the Geiger house would be like leaving home. Never having had a true one to practice such leave-taking, Jane was uncertain how she could do so with grace. Louise Street might be only one street down and three blocks over, but for Jane, it signified a whole other world.

Stating that covering walls in patterned paper was old fashioned, John refusing to consider samples chosen by Hannah and Jane from out of the catalogs, stripped, plastered, resurfaced the interior of his house, then, when every wall was primed, smooth as glass, allowed everyone to argue over what colors to paint them. As no one, except Johann and Henrietta, had ever lived in a house with painted walls, discussions got quite heated until one Sunday supper, John tapped the side of his water glass, waited for everyone's full attention, then announced, "My friends, the walls of the house will be warm cream, doors and molding two shades lighter for contrast. Those wishing to help after work may volunteer their services. The loan of ladders will be appreciated. Hannah has promised doughnuts and coffee and my wife, to show her gratitude, has offered to clean the brushes after each evening's session."

Although they all believed John would rue his radical departure from tradition by insisting on paint and in such revolutionary shades, all of them were eager to help. Even the wives got involved. Henrietta took care of baby Michael so Jane could work with the spirits of turpentine without Hannah worrying the fumes would affect him adversely. Dora, whose former husband had been a baker, brought flour sacking she had saved, arranged it into protective covering, Rosie pinned up her copper curls and, wielding a brush like a saber, went to work.

Feeling faint from the lead fumes, Frederika went outside, sat on the steps of the porch; calling over her shoulder that if she should be needed, they had but to call to her. Only Serafina stayed away. Stan, having finally made his move, asked for her hand in marriage, set a date, she and her overly large family were busy planning a proper Sicilian wedding.

It was Rudy who brought the shocking news. Actually, it was his wife who announced it in a voice quivering with rage after he barged into the Geiger parlor, shouting for Fritz. "What Rudy? What's happened?"

"The Archduke Francis Ferdinand has been assassinated!" answered Frederika as though proclaiming a death in her immediate family.

Fritz turned to Rudy.

"How?"

About to answer, Rudy was interrupted by his wife. "He was assassinated in broad daylight! Sophie, his wife, whom I never liked, also!"

"Frederika, shut up! Speak, Rudy! Who did it?"

"A Serb. They were on an official visit in Bosnia-Herzegovina, hell knows why . . . and one of those God-damned crazy Serbs shot them!"

"*Mein Gott!* Vhat is going to happen now?" Hannah asked as though dreading the answer.

Rudy shrugged, Fritz slumped into his chair. Frederika removing her gloves, spoke with imperious certainty. "We of the Austrian-Hungarian Empire cannot allow such an act of political murder to go unpunished!"

Rudy sighed, "It could mean war!"

"Of course! That is what they deserve!" stated his wife, surprised that any patriotic Austrian should hesitate.

"Fritzchen," Hannah sat on the arm of his chair, "do you tink dere could be a war over dis?"

"I don't know—a real one would be crazy. But, something has been brewing for a long time now, and—maybe this could start it going!"

Rudy nodded. "I think so too. Johann's coming with the others, said he'd meet us here. Okay, Hannah?"

"Sure. I go make coffee, get tings ready. Stan coming also?"

"Johann said everybody, so . . ." Hannah nodded, already on her way.

Far into the night they talked, none really believing that it could come to an actual declaration of war over this incident. After all, within the broad spectrum of European history, assassinations were not uncommon and one rather unpopular cousin of the Emperor of Austria, though tragic, would not be considered important enough to cause more than a minor stir. Still, the Serbian revolutionary might just have managed to light the fuse that had been ready-primed for centuries. Being so far away, there was nothing to fear for themselves, yet being of European origin, all were sensitized to repetitive border wars, had left relatives behind, so tensions remained.

Nervous that if something did develop, European mail routes might be affected, Jane wrote to Teresa her long overdue news.

Dearest Teresa,

You have surely taken your final vows by now, may I then still address you so? Or is such familiarity no longer permissible? Please, when you respond, do include some instructions as to protocol of your Order. As you know so well, I never paid much attention to such things in school and this is my first attempt at corresponding with a Benedictine nun.

Much has happened since last I wrote. I have born a son we have named Michele, which is Michael in American. I know this will please you for if not one of the Apostles, at least an Archangel will do. The boy is well named, I think, for whoever meets him seems charmed, immediately at ease, as though he truly had the gift to banish Lucifer. Please note how easily I use such an observation, although I have not changed, forgive me, I still can't. I do find I now make an effort not to insult the belief of others simply to prove my opinions. Our landlady, Hannah Geiger, is the truest human being I have ever known besides your sweet self. Though she is of Jewish faith, she is neither deceitful nor mercenary. A most astonishing discovery for we were taught they were. Remember? Not even her nose identifies her.

It is the purity of her belief that intrigues me. She seems to embrace all that is good, regardless of religious affiliation. Her God is a friend she trusts. In this simple trusting, she reminds me of you.

My husband has bought us a house. It is most ample luxury, with its own front porch. This protrusion before one's entrance door is very common here in America. Like our balconies one can sit on it to view what is happening in the street.

People here are given more to privacy than they are in Italy. I don't mean to imply that there is no curiosity or gossiping, there is of course, but here it seems more selective, more personal, not a daily occupation to be shared by the whole village as though it concerned them. I rather like this unusual personal sense of privacy.

Although he does not discuss such serious subjects with me personally, during discourses with his friends I listen and learn.

My comprehension of American is quite excellent. Though this may sound vain, it is the truth. I can also speak German now, but writing it gives me terrible problems. The pleasure it is to be writing this in Italian, you cannot imagine. Forgive me. I have strayed. The House. It has two bedrooms. Yes, two! Small, of course, but ample. Also a full bathroom, complete and inside the house on the same level as the sleeping quarters! So now you will understand my previous use of the word luxury. The downstairs contains the parlor, a room for dining and a kitchen. There is also another porch which leads to a small plot of land in back, that I hope someday to make into a garden—not simply a place for hanging wash out on the line—as it is done here. It already has a tree that now, being summer, has burst into flower. John says it's an apple but Hannah insists July is too late, so it must be something else. It looks pretty, no matter what it is. In a place so bitterly cold in winter, summer is welcomed here with great enthusiasm. At this time, they play a special game here that stirs men to frenzy. The participants in plus fours wear strangely shaped mittens of leather, catch and throw balls at each other—and run! When I have learned more of this, I shall write and explain it to you in more detail.

The alarming news of the assassination has reached us. Many are worried that this may lead to some conflict in the Balkans. The sanctuary of your Convent, as well as being in France, you of course are perfectly safe. So are those in Cirié, for John says no matter what may happen, Italy will never become involved. Still, many seem worried for their families' safety. John's company employs mostly immigrant laborers, so you can imagine the volume of concern. But surely, nothing will come of all this. After all, the assassination of one Archduke by an insane Serb cannot plunge the whole of Europe into a war! Remember the saying 'He that lies with dogs, comes up with fleas'? John says that's the Balkans, so let them scratch themselves and good riddance!

I must close, the baby cries and there is much that must be done before suppertime. So, dearest friend, good-bye. I will await your reply with longing and impatience. As we probably will be moving from here by the end of the month, I enclosed our new address.

Please write to me soon—oh, I wish I had a photograph of you in your habit, devout and perfect as you are.

Affectionately your friend,

Giovanna

The Great War would delay Teresa's answer by four horrendous years.

Having kept an eye out for a letter addressed to Zoltan bearing a Bulgarian postmark, the morning it arrived, Mr. Henry ran over, caught him just as he was leaving for work.

"Your letter! It's come!" panted the mailman excited he had made it in time. Zoltan ripped open the envelope, scanned the closely written lines, then sighed with relief.

"This is not from my mother, it is from her brother, my uncle. He says he will personally accompany her on the journey by train, then see her safely onto the ship that is scheduled to dock in New York City on the tenth of August. Mr. Henry, thank you." Zoltan shook the mailman's hand. "This was exceptionally thoughtful of you." Blushing, Mr. Henry touched the visor of his cap and, waving good-bye, hurried away. Zoltan turned back to Hannah in the doorway. "Of course, this was written before the assassination—still, with such an early date, no matter what trouble may develop, my mother will have gotten away in time. Hannah, I'm off! See you tonight!" Zoltan rushed down the street, hoping he hadn't missed his trolley.

Stan and Serafina's wedding day became a summer festival. In the small tented garden of her father's house, an Italian immigrant of affluence, more than forty close friends and family celebrated. Wine flowed, the pungent aroma of rosemary, sweet basil, oregano mingled with that of sun-dried tomatoes, garlic and cheese— re-creating Sicily in Detroit.

Only Jane and Hannah missed the fun. Baby Michael had colic and Hannah woke that very morning with a touch of lumbago. But, when the men came home, they were told all about it. The bride, the train of her white satin gown carried by her twin sister, Morgana, a mirror image of cascading jet curls and regal carriage. The groom, so nervous that the tips of his heavily waxed moustache seemed to quiver when he repeated the vows as though he might be having second thoughts. There had been a slight disturbance, when one of the stations of the cross fell off the Church wall—but . . . aside from that, all had been splendid abandon.

Later when they were alone in the kitchen, Hannah, who had been bursting to talk since hearing about the wedding, gave vent to her assessment of the incident in the church.

"Ninnie, you see? What did I tell you? A sign! Dat holy picture falling in de middle of de wedding? DAT was a sign! De saints were knowing what dat girl Serafina really is. All over dat Sicily dey got witches living. I know! Once I had a boarder from dere, burnt chicken feathers right in de room! When I caught him, said he was only curing a cold in his head, but I know dat was not de real reason. When he moved in, he nailed a big black crucifix over his bed—dat got loose, used to slip, turn upside down, so dat poor Jesus Christ stood on his head. Bad enough you get nailed up without being turned topsy-turvy by a Sicilian witch man!"

Jane laughed.

Hannah looked surprised, "Boy, dat wasn't funny. First he got a Mamma all special, mit a halo she walks around, den nobody believes what he tells dem, den at last, he gets some friends dat do; makes mit de fishes and de wine, walks around in sandals doing good and kind . . . and what he gets for it? Nutting but troubles and meanness! And den, one of dose 'goodie-good, we love you forever friends'—what's he do? He sells him to de bad peoples for silver—and not much even. In de end, he even forgives everybody for what dey do to him . . . can you believe it? Such a good boy!" And Hannah switched her attention from theology to concentrate on her perfectly risen bread.

Running dangerously low on cinnamon and pickling spices for watermelon rind and summer piccalilli, Hannah announced the time had come to once again journey into the city, not only to visit Mr. Hirt's Emporium but to make good on her promise to introduce Jane to the sublimity of another Detroit invention, the ice cream soda!

In her best summer muslin, wearing her mother's straw hat freshened up by a stylish length of new navy blue ribbon courtesy of Mr. Montgomery Wards Notions and Trimmings Department, Jane waited in the hall for Hannah to make her appearance. Looking every inch the regal matron in summer white, her winter bluebird concoction replaced by a stylish tricornered felt edged in black, Hanna strode down the hall, calling to Fritz. "As soon as Henrietta comes to get baby, we go. You hear me, Fritz?"

Her husband called down to her from the landing, "I hear you! I hear you! And before you start telling me again, I know what to do! John knows what to do! Zoltan knows what to do and, if Ebberhardt shows up—he knows!"

"Don't tink Ebbely coming today, yet. So better not count on him."

John joined Fritz on the landing. "Haven't got your sixth sense working today, Hannah?"

"Oh, I got it working honky-dory alright, Mr. Know-It-All-New-Papa. Our Ebbely is somewhere near, but not yet all de way. Maybe tomorrow he show or latest next day after." She pulled on her crocheted gloves. "Where *is* dat China Dolly?" Just then, Johann's wife and children arrived to pick up Jane's baby to look after him until she returned from her special outing.

This time, the Market Square was warm, its summer bounty bathed in sunlight. Everywhere bright colors in profusion, the perfume from freshly cut flowers vying with that of ripe berries and citrus. Inside Mr. Hirt's, nothing had changed, his Aladdin's cave untroubled by a change of season, except that filigree cones for ice cream replaced gingerbread and bins of tea for drinking iced stood towards the front, where tins of cocoa powder had stood before.

Their shopping done, Hannah took Jane to the promised rendezvous at Sanders Drugstore, made her climb onto a tall stool that, once balanced upon, made Jane feel very precarious, gave her order to a young man with pimples, and began her instruction on the complicated art of drinking through a straw. Jane, never having seen such a device, hoped she wouldn't choke and make a fool of herself.

"Sip, Ninnie, sip! And if a strawberry get stuck, reverse—blow de udder way!"

The tallest, most overflowing glass she had ever seen was placed before her. After a few timid tries of the straw, she got it right and tasted—ambrosia!

Beaming, Hannah was watching Jane's reaction to her treat.

"Oh, Hannah! It's delicious! Just like you said and it really *is* pink!"

"Now you nearly one hundred percent American. Next time, I show you hot fudge sundae, maybe even special banana split, but dis, mit de soda, dis de best. Next week when we have de big picnic for de birthday party, I introduce to you frankfurter mit all de fixins."

Jane licked her long soda spoon.

"Birthday? Who's having a birthday?"

"Dese United States of America, dat's who!"

"A whole country has a birthday?"

"Sure. Big important day when de King of England was kicked in de pants and dis wonderful country got free forever after! Everybody celebrates dis day, called Glorious. Red, white and blue—brass bands, no one go to work, everybody play—wave flags, have a good time, forget dere worries, eat till dey bust!"

"When, Hannah—when?"

"Next week. First we prepare, den we pack de wash basket wit de goodies, take de baby, all go out to Belle Island. Right in de middle of Lake Saint Clair it is. Missus

Henry Ford, she takes her family dere, so smart it is. What do Italians call, when you eat not inside? Your John once tell me."

"Al fresco?" Jane pronounced it slowly.

"Dat's it! John tells me, dat means in de fresh, right?" Jane nodded. "So, here, in de park, we spread out de tablecloth, unpack de basket, de potato salad, de deviled eggs, de crispy chicken, summertime huckleberry pies, big treat—all de tings we can have because dis country give us plenty and have grand Old Glory birthday in de American-Fresh!" For Jane, Hannah and Fourth of July picnics became inseparable. A special time not often repeated, yet held on to in memory as something precious, to be treasured.

10

O n July 28, the Austro-Hungarian Empire declared war on Serbia. A declaration was one thing, but an actual war seemed too far-fetched as yet. Allies on both sides watched, played their secret political games, and waited.

In Detroit, Henry Ford announced that if his company exceeded the sale of three hundred thousand Model Ts by the first of August of the following year, it would refund each owner a percentage of the purchase price. The first rebate offer in automotive history, this, once again, claimed banner headlines across the country; its impact on the public, reinforcing the opinion it had formed with the Five-Dollar-Day, that Henry Ford's generosity as well as his business acumen was unique, beyond all conception.

But, ever cautious Fritz was doubtful. "Wait till next year—then we'll see!"

"Oh, he'll do it. No doubt in my mind—whatsoever," declared John.

"You mean we'll do it," Fritz corrected.

"We, he, what's the difference?" John looked surprised.

Zoltan put down his newspaper. "In a way, John's right, you know. The Ford Company is us—the Ford men . . ." Leaning back in his chair, he mused, "Three hundred thousand Ts, sold by the summer of 1915 . . . you think that's possible, John?"

"For the Universal Car? The most reliable automobile ever built for the lowest price? You want to lay a small bet?"

"What are the new price cuts for this year's production?"

"The retail tag for the Model T Runabout is four hundred dollars. For the Touring, four hundred and ninety, and the Town Car is down to six hundred and fifty dollars."

"My God, that's a sixty-dollar reduction on each!"

"It just proves what a moving assembly system can accomplish." Fritz lit his pipe. "If we can deliver and the dealers do it, I still think this new scheme of Ford's will cost him a fortune!"

"No, he'll *make* a fortune! And, such publicity is beyond price!" John blew a spiral of perfect smoke rings.

"Yes, it's something all right." Zoltan folded his paper. "A man buys himself an automobile worth much more than he has to pay for it—and then gets a repayment for doing so? You're right, John, that is a terrific idea!"

As war clouds gathered across Europe and countries mobilized, President Wilson proclaimed the United States a neutral nation with no affiliations, cautioned the country to be impartial in thought as well as in action, and, for outings at his summer home, acquired his own Tin Lizzie.

Rumpelstiltskin returned quite exhausted, complaining that if John's patron saint didn't begin putting automatic starters into his motorcars as standard equipment, he would undoubtedly succumb to ruptures of various internal organs. Hannah fussed over her Ebbely, made him chicken soup, whipped a raw egg into a glass of hoarded port, made him drink it down, then tried to bundle him off to bed.

"But, my dear lady, how can you be so cruel! Order me to slumber before I have had a chance to see our baby still residing here? Never! Just a tiny peek is all, I swear, then—and only then—shall I obey, welcome soft oblivion between your deliciously lavender scented sheets!"

"Ah, my Ebbely! De house was getting so empty. Now you back, much better de feeling is."

The little man kissed her hand, wished everyone peaceful rest, scurried upstairs for his peek at the only member of the household smaller than he.

Shortly after Rumpelstiltskin's return, Hannah's nephew arrived, having made the journey from his home in Germany in record time. Heinz-Hermann had the look of someone newly scrubbed with a very hard brush, then rubbed dry with a very coarse towel without needing to have it done to him. His skin a natural raw pink, bristle corncob-colored hair, his bluish eyes so light they resembled watered milk.

Built like a tree trunk with as little agility, it seemed utterly impossible he could be related to Hannah.

"It's de papa. He comes from Prussia—dat's up in de north where all are so," she would explain whenever her nephew's appearance startled someone. Very resentful that he had been shipped off to a strange land when his country might need its young men to protect it from vile aggression from the decadent French, possibly even the arrogant English, Heinz-Hermann seethed, disguising his inner anger with outward servility. Rumpelstiltskin took an instant dislike to the young man who tried to please without selection, finding ever-new ways to ingratiate himself with everyone in the Geiger household. The unimpressionable little man presented an ongoing challenge to Heinz-Hermann's talent to fawn. He polished his little shoes, offered to wash his flivver, even ran to fetch Ebbley's evening paper for no recompense, but nothing deterred the traveling salesman from his original, almost instinctive aversion. What surprised Jane was that for once Hannah left this situation to simmer on its own, doing nothing to smooth it over as was her want.

With so many gone, in the evenings the parlor had an incomplete air, discussions few, mostly centered on giving explanatory answers to inquisitive questions asked by Heinz-Hermann from the hard chair he had chosen, saying that as he was employed as but a lowly sweeper on the machine shop floor, he should not rate one of the padded ones belonging to Ford men of higher station. Such servility usually made Zoltan sneeze, escape behind his paper, while Rumpelstiltskin gritted his teeth, already safely hidden behind his.

"Herr Fishbein," Heinz-Hermann, his knowledge of English sufficient to address him as Mr., never did. All men were *Herr*, all women *Frau*. When a German word would do, its English equivalent, even when known, was ignored. It was as though the young man did this on purpose, for what reason no one could fathom, except that maybe irritating others gave him a certain pleasure.

John and Fritz took as little notice of Hannah's relative as he made it possible to be. After all, he was still so young, surely he would grow out of this rather annoying phase of raw youth.

Suddenly, to have a presence that disturbed, permeate the comfort of her house, made Hannah irritable. Her nephew's ever-ready verbal dislike of his mother, even more so. She now kneaded her bread dough with an angry hand, as though she was slapping him, instead of it. When Jane asked why the boy should feel so towards his mother, Hannah shrugged, explaining that perhaps he was only mimicking his father's attitude. Being a Prussian with a Jewess for a wife had never seemed to please him; Hannah had often wondered why he had chosen to marry her sister in the first place.

"Strange man, dat butcher," Hannah sighed, as though the subject was better left aside. "He has a good shop. Makes de sausages perfect, wit gentle touch so careful he is, den, come home and hit. My sister Anna never say a word about it, but I know. Once, he smash her Passover plate our mamma hand down to her. Now, she never do de feast no more." Hannah shook her head as though to clear it of troubled memories. "Now, what you say—we make strawberry rhubarb pies for Sunday supper treat, get me cheerful! Okay?"

"Theophany!" cried Serafina as she stormed into the parlor, startling the men recuperating from their strawberry rhubarb pie consumption.

Always slightly embarrassed by his wife's dramatic entrances and exits, having been interrupted while in deep discussion with John, Stan glowered. Unfazed, his bride strode over to him and, jet eyes blazing, intoned, "Stanislav Bartok! Do you comprehend? Theophany! God has spoken onto a chosen one—ME!"

"Congratulations," murmured Zoltan from behind his paper.

Serafina whipped around in his direction. "Sarcasm? Was that sarcasm?"

"Stan, there is about to be a war, one that may eventually involve the nations of the world. I am *trying* to read the latest developments. Please, try to control this oracle!" Zoltan rustled his paper.

Serafina shrieked, "Control! I'll give you control! But first, I will offer a warning . . . hear me, Doubter! Watch your feet! Your FEET! Zoltan! When they begin to bleed, remember . . . !"

"Serafina!" Stan had a way of speaking in measured monotone to his excitable wife that reminded one of a trainer gentling a wild horse. "Tell me what has excited you. But, do it quietly. After all, this is Hannah's house and here we are guests. Even if the gods have chosen to do you the honor of speaking to you, let us remember our manners."

John suppressed a laugh, his eyes warning the others to do the same. It had amused all of them to see the revolutionary within their group becoming the Fatherly Sage by virtue of having acquired an erupting volcano for a wife. Sensuous mouth pouting, fires momentarily banked, Serafina curled herself into Stan's lap and, in a whisper that reached every corner of the room, an ever-astounding talent of hers, meowed, "Italy will remain undecided and next spring, we will have twins!"

"My God! She's right!" Zoltan exclaimed.

"Which one?" Rumpelstiltskin asked innocently.

"Italy—I just read it!"

As no one thought they could take this further without laughter, forced silence descended on the parlor. Serafina, recovered from her visionary epiphany as though it had never occurred, rocked Jane's baby, singing him songs in a dialect both savage and lyrical.

In anticipation of his mother's arrival, Zoltan moved to accommodations in the city, assuring Hannah he would never absent himself from her Sunday suppers.

"Zoltan, you sure?" Hannah already missing him, asked anxiously.

"Hannah, here was my first home in America. I can never forget it, nor you. I will come. I promise."

"And you bring your Mamma?"

"We'll see. Perhaps." Zoltan kissed her cheek and left. From the porch, Hannah watched until he disappeared, then reentered her house, closed its door, murmured, "Anudder gone," and slowly walked back to her kitchen.

By the middle of August, war was a reality. Powerful countries had chosen their allies, mobilized their youth who marched off to do glorious battle, believing God was on their side alone, making their cause just, themselves invincible. Euphoric patriotism was the order of the day—gallant bravery its password. The men of the Ford Motor Company, which employed immigrants from more than twenty different nations, became involved if not in body, by emotional ties to their homeland and families left behind who now faced a time of war, while they secure, well paid and safe lived the good life far removed from strife. As on the battlefields, national loyalties within the plant formed sides. Disruption of friendships, trust, the camaraderie so lauded previously so obvious that had existed on shop floors, began to erode.

Now during many evenings of their working week, the onetime boarders sought once more the Geiger parlor to discuss these disturbing times; seek comfort in old friendships.

Carl lit his pipe. "My Germans hate the French, the French hate them, my Russians hate the Germans, the Germans hate the Russians as well as every Pole. The Slovaks haven't decided who to hate yet, and so it goes all the way down the line . . ."

"Yesterday, someone called me an Austrian bastard who started it all," said Rudy, quite upset.

"Must have been a Serb," Ebbely commented.

"I heard someone sang 'Deutschland Uber Alles' on the loading platform." Stan looked around the room.

"Yes, and then others countered with 'God Save the King,' even the Rumanian anthem. We nearly had trouble out there," Peter shook his head.

"Where is this all going to end?" asked Fritz.

"We certainly can't allow any of it to interfere with production," answered John.

Carl relit his pipe. "I agree. We have to calm the men down."

Rudy turned to Johann. "Any trouble in your section? Anybody call you a name behind your back yet?"

"Little neutral Holland? I'm lily white—so is John, as long as Italy stays out."

"Well, I was called a dirty Hun and I don't like it! I'm American. I've got my first papers already."

"Fritz," John reached over to pat his shoulder, "don't let this get under your skin."

"Ja—we all have to ride this through. This war won't last long anyway."

Ebbely jumped down off his chair.

"If it is any consolation, my friends, remember that no matter what side they are on, everyone loathes the Serbs for starting this whole brew-ha!"

"Too convenient, Ebbely."

The little man stopped from exiting, turned. "What is that in reference to, dear Zoltan?"

"The assassination was a convenience—only a convenience, to a war ready to happen."

Ebbely saluted. "When Zoltan is right, he is irrefutable. I stand corrected. Oh, come on! Enough of this talk. I leave tomorrow to entice the fair magnolias of Southern pulchritude to encase their so soft femininity within the confines of my latest line of ephemeral corsetry. For this I need my thoughts to be pure, a pastoral landscape of idyllic symmetry. Speculations on human brutality tend to play havoc with necessary illusion. So I bid you all, adieu!"

"Ebbely!"

The little man halted, annoyed. "Now what?"

"WE LOVE YOU!" his friends chorused, laughing.

Bowing, Rumpelstiltskin acknowledged their affection, waved and went to bed. To avoid the buildup of August heat, he left at dawn.

Hannah and Jane saw him off.

"Farewell! Dear tall ladies, farewell! I shall return, possibly addicted to hogs' feet and grits. Who knows? All things are possible!" and was off to Georgia, the last bastion, as he put it, of true womanhood still more than willing to embrace whalebone and all such inhibiting restrictions laced tight against the invasion of their so useful repetitive virginity. Honking the horn of his shining Lizzie, Ebberhardt Isador Fishbein, salesman extraordinaire, wobbled off in style.

On a glorious late August morning, carrying their last-minute belongings, John and his wife walked to their new home, followed by Hannah carrying the baby, Fritz a jelly glass filled with sweet peas. Eager to get to work, John handed Jane the key, kissed her cheek, hugged Hannah and, calling to Fritz not to get held up, jumped on his bicycle and disappeared. Fritz shoved the jelly glass at Jane, kissed his wife and trotted after him.

"Couldn't even make a *little* fuss? Say something nice, like mazel tov? Carry you maybe across de threshold?"

"Carry me? Where?" Jane asked, confused.

"A man supposed to carry de bride into dere first home. Only right!"

Jane laughed, "What a silly idea. Anyway, I don't think John could!"

"What you mean? Your John, he's built like Gentleman Jim Prize Fighter—lick anybody!" Hannah shifted the baby to her other shoulder.

"Oh, I just meant with my size, how silly that would look. Here, give him to me, you open the door." Jane handed Hannah the key to her front door in exchange for her son.

"Not right, not right me doing *dis*. You, Ninnie—you are de mistress of dis house!" Hannah opened the front door of Jane's new home and they entered, closing it behind them.

By the time John returned from work, his house was spotless, his son bathed, asleep, supper ready, his wife in fresh apron, tidy and welcoming, everything in apple pie order, Ford Motor Company Sociological Department perfect. If he was surprised, even pleased, he did not show it; after all, Giovanna had promised him such service long ago and now he had given her her own home to give it in. Their marriage was a stipulated contract, demanding acceptance of its conditions agreed upon, emotions only clouded issues best left aside. Fortunately, the new household functioned as though this was true, neither partner aware that there could or should be more; and so a pseudo happiness existed that, though it did not fulfill needs, served the interim of their gestation.

Without Hannah's bustling presence, Jane's house was mired in silence. The baby, being one of those creatures that seemed not yet aware it was outside the womb and should therefore be complaining of being robbed of its encompassing delight, was docile. As she fed her son on a strict schedule, whether he was hungry or not, even a baby's outraged hunger cries did not disturb the silence of her house. Neither did the rattle and banging of pots and pans. Frenetic kitchen activity was not Jane. Except for the baking of pies, Jane rather disliked cooking, did not consider it an enchantment as Hannah did. Food was necessary nourishment, to be routinely administered, not an adventure with theatrical overtones. Sewing was as close as Jane got to a passion. Without a longed-for sewing machine, an activity in silence. If it had been knitting she loved, at least the click of needles might have filled the void of sound. At times she felt like a child playing house by herself, tidying her tidy parlor for the arrival of imaginary guests.

On Mondays, after the weekly wash was done and hung, the house swept, Jane would bundle up the baby and walk to Hannah's house, where home, coffee and fresh doughnuts awaited her. His special clothes basket lined with thick flannel ready to receive him, Hannah cooed and fussed over her baby, while Jane poured over the catalogs, her heart set on a carriage like fine ladies had to wheel their babies in. But, as four dollars and eighty cents seemed too high a sum for such a luxury when their house still needed more essential things, she realized she couldn't send off for one—so, just looked.

When Hannah decided that the making of noodles in two houses every Friday was plain silly, Jane made hers in Hannah's kitchen. Wednesday, being the day when Hannah beat her carpets, Jane went over to help with the task. Thursdays, Hannah visited Jane, kept her company while she did the ironing, wrote her special recipes into Jane's new household book. Saturdays, they baked together—no use wasting precious coal to heat up two ovens when one giant one would do just fine. As Sundays John and Jane were always expected to take supper at the Geigers', that left only Tuesdays for the two women to miss each other, which Hannah said was good because that made their Wednesdays extra special.

It wasn't all just routine, sometimes when Mr. Henry, in summer attire looking slightly undressed without his mittens, would deliver an illustrated postcard from Rumpelstiltskin, everything would stop, all work laid aside, forgotten, to appreciate it, tack it up on the inside of the larder door to join Hannah's impressive collection of picture postcards and trade cards. Coffee cup in one hand, the back of a kitchen chair in the other, they would make their way into the larder, close its door, sit down before it and admire the colorful display.

Receiving an illustrated postcard could put Hannah in a happy haze for days, preferably from her Ebbely, who often chose ones hand-tinted with delicate colors, of views from far-off cities, or more often depicting ladies of high station enjoying genteel pastimes. Due to his profession in sales, he was particularly partial to trade cards that advertised. Sipping their morning coffee, they would feast their eyes on the treasure.

Jane learned a lot about America and its ways from Hannah's illustrated cards. The Dutch were considered such prime examples of cleanliness that something called Old

Dutch Cleanser chased dirt by a lady in wooden shoes, wielding a big stick. Buster Brown wore only the very best shoes. A gentleman by the name of H. J. Heinz was America's Pickle King, and Lifebuoy soap was every sailor's preference.

"Ninnie, see dat one, de one where de pretty lady is conversing into a speaking machine? Dat's one from de Bell Company. Can you imagine? Your John, he told me it vorks. You shout into one place, but you hear from a receiver piece—see, she is holding it on her ear? De words an electricity vire up on poles, carries dem. Dis one not invention from de great Mr. Edison, dis one discovered from another smart man called Mr. Bell. Funny, no? Vit a name like dat, he invents something dat goes ring-a-ling?"

Of course, there was big excitement when Missus Adams, who ran just a rooming house, became the gloating owner of the first talking telephone in the neighborhood.

"Across de blocks she can speak wit someone who also got de special wires—and dey? Dey can hear—CLEAR! Now, dat's an invention! A marvel! Right inside de house it is, on de wall dey got it, like a picture. Over and over I tell Fritz I want, we should have one of dose where you speak into, to people not even wit you. Does he do it? No—he says first too expensive den no wires reach us yet and, second, not for simple people like us to need. For people like de Boss and his missus, de Vanderbilts and even de president, okay—but de Geigers? No! Now dat hoity-toity, Mrs. Adams nose-in-de-air woman, she got one and us, de best boardinghouse in Highland Park we still without, like nobodies!"

By the time autumn winds whipped John's shirts on the line, Jane was a well-schooled wife, mistress of her husband's house, mother of his son, well spoken, versed in the language of her new country, efficient, frugal, obedient and aware that in some subtle way, she had but exchanged inhibiting mountain granite for solid clapboard and domesticity.

In their parlor, still bare except for two armchairs, a side table in between, Jane sat sewing on the snake she was making to keep the draft out from under the back porch door, John read his evening paper. The cream-colored walls reflected the light from a single standing lamp, as though there were several about the room. At first, Jane had thought she would have trouble accepting John's unusual choice of color, but now that the days were shortening, the brightness within the house seemed to lessen the gray of approaching winter. I must tell him how his choice to paint—not paper—the walls in the burgundy I chose, is pleasing. I seldom thank him. *I must learn to do that more often. I wonder if it would make a difference to him if I do or don't?* She hoped that soon the ordered material for parlor drapes would arrive, for she planned to have them finished in time for Thanksgiving but, without the aid of a wondrous sewing machine, she might not manage to get them done until just before Christmas.

John put down his paper. "I'm off to bed. You coming, Ninnie?"

"I want to finish this first."

"*Buonanotte*, Ninnie."

"*Buonanotte*, John." In her pleasant beige parlor, Jane sewed on her snake in silence.

With Thanksgiving not too far away and already running dangerously low on precious spices, Hannah announced the time had come, once again, to venture into the city of Detroit. Her winter bluebird visible, announcing her long before she arrived at Jane's front door, Hannah was impatient to get going.

"You ready, Ninnie? Cold today. Dolly get de baby?"

"No, Rosie wanted to have him." Jane pulled on her gloves, looped a scarf around her neck. "I think now she is expecting she wants the practice."

"Our Carl—soon a Papa! Never I believe such a ting could happen. He is a good man—but lover type? He never was until dat hot blood Irish Rosie come along. She still mooning she have to give up her good work whit de typing machine because she marry?"

"Yes, a little, I think. I like her. She is not like Frederika."

"Nobody is like Frederika! Come, we go!"

Jane, now a matron in her own right, strode into Mr. Hirt's with confidence. Discussed the price of candied angelica for decorating her Christmas fruitcake, decided as almonds were much too expensive, she would do without—did not allow any of the many things she wanted to sway her from her resolve to remain beyond temptation; did purchase a small flask of rose water she planned to mix with equal parts of glycerin, so that no roughness of her hands would damage the surface of the velveteen cloth when fashioning the parlor drapes. Their purchases made, Jane treated Hannah to a Vernors float, a concoction of vanilla ice cream and Detroit's very own supreme ginger ale that she thought even more delicious than Hannah's strawberry soda—although she never told her, so as not to hurt her feelings. Afterwards, Hannah treated Jane to a just looking hour at Hudson's, Detroit's most elegant department store. No longer apprentice and teacher, the two tall women had become friends of equal stature.

While Henrietta's girls played with little Michael and the women helped with the dishes from Sunday supper, the men settled themselves in the parlor, enjoying the return to a male-dominated atmosphere enveloped in smoking tobacco.

Stan rolled himself a cigarette, licked along the edge of the paper.

"Well, my friends, the Dodge Brothers have done it, produced their own automobile without the mighty Henry Ford."

"The Boss isn't going to like his stockholders setting up a rival business."

"There you're right, Carl. After all these years, think he's going to try to buy them out?"

"Could be, Rudy. Could be. But, will they let him? With our profits so high, I don't know. What do you think, John?"

"I think he'll try. After all, it's his achievement. He should own it outright, when the time comes, let his son inherit . . ."

Zoltan smiled, "The new father of a son speaks!"

"But . . ." John continued, "if the Dodge Brothers would agree to sell, that's anybody's guess. By the way, anyone see the great Edison last week?"

Peter finished packing his pipe. "I hear he came with his family."

"Wife and son Charles. The Boss showed him his first fully automated continuous motion assembly! Just like a proud kid showing off to his Papa!" Fritz chuckled.

"And why not? You have to admit it must be quite an experience to have been a minor employee to a genius and then have him come to you to witness what has made you his equal." Zoltan lit a cheroot.

"Equal? I wouldn't go *that* far," murmured Stan.

"Our power house must have impressed the great man."

Johann puffed on his new ivory pipe.

"Considering it was he who oversaw its construction, no doubt."

Rudy leaned forward in his chair. "John, I know you—you saw him. Right? How did he look?"

"You know, I have been thinking about that. Do truly great men look so special because they are? Or, do we think they look special because we know they are?" John looked around for one of them to answer.

Zoltan cleared his throat. "John, when you get this way, you worry me. Does Thomas Edison look like a normal human man or not?"

"As a matter of fact, no. He could be your father!"

"Funny, funny," Zoltan smiled.

"Is the Boss still working on that farm tractor idea?" asked Peter.

"He has never stopped working on it," John answered.

"Does anyone here know why now Ford needs two thousand more acres along the Rouge River? That much land can't be just for his personal use." Stan looked about the room.

"I think he may be planning to build another plant," Carl observed.

"My God—what for? We just added two six-story buildings that will give us more than forty-five acres of floor space. We've got the new trolley lines hauling trucks from railroad platforms direct to factory floors. What more . . . ?" Fritz looked at John for an answer.

"But think for a minute, Fritz. If the iron ore and coal could reach us direct, brought to us on Great Lakes steamers, with a correctly configured plant, Ford could process . . ."

"Impossible!" Rudy shook his head.

"So was once building an automobile in twelve hours!"

"Ja, and now we can turn out a thousand in a day! But . . ." Fritz turned to John. ". . . if I understand you right, you're talking of from raw materials to finished motorcar—all within one plant?"

"Well, that would mean it would have to be an extraordinary operation, one of unheard proportion, revolutionary in design and concept, John."

"You're damn right, it would, Zoltan! We have done it once—every day, we are still perfecting one revolution, why stop there? Henry Ford has always looked beyond, never has he been satisfied with what he has achieved—only with what can still be done."

Sensing that John was about to be challenged, his enthusiasm deflated by Stan, Rudy thought it better to change the subject. "Hey! I heard a rumor—we may be going to support the British with equipment. Any truth in that?"

"Yeah, John, what's your Saucy Evangeline have to say about that?" Stan teased, an edge to his tone. Rudy gave him a warning look.

"Anyone have fresh news of the war?" asked Johann.

"I tell you who know," Fritz answered. "The Russians. One of my foremen gets a Russian-language paper printed in the East sent to him by his sister in New Jersey. Even days late, he gets more news than we do here."

"So? What did he tell you?"

"Well, there's supposed to have been a real battle in France, in a place called Ypres, with many casualties on both sides and there's been what the paper quoted as a 'dogfight' between a German and a British aeroplane that carried a sort of gun attached."

"Fighting in the sky? In paper held together with paste? Amazing," commented John.

"What speed can those things do now?" asked Carl.

"About sixty," answered Rudy, who loved aeroplanes, yearned to fly one.

"Whatever news I hear, it doesn't sound good. I have a feeling this war may last longer than anyone thinks." Fritz knocked out his pipe.

Zoltan fidgeted. Heavy silence filled the room.

"Hey, I got a letter from Jimmy."

Exclamations of "John, why didn't you tell us?" "What's he say?" "How is he?" "Well, you took your sweet time in telling us" bounced around the room.

"Okay, okay! I'm sorry."

"Well—read it, John!"

"Okay. It isn't too long."

> *Dear John,*
>
> *After an uneventful voyage, the Atlantic was smooth as glass, I arrived safely, made my way by train from Southampton, arriving home in time for my brother's wedding to the prettiest girl in all of Dorset. Spent a delightful week visiting with family, telling tall tales of my successful years in the 'Colonie,' being plied with innumerable pints of good old English ale in the local pub. Then left for Manchester, reported to Percival Perry, who is a combination of Sorenson and Couzens in his efficiency and administrative intelligence. He is both liked and respected for good reason, implemented the new wage structure and benefits quite some time ago—although the nine-hour day is still in force over here. The operation is highly efficient here, even if the scope is limited when compared to our Highland Park production. But then, ours can't be matched anywhere in the world. I do find hearing only English spoken all around me, despite the many regional accents, still the King's English—a bit unusual . . . takes getting used to . . .*

"I bet!" murmured Carl.

"Don't interrupt! Go on, John."

> *. . . Now that we are at war, with some ingenious redesigning, some of our Model Ts may be converted into ambulances. Let us hope they won't be needed too often or for too long. But, can't you just see our brave Lizzie, bouncing into battle, never getting mired in the abominable terrain of Flanders in winter, carrying our lads to safety across battlefields under fire, while the Huns, in their big heavy Mercedes are stuck in the mud, utterly helpless? Watch the newspapers for news of Lizzie's exploits. I am convinced if she is ever used, she will prove herself once again, the best, the most dependable automobile that exists, be a real heroine, make Ford even prouder of her than he is already. Actually I am looking forward to seeing her in action, for I am off to teach the Hun a lesson he'll never forget. My regiment is awaiting*

momentary orders. So, it may be some time before I can write again. Tell
Hannah not to worry and that I look quite spiffy in my uniform. Remember
me to our friends—there have been moments when I thought perhaps I
should not have returned to England, but then, I would have missed this
war and that would have been a pity. It is going to be a jolly great show. As
you say, 'Arriverderci!'
    Jimmy

For a while, no one spoke—then Johann asked, "When was it mailed?"

"Three and a half weeks ago."

"He could be fighting by now . . ."

"Ja," Fritz sighed, "we better not tell Hannah . . . wait a little till we hear further, okay?"

John nodded as the women arrived, announcing it was late, time to go home.

In time for Thanksgiving, Jane finished the parlor drapes. Up on the ladder, John waited for her to approve the height of the rod he had put up. Jane stepped back to admire her handiwork.

"Well? Are they hanging straight now?" John was getting impatient.

"Yes, thank you. It does require two to hang drapes properly, you're right."

"I want to take a look." He came down and stood beside her. "Ninnie, these are beautiful! How did you ever match the colors? And those folds—how they hang—as though they have weights!"

"They do! I found an old bicycle chain in Fritz's basement. He cut it in half for me and Hannah helped me boil it in Sal soda and vinegar to get the oil off. I sewed the lengths into the bottom hems."

"Great idea. It works. I'm proud of you, Ninnie! Beautiful work—just beautiful!" And he went to put the ladder away.

Jane stood where he left her, feeling very satisfied.

As their home took shape, so did their relationship. Imperceptibly, John began the delicate process of loving his wife. As Jane became accustomed to loving him for what he was, he loved her for what he needed her to be or thought she was. As with most such marriages, theirs resulted in benign comfort. Occasionally, he would make love to her—but not so often as to disturb. Actually, Jane found the term *making love* a strange misnomer for an act not in need of it to function. For sexual enjoyment, John looked elsewhere. It did not occur to him that this might be a breach of faith. He was a virile man in his prime, from a culture that made great distinction between the sanctity of the home, the wife's domain, and the relaxation to be found in the domain of an accommodating woman. America might change an immigrant's language, work ethic, and monetary stature but most likely not the accepted, approved behavior of his original culture. Happiness being dependent on individual perception of it, John and Jane were happy. That neither needed the other's happiness to achieve their own, this state as yet was a void they both were completely unaware of. Hannah, wanting, at least for their son, a home of discernible love to grow within, watched, worried it might never be.

11

I t was nearly Christmas, when Mr. Henry, his Casanova attractiveness once again hidden behind layers of wool, sounded his knock, smiled with his seductive eyes at Jane's eager expectation, handed her a letter from out of a woolen paw.

"Missus Jane, although sent to Hannah's, I have brought you joy at last! Now, I must run!" and disappeared in a swirl of fresh snow.

Chere Giovanna,

Do not faint from surprise. This is Eugenie, your French shipboard acquaintance. What a relief! What delirious joy it is to write once again my mother tongue, you cannot in your wildest dreams imagine. Why is it that Americans are still such barbarians as this pertains to the finer accomplishments of civilized life? Not once, since our arrival to these shores, have I encountered someone who has acquired the grace, the culture of speaking French. Oh, well, what one cannot alter, one must learn to accept. Though I find this a strain, I endeavor to follow my belle Maman's schooling and remain ever conscious that being a lady born, one must not be seen to complain, that being a weakness of the masses.

Oh, how I waited and waited that anguished day upon the quay and to no avail. Deserted, forgotten, poor little Eugenie me, abandoned, by one if not entrusted with my whole heart exactly, at least in possession of this pure maiden's trust. So, there I was. Well, you can imagine, quelle horreur, the utter tragedy of it. Me, in my beautiful rose-trimmed hat, forlorn, tears wetting my pale cheeks, not knowing what to do, where to turn, when suddenly, from out of the gathering dusk, a voice, a gentleman's voice asked my name and, looking up, I beheld an older man seemingly much concerned about my welfare. By the cut of his suit, he wore spats that were immaculate, carried a silver handled walking stick, it was obvious he was a gentleman of distinction and an affluent one at that. His advanced age added to my confidence to reply a soft "yes" to his question if he could be of service. We have been together ever since. I have my own apartment, two spacious rooms which I have decorated in palest pink with touches of lavender accents. I don't do much. I mostly wait. I would so like to journey to a place called New Orleans. Do you know it? They say there everyone speaks French, is very gay and devil-may-care. Perhaps some day, who knows.

If this reaches you, please if you wish, answer me to the name and address below. Here in Charleston, the newspapers talk of a Famous Henry Ford of Detroit. Is he the same man you told us employed your husband? If so, how nice for you. Money is so very important for a splendid existence.

Cordially yours,

Eugenie de la Rochemont

When Jane showed her letter to John, she couldn't understand why he frowned, asked if she planned to answer it and, when she said she intended to, told her it would be better if she didn't—for her not to get involved. Having shown her husband Eugenie's letter in order to share it with him, not be given advice on her subsequent action concerning it, Jane put it away—until she could find the time to write a nice long reply and when Rumpelstiltskin returned, she planned to ask him that should he ever be passing through the Carolinas to please stop off in Charleston to pay Eugenie a visit, for, judging by her letter, she surely was one who *lounged.*

Through its frosted windows, the Geiger boardinghouse had that special holiday glow. Despite the absence of most of her Boys, Hannah bustled about preparing for her Hanukah-Christmas celebration. It wouldn't be too lonely, for Johann with his family, Rudy with his wife had promised to come over for Christmas Eve, and of course, John and Jane with their Michael would be coming. Even Ebbely might return in time to join in the festivities, for he too had promised.

John and Jane shielding Michael wrapped in many shawls, plowed their way through the snow to the Geiger house. Hannah, watching for them, flung open the door as they reached the front porch.

"Quick! Unwrap! De others here already. Ebbely too. Wait till you see de big surprise I got! A wonder! Never in all de days of my life I ever dream to have such a present! Quick!" She pulled them towards the parlor. "Come! See what my Fritz give me!" And there, against the parlor wall, it stood in all its splendor. Rumpelstiltskin spun its stool, sat, placed his little feet on the pedals and, reaching up to the keyboard, launched into a clarion rendition of "Take Me Back to Ol' Virgini."

"An upright! How marvelous! Fritz, you old devil, you never told me you were getting one!" John exclaimed.

Beaming, Fritz took him aside, "Got it on time. But don't tell Hannah. You know how she is about owing. Great, eh? It's a Windsor. Came complete with stool and piano shawl. The keys are real ivory, but the rosewood casing . . . that's imitation."

"How much?" whispered John.

"One hundred and seventy!"

"Jesus!"

"It's forever! Don't tell your Jane—you know how those two are together, like sisters."

Rumpelstiltskin finished with a thundering flourish, spun himself up like a top, jumped off in mid-rotation, held out his arms for Michael, who, recognizing him, shrieked with delight. Hannah ran her hand over the shining surface of her treasure as though still not convinced it actually stood in her parlor, and wouldn't vanish in a puff of a conjurer's smoke.

"Hannah, it's magnificent! Now we will have music for Christmas." Jane wished she knew how to play.

"Ebbely says he knows all de carols, even de latest hits, also dat Mr. Stephen Foster and de new 'Naughty Marietta' one, like de bands play in de park in summertime. Wish de others were here . . ." Getting sad she turned, went out to fetch the frosted gingerbread and cider.

Stan's unexpected arrival was probably the highlight of this already most special evening. When a mighty honk reverberated down the silent snowbanked street, followed by putt, puff, groan and rattle—and something came to a halt before the Geiger house; despite the cold, everyone ran outside to have a look, see the cause of such a ruckus and there, by the side of his very own, still trembling Lizzie, stood a grinning Stan.

"Ach, *Mein Gott*! My Stan! Ebbely, look! Now you no longer Lizzie owner unique!" Hannah was hugging the proud owner of motor splendor.

"A Touring, no less! My, my!" Fritz was impressed.

"Stan, you son of a gun! You kept *this* a secret! She's a beauty!" John was running his hand along the fender, like a caress, brushing off a dusting of snow.

No one feeling the cold—everyone just stood and stared, rooted in admiration, until Stan pointed to the inner darkness of his automobile, laughing, exclaimed, "Look! Look, I brought presents!" And from out of the shadow of the back seat appeared the smiling faces of Carl, Peter, and Zoltan.

Hannah screamed, "MY BOYS! . . . But, de girls? Where?"

"With their families. We said tomorrow we are yours but on Christmas Eve—we are HANNAH's. Zoltan, we just kidnapped from his mother!"

"Come, come quick inside—get cozy. Enough cider and de gingerbread I got. I was hoping . . ."

So they were reunited, vowed the little tree was even better than the one of last year, admired the splendid piano, sang carols, drank a toast to Jimmy with Fritz's special Schnapps, settled themselves into their waiting chairs, watched the flickering candles and were home again. Fritz held Hannah on his lap, let her bury her face in his shoulder knowing she would cry. Michael, having enjoyed his first Christmas tremendously, cherub mouth smeared with the soggy remains of a gingerbread boy, slept in his wash basket between the menorah and the little tree, the picture of contentment.

Across the sea, battlefields lay silent. In the trenches, exhausted men on both sides rested on their guns, for a moment of suspended time, celebrating peace on Earth.

Not having been a disruptive presence during Christmas, Heinz-Hermann made up for it on the skating pond New Year's Day. Racing about bumping people, interfering as Rudy was trying to steady Frederika, spinning Johann's girls, until Hedwig, the youngest, threw up her breakfast. After that, Fritz ordered him off the ice, told him to go home!

Rumpelstiltskin, steering Jane in a careful waltz, his head just reaching her waist, looked up at her—a frown wrinkling his elfin face.

"That will have to stop. This can't go on!"

"Oh, I'm sorry. I know I am clumsy . . ."

"No, dear girl. You are doing splendidly! I meant that Luciferian nephew!"

"Heinz-Hermann?" Jane laughed.

"You see? You knew immediately who I meant!"

"Well, yes . . ." Jane was slightly ashamed that she had. ". . . but, that is a little exaggerated, don't you think?"

Rumpelstiltskin swung her around, making her skate backwards.

"Please! Ebbely! I can't see where I'm going!"

"Keep loose! Glide! I am in perfect control!" Pushing her in front of him like a wheelbarrow, the little man stretched a leg out behind him, skating on the other like a ballerina in *Swan Lake*.

Needing all of her concentration to keep the back of her skates from catching in her skirts, Jane had no time to appreciate the elegance of her partner's arabesque. Coming down to earth, both feet back on the ice, Rumpelstiltskin picked up his train of thought where he had left it hanging.

"Yes, that nephew must go . . . before he causes irrevocable damage to the superb equilibrium of Hannah's house. Don't you agree, Missus Jane?"

"I must admit I haven't given this much thought," replied his dancing partner, slightly out of breath.

"Well—think on it! Hannah needs our help on this, of that I am convinced! . . . AH! Here we are!" He slid to a halt by the bench. "And husband with babe awaits! Dear Lady . . ." Ebbely bowed, ". . . thank you for the dance. A winter memory to treasure. John, most kind of you to lend me your bride. Now, take her into your arms and go! The surface is divine today!" And, tipping his derby, Rumpelstiltskin was off—skates dug in, running upon the ice on tippytoes.

"Ninnie, you want to keep going?"

"Not if you've had enough."

John began unlacing his skates. Disappointed, Jane started to do the same.

"What were you two talking about?"

"Oh, Ebbely is worried about Heinz-Hermann. His attitude, his . . ."

"We all are. Fritz should insist he move. He's a troublemaker. The other day, he called one of the blacks a *coon*! There is enough bad blood already without some greenhorn kid stirring things up just to see where it gets him! He's got a vocabulary that he's certainly not learning at English school! . . . Ready? . . . Let's go." John put on his gloves, picked up his son, and started home. Jane, carrying their skates, followed behind.

Rumpelstiltskin stayed long enough to savor George Washington's sour cherry pies, then it was time, once again, to be on his way. His territory now included Louisiana and, having heard harrowing tales of dastardly ruffians lurking in the bayous, he bought himself a Colt Automatic Lady's Special, saying that although he was sure an occasion would not arise to actually fire it, the presence if its nestling power beneath his left armpit made him feel six feet tall. Armed, his hot-cold box stocked with Hannah's bounty, honking his horn, waving farewell, Ebbely and his Lizzie disappeared down the street.

The repetitive warnings that the Ford Motor Company would not approve men for profit sharing who herded themselves into overcrowded boardinghouses, or those whose wives rented out rooms to single men, became the topic for daily discussions. Apprehensive, Fritz told Hannah the time had come to close.

"But dey are talking of de bad houses! De ones where dey even got hanky-panky girls working!"

"I know, but . . ."

"Here, we never been crowded. Everybody always got personal bed . . . never we used same bed for different men on shifts. I don't have no flophouse! Everyting I make nice and clean . . . eat off my floors you can!"

"Hannahchen, I know. But we can't take the chance. Now, I tell you is the time to close!" Hannah looked as though he had slapped her. "Come, Liebchen, with all my profit sharing and the new pay, we don't need the money."

"I know . . ."

"So? Think of all the hard work you won't have to do anymore!"

"Ja! Me a real *Lady of Leisure*. What I do wit all dat lazy time? Go buy hats?"

"And why not? You certainly deserve to enjoy yourself!"

"So? We close?" Hannah said it softly, as though not wanting Fritz to hear her.

"Yes! We close!"

Furniture, bedsteads, mattresses, all the extras, everything was shoved into the no-longer-needed rooms. When all was stored away, Hannah locked the doors, hung the keys by the postcards in the larder, sat in her kitchen, and cried.

She, who was used to cooking for a crowd, dragging home a hundred-pound sack of potatoes, found that now twenty pounds lasted through a whole week. Making chicken soup for two threw her completely off balance, decreasing her recipes became an ongoing trauma. Every pan was too large, every pot too big! Preparing for those special Sunday suppers became a weeklong preoccupation, depending on them, a near obsession. But Hannah's Boys were men now, with homes and families of their own, their lives no longer inseparable, solely dependent on the roots formed in their first home in a strange, new land. They still came, but not as often and not always all together. Sometimes, even Hannah's Sundays remained barren.

To wean herself from daily mothering when the need for it is finished, Hannah knew was a woman's lot, yet the conscious effort that this required, she found somehow beyond her. She shuffled about the empty house as though it had become foreign territory, fell victim to vague afflictions, sometimes remaining in bed because of the severity of recurring headaches.

Worried, Fritz left his department, went down to the tool shop floor, where John was, to ask him what he thought he should do.

"Well, if you ask me," John shouted, trying to make himself heard above the din, "let Jane handle this—you? You relax!"

"John, you tell her?" Fritz yelled.

"Sure! Don't worry!" John yelled back, preoccupied.

"It's important! I don't know WHAT to do!"

"I'll tell Jane as soon as I get home. Now, get out of here!" Relieved, Fritz hurried back to his building.

With the help of Henrietta, Jane took on the task of seeing to it that Hannah survived the mourning period of her emptied nest. They visited at all hours, brought their children, encouraged them to be noisy, even misbehave, filled the Geiger house with happy chaos. Searching through endless catalogs for items they had no intention of ever ordering, involving Hannah in serious decisions concerning color, style, measurements, and price, were forever famished, utterly distraught if there were no freshly baked treats awaiting their arrivals, lugged home gallons of chicken soup that they convinced Hannah she had to make for them or their husbands would never speak to them again.

Jane had the feeling Hannah knew exactly what they were up to, but needed the game they were playing too much to want to put an end to it.

By early spring, the Ford Company's Sociological Department was a functioning reality, no longer to be taken lightly, casually dismissed as just another reformist's overzealous crusade. This pet project of Henry Ford's was now a well-run machine, consisting of precise components geared to doing its job efficiently, its charter duty the betterment of men and, consequently, the nation. Ford's determination to lead his immigrant workers to a better life, give only unto those truly deserving a share of his company's profits, strict adherence to the rules of hygiene, living habits and morality as set down by his Sociological Department, were tantamount to employment. To gather such information, the department employed inspectors who, with absolute autonomy granted them by the company, were free to question, interrogate, inspect, evaluate, make decisions concerning the household and its inhabitants of any Ford worker chosen for investigation.

As a worker's qualification for the profit-sharing plan, in some cases his very employment, depended on what an inspector wrote in his report, all questions had to be answered without evasion.

Ford investigators visited workers at odd hours to measure their home life against the *American* standards approved of by their Boss. Marital status was questioned, a written proof of it could be demanded, a man's religion, his home, was he in debt and to whom, had he money saved, where was it kept, his health, his doctor, his form of recreation, his wife, his children—all was scrutinized. Nothing, no one was exempt. Each answer was duly noted, written onto special forms. The inspector's trained eyes searched for telltale signs of bad habits, unsavory home conditions as well as neighborhoods. On the basis of these inspections, Ford workers were classified into groups: Fully Qualified, those approved of; Excluded, those not conforming to the rules of age, length of service, etc.; Disqualified, those with bad personal habits; and, finally, those Debarred because of unsatisfactory home conditions coupled with improper habits—such as excessive use of liquor, gambling, as well as "any malicious practice derogatory to good physical manhood or moral character."

So that there could be no misunderstandings, investigators carried pamphlets extolling the virtues of soap and water and damning such habits that could constitute a fall from grace.

Most men and their women were given another chance to "Cast Out Devil Dirt, Repent, Mend Their Ways," become the upright, God-fearing, sober, hygienic immigrants that America, with the benevolent help of Henry Ford, could be proud to welcome to its citizenry.

Those newly emigrated from ancient cultures, where women were chattel, their rights not even at issue, the memory of Ellis Island still raw, were far too intimidated to offer resistance to anyone in authority. Even those women already assimilated, by being denied the right to vote knew their assigned place in society was wholly dependent on the station achieved by the men they belonged to. In order to function within this confinement, they knew their place learned in childhood, that to struggle against it was a useless expenditure of will. Some not so readily subdued, strained against convention, but however women chose to loosen the yolk that held them, they did so cautiously.

Oppression and secrecy have a symbiotic relationship. During this time of the Sociological Department's power and the autonomy given its inspectors, the Ford women's primary fear was their utter helplessness. Not only did their men's loyalty belong to the company, their livelihood depended on them making a good impression.

Automobiles still a rare sight on community streets, the arrival of a Ford inspector's shiny new Model T could not be missed. With the help of Missus-Schneider-eight-blocks-over, and Missus Nussbaum, who lived not far from Jane, Hannah, fully recovered now her mothering skills were once again needed, organized some of the older women into a link-chain of "Watchers." With the help of Missus Sullivan to the east, Missus Kowalski to the north, Missus Martinelli taking over the perimeter, as leaders, their patrol covered an area of more than forty blocks. Every street in Highland Park had at least two watchers who, on spying an inspector's T, was instructed to stop whatever she was doing; if she still had young children, shoo them over to the next-door neighbor, put on her hat and shawl and, not to be seen running, arrive at the house of the inspector's choice as though just "a friendly neighbor paying a call." They had all kinds of ruses to gain admittance without causing suspicion of why they had come.

Jane discovered three daffodils making their way up into the light of spring when the Sociological Department came to inspect her. A man of smallish stature, dressed as though about to attend an internment, potbellied and jowled, his fleshiness far more curvaceous than hers, finding she spoke English, told his interpreter to wait outside in the car until he was through. Politely, Jane ushered him into her parlor wondering if it would be correct to offer him coffee or if that might be construed as an enticing gesture.

"Store bought?" Sensitive to his tone of censure, Jane hesitated. "How much?"

"The drapes? I made them myself."

"Really? They don't look homemade."

"Well, I made them—so they are."

Mouth set, he checked his notebook. "One child, a boy, born June of last year. Correct?" Jane nodded. "Any more on the way?" Jane shook her head. "Going to be?"

"I don't know, ask my husband!" The moment the retort left her lips, Jane regretted it.

The heavyset face before her, flushed, anger glinted in the eyes. The man licked the tip of his pencil, noted something in his book.

"How many bedrooms?"

"Two."

"Let's go see them, shall we?" The inspector started for the stairs.

Jane followed. "The boy is asleep."

"Good. Two o'clock we suggest is the correct time of the day for a child that age to nap." The inspector mounted the stairs, running an inquisitive hand up the banister, checking for grime.

"Walls this color when you moved in?"

"No. My husband painted them."

"Peculiar choice. One could even say a radical one. Husband's a radical?"

"I don't know what that means. He is a toolmaker, he designs them."

"That, I know, lady." His eyes roamed the immaculate bedroom.

"Clean as a whistle. You sure you're Italian? Usually you people don't know what a decent home is. Live like animals and seem to enjoy it . . . Okay, I've seen enough up here!"

Hand shaking, Jane closed the bedroom door behind him. Flipping pages, the inspector descended the stairs.

"Religion?"

"Catholic." Jane said the first thing that came to mind.

"Drink?"

"Excuse me?"

"Inebriating spirits! How many bottles have you got in the house?"

"None."

"Oh, come on. You people swill the juice of the grape like hogs do slop."

"My husband doesn't!"

"Okay. Let's just have a look, shall we? Let's see what's in your kitchen cupboards."

Jane was so relieved to be far from the bedroom, she led the inquisitor into the kitchen without a moment's hesitation. His search was swift and thorough. Seeming resentful that he had not been able to unearth the proof of expected Italian debauchery, remarking that even the usual stench of garlic was missing from her house, he tipped his hat and left.

Trembling, Jane leaned against the closed door gulping for air, not quite sure if she was doing so out of relief or fury. There was a knock on the door.

Fearful the inspector had returned, Jane opened it. A distraught Missus Nussbaum stood on the threshold.

"Dear Lord in Heaven, please forgive—I have come too late—my Elsa—she swallowed a button just when I see the automobile so I had to hold her upside down and shake her till the button dropped out before I can run over. You alright? He not try anything with you?" Pushing her way in, she held Jane's shoulders, searching her face.

"I'm alright." Missus Nussbaum, not convinced, held her. "Really, I'm alright . . . my knees just feel funny, that's all."

"Come, we go sit and I make you some coffee. What a watcher I am! Couldn't even get here on time! And I ran, which I'm not supposed to. Don't know what Hannah will say when she hears!"

"We don't have to tell her, Missus Nussbaum. I won't."

"Thank you, dear, that's real nice of you. But guilty I am. Just think of it—if something had happened . . . my goodness gracious me! I would never have forgiven myself!" She fussed, made a pot of strong coffee, they drank and talked.

When finally convinced that everything was really alright, Missus Nussbaum hurried home to see what else her Elsa might have found to swallow in her absence.

Of course, Hannah found out. First, without upsetting her, she switched Missus Nussbaum's post to cover further down the street, reassigning Missus Zovanovitch to watch the upper portion of Louise Street that included Jane's house, saying that as Ukrainians came from far deserted plains of endless vistas, their eyes were keener. Besides, now her children were grown, they wouldn't swallow things anymore.

"Ninnie, God was looking down on you for sure. Here, have some," Hannah cut her a piece of strudel.

Jane shrugged, "I was just lucky."

"What? You tink it was just a lucky ting dat exact morning you washed all de windows, scrubbed all de floors even?"

"Well . . ."

"'Well' nutting! You were being protected, you silly girl! One day you will learn dat God look out for you, even when you never tink He does. When dat day come, I want to be around to see your face!" She poured more coffee. "What I still wonder, can't get out of my head, is why dey come to John! He's a long time big shot. De Boss knows his name and everyting!"

"Maybe because we're Italian—or, maybe they made a mistake?"

"Dose kind of snoopers don't make mistakes . . . but maybe you got someting dere wit de Italian idea. I hear dey always examine dem first. Den it's de Low Irish, de Russian Jews, de Hungarians and everyone else like dat before dey get around to de Germans like us and all de others who keep clean."

Wanting to help, Jane decided to join the Watchers—in a roving capacity. On specified days, she deposited Michael at Johann's house into Henrietta's care, then made her way to the Italian sections clustered near the Ford plant, walked the streets looking for the signs of a parked T, its driver waiting.

With Frederika, who was so bored she welcomed any distraction as long as it was ladylike, and some of the other wives, Jane also began a sewing circle, stitching samplers that after Fritz framed them, were handed out to families at risk to be hung in strategic places to catch a Ford inspector's eye. *Cleanliness Is Next to Godliness* was, of course, the one they did mostly. But there were others. *Duty Before Pleasure, Err Today—Repent Tomorrow, Gambling Is Father of Despair and Son of Avarice.* Serafina, who sometimes found time to help, once blocked out one that read, *Lie Down with Dogs and You Get Up with Fleas,* but Henrietta stopped her just in time. Like schoolgirls attending an embroidery class, they often laughed together while thinking of proverbs they would prefer to be stitching for the suspicious eyes of Ford inspectors. Smiling, Missus Fillapelli looked up from her embroidery frame. "How about *Mention the Devil and in He Walks!*"

Henrietta rethreaded her needle. "I've got one—*Search Others for Their Virtues, Yourself for Your Vices.*"

"*Seek Not What You Should Not,*" volunteered young Missus Kretchmer.

"*The Road to Hell Is Paved with Good Intentions,*" murmured Missus Sullivan, to which, Missus Zweig added, "*What Can't Be Cured Must Be Endured.*"

After that, the women stitched in silence. As her husband continued in his blinded adulations of his God, Henry Ford, Jane began to see him in another light less sanctified.

Before Easter, Jane's flower border at the end of the yard rewarded her care by producing six tulips. Erect as soldiers, egg yolk yellow, she tended them like newborn chicks. Hannah had suggested she cultivate a vegetable patch, but now she was glad she had splurged—planted flowers instead of sensible green. Carl's Rosie gave birth to twins, turning him into a boasting Papa. On hearing the news, Serafina was terribly upset, wringing her hands, wailing that as her clairvoyant power had forsaken her, all was lost she would fling herself off the highest cliff as soon as she found one. But when Stan explained that all she had gotten wrong was who had twins, not their actual arrival, she calmed sufficiently to accept their birth, even bringing each a twig of thyme, suspended from a silver ribbon, assuring the new mother that if hung above their beds, henceforth her offspring would be protected from all infections of the eye. Frederika, who was now with child, was heard to whisper to Rudy that she hoped Rosie's fate was not due them—for if she had two, at one time, she was sure she'd die; to which Serafina, hearing her, prophesied that as she would produce only one, her death, though a tragic one, would not occur for some years yet, Frederika had nothing to worry about. Dora, who had wished for children during her first marriage to the baker, still had not conceived in her second to Peter, began staying close to Rosie, hoping her aura of proven fertility might benefit her.

Everyone, even Zoltan, came to see Carl's new family, complimented the proud parents on the beauty of their two little girls, asked what names had been chosen for them. When Carl replied that because his daughters resembled delicate flowers, one was to be Violet, the other Rose, after her mother, Jane was reminded of her first American friends, wondered how they were, if they were still flowers residing with their generous aunt in that pretty house in the City of New York.

Rumpelstiltskin returned, didn't even stop to say hello, rushed into the Geiger parlor, flung open the piano, spun up the stool, flecked his fingers, pounded out a lilting rendition of "When You Wore a Tulip," singing the lyric in an amazingly rich tenor for so tiny a man. Finished, he justified his explosive entrance by explaining to a startled Hannah that, having just been taught this salute to the Easter Season, he needed to set it in his mind and fingers before it eluded him. He had also learned the latest hit "Shine on Harvest Moon," but that he knew and would perform it after supper. Hannah hugged her Ebbely before allowing him to escape to unpack, take a nice hot bath in her Pride and Joy.

Everyone was asked to attend the naming of Carl and Rosie's twins. A Catholic christening in itself impressive, an Irish-Polish one in a cathedral during Holy Easter made it that much more of an occasion no one wanted to miss.

Having seen an illustration depicting Mrs. Rockefeller attending the races, Jane copied her ensemble, using genuine imported chambray in the shade of ecru.

Stan at the wheel of his Touring, Serafina beside him in Easter finery of deep purple trimmed with jet, came to pick up Johann and his family. He in a new suit of light gray and matching derby, Henrietta and the girls in identical dresses of white batiste with china blue sashes.

Rumpelstiltskin, resplendent in a vest of cobalt blue embroidered in tiny fleur-de-lys, having only room enough for one passenger in his Runabout, drove Hannah in her summer white to the church.

Frederika, not yet showing sufficiently to cause embarrassment, wearing her favorite shade of palest green with new bonnet to match, walked on Rudy's arm to catch the Inter-Urban trolley, with John and his family, accompanied by Fritz, following behind.

Having been asked to be the godparents, Peter and Dora greeted them at the entrance to the church. They waited for Zoltan's arrival which, when he finally appeared, slightly out of breath, was spectacular! In a moment of uncharacteristic abandon, Zoltan had bought himself a complete morning suit, striped pants, tailcoat and all and, in order to do its splendor justice, had added pearl-gray spats and matching top hat. People entering the church thought he must be the groom of a wedding no one had heard was scheduled to take place.

"Zoltan! If Jimmy could only see you now!" exclaimed Rudy. "You look like you've been invited to take tea with the king of England!"

"Too much? You think this is too much? Maybe . . . the spats?"

"Don't let dem kid you." Hannah looked him up and down. "Smart! Like a *real* millionaire, so handsome you look. Vhy you not married—still living wit dat grouchy Mama, I don't understand. Girls crazy for a nice-looking man like you! . . . Come, everybody we go in . . . or all de front places vill be full vit strangers."

It was such a special occasion, everyone so festive, at their best—even Violet and Rose accepting water splashed onto their little heads without complaining—that Jane never once felt the urge to escape, get away from the cloying dominance of consecrated ground. Afterwards, they all met up at Carl's home for Easter treats and wine. While the babies slept, Johann's girls munched hard-boiled eggs making sure Michael didn't eat the brightly colored shells he found so pretty, the women admired each other's clothes, the men crowded into the small parlor, drank wine and talked.

Johann lifted his glass. "Here's to your girls, Carl!" The others joined in the toast. "John, I heard you may be one of the men going to San Francisco to help set up the company's exhibit?"

Peter took out his pipe. "What exhibit?"

"Remember last year, when the Boss wanted to show off the moving assembly line at the Michigan State Fair?"

"Sure, but we couldn't get it working in time."

"Well, my friend—now it is, so now Ford is going to show off his famous baby to the whole world at the San Francisco's Panama-Pacific Exposition!"

Fritz turned to John. "True? You really going all the way to California?" Carl spoke before John could answer. "Listen. It's not only the line the company wants to show off, I hear the Sociological Department is planning a display of its own."

"What in God's name can those people show?" Johann refilled his glass.

"The before and after?" murmured Zoltan.

"You're kidding! What are they going to do? Make some poor bastard and his brood stand there filthy, then wash the whole miserable bunch down, right there in public—before all the people?" Stan laughed derisively. "The reporters will have a field day!"

Carl put down his glass. "I don't think even that department, with all its do-gooders will dare to go that far!"

"They'll do something, though. Ford has his heart set on showing the country his many achievements, not only his fast method of producing Model Ts, but also as philanthropic industrialist." Zoltan held out his glass to Carl, who was pouring more wine.

"The Motion Picture Department is preparing a film, showing the assembly plant in motion," remarked John.

"Now, that *will* be a sensation!" exclaimed Fritz.

"So will the actual line display! It will take up a whole building of its own. Ford wants to assemble eighteen complete Model Ts—maybe even more, during a three-hour demonstration every single day."

For a moment, even the Ford men were stunned by the idea.

"My God!" Rudy shook his head. "Can that be done, John?"

"To tell you the truth, at this moment I'm not sure it can. But, Henry Ford has his mind set on this and that means . . ."

Ebbely interrupted him. "And that means, my dear automotive geniuses, that in San Francisco, city of superlative elegance and elitist culture, your so famous, revolutionary assembly system will be spitting out little black Lizzies like shit from a goat's behind!" Laughing, the men raised their glasses in agreement.

Peter, who had wanted to be a musician before becoming a wheel man, asked, "Is the Ford Band going to perform?"

"You mean the March and Two Step or the Concert Band?"

"Either one will for sure," said Fritz. "The Boss loves his bands about as much as he does his fairs."

"You've got to admit, they're great for keeping the name of Ford before the people," added Johann.

"And *that* sells more Lizzies!" Rudy drained his glass. Zoltan looked at Fritz. "Think we're going to make it to Ford's goal, giving buyers a rebate if we hit more than three hundred thousand in sales?"

"Well, we still have some time to go before next August, so—yes, I think it could be possible. John, what do you think?"

"You know me—I think—with Henry Ford, nothing is impossible!"

"Here we go!" his friends chanted.

"Well—you asked me!" John countered good-naturedly.

"Anyone got the latest news on the war?" Carl looked over at his friend. "What about your Russians, Fritz? They know anything?"

"All they know was that in Flanders, there were terrible casualties. The British attacked the German line at a place . . . wait a minute . . . starts with a CH . . ."

"That's Neuve Chapelle, I believe."

"Ebbely? How did you know that?"

"Louisiana. Their newspapers keep up with the war as though their own people are fighting over there. In a way, they probably are, being mostly of French descent."

"Two of me younger brothers are in the fighting!" In all the years that Rosie's father had lived in America, his speech had not lost the lilting proof of his Irish roots.

"Where, Mr. Haggarty?" asked Johann of their host.

"Their regiment, the Irish Fusiliers, are said to be somewhere near Belgium."

"Have any of you gotten any letters from home?" Peter looked worried.

"My parents wrote, mail from Holland isn't affected," answered Johann.

"You're lucky." Rudy sighed. "Since war was declared, I've had only one letter and that was written before the fighting began. Don't say anything to Frederika—but I am really worried. And, let's face it, we, as Austrians, are the enemy." Rudy looked at Fritz. "And so are you, my friend."

"I got first papers—I'm not an enemy!"

"Well, if the war goes on and America has to take sides, you will be, naturalization papers or not!"

"I've had mail from Italy—and all of it is infuriating!"

"What's the matter, John, your family refuse to leave?" asked Stan.

"You're damn right. How did you know?"

"Mine are too scared to budge out of Rumania."

"Mine are too loyal to the kaiser and the Fatherland . . . if you can swallow that!" Fritz grumbled.

"Mine are just undecided—like the whole damn country."

"John please don't take offense, but that is so typically Italian!" ventured Ebbely.

"You're so right! I have a good mind to go over there and haul them out myself!"

"With German submarines now threatening Atlantic shipping, you can't. Fortunately for your Missus—if you don't mind my saying so." Zoltan got up. "Sorry, I must leave. My mother . . . well, you know how it is. Carl, Mr. Haggarty, it was a splendid ceremony."

Everyone agreed, went to thank Rosie and her mother, then collected their ladies and started home.

Having been impressed by Jane's Easter attire, Frederika visited her the very next day. Never one suited to the routine of a conscientious wife patiently awaiting a husband's return to give meaning to her day, she often walked over to Jane's to rid herself of a few hours of boredom.

Having hung up Frederika's hat and shawl, Jane preceded her down the hall to the kitchen.

"Come, I'm ironing—there's fresh coffee on the stove."

Knowing Frederika preferred conversing in her mother tongue, Jane spoke in German, welcoming the chance to practice.

Seeing that she was not going to be served, Frederika poured herself a cup, asking if there was cream.

"I'm sorry. I only have milk—it's on the back porch."

"I'll take it black." Frederika sat sipping her coffee, not enchanted by its bitterness.

Jane dampened a shirt. "How are you feeling? Yesterday I thought you looked a little pale, but that could have been just the reflection from your dress. That shade of green can do that, sometime."

"Yes, I know, but it never has done it with me. My complexion has always been perfect . . . until now!"

"How many months before you're due?"

"About five I think." Frederika's voice held little enthusiasm.

Not knowing what to say, Jane continued her ironing. Michael, distracted from unraveling a ball of twine, crawled over to examine the hem of Frederika's skirt. She snatched it away from his possibly grubby fingers. He gave her a startled look, then unconcerned by her rejection, crawled back to the fascinating tangle of twine.

"Does this child ever cry?"

"Not very often. Why?"

"I hope ours won't. I can't abide screaming babies." Frederika took another sip of coffee as though only good manners required her to. "The dress you wore yesterday—I thought was very attractive. May I inquire where you bought it?"

"I made it myself."

"Really!"

"We could never afford for me to buy such an outfit."

"Well, knowing from my mother, who only wears the very latest styles to be purchased in Vienna, how expensive high fashion can be, I believe you." Frederika extracted a lace handkerchief from her reticule, blew her nose without making a sound. Fascinated, Jane wondered how she managed to do that.

"Jane, would you ever consider making me a dress?"

"If you like."

"Of course, I should insist on supplying the material as well as paying you for your time and labor."

"You have such a petite figure, so well proportioned, it wouldn't take much time at all."

"Of course, all this will have to wait until after my confinement. Now doing anything would be just a waste of time."

Sighing, Frederika rose, gingerly stepping over Michael, put her cup in the sink. Jane folded John's freshly ironed shirt.

"I could let out the waistband of some of your dresses in the meantime."

"Yes, that would probably be convenient. Well, I should be going."

Jane saw her to the door. Putting on her hat and gloves, Frederika thanked her for her hospitality, told her she could come over to her house to collect the clothes she would want to have altered, and left. Jane returned to her ironing not disturbed by Frederika's blatant snobbery, for she was used to it by now.

Waiting for the iron to reheat, her thoughts took flight. If Frederika was in such need of a seamstress that she was willing to pay her, maybe there were others who required the same, would pay for her services. Then, with the money earned, solely hers, maybe she could someday buy herself one of Mr. Singer's splendid sewing machines.

The very next day, Jane went to pick up her work from Frederika, came to an amiable arrangement concerning price and date of delivery and, with arms full of silken finery, raced home, eager to become a genuine needlewoman to distinctive ladies. She thought of putting a discreet sign announcing this in the front window, but knew that John would never allow such degrading proof of a wife accepting payment for what other women of class did only for pleasure or acceptable recreation, would shame his manhood. So she altered Frederika's dresses as though doing a favor, put the cents earned inside her special shoebox, next to Teresa's letter and said nothing.

April was nearly over when fire destroyed the great bridge that connected Detroit with beautiful Belle Isle. Hannah, already looking forward to their July Glory Day picnic like the year before, was terribly upset—just couldn't believe it had happened!

"How in *Himmel* are we going to get dere witout dat bridge? Fritz, mit a boat, I won't go! Everybody get seasick—so special picnic don't mean a ting. What a tragedy! How could such a ting happen?"

For days, Detroit's newspapers covered The Big Fire. No one spoke of anything else. For a short while, the war in Europe, gaining alarming momentum, took second place to a tragedy closer to home.

The sinking of the British luxury liner *Lusitania* by a German submarine with the loss of more than a thousand lives brought it back into stunned focus. With 128 American citizens among the dead, the country began to take the European conflict seriously enough to consider renouncing its neutrality and enter the war.

"Now we go to war!" Zoltan was so convinced he was already worried about whom he could get to look after his mother when he enlisted. Johann agreed, "I'm sure of it. Now we have no choice."

"You? They won't take you—you're a married man with a family."

John, who had brought his friends home to discuss the shocking news, nodded.

"None of us may be allowed to enlist."

"What the hell do you mean?"

"If we do go to war the skilled labor force of the country will be needed to produce the articles necessary to wage a war."

"Are we ready for this?" Carl asked knowing the answer.

"No, I can't think how. How can we be?" Fritz turned to his friend. "We make Ts, John . . . you think the Boss will convert to war machinery?"

"I've heard that on the battlefields the stench of rotting horse flesh is sometimes worse than that of the rotting corpses. So . . ."

Carl interrupted, "John, what are you getting at?"

"I think this war will end the use of horses and mules and what will take their place? Motorized transportation of course and Ford will lead the way."

Fritz tapped out his pipe. "Well, my friends, I go home to Hannah—let's wait a little and see what the president decides."

Woodrow Wilson determined to keep his reelection platform intact, chose to fight through diplomatic channels—reprimanded the Imperial German Empire for its unwarranted brutality against innocent neutral travelers, warning that should German U-boats try it again in the future, the United States would then have no choice but to consider the possibility of entering the war on the side of the Allies.

Their confidence in the man who had vowed to keep the nation out of war reaffirmed, most of America heaved a sigh of relief—went back to work profiting from a war, for now, removed from them. Only natural that public opinion would favor England, a country part of its heritage sharing a common language, after the *Lusitania* tragedy, the hatred of Germans and those nationalities supporting them began to surface. A slow-moving current of public emotion at first, it now gained momentum, that eventually would become a raging torrent. The first to feel its fledgling impact were the immigrant communities.

America, a nation having absorbed more than fourteen million immigrants on a global scale, now found itself a Declared Neutral, with a workforce mostly comprised of nationals stemming from countries locked in deadly conflict. Popular hatreds, their reasons lost amidst the ages, resurfaced, played into ever-ready bias and bigotry. Those of German origin found that by changing their names to more Anglo-Saxon forms, now not only aided their businesses but their acceptability as well. Schmidts became Smith, Herrmanns—Herman. Most, not finding an easy way to retain the root of their name, changed it altogether, others simply translated it. Schneiders became Taylors, Wassermanns—Waters, Muellers—Millers. Hungarians and others hailing from those areas of Europe where men were more swarthy, shaved off their identifying facial hair, achieved a more acceptable clean-cut image which, in turn, pleased Ford's Sociological Department no end.

Whereas euphoric nationalism was the driving force behind Europe's youth, eager to do glorious battle, nationalism within America's immigrant communities was far more complex. Where did their loyalties lie? With their adopted homeland, the one that had welcomed, given them shelter? Or, as was true for many, the homeland they planned to return to with fortunes made? Or, should their loyalty first be to themselves, the struggle it had cost to realize a dream? Brave flag waving for old loyalties, though laudable, many had learned through hard experience that survival offered more lasting rewards than impulsive patriotism. Many did leave, later to die on some battlefield.

Most stayed, many torn by guilt yet more than ever determined to make America their new homeland. Those fortunate to have brought families over helped those who did not know what had happened or might happen to theirs. Everyone waited for news from across the sea.

During this time of political and personal turmoil, the thousands of immigrant workers on Henry Ford's continuously moving assembly lines began to welcome the numbing effect of its repetitive, hypnotic monotony.

For John, having a family left behind, even in a country not yet at war, geographically still close enough to it, was cause for constant worry. Since the very beginning of hostilities, he had been writing, urging his family to leave Italy, join him in America. His parents' refusal did not deter him from insisting that at least then his sisters should be persuaded to leave, come live with him and his family in Highland Park. Getting no concrete answer, he kept writing, hoping, until May 23, when Italy, having finally decided which side would be the most advantageous to join, entered the war.

"Ninnie! Damn! Damn! Now it's too late! Those stupid fools! Thank God, at least Italy has chosen to throw in her lot with England and France. But now my hands are tied . . . I can't do a damn thing to help! If it had been only Celestina, she would have come. She's got spunk! But, Gina? She probably moaned and groaned about drowning at sea—too, too frightened of everything just like that stupid Camilla and, because of Gina, of course, Celestina stayed. Wait till I get my hands on those two. Stupid! Just stupid! Women! Thank God you're not one!" And John stormed out of the house. Jane, closing the door behind him, wondered what exactly he had meant by that.

Just before his first birthday, Michael decided the time had come to explore life from an upright perspective and, slightly off kilter, under his own steam, walked out into the beckoning world and tumbled down the porch steps. He wasn't hurt but his agonizing screams convinced Jane he must be. From then on, her life was hell. Quietly sewing—an impossibility. As a matter of fact, any activity that did not include her son—a preordained disaster. Whatever caught Michael's fancy, he ran towards, oblivious to any and all obstacles that happened to be in the way. It was as though the little boy assumed things would step aside to accommodate him when seeing him coming towards them.

When tables, chairs, doors, walls bumped into him, he ricocheted off them, sat on the floor stunned, looking at the obstacle as though surprised at why it had refused to move out of the way. If Jane hadn't been so harassed, she might have found her so determined son amusing but, for some reason, his unfettered freedom annoyed her. John, working on an idea of how to restrict Michael's adventurous spirit, built a hinged four-sided fence around him. Hannah, on first seeing this pen, sniffed, "Your Michael—he is now a chicken?" But when she saw he didn't seem to mind, had toys to occupy him within this private, safe domain, she began to accept it, saying that as John's clever invention seemed to work, next year maybe, he should build one to hold Carl and Rosie's twins.

Most early mornings, after John had left for work and before it was time to begin her daily duties, Jane stood on the front porch waiting for Mr. Henry to come down the street. It had been months now, since Teresa's letter and, although she was sure a convent, even one situated in France, would not be desecrated by war, she worried, needed to have Teresa tell her that she was safe. Also, though she had answered both Bela's and Eugenie's letters, written Camilla and Antonia, even her father of the birth of a son and received no answers, Jane figured one of these mornings Mr. Henry, conscientious mailman that he was, would just have to stop at her house.

One sun-drenched morning, once again exposed, free of his winter cocoon, he came, looked up at her waiting on the porch, waved a slender milk-white hand in her direction, smiled his devastating smile and then, passed her by. Only Mr. Henry could make not getting a letter, though fleeting, a sensual experience. Sighing, Jane went back into the house to cook and clean. Maybe he would stop tomorrow.

Frederika, very satisfied with the results of Jane's work, recommended her to a neighbor who was also with child. A fat lady to begin with, at first Jane had great difficulty in finding enough in the seams to let out, until she had the idea to use the material in the hem, working it cleverly into inserts in the bodice then putting a false backing for the hem of the skirt. The blossoming lady was so pleased to once again fit into her Sunday best, she told her friend, wife of the coal merchant, all about the Italian woman on Louisa Street who was so skilled with the needle.

Slowly, Jane accumulated cents until they added up to a whole dollar—then two. There was no need to conceal her special activity from her husband, for John rarely took notice of what held no interest for him.

At times aware that he had probably made an excellent choice after all, John was very satisfied with his wife. Her respect for his work, her willingness to take second place to it, endeared her to him. She functioned independently, never needed tedious cosseting or cavalier behavior to keep her in a pleasant mood, as so many wives seemed to require. Hannah's influence had been as constructive as he had known it would be when first he had decided to bring Jane into her orbit to benefit from her example. John liked to have things turn out correctly as planned.

Now, after two years together, he had become used to her. Not necessarily in the physical sense, nor an emotional one, but simply that she existed. Though at times this puzzled him, it did not disturb him unduly. As with most ambiguities relating to human behavior, John did not delve, accepting their existence as though of no overly serious consequences. What he could see, could feel with his hands, that John understood—intangibles eluded him. His meticulous intelligence was focused on conclusion, not the intricacies of its process. As Jane became symbolic of his male achievement as breadwinner, husband, father, John began loving her as such. Jane, feeling affection, began to love him for nothing more than that—he seemed to like her. And so their marriage solidified, both oblivious to the nullifying direction this might take. Except for a war too far away to cause them any physical harm, their life had become comfortable. So comfortable that John, taking an obliging woman to bed now and then, did not disturb its grounded structure. John did not consider his sexual release as an act of faithlessness, and Jane, had she known, would probably have thought the same for, during these scattered interludes of not being her husband's focus of desire, the reprieve from that constant fear of another pregnancy she found a pleasant change.

Serafina, predicting rain for the Fourth of July, persuaded her father to set up a tent he had once used in his garden for a meeting of the Brotherhood, then told everyone to come and have their picnics there. Glory Day dawned, bright and sunny, but by noon the skies had opened up, drenching everything in sight. Serafina triumphant, swept amongst the picnicking groups beneath the sheltering tent, greeting friends, accepting their homage as their clairvoyant savior.

Rudy, watching her, turned to Stan. "She's amazing! How does she do it? Even when she's wrong, in one way or another, she's right. Of course, you know Hannah is convinced your wife is a witch!"

"Hannah isn't the only one."

"You're joking!"

"I'm dead serious! The whole family is strange. You think we Rumanians, with our werewolves and legends of crows that pluck out the eyes of fresh corpses are weird? We are as pure as the driven snow in comparison to a house full of Sicilians!"

Rudy roared with laughter.

"What's so funny?" John joined them.

"Stan agrees with Hannah. His Serafina has the Evil Eye!"

"All Sicilians do."

"See! What did I tell you, Rudy. The whole lot are touched in the head!" Stan wasn't joking.

John laughed, "They're not exactly, crazy, Stan. Just strange—full of macabre superstitions . . . and dark secret rituals."

"Must be that constant hot sun beating down on their heads," Rudy chuckled, "makes them a little peculiar."

"Well, you three are having a jolly time. What's so amusing?" Ebbely joined them.

"Stan was criticizing his in-laws."

"Oh, my God! Not here!" Ebbely looked furtively over his shoulder. "The place is full of them! Some look quite ferocious. I saw one, with a distinct bulge under one armpit!"

"It takes one to know one!" Stan grinned.

"Yeah, Ebbely, got your trusty cannon with you?" John asked.

"Now please," Ebbely lifted a tiny hand, "I don't mean to offend, Stan, but *never* would I be so foolhardy as to venture into your father-in-law's domain carrying a concealed weapon! Dangerous! Very dangerous! Not being Italian, even more so! Shall we rejoin the ladies? Hannah's huckleberry pies look divine. John, I have tasted your Jane's lemon meringue—bliss! Absolute bliss!"

"You staying awhile this time?"

"No. In three days I will be on my way, heading towards trellised balconies, painted women, steaming cocoa for breakfast with flaky croissants—in a town that wakes by night, makes love by day."

"Hey, Ebbely, where is this paradise?"

"Ah, my poor deprived! Prisoners of cold machines and endless precision—New Orleans of course! Pampered harlot of the South! Once she has seduced you, a man is never the same again!"

The morning Ebbely left, he reached up, pulled Hannah's face down to his, gave her cheek the softest of kisses, then allowed her to straighten up again, as he put on his driving gloves. "Dear Lady, have no fear! I shall return, this time bearing pecan pralines that, once tasted, one never forgets—and real cocoa powder just for you—I'll stop off at John's to say good-bye." And he vaulted over the fake door of his Model T, squirmed over to the driver's seat, calling, "Beware of somber men coming to do God's work in the name of our saintly Henry! Keep those Watchers alert! Farewell! *Auf Wiedersehen!*"

The repeated honking of Ebbely's horn brought Jane running out of her house into the street.

"Tall Lady! I have come to say good-bye! Give that delightful son of yours a chaste kiss from me. Tell John to treat you kindly—I shall return before the chestnuts fall! Now, stand back, no more cranking—observe how my new special self-starter springs this heap of tin into instant action!"

It was truly an amazing feat to behold! She shivered, she quivered, she shimmied, puffed, rattled and shook—then—exploded! Shouting, "*Au revoir!*" Rumpelstiltskin and his Lizzie disappeared in a cloud of dust.

Soon, Missus Schneider would no longer warrant her appendage of eight-blocks-over for, despite the many advantages of being a Ford man, her Walter, feeling his country needed him, had decided to take his wife and bank account back home to Westphalia to take up arms against the enemy. Hannah, returning from wishing them a safe journey, stopped off at Jane's. Stirring her coffee, she sighed, shaking her head, "Why? Will you tell me why? Dat Walter give up best job he ever can have? Leave a fine free country to go shoot peoples? And for what will you tell me? . . . And anudder ting—dere goes de best midwife we got! What we do now for when you get next baby?"

"There isn't going to be a next." Jane lifted Michael down off his chair.

"Ha! Dat's what you tink!" Hannah took a bite of Jane's apple cake. "Dis good, Ninnie. You make it wit de dried apples like I tell you?"

"Yes, and I added a little molasses."

"Nice . . . but dat woman going, can't get over dat! What are we going to do?"

"For what? Missus Horowitz lives on the same street, so she can take over her post as Watcher—and I'm certainly not going to need her."

"What, your John not sleep with you no more?"

"Of course he does."

"Well, den what you tink is going to happen? Such tings a woman decides? Or God maybe? What you tink you are? Magician maybe?"

"Please don't worry, Hannah . . ."

"Dis war, even so far away, make everyting topsy-turvy . . . everyting is changing!"

"More coffee?"

"A little too warm. De udder night, my Fritz he says maybe better we change, our name is too German. To what? I ask, and he says that some at the plant just translate— so I ask, you want we should be now Mr. and Missus Fritz Violinist? He laughed but, whole ting is not so funny." Hannah bent down to Michael, scooped him out of his pen, and onto her hip. "Come, my Bubbeleh, we take a nice walk in de sunshine and get happy." She started out the door. "Ninnie, you know—I just tink—dat Missus O'Reilly, de one mit de ten children? For sure she's got to know what to do."

Jane carried their cups to the sink, began to wash them. Hannah's conviction that a second pregnancy was only a matter of time, completely unavoidable, disturbed her.

Hannah insisted everyone attend the first graduation ceremony of the Ford English school, scheduled to be held on July 25. She argued that as her Boys had been such fine volunteer teachers, it was only right they witnessed the triumphant fruit of their labor. Besides, as Heinz-Hermann would be amongst the graduates, she was forced to go and needed company. She had confided to Jane that now her nephew had learned English, she hoped he would get himself other work—far from Highland Park, preferably out of the whole State of Michigan—IF she was lucky!

"I know it is not nice to say, but I can't help it! Now he makes friends with bully boys. Every night he goes—comes back—sometimes in de morning. When I ask—he snaps—none of your business . . . I worry—maybe he gets mixed up wit bad sort. Yesterday, you know what he says? Yellow peoples not civilized, dat's why not get ahead as good as white peoples. And colored peoples—dey come from Africa, where dey like animals in de jungle and dat white men brought dem to America so to make dem civilized. Can you believe it? And he says dis in front of Fritz—so you can imagine de trouble! But, you know what? Dat boy just kept right on insisting—shouting every word was true—because he was quoting direct what is written in de Ford Guide schoolbook. You tink dat can be true? I don't believe it. Fritz said in private to me, he is going to get one of dose school books and see if such tings really are written in dere."

Dressed in lederhosen held up by suspenders embroidered with stag heads, his Tyrolean hat sporting the obligatory boar's brush, Heinz-Hermann stood amongst Rumanians decked out as colorful gypsies, Greeks in white pleated tutus, Hollanders in perked caps and wooden shoes, Armenians in home-spun robes, Albanian goatherds in furry vests, Russians in banded tunics and tall leather boots, Italian organ grinders, only their monkeys missing, every nationality represented, garbed as though attending a theatrical costume party. The children amongst the crowd of spectators enjoyed it the most. Especially when the vast horde of adorned men upon the stage began to move down a makeshift gangplank of a cardboard ship, received diplomas, then filed obediently down into what looked like a huge black cauldron representing a melting pot, THE FORD ENGLISH SCHOOL written across its front, to be stirred with a mammoth ladle, only to reappear a short while later from out of its depth completely transformed. Every man now in a proper suit, shirt, and tie, all looking alike—newly reborn, waving little American flags in celebration of their joyous transit to Standardized Americanization, courtesy of Henry Ford.

Jane thought the whole spectacle hilarious but, as everyone was cheering, not laughing, she kept her amusement to herself. It surprised her that Hannah, even Fritz applauded as enthusiastically as the people around them.

After the ceremony, Heinz-Hermann preened, accepting congratulations, slaps on the back, as though he alone had achieved something truly laudable. Jane held back from the effusive mood, bothered by something she could not as yet name but certain that, when she could, it would turn out to be somehow disturbing.

Arrived home, she changed, put away her good clothes, gave Michael his bath, fed him supper, put him to bed refusing to read him a story because he had had enough excitement for one day. Calling to John to wash up for supper, she went downstairs. They ate in silence. Neither had much to say. Later, John read his paper while she mended, trying to sort out in her mind what was bothering her. She knew it wasn't just the rather ridiculous spectacle of grown men dressing up only to undress, then re-dress themselves. It was much more than that. Perhaps it was why they had done so, their acquiescence, their willingness to obey any dictum of Ford's even if that meant making fools of themselves? Had they no pride? Or, did they perhaps not even realize what had been demanded of them—that dressing up like children for a costume party, performing the ritual assigned to them, would make such fools of them? Frightened people desperate to conform, seeking safety in acceptance, allowed many abuses to be done them. Maybe that was what disturbed her so—the need of so many exploited that had made that day's entertainment possible.

John folded his paper.

"It's been a long day. I'm glad Hannah made us go, just goes to show what can be done if someone really cares. They'll all remember Ford alright!"

"Yes."

"I'm off to bed. Coming?"

"I just want to finish this."

"Don't forget the light. *Buonanotte.*"

Alone, Jane stitched by the light of the single lamp.

12

On the first of August, the Ford Motor Company announced that as 308,213 automobiles had been sold during the previous year, it would begin mailing out fifty-dollar rebate checks, representing about 9 percent of the purchase price of a Model T. The final tally would eventually come to more than fifteen million dollars dispensed—but, once again, Henry Ford had captured the nation's headlines, this time as the self-made millionaire whose word was his bond.

The first transcontinental telephone communication was achieved from New York all the way to San Francisco and Heinz-Hermann left to be an apprentice butcher in Chicago, Illinois. To celebrate all these wonderful happenings, Hannah invited everyone to a special supper. For such a festive occasion, Stan and John brought red wine, Rudy and Johann, white, Carl and Peter, buckets of beer, Zoltan a fine after-dinner brandy, Fritz, not to be outdone, opened a new bottle of his potent Schnapps. Only Ebbely was missing.

Zoltan never made it home that night, needed to be bedded down at Hannah's, Rudy and Johann, singing naughty schoolboy songs, had to be guided home by resigned wives, while Rosie and Dora herded their weaving husbands to the Inter-Urban trolley stop like unruly sheep. Stan couldn't even find his automobile, let alone the crank. Serafina, very furious, steered him to it, ordered him to get in. As he was valiantly attempting to do so, she lost patience, gave him such a shove he went flying into the back seat, where he remained—out cold. Putting on his duster, crank in hand, Serafina marched to the front of the Touring, started it on the very first rotation, clutching her skirts, climbed up, engaged the gears, trod on the pedals and drove off. Hannah and Jane, who had helped her get Stan out of the house, stood transfixed, watching the ruby glow from the tail lantern disappear. A woman driving an automobile? That, they had never seen!

"Dat crazy Serafina! She is really someting!" Full of admiration, not yet quite over the shock, Hannah went back inside to make sure Fritz could get up the stairs, find their room. Jane, very envious of Serafina's amazing accomplishment, wishing she too knew how to drive, followed—to lead John to his hat, and show him the way home.

Stan having volunteered to drive John and his surprise home from work, helped him carry it around to the back porch.

"I can't stay, John. We're having a meeting tonight."

John looked at his friend, "Careful, Stan."

"I'm always careful."

"Who's coming? Any of my men?"

"I know how you feel about union talk, better you don't know. I got to go. Say hello to Jane for me. She still angry about the other night?"

"I don't know. With Jane, you never know!"

"You're lucky. My wife hasn't spoken to me since! I'm off, see you tomorrow." Stan hurried back to his waiting automobile.

"NINNIE, I'm home!" John called through the screen door. "Come out here! I've got something to show you!"

Puzzled why he was at the back, dodging the long curls of sticky flypaper hanging down from the kitchen ceiling, Jane stepped out onto the porch.

"Ninnie! Here it is! Your Izze boite!"

"Did I ever pronounce it that badly?" Jane laughed, not quite believing what stood before her.

"Yes, I liked it."

"Really? But now I can say it properly."

"I know. Well? You like it? It's a Siberia, secondhand; I bought it off one of the Belgians going back."

"Oh, it is marvelous! Now the milk won't curdle and the butter won't melt! I can even keep meat! Thank you, John!"

"Well? Come on, say it." Jane, suddenly shy, hesitated. "Come on . . ."

"I-C-E B-O-X." She said it carefully, pronouncing it as though announcing a royal personage arriving at a palace ball.

"But first, I have to repair the handles, then you can give it a good cleaning. Don't worry, I'll be adding the extra cents to your weekly household money for the ice."

While John was busy repairing their latest luxury, Jane, so excited she forgot to put on her hat, ran over to Hannah's to tell her the news. Duly impressed, Hannah said she would inform Mr. Kennec that he had a new customer on Louise Street.

Repaired, its four brass handles polished with rotten stone until they gleamed, its zinc interior scrubbed, its oak exterior polished to a golden hue, commanding Jane's kitchen like a piece of imposing furniture; each time she saw her "izzbox," Jane felt a surge of prideful ownership.

The iceman and his polar bear–adorned wagon arrived the very next morning.

"Whoa—Molly! This here is a new stop! Here lives that Italian Missus we met, used to live at our friend, the German Missus. Remember? So get it set in your head—don't want to be having to pull you up each time!"

Mr. Kennec always talked to his shaggy Molly. Being a solitary man, Molly was like his better half. He relied on her easy companionship, her warm trusting nature to serve without complaint. Shooing aside the string of children that always trailed an iceman's wagon in summer hoping for watery chunks to suck, Mr. Kennec positioned a large block, raised his mighty pick and struck, showering them with the frozen bounty they had hoped for. Jubilant, the children scampered about, picking up pieces, licking them quickly before they melted away.

Having heard the clip-clop of his horse, Jane was ready and prepared. Porch and kitchen floor covered with newspapers, a tall glass of lemonade waiting.

"Good morning, Mr. Kennec. Nice to meet you again."

"Mornin', Ma'am." The iceman touched his cap with his free hand. "Much obliged. Missus Geiger, she says you'll be wanting twenty-five pounds, correct?"

"Yes, please. Are you going to give me a card—so I can put it in the window?"

"Got one right here!" Mr. Kennec rummaged in his jacket pocket, fished it out, handed the card to her with a flourish. The block of ice on his shoulder was beginning to melt down his back.

"Fine-looking box you got there. Mighty fine!" He stood back, surveying the icebox, taking its measure. Jane lifted Michael out of his pen onto her lap, telling him to watch the Big Man, both waited for the performance to begin. A breathless moment—suspended in time—then—a mighty CRACK! And silver fireworks spewed about the kitchen. Michael screamed with glee! The block fit like a glove.

"MO! Mo!"

"What's that little tyke yelling, Ma'am?" Mr. Kennec sheathed his weapon, wiped his face with a red bandanna.

"That's his word for more." Jane returned a very disappointed Michael to his pen. Being such an amiable child, he didn't cry, just gave his mother a look that spoke volumes.

"Please, I fixed for you lemonade. I hope it's how you like it." Jane opened her cookie tin and counted out the fifteen cents.

Mr. Kennec drained his glass, scooped up the coins. "Fine lemonade, Ma'am. Much obliged! Mornin', Ma'am."

"Mr. Kennec . . ." Surprised, he turned at the door. "Would your horse like a carrot?"

"You bet she would, Ma'am!" Jane handed him a fat one. "Maybe your little tyke like to give it to her? She's real gentle, my Molly. No cause to fear she'll nip him."

So, Michael, with a little help from the iceman, fed his very first horse, touched her velvety nose and was in seventh heaven. From then on, next to his father and Ebbely, both of whom he adored, Mr. Kennec became the man he most waited to see.

Jane had the best time with her icebox. Every day was another festive occasion. Just lifting out a bottle of milk, still pourable—not curdled to a gelatinous stinking muck—was cause for celebration, not to mention the taste of butter, not turned rancid. Now she could even keep meat for more than a few hours in summer and, after she had plucked and singed a chicken, keep it for cooking the next day! She found that just having food keep seemed to give her more time to do what before had to be neglected. Next to Hannah, Jane's icebox became her very best friend.

Not wanting to neglect her education, once she had finished reading Mr. Emerson, whom she secretly hoped never to have to read again, she borrowed a book from Zoltan by one of his favorite Russian writers. Now, each day, she finally had the time to read it. She liked the way it was written so much, she resolved to learn Russian one day so that she could read *Anna Karenina* in its original form and, perhaps then, understand more clearly why emotion, particularly the one of brooding passion, seemed so terribly important.

Jane didn't mention any of this to her husband, fearing he might discourage her choice of reading matter or, worse, replace it with another example of what he and the Boss considered suitable. She didn't question that Henry Ford was a genius, but if that necessarily encompassed intellectual acumen, she was beginning to doubt. Jane had her eye on a book that Rumpelstiltskin owned. The rotogravure on its flyleaf, of a man standing up on a thrashing whale in a violent sea had caught her fancy. Surely that had to be an exciting story but, when she found the chance to ask if he would lend it to her, the little man shook his head, saying that *Moby Dick* could not be considered proper reading matter for a lady, so, very disappointed, she asked Zoltan if he would lend her one of his Russians instead.

Mornings became crisp—the smell of fallen leaves was in the air when Jane finished her Russian romance, rather sorry she had been right about its central character. Killing oneself for love was not to Jane's taste. Suicide, on the whole, she thought was a self-indulgent act. This had nothing to do with the Church's condemnation of it. Jane's judgment lay in her belief that supreme egotism was necessary to execute such an act of self-annihilation, without regard to its tragic influence on those left behind.

Had someone told Jane that her intelligence did not always fit her simple origins or station, she would not have known what they were talking about, for she didn't know that she was intelligent. Her inner need to learn that drove her, she recognized as only an appendage to her need for self-betterment which, in turn, represented to Jane the logical progression to longed-for freedom. If once achieved what form such liberation would take, what she would do with it and why this should be so all-important in the first place, she did not analyze, nor would she have been able to. In Jane's day, one did not delve into one's psyche. Such indulgent, mystical elitism was the private realm of poets and philosophers.

Mostly Jane came to her conclusions through instinct, completely unaware that it was her intelligence that guided it. The nuns had taught her well, but as they so often seem to do, in reverse. By their very insistence that unassailable rote, not questioning, was education, they had taught Jane to always do so.

She kept most of her arrived-at opinions to herself, devoured any book she could get her hands on and wished she, like the men, had interested friends to discuss things with. She missed those stimulating evenings spent eavesdropping in the Geiger parlor. The boarders, talking about their work, the exciting things she had listened to and learned. John rarely spoke to her of his work and, except for his precious Miss Evangeline, probably considered all women lacked the mental capacity necessary to understand things mechanical and so Jane never asked, thereby avoiding him telling her so. At most Sunday suppers, she now found herself relegated to the circle of wives busy in the kitchen whose topics of conversation centered mostly around food, children, and household costs. Sometimes there were snippets of Ford gossip but these too concerned home and family. How young Mr. Edsel, so handsome, now all grown, would soon have to marry, have sons to carry on the great name of Ford, speculations on who he would choose to be his lucky bride and how she would have to be a most refined young lady of whom the Boss and his Missus Clara could approve. The latest news of the great Ford mansion fast nearing completion, that they were always eager to discuss.

Jane was far more interested in hearing about the great power house that Ford had built for himself to operate all electrical and mechanical systems for his vast estate. This marvel was rumored to be so magnificent, its construction and design so advanced that it was said even Mr. Edison, when taken through it, had been duly impressed. Sometimes, when the talk veered towards fashion, Jane's interest was caught but its range was limited to standard articles of clothing and what mail-order catalogs had to offer. Inquiring privately of the other Ford wives what their husbands might have told them of new and exciting things happening at the plant was useless. As Serafina was the only one who knew the art of driving, Jane had hoped she might be her best source for automotive news, but spells and potions were usually uppermost in Serafina's mind and now that she too was expecting, her concentration was fully focused on producing a male heir worthy of his awesome Rumanian-Sicilian blood line and the name she had chosen for him, Guido Salvatore.

Of all the Ford wives, Hannah would have been the best informed, but even she believed that machines and men belonged together, needing no female interference. Jane, left to her own devices, resolved to keep her eyes and ears open, find a way to keep up with what was happening at the Ford plant, all by herself. For Jane, a little house in Highland Park was not the world nor marriage a completed universe.

The chestnuts had just sprung from their spiked armor, when Rumpelstiltskin, true to his word, reappeared, his arrival heralded by the startling sound of a resounding Klaxon. Being Friday, their noodle day, both Hannah and Jane ran out of the Geiger house to see who was making such a strange noise and there, proud as a courting peacock, sat Ebbely behind the wheel of a brand-new Model T Sedan.

"Ah, both tall Ladies at once! Perfect! Step right up! Step right up! See the work of art presented here!" Imitating a sideshow barker, the little man waved a beckoning arm. "Behold, before your very eyes, this superb apparition—the Marvel of the Age, finally fully enclosed, therefore draftless—and it doesn't stop there! Observe—not one but TWO central side doors, the two-piece windshield, the high steel radiator shell—and this, the most astounding of all inventions," he paused for effect, "electrified headlamps! And now, cast your astounded peepers on this—the pièce de résistance! An OVAL-SHAPED WINDOW IN THE REAR! . . . Step right up Ladies, climb in—have no fear, experience the thrill! No need for scarves, hats or shawls, warm as toast inside . . . forget your troubles and take a spin!"

Eager to obey, Jane suddenly remembered, "Oh! No! I forgot the boy!"

"Well, go get him. The more the merrier!"

"Is it safe for a child?"

"Would I be sitting here if it wasn't? Hurry! I can't hold this beauty much longer—she's rarin' to go!"

Jane sprinted, grabbed Michael, ran back out, clutching child and skirts climbed into the back of the elegant sedan.

"Everyone in? Please note that cranking is no longer necessary! And we're off! . . . Coming through Winona, I heard a new poem . . . !" Ebbely shouted over the noise of the motor. "It's called 'The Big Cars Lament,' I'll recite as we go!

> *"I wish I waz a little Ford*
> *A-runnin' right along;*
> *I wouldn't need to wheeze and sigh,*
> *I'd sing a different song."*

Beside him, holding on for dear life, Hannah yelled, "Ach! What excitement! *Mein Gott!* Never have I gone outside witout my hat on! What will de neighbors tink!"

"They'll be gnashing their teeth bile-green with envy!"

"Ja, dat's for certain! What a tragedy Missus-Schneider-eight-blocks-over not here no more—can't see dis—knock her socks off!"

"Knock off more than her socks!" Ebbely giggled, enjoying himself enormously.

"Now don't you get naughty just because you got yourself a new so swanky Lizzie!"

"Ah! Just a little cuddle? See, I can steer with only one hand, so give me a little squeeze! . . . You two in the back, cover your eyes! Hannah and I are going to spoon!"

"Well, now we know! All dat fancy-prancy mit dose Louisiana floozies has got you crazy in de head! You take me home dis minute! I get out de castor oil, give you a dose to clean you out good! Never heard of such a ting! Cuddling and spooning mit a proper married lady in a machine dat's moving!"

A little daunted, eyes lowered, Ebbely peeked at Hannah, saw she was desperately trying not to laugh and, swinging his Lizzie around on a dime, announced that before returning Hannah to her domicile, he was taking Jane and the little prince home, for what he had in mind, chaperones were better not present. Then, in a high falsetto, burst into the latest flivver song, urging his happy passengers to join him. "Henry Ford was a machinist,

> *"He worked both night and day*
> *To give this world a flivver*
> *That has made her shivver*
> *And speeded her on her way.*

Now he is a millionaire,
But his record is fair,
He is humanity's Friend."

Everyone came to see Rumpelstiltskin's splendid sedan—the men asking their questions of how it performed, while the ladies admired the elegance of the oval window and opulent use of glass. Standing apart, Fritz glowered.

Ebbely, knowing why, walked over to him. "I agree, my friend. Shocking—simply shocking!"

"Ja! First it's leatherette—that was bad enough—now we work cloth? . . . What's next!"

"But, Fritz, the cloth upholstery is only used in the closed-in model . . . or so I heard!"

"Yes . . ."

"So?"

"Duesenberg doesn't."

"Oh, come on . . . you can't compare a mighty Duesenberg with a Ford!"

"I know—but there was a time when . . ." Fritz let the thought hang.

"The rich man's automobile and . . . what does your boss call it? 'The automobile for the common man'?"

"Yes . . ."

"Well, my friend, as in life, such are separated from each other by a social chasm far too wide to cross."

"Still . . ." Fritz looked longingly at the shining sedan, "build up the back trimming, if it was done in black cowhide, with a half-moon needle in French pleat . . . would look marvelous."

"Don't make me wish for it! Cloth it is and even for seven hundred and forty dollars, cloth it will have to be. Don't lose sight of the fact that, for every Duesenberg sold, Ford sells a thousand Ts. Just remember and be grateful that there are more common men in this world than millionaires."

"Ja, we make lots of money, give everybody 'The Universal Car.' But, I miss the old days when with our hands we worked, could make beautiful things."

"Never mind, Fritz." Ebbely pulled his sleeve, called to the others. "Stop fawning over my new sweetheart! Hannah is waiting . . . let's eat!"

Carl helped himself to more pot roast.

"You vant de gravy?"

"No, thanks, Hannah. I still got plenty. Sorry about Rosie not coming, but with the twins, it's not easy. I see Rudy and Frederika aren't here and Henrietta either—anything wrong, Johann?"

"No, no. Frederika wasn't feeling well, so Henrietta thought she better stay—just in case."

"Isn't she about due?"

"Still another six weeks, Carl," Jane answered him.

Ebbely giggled. Carl turned to him. "What's so funny?"

"You—the new father! Suddenly so aware of a lady's due date! I can remember a time when if something hadn't anything to do with your precious magneto, it just didn't exist! How the mighty have fallen! Ahh, the abyss of normalcy!"

Carl laughed, "Right you are! Ah, the good old days!"

Ebbely stopped eating. "You too? Fritz was just saying the same thing. What's wrong?"

"I don't know, maybe it's just like one of Fritz's feelings."

"My God. I hope not!" Zoltan reached for the beer pitcher. "I can't take any more trouble. My mother is driving me crazy. She refuses to learn a word of English, says she doesn't have to because she's going back to Bulgaria. I try to explain that she can't because there is a war raging—but does that make an impression? No! She's going and that's that! Yesterday, I came home and found her sitting on her trunk by the front door, ready, waiting for me to take her to catch a ship. Couldn't understand why I didn't take her. The way the war is going, there may not even be a Bulgaria when it's all over. You know, I am beginning to think I should have gotten married like all of you instead." Zoltan sneezed into his napkin.

Hannah came in, bearing a huge bowl of coleslaw. Ebbely clapped his hands, delighted.

"John," Johann helped himself to the slaw. "Have you heard anything from Jimmy?"

"No, not since that first letter."

"I hear that the Red Cross organization is going to help with mail from the front."

"Anyone see that item in the *Ford Times*?"

"No. What about, Fritz?" Peter wiped the last bit of gravy off his plate with a piece of bread.

Jane, on her way to the kitchen, stopped to listen.

"It seems some students at Harvard and Yale got together, raised enough money, sent seventeen Model Ts as ambulances over to France."

Johann leaned back in his chair.

"Remember? Jimmy predicted our Lizzie would go to war."

"Yes, she'll show them a thing or two!"

"Hope he gets to see her in action!"

"*Mein Gott!* Johann—you want our fine Jimmy to get hurt?"

"Hannah, not as a passenger . . . I only meant—"

"Wonder where he is," Fritz interrupted, voicing what was on all their minds.

Ebbely breached the ensuing silence by complimenting the cook, waxing euphoric over the sensitive seasoning in her onion gravy. The women cleared the table, the men, waiting for dessert, talked of war.

Across the sea, tough Lizzie was taking a mere war in her stride. Built to withstand, maneuver the gumbo mud, mire, ruts, gullies, furrows, the appalling conditions of rural America's roads, the scarred landscape of war in Europe didn't faze the Model T. Shell holes, mortar craters, torrential rains that created rivers of impassable mud, nothing stopped it. Where Tin Lizzie had to go, was needed, she somehow always managed to get to. In the front trenches, soldiers began to look for her, cheering her on as she sped across the battlefield under fire, picking up their wounded.

Whenever a new story of their Lizzie's bravery reached the Ford men, they thought of Jimmy Weatherby and his prediction that she would turn out to be a true heroine, wondered where he was, hoped no harm would come to him.

In the cozy kitchen, curled in his wash basket, now too small for him, Michael slept while Hannah and Jane added new layers to snakes, others waiting, curled in their basket at their feet. Winter would be early this year. Already the morning skies had that deadened look, as though they too dreaded what was in store for them.

"You wit child, child?" How did Hannah always know such things? Without looking up, Jane nodded. "When?"

"Easter, maybe."

"Good time, spring. Summer better, warmer but springtime okay too."

They worked in silence. Michael dreaming, smiled.

"John know already?"

"No. So early yet. I wanted to be sure."

"Maybe he not happy?"

"Oh, no. He accepts such things."

"What you mean wit dat?" Hannah rethreaded her carpet needle with button thread.

"He's sensible. Anything he knows he can't change, he learns to live with." Hannah, stabbing her needle through the belly of her snake, acknowledged this with an offhand, "Aha!"

Jane looked up. "I know your 'Ahas'! What are you thinking?"

"You got me, Miss Sharpie. What I tink is, 'sensible' don't make hot stuff between de sheets! Dere! You wanted to know? You know!"

Jane's perpetual astonishment at Hannah's gift for hitting any and all nails squarely on their head did not hinder her answering laughter. "Hannah, you're really naughty! What would Fritz say if he heard you talk to his John's Missus that way?"

"After ten years, he hear me plenty. So? You stop dodging and answer? Or what?" Silent, Jane fished out another snake needing repair from the basket. Hannah knew when not to push. "You know dat our China Dolly is also?"

"Yes. They came over to tell us. Johann was so excited—like this was his first! Henrietta too. Their girls, being excited, I can understand—but . . ."

"Johann is hoping dis time it will be a son. Every man want dat. And China Dolly—she just happy she can still have more."

"I suppose so."

"Also, dis new baby will be dere first real American! Dat make them happy. Even if it turns out dey get just anudder girl, American is American! No matter what!"

"Don't let the Boss hear you say that."

"And why, Ninnie?"

"Well, I found out that no women are included in the Five-Dollar-Day profit-sharing plan, because Mr. Ford said he expects women to marry."

"So? What's wrong wit dat? Every girl want to find a man to take care of her, only right! And what dat have to do wit being true American of which we were talking?"

"Well—oh, it's not important." Michael, having lost his dream, sucked his thumb. The women sewed . . . "I read . . ."

"Still reading? Remember when you first come, Ninnie? Such a young old country girl you were and I let you creep up to de attic to read . . . let on to nobody your secret? Nice time, dat."

"All the time you knew?"

"Sure, in my house—I know what people do."

"Now I can read new news. When John is finished with his *Free Press*, I take it!"

"He not mind?"

"I don't think he notices."

Hannah swallowed an *Aha!*

Jane picked up another snake. "The other day I read there is a woman who is making speeches about . . . the words they used was '*birth control*.' The paper said this woman is planning to start a place where she can teach women all about family planning."

"You know what, Ninnie? I tink sometimes you read too much." Hannah, finished with a snake's eye, cut the thread. "The name of dis crazy lady? You remember?"

"I think it's Singer . . . no, no, Sanger . . . that's it! Margaret Sanger. Would any woman really dare to go to a place like that, Hannah?"

"Not a lady for sure! But dat poor Missus O'Reilly? She could use some of dat *controlling*, whatever dat is."

Jane began to pack up her sewing box.

"I wonder what she teaches?"

"Don't you get any fancy ideas! It's got noting to do wit you. Now controlling— all over for you anyway!" Seeing Michael was awake, Hannah lifted him out of his basket. "Got to get a bigger basket for him . . . save dis one for de next . . . Bubbeleh, you want now a little applesauce?" Michael hugged her neck. "Ninnie, you making here with me de noodles tomorrow, like always?"

"Yes."

"Dora, she says she wants to learn—so I said sure, come—so we won't say nutting, okay?" Hannah, suspecting that Peter's wife might be barren, took extra care not to indulge in happy talk of expected babies whenever Dora was present.

While Hannah fussed over little Michael, Jane started to assemble their belongings in the hall. It was late and she still had supper to prepare. Rumpelstiltskin, coming down the stairs, saw her, whispered, "My dear, may I speak with you?"

"Of course, Ebbely."

"Not here. I have news of a private nature." The little man led Jane into the parlor, closed the door behind them. Jane wondered what might be wrong. "Please, do sit—looking up at you . . . my neck . . . well, you know." Jane sat. Ebbely settled himself on the footstool at her feet. "Now, that's better. Missus Jane, I will come right to the point. On my last trip I had the opportunity of making the acquaintance of your *friend*," he stressed the word as though wishing he could use another . . . "Mademoiselle Eugenie."

"Oh, Ebbely, I am glad—but I didn't know you were in Charleston?"

"I wasn't. The *Lady* . . ." Again he hesitated over the word. ". . . in question, now resides in New Orleans. It is there that we met."

"Eugenie *said* she wanted to visit there because everyone spoke French."

"Well, yes. As you say, that is the preferred language in the quarter." For some reason, Ebbely seemed ill at ease.

"And? Did she buy your peignoirs? I was sure she would be just the type to really appreciate them."

"Actually, she purchased three."

"Three! You see, I was right. She is the type to *lounge*."

"Undoubtedly the type." Ebbely squirmed, cleared his throat, "Miss Jane, may I speak plainly?"

"Of course." Jane had never seen him so unsettled.

"Your friend, Mademoiselle Eugenie, is employed . . ." Jane, about to speak, was stopped by his warning frown. ". . . as a painted lady of the evening in New Orleans's most frequented house of pleasure."

Rumpelstiltskin wiped his brow with his silk handkerchief.

Jane, wide-eyed, wondered if she had understood him correctly.

"A house of pleasure?"

"A brothel, dear Lady. A place of carnal pleasures where money changes hands!"

"Oh!" Though shocked, Jane's first reaction was that Ebbely was far more uncomfortable than she. "Poor Eugenie. She had such lofty dreams coming to America. Please, Ebbely—tell me—how is she?"

Very relieved Jane hadn't swooned dead away from such shocking news, the little man beamed.

"In excellent health. Most attractive. Quite the reigning queen of the whole establishment. All the girls so green with envy—they would like nothing better than to scratch her eyes out. That is, all except the high color ladies. Those cinnamon beauties are in a class of their own!"

"High color?"

"Octoroons. Gorgeous creatures much maligned. Degraded misfits belonging nowhere, they live with daily cruelty, so men can buy what society denies them."

"Really." Jane was fascinated.

"Goodness me! No, no! This is not a proper subject for a lady's ear. Please forgive me. I simply thought you should know under what circumstances your friend now finds herself. May I suggest that you do not tell John any of this. He would most assuredly be angered by your interest and, justifiably, upset with me for my part in it."

"Ebbely, could you give me that New Orleans address?"

"What? Certainly not! Very unseemly, not at all proper, Miss Jane!"

"Please! I promise no one will know. I won't even tell Hannah!"

"I should hope not! If she knew I even went close to such naughtiness, she'd flay me alive!"

"Ebbely, Eugenie may need a friend. Oh, I know—I could write, then give you the letter to deliver next time you go."

"Go? Go where?"

"To the house of pleasure." Ebbely jumped up, nearly toppling the footstool. "Well! Really! You believe I frequent such places on a regular basis?"

"Ebbely, I only thought . . ."

Hands on little hips, standing his ground, Rumpelstiltskin, eyes ablaze, challenged, "I know exactly what you thought! Miss Jane, though you are a lady, still here and now, I shall give you a piece of my mind. I may be small of stature but never, ever, have I had to purchase my pleasures. Always such have been offered me as beguiling gifts to accept or refuse as I chose. Only my wares I sell—NOT my pride!" Quite overcome, Rumpelstiltskin plopped back onto the footstool.

"Please! I didn't mean it that way! Truly! I only assumed that as painted ladies probably have to do a lot of *reclining*, you would go there often to supply them with your beautiful selections."

"My, my. I must humbly beg your pardon. Don't know what came over me. You are quite right of course. More and more, it seems that truly superb intimate apparel is being worn by women who entice and no longer by those who used to wear such loveliness simply because they found it beautiful. The world is changing—and people with it. Sad, very sad . . . Forgive me . . . Miss Jane, write your letter, and I shall deliver it!"

Hannah called from the hall. "Ninnie? Where are you? I got your Michael all dressed for going."

"Ebbely, I have to run. John will be home and want his supper. Good-bye and thank you."

"Dere you are!"

"Sorry, Hannah." Jane grabbed her son, hat, coat, and sewing box and ran.

Going to the parlor, Hannah surveyed Ebbely from the doorway.

"What you doing all alone in here?"

"Thinking, dear lady, just thinking. A brief moment of respite. Now—" Straightening his waistcoat, he walked over to her, smiling. "What masterpiece of culinary perfection are you serving this devoted admirer this evening?"

"Tomorrow you got goulash, because we are making de noodles. Tonight I made, just for you, chicken and dumplings."

"Oh, Hannah! Solace of my little heart—come, run away with me!"

"Always de kidder!" She gave him a gentle shove. "Go, wash up. Fritz come home any minute."

Jane was so eager to get to her letter writing, as soon as John had left the next morning, she collected writing tablet, ink bottle and pen and, full of good intentions, settled herself at the kitchen table, uncorked the ink, inserted the pen tip into the holder and, suddenly found that she didn't know how to start or what to say. Writing paper being far too expensive to waste, she decided to practice first in her copybook but, although she tried, nothing sounded right under the delicate circumstances. If she appeared to know how Eugenie was living, it would surely embarrass her and, if she pretended not to know, what would she find to say? Deciding it might be better if she took a day or two to think it through, she re-corked the ink, wiped the tip, put everything back in its place and got on with her morning duties.

Months later she would find her copybook, in it her laborious attempts and wonder why she had never written the letter, knowing that it was now too late to do so. In the old days, Teresa would have told her she had committed a sin, one of omission and, for once, Jane felt she would have agreed with her.

13

Winter winds whipped John's shirts on the line, long before Jane had prepared the kitchen for hanging the wash indoors. Hannah was already planning to make candied apples for the children at Halloween. Mr. Kennec was busy sharpening his cutting tools for when it would be time to harvest ice on Lake Erie. Mr. Henry had been issued real leather gloves, but continued to wear his rainbow mittens because, as he put it, mail tended to slip from hands encased in leather. Across the country, roads were being built and surfaced, streets paved with asphalt instead of gravel and sand. The City of New York had gotten its first motorized taxis. Polishtown, now such an important community, practically a small nation in itself, had become a suburb of Detroit, given its own name of Hamtramck. Highland Park boasted more than twenty thousand inhabitants, could point with pride to its first motorized fire engine. There were 7,882 different categories of jobs filled, full time, around the clock at the Ford plant.

The tough, yet respected, James Couzens, who many believed was responsible for the idea of the Five-Dollar-Day, had resigned as vice president and treasurer of the Ford Motor Company, "Young Mr. Edsel" had been elected to its office of secretary. Henry Ford was working on what was closest to his heart—to give the small farmer a motorized tiller of the soil, a tractor that he could afford to buy, could depend on to serve his needs.

The construction of a new Ford plant was under way on his vast marshland holdings along the Rouge River. His industrial power realized, Henry Ford was beginning to believe that his personal stature on both the national and international scene had reached sufficient importance for him to raise his voice for peace in Europe. He proclaimed and the press eagerly quoted him, that he would gladly "give everything I possess" if he could stop the war and prevent the amassing of arms in America, declaring, he would not allow a single automobile to leave his plant if he thought it would be used for warfare. Praise for Henry Ford's pacifist proclamations were legion. One influential newspaper calling him "one of the greatest benefactors of the human race," adding that "this modest mechanic-millionaire doesn't know he is a great man, makes him all the greater!"

When John brought this glowing tribute home to reread and savor, Jane, observing his obvious delight in his paper, dared to ask what it said and was answered by him reading the entire article out loud for her to appreciate; commenting when he had finished, that finally the Boss was being recognized for the superior human being he truly was—and about time, too!

Michael, covered by a cut-off sheet with two big holes to see through, that his father had painted with little flying bats, so he could be a ghost who flew amongst them, sucked on a big red candied apple, convinced he was in Heaven. On first seeing him before her front door, Hannah had screamed, couldn't get over that at only one and a half, her Bubbeleh seemed to know exactly what was going on—even to why he was suddenly covered in a sheet—even managing a scary "BOO!!"

"What a child! Never, in all my days, have I seen such a ting! Can't talk good yet but, a ghost—he is perfect! Even mit de booing!"

Hannah hugged him so often that Michael got a little upset, not because of the repeated attention but simply because each time she grabbed him, his sheet slipped and then his holes to see through ended up at the back of his head. Besides, he didn't want anybody to disturb his father's work of art! For Michael, John, with his magical hands that could make things for him to play with, was his very own deity, not to be desecrated by anyone's carelessness.

Now that he was finally protected from the elements, Ebbely decided to increase his sales by venturing into territory once unthinkable in winter. Wearing boy's long johns, two sets of them, one on top of the other, just in case he had to leave the sanctuary of his cozy Lizzie to patch a tire, he kissed Hannah good-bye, told her not to worry.

"But Ebbely! Even wit de New Lizzie—so nice closed up, in dat so far—Minnesota, Fritz tells me dis time of year dey got blizzards."

"What's a blizzard or two to a man with a closed-in flivver! Have no fear, for I must venture to where the dour Swedes await with their Viking cousins. None of them would know one of my gossamer negligees from a stovepipe—but those hefty immigrants from out of the frozen North, they'll grab up my double-thick woolen bloomers as though they were hotcakes! For two years, I have been trying to unload those hideous things and this time, I shall! . . . And, for your edification, I would like to add that in the whole country there is not a single traveling salesman of intimate apparel who can make that statement! . . . Now, thank you, my dear, for the roasted chickens, biscuits, multiple cakes and doughnuts—not to mention your truly divine divinity fudge. When, far away from home and loved ones, I shall think of you, shed a frosty tear and munch!"

As the elegant sedan wobbled down the street, he waved, calling, "Keep a light in the window for me—*auf Wiedersehen*!" And was gone.

After eighteen hours in labor, Frederika's exhausted body finally relinquished Rudy's son. He lived for a minute or two, then, too weak to struggle further, sighed, and was no more. The midwife wrapped him in a piece of flannel, handed him to Henrietta, ministered to the further physical needs of the mother, washed her hands, packed up the tools of her trade, and left the room. Downstairs, she informed the worried husband that a child had been born, was a boy and had died, wrapped herself in her shawls and, murmuring, "God's will be done," went home to her brood of ten. Frederika slept, Henrietta rocked the silent bundle in her arms, downstairs Rudy cried.

Not heeding anyone's advice, refusing all help, even her husband's, Frederika rose, washed, bound her breasts against the milk, dressed in black, packed away the ready baby clothes, then went about her daily tasks as though a child had never been born. Henrietta and the others, denied admittance to her grief, could only watch and worry. While Rudy allowed friendship to help him, Frederika shunned all attempts at it.

Fritz built the small coffin, Hannah lined it with a remnant of blue satin. Jane made a little pillow for his head. Standing apart from the circle of friends, Frederika watched the internment of her child, as though a distant relative attending out of politeness. Rudy, ashen-faced, seeking comfort from Johann and Henrietta by his side, didn't notice. Afterwards, coffee and reassuring food awaited everyone at the Geiger house, where friends murmured the timeworn words that are never actually listened to, nor truly helpful, yet still seem necessary to be spoken by those helpless to do more.

Jane, keeping busy in the kitchen washing dishes, was singled out by Serafina offering to dry. It was such an unusual gesture from this nondomestic woman, Jane looked at her surprised.

"You didn't go to the burial, Jane. Why?"

"Why do you ask?"

"It interests me. When I saw it, you were absent, yet you belonged."

"What *are* you talking about?"

Sometimes Serafina's habit of saying things that no one could follow irritated Jane.

"The other night, I had a vision. I saw the burial. It was quite distinct. Though not in color in shades of gray that fluctuated, the faces were sharp, quite startling! Yours wasn't there, but I FELT you!"

"Oh, really. These many visions of yours, they must take up so much of your time. How *do* you manage?"

Serafina rarely reacted to sarcasm, either because she considered it beneath her dignity to acknowledge it or, as Hannah thought, because that anyone would not take her seriously was simply inconceivable to her.

"Why did I *feel* your presence if you weren't there?"

"I haven't the slightest idea."

Serafina dried the last plate, handing it on to Rosie to put away.

"Jane, tell me. Have you ever been to a burial?"

Jane dried her hands, rolled down the sleeves of her dark dress, buttoning the cuffs.

"Once. My mother died. I was forced to go."

"That could be it! How long ago was that?" Jane wished Serafina would stop.

"Nearly twenty years."

"Much too long for a presence to remain so strong! So—it is still to come. Beware," and Serafina strode out of the kitchen in search of her husband to take her home. Left alone at the sink Jane trembled; despite her resolve never to allow Serafina's strangeness to affect her, it had.

Except for a heightened remoteness, Frederika seemed unaltered. Rudy aged but she remained the cool, superior creature she had always been, observing the world from her private parapet. Perhaps it was this very *sameness* that would eventually lead to her destruction, her so accustomed aloofness that had never allowed anyone to get too close to her, that now fooled everyone into believing she was alright, just being her usually composed self, so there was nothing special to worry about. Those isolated moments when the mask slipped, sometimes into irrational action, those were quickly explained away as just nerves, only natural after such bereavement; all she needed was time, for that healed all wounds. Innocent of what was happening to her, Frederika, suddenly unable to endure a husband's touch, revolted by the very odor of his maleness, withdrew to avoid him. Slowly, their marriage became one of harbored silence, its outward face benign, its reality hopeless.

Attracted by Henry Ford's fame, his monetary power, his repetitive ability to capture headlines and support for his pacifist views, Madame Rosika Schwimmer, an avid campaigner for peace, decided to make herself and her crusade known to the American hero who might be persuaded to offer much. Henry Ford, always putty in the hands of a strong, determined woman, quickly succumbed to Rosika's firebrand oratory, her conviction so equal to his, that peace *must* be achieved, *could* be achieved through positive action taken by powerful, respected leaders—men like himself, willing to dedicate themselves and their fortunes to ending the war raging in Europe.

The Boss's enthusiasm, bordering on infatuation with Madame Schwimmer and her peace crusade became the overriding topic in the Geiger parlor.

"Fritz, what do you think of this madness?"

"Now hold on, Carl!" John interrupted. "I wouldn't call it madness to want peace."

"Yes," Peter nodded. "What was it the Boss said to the reporters in New York?"

"I got it right here." Fritz read from the front page of his evening paper, "'Men sitting around a table, not men dying in the trenches, will finally settle the difficulties.'"

"Well, that sure sounds good to me."

"Okay—so they are all sincere, but you can't tell me that gypsy is just in this for bringing peace to the world!" Stan scoffed.

"Well Stan, it takes one to know one." Zoltan smiled, taking the sting out of the remark.

"You're damn right it does! That Hungarian Jewess is out for all she can get and it ain't just Holy Peace! Ford is being hoodwinked, good and proper!"

"Take it easy, you two," Johann intervened. "You can't deny that ever since the war started, Henry Ford has been talking out for peace. Now maybe he'll get a chance to really do something about it! It's time something was done . . . it's becoming a slaughterhouse over there!"

"What happens if the president won't do what the Boss says?" Peter looked to Fritz for an answer.

"The president won't turn down Henry Ford!" Zoltan lit a cheroot.

"Not a bad question though. What if he does—what then?"

"What do you think—then the Boss will do it on his own! You know him—once he makes up his mind . . ."

Stan interrupted, before John could go into one of his frequent speeches. "I agree! And with that Schwimmer woman, he'll have no choice but to. She'll make sure of that."

"They say the Austrians killed thousands of Poles advancing through Galicia. Carl, can that be true?"

"Peter, who knows? Every day I hear numbers no one can believe."

"Carl, you heard from your family in Lublin?"

"No. You?"

"No. Nothing." Peter sighed.

"Your parents, didn't they move in with your sister-in-law?"

"Yes."

"Well then, don't worry that far north they'll be safe."

"Carl, you think anywhere's safe anymore? It looks like it's becoming a world war . . . the Turks are in it, the—" Fritz was interrupted by Johann.

"On whose side? There's so many I forget whose side they're all on."

"The Turks?"

"Yes."

"On the side of the Germans, of course."

Johann shook his head. "I should have known, they've always been a blood-thirsty lot."

"I heard the czar is taking personal command of his Imperial armies. What do your Russians say to that, Fritz?"

"They're proud, Zoltan. Very proud."

"That Romanov tyrant will sit on his steed, decked out in jeweled orders to lead his starving serfs into battle to die for dear old Mother Russia." Stan lit a cigarette.

"Well, at least they are on our side. Is that sinister monk still wielding power?" Zoltan looked at Fritz.

"How would I know?"

"Well, as you are our Russian authority . . ."

"Lay off! Tell me, do any of you ever feel strange? What I mean, embarrassed that we are living here—while . . ."

"While back home they are drowning in their own blood?"

"That's a bit macabre, Carl." Zoltan blew his nose.

"No, it's not. If what we hear is true, it's worse!"

"Well?" Fritz looked at his friends. "No one going to answer me?"

"I do. All the time," Johann admitted. "But it's tougher on you, Fritz, because you're German. If Rudy were here, he'd probably tell you, as an Austrian, he too feels like the enemy."

"Fritz doesn't mean taking sides. He means all of us from over there, living over here, safe and sound, no one's life in danger, he sometimes feels ashamed."

"That's right, John. *That's* what I meant!"

"Sure, I do."

"Me too."

"Of course. But I try not to think of it. You can't allow yourself to—or your output suffers."

"Yeah, the morale of the men on the line is bad enough without their superintendents having a conscience."

Carl lit his pipe. "John, have you received any news from home?"

"Not a word. Everybody blames the U-boats why nothing gets through."

"Anybody know if it's true that the British used poison gas at Loos?" Johann looked about the room.

"I heard that, too—and that the Germans are now using a new one, even more lethal than their first."

"My God! Where is all this going to end?" Slumped in his chair, Fritz shook his head.

"We're going to be dragged into it! You mark my words—I said it before—it's got to come to that. We have no choice." Stan crushed out his cigarette.

"Not if we get peace before it's too late!"

"That's exactly what the Boss is trying to do!"

"More power to him!"

"Amen!" Zoltan crossed himself. "Stan, are you driving me home?"

"Sure. Anyone else want a ride?"

"You sure Serafina won't mind?" Peter asked, hoping Stan would be willing to go as far as Hamtramck.

"She's a good sport about me *chauffeuring*. Don't take this the wrong way, my friends, but don't you think it's time you got yourselves a motor?"

"Next year, maybe. I have my eye on our Coupelet."

"Swanky, Zoltan. Real swanky. Going courting?"

"Maybe, Johann. Just maybe."

"Fritz, what about you? Hannah would love it!"

"Ja, but first I spend my money to get her a talking machine—but don't tell her. Ever since Mr. Bell invented that, she has been dreaming of someday we have one."

"Serafina's father of course has had one for sometime. Now he complains to me daily that because I haven't installed one yet, he can't ring over to check on

Serafina's *delicate condition*. Hey, John, I hear your Missus is again in the family way. Congratulations!" The others joined in. "Know when?"

"Jane thinks early April . . . but one never knows."

"I'm not convinced they are as necessary as everyone claims they are," Fritz mused.

"What?" Heads snapped in his direction.

"Just a lot of unnecessary disturbance!"

"Fritz—what *are* you talking about?"

"Talking telephones. Fine maybe for business but inside a home, why?"

"Well, if you get one just so your father-in-law can ring through, I'm sure Stan will agree with you!" John laughed.

"I've told you once, John—and I'll tell you again—thank your lucky stars yours isn't on your neck!"

"What about all those look-alike brothers of his that play in that band, they give you trouble too, Stan?"

"I'm so busy keeping my nose clean with the father, I let those uncles fiddle all they want! Okay . . . Zoltan? You ready? . . . Anyone else who's coming with me . . . go get your wife."

Later, walking home, Jane asked, as though just making conversation, if anything especially interesting had been discussed in the parlor.

"Nothing much. Mostly the Boss's scheme for peace."

"Henry Ford is going to bring peace?" Amazement colored Jane's tone.

John shifted the sleeping Michael to his other shoulder. "And why not? Great men can achieve great things to better mankind."

Swallowing a retort, Jane decided to leave the subject of Henry Ford as Moses be. In satisfied silence, her husband led them home.

After a private meeting with a noncommittal Woodrow Wilson, Henry Ford left the White House, announced to the waiting press that to accomplish his personal "World Wide campaign for universal peace, supported by a one-million-dollar Ford endowment," he had chartered a ship, the *Oskar II*, henceforth to be known as the "Peace Ship," that would carry the most influential peace advocates in the country across the sea, first to Norway then on to Sweden—there to negotiate an end to war. "We are going to get the boys out of the trenches by Christmas!"

As it was already November 22, a most ambitious proclamation.

Waving Fritz's newspaper, Hannah ran over to Jane's with the news.

"Ninnie! No more war! De Boss is going to fix it! All de important peoples are going wit him and his Missus. His friend, de great Mr. Thomas Edison and his odder one, dat important bird-watcher. Even Mr. Wanamaker Department Store—dey all are going! What a wonderful ting!"

"You think it can really be done, just by talking?" Jane poured them both a cup of coffee.

"Well—shooting each udder hasn't done nutting." Hannah spooned sugar into her cup. "Fritz tells me dis Schwimmer woman she even convince de Missus dis is de ting to do. If Missus Clara she says okay de boss can go and she comes too, you can bet your bottom dollar, it's an okay ting! But . . ."

"But, what?"

"Just dis Hungarian ting. If dis Rosika Schwimmer lady, she was maybe even Rumanian, I wouldn't worry . . . but Hungarian? Dat's maybe a problem."

Jane laughed, "You and your Hungarians!"

"Hey—not so funny! If she's a real one of dose, den she is only making herself a big shot, not for de peace, only for de big importance . . . and de Boss's money."

"Didn't the papers say she's a Jewess?"

"Ja, and dat's anudder ting; so, if my hunch comes true and dis woman no good, all her Hungarian will be forgotten . . . and dey will say, of course, her badness is because she is Jewish! . . . I have to go—Missus Nussbaum—her Zellie is home because he got leg burned with de melted brass, so she can't do de watching. So Missus Horowitz, she has to find someone—maybe dat new Missus Tashner, the one whose husband works de emery wheels . . . you going to your Italians, see if anyting wrong?"

"I have to take Michael to Rosie first. Then I'll go."

"All dat way to Rosie?"

"I don't want to burden Henrietta. She's always so tired now."

"Ja, well—she's already twenty-eight, dat's old for having anudder baby."

"And I can't ask Frederika."

"Poor girl. Ninnie . . . you tink she is right in de head?"

"What do you mean?"

"Someting strange wit dat child."

"Frederika has always been a little strange. Remember you said so yourself when Rudy first brought her to the house that day."

"Yes—but cold stuck up is not like frozen dead."

"Hannah, you sound like Serafina!"

"Well, I tink Rudy's very unhappy and she too . . . and not only because de baby's gone."

"All they need is a little more time."

"I wonder." Hannah got into her heavy winter coat, put on her hat, wound a long scarf around her neck, pulled on her knitted gloves. "You coming on Saturday for de baking like usual?"

"Yes. Will you teach me to make your special rye bread?"

"We did it! Ninnie! Where are you?" John stormed into the house. "We did it!" Hearing his father's voice, Michael ran into the hall, flung his arms around John's leg, sat on his shoe, holding on like a monkey in a tree.

Jane, following, asked, "What?"

"There you are! Today, the first day of December in the year 1915, a Model T bearing the number 'one million' rolled off the line! With fifteen assembly plants working full out, we nearly missed it!"

"Every Lizzie has a number?"

"Of course. And today, we reached one million!"

Sensing his wife was not sufficiently impressed, he took her by the shoulders. "Don't you understand what that means, woman? Every one is spoken for, every dealership is screaming for more. There are a million—A MILLION satisfied customers! Our car has not only changed the daily lives, the very habits of a nation, it has captured its heart! Maybe—even its soul." Looking down at his son still clinging to his leg, he smiled, "You want a ride up the stairs?" Tightening his hold, the little boy nodded, ready. "Okay, here we go!" and stiffening his leg, John hoisted his monkey son up the stairs.

Four days later, amidst cheers, flag waving, bands playing "I Didn't Raise My Boy To Be a Soldier," well-wishers, some in the grip of patriotic hysteria flinging themselves into the icy waters to swim alongside, Ford's Peace Ship left the Hoboken pier. Neither Mrs. Ford nor Thomas Edison, nor most of the invited and announced important peace advocates were aboard; besides the real danger of being torpedoed, most had second thoughts on the advisability of the entire venture. The press, first so beguiled by Ford's sincerity, now viewed his peace mission as doomed to fail, resorted to ridicule in their coverage of it. When a dissenter sent a cage of live squirrels to the ship with a note that read "To go with the nuts" and another a large bag of raisins bearing the same sentiment, the press was quick to print the story; some papers, rechristening the Peace Ship "Good Ship Nutty," accompanying their editorials with biting cartoons to play up the absurdity of a bunch of Boy Scouts believing they could stop war as easily as leading an old woman across the street.

Waiting for the daily communiqués from the Peace Ship, the Ford men were described by their respective wives as being simply impossible to live with. Serafina even going so far as to inform her father that to preserve her nerves, she might have to return to the sanctity to be found under his roof until such time as Ford's peace had been achieved. Adding, that if his ship wasn't torpedoed, Henry Ford deserved to be for disrupting everyone's life with his crazy crusade; one of the few times Jane could understand her, even thinking she might agree with her.

Henry Ford was lampooned, dubbed a buffoon, a fool—Rosika Schwimmer a "Great spider weaving the web of her plans," and more. By the time the *Oskar II* was about to reach its destination, there were some amongst the reporters who actually felt sorry for "The Flivver King," had come to the conclusion that Ford had only acted like a gullible, well-meaning child and now might need their help to have his image of car-maker folk-hero resurrected for the good of the nation.

When, on December 18, the *Oskar II* reached Norway, an ailing Henry Ford was hustled off the ship by two of his trusted men. One, a Bible-thumping clergyman, head of his Sociological Department, the other a most obliging chauffeur-cum-bodyguard who was destined in the not-too-distant future to feather a most fortuitous nest as reward for private services done his Boss far beyond the call of duty. The "Spider," unsuccessful in holding her generous benefactor fast in her web, Henry Ford left his funded commission behind to do the best they could without him, and returned home.

By all normal standards, his return should have been one of public ridicule but, surprisingly, it was not. Once again, the country took him to its heart. Especially grassroots America, who regarded him as one of their own. Henry Ford had always put their needs first and just like the trusty dependable machine he had given them, had never let them down.

The Ford men were jubilant, though the Boss might have lost, in the end he had won. No man could be asked to do more than his best.

Having found adequate lodgings, even a warm stable to bed down his Lizzie in, Rumpelstiltskin decided to forgo the hazards of winter roads, lay over, spend the Christmas season among the hearty natives of St. Paul.

Out of the bowels of her larder Hannah called to Jane pulling off her galoshes in the hall. "Come! I'm in de larder pinning. You gotta see!" Intrigued, Jane looked in. "Come in, Ninnie, shut de door I gotta pin. Ebbely, he sent me new picture postcards, bad news written on dem but de postcards, dey are funny. I put dem up, den you can have a laugh!"

"Bad news?"

"Our Ebbely, he's not coming back for dis Christmastime."

"Oh, no!"

"Well, he says better he stay nice and cozy in a town in dat Minnesota and I tink dat's sensible. Iciness can make his Lizzie slip around and maybe he has den an accident. So, better we miss him so he stay safe . . . dere." She stepped back. "See, dey don't have picture like de others—dese are special funny drawing postcards wit Model T jokes . . . which you like best?"

Laughing, Jane picked the one that had little birds perched on the branch of a tree, chirping as a Ford went by. "Cheap, cheap, cheap."

"I like de goat wit de terrible stomach cramps, complaining, 'I ate a Ford and it's still running.' Many good jokes about our Lizzie so small but strong. Here," Hannah pointed to another card on the door, "dis one—see—a happy Model T passing a big limousine stuck in de mud, says, 'De big car fumes and throws a fit, but de little Ford don't mind a bit.'" Hannah sat before the larder door, relishing her collection. "You know of any udder motorcar in de whole world dat gets special postcards made of it?" Jane had to admit it was wondrous indeed. "And I hear dat in de big cities where dey have dose music halls, dere dey tell Tin Lizzie jokes—make people laugh . . . not to be mean, just give everybody a good time for dere money."

"You know any, Hannah?"

"Fritz tell me one, just like dey say it professional . . . see if I remember right . . . Policeman. What is de charge against dis fellow? Second policeman. Stealing a Ford car! Judge. Take de prisoner out—and search him." They both enjoyed that one. "Okay—we make de bread now. You got de kümmel?"

"The what?"

"De caraway—you said you wanted to learn to make de rye bread wit de seeds."

Together they baked their weekly breads, Jane being taught the secrets of producing a sour rye that was truly superlative. But, no matter how often she tried over the years, diligently following each and every step, Jane never did manage to turn out a loaf as perfect as Hannah's.

Their twins still too young to be exposed to the cold night air, Carl and Rosie decided to stay home on Christmas Eve. Johann and Henrietta's girls had caught a chill and so they too would have to remain home. As Dora's sister had come all the way from Buffalo to spend the holidays, Peter too had no choice but to stay, play host. Her pregnancy now well advanced, Serafina was adamant that when Stan drove her to her father's house, he stay by her side, the ever-attentive father-to-be. With no one to drive him, his mother in a fouler mood than usual, Zoltan cornered Fritz at work, made his heartfelt excuses, asked him to be sure to convey to Hannah how much it grieved him to have to miss her Christmas Eve celebration this year. Hoping that going to the Geigers' would bring a little cheer, Rudy persuaded a disinterested Frederika to make the effort, arriving at the welcoming house just as John and his family were being greeted by an excited Hannah.

"Quick! Get out of your tings! Don't ask questions!" Her tall frame tense with impatience, tapping her foot, waiting for them to peel off their winter layers, finally, unable to wait any longer, she grabbed Jane's hand, pulled her down the hall, calling to the others to follow quick!

"Look!" Hannah pointed to the wall next to the door leading down to the cellar and there, in all its glory, hung the oaken box and apparatus of a talking telephone! "Fritz, he gave me! Like a lady millionaire I am! Everybody, vatch! He show me how. First, you crank de handle couple of times—just like mit a flivver, den quick you lift off de important ting—for de hearing—den you crank again—den you shout nice and clear into dis, de speaking piece, tell de special number of de far away udder person you want to have speak wit you—to a smart nice lady who knows where to plug exactly de cables into de right holes so you get connected all the way to ring-a-ling anudder talking machine far away. All de way across town even, if you want!"

John put his arm around her, kissed her cheek. "If I had known a telephone would make you this happy, I would have gotten you one myself!"

"My Fritz, he knew. Anyway, only husband allowed to give expensive present like dis—so no smarty ideas from you, my Baby Boy!"

"You haven't called me that in years!" John hugged her some more.

"Dat's because you now a big grown-up papa. Where is my Bubbeleh? You forget him on de doorstep?" Hearing Hannah's special name for him, Michael ran to hug her skirts. Smiling, she bent down, picked him up. "Merry Christmas, little one. Now—first we go light all de candle—make de tree special—den we sing de carols, drink de Schnapps—you get milk! Don't make a face—it's good for you! Den, I have a big surprise I make for you *and* before your Mama and Papa take you home to sleep, you know what we do? I will turn de handle—let you listen to de ring-a-ling of my special Christmas present!"

Without Ebbely to tickle its ivories, the piano remained silent, but they sang the carols, remembered how Jimmy used to insist on singing the endless lyrics of those partridges sitting in that pear tree. All were enchanted by the fairy-tale gingerbread house and Michael's joy breaking sugar icicles off its roof to stuff his mouth with, drank the precious Schnapps, contented in the warm glow of the candlelight, watching it flicker. Michael, heeding his father's warning to be very, very careful, played with the carved figures of shepherds and kings, gently regrouping them around the baby lying in the manger. With Hannah, a Christmas Eve, even with so many missing, was complete, somehow.

After everyone had gone, Fritz put the Schnapps back in the cabinet, turned the key, blew out the candles on the little tree, made sure the lit menorah was well enough away from the curtains so nothing could catch fire during the night, called to Hannah in German. "Hannahchen, now I am going up. You are coming?"

Her happy voice reached him from the kitchen. "Go up, Liebling! Only a little bit still I got, den I come!" Listening for it, the instant she heard him open their bedroom door, Hannah scurried into the hall carrying a kitchen stool, sat herself down before the wall that held her wonderful Christmas present—just to gaze at it. With Missus Adams, once the owner of a talking machine, no longer in Highland Park having immigrated to Canada, Hannah knew no one who had a talking telephone. But she was sure she would some day and, when that glorious moment arrived, she would know how to ring-a-ling someone whole streets away and maybe even a someone would someday do her the great honor of ring-a-linging Missus Hannah Geiger, proud possessor of a talking telephone, in return.

Having made her usual quantity of Christmas gingerbread, Hannah had so much left over, the next day she packed it into one of her Glory Day picnic baskets, took it with her to the pond, handed it out to anyone who skated past her. This festive gesture was such a success, so appreciated, she told Fritz she planned to do it again next year, even if it meant having to do double batches.

Alone on the bench, Jane watched John skating with Michael perched on his shoulders, arms wrapped around his father's throat, holding on for dear life—scared stiff—loving every minute of it. By next Christmas, he would be old enough to skate on his own. Where had the year gone? She felt the baby move inside her, wished Rumpelstiltskin were there to ask her for a waltz.

14

As a New Year's treat, Mr. Henry actually stopped, one mittened paw waving a letter addressed to Jane. "Here, I got one!" His warm breath steamed. "Again this one was sent to the Geigers'! Doesn't *anyone* know where you live?" As though chiding a forgetful youngster his voice held a smile. Before she could tempt him to come inside, warm himself by the stove, the mailman turned, waved farewell, hurried off to his duties. Holding her letter like the precious gift it was, Jane returned to the kitchen before opening it.

In carefully formed words, placed neatly on lines drawn with a ruler, Megan had at last put pencil to paper.

Dear Giovanna,

> *Surprise, surprise it's meself, Megan, your shipboard mate, the Irish one. I hope you still remember me. Sure you're knowing how to read in English after so long is sure a welcome relief for me. So here I am writin' to say hello and give you our address so if you have a mind to answer, you can. Never did make it to where I thought I was goin'. Me Patrick havin' thought the better of it followed more advantageous opportunities up North. So here we are, still in the grand city of New York, livin' in rooms, boardin' in a house with other Irish folk just like us. Times have been hard. Oh, it's not that*

*me Patrick isn't ever willing to work, no matter what is—alright with him
but, no fine horses now to look after he follows the ponies. Never know from
one day to the next what will be, but as me dad used to say "You can't have
coal, peat will do as well." We manage. Me Patrick is away a good deal, his
so numerous business connections take him out of town. So I have taken day
employment in one of the fine houses on the 5th Avenue—just to keep from
sittin' home all alone twiddlin' me thumbs, mind. Here we hear all sorts of
talk about that Mr. Henry Ford and then I always think of you. Hopin' this
finds you well and you will answer in kind, I remain yours.*

    Sincerely, your friend,
    Megan Flanningan

Jane let the letter rest in her lap. How long ago it all seemed. The four of them, so different, who had forsaken familiarity to follow their men, so sure a better life awaited them in a far-off land.

Now it appeared as though only she had found a security worthy of their adventure. Sitting in her warm kitchen, Jane recognized her good fortune, at the same moment aware that the self-satisfaction this should bring eluded her. Once again, she chided herself for always being so hard to please, when all the basics for pleasure surrounded her, and felt confused with herself. As with most bereft children, never having experienced the dependability of love, Jane yearned for what she imagined it must be. Her birdlike eyes forever focused on far horizons, Jane rarely saw what lay at her feet waiting to be perceived.

During supper that evening, Jane mentioned Megan's letter and its contents to John, who replied that her cabin-mate's circumstances did not surprise him.

"When I saw that flashy automobile of his, I told you he was certainly no groom. So—he turns out to be a no-good gambler, doesn't surprise me in the least."

"Poor Megan, she had such lofty dreams—living in a great mansion, serving a fine Southern lady."

"All immigrants have dreams."

"But not all are disappointed." Clearing her husband's plate, Jane was struck by the thought that they were actually having a conversation.

"No, not if their original dreams, as you call them, were based on some reality."

Wanting to prolong this rare exchange, Jane asked, "Exactly what reality?"

"Hard work, determination, sacrifice, self-discipline, a passion, a true sense of purpose—not necessarily in that order but all of them necessary to achieve one's goal."

"You didn't include freedom, John."

"Freedom is the result of the others!"

"Is it really that hard? Was it for you?"

"Of course! Fritz, Rudy, Zoltan—all of us. The one thing about immigrants that unites all of us is our need, our initial courage to search for a better life. You are lucky you didn't have to do it alone, it was already done for you."

Although this was beginning to enter channels perhaps dangerous, Jane persisted. "Could marriage be considered a form of immigration?"

"Marriage?" John looked startled.

"Yes. Would you say it too needs all the things you mentioned to achieve its goal?"

Intrigued despite himself, John challenged, "Its goal being?"

"Success?"

"Don't be silly! A woman's success already lies in just *being* married. After that all that is left for her to do is live within its . . . boundaries to have what she wants."

"She may not always know what she really wants."

"Women as a whole don't know what they want! They blow like the wind—they need a man to give them direction!"

"Really."

Having noticed for some time that his wife seemed meeker, less argumentative when speaking a foreign language she had learned, John switched from Italian to English—his tone demanding. "Well? Are we having dessert tonight or not?"

Wishing she could, yet knowing she should go no further, Jane went to fetch the apple cobbler.

On Valentine's Day, Rumpelstiltskin returned, shed his winter coverings, grabbed Hannah's hand, pulled her into the parlor, positioned her by the piano, did his twirling trick with the stool and, smiling up at the object of his affection, launched into a buoyant rendition of "Oh, You Beautiful Doll," stressing the second line, *YOU GREAT-BIG BEAUTIFUL DOLL!* finishing his amorous performance with a delighted giggle. "When I heard it, I knew! Immediately! This song was written with you in mind. Bought the sheet music, learned it on the spot and have been waiting, fretting for months to serenade you with it! What's for supper? Whatever, smells delicious!" Hannah hugged him so hard, he squealed, "Enough! I'm delicate!"

"Ach, my Ebbely! Why you stay away so long?"

"Never again, dear lady! Never again! Barbaric, absolutely barbaric! But, they adored the bloomers and those latkes!? Ambrosia!"

"Latkes? You like dere latkes? Better den my German pancakes? So—I make you latkes!" Not having meant to make her jealous, Ebbely quickly kissed her hand and escaped upstairs to the safety of his room.

Though it was a weeknight, having heard their favorite shrimp was back, his friends came to welcome him home; picked him up, kissed the top of his head, chased him through the house, then, their game done, settled down in the parlor to listen to his stories, ask about the conditions of the roads, farther than many of them had ever been.

"Deplorable, my friends—still deplorable. Think of a freshly plowed field after a cloudburst and you get a good idea. Sometimes even a Model T can't get through and that's a shocking statement, as you will all agree. Have any of you ever heard of the idea they call 'seeding'?" Some of the men looked blank. Ebbely continued, "Sometimes, as you are approaching a town—the muck, rocks and ruts suddenly stop, and then, as though by magic, suddenly you are gliding on smoothest heaven! And you realize you're rolling along on a surface that has been paved! By the time you get over the shock, your aching bones just beginning to enjoy this astonishing sensation—BANG! You're back in the muck! . . . And you know why? You've just done a *mile*. Exactly one mile, of what is called a 'seeded road.' Some crafty bureaucrat has sold the idea of surfacing roads—one mile at a time, like planting flower beds, hoping these little seedlings will beget state funding and grow into long stretches of surfaced roadways. This scheme may not be as idiotic as it sounds—certainly something has to be done to wake up the legislators, convince those boobs that the horseless carriage is here to stay! Still, as of now, I can tell you—when you hit one of those seeded miles? It's a real shock—at both ends! But, I must tell you what I came across in Wisconsin. One bitter cold morning, driving through the town of Madison, I passed one of your dealerships—which I must tell you are springing up like mushrooms all over the country—when what do I see? With a great big For Sale sign? A Model T Two Seater!" Pausing a split second for effect, Ebbely intoned, "A *secondhand* Model T, my friends!"

Stunned silence filled the room. In those days, when things were built to last, fickleness to what served you well was nonexistent, and no one ever got rid of their beloved Lizzie.

"Aha—I see you are as stunned as I was by such an unusual sight. So, naturally, I had no choice but to stop and inquire the circumstances that brought this unique tragedy to pass."

"And?" the Ford men asked in unison.

"Hark. Well, my friends, for it is a sad, sad tale of loss and fickle fate. It seems there was an ambitious man of the cloth who, being convinced that the Lord had singled him out to spread the Word beyond his humble pulpit, go forth, search for his erring flock, roam the far reaches of Wisconsin to herd them back amongst the righteous—sold a pair of silver candlesticks and with the proceeds bought himself a Model T to do so in high style. By night, by day, through rain, sleet and snow, he toiled in the service of His Maker until, one dark and stormy night, he struck a large rock, his flivver bucked, he catapulted, struck his head on said rock *and* expired on the spot! The next day they found him, stiff as a board, his trusty T grazing by his side, still running!"

Hannah asked from the doorway, "Dis going to take long still?"

"You want us? Supper ready?" Fritz started to get up.

"No. A little time still. Just am wondering how long dis fancy story telling is going on." Rumpelstiltskin, knowing she was still fuming that he had dared to enjoy someone else's cooking, opted for silence. "Well, okay den—but make it fast." Heaving an exasperated, put-upon sigh, Hannah returned to her kitchen.

"Where was I?"

"They found him dead . . . "

"Ah, yes. Well, it seems he had a married sister, lived somewhere near Oshkosh, she and her husband came down for the funeral, afterwards, happy as two squirrels cracking nuts, they take possession of the Model T and are about to drive out of town, when lo and behold, the local sheriff stops them, claims it as the primary evidence in the theft of a pair of silver candlesticks belonging to the church! So after the usual ruckus, the car was put up for sale to recoup the loss. I'm starved! Let's eat!"

Moving into the dining room, Fritz still chuckling, asked, "Ebbely, how is Minnesota?"

"Oh, my God! First I must have sustenance before recounting you my experiences this winter. Have you ever had to live two endless months with nothing but snow and muscled women who walk like men? If not, you can have no concept of what that can do to a man. First—Hannah's magnificent libation, then I'll tell you—but let me warn you, it's not a pretty picture!"

"Sounds a little like Poland." Laughing, Carl took his seat.

Peter frowned, "We got pretty women!"

"Yeah, sure we have."

"What about that Temple dancer?" Peter sounded like a little boy determined to prove his point. "She's beautiful!"

"What Temple dancer? In Poland?" Zoltan sounded utterly confused.

Peter looked to Fritz for help.

"You know who I mean? Just a few years ago, she was the toast of Paris. Martha . . . something . . . if Dora was here, she would know."

Johann, rounding the table to his place, burst out laughing.

"You mean MATA—not Martha—MATA HARI!"

"That's her!" Peter beamed.

"She's not a Pole, you fool—she's a Hollander like me and her real name is Margaretha Zelle. I know, because my cousin was in school with her."

"Well, I once saw a likeness and she's beautiful!"

"But she ain't Polish, Peter! Hey, Hannah, your Ebbely says he's starving for your magnificence."

She, carrying in a platter of succulent brisket of beef, framed by egg noodles, gave Ebbely a look.

"Well, when you arrive, I tink you look special—scrawny—like dey don't feed you right—so? EAT!"

Having finished, Rumpelstiltskin sighed, leaned back in his chair.

"Now, my friends, while I digest, tell me what was all that hullabaloo about your Boss and his Ship of Peace? In the St. Paul papers, they printed some things he said at a meeting with the press that, begging your pardon, sounded as though he had gone and lost his marbles. Here . . ." He reached into his vest pocket. ". . . I cut it out just to show you."

"Read it, Ebbely."

"If you insist—but just the part that astounded me. Here, they quote Ford. Listen.

'*"Well, boys, I got the ship."*

"What ship, Mr. Ford?"

"Why, the Oskar II.*"*

"Well, what are you going to do with her?"

"We're going to stop the war."

"Going to stop the war?"

"Yes we're going to get the boys out of the trenches by Christmas."

"But how are you going to do it?"

"Oh, you'll see."

"Where are you going?"

"I don't know."

"What country will you head for?"

"I don't know . . ."'

"and so forth and so on. You must admit . . ."

Carl mumbled, "Ford might seem ridiculous to the press but for the people, he's still a hero. You should have been here when he got back! Detroit went wild, cheering him as Crusader."

"Ja, Ebberhart, Carl is right. At least the Boss tried, even if it turned out no good—you can't take that away from him."

"Well, it's more than Wilson is doing certainly," Ebbely stirred his coffee.

"Stan thinks we'll be drawn into it."

"By 'we'—I assume, Fritz, you mean the United States?"

"Of course, who else?"

Ebbely folded his napkin. "I happen to agree with Stan. But what troubles me is, when that day comes, what will be the country's attitude towards those of German birth. What is the feeling at the plant? Still under control would you say, Fritz?"

"Sure. A little blowup here and there, sometimes when the news comes in and it is really bad—like the poison gas—they get into a fight but nothing really serious. Right, Carl?" Fritz looked over at his friend.

"Yes, we moved the French and Belgians away from the Germans, shifted the Turks, Austrian-Hungarians and a few Bulgarians and Latvians into their positions on the line—seems to be working. How are your Russians?"

"As long as we group them with Poles, Rumanians, Ukrainians, and Lithuanians, they're okay," Fritz answered.

"I've got a rim man, a Serb, who got beat up—and he's on our side."

"Peter, that's because *no one* wants the Serbs, no matter whose side they're on!"

"It sounds to me, my friends, as though you've got your own war map over there." Ebbely finished his coffee.

"By the last count we have fifty-three nationalities speaking more than a hundred languages and dialects!"

"My God!"

"The end of this month, the Ford School will be graduating five hundred men who have received a sound education in reading, writing and speaking the English language," John announced proudly.

"Well, that should help!"

"What do you mean, Ebbely?"

"I would think, John, that the more your raw immigrants learn, become a functioning part of their adopted country, the more assimilated they become, the more they will be willing to let go of old loyalties. All of you are prime examples of that." No one spoke. "Do I detect a hint of guilt?"

"It's easier for you, Ebbely. You're a real American!"

"A real American? What's a real American? Only a Redskin can make that claim, and I wouldn't look good in feathers!"

"You know exactly what Zoltan meant." Appreciating the attempt to lighten the mood, John smiled, yet pursued the thought. "You, as the only born American at this table have an identity. By birth you belong here. No one can take that away from you. It's an inner certainty, an assurance of the future that none of us have—no matter how American we strive to be, we may become. But you? You, my friend, you ARE!"

"Let me get this straight. In principle, what you are saying John, is that you are but guests in a new homeland?"

"Yes."

"Most of you have taken out your first papers for citizenship—what then? Won't that make you real Americans?"

"No, that will make us proud, privileged Americans. Real ones, we can never be."

"Ja, John is right."

Zoltan put down his napkin, "I find he usually is, Fritz."

Having not far to go, Johann and John were the last to leave. Locking the door behind them, Fritz began turning off lights in the hall. Rumpelstiltskin, standing on the third step in order to reach Hannah's cheek, gave it a fleeting kiss.

"Dear Lady, I'm exhausted! Simply drained. Never again shall I be so foolhardy as to venture into the frozen tundras of this land. How Indians ever survived that climate covered only in deerskin, I shall never understand. Even wrapped in buffalo hide, one can freeze one's you know what off!" Fritz, passing, gave him a stern look. "Sorry, my dear. The master of the house objects . . ."

"De Mistress—she doesn't, so dere!"

Forgiven, Ebbely blew her a kiss and, calling, "Good night," scampered up the stairs to bed.

He slept for days, finally emerging from what he christened his personal hibernation, to play innumerable renditions of "In the Hall of the Mountain King" with such Nordic gusto, the piano groaned. When Hannah showed him her wonderful Christmas present, Ebbely sought out Fritz, bowed low before him, shook his hand, congratulated him not only on his generosity, but his "about time" acceptance of a modern miracle that for once had absolutely nothing whatsoever to do with the mighty automobile.

Of course, the little man knew many people who could be spoken to because they too possessed a talking telephone. Hannah placed a footstool so he could reach the apparatus, then watched in awe as her Ebbely made his connections, spoke with authority, conducted his business, ever the efficient knowledgeable salesman. Later Fritz built him a special step that was the perfect height so he could reach the mouthpiece more easily and hung a small coin box next to the telephone for payment purposes.

Each time the Ford men came over, Ebbely waxed rhapsodic, calling the talking telephone the "Marvel of the Age." Jane had the impression he did it on purpose for the fun of it, just to get them riled.

Especially John, who would rise to the bait every time.

"The Marvel of the Age? That contraption that needs another, a receiver, to make its existence worthwhile? Never!"

"Ja, Ebberhart," Fritz would agree. "And all those big ugly poles it needs—with all those wires all over going everywhere!"

"And don't forget about all those poor girls, who have to sit before those consoles all day, trying to figure out which holes to poke their cables into!" Often, Stan joined in for the fun of stirring the pot further.

John nodded in agreement. "Yes—it's dependent!" Certain there was more rhetoric to come, John's friends waited, resigned. "It is the automobile, and especially the Model T, that has offered the common man his individual freedom, to go where he wants, when he wants wholly independent, free to choose. Don't forget, it is *individual* freedom that defines this country!"

A look of mock wonder on his little face, Ebbely looked about the room.

"Isn't he marvelous when he gets going like this? Give John a soapbox and he could run for mayor. And, it takes *so little* to set him off!"

"You devil!" John was laughing. "You were having me on!"

"Forgive me, I couldn't resist! Calling forth your ever-ready oratory on your mania of the 'Liberation of the Common Man' is such a temptation!"

"But I'm right, Ebbely. You have to admit I'm right!"

"Yes! Now are you satisfied? I have great affection for you, John, but you can be—exhausting! Let's eat!"

Jane's second pregnancy, now in its final stages, was one of lethargic boredom. Having to repeat an act no more welcome than the first seemed redundant. *What is the matter with you, woman?* she would ask herself, deeply concerned by her unnatural reaction to something normal women accepted, if not always with total joy, at least with some resemblance of anticipation.

Both expecting to be delivered around the same time, Jane sometimes stopped off to visit Serafina on her way home from her Watcher duties within the Italian sections of Detroit. Her precious winter coat voluminous enough to hide her condition, she could still move about without causing embarrassment to others, whereas Serafina preferred to wait out her time in the privacy of her home. The two women, so very different in every way, now fashioned baby clothes together, united by their mutual status of approaching motherhood.

When Serafina's twin sister joined them, Jane would feel the disturbing strangeness in the presence of two beings so astoundingly alike, they seemed but one image split in two. Morgana did not prophesy as often as her twin, yet she too had a way of darkly smoldering, giving one the impression that any moment she would erupt, mouth what others might not want to hear. Morgana blind since birth, this did not seem to bother her unduly and, as her blindness was open-eyed, at first people did not notice, captivated as they were by her wide-eyed beauty. Jane often wondered what would have happened if these two strange and sensuous women had followed the ancient tradition of their origin, taken the veil, joined a Holy Order of nuns; what havoc these unholy twins might have wrought amidst a bevy of innocent virgins, their treasured chastity spoken for.

Crocheting baby bootees, Morgana holding the wool while her reflected image wound it off into a ball, Jane conjured up visions of them as Holy Sisters running, their heavy rosaries flying, as lightning was about to strike them down; breaking into laughter—when she realized that she was having visions in the presence of the two who believed these were their exclusive gift.

"Why are you laughing, Jane?" Morgana asked.

"Nothing, really. That's a pretty color of blue, Serafina. What are you planning to make with it?"

"A jacket with matching cap. Salvatore will look handsome in blue."

"I see you're still convinced your baby will be a boy."

"Of course. Morgana, put your hand on Jane's belly—tell her what hers will be." Imperceptibly, Jane recoiled. "She won't hurt you—she too has the Touch." As though she could see, the twin's hand found Jane's body, rested a feather-light moment, then returned to holding the wool.

"Well?" Serafina asked her twin in Sicilian.

Without expression, Morgana answered in the same dialect Jane could not understand. Feeling foolish to even be interested in their mystic covenant, Jane looked questioningly at Serafina, who replied, "You too will have a son."

"And?" It was obvious she had more to say but was reluctant to. "Serafina, don't be silly—tell me. Whatever it is, I won't believe it anyway!"

"He does not belong to you."

"Of course he does! Sometimes you two can really be—outrageous!" Jane tied off the toe of one white bootee, began the other.

Serafina patted her sister's knee reassuringly, turning to Jane, murmured, "You will nourish, he will feed but, as the cuckoo does, so will he be."

Sometimes, Jane couldn't get out of Stan's house fast enough, reprimanding herself for ever going there in the first place.

This time, no endless up and down, not even time for comforting chatter, Hannah arriving for her usual morning visit, took one look and ran. Having decided anyone with even a little experience in child birthing preferable to the callousness of Missus O' Reilly, she headed for the house of new Missus Tashner, who was rumored to have healing hands and, as her mother was a midwife back in the old country, one could safely assume she must know at least the rudiments of birthing. Swift, yet gentle, not given to ecclesiastical utterances, nor self-righteous fussing. New Missus Tashner delivered Jane of a healthy male child. His first cry, its anger controlled as though already a matured resentment, announced what he was to be. Hannah, cradling him as she had Jane's first, looked for a likeness to his brother and found none. There was a bland remoteness about him that resembled no one—as though an opinionated old man had been transformed into a newborn, his mental age intact.

"Well, that was a real easy one!" Missus Tashner exclaimed in quite passable German. "You did very fine, my mother would say you're made for having many children. It is still early—so—you can rest until it is time to get up and cook your husband's supper. Frau Geiger, I am finished here, so I will go now." Noticing Michael peeking around the door, she smiled. "And here is the big brother!"

Hannah placed the baby by Jane's side, beckoned to him. "Come, Bubbeleh, come in, see your new brodder—den we let your Mama sleep a little." Michael stood by the bed looking at his mother, captivated by her long hair lying open on the pillow. He had never seen it unpinned, it made her look so different, so soft, nearly a stranger. Jane folded back the shawl to let him see the baby and Michael was very, very disappointed. For months, everybody had been telling him how lucky he was, that soon he would have a brother or sister to play with—but this? This funny-looking thing? This was much too small to come out to play ball with him right now. He wished grown-ups wouldn't do that all the time, forget to explain things the way they really would be, it made life very confusing. Seeing Michael's disappointment, Hannah took his hand, bent to kiss Jane's cheek.

"I take Michael wit me. You sleep till John comes—and no getting up till de morning. After John see de baby, he eat his supper at my house, den bring Michael home." Expecting it might be a girl, John was very pleased Jane had produced another son. He kissed her tenderly, murmured, "*Grazie*, Ninnie," and, closing the bedroom door gently behind him, left to have supper at the Geigers'. Her body disencumbered, once more her own, Jane slept. The new life by her side stared into the darkness, as though it was familiar.

Because neither could think of a name that pleased them both, they named the baby John. Throughout his life, he was referred to by that name. Never a Johnny or Jack, even when a small boy, never held a nickname. It suited his character to be—a dour, impregnable John. Michael tried to adore his new brother but was not permitted to by the object of his affection. As with most, the baby shunned whatever contained human warmth as though mistrusting it. John was a child one remembered by the confusion one felt in his presence. His speculative gaze made most people uncomfortable, as though he knew their secrets and was willing to tell. Hannah, who schooled herself to love Jane's sons equally, found the effort this required unnerving.

Daylight had darkened, the threat of approaching thunder heavy in the summer air when, after a lazy labor aided by Morgana's infusion of sage leaves steeped in laudanum, Serafina gave birth to Stan's son. Overly large, already handsome, he resembled those chubby cherubs depicted on ceilings of ornate Italian churches. While her boisterous family celebrated, toasted the new father, stomped joyously about to the music supplied by happy uncles, Serafina, freshly washed and cologned, examined her child for signs of the Devil. Satisfied that he was neither marked by a clubfoot, nor a discoloration upon his flesh, she handed him over to Morgana, turned on her side to enjoy the still lingering effects of her potion and slept.

Believing it was his idea, Stan named his son Salvatore, after his father-in-law, earning that man's benevolence for relinquishing his Rumanian heritage in order to do honor to his. When Fritz and John spoke of this, they both agreed it was certainly a diplomatic move, but that Stan believed he needed to flatter, they found disquieting. At the musical uncles' insistence, the boy was given a second name in honor of the greatest living tenor and fellow Italian—Enrico Caruso and, just to make sure at least one saint was in his corner, they also added Anthony.

The boy's formative years were ones of confusion, his identity continuously disrupted. His grandfather called him Salvatore, his uncles Enrico, his father and those of his friends, Tony, his mother and aunt, having decided from the moment of birth that he was too perfect to be anything but an angel come to earth, called him Angelo.

In later years, Tony, as he thought of himself, could switch names with rapid ease whenever the need arose for him to stay one jump ahead of the law.

Flimsy peignoirs and lace-trimmed unmentionables restocked, Ebbely was ready, once more, to return to his Southern Route, explaining that only there, frail females still practiced the true art of delicate manipulation of their men with style.

"Give me a Southern belle and I'll show you a woman who knows how to entice a man, show him no mercy, while making him rapturously oblivious to his fate! I'd rather face a horde of Bengal tigers who haven't eaten a man in months, than one of those dainty damsels from South of the Mason-Dixon Line!"

"Den why in Himmel you go all dat way down dere, you silly?" Hannah challenged.

"Why my dear? Because those vixens are forever in need of new ammunition and, yours truly is just the man to supply them with it. Do with it what they will—I sell—they buy and let those that can, save themselves! Farewell! I'll be back in time to Trick or Treat."

"So long? It isn't even real summer yet?"

"I must. I have pretties to sell, places to see—you know me—the open road beckons and I must follow where it leads me! My God! I sound like John! Kiss his new babe for me and tell our Michael, no jealousy of new brothers allowed. I shall return sated with corn pone, hush puppies, and collard greens, ravenous for all you have to offer and I don't just mean your cooking! Adieu, Stalwart Guardian at the Gate—pretty postcards I shall send!" and Rumpelstiltskin was gone once more.

Apple trees were in full blossom, wild huckleberries would soon be in season, time for Hannah and Jane to make their summer trip into the city of Detroit. Leaving the baby in Rosie's care, this year they took Michael with them, so he could have his first taste of a strawberry ice-cream soda which, of course, he adored—even though at first it tickled his nose.

Now, all of two and rock steady on his chubby legs, he joined the band of boys that trailed Mr. Kennec's wagon, hoping for icy chips to fly their way. He would have followed even if there hadn't been any coveted rewards, for old shaggy Molly was still his first love and the iceman his very special friend.

"Missus, I notice your little tyke has joined my bunch of scallywags. Okay by you? I'll send him home if it ain't." Mr. Kennec pocketed his twenty-five cents.

"He never goes further than this street. He's very obedient that way."

"Well, if you say so, it's okay then." Pointing to the wash basket newly occupied. "See you got yourself a new one. Congratulations. Boy or girl?"

"Boy."

"Nice looker." He finished his lemonade. "Well, I'll be on my way. Good mornin' to you, Ma'am."

"Mr. Kennec." He turned. "Here, you forgot your carrot." Molly's treat had become an expected ritual.

"Much obliged as usual." Tipping his cap, the iceman left the kitchen, calling, "Hey, Mike, want to feed Molly for me?" This too had become a summertime ritual that to the little boy seemed forever new.

In the early hours of Glory Day, after a difficult labor bordering on complications, Henrietta's third little girl greeted the day. Thinking it a fitting name for a true American born on the Fourth of July, Johann named her Gloria. Again there were christenings to sew for and attend—and again Jane was relieved that John made no reference to wanting such for his sons. Hannah thought of saying something but then remembered what a sensitive subject religion as a whole was to Jane, so kept her mouth shut.

15

Rushing down the stairs, John called to Jane in the kitchen. "Can't stop for breakfast, the president is coming!" Wiping her hands on the apron, Jane entered the hall.

"What? What president?"

"Woodrow Wilson, president of these United States, that's all."

"He's coming here?!" Jane knew it was a stupid question but it just slipped out. John, busy putting on his bicycle clips, didn't look up.

"Yesterday they draped the whole Administration building in flags and bunting, put up a huge sign that says 'Hats off to the president who has kept us out of war.' Those are the Boss's own words!" He reached for his derby. "When he arrives, there will be more than thirty thousand workers assembled to greet him. Our photographic and moving picture departments are going to record it. We have been getting organized for days! Got to go! I don't know when I'll be home. *Ciao*, Ninnie!" and he was off.

Returning to her kitchen, Jane wondered what it must feel like to actually see the president of a great country—have him come to pay his respects for what you have achieved. It was a great honor to be sure! Maybe she could walk over, the plant wasn't that far away, just to catch a glimpse of him; but Michael wouldn't be able to walk all that way and, with the baby in one arm and him in the other, she wouldn't make it either. Oh, well, better put the water on to boil, start washing diapers and forget about grand excursions. Sometimes she felt as confined by motherhood as she had by the mountains of her youth.

At breakfast the next morning Jane couldn't resist asking if John had actually seen the president and what did he look like.

Focused on carefully decapitating his three-minute egg, her husband replied that Woodrow Wilson was a true aristocrat and that in his silk top hat he looked as distinguished as one would expect him to be.

"And Ninnie, you will have to curb your spending, learn to be more frugal."

"Excuse me?"

"Just what I said. I noticed you sent away for material again."

"I thought you agreed we finally needed curtains for the bedroom. We can't keep tacking up sheets, linen costs more to replace."

"Well, when Mr. Ford ordered his gardeners to dig up the dandelions on the Fair Lane lawns, you know what his wife said?"

"How would I know that? Michael finish your milk."

"Mrs. Ford said, 'Thirty men at six dollars a day picking dandelions! We can't spend that much money!' If a millionaire's wife can say that, surely you can do without bedroom curtains!"

"Eggs have gone up—used to be seventy-two cents for three dozen, now it's that for two."

"I wasn't speaking of essentials."

"I see. Michael don't squirm, finish your oatmeal. Hannah and I were planning while they last to put up some spiced peaches, but if you think these are unessential . . ."

"Is she planning to make her special baked ham for Christmas this year?"

"I think so—"

"Well then, spiced peaches are essential. Better buy two bushels. See you tonight. Michael! You heard your mother—finish!" And John was off.

Young Mr. Edsel became officially engaged to the pretty young thing that had first caught his eye when, as a youngster, he attended Miss Ward Foster's dancing classes to acquire social graces. Niece to J. L. Hudson, founder of the grandest department store of Detroit, the Ford wives fully approved of his choice, eagerly awaited any news concerning the preparations for the wedding announced for November; speculated on where the ceremony would take place, who would be invited, how many millionaires with bejeweled wives would attend, what color the so lucky Miss Clay would choose for her bridesmaids' dresses, how many she would have. Highland Park buzzed with the excited anticipation as did the other immigrant communities within and about Detroit that housed the families of Ford workers.

Prototypes of Henry Ford's pet project, his Fordson tractor, had been built, were being demonstrated at local and state fairs across the country, the Boss often appearing in person accompanied by his son, a camera operator to film the occasion for Ford's animated weeklies, and to make absolutely certain that no one could miss knowing they were there, bringing along the Ford Company's Hawaiian band strumming their ukuleles.

On the western front, the carnage accelerated. The battles of the Somme had begun and on the first day of the British offensive, forty thousand were wounded, another twenty thousand killed—Jimmy Weatherby among them. Shot through the heart, by the time a brave Lizzie found him, it was too late. His friends, not knowing Jimmy was already dead, waited for news of him.

On the first of August, the Ford Motor Company declared a one-million-dollar profit, and paid those workers who qualified for its profit-sharing plan the highest wage in the industrial world. John splurged—bought his wife a baby carriage. It was so grand it had real bicycle tires on its wheels, even sported an attached parasol. The whole neighborhood came to admire it. Missus Nussbaum pinched the tires, very impressed, Missus Horowitz marveled at the roomy interior, Missus Sullivan commented on the elegance of the fringed parasol; all the wives agreed that Jane's husband was both thoughtful and generous. Good-hearted Henrietta wasn't a bit jealous—only mentioned she hoped Johann would think they could afford one just like it.

The first morning Jane wheeled the baby over to Hannah's house, Michael in his sailor suit trotting proudly by its side, her gloved hands resting on the ivory handle guiding the tall carriage, Jane felt like one of the grand ladies she had seen parading their offspring along the flower bordered paths on Belle Isle. From then on, her days took on a freedom she had not known since becoming a mother. She went visiting, explored sections of Highland Park she had never been to, even took over Missus Nussbaum's Watcher duties when her Elsa came down with chicken pox.

When Michael learned to balance himself, straddling the carriage without crushing his baby brother, she was able to go all the way to the plant, showed him the wondrous world where his father *really* lived. In the warmth of summer, they could stay out for hours; whenever the baby needed to be fed, she nursed him beneath her shawl, hidden in a doorway while Michael munched a sandwich and the apple she had brought for him. Then it was back to showing him the exciting sights beyond the tall link fence that separated the kingdom of Ford from Manchester Street; the great puffs of billowing smoke that rose from the busy railroad yard, the fascinating noises that came from trains that the little boy couldn't actually see, far over by Woodward Avenue, more smoke rising high into the sky from a row of thin chimneys so tall they looked like giants on stilts.

Jane pointed out the great power house, the foundry, where they boiled the special steel that made the little Model T—and over there, that long, long building with all the windows—that was the Crystal Palace, where many men and their very important machines did their work better because they had so much daylight to see by. She pointed out the chutes, the walkways, the overhead cranes.

Excited Michael would ask questions and she, as excited as he, answered, tried to explain as best she could. They could have stayed all day and never had enough. One afternoon, arriving late at their special spot, they were caught as thousands of workers were leaving their shift and thousands more were arriving to begin theirs. Bells clanging insistently, endless streetcars arriving disgorging men, others departing with more, factory whistles blaring, thousands streaming out as thousands streamed in. Plastered against the fence, the baby carriage between them, Jane and Michael were too scared to move. But the second things calmed down a bit, they hurried home, got safely inside the house just as John's bicycle came into view.

One Sunday, arriving at the Geigers' just as Stan drove up, Michael pointed to his automobile and, in his childish lisp, piped, "Th-that's a Model T. I know where Papa makes it—Mamma showed it me!" and the cat was out of the proverbial bag.

Most of that evening revolved around John's little boy, his obvious pride in his father's work, the Ford men delighting in asking him questions, receiving his enthusiastic and amazingly knowledgeable answers. Beaming, Johann turned to John. "That boy of yours is going to be a master mechanic someday!"

"Damn right he'll be. You can see it's in his blood," Carl agreed.

"Never in all my days have I seen a youngster so interested—not even the Boss's boy!" Fritz preened, the proud godfather. Zoltan helped himself to another biscuit.

"Stan, as Serafina will be expecting you back early anyway, on your way, why don't you drive the boy home after supper."

And so, thanks to his uncle Zoltan, sitting by the side of his uncle Stan, Michael was driven home in flivver style. John lifted his son down from the car, was about to carry him into the house, when a sleepy little voice asked, "Uncle Stan? Is your motorcar a Touring?" Taken aback, Stan answered that it was. The little boy nodded, as if satisfied with himself. "Uncle Ebbely—he has a Sedan and Mamma and me, we have a carriage," and, putting his head on his father's shoulder, Michael fell fast asleep.

Now that John knew, Jane was afraid their exciting expeditions to the busy plant might be forbidden, but all he did was caution her never to go there when shifts were changing, explaining that could be chaotic and possibly frightening—which Jane already knew only too well. He made love to her that night, with a tenderness she hadn't felt for a very long time. Later, lying beside him as he slept, she wondered why this time had been so different.

The baby carriage became Jane's prized possession. She kept it polished, waxed and oiled, after every adventure she washed its splendid tires till they looked unused. Having freed her, she named it her Lizzie and, for a while, was content.

In New Jersey, German saboteurs blew up a munitions arsenal that the newspapers claimed was a staggering twenty-million-dollar loss and Stan felt vindicated. "What did I tell you? That much stockpiled ammunition? For what? Only one reason—we're getting ready to enter the war!"

Fritz disagreed. "That's not for us. We've been sending war materials over to England ever since the war started. That's why all those German spies are over here."

"Well, if you ask me we should be using it ourselves! How much longer are we going to just sit back and watch?"

"As long as President Wilson has his way."

"You mean, as long as we make a profit and the steel barons get even richer," snapped Stan.

Woodrow Wilson's reelection campaign running under the slogan "He kept us out of the war" was beginning to find opposition.

The Henry Ford trade school for teenage boys who, in the founder's words, "Never had a chance," had been "thrown on the world without a trade," opened to the approval of his men.

Margaret Sanger opened the first birth control clinic and was stoned.

Yellowstone National Park admitted its first automobile—a Model T, driven by its owner, a woman—and after excluding them since the windfall of 1914, the Ford Motor Company decided to extend its Five-Dollar-Day policy to finally include its women employees.

Tin hats proving too vulnerable to flying shrapnel, the first helmets made of steel were introduced by the Germans, and quickly became a part of modern warfare on all sides. In America, the Ford Motor Company was given a contract to produce them for the British armed forces.

Eager to fight for his kaiser, Heinz-Hermann left Chicago, secretly crossed the border into Canada, bribed his way aboard a Norwegian merchant ship, eventually made his way back to Prussia, to take up arms for the glory of the Fatherland.

September winds stripped the trees, early frost was in the morning air, the time had come for Hannah and Jane to get out the snakes, see who needed mending. Hercules had lost one of his button eyes, Goliath, who stopped the draft coming up from beneath the cellar door, needed his belly resewn, others, having given dedicated service the winter before, were leaking their stuffing. In the cozy kitchen, John sleeping in his basket under the table, Michael busy on the floor drawing serious squiggles on leftover paper his father had brought him from work, the two women sewed. The baby woke, began to fuss, Jane spiraled her mended snake into their basket, bent, picked up her son, put him to her breast. An automatic action of accepted duty without a trace of tenderness, that struck Hannah to the heart. An act so breathtakingly beautiful in its human simplicity had become mundane, even bovine. What demons did she hold so dear, that kept this young mother from being one? For Hannah, who either loved or hated, knew no middle-road emotion, the so hidden core of Jane eluded her; at times it felt as if she had bestowed her love on one who, though she needed it, accepted it, used it well, did not, in fact, exist. Like the fairy tales of her German childhood that doted on little children wandering lost, abandoned in dark forests, Hannah sensed Jane was too, wished she could find her, lead her home. Teresa had believed Jane's emptiness could be filled by recognizing God, Hannah by recognizing love—perhaps both were right—it was the same thing.

The morning Hannah's talking telephone actually rang, it startled her so, she dropped a big pot of boiling water, flooding the kitchen floor, screamed, *"Gott im Himmel!"* Not meaning the water—and ran! Out of breath, hand shaking clutching the earpiece, she yelled, "Hello? Hello? Somebody dere? I'm here!"

Through the crackle, she heard a faint giggle, followed by her Ebbely's voice, shouting, "Dear Lady—am I the first?"

"What?" she yelled back.

"The first! The first one to communicate through to your marvelous Christmas present?"

"Yes! I got such a scare, I dropped de pot mit boiling water!"

"Oh, dear! Hurt yourself?"

"No, just de kitchen has a hot flood!"

"I am relieved!"

"What?"

"Never mind. The reason I am telephoning . . ."

"Yes?"

"The reason I am telephoning . . ."

"You say dat already, dis costs money!"

"Precisely! I wanted to tell you that I shall not be coming back as promised."

"Oh, Ebbely—why?"

"Because, I am in love!"

"Where! Where you in love?"

"In New Orleans."

"You go crazy dere wit one of dose Frenchie floosies?"

"No, no, my dear. Nothing like that!"

"Den what? Who is she?"

"She's not a she—she's an IT."

"WHAT?"

"MY EARDRUM, Hannah—PLEASE! I'm trying to tell you . . ."

"So tell, already!"

"I have fallen head over little heels in love with a new thing that here they call Jazz. Utterly sublime! Gets into your blood, makes you tingle all over!"

"You in love with a girlie called Jazz who *tingles* you?"

"I should be home by Thanksgiving, I'll explain it all to you then. I'm taking lessons! . . ."

"You're taking lessons? For WHAT?"

"Tell Fritz and the others hello. Good-bye!" and the line went dead. Stunned, Hannah stood holding the silent earpiece, staring at it as though expecting it to come back to life, when it didn't, shaking her head, hung it back on its hook and, mumbling something about men and their consistent lunacy where no-good-Hootchie-Kootchie-harlot-hussy floozies were concerned, went to mop her kitchen floor.

This year, Michael wanted to go trick-or-treating dressed as a Ford but, after his mother convinced him even her skill with the needle didn't extend to fashioning motorcars, he consented and allowed himself, once again, to be draped beneath his ghostly sheet.

On the first of November, All Saints' Day, a strange choice for a wedding, in the splendid mansion of J. L. Hudson young Mr. Edsel married his love, disappointing the Ford wives who had looked forward to a big church ceremony that would have at least afforded them a peek, standing outside on the sidewalk.

Fritz, uncorking the Schnapps to toast the happy couple, couldn't get over that the Boss's boy was suddenly old enough to marry, have sons of his own.

"How time flies . . . seems only yesterday he was just a schoolboy, labeling his Papa's machines. Every summer he worked hard, always had a cheery 'Hello,' never was a snooty Boss's son. Now he will have a fine son of his own to carry on the business—make Mr. Ford a proud grandpapa. Here!" Fritz handed Hannah her glass. "To Mr. Edsel and his new Missus—the Good Lord give them joy!"

Everyone now talked of the frantic construction going on to enlarge the already giant Highland Park plant to enable the production of the next season's estimate for the manufacture of 540,000 Model Ts. Fritz kept shaking his head, remembering when they had made all of six in just one day and how proud they had all been to achieve such rapidity. One of Henry Ford's pet projects—a Model T as a one-ton truck—was about to roll off its own assembly line and his latest passion, the transformation of his endless marshland holdings along the Rouge River into the greatest industrial empire yet envisioned where (as he had with the common man) Ford intended to free the small farmer from the backbreaking drudgery of tilling his land by manufacturing an affordable machine that would do the work for him—the Fordson Tractor. John, who had been so enthusiastic when first discussing the advantages of such a manufacturing complex along the river near Dearborn, now when congratulated on his clairvoyance—smiled, accepted his friends' accolades, yet told no one that he was now involved in its conceptual design.

Woodrow Wilson was reelected by such a small margin, it seemed that the country might be growing tired of its isolationism and, to avoid a verbal confrontation, Rumpelstiltskin sent Hannah an especially pretty picture postcard depicting bluebirds weaving a garland of forget-me-nots above a dainty damsel being gallantly kissed in a gazebo, telling her in writing that alas he would not be able to return by Thanksgiving after all, promising on his most sacred honor she could definitely count on him to be back in time to waltz her on the pond on New Year's Day. Putting an arm around his wife's sagging shoulders, Fritz tried to comfort her.

"Ach, Fritzchen, I'm not so sad because I'm missing our Ebbely," she reassured him. "Only I am so vorried—vhy is he staying dere in dat naughty place so long? Maybe one of dose Juicy-Lucies has him all crazy mit all dat lounging and reclining dat he likes so much—and what den?"

Hannah baked so many doughnuts to keep herself from worrying, she started giving them out to her Watcher chaperones, telling them that whenever they found a poor misused woman, to feed her, as feeding in sorrow gave comfort to the soul.

With Henrietta's new baby next door, Frederika was nearing the breaking point. She could hear its cry through the thin walls that divided Rudy's half of their house from Johann's. At night, it sounded so like a stray kitten begging to be let in, she would wake wanting to do so, then realize it was only Henrietta's baby. During the day, the cry made her so nervous, she invented sounds of her own to drown out those that crept through the wall, often huddling in the closet amongst her leaf-green finery where she felt safe, once more untouchable. On days when even this did not help, she would have to leave her house, walk over to Jane's with a dress as excuse for doing so. Once arrived, instead of abating, her nervousness seemed to increase, as if she were confused by needing to escape what she couldn't endure.

Sensing her presence, John screamed his welcome, forcing her to pick him up to distract him. Jane had the impression she didn't want to hold him, did so only to stop the noise.

"That dress needs to be shortened." Frederika held the baby as though he was a bundle of dirty clothes whose proximity might soil hers. "I presume you know the correct length that is now fashionable."

"I heard because of the war—in London the new length is now all of five inches above the ankle."

"That will make dancing so much easier."

"I don't think that's the reason. I think it is to make it easier for the nurses at the front and for those who are taking over the work of men."

"Women—doing men's work—how ridiculous! Won't help. Anyway—we are winning!"

Scissors in midair, Jane stopped opening the hem of Frederika's dress. "We?"

Michael about to come in from the yard, took one look, saw who was in the kitchen with his mother, turned and bolted back outside. The boy had a healthy aversion to Frederika that at times Jane could agree with.

"The Central powers, of course. Who else? You don't honestly believe the British and French have a chance of winning against us, do you!" As this was said as a statement, not a question, Jane remained silent.

More animated than she had seen her for some time, Frederika strode about, carrying Jane's baby unaware she was doing so.

"If I were home, I would be at the front—nursing our brave soldiers. But in this country? What am I? Nothing! Just sitting in an ugly little house filled with sounds that you never know when they will come, having to live with a man who actually believes building automobiles is important work!"

"Frederika, do you wish you hadn't married Rudy?"

As if too much reality exposed, the question seemed to frighten her, which in turn fostered aggression.

"What? What do *you* know! You're so insufferably noble! Sewing, having babies like a sow—that's all you're good for—that's your life and, as far as I am concerned, you're welcome to it!" Without reluctance, Frederika shoved the baby back into his basket, picked up her hat and gloves and, ordering Jane to have her dress ready by the very next day or she wouldn't pay for it, left. Bereft in his basket, aware Frederika had gone, John began to scream. Jane, concentrating on her work, let him.

When Henrietta's baby next door developed an ear infection that caused the little girl to whimper incessantly, Frederika, robbed of all rest, began to roam aimlessly about the house, a sleepwalker in daylight, in the evenings greeting her husband's return as if she had forgotten he existed. Believing no other solution was open to him, Rudy made his decision to leave Highland Park, sold his half of the house, gave up his elevated position with Ford, to take a lesser one with the Packard Motor Car Company in Flint, whose advertising slogan "Ask the Man Who Owns One" rivaled "Watch the Fords Go By."

It was nearly Christmas when Rudy came to say good-bye to the people who meant the most to him. No longer the happy-go-lucky young Austrian, always ready for a joke, a good-natured prank, now a tired, strained man who had given up a nurtured dream in the belief that he could save a marriage already doomed, a woman's sanity already lost.

As if wanting to give of her strength, Hannah held him close. "Mazel tov, my Rudy. Here a home is for you—always."

Fritz wrung his hands. "We will miss you, my boy. So long it has been, all of us together!"

John embraced his friend, "Don't work too hard for the competition. Keep in touch," then stepped away, embarrassed by his own emotions.

Carl punched his shoulder. "Yes, you rascal. Keep in touch and, don't forget, tell us if they are doing anything on their big, heavy cars that we poor little flivver makers should know about!"

Peter shook Rudy's hand, holding it in both of his.

Zoltan just stood looking at him, not wanting to see him go. Stan, who had offered to drive Rudy to the station, took his arm. "It's getting late. Come on, we have to pick up Frederika. It's not forever! You can come to visit . . ."

"Sure! Stan is right, it's not forever. Well then, good-bye, everybody. See you soon. Maybe next year for Easter, okay?"

Stan pulled him towards the door. Jane saw Hannah shake her head, not believing she would ever see her Casanova Rudy Zegelmann again.

Now that winter darkness lasted into morning's icing streets without relief, Jane, as his friends had, ventured to bring up the delicate subject of John becoming the proud possessor of his very own Model T.

Straightening up from securing his bicycle clips, John looked at his wife as though she had suggested he buy himself a yacht.

"Do you know that every morning rain or shine the Boss rides his bicycle from his house to his front gate and back? And that's two miles and he's fit as a fiddle. So?" And he rode off.

Well, she mused to herself, *if I had known that* Henry Ford *rode a bicycle I would never have even thought of broaching the subject of John giving his up.* Jane shook her head. Everywhere one turned that man got in the way. Sliding the front door snake back into his position, Jane picked up John, who had crawled into the hall and took him back to his place in the kitchen.

Overcome by a sudden urge to be girlish, Mr. Henry's aging sister knitted him new mittens in alternating rows of Holly Red and Snow White to complement the Yuletide season. She had planned to add a tiny elfin bell to the tip of each thumb, but there the mailman had put his foot down, threatening to not wear them at all. Two days before Christmas, with paws resembling peppermint sticks, Mr. Henry handed Hannah a letter that had made the perilous journey across the sea, all the way from England. Knowing how fond her son had been of his American land-lady, Jimmy Weatherby's mother had written her of his death, enclosing a small photograph of him in his uniform, as a keepsake. Hannah placed it by the three kings and cried.

Nearly everyone received Christmas mail from home. From Poland, a letter from his father informed Peter of the death of a brother, the gassing of another. Carl's mother wrote, telling him his youngest brother, a mere boy of nineteen, had lost a leg, his father fighting on the eastern front was reported missing in action. From Flanders, Rosie's family received a conciliatory letter from the commanding officer of the Irish Fusiliers, assuring them their son had died a brave soldier's death for King and Country. Out of Rumania, now in German hands, Stan got news that his village had been razed to the ground, his parents fled, no one knew where. From Bavaria Fritz received a postal card from Hannah's brother-in-law, the butcher, decorated with grinning gnomes, dancing around a Christmas tree on which was written, in bold German script, "WE ARE VICTORIOUS," with his signature beneath, under which Hannah's sister Anna had added, "Where is my Heinz-Hermann? What have you done with him?" No mail had come through from Italy or Bulgaria.

When it was time and Fritz had lit all the candles on the little tree, they tried to resurrect the joy that once had been and failed. Christmas at the Geigers' had come and was gone.

※

All morning Hannah waited for Ebbely to appear until Fritz had enough and announced that if she didn't come immediately he was going skating without her. The first day of the New Year had dawned so clear and crisp, by the time they got to the pond it was full of people enjoying themselves. Still a little dejected, Hannah was lacing up her skates when from above her bent head came a soft whisper. "Well? Do you always keep your partners waiting?"

And there bundled in many scarves, one tied under his chin holding down his derby, stood Rumpelstiltskin bowing low before her.

"You are here! Ach, Ebbely! I was watching and waiting at de house!"

"Did I not promise? Happy New Year, Fritz! May I borrow your lady?"

Fritz grinned, "Happy New Year, Ebberhardt—you should have seen her—all morning she's been glued to the window looking for you . . . drove me crazy. Take her for God's sake—she's all yours!"

Hannah gave her husband a look, put her gloved hand into Ebbely's and off they swept.

Later, cheeks red, exhilarated, the dampening mood of Christmas dissipated by the lovely day, they all met back at the Geigers' for mulled cider and Ebbely in concert.

And how he played! The piano jumped, he jumped, the whole parlor seemed to syncopate as his little fingers tickled the ivories—coaxing, cajoling vibrant infectious rhythms. Those lessons that had kept him in New Orleans for so long had surely been worth the time.

Quite overcome by his virtuoso efforts, the little man mopped his brow. "Well, my friends . . . that's jazz! Capital J, capital A and a Z-Z-Zee! How do you like it?"

Carl scratched his head, "Well, Strauss it ain't."

"You want Strauss? I'll show you Strauss as a Southern Black—listen . . ."

And Ebbely launched into an intricate improvisation built upon the Blue Danube Waltz. If those in the parlor had actually understood what it was he was doing, they would have known how really superb their Ebbely was. Michael was so taken by the beat, he started to dance—stomping his feet, gyrating his little body—Ebbely was delighted.

"John, you've got yourself a real pigganinnie there—just like the ones that perform on the streets of New Orleans. Next time I go, I may kidnap your heir—show him off at a revival meeting. Next I'm planning to learn the banjo. As a matter of fact, I am seriously considering giving up unmentionables altogether."

Hannah was so relieved that jazz was only a strange noise that passed for music and not the name of a conniving, predatory *Juicy Lucy* who was out to ravish her Ebbely, she didn't care what he wanted to do.

While they drank their spicy cider, Ebbely entertained, finishing with such a thunderous rendition of "Alexander's Ragtime Band," they worried he might do himself an injury. Delighted by their applause, he swung around on his stool.

"Thank you, my friends. Now that you've approved my latest passion, what's new with yours?"

John laughed, "Well, America now has more Model Ts than bathtubs."

"How delightful!"

"Rudy left."

"What? You're joking!"

Fritz shook his head. "No joke. He's gone over to Packard."

Ebbely refilled his glass. "I can't believe it. For God's sake, why?"

"To get away. Take Frederika to a new place with no memories perhaps." Carl volunteered.

"Poor Rudy," Zoltan lit his pipe, "now with Jimmy . . . two are gone."

"Well, at least Rudy's still alive." Ebbely turned back to Fritz. "The war, what's the latest here? Of course, in New Orleans they are only interested in what's happening to the French—and with the carnage at Verdun all is gloom."

"Oh, Ebbely—no terrible var talk on dis fine New Year's Day."

"Forgive me, my dear."

But the subject had been voiced and now lay heavy about the room. Carl was the first to break the silence. "There isn't a man on the line by now who hasn't lost someone back home."

"We are already shipping enough war materials to England—why can't we just go over there and finish the job for them?"

"Yes, we probably should have gone to war when they sank the *Lusitania*," Ebbely agreed.

"Thus speaks our only neutral."

"In this bloody war there can be no neutrals—I don't give a damn what President Wilson says." Johann ground out his cigarette.

Fritz sighed, "Ja, we can't hold out much longer . . ."

Peter lit his cigarette. "The Boss said he will burn down the plant before he makes the machinery of war."

"Likely story," Stan scoffed.

John disagreed, "I think he means it."

"Henry Ford means whatever gets him a good newspaper headline."

Ebbely jumped into a brewing confrontation between John and Stan. "Talking about headlines—I read that Ford is blaming that woman for his Peace Ship fiasco. Says—and I quote—that 'she took him in, used him to gain importance for herself like all the money-grabbing Jews.'"

Hannah rose from the arm of her husband's chair. "Ebbely—you hear? Young Mr. Edsel is now a fine married man. Fine vedding they had?"

"And now because he's secretary of the whole company, last August he signed personally a thirty-four-million-dollar contract for our rubber tires with Mr. Firestone . . . at just twenty-two! Imagine!" added Peter proudly.

They were back to what suited them best—the subject they knew and trusted—and so talked shop, brought Ebbely up to date until Hannah announced, "Everybody! First supper of dis 1917 New Year! Ready! Come eat!"

Lingering guilt that it was he who had unthinkingly broached the subject of war, Ebbely asked Fritz in private, what if anything he thought he could do to help their friends. There had always been a sage closeness between the two, completely separate from the frills and flourish of the little man's affection for the other man's wife.

"Ebberhardt, my friend—I don't think there is anything anyone can do. But it must be hard—not to be in the fight. Over there helping. Now I don't have that."

"What do you mean?"

"Well, I come from the bad side—so I am not feeling guilty I'm not over there fighting for my old country. Here, this is my country now—for us Germans it is hard, but maybe also easier—know what I mean?"

"You mean it is easier to turn your back on what is bad than to desert what is good?"

"Ja, that's what I mean."

"You have a point. What about Rudy? He's Austrian—does he feel the way you do?"

"You know I think he is already fighting a war—his own war—so he has no time for the Big One."

"Poor boy—what a waste."

"Ja, just when he made supervisor the Boss even spoke to him, called him 'Rudy'—knew his name. Best Chassis Man I ever saw. Knows his trade."

"John seems to be doing alright."

"Ach, you know our John. Ever since he was a boy fresh off the boat—he never changed. He's designing now—I don't know what—but it's not just tools no more. Even young Mr. Edsel thinks John is going places."

"If Henry Ford were really God . . ."

"Our John would be a priest!" Fritz finished for him, laughing.

"You ever hear from that annoying nephew of Hannah's?"

"No. Never. His parents think we did something to chase him away. Now you know we didn't . . ."

"Of course not. But—you weren't sad when he went."

"Something about that boy—couldn't put my finger on it—just a feeling . . ."

"Aha—one of your famous feelings? A good or bad one?"

"Bad." Fritz said it softly.

"Listen, take my word for it. Never have anything to do with him again—if he ever comes back, lock the door!"

"Hey—I couldn't do that . . ."

"Well, you better! Because that's a Hun—a real Hun—even if you aren't!"

"You think we'll get into the war? Stan does."

"Well, of course the papers keep it quiet—but I hear rumors. There're so many being killed they're actually running out of men over there. If we don't send them reinforcements this war may last until everyone is dead or crippled."

"Where you hear that?"

"Here and there—I even heard rumors of mutiny—soldiers just refusing to go on killing, on *all* sides, just leaving the trenches."

"*Mein Gott!*"

"I've been seriously thinking of joining up myself."

"You?"

"Yes, me! Do you know, the British are so desperate for men they now have a special battalion for little men—five feet *and* under?"

"You're joking!"

"No, it's true! I heard it in Baton Rouge from a very reliable source. They're called the Bantams and in the trenches they dig a shelf for themselves to stand on so that they can see over the top to shoot!"

"Hannah won't let you."

"My dear Fritz—I admire, adore, even . . . cherish your wife—but there I would have to draw my masculine line."

"We come here because no war—then the Spanish-American start . . ."

"That was just a skirmish compared . . ."

"Ja—but killing is still killing. But I worry, so much is changing, know what I mean?"

"Yes, but tell me . . ."

"Well, first here our Highland Park—so nice a village it was—now even our big pond is too full for free and easy skating."

"Yes—I noticed—certainly more crowded than it was last year."

"See. And the plant—sure I know it's all great big business—we make lots of money—everybody gets rich—even us—but now just hard labor—standing—like Stan said long ago—what monkeys can do—but the men are not monkeys in the brain and . . . ! I see sometimes a sort of no complaining suffering—not just because of this war—something else—and that worries me. Ach, I talk too much!" Fritz smiled apologetically. Ebbely shook his head, motioned him to continue. "Well, I have this feeling . . ." Fritz held up a hand as Ebbely reacted. "Don't get excited like Zoltan. No, this one is not for one thing—this is like for everything. Hard to explain."

"Try."

"Well, like I said—here too many new people—at work too many—even in the city of Detroit too many now—and every day more come and more—everywhere everything is changing—even in the whole world after this butcher's war will never be like it used to be."

"True, quite true. I hear some say the mass slaughter over there will be the end to all war. Can you believe that?"

Fritz repacked his pipe. "Do you?"

Ebbely shifted in his chair. "I want to. What a human tragedy it would be if it isn't."

"In the old country I read too many history books."

Ebbely smiled, "Is that the German in you talking or the Jew?"

"Ach—you know Ebberhardt—I never think of that being separated."

"You should, my friend—I think you should."

"Why?" asked Fritz, his innocence startled.

"Just a feeling—mine this time, my friend."

Hannah slid open the parlor doors. "What you doing you two?"

Ebbely jumped out of his chair. "I know, I know—wash up for supper—right, my Lady Fair?"

"Right, my second favorite Bubbele and take dis Fritz wit you."

"Yes, Mama!" they caroled as they scampered up the stairs.

"Ah! It must be Noodle Day! There you are, Tall Lady!" Ebbely broke off in mid-riff.

Jane hesitated in the doorway. "I didn't mean to disturb you."

"You don't. Someone listening puts me on my metal. Come sit. Anything special you want to hear?"

"I like your jazz when you play it slow."

"That's what's called the blues. Got the blues, Jane?"

"I don't understand. What is blues?"

"When you're sad—and you feel low and your heart aches with too much longing of the hopeless kind."

"Then you're blue?"

"Then you're blue."

"Why music?"

"It helps. In your homeland don't people wail when someone dies?"

"What is *wail*? That's a word I don't know."

"A lament, a cry to the Heavens or to God, if you prefer."

"Oh. In Italy, down in the south they do that all the time—but that's not music."

"Still it's an expression of sorrow. Here in our South, slaves created glorious music out of their sorrows. Their music has words that tell stories—listen . . ."

When he was done, Jane—not knowing why she felt she must whisper, asked, "Ebbely, what was that?!"

"A spiritual."

"Not the blues?"

"A spiritual uplifts the spirit—reaches out to hope. The blues is a human complaint—a sadness that simply exists."

Jane wasn't quite sure what that meant.

"Have you ever seen a slave, Ebbely? What are they like?"

"Oh, child, where did you get your schooling?"

"The Benedictine nuns taught us."

"Any American history?"

"No! Oh, Christopher Columbus, of course."

"That's because he was an Italian no doubt." Ebbely chuckled running his fingers over the keys. "What about Abraham Lincoln? Ring a bell?"

Jane frowned, concentrating. "I think he was a very good American president."

"Right! You can go to the head of the class!"

"Please don't joke, Ebbely—you cannot imagine how I hate not knowing things I should know—that others know already. I wish I could go to school here—not Mr. Ford's—but a real one and learn everything. I thought when I came—but now . . ."

"You are just a dutiful wife and mother. So now you're blue?"

"Yes, I think I must be—but that's not right, is it?"

"Dissatisfaction with the mundane is never wrong."

Again Jane had trouble understanding the words and his meaning. Too shy to keep on showing her ignorance, she sat quietly in her chair and listened as Rumpelstiltskin played ragtime, which confused her even further.

16

Already her third winter as mistress of her own home, everyday life was becoming routine. The washing, mending, ironing, cleaning, cooking—interrupted by sequenced child caring—all had their allotted time, their necessary depletion of energy. As Jane had promised—she did it well, without complaint. Her marriage too had become set in its ways—a union based on conformity, a connubial friendship if not a sexual one; it sufficed. If this young mountain stranger ever needed raw emotion, her work as one of Hannah's Watchers at times supplied her a forfeit of it. Each time she left the stifling slums it resulted in reaffirming her gratitude to the man who provided for her and their children. Those nights when he took her—that persistent disappointment for what she herself could not identify the origin of—never compared with what John gave her in daily tangibles.

John was also unemotionally content. Never having loved a woman as wife and mother, the less complicated she made it—the more natural the result seemed. If he had been a modern man and therefore obligated by contemplative fashion to question his feelings, he might have become confused by the intricacy of being so comfortable within what had every right to be an uncomfortable union. But he was a man of his time, his expected duty, to provide, protect those in his keeping, once assigned, this difficult task accomplished, his male duty done, no one—least of all he—expected of himself further effort.

This early twentieth-century male knew exactly what society demanded of him. His lack of needing to continually search for inner confirmation bred a male confidence that at its best was utterly captivating to his women—at its worst could be indescribably cruel. Like most men of those times, he felt that being dependent on a man was preordained as a woman's destiny—except for a few mavericks who challenged it or those who obliged it only to survive.

But for Jane, freedom had been her sought-after lover and as with most romantic needs, what exactly the achievement of her dream would entail had been made opaque by the sheer desperate wanting of it. Now no longer a dissatisfied girl—simply a dissatisfied woman whose acquired responsibilities she handled better than her uncertainties, at the age of nearly twenty-one Jane was ready for love and didn't know it. If she had, she wouldn't have known what that required either. That the possibility existed that she could fall in love with the man who had married her for their mutual convenience was quite beyond her emotional capabilities. Yet he stood in the doorway of her future's maturity—and she, forever distrustful of what she needed most—saw only the provider not the man.

January was ending when Imperial Germany notified the United States that the forced, selective moratorium decreed by Woodrow Wilson on its submarine warfare was null and void. Therefore, on February 1 its U-boat wolf packs would resume their hunt, sink any and all Atlantic shipping regardless of nationality. Adding, as a magnanimous gesture, that neutral America would be permitted safe passage of one ship a week if it identified itself by displaying a designated ensign of red and white zebra stripes or if its hull was painted in a similar pattern. Left with no further diplomatic maneuvers or choice, President Wilson severed diplomatic ties and asked Congress for a declaration of war.

While the nation waited, Henry Ford announced to the press, "I cannot believe that war will come, but in the event of a declaration of war, I will place our factory at the disposal of the United States government and will operate without one cent of profit." And the Ford Motor Company increased the speed of its assembly lines.

Even before John could read of it in his Italian-American newspaper or Carl and Peter in their Polish ones, Fritz heard from his Russians that their czar had abdicated, and starving peasants rioting for bread had been shot down by the dreaded Cossacks. Mother Russia was in the grip of a fledgling revolution.

Finally on April 6, the United States entered the Great War as combatant—its president rechristening it the "war to end all wars," America's mission "to make the world safe for democracy." And overnight Fritz and Hannah became Huns. The zealot's cry "The only good Hun is a dead Hun" frightening them.

Within days, the Ford Motor Company stopped all civilian production, dedicated its workforce to the execution of government war contracts. As with the Five-Dollar-Day, once again Detroit and its Ford Motor Company became the beckoning pot of gold for desperate men. This time instead of an influx of mostly immigrants, now migrants from out of the deep South turned parts of the inner city and some of the surrounding outskirts into shantytowns.

"My friends, we are fast becoming a classless society," Zoltan settled in his chair.

John had invited his friends home after work to discuss the latest news and was about to answer him when Ebbely interrupted him. "That's a load of . . . how can I put this politely? Will crap do?"

"Ebbely, you actually don't believe that?"

"No, John."

"Well, from Stan I would have expected it, but from you, why? You're not a radical."

"What *is* a radical?"

"A troublemaker. A unionist . . ."

Stan was ready to challenge that, when Carl changed the subject. "The darkies are overrunning the city. One of my men told me in the rooming houses they now sleep in shifts. Three shifts, so, three men to one cot."

"What happens on Sundays?"

"The last Saturday shift man gets the cot and the others sleep on the floor."

"All single men?" asked Ebbely.

"Yes. Those that brought families are huddled in slapped up lean-tos."

"Well, that should supply our busy inspectors with righteous fodder!"

"Stan, why are you so dead set against . . . ?"

Johann interrupted, "He's not the only one, John. Have you seen that little black book they carry around with them?"

"No."

"Well, my friend, let me open your eyes . . ."

"Yes, John," Ebbely's voice held censure, "you really should investigate these goings-on before . . ."

"And what's so terrible in helping these people to a decent life? We've been doing it with the others for years!"

"Ah, that magic word *help*."

"Now even a word is wrong?"

Zoltan cleared his throat. "John, there is a dangerous chasm between helping and forcing."

"You too?"

"Yes, John—me too! Sometimes your blind devotion to Ford is simply childish."

Johann leaned back in his chair. "Okay—don't take our word for it—go ask some of the women."

"Oh, what would they know—they always exaggerate the least little incident and they . . ."

Stan interrupted. "Well, that is true—Serafina gives me blazing hell for the slightest . . ."

"You should live a day in my house, Stan." Peter joined a topic he was versed in. "I get the 'Well, my first husband didn't hang his pants on the bedpost—*he* knew what was proper behavior!' Nothing like a widow to make a second man feel no good."

"You think you've got something to complain about? Ever live under one roof with Irish temper? My God, my Rosie throws things—at me!"

"Come on, Carl—she *is* expecting again so she's bound to be a little nervy," Ebbely soothed.

"Nothing to do with it! She threw a shoe at me on our wedding night!"

His friends laughed.

"What did you do to her?" asked John.

"None of your damn business!"

"I'll tell my Jane to ask her. She and your Rosie are thick as thieves."

"No you don't—then she'll know I said something—and really give me hell!" Carl laughed.

"Hannah *never* exaggerates," observed Fritz.

To a man heads turned toward him in disbelief.

"WHAT? Hannah doesn't *exaggerate*?"

"Well, I mean about really important things—I know for a long time she doesn't—like with this inspector thing . . ."

"That's true," Johann acknowledged. "So ask her. John, I hear we're getting a government order for two thousand ambulances—with special storm curtains."

"Yes, and there's a rumor going around that we may be building warships."

"Ships? Where for God's sake?"

"The new plant in Dearborn," John said, lighting another cheroot.

"That monster? It's not even finished—the war will be over before that's up and running!"

"But the mouth of the river is there, Carl, and the draft should be sufficient for shipbuilding. If the war lasts another year, we'll be producing."

Zoltan looked about the room. "Anyone see in the papers that not enough men have volunteered for service so the government may have to institute conscription?"

"Yes," Fritz answered him, "and then they still have to be trained . . ."

"Well, it's perfectly clear the country isn't ready for war."

"Right you are, Zoltan, but we will be and faster than anyone expects."

"Oh, John!" Ebbely smiled, "You never disappoint. I think it's that unqualified optimism of yours that I like about you the most."

"Hey," Peter's voice held an agitated edge, "if we get conscription what will happen at the plant?"

"Well, some think women may take men's places in many shops—not just ours."

"Next thing they'll get the vote!" grumbled Fritz. "It's all those crazy women over in England that started all this. Troublemakers, all of them."

"Well, if you ask me, women and politics just don't belong together." Johann knocked out his pipe.

Peter agreed, "Yeah, to vote you have to know who to vote for and why you want to. When I get my citizen papers and I can vote, you bet your bottom dollar—I'll know."

"Well," Carl relit his pipe, "these women think all they have to do is push a piece of paper into a box and presto—they'll be equal. It takes more than that. But don't tell Rosie I said so."

"Evangeline thinks . . ." The mention of that cute bundle of bright-eyed feminine pulchritude instantly solicited comments from John's friends.

"Aha! So the fair Evangeline is still your private source, John?"

"Does your wife know?"

"You better watch out, she's the apple of the Boss's eye!" added Stan.

"Now don't get any ideas, my friends. She just got married!" John announced.

Zoltan sneezed. "All kidding aside, John, you still should watch out—from what I hear, that so convenient marriage has nothing to do with her still being the apple of the Boss's devoted eye."

Thinking that the subject of John as possible lothario competition to Henry Ford might be headed towards dangerous conclusions, Ebbely drew the men's attention away by asking had they heard that the territory of Alaska had just given women the vote, which made Fritz exclaim, "What? Eskimos vote? I tell you the whole world is going topsy-turvy crazy!"

Johann turned to John. "What were you about to say?"

"Well, Evangeline thinks that one day women will be on the assembly line."

"See! What did I just say?" Fritz felt vindicated.

"Can you just imagine a woman on the assembly line?" John laughed.

"Why is that idea so hilarious?" Ebbely asked.

"Oh, come on, she'd get so rattled—she'd have the vapors—be dead in an hour!"

"I agree," Stan got up, "I've got to go. By now Serafina has had a vision of me crushed beneath my Lizzie and will be out looking for my car and corpse just to make sure she was right. Say good-bye to your wife for me, John."

"Me, too," Zoltan sneezed. "Can you drop me, Stan?"

"Sure. Anyone else? Carl? Peter? You want a ride? Okay—let's go then. Good-bye, John."

Those who lived in Highland Park left to walk home. The front door closed behind them just as Jane came downstairs after putting the children to bed.

"Everybody just left, Ninnie—they said to tell you good-bye." John picked up his newspaper.

"It was nice having them come here after work."

"Yes—I think from now on we'll do it more often."

"I'm sorry I missed them. Did you talk about something special?"

"Oh, nothing of interest for you—just men talk. Supper nearly ready?"

Jane left to plunge the spaghetti into boiling water.

As more and more talk revolved around the influx of migrant blacks seeking work up north, Jane became interested in why that should cause such a stir. Never having seen people whose skin was different from hers before coming to America, she was intrigued by their very difference.

That they were human was obvious. That for some reason they were not regarded as such was also obvious. In her work as Watcher that now extended into the deplorable sections of Detroit—where Italian immigrants vied for living space with those from out of the deep South—Jane was familiar with the plight of those frightened by the stigma of the African savage who their old country cultures believed had a taste for the delicacy of white man's flesh. That color had such a potent influence on reactionary behavior bothered her. When she mentioned her confusion to Hannah it surprised her that this compassionate, generous woman who had taught her so much, with this, became so noncommittal, it bordered on evasion. Never one to allow sleeping dogs to lie longer than absolutely necessary, Jane went in search of her other mentor.

Rumpelstiltskin looked up from his book as she entered the parlor.

"Back so soon? No villainous Ford inspectors to thwart today?"

Jane shook her head. "Today I was translating—trying to explain . . ." Ebbely, sensing a need to talk, motioned her to take Fritz's chair. "May I ask you something?"

"Of course."

"Why is color so important?"

"Whatever are you talking about, child?"

"I know whenever you call me 'child' in that way you think I am really being stupid."

Ebbely reached over, patted her hands clasped in her lap. "No, not stupid, my dear—perhaps *surprising* might be more appropriate. What do you mean by 'color' exactly?"

"There are so many black men now and many of the people who had the beds before them are angry and afraid—today one of the immigrant women hid her children and wouldn't tell me where because she was certain the savages would eat them."

"That bad, eh?"

"Yes." Hesitating, Jane smoothed the broad pleat of her skirt. "Ebbely—is black always frightening?"

"What an intriguing thought. Possibly. But then we mortals are such slaves to color in general."

"How?"

"We identify the sexes—by pretty pink and very dependable blue. For morality, white always signifies good; black—evil. We mourn in black, yet shrouds are white. Because they have no pigment, albinos are frightening; Negroes perhaps because they have too much? If one's skin turns yellow, one's blood is tainted."

Captured by his own train of thought, Ebbely took fire. "Lavender is for sweet-scented sachets, but deep purple is for evil witches and sorcerers. To entice, sweetest sugar is white—coffee a bitter brown—perhaps just enough a degree away from black for us to accept it. Even red has its subtle connotations. Blood, bright crimson when alive, when congealed—becoming dark. The heart is pure red on Valentine's Day but the darkest shade of scarlet is given to women who have strayed."

Suddenly embarrassed, Ebbely avoided further questioning by asking Jane why she hadn't discussed such weighty concerns with her husband instead of him.

"I couldn't wait until he got home. Anyway—when you explain things I can understand the real meaning not just the words. Like that spiritual you showed me—I didn't just hear it—I *felt* it."

After the first wave of patriotic frenzy and while the nation waited for an adequate expeditionary force to be assembled, supplied and trained—most of the population resumed their daily lives with but minor adjustment to being at war. Wives saved extra pennies in pickle jars marked LIBERTY BONDS, made do with voluntary meatless days, even wheatless ones. As the latter concerned only the conservation of bleached flour, Hannah reigned supreme, offering to teach some of her more Americanized chaperone-Watchers how they too could make her famous rye bread and best yet, her blackest pumpernickel.

Morgana's sightless precision rolling bandages for the Red Cross encouraged both Rosie and Henrietta to volunteer. Not to be outdone and rather envious of their white uniforms and nunlike head scarves emblazoned with bright red crosses her sister Serafina sacrificed two mornings a week to join them, announcing that if she gave any more time to the victory effort her father's import liquor business would fail as she and she alone knew how to keep his books. When Peter wouldn't allow Dora to replace a man by becoming a trolley girl, she bested him by taking the vacated place of a young butcher's apprentice called to the draft. Soon her specialty of highly spiced pork sausages had a fame all their own in Polishtown.

Feeling it was time to do his patriotic duty, Ebbely gave up the road, went into partnership with the manufacturer of the ugly bloomers, secured a government contract to supply the US Army with its long winter underwear. His financial future assured, he decided to dedicate himself to lifting the spirits of the troops "*to be*," as he put it. Though music was supposed to calm the savage beast—henceforth he would use it to rally young men to fight for love and glory for this, his Promised Land.

Early one morning, his Lizzie impatient to be off and running, he kissed Hannah a fleeting good-bye, vowed to ring-a-ling, and with a bundle of sheet music and his new banjo by his side sped off to rouse the youth of America at Camp Funston—in the far-off land of Kansas.

As every woman now wanted at least a hint of visual soldiering, the uniform look became so fashionable. Jane was kept busy sewing military-looking edging on lapels and cuffs on travel costumes and day wear, shortening skirts to the new wartime length of one-eighth of an inch above a lady's anklebone. As the momentum of preparation for war increased—so did Jane's dressmaking business flourish.

Michael too caught the war bug. With an upside-down colander strapped to his head—a broken broom handle as firepower—he fought the good fight shooting Huns in the back yard. While his brother silently watched, Michael shouted waging war with his best friend Gregory from across the street.

"Bang, bang, you're dead!"

"No, I'm not!" Gregory shouted back.

"Yes, you are!"

"No, I'm not!"

"You're a Hun. Bang! Now you're dead!"

"No, I'm not!"

"But I kill-ed you!"

That evening when she told John—at first he laughed then frowned saying he did not approve of his son playing at war.

"But, John—everywhere—everyone is talking of nothing else. All the boys in the neighborhood are playing soldier and all the girls are Red Cross nurses."

"What the others do is not my concern—war is not a game and I will not have a son of mine thinking it is. Is he still awake?"

"Yes."

Having learned that even when not absolutely real any and all killing was wrong even when necessarily right, this last part of his father's lesson he found very confusing; still as his hero had said it—Michael knew it must be right and accepted with glee his father's consolation gift of new drawing paper, a whole box of watercolors with even a brush—and from then on busied himself painting colorful explosions.

As they had been doing since 1916, more and more university students left to join the British and French forces, becoming the first fighter pilots in the first war that reached its killing potential up into the sky.

Jane forever fascinated by what was beyond her immediate horizon wondered what it must be like to become a bird, see the earth below from its perspective. What an amazing concept—what a breathtaking invention it was that lifted men from their earth allowing them such borderless freedom. When she asked John what he thought of the new fascination of flight—his enthusiasm was as informative as it had been for the Paris sewers.

"It's reconnaissance, Ninnie, the first time in a war when photographs taken from above can be used for identifying the terrain. As the horseless carriage . . ." John smiled remembering her first use of the expression. ". . . has done away with horses, so will the flying machine do away with carrier pigeons."

"Pigeons—in a war?"

"Yes, Ninnie—everything will change after this—not just war itself but everyday life. The Boss and young Edsel are thinking of building these aeroplanes. They're even talking of a Ford airport. Well, with the mighty Rouge, now Mr. Ford will have the resources to build whatever he wants."

At the Highland Park plant, speed was now the master and mass production its perfected tool. The euphoria of entering the war in order to stop it carried the men to achieve their tasks, but the thought that nothing would ever be the same again—that from now on volume would be forever considered more important than quality—nagged. John particularly felt the disenchantment and the guilt for recognizing it as such. At work he remained his disciplined self. At home he allowed his moods full rein—confusing Jane and the children by the change in him. But as these were the days when wives knew their place, Jane did not question her husband's behavior, simply adjusted to it as best she could knowing she was not the only Ford wife who needed to cope.

By the end of spring, anti-German fever was running high—many of the German-language papers, so numerous before 1917, had dwindled down to but a few. The famous Harmonie Club—its music steeped in German tradition—was closed down. Everywhere those of German birth were suspect spies—their first-generation German-American offspring, if not voluntary soldiers, branded traitors. Even food came under suspicion. The innocent frankfurter was cleansed of any Hun association by being given the more acceptable name of hot dog, sauerkraut became coleslaw, and hamburger, Salisbury steak; all of which made Hannah exclaim, "Vhat dey got against cabbage? And tell me, why call sauerkraut dat is pickled, coleslaw dat is not? Even wit de meat dey go crazy. A hamburger dat is ground is a Salisbury steak, dat isn't? And a dog dat is hot—to eat? Vhere vill dis all end up?"

Hannah visiting Jane for morning coffee, put more sugar into hers. "Even our first papers no good no more for being good Americans! Mrs. Nussbaum, who has already de real citizenship because her husband already is, she tells me her Zellie is all worried because if dey have to change dere name, simply to translate dey can't because it's funny. Who do you know dat's called Mr. Nuttree? But even if, on dere okayed papers it says Nussbaum so, who can change a name on real already given citizen papers, will you tell me dat?"

From then on Jane noticed that Hannah rarely used German when speaking to Fritz—quickly catching herself whenever she did.

As Sunday was neither a decreed meatless nor a wheatless day, Hannah found solace still in cooking for her boys. The dinner table was never as full—still some came to talk and bask in the ever present devotion of the one who had sheltered them when life was still a young adventure.

"Did anyone hear the British have put in an order for six thousand . . . Fordsons?" Carl asked, helping himself to the coleslaw that was not sauerkraut but the real thing. "Because of the German blockade, England is so short of food their farmers are desperate for our light tractor to put more land under cultivation."

Fritz whistled, "My God, six thousand? Will the Rouge plant be ready for such an order, John?"

"Well, the new Ford and Son Company has been formed for the production of the Fordson 4-cylinder tractor and if nothing goes wrong, I think we'll be ready to ship certainly by early winter."

Now it was Carl's turn to whistle. "Jesus, Mary and Joseph! That fast? Now all they have to worry about is not getting torpedoed on the way over to England."

"I hear Ford is planning to buy his own newspaper." Zoltan helped himself to gravy. "Isn't our *Ford Times* good enough anymore? John, you are always up on these things, what does he need a real newspaper for?"

"To reach a broader readership perhaps. Evangeline—and if any of you say one word, I'll crown you—"

"Go on, mum's the word!" Carl laughed.

"Well, she said she thought it might be for political reasons."

"Don't tell me the Boss believes this talk going around about him running for office."

"Well," Fritz put down his napkin, "I heard someone say the other day if Henry Ford ran for president he could win."

"Every common man who owns a Model T would vote for him for sure," Peter agreed, "and don't forget the farmers."

"When do you think we'll be ready to send our boys over?" asked Carl.

"I don't think they can be armed and ready until late summer," answered John.

"Will young Mr. Edsel have to go?" asked a concerned Peter.

"No way. They'll find a way to keep him out." Carl was adamant.

"He will insist on going if they call him up," said John, ever the defender.

"It's embarrassing enough Ford has us out—at least his son should go," Zoltan countered.

Jane, clearing, ventured, "I heard young Mrs. Edsel might be in the family way."

Zoltan smiled up at her. "Well—if that's so—that would help to keep our young heir safely at home."

"No need for sarcasm, Zoltan."

"None intended, John."

With a war not fought on home soil, everyday life is permitted its normalcy, children's birthdays were celebrated—John's first and Michael's third amongst them and when it was time again for Molly to lumber down the street, his scalawags chased Mr. Kennec's wagon for their icy treats. Fresh strawberries were made into succulent jam, ripe currants into shimmering jelly, wash hung out on the line whitened under a summer sun. Even with restrictions—Hannah's Glory Day picnic baskets were packed, taken to Belle Isle, and even with some missing who had been amongst them the year before—it still was a happy time.

Under the command of its leader, the First Division, America's hastily assembled expeditionary force was creating havoc over in France, yet not in the trenches. Though the British were desperate for new cannon fodder as were the French, General Pershing was adamant that when America fought—it would do so within its own units, not have its fighting men integrated into the ranks of its needy allies back home. Not only patriotism made everyone want to attend liberty loan parades—they were exciting, offering marching brass bands playing rousing tunes accompanied by enthusiastic flag waving assuring glorious victory by investing in liberty bonds.

Hannah's first exposure to such joyful patriotism in the city of Detroit resulted in all future baking in the Geiger household being done to the vocal accompaniment of George M. Cohan. Beating a yeast batter was perfectly suited to a rousing chorus of

> *"Over der—Over der,*
> *send de word, send de word, Over der—*
> *Dat de Yanks are coming, De Yanks are coming . . ."*

Whereas making beds required Irving Berlin.

> *"Oh how I hate to get up in de morning . . ."*

For slicing onions Hannah's repertoire went British.

> *"Pack all your troubles in your old kit bag and smile—smile—smile . . ."*

She liked that one particularly because it had no *th*'s.

When Mr. Henry, the mailman, marched off to war—a Mr. Jeremiah took over his route. A somber man given to endowing the delivery of mail with a holiness that bordered on religious fanaticism, Hannah never warmed to him, never worried about his health or his love life, even doubted that he could have one.

"De Pope should have dat man for his letters!" she would grumble—as she concentrated on good toughts to keep her Mr. Henry safe from flying bullets and Oo La La French floozies.

Later in the war when "How You Gonna Keep Them Down on the Farm After They've Seen Paree" became all the rage and Ebbely loved banging it out on her parlor piano, Hannah would nod her head in rhythm commenting that song illustrated exactly what she had always feared from the very beginning for the future of her Mr. Henry the mailman-soldier.

Easter was long gone and as Rudy had not come back for a visit as promised, Hannah began to worry. It was already the end of August when Hannah answered the ring of her doorbell and there looking lost stood her Casanova Rudy. Pulling him into her house and into her arms, she held him welcoming him to safety. As he cried, she wondered what had broken him and why.

"Sorry, Hannah."

"What is sorry? Nobody home yet—so upstairs mit you. Remember Stan's room? Well dat's de one I keep always ready for whoever. You go now, sleep. In a couple of hours I wake you to wash, den you eat. Like a skeleton for Halloween you look. No, no argument. Later is plenty time for talking. Now, you go!"

And Rudy the broken man was shooed upstairs like the sad child Hannah knew him to be.

Through the efficient Ford wives' grapevine, Fritz was informed of Rudy's return—told to bring only John and Zoltan back for supper. The others would have to wait, for Hannah suspected Rudy would not be able to handle the curiosity of all of his friends as yet.

"Special good supper, Hannachen." Fritz, stretched out in his parlor chair, fanned the lit match across the bowl of his pipe. "Rudy? . . . You ready to tell us what happened?"

"Fritzchen . . ."

"No, Hannah—let him speak."

His voice monotone as though without its controlled bloodlessness he would bleed anew, Rudy began.

He had been late for work that day—why, he couldn't remember, but he was. Standing in the open door, clutching her shawl, Frederika shivered—so he told her to go back inside the house and get warm and left . . . without kissing her good-bye. He never left without kissing Frederika good-bye. But that day . . . that day he had. Rudy stopped—the silent room waited. "It was already dark when I got home. I opened the front door and called her name. She didn't answer. I called again. The house was still. I went to look for her. After a while . . . I found her. She must have been there all day—all alone—then . . . then I cut her down." His haunted eyes searched the room. His cry raw. "Was it only the baby's death? Hannah! Was it?"

Hannah ran, crouched before his chair. "No, my Rudyle. No! It was to be; a long, long time ago already, it was to be."

Though they all knew complete healing was an improbability, still within the ministering safety of their compassion, they gave him time in which to heal. Each day Rudy's friends tried to help him find his way back to life as he had found his way back home. Weeks later, deciding to visit his uncle Rudy, Michael ran the three blocks over to his second mother's house and found him sitting on the front porch staring at nothing. Receiving no *hello*, the little boy stared in return but seeing nothing that could demand such undivided concentration asked, "Uncle Rudy, what are you looking for?"

Rudy forced to acknowledge his presence tried a welcoming smile, "Hi, Michael— my God you have grown."

"Yes—I'm a big brother now—so I have to be growed."

"Makes sense."

"Uncle Zoltan say you are very sad and my Papa says so, too—why?"

"Because my wife has died. Do you know what death is, Michael?"

"Oh, yes—Mama says it's when someone is gone forever and ever. But I don't think so."

Rudy motioned Michael to sit next to him on the porch bench.

"Why don't you?"

"Well, when I was little . . ." That made Rudy smile. ". . . I found a big fat worm and he was dead and I buried him in the flowers—then I went back to look and he was gone! I think when you die you don't. You just stay living—not in the same place maybe and maybe you don't look like a worm no more—but that doesn't mean you're dead like Mama says forever and ever."

Like two sage men on a park bench, they sat and talked of life and its many ends until they both agreed they alone had solved the riddle—that longing for what was actually never ever gone was just wasted sorrowing.

Knowing her firstborn very well and where he usually could be found when he disobeyed her, Jane arrived at Hannah's house to scold him and found Rudy playing pick-up sticks with her offspring. She didn't say a word—just walked into the house to announce to Hannah that a small miracle was in progress on her front porch, shocking herself that the thought, even its designated word, had come from her.

Although Michigan had voted for Prohibition the year before—the law was not scheduled to go into effect until 1918 so, when on the fourth of September young Mr. Edsel became a father they all could toast his son properly—Fritz approved that he had been given the illustrious name of Henry.

"Now we have a Henry Ford the Second—how about that? Like real royalty, eh, Hannahchen?" to which his wife agreed it was the proper thing to do and Stan remarked that now the Boss's son couldn't be conscripted.

"Mr. Edsel's no shirker!" Fritz growled.

"No, but I bet the Boss is relieved he can now stop pulling strings."

John frowned. "He's been doing that?"

"Sure."

"Not easy for the boy."

"Never has been easy to be the only son of a great man."

"Yeah," Peter drained his glass. "A father! Just think of it!"

"Seems like yesterday he was a schoolboy in knickers home for the holidays," Fritz agreed.

Carl held out his glass. "Remember, Fritz, how he used to label the machines?"

"Sure . . ." Refilling his glass, Fritz smiled. "What a boy. And his little notebook . . ."

"Jotted down anything and everything that came into his head."

"Just like his father, Zoltan, just like him."

"Can't call him *young* Mr. Edsel no more, eh, John?"

"No, I suppose not—but now we have a young Henry." And all the Ford men agreed theirs was an American dynasty to be proud of.

17

Out of breath—eyes wide with outrage tinged with fear, Hannah rushed into Jane's kitchen. As the screen door banged shut behind her she gasped, "Through de window it came—BANG—CRASH!" and sank down on the kitchen chair, trying to catch her breath.

Worried, Hannah did not panic; Jane knelt down beside her. "What has happened—is Fritz . . ."

"Ach, no. No—tank de Lord for dat—but troo my fine front window—it smashed—a big brick—dey trow at me because I'm a Hun!" Hannah began to cry—not big sobs suited to her size and temperament but small hiccup ones, like those of a frightened child.

"Oh, no—that can't be the reason." Jane holding Hannah's hands patted them trying to comfort her.

"Sure it is! De note say so!" came out between half-swallowed sobs.

"Note—what note?"

"Around the big brick, tied on—oh—*Mein Gott!* Vhat vill I tell Fritz vhy de vindow is broken? If he tinks everybody hates us—ve are de enemy not American—he vill maybe do bad something so angry. He mustn't know—Ninnie, please, please no telling—keep mum, promise, not even John! I find a story, make up someting vhy vindow is smashed. But vhy? Vhy? Us good citizens have first papers already—even!"

After this, which became known in secret as *"de bad brick day,"* Hannah became acquainted with fear-expected; an inner nervousness that takes up residence within the spirit as though its pleasure is its destruction. She rarely spoke of it, perhaps was even ashamed, considering it a weakness of character. But it was there—and as with all insidious fear, it feasted on its host depleting it.

November brought its icy winds and the news from afar that Russia was in the possession of victorious Bolsheviks. Overnight those Russians on Ford's assembly lines who retained their ancient loyalty to the House of Romanov became designated White Russians; those in favor of the new order, Red. Suspect that anyone siding with revolutionary concepts would most likely be prone to also embrace unionist ideology, these were quickly weeded out from the employment roster of the Ford Motor Company. The Boss's vehement dislike of the very concept of workers banding together, empowered by a collective body to dictate to an employer, was a seething hatred throughout Henry Ford's life. The Ford Motor Company was a *free shop* and as long as he, as its caring father figure, benevolent benefactor existed, dreaded union free it would remain.

While impatient children waited for the expected magic of Christmastime, their elders worked to make it come true. Having kept the gingerbread house wrapped in baker's parchment, Hannah needed only to replace the sugar icicles that had been eaten off its roof and fashion a new marzipan witch to restore its perfection. This year it was Rudy who found the tree, perfect in its needle steady symmetry, brought it home on the trolley all the way from—of all places—Greektown. Hannah approved—but kept wondering why Greeks would have Christmas trees to sell and how had Rudy gotten the idea that they would. Taking Fritz aside she asked if he thought maybe their Rudy was regaining his Casanova talents. But Fritz shook his head saying it was much too soon and she shouldn't meddle, and to leave the poor boy be. Hannah chastised, gave her husband one of her looks and returned to her kitchen.

When Jane suggested baking extra loaves of dark flour bread for her to distribute amongst her tenement charges, Hannah quite upset that *she* could have forgotten those in greater need, threw herself into baking so many that Jane measuring and greasing tins, knew she would have to ask Rosie and Henrietta to help carry their pungent Christmas bounty and that it would take more than just one trolley ride to do so.

Now considered old enough, John, the younger, was permitted to join his brother in the very serious contemplation of where exactly the three kings should be positioned, then getting into trouble when he tried to eat the Baby Jesus. Being a child who preferred screaming to crying, he screamed when his father smacked his behind, but quickly refocused on the gingerbread boy that Hannah offered him instead. When Fritz and Rudy lit its candles, the tree glowed with the expected magic that seems forever new. Returned from his many adventures among the cantonment camps, Ebbely entertained a parlor sadly depleted of its former inhabitants. Though everyone ring-a-linged Hannah to wish those present a Merry Christmas and Happy Hanukah, even the excitement of hearing their voices coming over wires could not quite make up for them being all together as in days gone by. This year Fritz chose not to sing his "O Tannenbaum" considering such German tradition in questionable taste during wartime.

On New Year's Day it snowed so hard no one felt like skating; Johann went, but that was only because he was a Hollander and couldn't help himself, was how Hannah explained it. Fritz lit a fire in the grate, Hannah brought her special biscuit tin of marshmallows, John and Rudy cut sticks for the children, Ebbely played catchy tunes on his new banjo while Jane and Henrietta made sure no one burned their sticky fingers.

The beginning of 1918 held a singular glow. There were no factory layoffs this holiday season—America was at war and her unrivaled capacity to produce the articles necessary to wage it took precedence. Feeding this new army, Tuesdays became meatless—with an added meatless day mandated for every other day. Hoover, who believed that the world lives by phrases, had food messages printed in many immigrant languages including Yiddish. Those that appealed to Hannah, she pinned up among her postcard collection.

There was: "If U Fast U Beat U Boats—if U Feast U Boats Beat U" and "Don't let your horse be more patriotic than you—eat a dish of oatmeal!"

As fresh produce could not be shipped overseas and meat was needed for the training camps, one of Hannah's great joys stemmed from Mr. Hoover's Food Administration's zealous effort to retrain America's civilian palate for meat—to that of fish.

When Jane, having read "Catch the Carp; Buy the Carp. Cook the Carp and Eat the Carp" in one of John's out-of-town papers, brought her the news, Hannah dropped her turkey feather duster, ran upstairs, reappeared with bluebird hat secured and market satchel swinging, marched off to the trolley and Detroit to purchase that so-longed-for carp that surely had become affordable because her lucky charm was now a sanctioned *patriotic* fish.

Having taken another one of Mr. Hoover's dictums to heart—"Do not permit your child to take a bite or two from an apple and throw it away. Nowadays even children must be taught to be patriotic to the core"—Hannah had Fritz build Michael a wagon so he too could show his patriotism by collecting household garbage. On the government's solicited salvage lists were fatty acids for soap, glycerin for explosives, fruit pits and nutshells for carbon that went into gas masks, the rest was for pig food and fertilizer.

Michael was very proud of his wagon—especially after his father painted its wooden slats fire engine red—but when just plain grease was hard to come by and fruit pits in March were few, he changed his patriotic objective and collected wanted paper and string instead.

Although those employed in war work were exempt from rationing, by early spring of 1918, every household in Highland Park boasted one of the Food Administration's signed pledge cards displayed in their front window. Still, not every day was dictated by a war so far away.

Johann's older girls now attended school, left each morning with their father while Henrietta and her youngest kept house and when everything was done to Dutch perfection went visiting around the neighborhood, usually over to Jane's. Gloria—now a two-and-a-half-year-old bundle of flaxen curls and irresistible charm, aided by eyes that a summer sky could envy—thought Michael was the nicest boy in the whole wide world and never missed an opportunity to tell him so!

At first the little girl's cloying devotion had an adverse effect. Michael, very annoyed, tried to steer her in his brother's direction hoping John's usual sullenness would deter her from coming over all the time, but when one day John threw mud at her and Gloria, quite stunned stood there forlorn and cried, Michael feeling she needed protection went to her rescue, brushed the mud off her pretty pinafore dress—took her by the hand and whispering soothing words led Henrietta's daughter into his mother's kitchen for a nice apple to be eaten to the core. From then on Michael accepted Gloria as his unavoidable shadow—and both were happy. When Carl's Rosie on her day off brought their twins—all the children played together, but the unassailable unit of Michael and his Gloria remained intact.

Announcing that his company would refuse all profit from the manufacture of articles needed to win the war, Henry Ford stopped civilian production and Highland Park's assembly lines turned out Model T ambulances, Model T trucks, Liberty engines for use in flying machines, even experimented with the idea of using the Model T's chassis as a possible base for a two-man armored tank. While Britain's order for Fordson Tractors were rolling off the line in nearby Dearborn, Ford accepted a government contract to build a hundred submarine patrol vessels. Never before had ships been built indoors.

As a new colossus known as Building B began to take shape, its girders were adorned by banners reading AN EAGLE A DAY KEEPS THE KAISER AWAY; another, WARSHIPS WHILE YOU WAIT. Ford's vow that the first Eagle Boat would be launched in less than three months' time, accompanied by his rallying cry "AMERICA WILL DELIVER!" blazed across the nation's headlines.

War having arrested the influx of European immigrants, the migration of America's "working poor" now accelerated to feed the enormous need for manpower of Ford's mighty Rouge.

Now as the new plant with its accessible river began to demonstrate its astounding capabilities, the Ford men agreed that here, as when they had first come to know him in that secret room at the birth of the Model T, the Boss had triumphed—proving once again that the impossible could truly become possible. Though still in its developmental stages yet already acknowledged as possibly the greatest manufacturing empire in the world, the Rouge needed as many seasoned men as the Highland Park and the other Ford assembly plants could spare. Dearborn being closer to where they lived, Stan, Carl, and Zoltan transferred. John, having achieved what he had striven for when still a university student in Italy—now a respected engineer, went wherever he was needed. Be it bicycle, trolley, tram, when scouting the Rouge riverbanks, John was in his creative element—often remaining days in Dearborn when returning all the way back to Highland Park took up too much of his precious time. Ebbely and Fritz amazed at John's endurance were forever urging him to finally acquire a sweetheart of his own.

On hearing this, Jane wondered who, then remembering their first meeting beneath the chestnut tree, laughed. Wouldn't it be marvelous! If John did purchase his dream—she, Giovanna once village girl, would become the wife of a man who possessed a real live Lizzie. The sheer thought of it was so exhilarating, she nearby dropped a stitch of the army muffler she was knitting as one of her volunteer duties for the Red Cross.

Proud of her husband's achievements, when left alone Jane functioned as if he were in residence. Sometimes at night it felt strange having their bed all to herself, but she did not delve into why. When one is used to something and it is changed of course one notices, is how she explained her sudden reluctance to find comfort in a space usually now so welcoming.

By February Mondays had heatless added to their patriotic abstinence, tin was no longer permitted in the manufacture of toys, nor caskets adorned with bronze, brass or copper, the lapels on men's ready-made suits were narrowed to conserve wool needed for soldiers' uniforms, penalties for hoarding sugar were strict; yet despite the country's dedicated war effort—as no American unit had as yet seen battle—the actual consciousness of war remained what it had been, as the lending of help to others far away; a temporary emergency that would soon be ended once brave American boys were given the opportunity to make the world safe for democracy.

Avowing her Americanism, Mrs. Nussbaum left Hannah's Chaperone Watchers to become a part-time Munitionette remanding her younger children into the capable hands of her eldest who was a spinster in the making and therefore trustworthy to a fault.

As more and more women took up positions vacated by men gone to war, their outward appearance changed. Hairstyles too cumbersome, complicated and time consuming vanished as a female's once crowning glory was cut and bobbed exposing the slightly shocking nakedness of feminine necks. Having less hair to balance upon, hats lost their sweeping expanse, became smaller—their brims no wider than a sailor's boater. No longer soliciting outrage, ankles emerged from behind their curtained sanctuary, became fully visible as skirts shortened for easier maneuvering in a man's world. No long trains, no floating shawls, no overzealous adornment, even if left untouched within, a woman's outward appearance announced capability, dependability, efficiency, determination, as trustworthy a person as any man.

This transformation of women from hearth to workplace kept Jane busy sewing far into most nights. Her skill with the needle was becoming known attracting an appreciative clientele. She liked the feeling of importance this gave her. Suddenly through a competence all her own she existed as an entity without the necessity of first belonging to a superior male.

It was March when an exhausted Russia surrendered—made its separate peace with America's enemy, Germany. Immediately Russian immigrants be they Bolsheviks, Socialists or old-guard Romanov loyalists were looked upon and judged as dangerous traitors. As the majority of them were also Jews, this further fueled the anti-Semitism always already in place. It also laid the cornerstone of official distrust of all such labor movements led by the Socialist Party. With his close association with his Russians, Fritz was particularly concerned by the cloud of suspicion from others as they worked the line. Their country of origin's surrender had joined them to the enemy Hun, later this accusative distrust would spread to include all Slavic communities that already had the reputation of being devotees of the concepts of Socialism and judged instigators of industrial unrest.

"What is dis something new again?" Hannah exclaimed. "Now wit all de tings we do already to be good wartime Americans—we also supposed to save de daylight? And how, vill you tell me, we're going to do dat?"

"I don't know." Fritz was as confused as she.

When in March the very first daylight savings time came to Michigan, it confused many—especially small children. Carl's twins, Rose and Violet, cried in unison when put to bed before accustomed darkness decreed it. So did Johann's little Gloria while his older girls verbalized their opposition. Young John glowered a scream in the making, Michael tried to reason his way out of the ridiculous assumption that anyone could fall asleep in daylight, adding to his legitimate argument that his best friend Gregory from across the street would certainly not be asked to do so by *his* so very understanding parents. Jane's outstretched arm, index finger pointing up the stairs ended any further discussion.

At first Hannah burned, then undercooked a few suppers until her inner clock settled itself into the new time slot decreed by omnipotent man instead of God or as she put it, "de one who put de sun in de sky in de first place and who should know better!" and slamming the porch door behind her went, not for the first time to check her patch of victory garden—to consult with her carrots if they knew what had happened to time and if it disturbed them too.

When on May 1 Michigan became a dry state, it so pleased the Sociological Department inspectors that there were some who suspected Henry Ford had used his powerful influence in bringing temperance to Michigan a whole year before Prohibition became the law of the land. Those who had looked upon spirits as an occasional luxury for the celebration of special occasions now that such were forbidden craved their effect made desirable by their very status of illegality.

Just before Easter, Hannah came down with such a heavy chest cold that she actually took to her bed, where Fritz joined her a day later hacking and sneezing. Ebbely nursing them—concocted a very good simile of Hannah's famous chicken soup that he insisted on serving them within the privacy of their bedroom, dismissing their blushes as he scurried back down to *his* kitchen to try his hand at brewing curative chamomile tea from the dried buds acquired from Mr. Hirt's. Many became ill that spring, but as they recovered after a few days, thought nothing of it.

Morgana accepted a proposal of marriage from an earnest cleric of the Lutheran Church and Serafina predicted it would end in dire tragedy. Still, when all efforts of dissuasion failed she consented to being her sister's matron of honor and commissioned Jane to make her an appropriate dress for the doomed occasion. Intrigued by the prospect of a Sicilian Catholic joined to a dour Lutheran, Jane wondered what color she thought would be appropriate.

For once Morgana's twin was caught off guard. "Well, knowing what I already know, naturally I would prefer funereal black," Serafina paced about Jane's little sewing room. "But, whatever the color, the style of the dress must be severe—that way it will be useful to wear for any other somber occasion. I told our father to not allow this union—but he has been so certain no one would ever want a blind wife that when this strippant appeared he was actually grateful! No money, no proper religion and a GERMAN! The whole idea is insane! First, she will miscarry—then come to the brink of death giving birth to stillborn twins—and he? He will become a consumptive, a useless invalid for Morgana to nurse for the rest of her barren life. That's a marriage? What color for the dress do you suggest?"

Jane, caught up in this lurid prophecy, stuttered, "Pur-purple?" and was rewarded by a satisfied nod of approval.

While taking Serafina's measurements, she did venture to ask if poor Morgana had been informed of what exactly awaited in her marital future.

"Of course! I *always* announce. But she is so besotted she refuses all counsel. Besides, she claims her visions contradict mine and that she even knows something about me—but won't tell because I'm being mean."

Trying not to laugh, Jane rolled up her tape measure and set the appointment for Serafina's first fitting.

Morgana's impending nuptial brought a new dimension to Jane's structured world. A young woman blind from birth totally outshone by a domineering twin, Morgana had been transformed by unenvisioned love—into bubbling joy—all foreboding gone. While fitting her bridal dress, Jane was engulfed in a pervading aura of girlish flutter.

"Morgana, if you don't stop twitching . . ."

"Oh, Jane—just think, just one more week and then I will be Mrs. Emillian-Schmidt—I mean Smith!"

"Yes, that's why this dress . . ."

"Will he like it? Will he think I am beautiful?"

"Yes, dear—of course. Now please stand still."

"Did you know we will live in a big city called Milwaukee? And I will have a sweet house of my own with a rose garden and three happy children and servants!" All witchery gone from her demeanor, Morgana actually trilled.

"You will need them," Jane mumbled past the pins. "I'm done."

Stepping out of the half-finished gown, Morgana smiled in Jane's direction.

"Have *you* ever been in love?" Before realizing Morgana couldn't see her denial, Jane shook her head. "Well? Jane? Have you? Answer me! I know you're still here."

"I'm afraid I don't know how to answer you."

"Why?" Morgana, knowing her room, stepped to the chair holding her day dress.

"Let me help you."

"No, it buttons in the front—I can do it."

Jane turned to collect her things.

"Jane? You love your John—don't you?"

Back turned to her inquisitor, Jane answered the expected, "Of course."

With a blind person's heightened sensitivity to inflection, Morgana countered, "I don't believe you."

"Now don't be silly, Morgana. You are excited and a little foolish!" The bridal finery and sewing things packed, Jane put on her hat and coat, picked up the carton case, turned at the door. "Is there something I can do for you before I go?"

Buttoning the long row of her bodice in that assured fingering that always impressed Jane by its schooled precision, Morgana smiled, focused towards the door.

"Poor Jane—you will have so much sorrow and yet so much joy before you reach what is still shrouded."

Jane rushed home.

Now that noodle making was deemed one of many unpatriotic activities, Hannah and Jane had to find substitutes to comply with their weekly calendar of needed visits. Beating carpets seemed to fit perfectly into the time slot left vacant by the lonely noodle gone to war. On either side of a particularly resplendent example of Turkish artistry—they slapped away, creating clouds of dust that justified their decision to choose this activity over scrubbing the back porch.

Hannah coughed, "Oy—dis dirty I didn't tink it was!"

"Yes, it didn't look this dirty."

"Dat's de Turkish weaving—it's so deep, it holds de dirt, but doesn't show it." Hannah lowered her voice. "Ninnie, you don't think this is too German what we are doing for de neighbors to see?" Smiling, Jane shook her head. "How is Morgana?" Hannah lifted the narrow carpet from the line and replaced it with the similar one from before her side of the bed.

"She is so happy, she's completely changed. Oh, she still has visions, but . . ."

"Ah, no-ting so special as romance of de young."

Jane stopped in mid-slap. "What is that?"

"What?"

"That word."

"*Romance?*"

"Yes."

Hannah proceeded to conjugate the word in German, relishing Jane's confusion.

"*That* important that word is?"

"Yes, Ninnie."

"But, what does it mean?"

Trying to find the right explanation, Hannah stopped flagellating the Turks, indicated they needed to sit on the back porch steps to talk.

"Dis is not easy. But, de word is sort of de same, I tink also in your French you like so much."

"*Romantique* I know, but the nuns never explained it. I read it though, but still it wasn't clear."

"Well . . . let me tink. First, it means a feeling. A special feeling, a special feeling dat makes de heart beat faster, de breath sort of go away because of big happiness."

"Isn't that supposed to be love?"

"No, well maybe, yes, a little. But dis is different, not so serious like love is, more just happy, young and turtle-dovey." Not to interrupt this fascinating stream of information, Jane didn't ask what *that* meant, although she really wanted to. "When romance is in de air—you can feel it, all over. Like when a sunset is so extra special—you get goosepimples. Ever have dat?"

"No." For some reason Jane felt bereft.

"Or suddenly dere is music like de angels sing just for you. De first kiss you get from dat someone you really like and he tell you you are his little ladylove and de poem he puts den in your pocket so you can read it—quiet, before alone you sleep."

Jane trying to absorb all this abundance of emotion laid before her, stared. Hannah thinking she still was unable to understand, threw up her hands,

"Ninnie! De Saint Valentine's Day? Dat you *know*, well dat's it! Dat's when romance is in de air, in de fancy heart mit all de so fine chocolates!"

On returning home, Jane fished out the shoebox where she kept those things that mattered to her, unfolded Teresa's letter, lifted from its pages the rose that John had brought her on that first Valentine's Day in America. Careful not to harm it, Jane fingered its brittle petals, recalled the moment of its giving and felt again the unexpected joy of it—astounded that she had experienced romance when innocent of its very existence.

Ford's inquisitors now equally empowered by law as well as their Boss, increased their pursuit of those immigrant communities identified as having inherent national traits for drunkenness. High on their list were whiskey-drinking Shanty Irish, Italian wine lovers, beer-guzzling Germans. For once blacks and Jews were spared such lofty ranking. Jews because they were "misers—too penny-pinching to ever fork out for a drink" and "coloreds—because they were too stupid and lazy to set up stills, or know what to do with money even when they got some."

The temperance movement rejoiced—demon drink had been slain and saloons outlawed—and such Detroit landmarks of solace and humble comfort as the Bucket of Suds were shut down. Even famous Hatties and other brothels that depended so on liquor as companion enticement to purchasable sex could only offer the latter—that is until they became valued customers of Serafina's family business and those on the ground floor of bootlegging operations who were reaping the monetary awards of sheer audacity with little of the criminal brutality of later years.

"Poor Rudy—not bad enough he has a big sadness so young—now dey say dey won't take him for de war," was how Hannah, while serving a Sunday supper, announced Rudy's decision to volunteer.

John turned to his friend. "You're full of surprises!"

"Ja—Rudy, why not tell us? And why won't they take you?"

"I've got flat feet."

"They won't let you fight because you've got flat feet?" Fritz shook his head.

"Dat's what I said, Fritzchen—what has feet to do mit shooting mit de hands?"

"I presume it is because an army needs to march," Ebbely observed, helping himself to more coleslaw now renamed victory cabbage.

"Silly . . ." Hannah plunked down the potatoes. ". . . like Ninnie's bubbele—bang, bang—everybody killing everybody—like children and what for—I ask you?! I tell you what for—de gravediggers—dat's what for!"

"Hannah—you are a woman—you don't know what you are talking about. Besides . . ."

John thought it prudent to interrupt Fritz. "Men are dying for the principles of peace, Hannah."

"You hear yourself? What you say?"

Never had Jane heard Hannah so vehement—so defiant in front of men. Deep down she agreed with her—but knew she would never have challenged the men, when suddenly Hannah drew her into the fray.

"Ninnie—you hear what your so bright husband just say?" Jane nodded. "So? What you have to say to dat? You want your sons one day to bang-bang for real killing?"

"No . . ." Jane chose her words carefully. ". . . of course not. But our side is not the aggressor—America and its allies are defending themselves. When freedom is at stake—one must go out and fight for it."

"Even to die for it?" John watched her. Jane felt him waiting for her answer.

"Yes—John."

"Well said, Ninnie, well said."

Rudy changed the subject by announcing that what he really wanted was to fly and maybe if the war lasted he might get the chance. He had applied for a position in a fledgling aircraft company and had been accepted. After so many years he would once again be an apprentice—but that mattered little in comparison to being in daily contact with his beloved flying machines.

"Just what you need, my boy," Zoltan commented.

Fritz agreed, "Yes—nothing like interesting hard work to keep you from brooding over the past."

Zoltan cleared his throat.

"You actually want to fly one of those contraptions, Rudy? That's much too dangerous. I hear those things are put together with glue and sewing thread!" On hearing "sewing thread," Jane picked up her ears.

That evening, the talk of the parlor revolved around man's freedom of the sky, not the open road. Heated discussion of how effective such glued-together crates could be, where men shot pistols at each other amongst the clouds.

"No, no . . ." Rudy animated by newly acquired knowledge stimulated the room, "they no longer have to lean out of the cockpit to shoot at each other—a French flyer has invented a way to mount a machine gun that shoots straight ahead."

"Where is it mounted?" asked Zoltan.

"Directly in front on the top of the forward fuselage."

"Interesting . . ." Forever the automobile man, John seemed amused at the new terminology Rudy used with such ease. ". . . but it would seem that bullets traveling at their accelerated speed—towards the blades of a propeller, spinning at its accelerated speed—would surely strike the propeller blades, ricochet back thereby killing the pilot. Possible, don't you think, Rudy?"

Fritz and Carl tried not to laugh—Zoltan gave them both a warning look, Stan snickered. Jane, captured, looked to Rudy for an illuminating answer.

"Aha—now I've got you. Well, John, my clever, all-so-knowing friend—it's right smack in your territory! You said it long ago—with our moving assembly line—*you* were the one who said it!"

"What for God's sake?"

"Timing, my friend, timing."

Stan was getting impatient. "What the hell do you mean?"

"The gun and the propeller—their actions are synchronized! Speed, John, it's just a matter of timing—the speed!"

Fritz shook his head in awe.

"I can't believe it!"

"Well, you better—because that's exactly how they're now doing it over there. Now all sides are shooting each other's tails off instead of having to lean down out of the cockpit to kill each other with lucky potshots."

Zoltan cleared his throat, "Falling from the sky—what a death that must be."

"Ja—can you imagine?" Fritz sighed.

"I wonder how the Huns first got so good at it," mused Ebbely.

Johann put down his paper. "Well, I heard that years ago when one of the Wright Brothers was on vacation in Germany, he took their crown prince up for a spin. Who knows—maybe that impressed the future kaiser to take the future of flying machines seriously."

"I have said it often—and I'll say it again," Stan knocked out his pipe, "Americans can be so damn gullible—like children we give, give, give and think the whole world will love us for it. I've got to go—we've got trouble at the yard."

"Stan," John stopped him at the parlor door. "You've made up your mind? You're still leaving?"

"Who told you?"

"Never mind, are you?"

"Yes." His friends murmured disbelief. "Well, I was going to tell you all in my own way—but I guess now is as good a time as any."

"Come back—sit." Fritz patted the vacant chair next to him.

"No, I haven't got time—but try to understand, it isn't just because of the family business . . . it's other things much more important—I just have no other choice. Got to go. . . . Good night."

Their thoughts channeled, the men smoked.

Zoltan broke the silence. "I am worried, John."

"Yes, so am I."

"Me, too," chorused Fritz and Carl.

Ebbely seemed confused. "Why? Because Stan's leaving Ford after so many years?"

"That's not what's worrying us."

"Then what, Fritz?"

"Let John tell it—he's better and knows more, told me."

"Well?" Ebbely turned towards John.

"We think Stan has joined the Socialist Party and must leave the company before he is discovered. That's only one worry and one that some of us have expected for some time."

"What is even more," Fritz interrupted, "is that this liquor business of the father-in-law is now maybe shady business over the border, and *that* can get Stan into very big trouble."

"Stan's a bootlegger?!" Rudy was shocked.

"Shush! Not so loud. Hannah will hear and if she ever suspects I don't want her to get involved!"

"Involved? What do you mean involved?" Now even John sounded surprised.

"Oh, come on—you think I didn't know about her Watchers and the risks those women first took to go against the company's inspectors?"

"Watchers? Women? What are you rambling on about?"

Suddenly made aware that John knew nothing of Hannah's Watchers or Jane's involvement with them, Fritz tried to cover up his mistake. "Oh, you know Hannah—how she watches everything and how the women talk and they gossip all the time about the Boss and everything . . . hey, I hear we may be building a forty-pound tank on top of our chassis—is that right?"

"Experimenting, Fritz, only experimenting," John corrected. "It's the balance . . . it keeps toppling over. "

"Never in my life did I think I would see one day a flivver tank . . ." Fritz was laughing.

"Well, Rudy?" Ebbely extinguished his cigarette. "I must say I admire your decision. Up, up into the blue on gossamer wings—sounds like a title for a song."

"I'm not flying yet, Ebbely."

"But you will, my boy. I'm convinced that you will and be good at it. It takes spunk—and that you've got. Gentlemen, I'm off to welcome Morpheus. You all know how a good meal always exhausts me."

Later, rolling down her sleeves, making ready to walk home, Jane stopped Rudy as he was going up to bed.

"Rudy—may I ask you something?"

"Of course—what is it?"

"Well—remember you spoke of how flying machines needed gluing and their wings—the material of their wings, sewn?" He nodded. She rushed on so as not to detain him—but really not to lose courage. "Well—sewing is something I can do really well—and I was wondering—once you are working—do you think you could find out if there might be a position open for a sewer of wings?"

Jane never did get the chance to sew wings. In later years she often wished she had, for by then glue had given way to rivets, and gossamer magic to expedient transportation.

Instructing Gloria to hold the jam jar ready and not to allow his brother to snatch it from her, Michael was concentrating on finding worms. Hannah tending her vegetable patch grumbled that this year nature wasn't doing what nature was supposed to do.

"Ninnie, you tink it's dis light ting wit de playing around daytime?" Jane laughed. "Well, Miss-Know-It-All, you see snap beans like dis puny, maybe ever?" Hannah pointed with disgust towards her deserted string trellis that did look rather woebegone.

"Give them time, it's only the end of May. It's early yet." Jane nibbled on a twig of parsley loving its spicy taste. "Oh, I read in John's evening paper that many more troops have arrived in France, but they called them 'doughboys.' Is that what they're called now? What happened to the 'Sammies'?"

"I don't know. How dey spell it?"

"D-o-u-g-h, then boys."

"Dat's silly—dey gonna bake dem before dey go to fight? I ask Fritz—maybe he knows. You see what I say—everyting is changing—every day again someting new, someting not de way it was before, not de way it should be." Hannah pulled wisps of grass off her carrot patch.

"I found one!" Michael, jubilant, called from beneath the daisy bush.

"Fine," Hannah called back. "Let me see."

"No, I'm looking for another one—so he won't get so a-lonely." His voice trailed off.

"Hannah?"

"Yes, Ninnie?"

"That Miss Evangeline, the one who is now Missus Dahlinger . . ."

"Un-huh."

"Well, now that she is married and everything I don't suppose she's dynamite anymore—right?"

"Why you ask?"

"Oh, just curiosity, nothing important."

"Well, you just keep it dat way!" Hannah busied herself fussing around her turnips.

"Did she marry someone special?"

"What, you still at it wit de snoopy questions?"

"Sorry, Hannah . . ."

"Okay, you want to know—I tell . . ."

"I really don't have to . . ."

"Now you don't, before you did—I've got work to do." Hannah stalling for inspiration picked at the parsley.

"I didn't mean to make you angry—I only . . ."

"Enough already! Vell . . . okay, dat-oh-so-smart-I-got-de-world-in-de-palm-of-my-little-hand Miss Evangeline is now de Missus of Once-I-carried-all-de-money-for-de-Boss-chaffeur-now-I-got-it-am-convenient-husband Mr. Dahlinger—so der, now you know!"

Jane utterly confused by all the innuendoes of what she had no knowledge of thought it better to keep her mouth shut until another time was more propitious for the satisfaction of one's curiosity.

"Mama!" the outraged wail of her firstborn split the air. "John is squeezing my worm to dead!" ended any further conversation and not too soon where Hannah was concerned, who, stomping earth off her shoes, walked into her kitchen carrying two scrawny carrots as if they offended her.

In June war as an American reality swept the nation in a tidal wave of jubilant patriotism. At a place called Belleau Wood, an untried division of US Marines not only repulsed a German attack but drove the enemy back without the aid or participation of the more seasoned forces of their allies. At last brave American boys had proven their superior worth and the nation could be proud of its fighting men and of itself. There was even talk that now that America was finally in the war, it could be over by July.

What this victory might have cost in actual lives understandably was hidden within its incredible achievement. The country's morale was now too high and useful to deflate with unproductive truths. What had started out as a benevolent war, one based on ideology rather than actual need—now that America's youth was facing possible bloodshed, the hatred of Germans flared anew, this time encompassing all immigrant communities, be they friend or foe, aided and abetted by political utterances and gathering wartime hysteria.

Everyday hatreds never far from society's perimeter, now ran rampant—their destructive power legitimized by the addition to the Espionage Act, passed by Congress when the country was still neutral, of the new Seditions Act. A sweeping law that could and did imprison anyone for simply objecting to the war in any form and for any reason. As political utterances and gathering wartime frenzy accelerated, witch hunts materialized using the Seditions Act as legal justification. In a country mostly populated by immigrants whose origins were not yet completely distilled through generations, the very configuration of faces, customs, religions, accents, even attitudes were noted, judged solely on the basis of mostly unsubstantiated suspicion of friend and foe alike.

The process that was responsible for the grandeur of this enviable country of immigrants was being insidiously used to erode its still young and vulnerable structure. Those still without citizenship having the potential of being the enemy within the magnanimous country that had welcomed them, given them sanctuary, were particularly singled out.

A country settled, populated, its laudable stature gained though immigration was experiencing a self-erosion not seen since its Civil War. Only the fact that it was enmeshed in a war that was to end all wars, for all time, establish the freedom of its democracy across the world, kept most of the country's patriotism pure.

John, Zoltan, and Ebbely—perhaps the three most politically astute within their group—were appalled. On those evenings when voices were raised, private opinions aired, Jane managed to find acceptable reasons to be present in her parlor in order to listen. She who had by now devoured the writings of Elizabeth Seaton, followed the exploits and persecution of Margaret Sanger, Jane was no longer the starry-eyed young girl content with the crumbs of male enthusiasm for an automobile no matter how enchanting. First with her duties as Watcher, then with her own perceptive sympathy of what she had seen—she had educated herself sufficiently by now to be equal to the men's intelligence without seeming to be so, having added the new luxury of decision as to what to accept and what to discard from the process.

"This is utterly astounding—listen to this . . ." Ebbely began to read, "'. . . Enemy aliens'—this man's referring to Detroit's German Americans—'are not entitled to the slightest degree of respect from humanity. The sooner we perfect plans for the total extermination of such monstrosities in human form the sooner will this country and the world find itself again at peace.'"

"I tell you, my friends—I'm worried—where will all this end?"

"I think it has only begun." John lit his cheroot.

"What do you mean only begun—left and right people are being hauled off to jail for no more reasons than expressing their right, the right they came here for—the freedom to speak without fear of reprisal."

"That's just it, Zoltan—I don't think this will stop even if and when the war ends."

Knowing what John was getting at, Ebbely looked at Stan, wondering at his silence.

"Ja," Fritz shook his head, "I heard even the post office of the United States doesn't allow now any mailing of newspapers that say anything against the war."

"The *Michigan Socialist* is already barred from using the US mail," added Stan.

"You see! And on the line everyone is suspected—no matter who they are or where they come from—even the Negroes . . ." Stan's gaze swept the room. "That, my friends, is not the America I left my homeland for, nor, if you are honest with yourselves, did you."

The room was silenced. For some to agree with him would have seemed disloyal.

John flicked ash from his cheroot. "What worries me is that this Seditions Act is being used as a convenient tool to flush and imprison more Socialists than traitors."

"Well, well, John—what an interesting conclusion coming from you. You as a sudden sympathizer of Socialism?"

"No, Stan—freedom is a man's right, his greatest treasure. When that is threatened—by any organization regardless of ideology—"

"Don't preach, John," Zoltan cautioned.

"I'm not. Free to think, free to do—free to be—brought me to this country. Come on—as Stan said, brought all of us, and if that is *ever* lost—so are we."

"Well put, John," Zoltan acknowledged.

"As you so often remind me—as the only true American amongst you—do all of you support this war?" Ebbely looked about the room. Jane held her breath.

"Yes—if by that you mean to stop it."

"Ja, the killing must be stopped," Fritz agreed.

"By even more killing?" asked Ebbely making Stan smile.

"If that will do it, yes!"

"Yes, Fritz is right. It must be stopped and if we can do it thank God for America!"

"Amen."

"Mr. Ford says it's the bankers who started the war," Peter interjected.

"I thought he claims it's the fault of the Jews," countered Stan.

"Well, all bankers are, aren't they?"

Ignoring Peter, Stan looked around the room. "My friends, all of you must begin to realize that Highland Park is no longer your world nor Henry Ford your Messiah, there is a darker side to our dream and I for one . . ."

"And so you will join those that terrorize their own?" John challenged.

"Terrorize, John? Don't believe all you hear—the illiterate, superstitious *paisanne* of your country's South look to us for protection . . . they need us. You know the Irish control all law enforcement—well now they have even organized what they call an Italian Squad for the sole purpose of *keeping an eye on the dagos* and what has terror got to do with it?"

Zoltan stifled a sneeze. "Stan, you a Rumanian taking up the cause—the plight of the uneducated Sicilians—very interesting."

Having arrived to pick up her husband, Serafina heard Zoltan's remark as she entered the parlor. Ignoring the others' greeting—she stood before him annunciating his name as though the very forming of it was distasteful.

"Zoltan?"

"Yes?"

"My father's organization offers our people the services without which they would remain the shunned scum they are treated as. I am proud of Stan. He will be a fine soldier in *our* war!"

"So the Black Hand thinks of itself as justified benevolence?"

Serafina whirled in John's direction.

"How do you know its name?"

"My dear Serafina, such an organization cannot maintain its anonymity."

"Certainly not in these days." Ebbely enjoying Serafina's obvious discomfort, smiled in agreement.

Without another word, Serafina flounced out of the room—Stan, murmuring good-bye, followed her.

Zoltan squirmed. "There, my friends, lies a danger far more immediate than even a righteous union meeting."

"In a way I agree," John sighed. "If the Black Hand takes control of the illegal liquor business before Prohibition becomes law in the rest of the country, there'll be trouble—big trouble—"

"Well, for sure the micks won't like the wops getting too power hungry—sorry, John."

John laughed, "I love it, Ebbely—only you can get so downright American!"

Summer brought its accustomed activities, this year adding special occasions for jubilant news—the celebration of battles won, stretches of scarred land regained—marred only by the swelling lists of those sacrificed to do so. Death achieved in righteous battle was still a man's domain. Women as wives, mothers and sweethearts were certainly expected to mourn the result—but being politically educated enough to have an opinion and voice this progression to their grief was as unexpected as it was socially condemned. As the war progressed, women who had been assured by recruiting slogans that their loved ones would return *better men* began to think that a live return might be preferable.

It was rumored that Henry Ford would run for the Senate—that President Wilson had personally encouraged him to do so. Stating every farmer in America would vote for him, many thought that if Ford wanted to, he could run for the presidency and get elected. Those whom the Boss recognized, even called by name on the factory floors, were proud to be singled out, cheered whenever he appeared. Although he did not campaign, posters reading WILSON NEEDS HENRY FORD began to appear. In June, making good on his promise, the first Ford-built Eagle Boat was launched.

The day Rudy left to become a soldier in the sky—as Hannah described it—the Ford men gathered to bid him good-bye.

"You know you're crazy, boy." Carl hiding his emotion punched Rudy's shoulder while Fritz stuffed a pouch of his best tobacco into his coat pocket. Zoltan blew his nose.

"Good luck, Rudy—and let's hear from you."

"Yes—don't forget—write and tell us all about it." John hugged his friend. Michael, aware something was changing, clung to Rudy's trouser leg. Jane pulled him gently to her side. Hannah stood silent.

"Well-I-I-guess-I better get going . . ." The suspended hesitancy that always surfaces when good-byes could become eternal hung in midsentence. "Hannah?" Like a son leaving home, Rudy took a step towards her.

"You got de sandwiches?"

He nodded.

"And de clean underwear? De key to dis house in case you come one day back home and nobody here to let you in?" Again Rudy nodded.

"Well, den—so go already! But you just remember one ting—if you get yourself killed I'll never talk to you again!" And Rudy pulled Hannah into his arms and laughed. When he was gone—then, she cried.

Fritz's friend Mr. Horowitz took his Missus, said good-bye to their neighbors, left Ford and Highland Park, to journey to Massachusetts to be near their only son, Bruno, one of the forty thousand conscripts training at the hutted cantonment known as Camp Devens, before he was shipped out.

By the Fourth of July what once had seemed an impossible task had been achieved—an army of a million men fully equipped, trained and ready had arrived in France.

When at a fitting for a new summer dress, Serafina boasted that Detroit now had more speakeasies than any other city in the state, Jane just had to ask what that was.

"That's a place that sells hooch."

"Oh, Serafina, now what is that?"

"No wonder John calls you Ninnie! Hooch is booze is hard liquor—and a speakeasy is a place that sells it."

"But isn't that against the law now?"

"Of course—that's why there's so much money in it—and you know what . . . it's fun!" Serafina admired herself in the mirror. "You have done excellent work on this dress. When I brought you the material I thought it might be too delicate to stitch but this is very, very acceptable. Can you have it ready by Friday? Stan will be back then and we are going dancing."

"Friday? Yes, of course."

Without care, Serafina pulled the half-finished dress off over her head.

"Want to know how to spot a place that sells gin?"

Retrieving her delicate handiwork off the floor, Jane murmured, "Not particularly."

"Well, you just have to look if there is a potted fern in the window." At Jane's startled expression, Serafina chuckled, "That's the sign—they sell liquor. Once a week I deliver them to all our customers—our ferns are free but our booze . . . that's quite another matter." This last sally seemed to amuse her further. Putting on her latest acquisition, a splendid boater of lacquered straw, Serafina, gazing in the mirror squinted, her eyes drawn to Jane's accompanying reflection behind her.

"Why do I see you . . . as though duplicated? I wonder . . . oh, by the way, Morgana is expecting—so now all we have to do is wait for her to miscarry! I'm off—don't forget—Friday before the afternoon. *Arrivederci!*"

Frowning, Jane secured the pins in the hem of the delicate batiste.

Duplicated? She said duplicated! Really, that witch! Hannah was right—a real witch! She had a good mind *not* to finish by Friday. Still, Serafina paid well and Jane having seen a most splendid collar of real seal fit for her precious winter coat was determined to acquire it as well as a new pair of boots for Michael, who was growing so fast it would soon be time to make him another pair of knee pants. Sewing diligently, Jane wondered if her nest egg could reach to include a new invention—buttonhole scissors offered by Mr. Sears and Mr. Roebuck for the staggering sum of forty cents . . . a real luxury that she coveted even more than a fancy collar of real seal.

Both having been refused glory in combat—one because of a deaf ear, the other for being too old to pull a caisson into firing position—Mr. Kennec the iceman and his Molly came plodding along the streets of Highland Park trailing their usual gaggle of thirsty children as though this August was no different from any other. The first day of the ice wagon's arrival, Michael gave up his special privilege and allowed Gloria to feed Molly her expected carrot. In doing so, he felt very cavalier—especially when he saw how much the little girl enjoyed it.

As the first death lists began to appear, the hatred of all things German intensified. Aided and abetted by the propaganda needed to rally a nation beginning to go sluggish by its very distance to actual combat—by many means the enemy was brought into focus to invade the consciousness of the country if not its actual terrain.

As always, rumor was an effective tool for accelerating hatred. It was whispered that those of German origin were putting ground glass into food, poison onto Red Cross bandages, explosives into every conceivable aperture for the sole purpose of killing as many innocent American women and children as possible. The evil of the Hun was graphically illustrated in a moving picture entitled *The Kaiser, the Beast of Berlin*. The teaching of German was banned as was the music of Beethoven. Regardless of citizenship all of German origin were suspect. Some were forced by riotous mobs to kneel, salute, kiss the American flag. Many were beaten, in Kentucky one was lynched. It was even rumored that the black radicalism that was beginning to surface was solely due to German agents.

Hannah believing herself tainted by her origin, and therefore rife for other's punishment of her—rarely left her house. Especially nervous when visited—she cautioned those who came, to be careful if seen, perhaps not come at all for it could mean they too might become suspect of terrible deeds to destroy the glorious freedom of America. Fritz at a loss of what to do with her, yet equally apprehensive when going out amongst the people taking his tram to and from work—tried his best to assume the air of normalcy that had been, believing that as soon as the war was won, it would be again.

Jane now needed to knock on Hannah's door to gain admittance. And even then she was usually made to identify herself before the door was opened. She had the feeling that if she had been other than a safe Italian—despite their long and binding friendship, Hannah might not have let her in. When together their speaking in German was strictly forbidden. Even if rationing and the inflationary prices had permitted it—Jane somehow knew neither jelly doughnuts nor ginger-bread houses would ever emerge from Hannah's kitchen again. If Ebbely hadn't been in residence those who loved Hannah would not have known what to do. But he was and despite it all he made her smile, even laugh at times, played jaunty tunes upon her lovely Christmas present filling the house with jazz—even suspect Mendelssohn—recalling happy times and joy-filled days when all her immediate worries were kitchen bound, easily solvable by a pinch of salt, the addition of a bit of spice. To feed the ones one loves is such an all-embracing sanctuary that after so many years of having it, now that it was allowed her but rarely, Hannah felt its desertion at a time an exterior danger was threatening to strip her of herself. As a Jewess she knew hatred. As a German who was about to become a citizen of the country she adored—it tore her to pieces.

Often, when Hannah voiced her need to be left alone, by saying, "A little time in my kitchen for just peeling whatever mit nobody—okay, Ninnie?" Jane would use the luxury of time gained to seek out Ebbely, draw from him what had become important to her to analyze from. His ever-generous availability gave her that gift so unusual, the respect of her right to intelligence. Sometimes not to interrupt, she would simply sit and listen while he played—at other times pick up a thought that might not have been concluded to her satisfaction days before.

"Why are people judged before they are known?"

"In what way?" Ebbely fingered the keys at random.

"I'm sorry, am I disturbing you?"

"No, continue—you usually have a purpose." Knowing how he liked to tease, Jane acknowledged this with a smile.

"Well . . . now that Russia has surrendered, suddenly all Russians are bad—where before when they were fighting with us they were good. What if Italy has to surrender—will that make all Italians into enemies?"

"Mob thinking needs to generalize to make a mob."

"What is a mob?"

"An accumulation of humans who generally have forsaken their humanity."

"Why would they do that?" Jane sounded like a child at school.

"Mostly it is done *to* them not *by* them."

"Remember that day when John and Hannah were talking of war and freedom? Will we win the war?"

"The *we* being?"

"America, of course!" Jane sounded surprised.

"I think we must at least try." Ebbely ran the scale of E-flat. "Soon Europe will have lost a whole generation to this terrible war."

"I think freedom is more important than death."

"Even if death *is* freedom?"

"We don't know that."

"But what if it is?" asked Ebbely, leaving "The 'Jelly Roll' Blues" for another day.

"Then I suppose all of us would court death and be done with living."

"Sometimes, my child, you startle me, and I pride myself on not being startled easily."

"I'm sorry."

"Don't apologize—after strumming a banjo for the entertainment of pimpled youth about to be brave cannon fodder on some foreign field, I welcome theological dissertation, especially with you." Ebbely patted the footstool by his chair. "Sit, Tall Lady—sit. We sages hate looking up at our interlocutor—kinks the neck muscles."

Settling herself, Jane wondered where their talk would lead. From above her head the question came.

"Do you believe in God?"

"No," she whispered—half-afraid for having voiced it.

Bending down, Rumpelstiltskin placed his small hand beneath her chin, lifted her face to look at him. "Aren't you terribly lonely then?"

And the sobs came. As if contained too long of a childhood warped—loving denied—yearning ridiculed by too strict reality, all was there . . . yet nothing salvageable to build upon, give ballast to a spirit made vulnerable by too much need.

Enfolding the child he knew her to be, Ebbely wished he were tall and handsome.

"Dear friends, those within the delightful proximity of me, even those long gone and sadly too, too far away" is how Ebbely began the announcement of his planned departure during a rare Sunday supper. "No, no, do not stop partaking of this magical concoction—only Hannah can make a soup out of nothing and triumph. Herbert Hoover should have hired her long ago. Now . . . where was I? Ah, yes— before the leaves fall, carpet their russet beauty upon newly glacial ground, I and my trusty T must once again sally forth to cheer the fuzz-cheeked youth of this my promised land."

Zoltan twitched. "Where to this time?"

"I've been trying to make up my mind. The camps are mostly all alike, just row upon row of endless makeshift huts, their perimeter clustered by the usual whore-houses and booze joints."

"I heard that army doctors have been so overwhelmed by the rampant rate of syphilis that the government has given orders to burn the houses down. So at least those will be gone."

Ebbely smiled, "You want to make a bet on that, John?"

"No—not really."

"Well, at least here in Michigan all the saloons are gone," Zoltan observed.

John laughed. "Ebbely will probably want to bet you on that, too!"

"You know the clap and all its happy handmaidens is not, as the traveling salesman said to the farmer's daughter . . ."

Seeing Hannah enter the room ready to serve her perfected vegetable stew, Fritz barked, "Ebberhardt, not this talk. Hannah is here now."

"Sorry, dear Lady." Noting Jane had followed her in, Ebbely amended it to "Ladies."

The women served—the men ate in silence. Despite Fritz's possible objection, John reopened the subject knowing his friend had more to say.

"Ebbely, tell me, regardless of such commodities that have existed since the days of the Caesars as part of any military installation, what are these military cantonment camps really like?"

"Besides the obvious deplorable conditions? The mounds of garbage no one has figured, nor possibly can figure out what to do with? The absence of proper sanitation and often nonexistent viable disposal of the human waste of more than twenty thousand men? The astounding illiteracy of our backcountry recruits? The cruelties of those who are in charge as well as those who receive, who then turn on their own kind in impotent revenge? The indiscriminate use of the Chihuahua Weed supposedly smoked by Mexicans of the lower classes that the army claims produces insanity and homicidal mania. So especially convenient for war, might one agree? Sometimes when the handlers infiltrate the camps—I have seen men line up just as they do for vaccinations . . . for injections of morphine."

"For God's sake, why, Ebbely? Why is it allowed?" If Zoltan hadn't asked—Jane nearly would have.

"Why, my friend? You may well ask. Lonely? Desperate? Far from home? Uneducated? Scared? Lost or just plain dumb? Youngsters being taught to kill having not the slightest notion what that will entail. The natural euphoria of the young for war needing a reinforcement to keep the excitement of it going until it becomes real? Take your pick. General Pershing has asked for four million men and he will get them. How many of them will *be* men in our sense of the word, or how many will return alive and sane after their baptism by fire turns them into so-called men—that's up to whatever god suits you."

The women stood waiting in the shadows. The men ate their supper in silence. To lighten the mood, Ebbely ventured, "By the way, in Kansas and Missouri so many conscripts go into Kansas City that its notorious Twelfth Avenue has been renamed Woodrow Wilson Avenue, a *piece* at any price!"

Fritz barked, "Enough! Hannah, Jane—now please leave this room." John covered a smile behind his napkin.

"Really, Ebberhardt," Fritz spluttered, "such talk in front of respectable wives!"

"I agree and I am terribly sorry—I don't know what got into me." Noticing John's expression, Ebbely added, "And I was about to tell you of the posters hung everywhere that proclaim in overly large letters . . ."

"What?"

"Well, if Fritz will allow, now the course is clear . . . I'll quote, 'A German bullet is cleaner than a whore,' and one I particularly found enchanting, 'You wouldn't use another man's toothbrush. Why use his whore?'"

Putting down his napkin, John looked at his friend. "You are in one of your naughty moods tonight, Ebbely—any special reason why?"

Caught off guard and startled that this should so discomfort him, Ebbely changed the subject. "As to my imminent departure, in all the years you've known me I bet none of you have figured out how I find my way around this land."

Zoltan rose to the bait. "Well now that the first maps of real roads are being printed to be sold I assume your bloodhound senses will no longer be necessary."

"Regardless, I venture to assume that you dyed-in-the-wool Detroiters don't even know that the Lincoln Highway—that excellent example of navigational surface—carries the identification of its amazing lengths by painted colors of red, white and blue. Aha! Just as I thought! And for those roads less auspicious, 'Follow the telephone poles' is now the motto of the open road. For these and only these will lead you into the heart of civilization, or what passes as such. John, my boy, when *will* you acquire a T of your own? You of all people—without one—seems practically blasphemous."

"Soon."

"Well, don't tell me your miracle car suddenly can't maneuver your favorite riverbank. After all the years we have had to listen to you expound on the dependability of your unstoppable heartthrob, I should think you'd be ashamed to have your Lizzie at times see you use a real horse. Shocking, John—really shocking!"

"After the war—time enough." John rose.

Following him to the parlor, Ebbely murmured, "Just be loyal, John!"

When Ebbely stopped by her house to say good-bye, Jane felt it was somehow different from the many such times before. As the little taillight of his flivver disappeared in the haze of early morning, it was as if suddenly all of him was gone. Even Michael must have felt deserted—for he began to cry until she took his hand and walked back into the house.

18

By the time Jane stepped off the trolley it had begun to rain—a penetrating drizzle that seemed to herald yet another brutal winter. Hugging her cape, she tried to shield her Red Cross uniform. She had marched in a victory bond rally in the city, rolled bandages, then missed her trolley, and had to wait for the next—it had been a very long day.

Pulling her shawl closer across her chest, she rose from her chair, extinguished the lamp—and in a voice that sounded her exhaustion said good night to her husband. "*Buonanotte*, John."

Looking up from his evening paper John replied, "Go ahead, you look tired— *buonanotte*, Ninnie—I'll lock up." She smiled her gratitude and went upstairs.

When he moved, she half-asleep, as accustomed turned onto her back accepting his weight. His hands gentled her face—one slender finger traced her mouth, descended to the hollow of her neck, where it remained, stroking lazily along the line of her collarbone as though hesitant of reaching the pleasure of her. Something stirred in the woman he was fondling and John felt it. A response so unexpected—so new it arrested his exploration of her. She moaned—that primal entreaty calling him to her, he entered her as though his need to explore her newness overpowered him and she gloried in it. During the night his hands once more caressed—first choosing her small breasts, pretending aimless direction as they slid down between her thighs and Jane reawoke to being woman.

In the morning, he was gone and she was lost. Utterly confused—slightly ashamed, even shocked . . . her body no longer an ally, now an incomprehensible stranger—Jane surveyed her nakedness as if it belonged to another woman she had yet to meet wondering who she might be. Hearing her children calling, she dressed quickly knowing that whatever had happened to her during the night would have to wait until she had the time to think it through. With legs strangely unsteady, stirring a memory quite shocking in its delight—she hurried to her daily duties.

Being a rare pie-making day she couldn't avoid seeing Hannah unless she pretended one of the boys was ill—Jane never liked to tempt fate with such lies and so arrived at Hannah's as expected. Having been admitted, hanging her and the children's coats and hats on the hall tree, she called to Hannah back in her kitchen, "I'll be right there. I'm just taking off my galoshes. I brought the apples," and wondered why her voice sounded so girlish. Securing an imagined strand of hair back into her sensible bun, Jane entered the kitchen and Hannah dropped her rolling pin! Bending down to retrieve it hiding a smile, she murmured, "It's de grease on my hands make it slip." And without further explanation continued to roll out her dough. "You look nice, Ninnie—have a good night?"

Blushing Jane nodded.

Those nights when her husband explored her, she who had always found his hands beautiful—now savored their knowing touch—waited—heart pounding—breathless for that moment when his need of her overwhelmed—demanded her willingness to welcome him inside her—where his passion resided—and her loving began.

Those nights when work kept him from her—she sewed. Wanting him became the catalyst of her days until his return to claim what was his.

Riding along the riverbank John's thoughts were of his wife. Jane's surprising response had unsettled him. No, he corrected his thoughts—not actually unsettled—confused perhaps—certainly surprised. As the horse stumbled he pulled it up, steadying its gait. It was the feel of her that lingered—that clung, its memory too pleasant to be ignored as simply sexual. Women as such had never bothered him beyond the confines of enjoyment. Certainly a willing woman be she a professional or simply accessible, was a normal man's bodily relaxation. Making *love*, that misnomer of all time—had never been a part of John's sexual affiliations. Love was such an intangible emotion—so multifaceted as to its very origin, dependent on so many individual concepts as to its source that very often when *love* was used as convenient catalyst for sex it could impede the very enjoyment sought of it. For most men *love* really had a way of getting in the way of a vigorous enjoyable form of exercise needing no further impetus. To find sudden recognition of physical delight within his marriage rattled John sufficiently to shy away from the woman who had fostered it, seek out those who had gained his confidence by allowing the game to be played without interfering emotion. Adjusting his grip on the reins, John lit a cheroot. Shielding the flare of the match against the slight breeze coming from the river he heard its approach. Often when riding this stretch of the Rouge—he caught the soft rippling sound of the electric boat that Henry Ford had given his wife when their Fairlane estate was first completed. John had heard its silent gliding approach often, never taking much notice of its passing, its intended destination, nor who was its captain.

As Jane's body yearned and waited, her mind forming excuses for John's many absences—death prepared itself for a global feast.

It came, as death so often seems to enjoy, first disguised as casual discomfort. A slight fever, a minor headache, a rolling cough that though it seemed strangely persistent, all were to be expected at the end of a particularly raw September. From Boston, where he had entertained recruits at Camp Devens, Ebbely telephoned the Geiger house, sounding the first alarm.

"Fritz?"

"Ja, it's me." As all who need to speak in a language not their own, Fritz didn't like talking to a face he couldn't see.

"Fritz, listen to me and listen carefully . . ."

"Ebberhardt, Hannah is not here . . ."

"I don't want to speak with Hannah . . ."

"Oh—why not?"

"Because what I have to say may frighten her—but it must be said, so please listen!"

"I'm listening."

"Something very strange is happening here. Healthy young recruits are suddenly becoming ill, and no one knows why—the army doctors are going crazy. So many sick here—not enough cots, not enough sheets, they are lying in hallways, in the mess halls, everywhere—all as sick as dogs . . ."

"Why—Ebberhardt—what is it? Typhus?"

"No—nor cholera either, nor yellow fever. It's like some monstrous pneumonia—but even that doesn't fit—although the doctors think it could be because something like this has started in Spain. Fritz, just in the past twenty-four hours, there have been a hundred new cases and more than fifty deaths!"

"Deaths?!"

"Yes! Young men in the prime of life and remember they have been conditioned as fit soldiers—are dying as fast as exhausted personnel can strip the sheets, make up a cot to receive still another. And on top of that, they are shipping out a thousand men a week. It's a nightmare here! Fritz, I have a feeling whatever this is, it may spread to the other camps—perhaps, even God forbid, into the cities . . . be careful—tell Hannah to get out her trusty barrel of vinegar and wash down everything!"

"Ah, come on! You talk like it's the Black Death . . ."

Ebbely interrupted him by yelling, "Very, very like it! I warn you! Have the women be extra careful. Especially watch the children—this horror seems to target the young and healthy. I am leaving here tonight for Louisiana . . ."

"Ebberhardt—you're okay?"

"For now, yes. Don't worry for me. Just do as I say. And, Fritz! Watch for the signs! Have Hannah tell Jane and the others. First it appears like a bad grippe. High fever, sweating and so on. Then very, very quickly it's like serious pneumonia, only worse. The lungs seem to drown in their own phlegm and then . . . Death! It can take only hours! It's unbelievable, Fritz—it's bedlam here! Warn everybody—I'll telephone again when I reach New Orleans."

Half certain that Ebbely had exaggerated as was his style, Fritz returned the earpiece onto its hook, cranked the handle, wondered how much to tell Hannah.

Within weeks the killing rampage of what was now thought to be a previously unknown virulent strain of influenza was in full bloom. Cities were under siege, their populations sickening and dying at an alarming rate. Wherever people gathered—churches, schools, those factories not involved in war production—were shut down, those left in production replacing their stricken workforce whenever and from wherever possible. In the first months of what was quickly an acknowledged epidemic—Ford's Highland Park plant needed to replace ten thousand men.

No one ventured into the streets without a homemade face mask—firemen, policemen, conductors, shopkeepers, clergy—by October, every man, woman and child wore this protection that couldn't begin to protect them.

Philadelphia, out of coffins, had to instruct its citizens to leave their shrouded dead on the front steps for collection by the city's roaming death carts. Undertakers overwhelmed, no longer able to perform their expected duties, stored their overflow in makeshift sheds.

Those cities hardest hit made do with communal graves, their trenchlike appearance a macabre reminder of another war being fought far away, where thousands of already infected American troops were arriving daily—soon the death count from influenza would outstrip that of war on all fronts.

As no medicine seemed to exist that could hold out any hope, desperate people began to concoct their own. Turpentine was sucked on sugar cubes, a brew of kerosene flavored with garlic and honey was tried. The more potent the smell, the more vile the taste, the more medicinal was the popular consensus, but nothing helped. One either died or for some inexplicable reason lived. There seemed to be no middle ground. In Chicago, a man claiming that he had found the cure cut the throats of his wife and children before slashing his own.

Many believed that with their use of mustard gas in war, Germans had already proven themselves to be monsters—it followed they were certainly capable of unleashing disease across the sea in order to destroy America on its home ground. Some barricaded themselves within what they mistakenly believed was the safety of their homes, others faced the inevitable, helped to nurse those in need—most did battle with death within their immediate families.

Her sodden lungs no longer able to cope, Carl's Rosie died two hours before their child. As by now coffins were hard to come by, Carl buried his wife and daughter as one. At the age of only three, his Violet was small enough to fit snugly by her mother's side. Quite lost without her twin, little Rose cried incessantly. At just thirty-three, a widower left with a small daughter to raise, Carl felt quite lost himself.

Zoltan buried his mother without ceremony—by October funerals as a whole were so numerous that the sheer necessity to get the dead underground took precedence over sanctified occasion.

With schools closed and adults too sick or too busy nursing, unsupervised, still healthy children played. Michael and his best friend, Gregory, thought climbing on caskets stacked on the latest sidewalk waiting for transport a lot of fun, until Jane, on her way to nurse Mrs. Nussbaum and her eldest daughter, scolded them—then they switched to the latest activity for children in many neighborhoods—a simple game, its rules requiring only the search and counting of front doors hung with crepe. Black crepe meant a grown-up had died within, white crepe—a child. As it was the hardest, whoever could find a crepe-less door won.

A light rain had made the white crepe limp the morning John took Michael to pay their respects to his best friend's parents. Laid out in the parlor, his Sunday sailor suit making him appear quite smart, Gregory posed by the living, slept as though he could wake. Never having smelled death, Michael now had its fetid odor of warmed wax and formaldehyde imprinted onto memory. While Jane's stirred to a time and place never forgotten, rarely revisited, mostly shunned.

Michael stayed properly attentive until the Gregorian chants had faded and the procession for viewing of the corpse was about to begin, then plucked at his father's sleeve and urgently asked permission to leave. Holding hands, Jane and her son walked home in the rain.

With his best friend's death, Michael began to wonder about his comforting theory of nondying worms. It had seemed so simple a solution; but now with Gregory gone, *forever and ever* loomed as a frightening possibility and he wasn't so sure anymore if he or his mother was right. So many were gone, referred to as dead, that for the first time, Michael's world tottered on the brink of uncertainty and he didn't like it at all. Michael being what he was, believed life was supposed to be fun, full of wonders, exciting, adventure and all the sticky candy one could eat. Crying and worry, hushed whisperings, grown-ups being scared and sad was really very unsettling. Being all of nearly five and therefore grown-up in his opinion, Michael felt it his duty to set a good example—decided for now to be extra kind to all those who had someone gone forever but to pretend that Gregory was only on a journey and would return whenever he was able.

Jane always wondered how her firstborn managed to be so brave. He allowed her so little input into the formation of his character that she often felt as compliant outsider to one in no actual need of a parent. If she had been a clinging woman, this might have upset her, at least annoy her for the absence of control this afforded—but cloying motherhood did not suit Jane's character. Despite restrictions, she was her own compass and as such admired those who thought for themselves, resolved their own confusion or at least attempted to gain a freedom from convention.

But then she was not to know Michael's course had been charted and as such his time was limited, his impact on the lives affected by him therefore at a premium.

Morgana never did have to fully experience Serafina's demonic prophecy, for while still a blushing bridegroom, her Emillian succumbed to influenza. A widow before a real wife, Morgana returned to Detroit and her father's house to find a hysterical Serafina convinced nothing and no one could save her son from certain death. Without sleep or rest, Morgana nursed her sister's child until he was out of danger. Having told no one she was with child—when she miscarried everyone assumed her ensuing weakness to be due to the grueling hours spent by Angelo's bedside to achieve his resurrection.

Little Gloria, her eyes no longer pristine blue, already dimmed as though they knew what their host had yet to learn, died in her mother's arms, before her father could reach home.

The death of Gloria affected Michael in ways not immediately apparent to those whose duty it was to be aware of them. At a time of great anxiety even good people lose their intuitive ability to fathom others' needs. Later, when prodded by an insistent Michael, Johann explained his child's departure as one resulting in permanent residence among angels. Hannah hugging him, murmured that his little friend was now happy sleeping among the stars, Fritz explained that the great sickness had taken Gloria as it had Gregory to a nonsuffering place. Home on leave, resplendent in aviator's regalia, his uncle Rudy counseled him to remember his worm.

Michael's first encounters with mortal death hurt so much it confused his once comforting theory of resurrection. For Gloria was not a worm and when taken to where she was buried, she remained beneath the marble angle placed there by weeping parents who seemed convinced she would stay where she had been put. Wherever everyone said Gloria was—Michael hoped she was okay—but wished she had been a worm, for then he would know exactly where to look and find her again. What worried him most was her enclosure. He didn't like her being locked inside such a sturdy-looking thing. One night when John was home putting him to bed, Michael decided it was a good time to ask.

"Papa, why did Uncle Johann put Gloria in a box?"

"What? What are you talking about, Michael?"

"The box, Papa."

"What about the box?"

"It's so big, Papa! Maybe Gloria can't get out! She's very, very little, you know—littler than Gregory even."

John put his arm around his son, pulling him to his side. "Michele," John often spoke Italian when in intimate discussion with his firstborn. "You mustn't be afraid. Do you know what a soul is? Has Mama explained this to you?"

"No. I don't think Mama likes souls, but Uncle Rudy—he told me they are extra special and once Gregory said God made them, maybe." Michael snuggled into the crook of his father's arm. "You know, Papa? You know everything!"

"No, not everything. Your Uncle Rudy and Gregory—they are both right—a soul is *so* special only God knows how to make one, and when someone dies it is their soul that goes free . . ."

"Why?"

"Because only your body is dead—not the real person you are." Eyes riveted on his father's face, Michael swallowed a sigh. "Michelino, you mustn't worry so! Death isn't really bad. Some even think it must be beautiful—like a long sleep with no need to wake."

"Oh, I know that, Papa . . . but . . ."

"No more buts—go to sleep. Don't wake your brother."

Left in the dark, snuggled down in his warm bed, Michael wondered if Gloria was cold, hoped she had already gotten out of her box and was gone to wherever souls lived.

This year the casual search for enjoyable fear was abandoned. With life and death playing their own ghoulish game of trick or treat, Halloween was unnecessary.

Jane woke more tired than when she had gone to bed exhausted. During the night it must have snowed for the intensified brightness of the morning light hurt her eyes. Dressing, seeing to the children, everything seemed such an effort, she gave in to their clamor to go out and play, returning to the kitchen that seemed overly hot, she shivered. Silly to feel so tired with the day just begun and so much to do, sinking onto a chair, Jane rested her head against the cooling surface of the kitchen table and without being aware of it slipped into oblivion. A half hour later Hannah found her semiconscious, drenched in sweat.

"Ninnie! Ninnie! Oh, *Mein Gott!*" Cradling the limp figure, Hannah began to cry. Death loomed large in that small kitchen—then Hannah collected her courage, took charge and the ominous specter receded into the shadows to wait for who would win the battle for Jane's life. Half-dragging, half-lifting Jane up the stairs, Hannah covering her fear crooned, "Come, child, come. We do it, you and me togedder. Okay? I hold—you step—you can do it, Ninnie! We do it slow—see? You can do it!" Propelled more by her love of Hannah than her willingness to move, Jane tried to focus on lifting one foot after the other. "Good, child! Good! See—up we go to a nice bed and a nice cold compress on de so-hot head. Don't worry about de children. I take care of everyting—get de doctor, get . . ."

"Hannah!" The cry was low, its fear raw. "I think I am with child."

"Oh my God—how long?" Hannah stood white-faced before this new calamity.

"Two months, maybe." Jane's cough rumbled up from a phlegm-filled chest. Hannah, trying for an encouraging smile, failed.

"Well, okay, so we got to nurse one outside, one inside. John know?"

"No, I wasn't sure enough."

"So, we won't tell. Better he worry just for his Ninnie now—later if dis baby not leave—stay mit you—den time enough for him to know good news all together at once. Now you sleep. I take children away from dis sickness to my house. First tell John where and what—den get doctor, come back here and we will see what we gotta do. Don't be frightened, Vifey—I'll be back."

By nightfall Jane was delirious. Having scoured the neighborhoods, Fritz finally found a doctor, Hannah hurried him up the stairs.

"Doctor, she is in de family way."

"How far on?"

"She tinks two months, maybe."

"How old? First baby?"

"Twenty-two and no, dis is number tree."

"Only the young—why only the young and healthy? God damn this thing!"

Later after a much-needed steaming cup of heavily sugared coffee, they spoke— their voices low, their fears apparent.

"Mrs. Geiger, that woman upstairs may not survive. If she does—I have grave doubts she will hold the child. She can't be moved. All the hospitals are full. Compresses—sponge baths—try to break the fever if you can—and drink—make her drink—you know what to do—fluids, fluids—we have nothing. Nothing helps." Nodding, Hannah helped him into his heavy overcoat. "There is a husband?"

"He is away working for Mr. Ford in Dearborn—my Fritz is getting him."

"Well, just remember, keep everyone away—if possible." The harried doctor and his trusty Model T disappeared into the winter night. The dreaded word *influenza* had not been spoken, both knew the enemy they were facing.

Like Gregory and Gloria and all the others, Mama would die—Michael was sure. He prepared himself for this ultimate of losses by pretending that his mother was well and that the whispered worry about the house was only grown-ups being overly excited about absolutely nothing. When Hannah moved him and his brother to her house, he left his home willingly without hesitation or defiance and did not question why he was not permitted to say good-bye.

The sudden realization that any moment his wife might be lost to him panicked John. For the first time since Jane had thrust herself into his life, despite its alarming beginning, John felt more than just having made a comfortable bargain. For some reason she had become precious, a woman of worth that belonged to him, who he wanted to keep, even love, if given the gift of time to do so. Looking down at her, knowing she was far too ill to recognize him—he growled, "Ninnie! You get well! You hear me?! I order you!" Grabbing her shoulders, pulling her close—he shook her. Hannah screamed.

"You crazy? Shaking a so-sick woman!" and smacked him.

"Well—you better make her well because I need her!" and shoving an outraged Hannah aside, John stormed out of the room.

"Was that John? Why is he angry?" the exhausted whisper brought Hannah back to Jane's side.

"Because your so-scared husband—he loves you and don't know what to do—how to help. No more talking now, Vifey—sleep—fever is down a little—so dat's good news—sleep, Ninnie, sleep. He loves you, child—finally—he loves you."

And Jane slept.

Downstairs, hands shaking, John poured himself a stiff drink. The possible loss of her had never entered his mind. He had acquired her as unavoidable convenience, a commitment made into a common reality accepted by both without complaint by either party. True of late it had become pleasurable in ways hardly envisioned before—still this slight adjustment in their relationship could not account for this sudden wrenching, this terror at the possibility of losing her. John was not a man who questioned emotion. Impatience with himself did not permit introspection. He loved, he hated, he liked, he disliked. Life was an exterior battle to be won, not an interior one to mull over. It therefore shocked him that seeing Jane's face drained of life made him want to grab her, shake her back into life to allow him to love her. Knowing he had duties as a father before those of a husband, John downed the whiskey, and left to seek his sons at the Geigers'.

"Hannah—" the whisper sounded stronger.

"Yes, child?"

"Please, cut my hair." Thinking Jane was once again delirious, Hannah replaced a compress without comment. "Please, it's so hot—all this hair is so heavy." As she drifted, Jane's voice faded.

Two more such entreaties during the night and Hannah took Jane's big dressmaking shears and cut off her long hair—quite shocked at herself for having the courage to do it. Receiving a sigh of relief as her reward, she settled back into her chair to watch over the sweet woman she loved.

Eight long arduous days the specter did battle with Hannah, then accepting defeat slunk away ashamed of himself for even having tried. Triumphant tears streaming down her face, Hannah stood in the doorway of her own house.

"She will live! Our sweet Vifey will live!"

Fritz caught her as she collapsed.

As though both scourges decided they had achieved their proper importance in the annals of history—the Great War and its companion, the Great Influenza pandemic, ceased their monumental killing spree by the middle of November 1918. Between them they had wiped out most of the youth of the world. In time, the war would be easily remembered—the other quickly forgotten within the euphoria of peace achieved. A collective amnesia within jubilation quickly blocked out the memory of a worldwide scourge as though it had never existed. Unaware they were statistics of history, people buried their dead, grieved, then forgot what was forgettable. Those who survived the Great War and its virulent companion acquired the inner scarring of both. Wounds seen and unseen—that for the remaining lifetime granted them were forever their own burden. As with all tragedy—those on the perimeter equally affected, needing help themselves, were expected by society as well as their guilt of survival to aid those who were beyond helping themselves. In all nations—those defeated and victorious, healing was assumed automatic through peace recaptured; that it couldn't be—later generations would have to pay for.

The first arrival of overseas mail brought new tragedies for some—relief and comfort to others. New hope and unbridled joy gripped the nation—its brave boys had done what they had promised. They were coming home because it was over—*over there*. And the American parlor that had seen so many loved ones laid out to mourn over was rechristened, given the new hope-filled name of *living room*.

"Dat's nice, I like dat," was Hannah's reaction when first informed by the *Ladies' Home Journal* of this monumental change. "We dine in de dining room, now we *live* in de room for living—so what we do now mit de bedroom?"

This year Thanksgiving was one of true gratitude—whatever the cost, world peace was assured for all time. For those who had survived whatever battle, being alive was sufficient unto itself.

After months of worrying, not daring to even think of what might have happened to him—Hannah finally received word from Ebbely. In that flourished penmanship so suited to his flowery speech, he informed one and all that the mighty Spanish influenza had clicked its castanets in his direction and he its innocent victim had succumbed, been hospitalized on the very day of his arrival in New Orleans. Weeks at death's pearly gates, he had struggled against Lucifer's avarice to survive—the remembrance of Hannah's glorious suppers his only talisman. Still too weak to attempt travel, his body would therefore not be present for the holidays, but his undying devotion—that would certainly be, always. Hannah was so happy her Ebbely was alive she didn't even shed a tear at his absence.

By Hannah's orders, Christmas this year was moved to Louisa Street so John put up his tree, Fritz carried over the manger, the menorah and decorations, Hannah the gingerbread house—and everything else. No one came—but then no one was expected. For the children, normalcy was attempted. Familiar songs sung, candles lit, sugar icicles sucked—sad thoughts held at bay—while Michael and Little John concentrated on generous wise men and suppliant shepherds . . . Jane, carried down to sit amongst cushions engulfed in blankets, joined in the manufactured mood. So much had been lost—so little won. Death had claimed 1918 as its personal trophy. Grateful they had been spared, Christmas on Louisa Street lay becalmed.

As many had before it, the New Year dawned crisp, white and very cold. Only the pond was changed—its glistening surface uncrowded—practically deserted. His head bowed, lacing up Michael's very first skates, John murmured, "So many dead—war and pestilence—what a combination."

Always intrigued when his father was being serious, Michael asked, "What, Papa?"

"Never mind—now stand up—careful. Put your feet together—don't wobble . . ." and holding each other, they slid away.

Watching them with a doting mother's pride, Hannah smiled.

"Fritzchen, so big he is—already first time skating and no Ebbely, no anybody to see dis big moment!"

Holding her close, Fritz waltzed them onto the ice.

Alone at home, bundled up by the fire, Jane her short hair making her look even younger than her youth, watched as little John played with his telescopic picture blocks. She felt fragile; with the child still alive inside her, even more so. There seemed such a chasm between the year that had been and the one just beginning. Somehow life, the very concept of it, had changed and she carrying it, wasn't sure what that meant anymore or in what direction to steer her gratitude for being granted it.

"John," her voice hesitant, the importance of her announcement making her stand overly straight as though fearful, Jane touched her husband's shoulder as he undressed.

"Ninnie? Are you alright?" His concern for her still delicate health was immediate.

"Oh, I'm fine! But . . ." she hesitated again.

"Well, what?" As nothing but her health was important to him, this sudden timidity annoyed him.

"I am again with child and I thought you should know."

The unbuttoning of his trousers forgotten, John grabbed for his wife. She thinking he was going to shake her again, backed away; he laughing pulled her into his arms.

"When, *Tesoro*?"

Relishing him calling her his "treasure," she nestled against him.

"Summer. Maybe July, but I'm not sure—the sickness . . ."

"You're worried?" He pulled her from him to see her face. She nodded. "Oh, come on, nothing to worry about. You feel fine, you said so yourself—anyway, you're strong as a horse, nothing ever fazes you. Besides, when a Ricassoli finds a woman to cling to, he stays put. Told the boys yet?"

"No."

"Hannah knows of course," John pulled on his nightshirt.

"When I was so ill, she had to know."

"Come to bed, Ninnie. You need your rest—especially now. I won't touch you."

Hiding her disappointment at that last remark, Jane went to brush her teeth.

Her recuperation now linked to a pregnancy if no longer in actual danger of aborting, still at plausible risk of producing a damaged child, Jane became self-protective. Having been conceived within pleasure, even possibly love, this new being demanded her devotion as none had before. Beginning to love its father, she loved it, agonized over what might have happened before it was fully formed. Her fears hidden by an outward assurance that bluffed its daily way as though all was natural—Jane achieved the visual lie that she was whole, in benign charge of her female destiny. John just grateful his wife was alive, handled Jane like a breakable treasure, dared not touch her for fear he might do whatever harm men were supposed to be capable of at such times. Hannah knowing exactly what Jane was afraid of—prayed.

The end of war did not bring the return of all-encompassing peace as everyone had expected. Too much garbage, both political and social, lay heavy upon an isolationist land forced by a world war to grow up before its national maturity had fully developed. Being geographically so vast, before the age of radio, America was capable of absorbing inner upheavals, often making it appear when viewing the whole that nothing of great import was happening at all, but the Ford Motor Company on its home turf would soon feel the backlash of the social turmoil already sweeping the rest of the country. But not yet—for now those whose lives were irrevocably joined to Ford and his magical little motor—the glorious dream could continue, for a while at least.

Everyday life resumed its recognizable patterns. It was time to resurrect the snakes, their bellies restuffed, their loosened eyes resewn. This year it was the fate of old faithful Hercules to be disemboweled then reshaped into a younger version of himself.

With so many women needing widow's weeds to symbolize their new station in society—Jane's sewing room was engulfed in black moiré, black alpaca, black braiding and so many boxes of jet trimming that she had to move some of this somber bounty into the children's room to have space for her dress form and cutting table.

Freed by death of his filial duty, Zoltan became enamored of a young woman employed as assistant librarian in the city's central circulating library. Russian literature being her passion, they had met, late one afternoon just before closing time, between the rows as he was searching and she was at that very moment replacing a volume of plays by Anton Chekov that he was looking for.

Their mutual interests soon led to courting—but before committing himself, Zoltan asked permission to bring the young lady to a Sunday supper so Hannah could give her opinion of whether he was simply being a romantic fool or not.

The evening Zoltan's first romantic fling was expected, his friends on their best behavior waited with trepidation for the woman who seemingly was willing to cope with repeated sneezes, coughs and wheezes.

Standing beside him, prim and proper, not a mouse brown hair out of place, Agnes Hepplewhite looked the strictly educated young lady that she was—until she spoke and a vivaciousness quite unexpected usually kept in check by necessity, bubbled forth and overflowed, the slightest of lisps only adding to her charm. Convinced that she was destined to be an old maid amongst dust gathering tomes, to have found a well-read gentleman who wished to join his life with hers seemed a romanticist's dream from which she feared to wake. Everyone glad that he had waited so long before committing himself, approval of Zoltan's choice was unanimous. Jane hoped she would be asked to make the wedding finery—but Zoltan in a hurry eloped, married his Agnes across the border and so though happy for the newlyweds, Jane, disappointed, resumed her work amidst her funereal hues.

By February, having been put in charge of the retooling of Building B, that colossus erected for the construction of wartime submarine chasers now being converted for peacetime manufacture of Fordson tractors as well as the bodies for the latest Model T Sedan, John was absent from Highland Park and home for days at a time. Though she missed him, Jane occupied with children, work, overlaid by persistent apprehension, welcomed the respite from having to appear an untroubled wife to a deserving husband. While her body recovered, her inner strength was struggling to regain its equilibrium. Faced with the probability of bearing a damaged child, even one stillborn, Jane had need of whatever strength was available to her. As her pregnancy stretched before her, its remaining time became a term of anguished imprisonment awaiting calamity.

With the first faint flutter, hardly discernable unless one's anxiety was fine-tuned for its arrival, Jane's association with the being coming to life inside her took on an emotional closeness never felt before. Whenever it moved, its very liveliness seemed to prove a determination to survive that pleased her. Where as before she had never speculated on what she carried, now Jane found herself wondering if this feisty stranger was male or female even thinking of possible names though not actually daring to voice them. Watching the new softening awareness in a woman who though she had borne children before had done so simply as expected rote to the duty of marriage now actually wanting the one possibly denied her, convinced Hannah that this, the third child Jane carried was the first conceived within love and therefore uniquely precious.

Jane waited, sewed, and feared. On those nights when her husband was home he held her with infinite care. A man of his time, John knew the rules. Once in *the family way* a woman became untouchable, no longer useable for pleasure, now a life-bearing vessel to be guarded not invaded.

Licking the end of the silk thread, Jane poked it through the eye of the fine needle, thimble in place her skilled fingers took up their task. Sewing a wide, black satin border onto a mourning veil for one of her clients, she needed to concentrate on the delicate stitches this required, yet her thoughts took their own direction.

I feel so heavy today—why? If it's born too early it will be blind . . . always in the dark. I wonder what that must be like. Teresa always said, "God's light shines within, one has no need of sight." Ha! Tell that to Morgana! Don't be so stupid, Giovanna—all babies born too early die anyway.

Reprimanding her thoughts, Jane rethreaded her needle.

I suppose now that I'm showing I'll have to lock myself away again—just so that my condition won't shock the sensibilities of complete strangers—what stupidity! Unattractive? Well that, maybe so to some—but shocking? Why? I wish Mrs. Kowalsky had preferred grosgrain instead of this—I hate working with satin! Zoltan's new wife is nice—I like Agnes. When I mentioned Margaret Sanger right away she knew who she was. Do this, do that, don't do this, it's not proper, behave—rules, rules, rules! What does it get you? I wonder if Agnes is one of those suffragettes who want to vote. It wouldn't surprise me. If I was one, I'd chain myself to city hall, bulging belly and all!

Feeling rebellious, Jane put down Mrs. Kowalsky's widow's weeds—to continue reading a saga by Mr. Walpole that Zoltan's Agnes, the librarian, had lent her.

Though Henrietta tried valiantly to come to terms with the loss of little Gloria, each day she failed. As though everything about her was fading, she turned pale, her corn silk hair now touched more by moonlight than summer sun, the deep blue of her eyes, bleached; nothing left over from the luminous China Dolly except the palest memory of what had been. Whenever Jane visited, she was reminded of her Valentine rose. At a loss himself, Johann watched his wife's struggle and worried. As time passed Henrietta's longing for the remembered shelter of her homeland increased. She needed her mother's strength, yearned for her comforting presence, to help her to return to herself, to function once more as mother to her two remaining daughters, wife to the husband she loved. Finding no solution, Johann made his decision, negotiated employment at a Ford plant in Holland, sold his half of the house he and Rudy had bought so long ago, booked passage, and prepared to take his family back home.

After an extra special Hannah supper, the Ford men gathered one last time. As they smoked, there was a hesitancy about the room—as though each was waiting for another to speak. For years they had held each other's friendship, relying on it—building upon it—their shared immigrant quest binding them, forming their union within their world of Ford. The future they had once known, had been so certain of seemed suddenly in transit—its destination in question. Their memories lay upon the room like a child's necessary blanket.

Finished helping in the kitchen, Jane entered, went to sit in her corner. Fritz cleared his throat. "When are you leaving?"

"The *Rotterdam* sails in two weeks," Johann answered relieved that someone had begun.

"Hah, lucky fella! No more U-boats to worry about!" Peter's attempt at a little humor failed.

"Who you sell your part of the house to?" Carl lit his pipe.

"A Latvian, works in the paint shop. He's a relative of the one who bought Rudy's part."

Zoltan blew his nose. "Good deal?"

"Fair."

Jane watching their faces wondered why they were so bland.

"Tell me . . ." Johann leaned forward in his chair. ". . . now that the war is over will any of you go back?"

"No." Zoltan was adamant.

Carl sighed, "I can't go back. Everything is gone."

"For just a visit, maybe." Peter sounded unconvincing even to himself.

"Well," John flicked ash from his cheroot, "I would like my parents to meet their grandsons."

Jane never having envisioned returning to the origin of her escape—John's response startled her.

Turning to the chair next to his, Johann asked, "What about you, Fritz? Could you go back? Not stay of course—just see it all again?"

"Maybe."

Tinged with the hurt of having been so hated in the new homeland he loved, his "maybe" lingered in the air.

Determined to alter the prevailing mood, Zoltan changed the subject. "Hey, anybody here find out yet what's happened to Rudy?"

"Well, he's back," volunteered Peter.

"We know *that*!"

"And, listen to this—shot down two Junkers, and got away without a scratch!"

"That, Peter, we also know—but where *is* he? You know, John?"

"I heard he was barnstorming."

"What in God's name is that?"

Jane was glad Carl asked for she was dying to know.

"It's something these young daredevils back from the war are doing all over the country. At county fairs—they perform aerial stunts . . . something called a *barrel roll* and *loop the loop* over the heads of dumbstruck locals."

"For money?" asked Peter.

"Well, if you're crazy enough to risk life and limb for entertainment . . . I should hope so!" countered Zoltan.

"Do you know why it is called barnstorming?" whispered Jane in Carl's direction who whispered back, "Beats me."

John answered them both.

"Part of the many amazing tricks these men are able to put their flimsy crates through—is fly them so low to the ground that often they can't pull up in time and then crash into farmer's barns killing cows, pigs, chickens, even themselves."

"Apart from the killing, *that* I've got to see!"

"My Hannah know about this crazy business?"

John shook his head. "Not yet, Fritz—I didn't want to worry her."

"Ja, better we keep it from her."

Johann knocked out his pipe. "I've got to go. I don't like leaving Henrietta and the girls alone too long—especially after dark. Anyway, we'll all see each other again before we leave. So . . . I'll be on my way. I'll say good night to Hannah on my way out."

The morning Henrietta went to say a last good-bye to Gloria—Jane accompanied her to the cemetery. Standing apart, not to intrude—Jane watched a mother trying to justify the desertion of her dead child, and wondered if she, in a similar situation could ever manage to do so.

Troubled by her thoughts, Jane knelt by Henrietta's side and tended the periwinkles nestled against the small white cross.

The admonitions to write, to take care, to keep in touch, to not forget, all said, in the bright sunshine of a Great Lakes summer, Johann and Henrietta bid good-bye to dear friends, a country that had embraced them, one last time stood before the small plot of earth that covered their child—then returned from whence they had come. Through the years Hannah often remembered that first day when China Dolly had stepped into her house and brought such unbridled joy to their pining Johann, the Hollander.

19

Newly returned from yet another clandestine sojourn across the Canadian border, Serafina now was mistress of her very own Model T. She stayed long enough to voice her opinion on Johann's exodus, claiming that now she saw nothing in his Dutch future that could be interesting to anyone. Then she dropped two additional items of news—one that Morgana, her twin, was not well—but that Guido Salvatore Antonio, her angel son Angelo was, and sped off.

With life resuming its habitual rhythms, the time of war became an aftertaste. In sun-drenched France the splendidly mirrored hall of the opulent palace of Versailles was being turned into a shrine to legal peace. Great minds of great men were eradicating war for all time on signatured paper, believing in what was beyond belief—fostering callous innocence turned inward into evil born. Henceforth, without fail the world was expected to behave itself—abide by the sage words written and attested to, not by the more than ten million men who had shed their blood, but, as in all wars, by the few who had led them so they could.

Hannah's battlefield, forced on her by both birth and war, remained. She was still a German and still a Jew. The war had brought the shame of one into focus while partnering the other. Somehow self-guilt had entered her equation as though she herself had fostered it. Whatever the reasons, once spat upon, such remembrance becomes permanent injury. Hannah did not know why she was troubled only that she was. Concerned, Fritz turned first to Zoltan then John for advice.

"One of your feelings? You're having one of your feelings?" Zoltan nearly choked on his own nervous excitement. "The plant? I knew it! Something is going to happen at the plant. God knows there's enough going on at that behemoth anything can happen!"

Fritz shook his head, "No, Zoltan. Nothing like that—get a hold of yourself, my friend. Marriage should have calmed you down—it's supposed to."

With John the result was only slightly more encouraging.

"For heaven's sake, that wonderful woman of yours—after all the nursing she did, the terrible worry not only for my Ninnie—but Ebbely too, all of us. My God, that woman was never off her feet! Don't worry—she's just exhausted—the best thing *you* can do is take good care of her—see she gets a lot of rest. Giving her a nice kiss now and then wouldn't be a bad idea either."

"I kiss her all the time!" bellowed Fritz in self-defense.

"Well—then do it . . . better! *I* don't know. Why are you asking *me*—she's *your* wife! Anyway, soon we'll all be citizens—then you'll see how Hannah perks up!" And swinging one leg over his precious English Humber John bicycled off to work.

Henry Ford and his Clara having traveled to far-off sunny California for no apparent reason other than to indulge in a well-earned vacation, no one knew what to make of the sudden rumors circulating that Ford was deserting the Model T, planning to form a new company that would manufacture an automobile he supposedly claimed would not only rival the T but undersell it by more than two hundred dollars.

Fritz cornered John as he was coming home from work.

"We're stopping production on the T. Is that true?"

"No, we're not."

"Who says?"

"Evangeline hinted it may have to do with the Boss's plan to buy out the Dodge Brothers."

"You're sure, John? He's not giving up on Lizzie? After all our great success to change, now start up all over again with another sounds crazy!"

"I agree, it doesn't make sense. There is absolutely no reason for the company to change now or to sell it. We can't even fill all the orders for the T that are coming in."

"Then why all this talk of a new company to make a new model? Mr. Edsel say anything?"

"Not to me. Let's wait and see—Evangeline usually knows what's really going on. If she believes it may be just a clever stunt—her word not mine—to scare the shareholders so they'll sell, I'll bet she's right and the Boss *is* up to something."

"You'll let me know?"

"Of course. Don't worry, Fritz—I'm sure our Lizzie will be rolling off the line for years to come in 'any color you want as long as it's black.'" That now famous Henry Ford statement got a laugh out of Fritz.

By the beginning of July Henry Ford achieved what he was after; had maneuvered the buyout of his company's stockholders, his original partners, and with a little help from those Jewish bankers that he never trusted until they were of use to him, now owned the Ford Motor Company outright, lock, stock, and proverbial barrel and the rumor of that new Model Ford vanished. With his railroad, forests, mines, newspaper, hospital, schools, motion picture department, ever-increasing dealerships and assembly plants, his ships and barges hauling their endless spectrum of raw materials to his vast empire on the Rouge River, the Flivver King of Detroit was truly the monarch of Michigan.

Two days after Glory Day, Mr. Henry, the mailman, returned. No longer garbed as guardian of the United States Postal Service, he, in vested store-bought suit and silk cravat, stood in Hannah's hallway smiling his devastating smile, as she screamed her delight at his being still among the living, then noticed his left sleeve and the large safety pin that anchored its emptiness to his side.

Confused, not knowing what to say, hands covering her mouth afraid of what she might blurt out, Hannah looked at her friend imploring him to excuse her stare. One slender hand touched hers in a gesture of forgiveness and Hannah began to cry.

"Now, now," sounding like a concerned family retainer, Mr. Henry patted her shoulder. "Dear Lady, do not upset yourself—a small sacrifice for victory." Lifting the corner of her apron he proceeded to dry her tears as though she were a child of three. "Besides, it's only my left and you *know* I do my best courting with my right." Mr. Henry had learned to joke. It made those concerned for him more comfortable in the presence of his affliction. Continuing his ministration, he asked if she wasn't going to feed him as always.

Soon coffee brewed, pie, cookies, pastries, anything she could find, spread before him, they sat and talked.

"You know dat cutesy redhead de one you fancied? Well she got married . . ."

"To that boozer?"

"Yes. He got out of de war for something he did bad in it and now is someplace in jail."

"And the Nussbaums?" Mr. Henry asked questions answerable, avoiding those unanswerable.

"Oh, dey had big trouble when de sickness came. De eldest girl, her you remember?"

"Yes, a real mother hen, with all those sisters and brothers."

"Well, dat poor girl, she died. Her Mama and de udders dey all got sick—but now everybody okay again."

"The influenza hit you hard here?"

"Yes—hit us hard—you too over dere?"

"Yes—in November just before the Armistice, we didn't know who was killing us faster—the Huns or the fever."

"Anudder cup?"

"Yes, please."

"Johann our Hollander? He and his China Dolly—dey lost dere little girl. So now dey gone back to dere old country and forget. Horowitzes? Dey now live in Massachusetts where dere Boris was in a camp. Den when he was killed over in Flanders his folks stayed."

"Everything has changed, eh?"

"Yes. You got a job?"

"Not yet, not much work for a one-armed paper hanger."

"A paper hanger you are now?"

"No, it's only an expression. A kind of joke."

"Not a funny."

"Better to joke than cry. Anyway, girls don't cotton to a beau with too much war still inside him."

"You still a rascal?" This was asked with the faintest of sighs.

"Yep. Gotta be."

No need for further explanation, Hannah understood his need to be what he had been, regardless of what he had become.

"Your knitting sister, she okay and all de children?"

"Yes, she found a man to marry her, moved to St. Paul."

"Where you live now, den? More coffee?"

"Bunking in with a friend. Thanks."

"Lady friend?"

Mr. Henry laughed, "No, ex-army buddy." Pointing to the plate of crullers, "Can I have another?"

"Eat! You want I should make you maybe a nice bologna sandwich to take?"

Busy munching, Mr. Henry shook his head. A second's hesitation, then Hannah spoke what had been forming in her mind since the moment Mr. Henry had appeared, seeming so alone, covering his need with attempted joviality.

"I got plenty empty rooms, you want one? Come stay? For a while, until you find work? Fritz and me happy to have you . . . but, maybe . . . maybe you don't want to because we are German—maybe?"

All veneer gone, Mr. Henry brushed away a tear, smiled his devastating smile and that was that.

The very next day the mailman moved his meager belongings into what once had been Stan's room and in no time at all, it seemed as though the Geiger house took back some of its aura of bygone days. Michael very impressed being acquainted with a real, brave soldier became his ever-willing sidekick, ready to be of service whenever his new friend needed anything complicated like opening jars of Hannah's special strawberry jam that Mr. Henry seemed particularly partial to.

Conferring in private with Jane about her new boarder—Hannah allowed her concern for him to show.

"Dat poor man. What girl will look at him now? And him always used to dem all crazy lovey-dovey over him. What he do now wit no two arms to hold dem? Many girlies will tink dats ugly, you know, not know any better, not see what a good man he is." Hannah ladled sugar into her coffee—forgetting she had already done so before. "Fritz, he says, 'Give him time.' Well dat's okay for de oldies but for de young? I don't tink. Not so good. What you tink?"

"Hannah, exactly what's an oldie?"

"Well, like me. Thirty-two nearly already."

"That's really not so old."

"Well, if I was not married to Fritz—and I was an old maid—den I would be!"

Laughing, Jane refilled Hannah's cup.

"Don't worry. If someone really loves your Mr. Henry, she won't mind about his arm."

"Ha! You de innocent! De *so in love already safe lucky Vifey*—you tink doze floozy ladies he always find will be so good like dat? I got to hurry. For tonight I'm making fluffy potatoes wit real butter now allowed also a nice cabbage mit de Kummel and gravy mit real cream. If I got time, maybe even a little someting for just on de side to nosh. Before I came over I make already de shortcake to go mit de nice strawberries for after." Hannah pinned on her hat. "You come too, Ninnie? A little strong walking good for you now, bring de children! WE EAT . . . AS USUAL!"

And in a whirlwind of joyous anticipation Hannah was gone.

Back in her element once again caring for multiple people, Hannah blossomed, Fritz seeing her happy—was too. Now all that was needed to complete this rosy picture—was the birth of a healthy baby and Ebbely's safe return.

Her labor began on a warm summer's eve. This time aided only by experience and Hannah's care, at dawn Jane gave birth to a son, unmarked yet with a quietness that first alarmed. When slapped, he did not bellow, only meowed. As if still bewildered by his harrowing journey into the light, he remained silent as if contemplating where he was and if he would like it once he knew. Then resigned, he allowed Hannah to cut his lifeline, clean and swaddle him, hand him in his latest cocoon over to the woman whose heartbeat he was accustomed to. As Jane looked down at him—he looked up at her—and she saw Michael in his eyes. Hannah too had seen the resemblance.

"Ninnie! You got anudder Bubbele! Just like our Michael he looks."

Jane tore her eyes off the bundle.

"He's alright? You're sure? Did you look? Really look?"

"Nutting wrong, child. Nutting missing—everyting perfect—a healthy boy! I swear." Relief overwhelming her, Hannah sobbed, "A healthy boy, Ninnie! A healthy boy—God loves you, child. God loves you!"

The baby slept. They had been through a lot together she and this helpless being and survived. Jane liked the feeling of accomplishment this gave her, a bond, a sort of victory united them. Holding him close she slept.

Without stopping to take off his riding boots, John sprinted up the stairs, hugged Hannah, kissed his wife, cradled his new son, then kissed her again. Hannah quite overcome by the picture of such marital bliss so long in coming exited the room to preserve its impression before anything could alter its perfection.

"Michelino, that's your new brother." John pushed him towards the bed. Jane pulled back the swaddling blanket as Michael took a look. Having gone through the arrival of his brother John, he was careful not to touch the bundle in case it too would screech, but this one only looked at him, and sucking his fist fell fast asleep. Michael decided he would do. Little John climbed up onto the bed and tried to sit on his new brother but was caught in time. Kissing his wife, John scooted the children out of the room. With the heady thought how nice it felt to be a family, Jane fell asleep.

Being a woman, Jane knew the exact moment she fell in love. Being a man, John did not; knew only that he loved the woman he happened to be married to and that sufficed. It would take more time before Jane would learn the difference between being in love and actual loving and then know to put them into the rightful category of either. But for now, she was content, basking in being treasured, a healthy son, who for the first time she wanted to nurse, actually enjoying his need of her.

Early the next morning though it was time to resume her duties she lingered, wanting to get something settled before starting her day.

"John."

"Yes, Ninnie?"

"I was so sure it would be a girl I wanted to name her for Hannah but now . . . I think it should be Fritz."

"Fritz? Do you like Fritz?"

"No, not particularly. But . . ."

"And it doesn't translate into Italian."

"I know—but without Hannah I wouldn't have been alive to have this baby so it has to be for her—Fritz."

"What about using his middle name—Wilhelm?"

"John, that's the name of the German kaiser!"

"Not in English. In English it's William and in Italian it's . . ."

"Guillermo! That sounds nice. Yes, that will do. It's decided then?"

"For you, Ninnie—anything!" And laughing John left to tell his friends the news of their choice.

Though William it was decreed—Billy he became. It suited him. Hannah often explained his exuberance for life as being the natural result of nearly having died. Just as everyone was drawn to Michael's gentleness, as he grew Billy captured everyone's heart by being such a happy little boy.

Michael put this new brother into the place in his heart Gloria had left behind. Rocked him when he was teething, shooed flies from him on the back porch, waited with harnessed impatience for him to grow, become his pal. Billy did not disappoint him—by the time he could crawl he was the acknowledged shadow of his eldest brother, as though one breathed for the other they became inseparable. Young John, the solitary, was content to be what he was, the judgmental onlooker of life not its gullible participant.

Their parents' loving resumed as if birthing had never interrupted it. When John was home, he loved Jane. When away, though his body enjoyed other excitements, he loved her still. Men are capable of such separability, often women wish they could so divide emotion, keeping one from the other without destroying either.

Even when only felt not overly displayed, Jane's love for her husband sweetened their existence. She softened, smiled more often, he finding a new sense of comfort in a home though always efficient usually devoid of much feeling, relaxed with new appreciation.

Children always acutely aware of the emotional currents within which they must exist, Michael even John allowed their self-protective guard to slip, became younger, less self-contained. Of course Billy never having known any other atmosphere but one infused by love—went right on blossoming—certain the whole world was made of it.

Their first camping trip having been such a rousing success the summer before, annual Ford-inspired camping trips captured a new wanderlust of the common man that through the freedom and heretofore unenvisioned possibilities of his Model T, had become possible. Whole families began *Fording* into nature there to eat, sleep and frolic as untroubled creatures of the forests, until duty to hard work called them back. Soon small cabins began to sprout by the wayside of those roads mostly traveled, one astounding establishment even permitting its patrons to consume food without ever having to exit their automobiles, dispensing a beverage named Coca-Cola that promised "to refresh the parched throat—to invigorate the fatigued body and quicken the tired brain." One could of course also refresh oneself with Prohibition's favorite, a very dark brown brew known as root beer.

As the country's expanding highways took on their latest enticements, the once so astounding way stations that had been invented to dispense the fuel necessary for the feeding of the horseless carriage lost their awe-inspiring uniqueness that, only a short time ago, had been theirs alone.

Fall was beginning to strip the trees when Jane was handed a letter by the dour Mr. Jeremiah, who requested that if she was not a collector, at her convenience of course, he would appreciate being given the foreign postage adorning her envelope. Assuring him it would be his, eventually—once alone, hands trembling, she tore it open. This time Teresa had written in perfect French.

Giovanna, Ma Chere,

As celebration of the Armistice we have been given permission to write. Not knowing if a letter would find you, at first I hesitated to write it at all, yet concern overcoming uncertainty I pray this will reach you.

The wounds of war lie heavy upon the land. Memory of its carnage dismays the soul. Now many question the very root of their faith, finding no satisfactory solace to their need in prayer, many are convinced all is a lie. Nursing Sisters, such as we who attended the wounded, were often placed in juxtaposition to what we represent and what the maimed and dying expected, even demanded of us. Not simply the ministering to their flesh but for answers that in some way might restore their faith; if not in the goodness of man, then in the Almighty Saviour of man.

A nun's habit is such a visual presence of the Church that often we in ours represented an affront to soldiers who had come to doubt its very existence. Over such destitute souls one cannot pray. Having care that our rosary did not swing against their mattress, for by chance if it did it so upset them, they cringed from our touch as though repulsed by our advertised sanctity. Yet during these endless years of war whenever that ultimate moment came to summon the priest—they welcomed his presence with the need of innocent children, afraid to be left alone in the dark.

Now, we search for food for the many who come to us for bodily resurrection. Their physical hunger is such that it obliterates all other hungers. I am afraid it will take much time before we are once again able to feed their faith. A starving child makes mockery of cloistered sanctity. A sin to voice, yet one that propels me on, to prove it is not so. Four years of war have only strengthened my faith in the innate goodness of man and his creator, not destroyed it.

The Spanish Influenza appeared so rapidly amongst us that we were often helpless in the face of two calamities at once. I pray that you and yours were spared—though being so far away you may not even be aware that such happened. Here two of our Sisters died of the infection, six others were spared and are recuperating blessed with a resurgence of health through prayer.

Do respond, tell me of your life. The war did not touch you, I believe and that is good. We all cheered the arrival of your brave American boys were so grateful that they had come. We nursed many here. One who was blinded said he came from the city of Detroit and when I told him my very best childhood friend lived there he told me of all its many splendors. I know I'm not allowed to remember, but it cheered him to speak of home.

Your letter announcing the birth of a son reached me before war was declared. He is included in my prayers. Now that postal service has been reestablished—please respond—I await impatiently for news of you and yours.

Yours in God,

Sr. Marie Luke, O.S.B.

Jane placed Teresa's letter into the shoebox next to the first, looked to the children, her house, finished Mrs. Sullivan's and her newly engaged daughter's party dresses—and when the day was done—everything tidy—everything accomplished—all the children asleep—she took out her precious letter and read it again.

Michael, spinning his top on the front porch, saw him first, ran the three blocks over to tell Hannah, who having sensed her Ebbely's approach was already outside looking for him.

"Ah! Two of my favorite people! The smallest and the tallest!"

"Ebbely! Ebbely! So long you take and so tin! Come, come quick put down de patchkas—first a nice cup of tea exactly how you like. Den I got still warm just-out-of-de-oven strudel, time enough to schlep from de Lizzie to inside later." Propelling him down the hall towards her kitchen she suddenly stopped, bent down, threw her arms around the little man, gave him a crushing hug, set him back on his tiny feet and pulled him into the kitchen.

Trying to catch his breath, Ebbely gasped, "Sparta! Sparta would have made of you a goddess! My dearest Hannah either you have gained in strength or I have become even more depleted than I knew. I brought you some things, just allow me to . . ." And he started back towards the hall.

Hannah barked, "No! First you sit!"

Ebbely knowing that tone, sat.

"Ah, it's good to be home."

In one big rush of welcoming breath, Michael lisped, "Uncle Ebbely, I have a new brother, his name is William, I call him Billy—he is too small and I have to wait 'til he's growed to play—Gregory is dead and Gloria is dead, Mama is not and Papa is working and Uncle Johann took everybody far away and I got a new string for my top, want to see?"

Ebbely said of course, a spinning top was just the thing a weary traveler needed to celebrate his return to those he loved. And so with a deft flick Michael demonstrated the gyratory magic of his wooden toy, beamed at Ebbely's enthusiastic appreciation of his skill, then calmed down significantly to consume a healthy portion of still warm strudel.

The news of their favorite shrimp's return spread so fast that by suppertime Hannah's dining room was filled once again with her boys, expectant of her superlative cooking and Ebbely's oratory talents.

Neither disappointed them.

Ebbely held court as only he could, but, remembering the last such occasion, only after clearing the subject of his dissertation with the master of the house.

"Fritz, my dear friend, knowing your penchant of the proper, the utterly pure in all things, I hesitate to recount my Iliad for fear you will deem it your necessary duty to interrupt such sections of it that might disturb, even be considered slightly shocking for the shell-like ears of your Lady and John's so admirable wife. Although I personally find nothing that could in any way distress, remembering our past encounter, I must defer to your judgment before I can commence." And turning away, Ebbely helped himself to more stuffing.

His friends groaned. Knowing exactly what Ebbely was up to, John ate, trying to look serious.

"Well, really Ebberhardt, such a fuss you make over nothing!"

"Nothing, Fritz? You call, though inadvertently, shocking your sainted wife and an impressionable Jane *nothing*?" Without looking up Ebbely continued eating.

Thoroughly flustered, his friends looking daggers in his direction, Fritz capitulated, "Okay—so tell already whatever you have to tell, I won't stop you. But . . ."

"Yes . . . Fritz?" Ebbely's tone was ingenuous to a fault.

"Oh, nothing." The table exploded into laughter. Relieved that they had escaped banishment, Hannah and Jane sat down with the men. Both having noticed a new fragility about Ebbely that worried them, they welcomed this display of his usual pixielike teasing—its exaggerated liveliness seemed suddenly necessary.

"Well, how shall I begin? Tragedy never suits the retelling of it. One must experience it to know it well! And from what I have been told it has touched many of you at this table—far deeper and far more heart-wrenching than my saga of personal survival." As though not wishing to insult the sorrow of others by his less sorrowful tale, Ebbely hesitated.

Carl cleared his throat, "It's okay, Ebbely—tell us. We heard you were in a hospital."

"I arrived in New Orleans a few days after my telephone call to Fritz. Though our Lizzie performed perfectly, an unpleasant journey, for already then I was feeling lackluster, weary, apprehensive, certainly not myself. On entering the city a strange exhaustion decided me to book myself into the very first reputable-looking establishment I came across, where I must have collapsed—for when I awoke I found myself garbed in but a flimsy shift—between overly boiled, rock-hard sheets in an overly long room filled with similar beds to mine containing wan corpselike creatures similar to me. Actually considering the way I felt I thought I probably would expire any minute. Raising my head for what I believed would be for the last time I surveyed the long rows of my fellow sufferers and found that I was one of many *children*. My friends, I assure you, had I been placed in an adult ward where I belonged I would not be here now. How long I remained—I have no recollection of. Finding myself to be still amongst the living is as surprising as it is welcome. But though one may be fortunate to survive within a hospital—to fully recuperate in one is problematical. And so I chose resurrection within the silken folds of a dear friend and longtime customer."

"Aha, here comes the good part." Peter leaned forward in his chair.

"You have no conception of *how* good."

"Well? Go on." Despite still being in the dining room John lit a cheroot.

"As a matter of fact, I am indebted to a shipboard acquaintance of yours, John, a Mademoiselle Eugenie de la Rochemont, a lovely young thing who with heroic dedication nursed me for many weeks, to whom I am convinced I owe my life. A treasure that Gaelic beauty, a real treasure."

Waiting for what John might say, Jane held her breath, but it was Zoltan who spoke. "So let me get this straight—you nearly died, but you were saved through the devotion of one of your former customers of your unmentionables?"

"Yes, I must admit to be nursed by a bevy of caring damsels who finding themselves with sudden time on their hands due to a lack of living customers, has been an experience not soon to being forgotten. I felt and still do like some newborn babe, pampered and cosseted after a grave illness. As all women are mothers at heart regardless of their profession, I was in excellent hands."

"Ebbely, you're incorrigible!"

"Thank you, Carl—I try to be."

Having kept quiet long enough Fritz wanted to know how New Orleans had withstood the epidemic.

"War and disease an unholy union you must admit—yet, admirably suited to each other's rapacious appetite. Never having forgotten nor freed itself completely from the horrors of the Black Death, New Orleans is a city mired in theatrical doom. Every tragedy magnified then celebrated as though death itself is a sorcerer's familiar to be placated, resurrection assured if one but knows the mumbo-jumbo and is then willing to believe it."

The entrance of dessert, a towering chocolate soufflé exuding its enticing steam, ended any further gloom.

Jane was putting on her hat preparing to leave, when Rumpelstiltskin after saying good night whispered, "Eugenie sends you fond greetings and hopes you are well. I promised I would give you her message."

Jane whispered back, "Oh, I was so surprised when you said her name—how wonderful that it would be she who took such good care of you. I must write and thank her. Does she know English now?"

"Oh yes—she's quite proficient in everything." Noticing John's approach Ebbely repeated a loud good night and scampered upstairs.

When first informed of Mr. Henry's residency, Ebbely ignored its implication. But the first morning when he came down for his expected breakfast, Mr. Henry, the mailman, already in place, rose, extended his hand and introduced himself as though he belonged. Two roosters circling the henhouse might have been a perfect description of Rumpelstiltskin and the Casanova mailman's first encounter—later finding they had much in common, jazz being one of their mutual passions, they became friends—but this their first social encounter though correct was extremely frigid. Completely oblivious to anything but the German pancakes she was making, Hannah told her boarders to sit, and start eating before their breakfast got cold.

For the great day John bought a new suit, Jane made him a splendid shirt, Michael polished his father's shoes until they shone like a brand-new Model T. Fritz wore a new vest and bowler that made him look most distinguished. Pride illuminating her whole being, Hannah kept straightening his tie.

"Enough, Hannahchen—enough. We go now."

In new frocks sewn especially for this once-in-a-lifetime day, Jane and Hannah drove with their husbands to the city of Detroit to pledge their allegiance as true citizens of the United States of America. At last that longed-for dream had become a reality.

On their triumphal return they were greeted by family, friends, children and neighbors all waving little American flags—courtesy of Mr. Henry, the mailman.

What a prideful day that was! For such a day, breaking the law seemed essential. From some dubious source Ebbely produced pre-Prohibition champagne. Not one but three whole bottles, popped their corks with ceremonial flourish and pronounced the toast.

"To my dearest friends, welcome to my country as the best example of its citizenry!"

Michael very impressed by the jubilant proceedings—went amongst the well-wishers announcing that as he was already *a real borned American* he was glad his Papa and his Mama were now too.

The very next day was the day of Jane's great surprise. Ebbely drove it home, John struggled to get it into the house, where, clumsily wrapped in thick brown paper, it stood in the center of the living room waiting for Jane to unwrap it.

"Ninnie! I'm back. Come down."

Wondering why he was home in the middle of the day, and why he sounded so excited, Jane came down the short flight of stairs—the children following her. Taking her hand, John led her to his gift.

"For you, Ninnie—open it."

Telling the excited children to behave themselves, he sat down with the youngest on his lap—watching his wife's face. Puzzled, wondering what such an odd package could contain and why John would give her another present when becoming an American was already the best of all gifts—she pulled off the thick paper—and gasped.

At first she just couldn't believe it—looked over at John—saw his joyous grin—then back at the marvel standing right there before her in her very own living room. Running, she threw her arms around her grinning husband giving him a fast kiss before returning to her breathtaking surprise—a high-arm, five-drawer, walnut woodwork, model No. 5 Singer sewing machine just as she had seen it illustrated in Hannah's mail order catalog of the Montgomery Ward Company of Chicago.

"Ninnie, it's only a secondhand—but I checked out all the parts, they work fine. The foot pedal needed a little readjustment but otherwise everything works as it should."

"Oh—John—it is the most beautiful machine I have ever seen! All I have ever wished for. Now I can make your shirts in a day—even suits and all the children's clothes in only half the time. Does Hannah know? I must tell her!" At the door she turned—rushed back, kissed him again—murmured a shy "Thank you" before grabbing her hat and running down the street with her exciting news.

Laughing, John began tidying up the wrapping paper, his sons watching still astounded by so much affection—such enthusiastic kissing on display between such usually self-contained people puzzled them as much as the weird-looking contraption that had caused the fuss.

That Singer magnificence must have been the most pampered machine in all of Michigan. It was stroked, touched ever with reverence, oiled, polished, every screw promptly adjusted with care, at night covered against possible cold, in the daytime when not in use, which was rare indeed, covered against possible dust. Although her loyalty to Lizzie demanded she be foremost in her regard, in private Jane's devotion to her sewing machine even eclipsed the Model T.

Before Thanksgiving Jane received yet another luxury. A real crib. Though used, it was like new with its iron rungs painted glossy white without a single chip. A generous gift from young Mrs. Ziewacz, once a fellow Watcher, whose husband having fallen at the Battle of the Somme had no more need of it. When first put inside this new enclosure—Jane's baby looked about him, assessing its restricted boundaries. After a while, as if a conclusion reached, fell sound asleep. Jane had the feeling that cages did not trouble Billy.

This year Michael got his wish to be a Model T. Jane sewed him one out of black felt to go trick-or-treating in. His brother John got the ghostly sheet, which he rather liked for it hid him from the world.

By Thanksgiving mail from Europe was once again arriving regularly. Finally having received a long account from his family, John was full of plans.

"For the New Year, I shall have the means for Celestina to make the journey, bring her to America. Now that Gina has stolen her rich beau right from under her nose—of course who can blame him. Once my pretty sister made her mind up to get him he was lost anyway—so, much better to get Celestina away from there before she cries herself into a decline and pines away—driving my parents crazy." John chuckled visualizing his so inseparable sisters now at loggerheads over a mere suitor. "And Ninnie, once you have taught her English—I'll find her a good reliable husband to take care of her."

Having known her sister-in-law since their childhood, Jane thought it far more likely that Celestina would find her own, but said nothing.

Motoring down Prospect Avenue, Ebbely saw it first. A working-class house, like all the others in Highland Park, this one exceptional by a dormer window tucked beneath its gabled roof signaling the possibility of an extra room.

"John, I found you a house! Couldn't resist investigating, rang the bell and lo and behold find a Dalmatian returning to a country that doesn't even exist anymore, but still wants to sell!"

"What house? What are you talking about?" Parking his bicycle on the back porch, John motioned Ebbely to follow him into the kitchen. At the sink—Jane moved aside to allow her husband to wash his hands.

"Good evening, Tall Lady of multitudinous brood," Ebbely acknowledged her smiled welcome, "and that is exactly why I am here, John. Ask your Lady. Ask her where your latest offspring resides. Well—go on."

"In my sewing alcove," Jane answered for her husband, who appeared utterly confused.

"Aha! Just what I surmised. Your wife whose dressmaking skills are known far and wide and duly admired has sacrificed her very own sanctum for the sole benefit of your latest without a murmur of dissent. A jewel, your wife—a precious jewel!"

"And?" John dried his hands.

"Well, my friend, what you need is a house that will not only accommodate your growing family, but offer the mother of your children a space of her very own in which to practice her admirable profession of superlative seamstress. For heaven's sake, man, you gave her that magnificent sewing machine—now give her a room to use it in!" Receiving no answering enthusiasm, exasperated Ebbely stamped his foot, exclaimed, "Well? Are you coming? I told the owner I would bring you around this evening." And pulling John out of his kitchen—Ebbely got his way.

Far into the night they talked, by morning having agreed that Ebbely, as was his want, had been as sensible as always, John began the necessary preparations to sell one home in order to acquire another.

With everyone pitching in during the resumed layoffs, John's family was moved and settled, in time for the holidays, and for a while that little room tucked under the eaves became Jane's very own luxury.

Like a proud teacher taking perfect attendance, Hannah looked about her crowded living room and beamed. Over there was Peter and his Dora, Zoltan and his nice Agnes, by the tree Carl's little Violet in a new party dress holding her father's hand. John with his Ninnie, the little one cradled by her heart, their handsome sons in their brand-new, just-finished-in-time sailor suits, Rudy returned, a new man full of life, all sadness gone, even Stan with Serafina, their Angelo intrigued by the menorah wondering what it was for, Morgana explaining it to him. By the punch bowl Mr. Henry ten pounds heavier, looking fit, her Ebbely in his Christmas vest of scarlet perched, ready on his piano stool. Looking up at Fritz, she whispered, "Everybody! Dey all came, Fritzchen. All our children and dere children dey came. If only Jimmy and Johann and . . ."

"Now, don't start, I know." Giving her a reassuring squeeze Fritz went to light the candles on the tree. They sang, they ate, they drank, they even danced. What a Hanukah-Christmas this was! Better even than all the ones that had gone before. A celebration of so many things; a war won, an epidemic survived, the glorious dream of citizenship realized, a healthy baby born, yet beyond even such milestones, there stood what mattered even more, had always mattered most, their friendship, their love for each other that had brought them back together, memories of those now absent, making them a part of theirs.

On New Year's Day this feeling of a family reunited persisted. The pond's glistening surface echoing their laughter, no one acting their age except the children, they waltzed, played upon the ice using the children's boisterous glee as excuse for their own abandon, everyone was certain that 1920 would be a special year.

Industrial strikes that had started the previous winter, most for legitimate grievances too long endured, swept the nation—were branded as the obvious result of organized, subversive Socialism. Justified or not, all such rebellion painted the same color—the *Red Scare* soon took its toll. Ever the malevolent opportunist, The Ku Klux Klan watched, and waited for its turn.

Yet in Highland Park all remained serene. With its patron saint dedicated to the betterment of his workers' lives, morals and efficiency—organized and executed by a company wholly committed to the ultimate well-being of its workers at the Ford Motor Company everyday life was as fluid, uninterrupted as its now internationally famous assembly lines.

It was January 8, a bright invigorating morning, when feeling guilty that due to illness and birthing she had neglected her monthly visits to the Italian settlements, that Jane took the trolley into the city of Detroit.

As she stepped off into the street—a woman running past her stopped, clutched her arm, dragged her into the gathering darkness of a nearby alley. Desperation, overriding the usual deference shown to one of a better class, urgency making her Italian a jumble, she gasped, "Help me—I know you—you must help me—you can, you speak American they will listen to you—please *Signora*! Please! . . ." The child clinging to her skirts began to cry.

"Tell me," Jane said calmly, feeling far from calm.

"My husband—Enrico—he works on the line—you know him—remember that day you come when . . ."

"Yes—I know him—go on . . ."

"They took him!"

"Took him? Who? Who took him?"

"I don't know! Many, many women like me are looking—they say government men—they came and took all the men they found in the club and arrested them—now policemen have them."

"How many—do you know?"

"No—but many, *Signora*—many, many are looking like me!"

The little girl tugged at her mother's skirts. "Mama, I'm hungry!"

"Three days, *Signora*—three days now my man is gone—he left to go to work and never came back! Where is he?! Three days! He has no razor—no clean shirt. I never got his wage packet, I have no money for food, for heat—PLEASE, PLEASE, *SIGNORA*—HELP ME!"

The federal consensus being that if one arrested the lot it would result in a sufficient number of subversives they were actually after, on January 5 the soon-to-be notorious Palmer Raids named after the secretary general of the United States who ordered them—struck without warning or legal warrants the meetings halls, card clubs, social centers of Detroit's immigrant workers. To keep their illegal catch completely incommunicado, to avoid any snooping of the press, like a clandestine cattle drive, federal agents aided by the Detroit police, herded 150 frightened men from precinct to precinct—finally penning them in a windowless room sized for no more than possibly 60—lacking bathroom facilities.

By the time Jane found this despicable holding pen, her fury had grown as had a group of desperate women and children trailing behind her. Blazing fury making her appear even taller than she was, Jane accosted the policeman in charge. A burly Irishman unaccustomed to having a female other than a whore in the station took a startled step back. Fists clenched, her English distinct, precise and wholly accusative, Jane advanced towards him speaking her mind and constitutional outrage. Huddled in the doorway, her group gasped. For most immigrants having escaped persecution in their homeland, uniformed officialdom represented not only imminent danger but certain defeat, now witnessing their only champion—a woman—not only threatening a man but one wearing a uniform, convinced them that now all was lost—they would never see their men again. Women began to pray, their children cried as Jane continued laying down the law to the Detroit constabulary.

With her status as United States citizen, her command of English, her imposing stature as well as her seething outrage, Jane managed to negotiate not only the release of a badly frightened, bedraggled Enrico, but also a select few of equally innocent kinsmen, among them two ex-soldiers, their honorable discharge papers in their pockets, who had volunteered to fight for their adopted country and been decorated.

It was Zoltan who finally found her, drove Jane back home to Highland Park and a frantic husband.

"John, go easy on her—she's exhausted—a courageous lady your wife—you should have seen her . . . well, she will tell you herself—have to get back—Agnes had supper ready when you telephoned."

"I'm sorry . . ."

"No, no, happy to help. From what I saw you were right to be worried. Well, good night." Consulting his pocket watch Zoltan changed that to "good morning" and left.

Until dawn they talked—husband and wife suddenly equals—brought into balance by mutual anger. This night would add new dimension to their relationship—she for having convictions and the moral courage to act upon them—he for admiring and approving of her defending what she believed in.

For Jane this night would often conjure ghosts. This first need to censure her new homeland disturbed her. A nirvana so all-inclusive of perfection had suddenly become marred by the actions of its own government and Jane felt a loss for what had been thought inviolate, perhaps too readily taken for granted. Taking herself to task whenever thoughts weighed too heavily—Jane turned her emotional back on the outrage of the Palmer Raids and faced what was faceable. This experience left Jane forever wary of the Irish and their penchant for embracing whatever municipal power could serve them.

This year changes were everywhere. The Ford Company's famous profit-sharing plan was discarded and the bonus and investment plan took its place. Most of the men, not understanding the change or how this would affect them, simply accepted their boss's reminder that "thrift is an index of character" as readily as they had so many other homilies. The feared Sociological Department suddenly became the Educational Department, its ominous *inspectors* rechristened benign *advisors*, and so after much soul searching Hannah disbanded her Angel ladies and the Watchers were no more. The factory newssheet printed enticing advertisements extolling the advantages of purchasing not only one's grocery goods but also the latest men's clothing at the Ford Company store, guaranteeing the wise shopper that "a dollar saved is a dollar earned" which then could be placed within the safety of the company bank.

On the morning of January 18, in pressed suit, high starched collar and band box bowler, the 1920 census enumerator appeared at 398 Prospect Avenue to record that its inhabitants were bona fide citizens, two by decree, three by birth. This first official documentation of her new identity so pleased Jane, in a rush of unusual familiarity she invited the so earnest gentlemen in for Prohibition's latest stepchild—a glass of bubbling root beer, which he politely declined, stating he was strictly scheduled. That evening, feeling newly important for being recorded within her new country's historical archive, Jane greeted her husband with "John, today a gentleman from the government came to take what he called 'the census.'"

"Did you answer all his questions?" John dried his hands on the dishtowel she handed him.

"Yes—they were very simple ones. Only the one about your work—what you do—I wasn't sure of. But I didn't let him see that."

John smiled. "What *did* you tell him?"

"Well, I said my husband is a special machinist for Mr. Henry Ford. You once told me that. Was that alright?" Jane ladled out the soup for their supper.

"Good enough—such things are not that important anyway."

Carrying the soup plates to the table, Jane thought that such a momentous occurrence of historical significance warranted more than such a dismissive remark.

When new laws were proposed setting forth immigrant quotas—the mood around Hannah's Sunday table smoldered.

"You hear, now they say Jews, also Slavs can only come, only a few?" Peter, troubled, looked over at Fritz.

"Ja—they say every country now will have a limit."

"I heard also no more than a hundred darkies are going to be allowed from any African country."

"Well that will be a new one!" Zoltan's sarcasm dripped.

"What about all the others?"

As though wishing to finish the subject, John answered, "Germans, English, Irish are to have very large entry quotas—Lithuanians, Russians, even Italians, theirs have been drastically reduced. It seems that despite the war and now President Wilson's lofty dream of a unity of nations, America may choose isolationism after all. Time will tell. Fritz, please . . . pass the gravy."

John's overly casual comment surprised Jane. It was unlike him to choose to evade a discussion that could lead to an invigorating battle of diverse opinions. If Ebbely had been present he would not have allowed such a withdrawal—but as he was absent pursuing what he referred to as an "evening of profound insight," no one challenged John's opinion.

What or where Ebbely was being *profound* and in what specific direction of *insight*—no one knew. Not even Hannah, although she tried her very best even resorting to jelly doughnut bribery—Ebbely divulged nothing of his "One Sunday Evening a Month Sortie" into the city of Detroit.

"You tink maybe he has a woman, Ninnie?" asked a troubled Hannah trying not to sound a bit jealous and failing.

"Oh, no! Ebbely wouldn't do that in secret." Dodging the subject, Jane made herself sound very convincing.

"Ya—I suppose. But why den so punctual—on de dot—he goes and all dressed up in his fine three-piece suit with de silk cravat, yet. I don't like it—looks like hanky-panky to me!" Hannah rattled her pans—Jane opted for silence.

Later that evening as they were walking home John stopped suddenly, startling his sons following behind, turned to his wife carrying their youngest—and in a voice full of command and irrevocable decision announced, "Before that miserable Italian entry quota becomes law, I am bringing over my sister. Celestina can live with us—until I can find her a suitable husband."

Ever since influenza had felled Ebbely then permitted continued living, a magnanimous gesture wholly unexpected, he had become introspective. As though weighing his past in order to rebalance this gifted future, he seemed preoccupied. Though he continued to play himself, he no longer believed in the role.

Army long johns long gone, newly emancipated women thumbing their noses at frills and finery—Ebbely now contemplated the beckoning charm of becoming a player of tunes.

"What you mean tunes?" on first hearing this Hannah asked, giving the utterance of tunes as though he had decided on becoming a rat catcher.

"Music, dearest Lady. I have come to the conclusion that the time has come to indulge *myself*. Life is tenuous, its very fragility demands one to look beyond those horizons decreed by need and convention to those that only beckon, their perimeters yet unexplored, those so virgin vistas of the perhaps still possible . . ."

"Maybe you still know plain English?" Hannah sat in Fritz's chair ready to do battle.

"Oh, dear Lady—I am a little man . . ."

"No, dat's just silly. After my Fritz—you are de biggest man I ever know."

For a moment silenced—Ebbely murmured, "Thank you, my dear."

"It's true! So? Why you suddenly want to be a somebody dat plays in a honky-tonk place with no respect?"

"Is that what you think?"

"Dat's what I tink, yes!"

"I don't play well?"

"Oh, you play very beautiful—even on dat so funny banjo you sound nice—but . . ."

"But what . . . ?"

"Well . . . see how good I now say de double Us?"

"Hannah, you're stalling . . ."

"Okay—playing for de joy it gives is one ting—playing for nickels and dimes is not."

"Even if I enjoy it?"

"Even."

"Hannah, I still have to earn a living."

"Not dat way."

"Well, of course I could always become a sporting man, wear a long feather in my hat."

"What's he do?"

"He runs a racy stable of obliging girls—the feather in his hat is a sign that he has personally tested them all."

"You making wit de jokes again?"

"No, sage Lady—in New Orleans such men are very prosperous and duly respected."

"Now you mention dis—dat so almighty place you love so much—is a place you shouldn't be in also!"

"Oh my Juno! Now that you have stripped me of all my earthly pleasures—what divine concoction do I get for my supper?"

"Aha—mit de jokes—just to get out from under de serious—that you never like. I know. Okay, now I go make you stuffed cabbage how you like—but you better remember what I was telling you!"

When Rumpelstiltskin happened to casually mention the subject of his desire to change professions, Jane's reaction surprised him by its enthusiasm.

"Oh, Ebbely will you really?"

"I am seriously contemplating it."

"That New Orleans—you really like it there."

Though it was a statement of fact not a question, he answered, "Yes—possibly even more than simply like. It's a comfortable city."

"Comfortable? You always tell me how exciting everything is there. 'Comfortable' seems an odd word."

"A place attractive to variant misfits allows those of us imperfect to blend into its diverse brew." Catching himself Ebbely apologized for perhaps sounding a trifle maudlin.

Jane reached out in a gesture of automatic compassion. Permitting her touch Ebbely patted her hand where it lay upon his arm.

"Are you that lonely, Ebbely?"

Remembering their time when he had seen her cry—Ebbely jumped up, walked over to the piano and played Jane a rousing chorus of "Oh! Susanna."

Somehow spring seemed early this year. Bulbs for hoped-for daffodils that had been buried with such tender care back in September showed their appreciation by decorating Jane's back yard border before she had anticipated their arrival.

Carl's new marriage was beginning to heal his sorrow. Peter still grumbled at having to put up with a wife that insisted on working. Rudy, his injured spirit always lifted amongst the clouds, was flying again. From Holland, Henrietta wrote long letters telling of joy regained in a homeland loved.

Having taken over the family's flourishing bootlegging business after her father's death, Serafina was running it with an iron fist, a bookkeeper's sterility of purpose. Stan somehow having lost direction, followed her orders regardless of where they might lead, while their son entranced by his mother's power watched, learned, and waited for that glorious day when he too would flaunt armed bravado in the face of the law.

Having taught himself to read, young John now existed within the satisfying safety of books. Whenever necessary he emerged—but always with that smoldering resentment so common to the self-jailed, while Michael discovered that within a cardboard box containing brownish flakes that were proclaimed edible one could find hidden treasures, munched Mr. Kellogg's new stressed corn with anticipatory glee, until one morning his father found the kitchen floor crunching underfoot.

"NINNIE?! How did the boy get this? Don't tell me you spent good money on this!"

"Blame Ebbely. It's his latest enthusiasm—gifts hidden amongst nutrition—don't ask me why, but he adores it. Even has Hannah enthusiastic." Jane poured her husband's coffee.

Michael watched with apprehension as his father scrutinized a flake.

"It's nothing but hardened corn shells. But the idea of flaking it, then selling the public the idea that it's food, that it's good for you, needs no preparation . . . that's genius!"

"Well genius or not tell your son he has to eat what he spills or no more surprises!"

Winking at Michael, issuing stern orders to eat first, then search, John examined the day's discovered treasure—a miniature flipbook that when riffled created comic antics in motion. "Ingenious!" One of the things Jane liked most about him was John's unguarded delight, that instantaneous exuberance, whenever inventive skill, perfection in any form presented itself. "Ninnie, look—just a flip and the figures seem to move just like a moving picture show. What will they think of next! Good company—W. K. Kellogg. They have a knack for simple innovation."

"Well, I still think it makes a mess and a bowl of cooked oatmeal is healthier."

Putting on his overcoat, John offered his son an improbable fantasy as further incentive for tidiness.

"You know, Michelino, perhaps one day the gentleman who invented this will hide a little automobile inside with real wheels that spin and everything—so, you don't want Mama to stop buying this, do you?"

Eyes aglow at the possibility of such an amazing treasure, Michael shook his head, scooped flakes off the table, threw them back into his bowl and wolfed down his noisy food.

"I don't care—I *still* think eating and playing are two separate things."

"So beware, boy! Mama is *very* serious today." Laughing John kissed her cheek, hugged his eldest and left for work.

Easter had been, Passover had passed when John and Ebbely became disturbed by various newspaper reports of two Italian immigrants, tarred with the inflammatory label of anarchists, arrested for armed robbery and murder, that to them seemed to have all the earmarks of another immigrant witch hunt in the making. When discussing this with their friends they all agreed—Zoltan even remarking that the whole story smelled fishy to which Fritz added, "I have a feeling . . ."

Ebbely threw up his hands in mock horror, "Oh my God one of his feelings . . . !"

"Ebberhart! No joking on this. If these two men are accused of a bad crime only because they are foreigners—then that would be a terrible thing."

"Possibly even more dangerous than the supposed crime I would venture to say," Ebbely injected.

"John those two . . ." Fritz searched for names.

"Nicola Sacco and Bartolomeo Vanzetti. It says here when the police caught them in Brockton, both were carrying guns."

"Where's Brockton?"

"Near Boston in Massachusetts," John answered.

"This holdup was in Massachusetts and our papers here are making a big story out of it? Why?" Zoltan lit a cigarette.

"Ja—that's right."

"It's headline-worthy in my Chicago paper too," volunteered Ebbely.

"There too? I tell you, friends—nothing good will come of this—from now on all Italians will be 'murderous anarchist wops.' Sorry, John." Zoltan ground out his cigarette, and decided it was time to go home.

The Geiger parlor was rife with troubled talk this year. Clutching the *Dearborn Independent*, Fritz stormed into the room, closing the door behind him. "Good, you are already here. John! Have you read this? In God's name how can the Boss say such things?"

"It's not the Boss."

"It's *his* newspaper."

"It must be Liebold. Everyone knows he has always hated Jews."

"And since when does the mighty Henry Ford permit anyone to think for themselves, let alone write his column?" Sounding particularly sarcastic Ebbely settled in his chair.

"It is terrible! Absolutely terrible, just terrible!" As if incapable of finding another word that could ever suit—Fritz kept repeating, "Terrible! *Furchtbar!* Just terrible!"

Carrying the *Ford Weekly* as though contaminated, Zoltan entered. "This is insane!"

Ebbely corrected him. "No, it is much more than that. It is *meant* to be inflammatory and therefore highly dangerous. The hatred of Jews is nothing new—they have always been hated—and always will be. But this glaring Jew baiting by the public tool of an American folk hero compares, in my mind at least, to a well-orchestrated public lynching of satanic possibilities!"

"Aren't you exaggerating a bit? Who knows, there may not be any more such attacks after this one." Zoltan tried to sound convincing.

Waving his paper like a truncheon, Carl rushed into the parlor. "Have any of you read this . . . garbage?"

"Ja, we're just talking about it—close the door, Carl. I don't want Hannah to know."

"Jesus! Someone is bound to tell her . . ." Carl turned on John. "Well, and what have *you* got to say to this . . . outrage?"

"He thinks it can only be Liebold." Fritz was quick to protect his friend should such be necessary.

"Impossible! Sure everybody knows Liebold hates Jews—but it's Henry Ford who rules—he gives the orders."

"That's what Ebbely just said."

"The man has gone mad—that's all there is to it!" Carl flopped down in his chair.

"It may be all Edison's influence. Have any of you thought of that?" Ebbely watched for the reaction he was certain this heresy would cause.

"Edison? Thomas Edison?!" John was incredulous.

"Yes, my dear still-wet-behind-the-ears-idealist Italian! The great Alva E—the idol, the divine god of your so equally bigoted Henry. For God's sake, wake up, John! None of this is new—only now the shit is out—the stench proclaimed in print by the symbol of the American dream, the self-made millionaire whose so *common man* looks up to, believes in and will follow *wherever* he leads!" Explosive anger so foreign to Ebbely's character—it now silenced those who heard it.

John's continuing silence making him nervous, Fritz repeated, "Terrible! *Mein Gott!* Hannah! Hannah mustn't know! All of you—you all have to promise me not a word! Maybe Zoltan's right, maybe this is only one time and next paper nothing."

The next edition of the *Ford International Weekly* and the *Dearborn Independent* had much more and the next and the next. In all, ninety-one articles of such vitriol, such extreme anti-Semitism that years later when these were published in book form under the title *The International Jew*, financed and distributed worldwide by Henry Ford, Adolf Hitler already enamored of the assembly line concept which he used in the rearmament of Germany, hung a portrait of Heinrich Ford in his office and saluted it.

20

The Nineteenth Amendment granting women the vote now law, Jane conscious of her civic duty as well as the heroic struggle waged to secure this right, approached John for some political insight. As usual when alone they spoke Italian.

"Now that women have been given the right to vote—does that mean I shall be allowed to do so?"

"Of course. That is if you want to." John, concentrating on his evening paper, replied without lifting his eyes.

"A right so long fought for should be honored. Don't you think?" Jane threaded her darning needle.

"Uh-huh." Turning a page John added, "Do you think you know enough *to* vote?"

"Oh I intend to study—to inform myself on all the issues presented by . . . what are they called?"

"Candidates."

"Please also tell me the names of the what is called *the parties*."

Rather amused by his wife's earnestness concerning political matters that were surely quite over her head—John put down his paper smiling. "Well, first and foremost there is the Democratic Party. Then the Republican. Those two being the most powerful, rule. But as this is a democracy, other parties exist and are permitted. There is the Socialist, the Reform, the Federalists, the Whigs and others—but of course, if you vote, you will vote Democratic."

"Why?" Though an innocent question—it seemed to annoy him.

"Why? Because they are the only ones who know what they are doing and the Boss expects us to."

"Oh, Mr. Ford approves of the Democrats?"

"Mr. Ford is a Democrat."

"President Wilson is one too. But now Mr. James Cox is running, why?"

"Some say Woodrow Wilson is a sick man—his obsession for the formation of a body of many nations collective to ensure peace for all time is doomed and so is he. Some think his playing God has gotten out of hand anyway."

"Does that mean that the Republican Party might win?"

John shrugged, "I am afraid so," and went back to reading his paper.

Picking up her mending Jane murmured, "Oh, dear, Mr. Ford won't like *that* at all."

Hannah and Jane took the privileges of their new citizenship very seriously—they pored over newspapers, on their daily excursions to tradespeople questioned whomever they encountered. Discussed amongst themselves whom they liked—whom they didn't and why. For some reason both were partial to the Democrats' choice for vice president. Though Hannah thought him to be a trifle young for such a lofty office she liked Franklin D. Roosevelt's looks—because they were so aristocratic—"Just like a real prince from the old country," Hannah said. Jane thought so too—adding, "An *intelligent* prince" and wished he was running for president instead of the so less interesting Mr. Cox. Both had no trouble at all dismissing Warren Harding and Calvin Coolidge and their Republican platform of *America First.*

It was on a bright summer morning that Ebbely announced that before the year ended he would be leaving to prepare for a new profession—that of musical entertainer for hire available for nuptials, births, funerals, and other such frivolous occasions. As this latest endeavor necessitated forceful advertising, to accommodate the limited space for this purpose on sandwich boards he decided to drop *Hardt, Bein,* and *Isadore* from his given name leaving a simple, straightforward, no-nonsense Ebb Fish—"that's with two *b*'s as in *tide*" in its place. Well, how does that strike you?"

No one knew what to say. Ominously calm Hannah inquired, "So . . . your good name no good no more?"

"There are reasons, my dear."

"Reasons? What reasons?"

Fritz jumped in. "You have a date to leave?"

"It has to be before the winter sets in and makes the roads impassable."

"Reasons—what reasons?" Hannah persisted, tone glacial.

"Now, my dear, is not the time to go into them. Trust me."

"Oh, I trust you. I tink you have gone crazy in de head, dat you running away will solve notting—dat you, a once-upon-a-time so smart, educated, by-everybody-envied gentleman, are all of a sudden a crazy *meshugah*, but . . . I trust you."

Jumping up Ebbely hugged her. "Dear Colossus of my tiny heart, how I shall miss you!"

Looking down at where he knelt by her chair, the object of his adoration retorted, "Aha! If *already* you know *dat* much . . . stay!"

Fritz cleared his throat. "Ebberhardt?"

"Yes, my friend?"

"You are—sure?"

"Yes, I am sure. There are changes in the winds and I must follow where they blow. It is in my nature to be facile you know."

John lit a cheroot. "Whenever you get this theatrical, Ebbely, I know you are hiding something." John's remark surprised Jane. She had not been aware that he knew Ebbely that well or had ever taken the time to discover his so carefully hidden vulnerabilities.

"I am not! John, I assure you, I am not!" Turning to Mr. Henry, now a rosy-cheeked mailman of expanded girth, Ebbely inquired, "Well, my boy, have you made up *your* mind yet?"

Spinning around, Hannah focused on her Mr. Henry.

"What now?! Has he got you crazy too?"

"Well . . ." Not wanting to hurt her, Mr. Henry searched for kind words. "Please don't take this the wrong way, Mrs. Geiger, but when Mr. Fishbein said he was motoring all that long way and wouldn't mind some company . . . well I thought to myself, 'What a grand adventure! To go fording out into the wide-open spaces, sleep by the side of the road under the stars!' I'd sure hate to miss a chance like that."

"You planning to go all de way to dat shame-on-you place, he's going?"

"Hope to, Ma'am. Sounds real lively—plenty of possibilities for a one-armed *rascal man* like me." Using Hannah's old affectionate nickname for him, Mr. Henry tried to soften the blow of his defection from her generous care.

As he would be long gone before the holidays—the new Mr. Ebb Fish proclaimed that he was choosing Glory Day as his Giving-of-Gifts Day. Everyone dedicated to shielding Hannah from the evil being manufactured along with their beloved Model T, Ebbely's announcement to celebrate Hanukah-Christmas on the Fourth of July was greeted with enthusiastic acceptance. Hannah was relegated to her kitchen to get busy making gingerbread boys, the children the important task of decorating the rubber tree plant that stood in the parlor, with imagination and cut-out shapes of colored paper. Fritz set out the nativity scene—even the menorah saying, "God wouldn't mind, for after all the calendar was man's idea." Jane clipped the candles onto the rubber tree. When lit, it looked so splendid—Hannah said maybe she would keep the candles there for good.

Trying not to cry, determined to be brave, Hannah baked so many festive delicacies that the house began to smell of warm cinnamon, nutmeg and precious clove, just as if it were really December.

For an early farewell and holiday party combined, everyone joined in the sunlit festivities. Excited, the children waited for Ebbely's giving of gifts. No one was forgotten. There were hoops and Erector sets for the boys, delicate porcelain-faced dolls for the girls, pretty will-o'-the-wisp mementos for the ladies, pungent, rich tobaccos for his friends. Then came the moment everyone had been waiting for—Hannah's gift. What would it be? What could it be?

Ebbely wheeled it into the parlor. Hidden under a large bedsheet it stood like a pylon—shortened to the size of its procurer as if waiting to be disrobed.

Like a salesman giving a demonstration, Ebbely stood before his curious audience holding out a tiny metal box.

"Ladies and gentlemen and Lilliputians, here in my hand you see a vital necessity to the one standing hidden before you. This tiny receptacle made of tin, its hinged lid adorned with flourished script indicates the manufacturer of its contents of needles and their graded sizes of soft, medium, medium-loud, and extra-loud. 'Needles?' you'll say. 'For what?' You'll mutter, 'The man is mad!' But stay—take heart for we have but begun. Assembled friends—as yours truly cannot be with you this year to enchant, transport, delight you with his sublime musical renditions, I hereby present you with a more than worthy substitute."

With the dexterity of a flamboyant conjurer, Ebbely whipped off the sheet.

"Voilà! Behold! Here before you stands the latest marvel, a Victrola! Housed in its own cabinet of finest black chinoiserie. I shall now demonstrate." Cranking the handle on its side, pushing a lever, Ebbely carefully lowered a peculiarly curved pipe, positioned its head into the grooves of a glass plate rotating at an alarming speed and suddenly a man's voice enveloped the parlor in rapturous beauty.

His audience gasped.

Having achieved the impact of his surprise, Ebbely bounded about the room chanting, "Caruso! The divine Caruso—listen! What passion! What tonality!"

"Who?"

Ebbely, in midhop, froze—aghast.

"You *must* be joking. You are, John, aren't you?" Taken aback by the shocked faces directed at him, John shook his head.

"My father-in-law just bought one of these new Victrolas just to hear the great man," injected Zoltan.

"You hear that? Zoltan, a Bulgarian, knows who Caruso is and you—a landsman of the great man, a compatriot, a true Italian—you don't? You asked, 'Who?' You should be ashamed of yourself, John! You should hang your head in abject shame!" Ebbely shook his head.

"So, hang me by my thumbs!"

Everyone crowded around the splendid Victrola—examining the phonograph— discussing the great man. Caruso kept singing his heart out.

Still not a word or sign of joy from Hannah. Ebbely, concerned by her silence, approached her. "Well, my dear? Was I wrong? Don't you like it?"

Eyes half closed—her body as still as a sunset—Hannah whispered, "Shhh . . . I am listening."

And Ebbely had his answer.

"Ebberhardt—what a gift!" Fritz shook his hand. "You shouldn't have spent that much money but I thank you anyway."

Later as the party was ending, Ebbely handed Jane a book wrapped in white tissue tied with red string.

"For you, Jane. A courageous woman wrote this—I think you will understand what she had to say."

Throughout her life Jane kept her special gift. *Uncle Tom's Cabin* became a sort of talisman—a reminder of those early years and all that Rumpelstiltskin taught her.

The red maples had turned—clocks and nature had reverted back to where they belonged when Zoltan announced that his Agnes was expecting. Everyone was delighted—especially Hannah, who was heard to remark, "Now finally dat poor alone man—he will have a family—a real home!" Mr. Kennec and his Molly had said their annual farewell when John stormed into the house calling for Jane.

"Ninnie! You will have to go! I have been assigned to the Rouge on a special project—so I can't go."

Jane looked up from mashing potatoes.

"Go? Go where?"

"To New York—in three weeks when Celestina's ship gets in." Jane stared at her husband. "Well my sister can't be expected to travel halfway across the country by herself." Taking off his coat, John began washing up at the sink. Still no word from the woman frozen behind him. "For God's sake, Ninnie, you're capable, intelligent, you know how to handle yourself and you speak the language. Who else is there?"

"Me? You want me to travel to the city of New York all by myself?"

"Hannah will take the children, I'll make all the travel arrangements, an exact schedule for you to follow, where you have to change trains, where you have to go— what you have to say and when. Both for going and coming back. You're lodging . . ."

"Lodging?" Though it was but a breathed question its panic was poignant.

"Yes, you must overnight. It's the only way you can be on the dock in time the morning of Celestina's arrival. Of course I shall send you first class all the way. So you really have nothing to worry about."

Her '20s bob contained by the latest fashion, a head-hugging soft felt she had made to match the shade of dark plum of her perfectly tailored traveling suit, Jane positioned herself by the window of the First Class railway carriage. For this her first adventure solely dependent on herself, she had permitted herself the luxurious affectation of a small velvet muff for added courage. That John trusted her to accomplish this mission contributed much to her determination to succeed. That it also scared her gave her the incentive not to let it show.

Elbow resting on the windowsill, gloved hand cupping her chin, a remembered pose observed so long ago, Jane gazed at the passing countryside as though genteel nonchalance was not new to her.

A twilight arrival to a great city begets its own magic—that spectacular shimmering of lights before real darkness requires them, so different from any other times of the day or place. Caught by the wonder of having actually managed to arrive in the city of New York, Jane longed to explore its magic but as her explicit instructions made no mention of such wayward excitement, she lifted a gloved hand to hail a taxicab, handed the driver the piece of paper on which John had written her destination. Having given the cabbie sufficient time to familiarize himself with it, she inquired, "Do you know where it is?"

He hesitated.

"You sure that's where you gotta go, Lady?"

"Oh, yes—my husband wrote it."

"Yeah—sure!" He smirked—making Jane wonder if this somewhat sinister man might finally be one of those white slavers she had feared so very long ago.

Thinking it a wise precaution, Jane ventured a soft, "On the way, I may wish to stop at the nearest police station—but I will let you know."

Still reeling from the shock of stormy seas and endless travel, Celestina close to tears in headscarf and rumpled coat, sat dejected on her battered case, when suddenly an elegant stranger advanced towards her, and she cringed.

"Celestina! Don't you know me? It's me, Giovanna! I am Giovanna, your brother's wife!"

"Oh, dear . . ." gulped Celestina all flushed and trembling, "can we go home now? Please! All these people! And the noise and when I stand up—the ground moves and I have to sit down again." This time the tears gushed. Jane held her close.

"I know, I know. I felt just the same—everything wobbled. Don't cry, in a few days it will be gone, but the many people and the noise, that won't go away—you just get used to it." Jane steered her sister-in-law through the crowds to the tram that would carry them to the station. Celestina recovered enough to be very impressed by Giovanna's command of American plus her astounding expertise when choosing the proper coins to pay for their fare not to mention knowing where and when to alight from the strange but rather attractive wagon tinkling its bells with its shovel-like grate in front that Giovanna informed her was called a Cow Catcher—but though she looked, as she saw not a single cow, this confused Celestina even more.

"Look!" Jane pointed, "look there—that's a Ford motorcar—a Model T. It is the most famous motorcar in the whole world—the one Giovanni builds."

Celestina trying to take it all in—awed by so many wonders knew that if she lived to be a hundred she would never be able to do so.

In their girlhood Italian they chatted—enjoying each other as though no time had passed to turn them into women. When changing trains and other such serious maneuvers, Jane was in charge—when on their way again it was Celestina's turn to bring news from home.

Flirty Antonia, betrothed to a successful elderly merchant from Milan, a splendid match that the whole village approved of without reservation, had run off with a common soldier, disappeared—no one knew where. "She chose a common foot soldier! Not even an officer with a horse! Imagine!" is how Celestina put it, after months still shaking her head in disbelief.

"Broke her father's heart. Since then it's rumored that the accuracy of his treatments has waned alarmingly, some even suspect that our good doctor drinks."

Camilla had born twins, girls, now expecting once more was so big it would surely be twins again. "Remember the Rossini twins? Well, she married Mario the one with the big hands so it's no wonder she keeps having two of everything! Giovanna, if you saw Camilla now you'd never recognize her. She already looks worn out, old and behaves just like her mother—always cooking, washing and having babies." Taking a quick respite, Celestina nibbled on the tangerine Jane had peeled for her. "Last winter after spitting blood for goodness knows how long, Sister Bertine finally died of consumption. Her funeral was splendid! Everyone stopped work to attend, dressed in black. Even the horses had crepe ribbons tied on their harnesses. Father Tomasso was at his most inspired—listening to him everyone had the distinct impression they could hear angels singing the *Requiem*." Removing her headscarf, Celestina used it to wipe her fingers.

Jane thought, *I must remind myself to tell Celestina that in America ladies wear hats.*

"Oh, even your father attended, which shocked quite a few of our village as you can well imagine. He has a peasant girl from the South—a Calabrese keeping house for him now. Have you ever heard from him?"

Busy stowing their suitcases, Jane answered, "No."

"Oh well." Celestina yawned.

"Oh, please don't go to sleep yet. Tell me, how is Teresa? Has anyone heard from her?"

"We certainly haven't—and I don't think anyone else has either. Most of her brothers were killed in the war—the one who became a Franciscan—and her mother they died of the influenza—but no, no—nothing else." The train wailed into the night as Jane's heart echoed its lament.

On a grim October evening, arctic winds whipping across the Great Lakes, teeth chattering like castanets, a very miserable, travel-worn Celestina was finally enveloped in Hannah's welcoming embrace, given that instant loving safety that Jane remembered so well.

Everyone came to meet and welcome the new immigrant come to stay. Confused, yet delighted by their generous acceptance of her, Celestina beaming kept repeating, "*Gracia, molto pecharie, molte gentile,*" asking her brother to please translate, assure his friends that she had made up her mind that she would speak good American by Christmas.

Ebbely liked Celestina immediately. He called her his "Raphaelasian cherub" and delighted in her old world charm, her unabridged enthusiasm for every new discovery, every new experience.

The children had great fun introducing their new aunt to the rituals of their country. There were so many things to learn, decipher, absorb that at times Celestina felt quite undone.

Though this year young John refused to dress up, Michael ever loyal to his black felt went as his model T, and allowed Billy to borrow his ghostly sheet to spook in. Not one to be left behind, Celestina went as Bo Peep. Of all the new things she came to know, Celestina always liked Halloween the very best.

As Ebbely's exodus approached, Hannah hiding her broken heart helped him pack up his belongings. Each bibelot carefully wrapped, a reminder of a time, an occasion linked to their years of friendship. She did not begrudge Ebbely his decision just missed him long before he was ever gone. Jane was far less successful in hiding her loss of him.

Autumn was fading into white, when one last time the famous hot-cold box was packed with Hannah's loving provisions for a long journey. His trusty flivver piled high with his belongings, Ebbely bade farewell to his Michigan home and those he loved who had made it one. Vowing to return for occasional visits, especially for those that required his terpsichorean skill upon the icy pond, he kissed the foreheads of the children, both cheeks of his favorite Tall Ladies, was lifted up and bear-hugged by his favorite husbands and waving a last good-bye, Ebbely and his companion bachelor vanished into the winter gloom. With the departure of Ebberhardt Isadore Fishbein now but a simple Ebb Fish, it felt as though an era was gone as well.

That once alone Hannah would cry, everyone knew; that Jane would, some expected, others not. Thinking this was only one of their Uncle Ebbely's many absences that always culminated in his certain return, the children went inside to play.

"Good for Ebbely to have company." Hannah closed the front door.

"Ja, good for both of them . . ." Fritz agreed. "Only hope Ebberhardt doesn't get your postman into too much trouble with his fancy ladies."

"My postman? Where you get dat wit *my* postman—dat poor boy what he needs is a little cozy business wit a nice-to-look-after girl, and so Ebbely promised me to find a special one who fits him. Fancy ladies? Where you get such talk?" And grumbling censure, Hannah escaped to her kitchen to prepare supper for those who were left.

Despite all their studying, neither Jane nor Hannah voted this first year of being allowed to do so. The right of women to vote was still so new, so startling a concept that many chose to enjoy, glory in this right finally granted them without having the courage to actually do so. Women empowered by legislation passed by men—was a future to get used to in easy stages.

Michigan and winter, so suited to each other, began their tryst. The snakes took their accustomed positions, wash hung steaming in kitchens, mittens were sorted, sleds sharpened, excursions to the grand city of Detroit for the vital aromas for the holiday season a must, this year with Celestina the willing awestruck convert to the treasures to be found within Mr. Hirt's Aladdin's cave.

Old enough, Michael liked to be taken along, especially when such rare expeditions included visiting his Uncle Stan's wife's twin. He liked her storytelling, the way by her voice alone, she could paint pictures for him to visualize.

Now a stereotypical old maid wearing a wedding ring, Morgana had acquired a gauntness that troubled Jane. Those sightless eyes so luminous even in their locked imperfection, now seemed suspended in sockets appearing too large to retain them. No longer the reflected image of her twin, now Morgana resembled a Serafina destroyed.

It was on a winter afternoon when the little boy saw her after an absence of many weeks that Michael sensed in her, finality.

"Aunt Morgana—it is me—Michael," he announced on entering her private sitting room.

"You have grown."

Michael moved to her side. "How do you know I have?"

"I hear it in your voice—it has a growing-up sound and your walk is heavier." Morgana patted the place next to her on the settee. Michael climbed up and sat. The slight shifting of weight made her wince.

"Is it very bad being blind?"

"Sometimes, when you want to see."

Michael reached for her hand. "What?"

"Oh, things"—Morgana moved her hand to clasp his—to the boy its touch felt like a fallen autumn leaf.

"Why are you sad?"

"I am not sad, child—not really—just tired."

"No, you are sad first!" Michael's voice held the tone of masculine conviction. Stroking his hand, Morgana smiled.

"I am the one who has visions, not you—you scamp."

"If I give you a hug will that hurt you?"

"Why do you say that? How do you . . ." Morgana let the useless words trail.

Michael looked up at the haggard face that could not see its own destruction.

"I'll be careful, Aunt Morgana—really I will, I promise." Carefully his small arms encircled her waist. His head resting on her protruding rib cage, they sat—child and woman, and Morgana wept while Michael listened—feeling it was their moment of farewell.

When Morgana died in the agony of rapacious cancer everyone wondered why no one had guessed her suffering. Dry-eyed, Michael stood by the open coffin remembering Gregory, wondering why grown-ups felt it right to fix dead people into strangers. Looking up at his father beside him he whispered, "Papa?"

"Yes, Michelino?"

"Papa . . ." he hesitated.

"You're disturbing people—what is it?"

"When I die don't fix me."

"Fix you?" John's whisper held impatience.

"I don't want to look funny like Gregory and Gloria and Aunt Morgana. Okay, Papa? Promise?"

"He means strange." And taking Michael's hand, Jane took her son out into the soft snow.

It was not because they had celebrated Hanukah-Christmas in July that when it was time for the real ones—it seemed like a memory no one wanted to remember. For Celestina and the children the rituals were re-created—the festive mood pretended— the prevailing sense of emptiness hidden from those whose lives were still in their beginnings. The sumptuous Victrola spun its lyrical magic—yet Ebbely spinning his piano stool would have been preferred.

On New Year's Day, certain she would plunge and disappear, Celestina refused to set foot onto frozen water assuring her new friends in most passable American that watching everyone else slip and slide amused her far more. Somehow the old year was gone, as though it had never been.

John started off the New Year by looking for a man to marry his sister. Jane didn't understand why this should be so vital a quest, so imminently necessary. Most willingly she had given up her sewing alcove, making it into a small but cozy and quite ample enough bedroom for Celestina to feel at home in. Basically a happy person, who loved children, ever eager to learn, willing to help about the house, Celestina was a joy to have around—so why this haste to get rid of her? When questioned, John patiently explained to his wife that a woman needed a man to protect her, feed her, house her, by the gift of his name assure her the respectability necessary to be accepted into the community and most importantly, fulfill her womanhood by giving her children. Certainly there was no quarreling with that. Even if one wanted to, which Jane most earnestly did, all such rebuttal would have fallen onto the stone-deaf ears of any early-twentieth-century man. Knowing that Celestina had a sharp mind of her own—Jane decided it would be prudent to wait and keep her mouth shut. No use getting a husband riled up over something that was obviously beyond his comprehension.

As head of the family, John took his duty of marriage broker very seriously. He felt it was his responsibility to set his sister on the proper path towards matrimony. It was time for Celestina to become a wife, care for a husband of her own. With his usual thoroughness he searched the Ford employment rosters, eliminating Latvians, Croatians, Turks, Dalmatians and other such fringe nationals for being too low on the wage scale. In view of the Red Scare and increased deportations, Russians were definitely out, as were those mostly from the Balkans. The really dependable Germans, these were either already married, about to be or since the war now eager to return to their beaten homeland. The Irish could read—but they drank, were known to beat their women on a regular basis—married their own kind and their hatred of papist Italians was known by all. Of course as a Torinese fond of his innocent sister, choosing a worthy Italian would have been the obvious choice, but this year with both Sacco and Vanzetti finally going to be tried for murder, John was worried. Why he couldn't quite put his finger on, as he tried to explain to Fritz when discussing the somewhat shocking, even violent, reactions in the press to these two Italian immigrants.

"It's like one of your feelings, Fritz. I don't know why, but something . . . something is going to happen from this. Something bad, very bad." Of course Fritz had not taken him seriously, said he was only worried because he too was Italian—but John knew that wasn't the reason.

Having exhausted most of the sixty different nationalities employed by the Ford Motor Company—at the end John was left with the stoic, nose-to-the-perpetual-grindstone Poles. Granted a boring lot at times, still on the whole they took care of their women, were frugal, hardworking men any woman could be proud to belong to.

While John was searching for an eligible Pole, Ford's giant workforce waited out their seasonal layoff.

In Dearborn, the Rouge, that mastodon of production power in the making, was beginning to sap the creative strength from Highland Park. The continuously moving assembly line, such a revolutionary concept just a few years before, now an accustomed presence in most factories, requiring only unskilled laborers to feed its stupefying repetitiveness, Henry Ford began transferring his best men over to Dearborn and his industrial behemoth, the Mighty Rouge. Zoltan and Carl were reassigned—Fritz and Peter remained, while John divided his designing skills between the two factories.

For some reason Agnes didn't show. Five months into her pregnancy, Zoltan's wife still worked at her enviable post of trusted librarian without visually embarrassing anybody. Now that Celestina was there to look after the children, once a week come rain, sleet or icy storm, Jane took the trolley into Detroit to visit Agnes at the library. To have a friend in the big city, one who had unlimited access to books, was an anticipatory joy that Jane treasured. Zoltan's Agnes, a gifted shepherd, led Jane to regions she would never have discovered by herself amidst the vast riches of beckoning shelves. Sometimes their tastes came into conflict as when the earnest librarian suggested Thackeray openly disapproving of Jane being stirred by Upton Sinclair.

"Jane, how can you?! You mustn't read such shocking prose! Even I haven't—*The Jungle* is not proper for a lady. A violent man, with violent ideas, violent places and so brutal! If you must like the *macabre* then at least read Edgar Allan Poe but not such a radical as Upton Sinclair!"

Seeing her friend so disturbed by her taste, Jane quickly snatched one of the sisters Brontë off the shelf hoping she would do—then took back Mr. Sinclair and his brutal reality as soon as Agnes's back was turned. During this year of literary discovery, Jane became engrossed in what would become a lifetime interest in those, who using the weaponry of words, fought against the wrongs they perceived as such. Later this would aid her to endure her destiny—but for now it simply intrigued her view of life.

Jane was maturing, her self-awareness more stringent than when untried youth had governed her perception. Dutiful marriage had given her its grounding, motherhood its pride of achievement, sex its physical discovery, love though still in its infancy, an awareness of its necessity. Without realizing the implications, Jane was becoming herself; no longer wholly dependent on those categories that had made this transition possible. Though her era and its set priorities might demand obedience, even subservience, Jane would travel her own roads, seek her own horizons—ever convinced that freedom was her quest though its applicable meaning still eluded her as it related to herself.

By spring, life and the living of it had settled into its accustomed patterns. Children grew, their expanding individualism separating them from homogeneous babyhood. Under the sheltering attention of a replaced mother—Carl's little Rose shed her sorrow, reawakening the Irish joyousness that was her true mother's legacy. Serafina's Angelo honed his skill of truant of all authority that would shape his violent future. Jane's sons simply embellished what they had always been. Michael—The Romantic; John—The Sullen; Billy—The Happy. Still childless and resigned, Peter and his Clara adopted a stray kitten and named her Lizzie.

It was summer when Agnes presented Zoltan with a daughter and transformed him into the young man he had never been when young. A spring in his step, a grin on his face—not a sneeze, cough or fidget in sight—he became actually handsome in the process.

Overjoyed, Hannah couldn't get over that a baby had been born in a hospital—a place designated only for sick people who were going to die.

"Can you imagine—a new life in such a place. What will dey tink of next! Dat Agnes I have to admit—courage she has! You going to do dat too next time, Ninnie?"

Jane preparing to help lay the table for a Sunday supper smiled, "There won't *be* a next time."

"Aha—you sure?"

"Yes—Hannah, I'm sure."

"Well, la-di-da, you getting to be like one of dose real so modern ladies who know so much but don't tell—keep dere secrets so dere figures stay?"

Blushing, Jane admitted she had been reading the latest writings by Mrs. Sanger.

"You know, Vifey—I tink someday that lady maybe right—but nature is nature—maybe not so smart for people to play around wit it. God he knows—but plain people? I am not so sure."

"Don't worry—it's simple and not at all dangerous."

"Aha . . ." Hannah poured the creamy soup into her cavernous tureen. "But . . . a woman's body is for making life—so maybe not good to stop it."

"A woman's body belongs to her. *She* decides what to do with it!"

And that shut up Hannnah forever on the subject of birth control.

Finally having found a worthy candidate that suited a brother's strict requirements—a strapping Pole whose bulging muscles attested to his awesome skill as a smelting boss—one late summer evening John brought him home for supper. Jane had arranged Celestina's hair in a more becoming way, made her a new blouse of finest muslin, its small blue flowered pattern repeated in the piping on collar and cuffs, splurged on a chicken roasted with three vegetables—even some store-bought cheese from Mr. Hirt's in the city. The two for whose benefit all this finery was displayed never so much as looked at each other nor said more than two words—these being *good* followed by *evening* which two hours after excruciating intermittent silences became *good* and *night*.

John stormed into the kitchen where the women were washing up.

"Cillie! What the hell got into you? You the chatterbox—I go and find someone suited—you think perhaps that is easy? There are more than twenty thousand men

I had to go through! Ninnie works, decks you out, puts a festive meal on the table fit for a king and you, what do you do? You just sit there—as dumb as the village idiot. I'm going to bed!" Disgusted he turned to go.

Celestina's "He wasn't bad" stopped him. "His neck was huge and with those shoulders he looked like an ox—but . . . he wasn't bad."

"Then why? You could have at least smiled—once!"

"Actually, if you must know, I was trying very hard not to giggle."

"You *what*?"

"Just what I said . . . giggle." An unperturbed Celestina began putting away the dried dinner plates.

"I don't understand you," spluttered her brother.

"Oh, I know you don't. You never have you know, not really. Gina, yes—but me, no."

"And what is that supposed to mean? I suppose you think being an old maid will satisfy you? Well, let me tell you my fine girl—" John got no further.

"Well, let *me* tell *you* my so important Mr.! I did not come across a whole ocean to become a wife of an ox—as a matter of fact, I didn't come all the way to America to be a wife to just anybody—especially someone my brother has to get for me. If I marry and please note the *if*—I will marry a man *I* have found, that *I* want to marry who really wants to marry me! And if he doesn't work for your Mr. Henry Ford—who cares!" And with that last salvo, Celestina marched out of the kitchen.

Stunned John looked at Jane, who absolutely delighted, was trying very hard not to laugh.

"Ninnie—did you hear that? That ungrateful urchin has the gall to tell *me* off!"

"You must admit, John—she does have a point—Mr. Polansky may be nice, but attractive he is not." Jane busied herself setting out the breakfast dishes.

"Attractive? What's that got to do with finding a good provider?"

"Oh—you know, marriage is frightening enough without also having to do it with an ox." And this time Jane couldn't stop the laughter as her exasperated husband flounced out of the kitchen.

Determined to find herself a husband, within the month Celestina had one. A roly-poly Bavarian who owned a tiny candy shop not far from her brother's house. A childless widower who being already broken in, a practiced milquetoast, he suited Celestina's managerial character to perfection. He, craving a determined woman who could tell him what to do, she being one, looking for a man to manage, for both of them it was congenial need at first sight.

As usual Celestina wasted no time, informed her smitten candy man that a lengthy courtship was unnecessary and holding his hand marched him into her brother's parlor fully confident that his wrath would have no effect on her decision.

"John, this is Mr. Josef Ritter. He is the proprietor of his own shop, already a citizen of l'America and I will be his wife. I will sell his candy, make American change. He has promised to teach me everything I need to know and be good to me."

That left nothing more to say. Jane brought glasses, John secretly relieved, uncorked the bottle of illegal spirits, toasted the betrothed. Later that evening a slightly dazed Josef returned to his rooms above the store, content that soon they wouldn't seem so lonely.

The wedding was brief, a honeymoon nonexistent. It took no time at all before the new Mrs. Ritter had the corner candy store organized for optimum efficiency.

Soon her jolly manner, her welcoming smile that lit her whole being whenever a child's entrance activated the tinkling bell above her door, became the magnet that drew children to Aunt Cillie's sugared heaven. They would stand transfixed before the wonders displayed, undecided—hesitant what to choose from amongst the endless bounty. Celestina loved these moments of indecision—of mittened fingers clutching precious pennies—eyes staring in profound concentration—small mouths already making sucking sounds in delicious anticipation.

Sometimes, with those she knew had walked the distance from poorer sections, she would make up a *special*, and announce that today one penny had the buying power of two. Every child in Highland Park adored Celestina and she loving them—became a mother every afternoon when school was out.

Now that she had her sewing room back, Jane was able to resume her private dressmaking business. She had missed the work she loved and now that everything cost twice as much as before, more than ever its financial rewards were welcome. So rarely was John at home that Jane could pin and sew far into most nights without being needed by anyone.

21

Today John was homesick. Italy—that malleable illusion when all else pales; he knew her for what she was, yet longed for her. She was so easy to love. Her generous beauty, her power to treat time as mere interruption—decadence without guile. The touch of ancient stone, the sudden stillness of an empty square, the light—that unrelenting light that forced all color to be true, shadowed sienna, empowered umber. The scent of rosemary growing wild—its pungent oil the bane of seductive witches. What was it really that he missed to such a degree as to feel a sudden disloyalty to the country of his choice? It confused John that he found no satisfactory answer to the question he asked of himself. It was not like him to accept loose ends. He found himself wondering if Jane would understand.

Protesting their complete and provable innocence which they had done both verbally and in print since their arrest and imprisonment without bail the year before, in July both Sacco and Vanzetti were judged guilty of premeditated murder and under heavy guard taken back to prison to await sentencing. International as well as national newspaper headlines predicted that these foreign anarchists would surely be given and deserved the electric chair. In Italy and France as crowds demonstrated against the guilty verdict, in America anti-immigrant feeling accelerated, especially against those of Italian origin. As John had intuitively felt, in the prevailing atmosphere of *get rid of all foreigners* this case of two immigrants could easily develop into a scapegoat trial. Though none of the Ford men actually believed that these men would ever be put to death—still they agreed with John that if ever this should be proven to be the case, not only would it be a travesty of American justice, it would do irreputable harm to both the nation and what America stood for in the eyes of the world.

When a letter finally arrived bearing a Louisiana postmark the call went out for everyone to come have their supper at the Geigers' and attend the public reading of Ebbely's news.

Knowing full well that Hannah would share his letter, with an audience in mind—he gave his already theatrical style added flourish.

> *Dearest Hannah and all such friends who having congregated to hear the latest from him who though gone amidst the bayous, yearns for sight of them,*
>
> *Let it be known that one Ebb (remember as in tide) Fish safely arrived in New Orleans, first bedded down his valiant Tin Lizzie, then his most congenial traveling companion in a lodging house unmentionable here . . .*

Hannah stopped Fritz reading long enough to exclaim she knew exactly what kind of a *house* and that Ebbely should be ashamed of himself—then allowed him to go on.

> *. . . Ah, the rapture, the softness of a real bed after so long an absence, sublime. Since then I have procured a domicile more suited to my needs. It comprises a small bedchamber, an even smaller sitting room with an adequate alcove for sparse cooking. Its pièce de résistance . . . a small Juliet-like balcony that looks down onto the quartier where most days peddlers roast pecans coated in raw sugar and dark molasses. Divine! Simply divine! That aroma must surely be the perfume of all the best goddesses on Mount Olympus.*
>
> *Now to the latest news of our brave soldier, ex-postman. Yes, my dear Hannah, I have kept my promise—found him a nice girl. Be assured that when I say "nice"—I mean exactly what that simple word implies. Though not untouched—untarnished, with a pure heart and a happy disposition, she will make him a good wife—they are to be united as soon as I, their honored best man and organist, have Lohengrin's "Bridal Chorus" set to memory.*
>
> *As I predicted and anticipated, my sandwich boards have been most effective. Astoundingly generous requests for my services are an ongoing delight.*

Mostly piano for now—but soon I hope banjo, even the Spanish guitar for which I am taking instructions from a tempestuous lady, the fire in her blood when she strums is quite overwhelming.

Here, there is much heated—sometimes even inflamed resentment, with fisticuffs and such—discussions both pro and con of the Sacco and Vanzetti debacle. For some reason the French here are as incensed as the fewer Italians who have more reason to be.

Well, now that we have Mr. Harding at the helm of our national, lagging ship, let us hope for better times—although without the ethereal Mr. Wilson I am afraid it may simply become boring.

I must stop—my impetuous lady awaits her pupil. I send you all my deepest affection—born of memories cherished, held with reverence.

Ever your devoted,

Ebberhardt, Ebbely

And for Jane, Rumpelstiltskin—for I have always known her secret name for me.

Pulling her handkerchief from her apron pocket, Hannah blew her nose—Fritz handed on the letter for the others to reread.

Another autumn—another summer gone. Having said his annual good-bye to Molly, given her the last carrot, Billy wandered over to the Geiger house to drown his farewell sorrows in milk and Hannah's sugar cookies. Soon it would be cold again—the long wait for snow and exciting holidays would begin. Now that Michael would be going to school, Billy felt threatened by the strange new world his favorite brother was about to embrace without him. Feeling deserted, Billy climbed into Hannah's lap while she peeled the apples for a brown Betty.

When Michael came home, he marched into his mother's kitchen to announce that in his opinion, school was "real Jim Dandy."

"Where did you hear such language?"

"Oh, Mama, nobody speaks English good."

"You mean *well*—nobody speaks English *well*." Jane corrected her eldest, who thought it was safer and probably prudent to continue in their at-home language of Italian.

"All the boys in my class have accents because they haven't been here very long—and the real American boys—they speak funny too. I wish Gregory wasn't dead so he could go to school with me. Today I learned one plus one is two but two plus two

is four and you know what? Cat starts with a *c* not with a *k*. Isn't that interesting?"
And Michael marched off to draw a Model T for homework.

Snakes were mended—windows corked, children bundled, coaxed to go play
outside watch their breath turn to smoke, holiday baking begun. This year Fritz and
Carl having joined a group of hunters who cut their own Christmas trees—brought
home such a lovely spruce Hannah said it was so regal in its naked state decorating
it might spoil it. But later she relented not to disappoint the children.

Proud that he was considered old enough to be given this enviable task, Billy placed
the three kings into their correct procession, laid Jesus in his bed of straw. Showing
off a little, he glanced over at Natasha in her cradle, to see if she was watching.
Much too young to really be seeing anything but her own thumb, still Zoltan's new
daughter appeared attentive which satisfied Billy's need to preen. The women brought
in Hannah's baking bounty, Michael, finally allowed to use matches, lit the candles,
Fritz placed a new platter its grooves filled with many selections of Christmas music
on the splendid Victrola, everyone sang—Zoltan and Agnes even danced. That this
would be their last time together no one could know—Hannah sensed a loss, yet
unable to find any reason why she should be troubled, pretended that she wasn't.

Early in the morning of New Year's Day, when Hannah's telephone rang she nearly
dropped the coffeepot. Ebbely had not forgotten to ring-a-ling.

"My dearest Lady, Happy New Year! Getting ready to trip the light fantastic?"

"Oh, Ebbely, please speak plain English—dis costs."

"I was."

"No, dat was your special *I am so perfect show-off talk*!"

"And *you* say to me 'dis costs'!" Ebbely was laughing.

"Now stop. Very nice of you telephoning. Here everybody is missing you—even
my special doughnuts don't know why so many left—not eaten. Oh, quick, I got
to tell you—my Victrola—it works beautiful—Fritz bought a new platter and wit
special holiday songs we all sang along!"

"Did you dance?"

"Zoltan and his Agnes—yes, my Fritz and me—no. Dere were no waltzes—just
carols."

"I will send you some new fox trot, you will adore it."

"Fox trot? What is wit de foxes suddenly?"

"No, no—fox *trot*—it's the latest dance—fast and fun!"

"Oh. You behaving?"

"Perfectly, my dear. Is Fritz there—let me speak to him."

"You got enough money for dis?"

"Yes, Hannah—put him on the telephone."

Gingerly Fritz took the earpiece, positioned himself at the mouthpiece. "Ebberhardt—I'm here. Happy New Year! How is the weather where you are?"

"Happy New Year and the weather is weather—listen—I don't want Hannah to hear you so just answer yes or no. Is Ford still at it? I mean about that madness that only Jews are responsible for all the wrongs of the world?"

"Yes."

"Has Hannah gotten hold of any of those hideous articles?"

"No."

"Thank God!"

"Yes."

Hannah pulled Fritz's arm, whispered, "What are you doing? Yes, no, yes—dat's a conversation?"

"Well, Ebberhardt, I think I better finish now. This has been a long telephone call—costing money."

"Fritz, write me—let me know what is happening—and if Hannah ever finds out what that bastard is up to you must telephone me immediately—I will send you the number of the coffeehouse I am calling from, maybe I'll be able to help."

"Yes."

"Again wit de yeses?" Hannah hissed.

"Who is there with you?"

"John and Jane and of course the children. Carl and his family came and what do you think, Zoltan and Agnes—in the motor in the snow they brought the baby, said because it's her very first Hanukah-Christmas-New Year, they wanted her to start it here with us."

"And right they are! Wish everyone a prosperous 1922 for me and to celebrate properly you have my permission to kiss your wife! *Auf Wiedersehen.*"

It was February when a great ice storm froze Michigan and made Michael angry. First his beloved school was closed down, then everyone was forbidden to leave their homes because it was too dangerous being outside. His brothers didn't mind, John with his books, Billy with his blocks were quite content, but Michael, accustomed to running over to Hannah's whenever he wanted—thought that such a short distance should be possible despite the cold. His father, also a captive of the weather, would be the one to ask. He found him in the cellar stoking the furnace.

"Papa—if I put on *all* my sweaters—all of them, maybe even *two* pants and my gloves and *two* hats—can I go to the Geiger house and not get frozed?"

"No. Everyone has been told to stay indoors."

"Even if I . . ."

"I said no, Michelino."

"Okay, Papa." Michael sighed.

"Have you nothing to do?" Knowing his father disliked idleness, Michael just nodded. "You know even some of the big ships that bring the raw ore to the Rouge can't move because they are locked in the ice of the big lake—come, I'll show you where." And Michael learned what a map was—and where within it he lived.

This year, as the commercialization of radio made its appearance, everyone talked of nothing else. How it worked no one really knew but the very idea of sound being carried on waves of air across distances then finally emerging from a box containing glass tubes that glowed—was such a startling concept that knowing the scientific intricacies of it was quite unnecessary—wonder and awe were sufficient. Soon there would be mail order crystal sets for the avid young to build at home, the marvel of a disembodied voice telling them things they had not known before. Even the unrelenting static was exciting for it too was sound coming from out of nowhere.

The very idea of maybe someday being told the latest news instead of having to read it fascinated Jane. Music, maybe even learning—would this too one day come from some place far away, fill a room with beauty and intelligence? She wondered if by next year she might have enough in her cash box to send away for a *Radio Phone Crystal Set* of her very own.

Spring hadn't quite recovered from its frozen delay when John, throwing hat, gloves and bicycle clips in all directions, stormed into the house shouting, "We are leaving! Ninnie! Where are you?" His youthful face alight—a conquering hero in his step, as he entered the kitchen, Jane saw his pride before he made his announcement. "I've been promoted! The Boss has put me in charge! I am going to build his factories for the production of our Fordsons! In six weeks we leave for Rumania!"

"I won't go!"

"Oh, yes you will! You are my wife!" The Italian language lends itself so well to such emotional conflict.

"I became your wife in order to *get* to America—not to leave it!" As the words left her mouth, Jane knew they were a mistake.

"What? What did you say?"

"I said I won't go and you can't make me!"

"Oh yes I can!" For a suspended moment John battled his wanting to do her physical harm.

"I am an American citizen, I belong here and so do the children!"

Incredulous at her violent rejection of what he considered glorious opportunity, John retorted, "We are going. My wife and sons are to accompany me, Henry Ford says so."

"Well, for once your mighty Henry Ford is not going to get what he wants!"

"Giovanna!" That tone of command, the use of her given name, silenced her. "Because of the Boss's generosity all our travel expenses, our housing, even the boys' education—everything is being paid for. As the wife of the Ford Company representative you will have a life of luxury—a maid, maybe even two . . ."

Though feeble, Jane made one last attempt, "But, I don't know Rumanian!"

"Oh, that! With your talent for languages you'll pick it up in a week—anyway it may be Egypt!"

Where? Jane never forgot that moment when her tidy life unraveled leaving her stunned and newly afraid. Would she be allowed to bring her precious sewing machine? was the first anxiety that popped into her head until she quickly chided herself for such selfishness in the face of much more serious calamities. Searching for her hat, corralling the boys, Jane hurried over to the Geiger house.

"Hannah—John is taking us back—he says in six weeks we sail!"

The Ford wives' grapevine always a swift and reliable source, Hannah was not surprised. Putting the children on the back porch to play she propelled Jane into the kitchen shutting the porch door behind her.

"Ja! I heard someting like dat. Here, sit—have some nice coffee."

"But . . . Hannah?" That sounded like a sob beginning.

"Now, Ninnie—not de end of de whole world if de Big Boss believes so much in you—he gives you his trust, makes of you a so important Boss—"

"But Rumania?!"

"Oh, is dat where? Well—dat is of course not de fanciest place in de world—for becoming de fine lady of a new Boss."

As if this visit was no different from the hundreds of others of their friendship, Hannah poured their coffee, added condensed milk to Jane's, sugar to hers, the slight tremor of her hand hidden as she stirred. Her kitchen, that symbol of constant comfort held a sudden alien silence. Knowing what she must do, that it was she who first having taken John's fledgling under her wing—now needed to let her know she could fly away, Hannah began, "Vifey—"

"Yes?" There was so much desperate need in that *yes*, for a moment it stopped Hannah from what she had to say.

"Now, child—now I will say all dis in German dat you understand so good—so no mistakes—because it is important. So . . . first and foremost—the man you love . . . no—no interruptions! Because you do and someday you will wake up and say, 'Hah! Hannah was right—she knew—she told me so a long time ago.' So—you love this man who before today was losing his dream—the dream that pulled him across the great sea; oh, it was fine for a while, for all of us it was fine, but now it is all changing. Only money and power and more money and more power—like sausages in my sister's husband's butcher shop. Very good for a business but not good for a dream. Now, all of a sudden your John has, out of the blue, been given a chance to dream all over again—in new lands, honored and protected this time by the most important motor company in the whole world—and what do you know—surprise, surprise! He wants *you*, his wife, to share it all with him. How can you even *think* of denying him?"

"But the children?"

"What about them? Just think, someday they will be men very smart who can speak many languages, know more of the world than just here our Highland Park."

"Hannah, I can't leave. I can't leave you."

"Oh—now you stop right dere—dis minute. Of course you can. You? You can do anyting! If you can survive the big influenza, for sure you can survive Rumania!"

Hannah's methods were so skilled that when John returned that evening Jane was calmed sufficiently to make logical inquiries—turn to him, discuss his plans for their departure as though this upheaval was no more to her than a summer outing to Belle Isle.

When John explained to his sons what awaited them in August—young John got his atlas—had his father trace their long journey in pencil. At first Michael too was excited over their great adventure—then thought better of it when he heard it meant leaving school. Still too young to fully understand how his childhood was about to change, Billy accepted the busy preparations, as though the packing, the general chaos, the harried to and fro, this summer like the last, a big Hanukah-Christmas was probably the reason.

At first John had planned to rent his house to a man on the line but after being told that darkies were not allowed in Highland Park—he sold it to an Armenian friend of Zoltan's, lock, stock, and barrel.

As summer progressed, for Jane the days became a blur. Packing up an existence to exist somewhere else unknown presents an uncertainty quite unique to it. For Jane, ever the willing adventurer yet in need of roots for a sense of place within her universe—the finality of packing up a home that had become a steadying frame of her life upset her more than she had thought possible. Too many good-byes, too many "take cares," too many tears. Having to leave her life Jane could school herself to endure, having to leave America and Hannah was quite another elimination. In the years to come, Jane could never precisely remember that final summer's day, luggage piled high, locomotive steam enveloping her visual memory, turning emotion opaque, sorrow defused. What did remain, haunted—Hannah's face, all control gone as she ran beside the moving train calling, "Ninnie! Write! Don't forget—write! God bless you! Kiss the children! Good-bye Vifey! Good-bye!" And then suddenly as though she had never existed—Jane lost her.

Eyes fixed on America, Jane stood by the railing of the ship that was to take them across an ocean through the Straits of Gibraltar and into the Mediterranean Sea.

Now as she was about to return from whence she had fled when but a girl, this conjured up so many childhood memories that she feared her newfound maturity might not be secure enough to combat them.

Really Giovanna after all these years what have you learned? One farewell and you are right back where you began—a willful child with no direction looking for what? And at any price? Remember, an adventure is an adventure no matter where it leads you! Taking herself in hand, she turned her back to the coastal breeze, and faced the sea.

Coming up behind her, John put an arm around her waist, pulled her against him.

"Don't be sad. We'll be back—someday. And then I'll buy us another house." He searched her face. "Okay? Tell you what—then, I *promise* I'll find one even closer to Hannah." Jane began to cry. "Tesoro, it's not good for the boys to see you crying. For them all this is a glorious adventure."

Jane blew her nose on the elegant white linen handkerchief she had made to match her traveling outfit.

"You're right, I'm sorry. It *is* a glorious adventure."

"Remember our first? It's not *that* long ago."

"Yes—I was frightened then too."

"But you didn't cry."

"Then I was frightened just of you—not of what might lie ahead or what I was leaving."

"Were you really frightened of me? Why?"

"I didn't want to be a disappointment, after all you really wanted to marry Camilla not me."

"I'm glad I didn't."

"You are?"

"Of course!" Astounded, John turned her to him. "I love you, Ninnie, don't you know that?!" Embarrassed to admit she didn't Jane shook her head. "You're a *fine* wife, Giovanna." And wishing to lighten the moment John added, "And I am very grateful that you forced me to marry you." That made her giggle.

"I didn't."

"Oh, yes you did!"

Standing close together they watched America begin to fade.

22

*W*ho was it who said, "See Naples and die"? Die from sheer relief of having arrived? Or succumb to disappointment? This overly romanticized harbor reminded Jane of a Breugel lithograph she had seen at the library, its insane chaos generated by a crazed multitude utterly convinced they were sane, here overlaid and abetted by that Italian frenzy indigenous to a port city in the south. Jane had no time to see if her first impressions of Naples could be modified for John hustled family and baggage onto the first train headed north.

Rumania, that mysterious land of somber fables, superstition and roaming wolves, in reality—though dark and somewhat brooding—left such fears undisturbed, except for one's exasperation at its lack of modernity. Its culture might be colorful at times even theatrically romanticized but for a woman fresh from industrial America with three children and a busy husband to care for Jane could happily have done without ancient trappings in exchange for a bathroom that worked, and a toilet that flushed. No longer a European, who immured in antiquity respected without reservation the old, Jane had become an American who once dissatisfied thought it only natural to fix whatever didn't work, making it better. In future years she would always travel with her private supply of handy tools and toilet paper.

Children being adaptable if their basic foundation remains intact, the boys took Rumania in their stride. Though everything and everyone was strange to them they coped—or seemed to. At least the two youngest being of an age still judgeless were content. Michael who had the tendency to discipline his feelings in order to assuage the possible guilt felt by his elders, having learned to perfect this trait through coping with the deaths of his friends—used it—fooling his parents into believing that he was not overly homesick, which he was. If anyone had thought to ask him, penetrated that perfect shield of subterfuge that only children seem to have the ultimate talent for, Michael would have sobbed out his longing for Hannah, uncles, iceman, even shaggy Molly and Highland Park. Nearly eight is not a good age to feel deserted. Though no age ever fits imposed loneliness, after three and before ten can be the worst. With years left, time given to recuperate, such hurts can be erased. That Michael had used up all the time allotted him, no one could know.

Within weeks John knew his assigned task was hopeless. After such a devastating war it was still much too early to consider building a factory let alone find enough able-bodied men left alive to work it. Leaving his family behind until new decisions could be made, John left Bucharest to consult with the men in charge of Ford's European operations in Manchester.

Jane was relieved to stay behind and wait. All the boys were just getting over heavy colds—Michael, his having settled in his chest, was still coughing, a winter crossing of the English Channel would certainly have been unwise.

She first thought it was the wind rattling the leaded windowpanes that must have awakened her, for she heard it as she woke. She felt uneasy.

"Mama . . ." The cry faint—its fear raw—Jane hurried down the corridor to the children's room. His head lolling over the side of the bed, Michael vomited, began to cry.

"Shhh, Michelino, it's alright—you can come into Mama's bed." Wrapping him in blankets carrying him close, she felt the raging heat from his body burn through into hers.

"My throat hurts," he whimpered trying to be brave then gagging, buried his face against her. As though something was blocking his windpipe, Michael was having trouble breathing.

"Michelino, here, try to drink—even if just a few drops." He tried—but it hurt too much. She sponged him down, changed him, lifted him to help his labored breathing—fought the consuming fever with the fury of mounting desperation.

He is too small to have to suffer like this. Like a frenzied bat, her thoughts flew about searching for direction. Could she leave him, run downstairs, wake somebody? No, they were the only tenants in this new apartment building—there was no one to wake—ask for help. A telephone! If only they had a telephone! She could call . . . but who? They had no friends yet, knew no one, they were still strangers in a foreign land. She didn't even know the language.

Fighting for air, Michael began to thrash—she patted, kneaded his back—it seemed to help—it calmed him a little.

The American embassy! Yes! They would understand—know a doctor—they would help—but it's the middle of the night—they are closed! Antonia! What did Antonia's father say that time when one of Teresa's sisters had the croup? Steam! Boil water for steam!

Jane ran to the small kitchen put pots of water on to boil then returned. Michael looked so small, so lost in that vast expanse of rumpled sheets. When she placed his head near the steam rising up from the pots on the floor—it helped him a little but only for a short while—as the night dragged on Michael's struggle to breathe intensified.

I can't leave him—maybe if I wrap him up and carry him outside to find somebody? No—it's freezing! It's winter, nobody is out, and where could I go? . . .

Against her Michael whimpered. Suddenly the sound of a horse's hooves on cobblestone penetrated—running to the window she flung it open—called down to a coal merchant who was passing, "DOCTOR! Get Doctoré! I need Doctor! Help, *please!*"

Startled he looked up—touched his cap and switched his horse to go faster.

Thank God! Jane's heart sang, *Thank you, God! He understood! Now a doctor will come!*

Taking Michael back into her arms she waited. She sang him songs of bluebell fields and golden sun where goats played their bells amongst mountain crags, rocked him, cleared the catarrh as best she could, kept him awake fearing that if he slept he might not wake. In that small room of impending tragedy, death hovered, watching her.

The night wore on—child and mother waited. He for an end, she for rescue. Sometime before dawn, Jane began to pray. Surely God would not forsake a child so much in need of him. A little boy so good—who possessed such magic all his own. Not wanting to prejudice her plea she begged forgiveness for her terrible sin of rejection, implored God to listen. Michael's labored breath feathered.

Daylight and Death arrived together—Jane felt its irrevocable silence and knew her child was dead.

Slowly she released the small body from her arms—laid it back onto the bed. John should have kissed him good-bye—Michael would have liked that. As though the task that awaited her needed more time in order to perform it, she stood looking down—focusing on nothing. Then, she prepared him, washed him, combed his hair, arranged his limbs, wrapped fresh sheets around him to keep him warm, oblivious as to why this should be so important to her, drew the curtains against the day, lay down beside her shrouded child and wept.

The doctor signed the death certificate, wrote *Diphtheria* in the space provided—pronounced the living children free from harm, handed the address of a reliable undertaker who understood English to the mother whose calm demeanor he judged cold and definitely unaffected by a tragedy that would have destroyed a warm and loving one.

Having found the building that housed the Central Telephone Exchange, she waited on one of the many benches while they routed her long-distance call, trying to think of how she would say it, tell John.

The morning of his return, John rushed to meet her at the mortuary. There was a body to be assigned its fate a decision to be made. In a taper-lit anteroom—its odor of intrusive formaldehyde a dour reminder of where they were and why, they faced each other as though they had never met. Having convinced herself all was her fault Jane stood before him, helpless. Reaching out John pulled her into his arms. They held each other arresting time, until she whispered, "They say we must decide."

"No coffin! I won't have my son put in a box! It's cold and dark—it frightens him—he told me . . . he . . ." and John broke—sobs draining his body he leaned against the doorframe of the undertaker's—abject misery incarnate. To bury one's child in foreign soil to which one might never return—was too wrenching a leave-taking even in death. Jane had learned this long ago from when Henrietta had left her Gloria behind, and so cremation, that procedure so often condemned by true believers, became their only solution.

For his Baptism of Fire Jane dressed him in the new suit he would have worn on the first day of school. On his return Michael resided in a delicately hammered tin urn in which he would travel the world. For the rest of her life Jane kept it with her, as duty and love combined.

Though he must have been affected if only by the absence, young John behaved as if nothing had changed. Billy, confused, searched for his brother—until he came home in his urn—after that Billy knowing that Michael was no longer lost went about being a little boy who had learned what death could do. John hid his sorrow in his work, the panacea of his life.

Where one might expect a bereaved mother to become timid, overprotective of those of her children remaining—Jane did not. As though challenging God, daring him to continue his destruction of those she loved, Jane fought him, vowed never again would she give him another chance to make it up to her. To be free was no longer simply a physical necessity—she now demanded of life an unconditional pardon of the soul. As though she had voiced *Smite me if you can—I dare you*, Jane challenged God's very existence.

Expected next in Denmark, John first moved his family to the home of his parents—outside of Turin. John's father, a proud man, accorded dominion over a prolific family—though rarely seen except at mealtimes, he ruled with an assured nonchalance often present in Italian men who believe there is no reason to exert their limitless authority until such time something of real import occurs to warrant it. His wife also a Piemontese and therefore just as respectful of class and those sought-after advantages connected with it—ran the villa, which was never referred to as a "house," the servants and anyone else within her radius of patrician interest. Celestina's pretty sister, Gina, having married well, now a fussing mother of four, divided her time between overseeing peasant nursemaids and cutting flowers for the decorating of side tables. Expending energy on anything else being far too exhausting she conserved it, this contributed to her being bored—and being boring.

In this aura of strict gentility, amidst planned flower beds, tended gravel paths that fanned out from a villa that was just weatherworn enough to make it ancestrally attractive, Jane felt like an interloper discovered in the wrong garden.

As always she blamed herself, assuming the negative that it must be she—who having little talent for being a guest made the situation uncomfortable for herself not they for her. She was aware she was being treated with as much kindness as a grieving mother could expect, yet as her grief was anger not gentle tears—how could they understand her? She was such a private person that even well-intentioned commiseration being Italian and therefore overly effusive, disturbed.

As families will, Jane was accepted as the wife of the son who though he had chosen to turn his back on the country of his birth, had made them proud by his achievements. She had added to that assessment by having produced sons. To conform, cause no rift within time-honored custom, she dressed as expected, wore funereal black. Being Jane, whose sense of fashion was acute, this was no great acquiescence on her part, black was an elegant color and it suited her.

Head to toe in mourning—every inch the acceptable Italian matron—her bobbed hair that shocked, her only individuality, Jane moved about her husband's boyhood home as if she belonged.

With language no obstacle, the boys made friends, enjoyed the freedom of a small town where they were looked upon as foreigners, a rich man's sons and therefore special.

Proud of his new position as the eldest son, young John blossomed—less withdrawn, he became approachable. It was during this time of personal transition that the exposure to papist Catholicism established its lasting beachhead on his character. The Bible became his favorite reading matter, daily prayer and regular churchgoing a part of who he would become. Billy too liked the smell of incense, the tinkle of bells that came between solemn parts but really he looked forward to Sunday churchgoing because afterwards everyone got to eat cake.

John came home for Christmas, just in time to explain to a very disappointed Billy—that no, Santa Claus had not forgotten him, had only handed on his duties to a funny-looking old crone who also could fly over rooftops—but because she used a broom that was much slower than a whole bunch of reindeer—he would have to wait for presents until she arrived on the Day of the Three Kings, which young John immediately declared was Epiphany and proceeded to give a dissertation on its religious origin. Then and there Billy decided that although Italy was okay, for a real Hanukah-Christmas, America was much much better. He did question his new grandmother why she hadn't put out the menorah—but when she scolded him saying that it was "a Jew thing" and that these terrible people had killed the Son of God—nailed him to a cross, left him to die a slow and terrible death of unspeakable agony, frightened, Billy ran from the room and never mentioned anything connected with Hannah ever again. It was his way of protecting her, from what Billy wasn't sure—only that he felt he had to.

The family being in collective mourning the arrival of the New Year hardly created a stir. Jane wondered who had danced on the icy pond, had Ebbely returned as promised—*tripped* his light fantastic with his favorite Tall Lady, had Hannah resurrected the gingerbread house for Zoltan and Agnes's little Natasha, who had placed the three kings into their correct procession now that Michael was gone? Then, she sat down to write her sad news to those she missed so far away.

Michael's ashes often drew Jane's thoughts to speculating on where he was. As God did not exist as benign harvester of souls—where was Michael's? what had become of his? She did not believe the grit of incinerated bone that had once been her child contained still his essence—yet something made her keep them by her as though afraid if she forsook them, he would be lost even more than the death that had erased him. She didn't like this unintentioned returning—this interruptive revisiting of death that she seemed to have no control over.

For John, the little urn represented a son—no longer earthbound for loving and he had come to terms with it. But then he was not the one who had heard the sound of that last strangled effort to survive—that would haunt Jane for the remainder of her life—perhaps even beyond that insidious threshold.

Grieving her way—no one was aware that she was. The inhabitants of the villa were quick to accord her courage—yet reserved their communal opinion as to Jane's capacity for motherhood. As their concept of this most revered state of womanhood equated with that of the Virgin Mary, Jane came up lacking. She knew it—sensed their polite disapproval and ignoring it, allowed them their opinion.

Having found a small sewing room set up for household repairs, as she had done often, Jane took refuge in her skill. An old but serviceable sewing machine offered her its sanctuary and she took it like a drowning man a buoyant life ring. In her new world at the top of the house—repairing the villa's linens, sewing for its inhabitants, Jane became herself again and healed, at least sufficient for existence. As her hair grew and she allowed it—so did her assimilation. The daily rhythm of structured routine created function and with it a casual contentment she did not wholly understand.

After Gina mentioned that Camilla now lived in Turin, Jane wrote her suggesting a teatime rendezvous.

They met in one of those high-class British-type tearooms that Italians seem to have such affection for—that suited this city. Once the capital of Italy, Turin exuded that pompous nobility often found in displaced monarchs who wear their crown convinced it still belongs to them.

Camilla's welcoming smile struggled to emerge from behind rouged lips in a fleshy face framed by pin curls and a baby blue felt adorned with an overly large cabbage rose. Although the thickness of her body cried for concealment—she wore what flat-chested fashion decreed and looked ridiculous thinking herself beautiful. Her life had become a parody—and her looks suited it. Jane in her perfectly tailored navy blue linen, feeling a little as though she was about to interview a new cook, sipped her coffee—and wondered what to say. Poking the straw in her lemonade as though it were a plunger—Camilla lifted eyes ringed by sad shadows surveyed her childhood friend as though she were a stranger.

"Two sons—you say?"

"Yes, and you?" Jane wondered why she had wanted so to meet Camilla again.

"Five—all girls—of course Mario is very disappointed. So important for a man to have a son. Especially if he owns a successful business." Sighing, Camilla poked the lemon slice in her glass.

"And your parents—your brothers and sisters—all well, I hope?" Jane asked remembering.

"Mama died—a growth they said in her female parts—Papa remarried soon after. A widow who had her eyes on him. Remember my eldest sister? The one who wanted to be a nun like poor Teresa? Well, she was made pregnant at a fiesta—so she had to be married off Papa said. But the rest of us, we all got married correctly in a church—some are happy—some are not. Some died from the influenza. Of the boys, Stephano, the eldest, ran away to sea. We don't know what happened to him. Franco, the youngest became a Dominican—goes around preaching poverty—Mama before she died was very upset. She kept saying, 'If God had wanted only poverty he would not have sanctioned the lifestyle of the Holy Father and the riches of the Vatican.' It shocked me to hear this—but when I brought this up in the confessional I was absolved of 'censure'—so I said my beads and then I felt relieved. Yet, I often wonder if Mama's affliction wasn't visited upon her as punishment." Jane swallowed her coffee to drown the smile lurking to emerge. "Like Papa, my husband has a woman. He goes there twice a week—sometimes more. It is expected—and I don't mind—I have enough to do—I have a big house to run—one has to watch the maids like a fox!" Snatching a cream puff off a passing tray Camilla stuffed it into her mouth.

"What exactly is your husband's business?" Jane asked, trying to be polite.

"He deals in the latest bathroom fixtures." The tip of her tongue recapturing a dollup of errant cream, Camilla continued, "Of course nothing shoddy, only the latest designs. We own two stores and by the first of next year we will have another in the most prominent section of the city. Last summer we had our very own seaside apartment in Viareggio, where only the best people go. And Giovanni? . . . Still a happy mechanic?"

"He builds and establishes new factories for the Henry Ford Motor Company," retorted Jane.

"Oh—" Camilla's pout hadn't changed from how Jane remembered it from when she was seventeen and in a snit. "Well, I really should be going. Julietta and Faustina have a piano lesson."

"Wait—please—I can't find Teresa—do you know where she is?"

"Oh, I heard she was somewhere in France—no . . . maybe it was Belgium, I really haven't the slightest idea. I know that Antonia—she is still in Milano with some man—but Teresa—who knows?" This last was said with such an intonation of *and who cares?* that Jane wanted to slap her. "I must go—it was really a delight to see you again Giovanna, after all these years. Maybe the next time you are in Torino—we must all get together—perhaps you can join us for one of our dinners—we entertain a great deal—it is so important in business you know. Mario is considering going into politics. He thinks his friend Benito Mussolini, only he can bring our country back to the glory of the Caesars."

Jane paid the check, while Camilla objected in that exaggerated, effusive denial that usually denotes a serious lack of sufficient funds to do so, then quickly capitulated with the time-honored "Well, if you insist! And now, I must run. Give Giovanni a little kiss from me—just for old time's sake—nothing serious!" She giggled, "*Ciao!*"

And Camilla heaved her spreading body off the café chair and waddled off in the direction of the tram stop.

Letters from Ebbely—one for Jane, the other for John forwarded from Rumania arrived in Italy in late July. As they had been written before receiving the news of Michael's death—they were filled with snippets of news not condolences.

> *My Dear Child,*
>
> *I hope this finds you well despite lascivious gypsies and salivating wolves that have a tendency to circle innocent damsels lusting for their blood in the flickering light of lonely campfires in deep, dark forests. Composing this, I've frightened myself. Still do be careful—Rumanians, even those not of gypsy lineage are notorious scoundrels as everyone knows.*
>
> *This is but a short epistle to inform you that all goes well with your so humble servant. I play, they applaud, I am paid, then partake of a succulent repast superbly prepared by my employer and then I am off to welcome Morpheus. A repetitive existence but one that having chosen it over all others, satisfies at least that part of me that craves attention. I herewith enclose my address in case you should wish to send me news from that far off continent where your husband transported you despite our wails of woe.*
>
> *Remember me to those delightful sons. I am as ever your devoted friend,*
> *Ebbely*

> *Dear John,*
>
> *Here all is as expected. Life is lived as though a beginning and an end are unnecessary. It takes a great deal of energy to live in the moment and so I am usually exhausted.*
>
> *Our brave soldier postman having succumbed to the tall tales told of waiting wealth, took his bride and left to pan for gold amidst the rugged rocks of some heathen state out West. A one-armed prospector he was determined*

to be and nothing I could say could dissuade him. I really do not know how I shall ever explain this to dear Hannah—who will surely blame me for not doing my proper guardian duty by her sad lothario.

As for me, I now play the Spanish guitar with such skill that I even amaze myself and getting recompensed for enjoying myself, that astounds me even more.

By the way, thought you might like to know, the fair Evangeline has become a Mama. On the ninth of April she gave birth to a bouncing baby boy that the Flivver King simply dotes on. So much so, and so publicly that gossip abounds. They say he is so besotted Ford is in constant attendance at the Dahlinger spread, lavishes gifts upon the babe as though it were his very own. Even insisted the boy have the cradle he himself occupied. As you can readily imagine not only Detroit, the whole of Michigan is buzzing. Evangeline named the boy John—known far and wide as Johnny—a most interesting choice, wouldn't you agree?

I am afraid that what we all feared, tried to hide was all for naught. Hannah read one of Ford's venomous tirades and took to her bed. As I had instructed Fritz to telephone me if and when such a day came—he did and I spoke to her at length hoping to cushion not only her shock but her understandable fear. With a rejuvenated Ku Klux Klan marching to its racist drummer and Ford to his—I have the distinct feeling the time may not be too far off when the Geigers will perhaps make the once inconceivable decision and leave this country for their less prejudiced homeland.

What about this new prime minister in Italy? Isn't he the one who led the fascist on their march on Rome? That's a strange bedfellow for King Emmanuel. Over in Germany it seems no better but at least there that Austrian rabble-rouser is safely in jail. Here anything political happening in Europe is hidden on the back pages—if then. But how is it there? Do let me know, for it seems to me that the pot is beginning to simmer all over again despite a so recent war won.

You are missed dear John, you are sorely missed for many reasons.

As ever,

Ebbely

While in England having been made even more aware of the political situation developing within Italy on his return, John confronted his father in his study.

"Damnit! Why wasn't I told?"

As she passed the closed door hearing John's anger, Jane stopped to listen.

"Told? Told you what?" John's father sounded equally annoyed.

"The riots! Last year you had riots—the Socialists, the Bolsheviks—right here in Torino—and a march on Rome by radicals calling themselves Fasci di Combattimento—and no one thinks of writing me about it? My God! What is the matter with this country? Are you all so used to political chaos that no one gives a damn anymore?"

"Don't use that tone with me. I am still your father."

"Well then if you insist, as a *father* it was your duty to warn me before I took my wife and children away from the safety of America."

"Safety? You have Bolsheviks, you have Socialists. You have strikes."

"Ah, but being a democracy we still choose our leaders."

"So do we."

"You may think you do—but achieving political power through organized violence, intimidation even murder can't survive in a true democracy."

"So now the country of your birth means nothing to you?"

"Don't be ridiculous! I love Italy. If I didn't I wouldn't mind it going down the shit hole, the way it is."

Looking for a match to light his cigarette, John's father remarked, "You know, Giovanni, America has made you coarse."

"Not coarse, Papa . . ." John offered him a light, "only honest. True democracies have a way of fostering that."

"You do know that these Fascistas are now a recognized party and that their leader is our respected prime minister."

"Oh, I know. Remember I am about to build an American factory—financed by an American company in a country run by Fascists who now demand that grown men no longer shake hands but salute each other as if they are playing at being Roman soldiers. How I'm going to train men to work a moving assembly line who every time a Fascista walks by have to raise an arm—is just one of the thousands of impossible problems that your—what do they call this Mussolini now?"

"Il Duce and don't think you can just dismiss him. He says he will bring discipline and order—and even you will have to admit that this is what Italy needs now. We must clean house—become a united country for the good of the people."

As though their discussion was at an end, John's father put on his coat he had draped over the back of a chair.

"Through a revolution?"

"What? What are you talking about now?"

"Control, Papa. Control. Control is power and power is control—that's what these Fascists are after. Make the Poplulari, the Catholics, perhaps even the Vatican dance to your tune and *only* your tune and what you have is ultimate power. I have seen it for myself and I know."

"You are exaggerating as you have always done whenever you can't get your way."

"I thought coming back would be exciting. A positive challenge, a chance to demonstrate American excellence, renew confidence after a terrible war in the dependable abilities of an Italian labor force. But all I see is that besides the killing, the war achieved nothing. Nothing has changed—it's still the same old, never-ending political shit!"

"I told you I won't have this kind of language in my presence."

Sensing John was about to storm out of the room Jane fled.

The chestnuts were coming into their special season when John returned from England this time with news that they would be moving to the far-off city of Trieste that overlooked the Adriatic Sea.

"I found a nice house. It sits on a bluff—from the front door you can see the sea and there are climbing roses and a fence around the garden where Billy can play and John will be able to walk to school."

To be mistress of her own house again—Jane would have happily gone to Timbuktu. Trunks were repacked—farewells said—and John prepared to shepherd his flock across Italy.

Trieste, that beauty queen serving many loyalties, conquered by many, belonging to none, having been a sought-after pawn of war had been returned to Italy in 1919 as war booty for having chosen to cast its lot with the winning side. Its Austro-Hungarian Empire past having imparted a certain sophistication, where one might expect a major seaport to be rough and ready, Trieste behaved as though its acclaimed position on the Adriatic was solely due to the imposing perfection of its coastline—the elegance of a harbor adorned by buildings reminiscent of Roman glory embellished by the Greeks. Just as Venice, its glorious cousin across the water, anything as mundane as trade seemed but a sideline to its existence.

Though small their little house was comfortable—in the summertime its shaded garden a perfumed pleasure. It seemed in no time at all—it felt like a home.

During these years like the sea below, Jane's life seemed to take on the rhythm of the sea. Young John started school, then it was Billy's turn to feel grown-up. Because their daily language was now Italian, Jane decreed that now their at-home language would be English. Billy was particularly pleased with that new rule. Through the kindness of Agnes and her talent for scrounging, Jane and the boys received a steady supply of books in English to read and be read to. Her librarian talents challenged by what would interest growing children as well as a homesick mother—some Edith Wharton arrived, a little O. Henry, Poe and London for the boys and Mark Twain for all of them. It was fortunate that she did for it would be many years before the boys would once again face American schooling and by then having been exposed to only English literature, without Zoltan's Agnes, Jane's son's would not have known their own country's masters.

Ebbely's letters together with news snippets from Hannah and Agnes kept Jane from losing touch with America. What intrigued her often were the different perceptions—of three such opposites when writing giving their opinion on like subjects. Mentioning the recent publication of Henry Ford's autobiography, Agnes referred to it as "not at all well written," commented as to its lack of literary quality, while Ebbely concluded that "after the boycott of the Jewish Community of the carmaker's Model T, probably someone in his public relations office had the bright idea to polish Ford's somewhat tarnished image by refocusing the public on his rural beginnings and the hero of the common man." A disenchanted Hannah simply ignored it as she now did the man she once had respected—even idolized.

Often in the evenings after supper John would share his letters with Jane—and she hers.

Peter's were always centered on the latest improvements of the Model T, his unbridled enthusiasm of the latest, the balloon tire took up two whole pages that ended with the proud remark "of course our Lizzie is the only motor car in the whole wide world who has 'em!" Carl too mentioned such possible innovations as "wipers" that when it rained could wipe the windshield, an idea for a mirror for seeing to the rear, even a light that would indicate whenever their Tin Lizzie stopped. He wanted to know what conditions were like in Europe—how the building was going, how soon production could begin and what John thought of the men; while his wife informed Jane that Hudson's Department Store had unfurled the biggest American flag ever made and that all of Detroit was agog.

Like Ebbely, Zoltan was mostly interested in the political climate—but even he could not resist a little bragging about the little machine they all loved so well . . . that to celebrate the fifteen millionth Model T built, a transcontinental publicity trip on the great Lincoln Highway was being organized with *15,000,000* emblazed on the side of Lizzie's black body in thick white paint.

Having heard of Michael's death, Rudy had written his deep sorrow then added the news that Ford was preparing to build *aeroplanes* including a Ford Airport to fly them from. The news of a five-day workweek everyone celebrated. The Prince of Wales had actually paid a royal visit to Highland Park and the Ford Company having bought out Leland Motors—was now in possession of their magnificent Lincoln, truly a car for the most uncommon man.

Despite the invigorating challenges and subsequent rewards of his new position, there were times when John felt he might have made the wrong choice by accepting Henry Ford's promotion—then reminding himself that such a choice had actually never been offered him, he quickly schooled his budding frustration and got back to work.

Removed as they were from the daily political turmoil that was turning the rest of Italy into a Fascist dictatorship, for Jane these first years in Trieste held a certain benign unawareness until Billy was old enough for fourth grade and rebelled. Well, not actually rebelled but put up a mighty fine fight against the latest dictum—having to wear the regulation black shirt to school. The Roman salute—that he didn't mind so much . . . it had a history and seemed brave—but the symbolic black shirt; *that* he hated. Of course it didn't help his case that his brother wore anything even remotely connected with Fascism, with obvious pride and flourish.

At first Jane reprimanded her far too outspoken son—then tried to explain the rituals insisted upon by Mussolini, whom she secretly objected to.

"Billy, you know what a king is?"

"Of course, Mama, he's the Big Boss, like Mr. Ford."

Jane hesitated, wondering if she should tackle *that* misconception, then deciding that one could wait, went on, "Well, here in this country there is also a Big Boss, who wants everybody to do exactly what he says and gets very angry if they don't."

Interested, Billy asked, "And he is the one who wants scratchy black shirts?"

"Yes."

"Why?"

"Well, I suppose—it's like soldiers. They always have to wear what others tell them they must."

"If I wear my black shirt I'll be a soldier?"

"No—no one can make you *be* a soldier—your black shirt will only make you look like one."

"And then the Boss will not be angry?"

"And your teacher won't get into trouble."

"But it's hot!" Billy stamped his foot.

"But it is now the law—and so you will obey," countered his mother.

"Why? Why is it the law?"

Already dressed for school, John, now a self-assured eleven-year-old, entered the room.

"Because, stupid! The leader of the ruling Fascist Party has ordered it."

"Okay if you're so smart—what's a Fascist?" Billy challenged.

Eager, John rose to the test. "A Fascist is the best, the strongest, the bravest soldier 'for our glorious cause.'"

Adjusting Billy's schoolbag on his back, Jane remained noncommittal.

"I'm not a soldier! Mama said so!" retorted Billy.

"Yes you are—every boy is—Il Duce says so . . ."

"John—you know what?"

"What?"

"You're stupid!" And knowing his brother would hit him, Billy ran out of the room.

The very next day Billy had another problem.

"Mama?"

"Yes?" In a mood of frustration against the coastal winds, Jane was tying up the rampant roses for what seemed to be the hundredth time.

"Mama, is John going to feed me castor oil if I don't do what he says?"

"Feed you? What *are* you talking about?"

"Put a big hose into my mouth so he can pour castor oil down my throat!" Billy sounded exasperated with his mother's innocence.

"I have never heard of such nonsense! Of course he isn't! I know your brother often teases you—but he is not cruel."

"Well, he says that's how they do it to everybody. If you don't do what the Fascists say, then you get a liter of castor oil pumped into you. So? If I don't do what he says will he do it to me?"

"He better not try! He won't be able to sit for a week! No—a month!"

Satisfied he had gained protection—Billy left for school.

Overseeing the construction of Ford's Trieste plant, John was seldom home to aid Jane in regulating these disputes between her sons, defuse the rising animosity developing between them. Not a weak mother or an ineffectual one, though Jane was strict—she lacked the intuitiveness necessary to understand what lay beneath a child's exterior behavior and so she punished what she perceived as punishable without involving her intellect for understanding its deeper cause.

While Billy continually challenged and John resented and smoldered, the brothers' lifelong misunderstanding of each other took root and grew—later, when matured, it would separate them.

Her allowance more than ample, the boys now relegated to a strict uniform, her personal wardrobe replete, no ready clientele requiring her seamstress skills, Jane sat in her little garden at a loss for what to do. Of course there was housework, the children's homework, marketing, cooking and other such necessary tasks required and expected of a wife and mother—but these being rote had never been enough to exhaust a woman like Jane. As much as John craved challenge she needed reasons to justify indulging her creativity.

Hannah's letters always in German that she maintained was done on purpose so that Jane wouldn't forget, were always full of news. When in 1928 Herbert Hoover was elected president, she lamented that her first-time vote had done little to save America from a Republican who maybe could make up nice sayings like those he did in wartime about carp and eating apples down to the core—but such a talent was *that* enough to run a country? They should have made that nice-looking young man who flew that aeroplane all alone across the ocean—him they should have elected. But then with a name like Lindbergh maybe they thought he was Jewish? She wished Jane could hear her favorite new song. Everybody was singing it— even Ebbely when he ring-a-linged had said he was learning to play "I Found A Million Dollar Baby in a Five-and-Ten-Cent Store" on the piano and did Ninnie remember the first time they had traveled into the big city and she, Hannah, had pointed out a five-and-ten-cent store? Did she remember that day? There were always sections of Hannah's letters that made Jane stop reading to blow her nose.

She was so lonely for Hannah that sometimes the days seemed endless—filled with nothing but memories best left alone, avoided before they could cause further harm. After a while even the writing of letters back became inhibiting—for her news was repetitive, her longings already too well known.

It was a sad day when the news arrived that the great assembly lines were stopped—Highland Park shut down for retooling for the future production of a new king of the road—the Ford Model A. Oh, they had known the day would have to come, that this would become necessary. Their Tin Lizzie had reigned so long—she could no longer compete in the mighty automotive market that she had spawned, that had developed because of her unique excellence, her loyalty, her indomitable courage, the enduring symbol of a nation of common men forging their dream of personal freedom.

Fritz wrote of a lady in New Jersey who was so upset at the Model T's demise that she had bought seven new Lizzies as reserve for her future existence. Although Ford of England would be producing the T for a little while longer, still John felt his youth so entwined with the T's fate and mourned a little for the both of them.

In her pretty garden—writing endless letters to Teresa that were never answered or returned, Jane floundering, began to feel sorry for herself when in the spring of 1929 John came home and announced that as his work was done, they would be moving to Turkey.

"We are getting the hell out of Italy! Thank God for the British—they know what's coming . . ."

Having recovered sufficiently to speak, Jane asked, "What? What is coming?"

"Another war Goddamnit! Or another revolution—whichever comes first."

"John—you can't be serious."

"Oh, it will come—it may take a few years, but it will come—another bloodbath and for what? Look what's happening here—I told them as soon as I'm done I want my family out of Italy! Even Turks are better than strutting Fascists!"

"The boys—their school . . ."

"That's the best part—now they will be able to go to an English school—get a *real* British education—the best in the world!"

"But I'm not so sure of John—he sort of hero worships his Il Duce."

"So I've noticed and that's one of the reasons . . ." John let the rest of that thought evaporate. "No more black shirts. From now on my sons wear blazers."

Jane laughed.

"Oh—if for no other reason Billy will love Turkey! Where are we going to live?"

"Constantinople."

Jane nodded and started for the kitchen.

"Ninnie . . ."

"Yes?"

He came up to her, holding her shoulders turned her towards him. "You are one in a million."

"I am?"

"Any other woman would have thrown a fit."

"Why, for heaven's sake?"

"Another house, another move, another country, another language, another life. But you—you take it all in your stride, without a single complaint."

"Oh, that." The warmth of his touch through her summer blouse made her breathless. "Where you go—I go. That was our bargain."

23

Constantinople once the suspected repository of the Holy Grail, this glorious city of ancient mosques, synagogues and Christian churches—seemed to have acquired that assured worldliness that only centuries of assimilation of many rulers and many religions can foster. Whereas the Ottoman Empire had given it power, the Byzantine its culture, its unique geography outdid them all. Lying on both shores of the Bosporus Strait that divides Europe from Asia Minor, allowing the waters of the Black Sea to join those of the Sea of Marmara that eventually find their way to the Mediterranean, this Scheherazade city of soaring domes and spindle minarets adds another breathtaking jewel of its own to its already laden crown—that of light.

Leaning out of the window of the company automobile that had met them at the railway station, at the sight of the Blue Mosque Jane caught her breath and didn't exhale again until they arrived at their destination. The British, those most practiced colonizers know how to take care of their own, Ford of England now being John's immediate employer, their new home was a rooftop apartment complete with cook, maid and cooling terrace from which one could view the quicksilver sheen of the Bosporus by moonlight.

Within hours of their arrival, John with his new mentor Mr. Thornhill Cooper, whom Jane took an immediate liking to because in his so gentlemanly way he reminded her of Jimmy Weatherby, left to inspect the chosen site for the new assembly plant.

Those first weeks in this glorious city were magical. Everything about it was exciting, unusual, intriguing—its overwhelming opulence at moments hypnotic. With John preoccupied by the demands of his work—a sort of camaraderie emerged between Jane and her sons. Her enthusiasm, her avid interest in all things new, her love of learning matching theirs—together they explored this new and exciting city. All being natural linguists soon they knew enough conversational Turkish to venture even further—take short trips afield, board the passenger boats that meandered up and down the Bosporus like crowded trolleys along Detroit's Woodward Avenue, saw the famous tulip parks on the Asian side, the Golden Horn, considered the most beautiful natural harbor in the world, on the European side, the magnificent palaces of the many sultans, the vast rose fields—Turkey's main export. By the time school was to begin, these three intrepid adventurers were well versed, knew how to buy a precious drink of water from the water vendors that moved within the milling crowds their silvered tanks strapped to their backs, could recognize an intricate mosaic of the twelfth century from one of the fourteenth—could even tell time from the echoing calls to prayer from filigreed minarets.

When it was time for the boys to be registered at their school they were fitted for that time-honored British schoolboy uniform of gray flannel knee pants and crest-adorned navy blue blazer. The only concession for being in Turkey was that the usual obligatory tie and thick knee socks were omitted because of the heat.

Young John now had a bedroom of his own, created within it his own universe and was marginally content, while Billy having discovered halva was ecstatic. After she discovered how much he enjoyed Turkish delicacies, Selma, their cook, became a sort of surrogate Hannah. Whenever Billy told her in his halting Turkish that a particular dish was even better than the one she had made for him before, she preened. In no time at all it seemed she cooked for him exclusively—the other members of the family she fed—but her Billy, him she catered. When he came home from school, böreks—little paper-thin pastry pockets filled with spinach or meat, waited for him, baklava dripping in rose syrup, dimpled pastry balls with clotted cream, powdered Turkish sweetmeats covered in pistachio nuts, thick golden humus, blackest figs fresh from the street vendor.

Early mornings in Constantinople were *especially* exciting. The din of street vendors hawking their wares filled the air already pungent with the powerful aromas of just ground coffee. When the bread vendor, his tall pole stacked high with breads in the shape of small Christmas wreaths, shouted, "*Simit,*" Jane ran out, always the first of her apartment block to buy those delicious sun-warmed circles covered in freshly roasted sesame seeds. The daily purchase of yogurt—that took skill and strict concentration. Jane and the boys would wait for that special singsong call, then quickly lower a basket containing a bowl, their order, and correct change down to the street, where the yogurt man would slice their required amount off a block of shimmering, quivering solidified milk, place it into the basket, tug on the rope, call up to his customer to haul it back up. Rarely did this unique yogurt so pure, so delectable make it to the kitchen icebox.

With John completely occupied, the boys being educated by the most elitist form of education in the civilized world, a staff running her home far better than she ever could—Jane was free to do whatever took her fancy—and at any given moment. A heady position to be in—if one knows one's fancy. With money now no object, Jane went exploring the Grand Bazaar and shopped. In this true Aladdin's cave she wandered enchanted and splurged. Like a drunk after the first forbidden drink— she reveled in the euphoria of irrational self-indulgence—then, sated, looked about her impulsive purchases with concern knowing she would now have to actually do something with them.

Jane who never enjoyed cooking—often astounded by Hannah's undying love of it—now under the influence of a visit to the endless spice bazaars embraced the exotic culinary history of Turkey that melded the flavors of Syria, Greece, Arabia, Jewish Palestine, Persia, Armenia and most of its neighboring Bulgaria into its daily repertoire. She acquired a large selection of traditional receptacles to serve them, do honor to their ancient histories. As her collection of decorative plates, bowls and platters for simit, pilâr, taramasalata, yufka, halva, baklava and that truly superlative Turkish yogurt grew, so did her historical knowledge.

Now accepted within the exclusive circle of the reigning British colony, Jane was expected and complied in attending their numerous gatherings for tea and bridge. Especially appreciated for the obvious dedication to the success of their many bazaars, her beautifully stitched handkerchiefs, tea napkins and lace doilies were prized. Courting social status Jane enjoyed being so magnanimously accepted by these ladies of the British upper class. Though at times she found their circle rather insular, even antiquated—the nonarrival of a shipment of a Fortnum & Mason chest of tea could cause vapors of alarming proportion—still by and large, these were valiant women far from country gardens, doting nannies and secured pomposity, tending to husbands in a *heathen* country with noteworthy fortitude. To fit, to become acceptable, Jane took note of their rigid code of expected attire by copying it—the small fashionable changes she incorporated, when noticed, were praised and quickly envied. Some ladies even had the temerity to inquire if the Italian woman in their midst, having so skillfully managed to produce her wardrobe, would consider improving the less than perfect examples of their local seamstresses' efforts. By the end of her second year in Constantinople, Jane's dressmaking business was flourishing. Not wishing to exchange her position of club lady for that of employee, Jane let it be known that any recompense for her sewing skills should be given to the ladies' charitable causes.

When finally assembled, Jane's Turkish *Salon* as it became known by one and all, could have done a sultan proud. A bit theatrical, though being Ottoman it couldn't help but be—whenever Jane entertained within its draped silks and harem splendor, the ladies of the British colony sipping thick sweetened coffee from tiny gold-encrusted cups, their fingers sticky from honey-drenched baklava, being offered rose water in alabaster to rinse them in—came away from such cordial visits with nothing but praise for this most interesting American lady who not only had become proficient in that most difficult language of the new Republic of Turkey but had diligently acquired a most profound knowledge of its ancient history and tradition.

Yet aware they might be ridiculed the ladies omitted to relate their fascination with Jane's aptitude for fortune telling. How skillful she was, when their tiny coffee cups emptied—only the thick residue remaining—she, having learned the time-honored Turkish procedure, took them, inverted them onto the saucer, turned them three times in a slow clockwise motion . . . then lifting them carefully could read the black shapes that had formed inside—interpret their meaning.

Without real friends or observant husband, Jane, forever seeking self-betterment, now entered that period of her life when choosing the wrong direction seemed to her the right one.

Unconditional belonging became more important than choice, to be thought of as a grand lady more important than being one. She acquired the trappings of beauty parlor hair, a perfect silver fox, shoes made to order of the finest black and white calf, an expensive milliner's creation its small veil giving it a tantalizing slant and a lover's interest, for having made herself a most becoming riding habit for fashionable morning canters under the watchful and appreciative gaze of a handsome riding instructor—their few encounters in the taproom were brief and wholly unemotional as to love. Not shocked at herself—more surprised—this interlude gave Jane an added dimension, an awareness of her gender, for the first time completely separate from her status as acquired wife-mother. Being a party to illicit passion was so foreign to her that at first she did not recognize it as such. Being wanted by one who yet attracts is the elixir of women. Whether consummated or merely anticipated—it is the wanting that attracts and when cloaked in romance—irresistible. For some reason she could not explain to herself she suddenly felt attractive. A most startling realization for one who knew she was plain.

Jane's excursion into forbidden territory lasted until John's return and then was done.

There was an aliveness about her that John had never noticed before. An awareness of herself as a female that intrigued, enticed. He wanted to touch her as though she were an unknown landscape to explore. She was his accustomed wife yet all at once had recaptured a mystery that she had never even possessed.

Jane, sensing his interest was confused by it—it disturbed her guilt—making it into a means to an end she had never expected, was uncertain if she had ever wished it at all. He made love to her that first night and she responded with abandon that captivated him beyond questioning its origin. For her it was as though she had yearned for him without her sensing its need. Now the hands that caressed her were familiar—their touch a homecoming, passion became love and with it, safety. Jane had never thought of copulation as a beginning process, the act itself as being more than just a purely physical progression to a physical climax—then when reached—an automatic retreat back into oneself, emotion untouched. That she could have been so completely wrong astounded her—that so long ago Hannah had been right did not.

As with many marriages based on logic instead of love—passion once ignited by an outsider now served to erase the years of accepted companionship, replacing it with a willingness to love, to become vulnerable to another. For Jane sex became beautiful and the man who had married her knew how to harness its beauty.

If Jane had been more cathartic she might have ruined it with guilt-ridden shame. As it was, she flung herself into the rapture of being shameless without regret. He never questioned, she never confessed. They loved each other and were in love. The age of noncommunicative exposure of self had its advantages. After all, there is nothing more stimulating to a mired relationship than a satisfactory sojourn outside of it. Like an electrical charge it jump-starts sagging sensibilities to once again be willing to appreciate what one already has. If there is love and if one doesn't kill the effect by confession first or discussing it to death in order to clear one's conscience or be magnanimously forgiven—everything's fine. The children enjoyed it too. For them their mother was less strict—her criticism less frequent—a new leniency in her approach to mothering, and now most evenings their father came home in time for supper.

As this marriage meandered through the time mazes that filter emotions, theirs became a quiet love, one of those rare unions that had within its passions a peace; as though once born and believed, love so assured needed no further proofing. Rarely understood except perhaps by those in love with God, in whatever guise their surrender requires Him to be—such love once recognized, its utter truth accepted, exists—no further reconfirmation is necessary; it simply *is*. Possibly, the only force that can and does do battle with the planned forgetfulness of death and most often wins despite it.

It was in Constantinople that Billy too fell in love. It was one of those perfect loves of sighs from afar that valentines are made of. Even her name suited this pure, untouched, untarnished romance. The object of Billy's first adoration was called Miss Peach and she was his teacher. This English schoolmarm must have been truly wonderful for he never forgot her—kept her close, as gently harbored when grown as when he was just a boy, daydreaming in class.

Young John, now referred to as John Jr., though still resentful at having to leave Italy, excelled in school—became a leader within those student groups that attracted boys with opinions judged radical by others.

Cricket and rugby were the sports everyone wanted to excel in. Some like Billy played excellent tennis hoping to someday captain the school team.

Appreciated and respected, John was happy in his work. Despite being involved with his duties in Turkey his talents and expertise were often solicited for the new assembly plant being erected for Ford of England, this one in Degenham. At times it seemed he was forever in a hurry to catch a train to somewhere.

When by decree Constantinople was renamed Istanbul no one who lived there took the slightest notice. Particularly the reigning British colony, who thought it an affront, blamed President Kemal and his young republic for trying to modernize a city that by its so glorious antiquity represented all that Turkey was, had been and should remain to the outside world. That image of being removed from the rest of the world was a pervasive norm in that part of the globe. Back in America the Great Depression was beginning its terrible journey—yet on the cusp of Asia Minor every day seemed to overflow with riches to be savored, enjoyed, held dear, remembered forever. If it hadn't been for letters from home, no one would have been the wiser.

Zoltan wrote informing them that Henry Ford had stated publicly that hard times were a wholesome thing, a purge against the debauchery of the Jazz Age, then commanded his workers, who were now forced to work below the celebrated five-dollars-a-day standard—to go plant their own food on his four-thousand-acre farm.

. . . because of this royal decree and because everyone is frightened of losing their jobs some are actually doing just that. Secretly they call these plots

shotgun gardens. Every day now we hear of another suicide and the Boss, he tells them to eat more vegetables! Of course with the unprecedented success of our new Model A, even our Lizzie didn't have that at first, Ford is once again king of the open road and he knows it. We know it was Edsel who forced him to finally bring a new model to the marketplace but of course he will never be allowed the credit he so deserves. Times are really bad over here—newspapers are now called "Hoover Blankets" because so many homeless men use them as cover to keep from freezing to death.

In his letters, Carl too spoke mostly of what was happening—worried for the country as well as his continued employment with Ford he mentioned that the "Cork Towners, those Irish ruffians always such troublemakers" were forming unions and he suspected had placed informers in the Ford railroad yards because federal Prohibition agents were staging too many successful raids at the plant. He added that although no one knew for certain what had happened to Stan, he had heard from a reliable source, that he could have been among the victims of a shoot-out between rival bootleggers that had occurred in Chicago on Valentine's Day, because the very next day, Serafina was seen wearing widow's weeds accompanied by their son and most of her uncles, had left to return to Palermo.

Letters were the threads that connected Jane's new home with the only one she called home. After hearing of Michael's death, Ebbely had taken on the task of being amusing when writing Jane saving anything disturbing for those letters he addressed only to John. Sometimes, at breakfast when John was home, Jane enjoyed reading passages from Ebbely's latest.

"John, listen to this . . . 'Oh, dear, oh dear how the mighty have fallen! Our Lizzie—our goddess of the muck and mire—our heroine of the oh so common man—gone—abandoned—forever lost to progress, greed and ever pallid tomorrows . . .'" Jane laughed. "Isn't Ebbely wonderful! I do so love his exaggerated use of language!"

"Still, there's much hidden within that exaggeration."

"You noticed?"

"Of course. I miss him."

"So do I. Do you think he is really happy in his New Orleans?"

"Why do you ask? You think he isn't?"

"It's hard to explain—sometimes I think he sounds too happy, as if by trying to convince us he is hoping to convince himself. Do you ever feel that?"

"Often—that's very astute of you, Ninnie."

Basking in his approval, Jane poured John his morning coffee. "In his letters to you, John, does he ever say anything . . ."

"No—his life, that's for you, for political and economic chaos, it's me. He doesn't like what is happening in Germany and neither do I—told me that Mussolini is a bigger gangster than a hundred Al Capones put together which I also agree with. Over the years I have learned that our Ebberhardt is right about everything and that I usually agree with him." John finished his coffee. "Ninnie, they are having some timing problems in Cologne that I have been asked to check on—so I'll be leaving for Germany by the end of the week. I shouldn't be gone for too long."

"Will you be needing your good blue suit?"

"Probably—you know the Germans—business discussions in restaurants over food is their specialty. Oh, and I'll need those special shirts you made for me with the French cuffs—I find the Germans rate a man's success by his cuff links. Have I got any worthy of them?"

"No, but Mrs. Cooper showed me the store that carries them."

"The Coopers like you."

"I'm glad—because I like them."

John kissed her "I'll be home for supper" and left.

In his first-class compartment on the Orient Express John read the letter from Fritz that had arrived just that morning.

Dear John,

We are no longer needed—the Boss has forsaken us and Highland Park. That it should come to this—after all the years, after all we accomplished together is so unbelievable that I cannot believe it. Everywhere men, good, hardworking men, men we know, we trusted, who gave more than just good work, gave also their loyalty to Mr. Ford and his company—now are good listeners to the straw bosses who talk strikes, and only because they are hungry and afraid. Suddenly our Peter was let go—but nobody knows really why—but everyone thinks probably because here we will not be assembling anymore—just making parts, and it seems Highland Park men are not wanted at the Rouge. Who knows? Carl, Zoltan and me—we have talked a lot about the new orders and changes, and we think maybe we should go too before, you know, before it's too late and maybe we lose our jobs too. Carl talks of taking his family— getting a job with Buick and moving to Flint. Zoltan, with Natasha still so young and Agnes again in the family way—says he has to hang on—he has no choice—and me? Well Hannah and me—after long talks and much pro and cons—we have decided to go back where we come from, maybe even safe. I have enough saved up to give my wife not maybe an American luxury life—but a nice comfortable one until I find good work again and the money we get for the house will help for the journey, and finding a small house with a garden maybe near her sister. So, dear friend, this is my news—sad and good together. Sad because a so special dream and a wonderful American life must be ended—good because as Hannah says, "you and your Jane and those beloved boys won't be so far away anymore" and that is why Hannah cried not so very much after we decided. Of course I will let you know when all is arranged.

Your friend,

Fritz

On his return from Germany, John—tired and strangely angry—let off steam in the safety of his home.

"Ninnie, the world is going crazy! Back home bread lines and soup kitchens! Now wild inflation in Germany with the National Socialist German Workers' Party thugs just waiting for the old Hindenburg to die, if they don't assassinate him first so they can put their Adolf Hitler in his place—Italy is in the clutches of an egomaniac—in France they are building that subterranean Maginot line—and for what? Spain is ready for a civil war and there is famine again in Russia and you know what *that* means—and what do *we* do? We build plants in every one of those countries and are teaching them mechanized production at speeds no one even knew were possible before Ford! Right now he is in Germany on a goodwill inspection tour. You know what, Ninnie? I am beginning to think the Boss may be as mad as the rest of them!" Shocked by John's sudden so uncharacteristic disloyalty, Jane remained silent though attentive. "It's a cesspool everywhere I've been—Cologne, Berlin, Barcelona, Bordeaux, of course Cork is a disaster already—and now Fiat wants to coproduce Fords for Mussolini. Only England, Holland and Denmark, even Belgium, are sane and here . . ."

"I just heard from Mrs. Cooper that young Mr. Roosevelt—the one Hannah and I liked so much—he has been elected as our next new president—is that right?"

"Yes."

"Would you have voted for him?"

"Yes. Let's hope he can save us."

"Save us?"

"Ninnie, there was a hunger march on Washington—thousands of men sleeping in cardboard boxes that are known as Hoovervilles! All over America men ready and able to do a good day's work are starving! Hunger in America? Ninnie—in our America?—the land of prosperity and endless opportunity?—it is inconceivable! Where will it all end? Who *is* there to end it?"

"John, do you want to leave? Go home?"

"If I was alone I would—I'd take my chances—but—"

Jane interrupted him, "Even if Highland Park does close down Mr. Ford would never let you go—there is the Rouge—and I could help take in sewing and—"

"No, my work is here—besides, Mr. Cooper has been good to me—I would never let him down." Jane took notice that this was the very first time John omitted Henry Ford's name when referring to his duty to the company.

John lit a cigarette—its Turkish tobacco burned with a pervasive sweetness that Jane missed whenever he was away. "While I was gone did you receive a letter from Hannah?"

"No—why?"

"I had a letter from Fritz—I think you better read it—" He handed it to her. Sensing it must be something important Jane read it carefully—then taken aback, read it again. "Well, what do you think? Does it make any sense to you? No matter how terrible things are—leave America, leave Ford—for what? I told you everyone is going mad!"

"They are coming? They are really coming?"

"You read the letter."

Quietly—as though she didn't dare to say it out loud in case it might not come true, Jane said, "Hannah," it sounded like a prayer.

John took her in his arms. "Yes, *carissima*—Hannah is coming."

Shy at exposing her longing, Jane buried her face against him, grateful that he understood.

When Hannah's letter arrived it was full of similar news—tinged with an overwhelming regret even a sense of defeat. Having been an enemy Hun during the war couldn't compare with what had happened to her dearly held respect for Henry Ford. For so long he had been Hannah's idolized benefactor that now that she knew he hated her by being a Jew, it was as though she doubted her own worth. Reading between the conscientiously executed lines, Jane knew it was this disenchantment that had made Hannah agree to leave, return to a home she had left so willingly when young.

. . . Fritz, he has promised me that after a little while if we get too lonely, miss our America too much, we will go back and try again. Maybe have another cozy boardinghouse somewhere nice. So if now this is just like a long visit to see again old friends, then the sadness of saying good-bye to our Michigan is not so bad.

Quick, I must tell you big news from here. First that nice Mr. Roosevelt we liked now is our new president and because he is—he has ordered no more Prohibition—so of course everybody is happy toasting him. And also because he is so smart all the poor people will have work again and food on the table and not be sad hobos anymore. Oh, and another thing—now we have a real station that beams (that is how they say it) speaking and music out into the air. The new Mrs. Polansky, two blocks over—she has a big beautiful radio in real wood with knobs and I heard out of it myself. What will they think of next?

Having sold their furniture to friends, their house to strangers, in the late spring of 1933 Fritz and Hannah boarded the SS *Bremen* for Bremerhaven, at the same time that John having been called to Alexandria, and it being half term, took his family with him to Egypt. After their boat docked, John left them to enjoy Cairo while he continued on.

Learning to know and understand Turkey and now Egypt very nearly made having to leave America worthwhile. Even when missing many of the modern conveniences, Egypt so mesmerized one's imagination that after a while when such happened to appear, Jane resented their intrusion. Automobiles really had no business on roads that camels trod. For her the Industrial Age had no place in this overwhelming, somehow indestructible glory of pharaohs and their omnipotent deities. In this awesome land of constantly moving sand, its aura of permanence so quixotic, every dawn was a wonder, every twilight a yearning for repetitive tomorrows. When the hot winds blew Jane could smell the Sahara, Jane, who had never thought of Egypt as conjuring romantic visions was surprised that such profound magnificence could make one feel so human.

John Jr. just seventeen graduated from the Sixth Form and now looked forward to returning to Italy to join the black shirts of his hero. Worried for his son, John made immediate arrangements to send him back to Michigan to live with Celestina, while attending university. Many heated arguments later—too angry to even say good-bye, John Jr. left Turkey, hating his father. Billy, who thought that going home, all grown up alone on a big ship was the ultimate prize for being an A student, buried his nose in his schoolbooks determined he too could achieve such a gift.

Billy, as he would be known until true maturity required the disengagement of the *y*, was becoming an interesting boy. A jigsaw puzzle of many parts garnered from heredity as well as the kaleidoscope that life had spread before him, he encompassed the tenderness of Michael, the idealism and artistic courage of his father, the innate perception and profound respect of all beauty of his Italian heritage, the patrician discipline of his mother which made him already by the age of fourteen an intriguing, complex character.

It was already September when a letter arrived from Fritz bearing a German stamp.

> *Dearest Friends,*
>
> *Well, we are here. The fields are still full of fat cows—the mountaintops are full of snow—the air is so clean—so sharp sometimes it hurts to breathe it. We are grateful to have made the long journey in safety and good health. Hannah's sister, Anna and her husband have been most welcoming—kind to let us stay here in their home until we find a place and our so many belongings coming over by cargo ship arrive. Remember Heinz-Hermann—Anna's boy, the one who stayed with us before the war? He is here, is now an important member of the Schutzstaffel—in English that is "Protection Squad" but here it's just known by initials, S.S. His father, the butcher is of course very proud—his mother too, I think, though Anna hasn't said much about it.*
>
> *When she thinks I am not looking Hannah cries. Bavaria is not Highland Park—but then Highland Park was not Bavaria either. I am sure that once my Hannah has a home again and her own kitchen—everything will be fine.*
>
> *Here is the address where we are now. Anna's husband prefers that I give you the address of his butcher shop downstairs and that any letter for us is addressed 'in care of' Herr Wolfgang Streicher.*
>
> *Ever your old friend,*
>
> *Fritz*
>
> *PS. Hannah says she is writing to your Vifey herself.*

When an assembly plant for the Fordson Tractor was deemed finally possible in Rumania, John wanting to spare Jane the misery of returning, arranged to live and work in Bucharest, leaving her and Billy to the comfort of their accustomed life in Constantinople, arriving in the capital just in time for the widespread anti-Jewish riots that no one had expected. Newly loving him, for Jane these would be the lonely years, waiting for John's infrequent returns, a repetitive discipline.

Hannah's letters as always in German were frequent.

8 Juni 1934
Großnöbach
Bei Dachau
Dearest Ninnie,

> *Now it is here so pretty. Cornflowers and daisies all mixed up—like a*
> *flower carpet . . .*

Little bits of gossip followed, some description of who and what she was beginning to know, get reacquainted with—then there were moments when Jane felt her
need for a real friend—one that could be trusted to whom Hannah could confide,

> *. . . Heinz-Hermann, he visits often—in his smart uniform and he makes*
> *speeches—said that the Jews are a race not a religion group and that*
> *because they are ones that lost the war they must be punished. But I don't*
> *know what kind of punishment. So I worry a little if his mother, my sister*
> *Anna, is going maybe to be punished. You think so? I asked Fritz but he*
> *said it is all just politics and anyway her husband is a good Prussian so why*
> *worry. And us—we are good American United States citizens. But still I*
> *don't understand why they burned books. Did you hear? Even our Mr. Jack*
> *London and that nice young Ernest Hemingway that Agnes likes so much,*
> *they burned. Why? They didn't do anything wrong—they just write special*
> *and they are good Americans also.*
>
> *I better stop. Heinz will be home soon and I think he doesn't like me to*
> *write letters. Last week I think he tried to steam open a letter Fritz wrote*
> *to Zoltan—but I am not sure. But now because he snoops I pretend I go for*
> *a walk down the hill and then I send this from the post office in the little*
> *grocery store in the village.*
>
> *Oh, quick—we found a little house not too far from here—with a*
> *small garden to grow vegetables and maybe even flowers. It has a tree for*
> *shade and real plumbing inside. Anna's husband says maybe they won't let*
> *Fritz buy it because he has a Jew for a wife, me, but Fritz said that is just*
> *ridiculous—good American dollars are still the best money in the whole*
> *world—so, maybe by Thanksgiving we will be in our own home again. This*
> *year I will have to make just a chicken or maybe a fine goose to celebrate and*
> *use* preiselberren *(like little red currents in case you do not know what those*
> *are) for our cranberries—but—the thankfulness will be as it always was for*
> *our special Thanksgivings back home in the good old days.*

I send as always and forever to the boys many hugs and kisses, and warm
loving thoughts to you, dear Vifey and your John. Soon—maybe soon we
will be together again and then we can talk a blue streak.
    Your friend,
    Hannah
    P.S. I have not heard from Ebbely, have you?

On one rare occasion when John was back Jane seized the opportunity to voice a growing concern. "I am worried—it's been months now since Hannah's last letter. It's not like her—and you haven't heard from Fritz either."

"I know." Reluctant to pursue the subject, John turned the page of his British newspaper. Jane put down her darning.

"John? What is it? Do you know something?" After years of marriage she knew whenever he evaded something.

"Leave it, Ninnie." He spoke Italian, which made his order even more commanding.

"No. I won't 'leave it, Ninnie!' These are our friends—people we love—if you know something you are going to tell me!"

"The Germany of today is not the same homeland that Fritz and Hannah left. I always thought they should have never left America and I told Fritz so. Ebbely did too. He of course was prompted after Ford's *International Jew* was translated into German and sold more copies there than anywhere else in the world—he said then it was madness for *any* Jew to return. But you know them—Hannah was a little homesick and scared by the wartime Hun thing and Fritz was worried by the layoffs—wanted the pride of returning having prospered."

Darning forgotten, Jane watched her husband's face.

"You have never spoken like this before."

"I have never had to work within the structures of Fascist regimes—it is only my American citizenship that protects me."

"Ford doesn't?"

"Ah, yes—the great Henry Ford and his ever mighty industrial power—which is now being offered to whom and for what!"

Never had Jane heard such a note of cynicism when mentioning the man and his company that had been the core of John's existence for so long. Though her husband's awakening from what she perceived as an overly idealistic hero worship pleased her, still Jane had the strange feeling that if ever a complete disenchantment should occur, it might eradicate the boy, the dedicated dreamer—leaving a desolate, hopeless man in its place. "Listen, *cara*, I have been told to inspect a proposed sight for a new Ford factory outside of Hamburg—you know Ford's credo . . .'No water, no factory'. . . well, Hamburg sure has water. So I'll be back in Germany . . ."

"When?"

"Next week, maybe."

"For how long?"

"Haven't the faintest idea."

"I'll go with you . . ."

"Oh, no you won't!" The vehemence of his denial startled her.

"Why not? Billy is . . ."

"It has nothing to do with Billy."

"Then why not?" The sudden suspicion of another woman as beguiling traveling companion entered the atmosphere and John felt it.

"Giovanna!" When he called her that—Jane always knew she had overstepped her mark of obedient wife.

"Yes *John*!" she challenged back, getting nowhere.

"*Carissima*, give it time—it's nearly Christmas—we will certainly hear something by then."

It was long after Christmas when Jane received the present she had been hoping for, a letter arrived from Hannah, this one written in English bearing no return address.

> *Dearest American Friends,*
>
> *Here everything is fine. Everyone is just like our old Boss back in Michigan. I wish I could take a little trip—a short visit to visit old friends. But as you know my rheumatism is very bad and with my Fritz's poor eyesight—well all that is not so good for making a journey. Maybe next year. Please understand.*
>
> *Fritz and me, we wish you a Merry Christmas and a very Happy 1935. When this reaches you.*
>
> *Your forever friends,*
> Fritz and Hannah
> *(the boys—kiss the boys)*

Jane stormed into their bedroom, where John was putting on his shirt.

"John?" Body tensed, eyes blazing, she stood before him shaking the single sheet of paper. "Did you read this? It arrived already open."

"Yes—it was addressed to both of us." Knowing what was coming John stalled for time.

"Well? Rheumatism?! Hannah has rheumatism? Since when?!"

"Perhaps it was the mountain air?" Putting an arm around her—he sat on the edge of their bed, pulling her down next to him.

"Don't make jokes," she admonished.

"I'm not, *carissima*—I'm not."

"You know something." It was a statement not a question.

"No, not really . . ."

"Oh, yes you do—tell me!"

"It's the letter, Ninnie. I think Hannah is trying to tell us something in the letter."

"Tell us? Tell us what? I don't think she even wrote it—it's not the way she writes—it doesn't sound like her—and in English! She never writes me in English."

"I know . . ." John tried to sound comforting. ". . . read the first sentence."

"Which one? The one about Ford?"

"Yes."

Silently Jane read it again.

"You think . . . Oh no!"

"Yes, Ninnie I think they both may be in some trouble."

"But, John—they are American citizens! And Fritz, he isn't Jewish!"

"With the new Nuremberg Laws just being married to a Jew is trouble enough—it makes him a *Mischlinge* and therefore tainted. As for their papers and passports—they could have been confiscated by now."

"They can do that?"

"Just like Mussolini, this Hitler is now the proclaimed Führer of his Nazi Party and can do whatever he wants. It may be that Prussian brother-in-law butcher—or that opportunist nephew—but something, something must have happened for Hannah to write in this veiled way making up lies so we would understand."

"But why Fritz's eyesight?"

"Perhaps she means that Fritz doesn't see or want to see?"

"What can we do?"

"Nothing. No—let me finish—next month I am expected back in England. Maybe I could arrange a detour to look in on the Cologne plant. Once in Germany, maybe I can . . . in the letter doesn't she put what town they are near?"

"Not on this one but on the others she had Großnöbach near Dachau."

"Dachau—that's just outside of Munich—that'll be easy—all trains stop there."

"But what real trouble can there be?"

"No one seems to know exactly—at the Ford Werke . . ."

"Why do you always say it like that?"

"*Werke*?" Jane nodded. "Because Ninnie, by new directives everything must now be exclusively German. Plants may be built by Ford—produce Fords—but by order of the National Socialist Party it must be a German enterprise—run by Germans certified to be of pure-blooded Aryan stock. Anyone even suspected of being any different is let go—very often they just seem to disappear."

"Oh, John—why did they ever leave America!"

"Yes—I always thought it was a foolish thing to do. I wonder why Ebbely allowed it."

"Shall I write him?"

"No—now it's too late anyway—let's wait—maybe I can find out more . . ."

Though John inquired—even using the importance of the Ford name to make people talk who wouldn't to a mere individual, it seemed that the Geigers had somehow vanished. The little house they had chosen was no longer available—had been sold to an Aryan couple with an impeccable pedigree. The brother-in-law butcher, a very recent widower, although the cause of his wife's sudden demise seemed clouded, insisted the Geigers had simply decided to live somewhere else, possibly in Austria, and though the grocery store postmistress confirmed this, there was no forwarding address.

Weeks, then months passed without a word, then one day its stamp of origin completely obliterated, a smudged, dog-eared postal card arrived, on which Hannah had written in English that they were happy, well and sent regards, signed, "Your friends, Mr. and Mrs. Fritz Geiger." Throughout the months that followed such cards kept arriving periodically bearing the identical message written in pencil in Hannah's recognizable hand. Somehow Jane clung to these cheap cardboard tokens as though they were true. John who in his searching had been in Dachau, that rather quaint Bavarian town full of smiling inhabitants, suspected much but had no proof—allowed Jane her fantasy hoping it would sustain her.

Thumbing its nose at the Treaty of Versailles that forbade its rearmament, by 1937 Germany had reinstated compulsive military service, enforced the racial laws created in Nuremberg that would affect all aspects of Jewish life, and formed its Axis bond with Fascist Italy. Having raped Ethiopia, Mussolini was helping Franco accomplish his of Spain and Billy, eighteen, graduated with honors.

His work in Rumania and Turkey done—now considered a valuable tool for possibly enhancing mass production, John was ordered back to Italy. Still believing that the power of the Ford Company as well as his American citizenship would protect him, he moved his wife and son back to his father's home in Torino—then faced a situation that no one could have predicted just a few years before.

He was about to learn a disturbing truth that within the psyche of all naturalized immigrants a pervasive uncertainty exists—that being once so accepted does not irrevocably guarantee one's belonging to the country of one's choice. This is not as much of a paranoia as it might appear for there are many countries and many governments who are totally convinced that once born within their realm both blood and birth will conform—making them eternally theirs. Regardless of personal choice, *once a German, always a German—once an Italian, always an Italian* was as prevalent a belief in the twentieth century as it was in those past. That tenacious sense of insecurity in all naturalized Americans is not as completely imaginary as it might seem. In Italy his American nationality ignored, John had resented the assumption that he was a willing Fascist simply on the basis of having been born an Italian. Now while he secretly struggled with a situation he was ill equipped to handle, Jane, confident that his integrity was intact, expected that any day John would probably announce that they would be leaving again to somewhere exotic where he was again needed.

Teresa wrote, once again, in perfect French.

> *Giovanna Ma Chere,*
> *Have you found what you were searching for?*

Jane could imagine her voice, feathered into a smile.

> *Have you lost your inner fire, Giovanna? Dearest friend, you cannot go through life blaming God for everything. Blame is a coward's tool for self-evasion. You really think you have the right to judge? To stand in judgment of God is to question faith—to question faith is to lose the very foundation of human hope. Be very careful, Giovanna—to deny God is to deny man. To deny man is to deny life. To deny life—is Death without recourse for salvation as the ultimate peace. The acceptance of unconditional, all-encompassing love.*
>
> *Remember when we were children and Sister Bertine spoke to us of the Divinity of souls? Remember no harm can come to a soul given to God. You have always had it in your very rejection of what you crave. You believe you have lost first a mother, then your child. Yet they live within you—they are a part of you. Every breath you take they take—every joy you feel, they feel. Every sorrow, they weep with you. To love is to become one with one's beloved.*

Peace, child, I shall pray for you—I always do. We may not ever see each other again . . . I do not want you to mourn—remember I shall be where I want to be—have hoped to be since we were children—so no mourning—for the tears you will shed will be for yourself if you do—not me.

Remember all I have said. It was not the Church—it was my heart that writes and speaks to you. May the Lord watch over you and yours. You are always in my prayers.

Jane placed Teresa's letter into her special shoebox next to the others. Through all the many stages of her life there had been one certainty, one purity to hold on to, worth believing in—Teresa, as dependable in her faith as her friendship—she and she alone by simply existing had left the door ajar to Jane's faith, a chink in her armor against the God she no longer trusted. *Oh, Giovanna, what will happen to you now?* Jane shook her well-coifed head as though to stop her self-involvement. *You really should be thinking of Teresa and her suffering—not what will become of you when she no longer exists for you to lean on.*

That summer the Ford Motor Company terminated John's employment thereby releasing their American-trained Italian-speaking specialist to be available for service to the industrial needs of Fascist Italy. That John should have been informed, even asked, was considered quite unnecessary. He had always been such an exemplary employee, it was assumed he would certainly welcome any and all decisions made by the company he had been loyal to since his youth.

His vehement antifascism not yet fully comprehended by those he now considered his probable enemies—realizing that when they did, his political stance might endanger not only himself but Jane and his son, John began to make furtive plans to ensure their safety. Under an assumed name he booked passage to America for two on the SS *Saturnia* due to sail from Genova within the month.

"Ninnie!" The urgency in his voice giving his name for her a strange cadence, John closed the door of their bedroom. Expecting the anticipated announcement of yet another move, Jane stood waiting wondering what country they were being sent to this time. "Listen and listen carefully. You and the boy must leave and you must leave now. I have booked passage—you sail on the fifteenth out of Genova. Go home, Ninnie! I beg you—take the boy and go! I'll follow when they let me."

"I won't leave you!"

"Yes—you will!"

"No!"

"Don't, please. I want you and Billy away from here. Do you understand what I am trying to say? You must leave and now! My passport has been commandeered—but yours . . ."

"Why? They can't do that!"

"This is a dictatorship, Ninnie—how many times must I tell you they can do anything they want . . . anything! There is no one who dares to question Mussolini's actions."

"But . . ." Now she was frightened. ". . . why? You work for Henry Ford, everybody—"

"No—I don't, not anymore." Jane just stood there and stared. "I have been relieved of my position—no pay and there's no guarantee that my back salary—which has been frozen—will be released, unless . . ." Not wanting to worry her further John stopped himself from voicing what he suspected—that once he agreed to Fascist demands—only then would his bank account once more be made available to him. "Ninnie, please do what I say." He held her against him wishing he could spare her.

"Will you follow? Will they let you?" For just a second he hesitated then assured her of course—after all he was an American citizen—if Ford no longer protected him the American embassy certainly would. His main worry now was getting her and Billy out of Italy and as quickly as possible.

"Ninnie, please listen—if you stay they might try to force me, use my family and then I would be helpless. Please understand!"

That note of pleading disturbed Jane more than the words.

"Where will we live? Our house is . . ."

"All is arranged . . . I . . ."

"It is?"

"Yes, when Mr. Cooper warned me . . ."

"He did?"

"Yes, before we left Constantinople, he found out that the Boss might be letting me go. So when it happened I immediately wrote Zoltan that we would be coming home and to find us a house . . . he immediately wrote back, said because of the hard times there were a lot for sale and Agnes had seen one over on Pilgrim that she said was exactly like our old one so I told him—buy it."

"That's crazy! You just can't buy a house like . . . like buying a new hat! Why?"

"I HAD TO! Hannah wouldn't be there, Fritz wouldn't—I didn't want you to have to live with strangers. I want you to have a home of your own to come back home to."

Never having seen her husband's pride laid bare, this silenced Jane into acceptance.

"It's on Pilgrim?" Her voice reed thin held a hint of tears.

"Yes. Zoltan and Agnes are ready to help all they can. They say the house will need a little fixing but Rudy says . . ."

"You even contacted Rudy?!"

"No, Zoltan did. The moment he got my letter he telephoned everybody. Rudy said that Sundays he and the others can give the house a fresh coat of paint inside and out and it will look like new. When Ebbely heard he deposited a sum of money to see us through the first few months until . . ."

"Ebbely lent us money?"

"He insisted. And I have to accept. I have no choice—of course I will pay him back the moment I find employment." Ashamed, John sounded like an earnest boy explaining his intention to be good.

"John . . ."

"Yes, Ninnie?"

"You *will* follow?" Her eyes searched his face.

"Of course."

"When?"

"*Carissima*, I don't know! I don't know." It was such a cry from the heart that Jane reached out, took her husband's hand to comfort him. "Agnes says she has extra furniture, not to worry and you are so wonderfully frugal I know you will manage."

"Just come home."

"The house, Ninnie—I used all my savings—it's all we have left—try to keep the house. I know it will be hard—but try."

"I will, John—I promise."

24

Milling crowds, the chaos of an imminent sailing, worried someone might jostle it, Jane adjusted her grip on the travel bag that held Michael's ashes. The noise all around them was so deafening they had to shout.

"Billy . . ." His father sounded so strange. ". . . remember, take care of your mother. Promise me you will always take care of Mama."

"I will, Papa. I promise."

"Ninnie—I am sorry—about the cabin. I promised you a good life and now I can only afford to give you a third-class passage to go home. Forgive me."

"Oh, John—" She flung herself into his arms. "I don't care, it's been a wonderful life—it has—really it has."

"Here Ninnie, I bought this for you long ago. I wanted to give it to you when we returned home—as a reminder of our years away—but now . . . take it, Ninnie—they say amber brings luck." He placed the necklace of purest living beauty around her neck. "I love you," he said and for the very first time of their many years of marriage—she believed him completely, without question or hesitation. "Good-bye, boy, take care of your mother. You're the man now, Billy—I'm counting on you." Sensing his father's despair, Billy moved towards him. "No, Billy—time to go—be a good boy, work hard at school—you'll love America—you hardly know it, but you'll love it. It's the best country in the whole wide world. There is none better. It's *your* country—remember that. It belongs to you and you to it." A last kiss, a whispered "*Carissima . . . ciao.*" Then he pulled away allowed himself to get lost in the crowd.

Knowing for his sake she mustn't run—call his name, she stood where he had left her and cried.

"Come, Mama—" Billy led his mother up the gangplank and onto the big ship that was to carry them home.

For the first time feeling like a true immigrant, she watched Italy become a leave-taking memory. Was John still there on the quay or had he refused the memory? She knew so well his need to negate all that might have the power to weaken him—drain off what he believed he had to be—he had to retain to survive—be the man he thought he was. He who had taken her with such assurance from Italy, now was forced to remain behind—and as the land of her birth receded in the morning fog she had the strangest sensation of loss quite unrelated to homeland or memories of it. Feeling strangely bereft as though deserted by what she couldn't identify, she turned her back, walked along the overcrowded third-class deck in search of her son.

This journey to America was uneventful except for the reawakened memories. Bela guarding her precious salami for her Lotar, Megan, in her servant's cap dreaming impossible dreams, Eugenie, her fantasy world adorned by paper roses—where were they now? What had become of these fellow immigrants to the promised land, its wonders when still unreached yet believed, depended upon? The remembrance of John teaching her to speak American, Jane did not dwell on—it increased her longing, weakened her determination to be what he expected of her.

On a stormy autumn evening Jane and Billy arrived in Highland Park to find it had acquired a forlorn look. Without the welcoming lights from the Geiger house and Hannah's embrace everything seemed barren as though a new poverty of spirit had settled in. Soon good friends, forever kind, rallied, made every day at least bearable. A fresh coat of paint, some floorboards nailed down, a door or two rehung, everything scrubbed, polished and repaired, and daily life in the little house took on an optimistic shine of its own. Billy entered Wayne University on a scholarship—to help out, did odd jobs, shoveled snow, delivered papers, after school worked the soda fountain in Mr. Kline's drugstore. Advertising her dressmaking skills Jane convinced the alterations department of Detroit's most elegant depart-ment store to hire her. On her days off and for most special holidays remembering all that Hannah had taught her, Jane became a hired cook for a well-to-do family in Dearborn. Within structured discipline, life took on expediency; emotionally every day was a waiting for John, every extra dollar earned was for the house she had promised him to keep.

Not being able to afford the luxury of a telephone, a weekly ring-a-ling to Ebbely became an anticipated evening walk down to the corner drugstore.

Necessary nickels carefully counted—laid out before her, as always slightly nervous going through the required procedure of placing a long-distance call, Jane waited for that savored moment when he accepted her call with his usual assured "Yes? Yes, this is Mr. Fish . . ." and the subsequent joy of Ebbely's "Hello? Is that you, dear child? Well, and how is life treating you today?" When she was sad, he refused to allow her the luxury of complaining, usually stating that sadness being the robber of one's resilience which was bad enough, paying five cents for discussing its presence was just money thrown to the winds. When she told him of becoming a cook, Ebbely's shock radiated all the way up north from Louisiana.

"A cook? You? Amazing!"

"Yes—and they pay me for it!"

"But . . . but, dear Lady, you hate—no, if I remember correctly, you *abhor* cooking!"

"Oh, I do! But it's the only extra work I could find—and I have the copybook Hannah wrote out for me with her . . ."

"Jane—we will not speak of Hannah."

"But, Ebbely, I was only going to . . ."

"Did you hear me, Jane?" Ebbely's voice had lost its gentleness.

"I'm sorry—I know we agreed . . ."

"We did, didn't we."

Her nickels running low, Jane hurried to another subject.

"Eugenie wrote me. She sounds so happy—now that she is working for you."

"She runs my humble establishment with a devotion at times bordering on embellished adulation."

"I am so glad you found her."

"Thanks to you, dear child, thanks to you . . . now . . . this telephone communication—is it for a constructive purpose or simple need?"

"Need."

"Which is?"

"If I could answer that . . ."

"You wouldn't have to telephone me in the first place!" Ebbely finished for her, laughing. "Repartee! Delicious! You are growing up, Vifey . . . you are growing up." Catching his use of Hannah's name for her, Ebbely bid Jane a hasty good-bye and hung up.

Most nights when the day was done and she was tired, then longings intruded that she could not allow during work. *Where was Hannah? Where was John? When?*

John waited for a sunny autumn morning when everyone would leave the villa to enjoy its unexpected warmth, then alone and undisturbed, cocked the pistol, and blew his brains against the bathroom wall.

By its very arrival the cablegram caused anticipatory anxiety even before being opened. Hands shaking, Jane unfolded it and learned she was a widow.

Profiting by financial inability as well as the length of time it would take a ship to reach Italy to bring his widow to attend—John was buried quickly. They could have waited, sent the necessary funds, but these were not forthcoming—neither was compassion. Jane had been deserted before—known its demand for an acquired emptiness of both spirit and feeling—she was well versed in helplessness. Having been a participant of life, not an instigator of it, Jane now found herself alone once more as spectator to her own void. Her life that lay behind her seemed fallow by things neglected—emotions perhaps disregarded, so undervalued that their extinction seemed guaranteed. What had she done to lose so much? As her grief increased so did her guilt that such intense grieving deserved a greater love as catalyst than what had been shown the living.

Had she loved him enough to bring him joy? Was she even capable of a loving that could enrich another's very existence? Somehow she doubted it—the guilt, though unacceptable, was self-erasure. She felt she had deserted him by leaving—he had deserted her by dying. For John Jr. his father's death seemed to hardly register. Billy confused by a sadness untried, thrust upon him by one he had believed loved him— still too young to know one could still love one who disappoints, felt anger mingled with his sorrow and resented his need to understand the why of another's action.

Highland Park
December 4, 1938
Dearest Teresa,

I am a widow. On the seventeenth of October my husband took his own life—and I was notified of this by cablegram. For you this is a terrible sin—for him I believe it may have been a valiant act of freedom. For me a numbness that even after almost two months still envelops—sits in me like one of our thick mountain fogs. I should be weeping—but can't. For the boys it must be the same—although I can't be certain as John, the eldest rarely shows his feelings—lives in such a world of his own that sometimes I have the fear my mother sits in wait for him. Billy is brave, looks after me—cries when he thinks I do not see. Although I continue to write to my dear friend

Hannah hoping that mail will be forwarded to wherever they may have
moved to—I never get an answer so I worry every day a little more and now
that I know John will never come home, I sometimes even worry about me . . .

By her selfishness not wanting to burden Teresa's selflessness, Jane folded the unfinished letter, tucked it away in her precious shoebox that nestled against the urn where Michael slept.

It took Billy many months to earn enough to fulfill his need to see his father's grave.

"Mama, I am going." They spoke Italian when they were friends but this he said in English, for he expected his mother to disapprove. When she didn't, they discussed his travel plans but in French because as Jane so rightly pointed out he might be in need of it and though he spoke it fluently, needed a little practice. German she never spoke—that language belonged to Hannah.

What Billy finally saw, what he thought, even what he might have discovered, learned from his sad pilgrimage was never voiced. Like those, years later, who knew Hell and could not speak of it, describe it to the uninitiated, could be a possible reason. In later life those who knew and loved him, needed to live with the terrible scars this journey left.

Still in Italy and out of money, when European war was declared in September, Billy sold his American shoes for train fare, escaped to Paris and barefoot sought sanctuary in the American embassy—and as a born citizen stranded in wartime Europe, was given passage home.

As war was once again dismembering the old world, the new hugged its treasured remoteness closer hoping it would not be called upon to again spill its blood for distant strangers. That this hope would be obliterated on a beautiful sunny morning just twenty-three months later—no one could know.

Escalating strikes and slowdowns, riots, and clandestine brutality began to turn Detroit into its own battleground. On the gates of the mighty Rouge, a giant swastika was erected, placards proclaimed UNIONISM NOT FASCISM, FORDISM IS FASCISM. The Ford Service Department comprised three thousand men, that the *New York Times* declared was the "largest privately run Secret Service force in the world."

Billy continued his youth, John Jr. married and forsook his. Having lost their candy shop during the Depression, Celestina and her Josef now worked for the man who had bought it. Agnes presented Zoltan with a son they named Fritz. Rudy became a tester at Ford's aircraft plant, remarried and closed his wounds. With his wife's approval, Peter became a unionist, joined the UAW, Carl having found work with Chrysler moved his family back to Detroit. His generous loan repaid, in a moment of wild abandon Ebbely bought a small hotel off Bourbon Street where most evenings in its corner lounge he entertained his guests with such soulful renditions of the blues that soon all of New Orleans knew of him—some even going so far as to insist that if the great Mississippi bluesman, T-Model Ford, heard him—he too would agree that their Ebb Fish was grand. Before Holland was lost everyone received news from Johann and Henrietta telling them they had become joyous grandparents.

Early 1941 Billy volunteered for military service and by the spring of 1942 with America at war, was home on leave before being shipped overseas.

Jane, not knowing how to say good-bye, fussed.

"A disgrace to send fine American boys to win the war in such sloppy workmanship!" She settled the shoulders of his uniform, smoothed a buckling lapel, murmured, "I wish we had more time, I could take the whole thing apart and fix it right."

"Yes, Mama, you and your magic needle that never rests." Billy laughed.

"We kept this house like I promised Papa."

"Yes, I know, Mama." He had heard these exact words so often it had become a family saying.

"Billy . . ."

"Yes?"

"If they send you over to Europe . . ."

"Mama, you know I . . ."

"Oh, I know, but if—if—it's that side will you try to look?"

"Mama, in the middle of a war?"

"I know—but . . . please, please try . . . Now, you have the sandwiches for the train? And the apple?"

"Yes, Mama—" Even in English, the way he gave it an Italian inflection always reminded her of John. He was so like him. Knowing she couldn't keep him much longer, she rechecked the sergeant's stripes she had sewn on his sleeve.

"You know how to put these on when you get promoted?"

"Mama, who taught me to sew?"

"Me!" Jane smiled, "I forgot. With all you know you will make a fine husband some . . ." Her voice caught at the possibility he might never be one. "Billy . . ."

"Yes?"

"You will be careful?"

"I promise."

"No—don't promise—I have a fear of promises—and no good-bye—I don't like that either."

"Well, will *arrivederci* do, or *au revoir*?"

"Yes—" Not knowing if he wanted to be kissed, she stood looking at him, uncertain. For a moment he held her—then walked out the door.

Most Dear Teresa,

Today my youngest left for war. Here—one hangs a red star in the front window to announce it to the neighbors. The color of the star changes to gold when they are killed.

I had a sudden urge to acquire a picture of St. Anthony, slip it into the pocket of his uniform, but then thought better of it. It seemed somehow blasphemous to ask protection out of sudden need when having shunned all forms of belief for so long.

I only tell you of this because I tell you everything—even those thoughts I am later ashamed of having thought you hear. If you were a priest—I think I might even be willing to go to Confession. How I ramble on—forgive me, I must be lonely—the house seems empty—so still—memories have room to invade. A lifetime of so much and yet so little to show that it was worth the living of it. Sometimes I see me—as I was in the shade of our tree—all youthful dissatisfaction, welcoming escape at any price and wonder was it worth it? And each time I am forced to admit even to myself—that yes—it really was after all, all of it. That lifts my spirits no matter how far they have fallen and allows me to start up my sewing machine with renewed determination.

It seems that all my life I have been searching for what exactly, I do not know . . . and so should it ever come my way how would I recognize it—not knowing. There is a persistent fear that it might actually have come, but then left because of my lack of trust in its existence. I who was so certain that freedom was one of place—now think that perhaps I have been wrong and it is simply one of self.

Even now I seek a comforting embrace in which to lose my reality. Perhaps someday if war does not destroy all future—I will bring Michael's ashes to let them lie with John or perhaps someone else will mingle mine with his— leaving John his own peace. Still time has a way of nullifying energy—until even dreams can no longer survive.

Forgive me, I am tired and therefore foolish.

I wonder if this letter will ever reach your cloistered world—they may have moved you to a safer place. I wish I could be certain that you are safe and war will not touch—reach you—that is I mean only the physical part of you—your soul I know has always been in safe regard. Pray for Billy—you have the right that I forfeited.

Know that I love you and love does not become me as I wish it would. All you have taught me—I remember and I try. Will our chestnut tree survive this war as well? I wonder.

Jane put down the pen. The house so newly silent—beckoned rest. She sighed and smiled, caught herself slightly embarrassed. *Billy has promised to return* and for some inexplicable reason, she was now certain he would. Despite all odds he would survive—as she would, as she must—to welcome him home.